Raves for *The Dragon Quartet:*

"Enchanting fantasy, filled with adventure, villains, romance, and hope . . . a heroine with some spunk . . . a magical tapestry of intrigue and daring . . . weaves a spell over the reader. A must for all those dragon lovers of other writers like Wrede and McCaffrey. I can't wait for the next book in the series."   —*VOYA*

"Dragon fans are really going to love *The Book of Earth* . . . the dragon is absolutely irresistible. When he's on stage, sparks of excitement leap through the pages. By the end of the book and the dramatic introduction of Water, you will indeed find it hard to wait for the next tale."   —*Romantic Times*

"Entertaining. . . . Kellogg's characters make a delightful quartet, neatly balances Erde's fish-out-of-time experiences with N'doch, a modern man who encounters real magic for the first time with a sense of awe."   —*Starlog*

"A fun romp with some creatively surreal moments, and a frightening view of a too-possible furture."   —*Locus*

THE DRAGON QUARTET

By Marjorie B. Kellogg:

The Dragon Quartet

The Book of Earth
The Book of Water
The Book of Fire
The Book of Air

By Marjorie B. Kellogg with William Rossow:

Lear's Daughters*
(The Wave and the Flame; Reign of Fire)

*Coming in hardcover February 2009

THE DRAGON QUARTET

VOL II

THE BOOK OF FIRE

THE BOOK OF AIR

MARJORIE B. KELLOGG

DAW BOOKS, INC.

DONALD A. WOLLHEIM, FOUNDER

375 Hudson Street, New York, NY 10014

ELIZABETH R. WOLLHEIM

SHEILA E. GILBERT

PUBLISHERS

www.dawbooks.com

First Paperback Printing, January 2006
5 6 7 8 9

DAW TRADEMARK REGISTERED
U.S. PAT. OFF. AND FOREIGN COUNTRIES
—MARCA REGISTRADA
HECHO EN U.S.A.

PRINTED IN THE U.S.A.

INTRODUCTION

It is to be hoped, by this writer at least, that you, the Reader, have opened this book because the previous two novels of *The Dragon Quartet* stand bright and clear in your mind.

If not, don't worry. Much is done in the world of series creation to assure that each book, no matter how tightly connected to its fellows by grand theme or superplot, retains equal value as a stand-alone tale. After all, given most booksellers' current practice, a reader first must be lucky enough to happen upon the first volume of a series, and then be alert enough to catch the succeeding volumes before they, too, vanish from the shelves. So, I have done all I can to honor the stand-alone tradition.

However . . .

What writer would not prefer that her readers partake of the entire rich feast she has prepared for them? Gathering up four books scattered over years into two published more or less together is intended to encourage this literary gluttony. If you don't mind starting with dessert, please read on. But if, like me, you want your meal presented in a proper order, set this book aside for long enough to search out its companion, and then, begin at the beginning.

Bon appetit!
Marjorie B. Kellogg

THE BOOK OF FIRE

To Lynne Kemen and Bill Rossow

Who have found so much time in their busy, busy lives to give tirelessly of their expertise and help an anxious writer see what she's written.

Who appreciate the necessity of a dry white wine and fresh coffee from Zabar's.

Endless thanks.

In addition: much praise and gratitude to my tireless editor and publisher, Sheila Gilbert.

Thanks also to my agent Joshua Bilmes, to Allen and Annie Rozelle, and to Antje Ellerman.

PROLOGUE

The Creation

In the Beginning,
and a little after . . .

In the Beginning, four mighty dragons raised of elemental energies were put to work creating the World. They were called Earth, Water, Fire, and Air. No one of them had power greater than another, and no one of them was mighty alone.

When the work was completed and the World set in motion, the four went to ground, expecting to sleep out this World's particular history and not rise again until World's End.

The first to awaken was Earth.

He woke in darkness, as innocent as a babe, with only the fleeting shadows of dreams to hint at his former magnificence. But one bright flame of knowledge drove him forth: he was Called to Work again, if only he could remember what the Work was.

He found the World grown damp and chill, overrun by the puniest of creatures, Creation's afterthought, the ones called Men. Earth soon learned that Men, too, had forgotten their Origin. They had abandoned their own intended Work in the World and thrived instead on superstition, violence, and self-righteous oppression of their fellows. They had forgotten as well their primordial relationship with dragons—all, that is, but a few.

One in particular awaited Earth's coming, a young girl who knew nothing of the secret duty carried down through the countless generations of her blood. Her name was Erde, and she knew her Destiny when she faced a living dragon and was not afraid.

Thereafter, Earth's Quest became her own, and together they searched her World for answers to his questions. Some they found and slowly, along with his memory, Earth's powers reawakened. But the girl's World was dark and dangerous and ignorant, and the mysterious Caller who summoned Earth could not be found within it. One day, blindly following the Call, Earth took them Somewhere Else.

In that Somewhere Else, they found Earth's sister Water and her Companion N'Doch. N'Doch's World was hot and crowded and full of noise, and mysterious to Erde until she understood that she had traveled to Sometime, as well as to Somewhere. It became her task to teach N'Doch about the dragons and their Quest, for he did not know his Destiny and did not join them willingly at first.

Water, too, had heard the Caller. She could answer some of Earth's questions about the Work, but added many of her own. Soon, the dragons were convinced that an unknown Power not only blocked their Search, but threatened their safety. Evidence pointed to the dragon Fire, but why would their own brother conspire against them?

When the dangers of N'Doch's world, both human and inhuman, closed in around them, the four in desperation returned to Erde's time, with nothing but N'Doch's recurring dream of a Burning Land to tell them where to go to continue the Search.

And in Erde's time, conditions were deteriorating. . . .

PART ONE

The Summoning
of the Hero

CHAPTER ONE

It's the wind, she tells herself. Only the wind. Making a little adjustment, minute but perceptible, like a singer sliding off-key. But she stills her breath anyway, to listen around the hard dry corners of the wind's howl for whatever might have waked her.

"Only the wind." Paia whispers it aloud. An incantation of hope: the wind, and not some herdsman famished into an ill-advised grudge. Not the murderously disillusioned acolyte that she's always fearing will hack a path through the several layers of her bodyguard and gain her inner sanctum. Perhaps a timid servant, then, one of the newer ones, stumbling upstairs in haste to inform her of the God's return.

But the door does not burst open. There is no warning clatter down the hall. Just the wind. It has to be.

Paia eases one hand beneath her pillows. The move is slow and noiseless, through folds as silky as feathers, glimmering in the dull red night. Whoever it is might already be in the room. Her hand is a wave under sand. It's only the wind, but with the little gun cradled in her palm, almost cool against her heated skin, she feels much better.

Paia resettles herself. If she can make herself stop listening, she can will sleep to come. She has learned to sleep with the gun. She's trained her right hand to rest on it lightly, immobile, relaxed but ready. The God insisted, when he presented it to her: she must keep it close by at all times. At *all* times. Especially at night. At first, it was like carrying a live scorpion around. She hated it. She did everything she could think of to convince the God to rescind this command. She accused him of being paranoid and overprotective. He assured her he had good reason.

She implied he was afraid someone would steal it—such a rare relic, priceless, really, a functioning firearm. The God waved a gold-ringed claw and snorted. She threatened to sell it. Another snort, and a reminder that while the little weapon might be *her* most valuable possession, he—the God—was magic and could simply conjure another. And by the way, he noted, it would only take the one time she needed it and didn't have it on her for all her protests to be moot.

So that was the end of it. The God would trust no one to instruct her, which was awkward, as the only training he himself could supply was verbal. Paia taught herself by experiment how to care for the thing, and how to shoot it. She had a soft leather harness crafted, part garment, part holster—and learned to live with it.

And now she feels half-naked without it.

She's stopped listening, she realizes, except in the usual reflex way. There's nothing to hear, nothing but the incessant wind, swirling past the upper terraces, moaning among the steel balustrades. But Paia is wide awake, and her body is taut with an odd, restless energy that cannot be accounted for as mere adrenaline rush. She rolls over and runs an inventory: not thirsty, no hotter than usual, no need to visit the privy. She rarely has trouble sleeping, except in the early hours before a major festival, when her brain won't cease rehearsing every step and detail of the coming ritual. But tomorrow isn't even a minor holy day. In fact, tomorrow her temple calendar is practically empty. So what is this? She feels like she's downed a big swallow from the Sacred Well. It's the same sort of liquid invasion, power and pure sensation coursing toward the very ends of her extremities, pooling in her toes and fingertips: alien, sweet, and chill. She wonders what it means.

She flips aside the pale sheet and sits up. An unlit lantern waits on her bedside table. When the lectric first went off, she kept a flame burning through the night. Then the God pointed out that the light left her just as visible to any potential assailant. So, as she learned to live with the gun, she learned to sleep in darkness. It's never total darkness anyway, not in any room with a window. Paia squints into the deeper shadows at the corners of the room. She considers waking the God, to solicit his opinion of this peculiar sleeplessness. The God has an answer for everything. Paia can't recall him ever saying, "I don't know." Then she remembers he's not at home. Off on one of his mysterious week-long expeditions. He'd be irritable as a viper anyway, having his sleep broken without (what he would consider) due cause, like if the Fortress was under attack, or if it began to rain.

Sitting alone in the hot red gloom, Paia allows herself a moment of self-pity. If only she had someone to talk to. Not just servants and acolytes, or her subordinate priests, always jockeying for position. A friend. The God, of course, would insist that he's all the friend she needs. When he's around, he encourages all manner of intimacy. But Paia knows he doesn't really listen unless she's talking about something that directly concerns him, such as the accounts of the monthly tithing, or his own participation in the next Sacred Festival. He does show a keen appetite for news of her meetings with the various Official Suitors. He demands the finest details, yet leaves her with the distinct impression that he considers this pretty tame stuff—as if, each time, he's hoping for something racier. When he instituted the requirement that all Suitors disrobe, Paia assumed this to be another of his endless security measures, or a (typically) crass way of allowing her to fully inspect the goods on offer. But she recalls him chiding her sternly for exempting Suitors she knows she will reject the moment they enter the Hall of Audiences. She wonders now if what the God *really* enjoys is the full spectacle of each poor man's vulnerability and abject humiliation.

She gets up abruptly and lights the lamp, as if its pale spot of flame could dispel the shadows left in her heart by the last such encounter. She might have favored that one a little, if not for the dull gleam of hatred he could not keep from his eyes as he dropped his robe and stood before her. She wanted to say she would not ask it if the God did not insist, but that would be questioning the God's word in public, a dire offense. As the God has told her many times: he is the God. His word is law.

Paia turns up the lamp flame. The light throws the coffered ceiling into high relief and deepens the folds of the velvet draperies into columns of mystery. She quells her rush of resentment with a sour, quiet chuckle. One day

soon, she vows, I will begin to embroider my reports. Catch
the God by surprise. Describe in painstaking detail all the
clothing *I* took off, and then what happened after. She wonders: would the God be jealous?

She leaves the lamp burning on the table, her emphatic
stride muffled by the layers of antique and threadbare carpets strewn across the slate floor. In her cavernous dressing
room, her hand finds the dead light switch by instinct, pressing it before she can stop herself. Paia grimaces. She prefers
not to be reminded that the lectric is now a precious commodity, reserved for an hour or two of pre-curfew darkness,
or for any and all Temple ceremonies. Better to pretend
that it's always been this way. She grabs the nearest robe
and throws it on. When she was a child, the House Monitor
ran twenty-four hours a day . . . well, at least when it wasn't
broken. Climate control, music and light, intercom and
sonic cleanser, ice water, hot water—all this in every one
of the hundred or so rooms in the House. That's what they
still called it then, a house, even though it was already
becoming a fortress. When the God came, he deactivated
the Monitor and gave all of its functions to people. But
people, Paia is just old enough to remember, are not nearly
as reliable as machines. And it's hot all the time now, whatever season, whatever time of day, though cooler in the
Citadel than outside, due to the interior temperature of the
bedrock, and the giant circulation fans turned by the windmill array at the top of the scarp.

She wraps the robe around her, and then her arms as
well, hugging the thin fabric against her ribs as if its embroidered sheen could smooth away her unexplained restlessness. Halfway to her favorite window alcove, she stops,
turns on her heel, and paces back to the dressing room,
shedding the robe as she goes. Rooting in drawers, she
tosses out fistfuls of clothing behind her—sheer, clinging
silks and brocaded robes, cloth-of-gold vests and gowns
studded with seed pearls, strewn all across the floor in her
search for the garb she can wear only when the God is
not around: her old sweatpants, worn soft with use and
laundering, and a tunic-length T-shirt. Her chambermaid
disapproves of these garments as much as the God does,
and tries to hide them from her. But Paia uncovers them
with a quiet whoop of victory and slides into them, grateful

for the rare opportunity to be unaware of the shape of her body.

Now the odd surging inside her feels good. Strong and positive. Purposeful. She's awake and comfortable; so far, she's roused no one with all her moving about, and suddenly she knows what to do. The restlessness has left her extremities and withdrawn its force tidelike into her interior. Images are washing up on the shores of her mind in waves of white and green and blue. Nothing specific yet—that will come only when the right language is available, when she has a brush and colors in her hand.

Her fingers are on the doorknob when she remembers the gun. She races back to the bed to snatch it from under the silken pile of pillows and shove it into a pocket. Across the room again, Paia twists the knob soundlessly and hauls on the door. Chances are good that the sentries outside in the hall will be asleep, due to the God's absence and to an archaic and inefficient system of seniority that, for his own private reasons, the God has chosen not to overturn. It makes a certain kind of dull sense, Paia admits, to station the youngest and most vigorous downstairs at the points of entry into the Citadel. But she doubts that the God is aware that higher rank also means high priority for the booze ration. She would complain, except that this tends to work in her favor, granting her an extra measure of freedom now and then, as long as she's quiet about it.

Another thing she's learned since the God came: to move about the endless stairs and corridors in near total silence. And because she's positive that her guards try to cultivate a convenient layer of rust on the hinges, she foils them by oiling them regularly. Twice as tall as she and two arms' lengths wide, the heavy slab of paneled oak drifts toward her without so much as a murmur.

"Ha," Paia grins.

A soft chorus of snores floats through the narrow opening. A discord of drunken slumber. Paia pokes her head around the edge of the door. There are four of them, two men and two women—the God thrives on symmetry. There's not a booze jug in sight, but the sweet-sour aroma hangs heavy in the still air. They've all loosened their braided formal collars and drawn up the most comfortable of the stiff, half-upholstered chairs that inhabit the corridor.

Their single lantern is burning low. Paia marvels at their bravery. If the God were to materialize here suddenly, their lives would be ended. But the God is not home, and besides, he'd be forced to appear in man-form in order to fit in this human-sized space. For reasons that Paia does not comprehend, most people find the God less frightening in man-form. Perhaps these four have told themselves that as a group, they could take him if they had to. They would be wrong.

It's the implied presumption, even more than their lack of proper discipline, that rouses Paia's ire. Who do they think they are, sleeping on the job? Is this how the Honor Guard of the Temple protects its High Priestess? When her father was alive, she would have reported such insubordination without a qualm. Their sodden snores abruptly disgust her. She thinks she might report them after all. She draws herself up in the doorway, ready to end their careers, if not their lives. Then she remembers her sweats and T-shirt. How can she appear before these men and women, her servants, her Faithful, dressed no better than they would be in their own homes? Her hair isn't even done. What would they think? Even worse, what would the God say if he found out? Paia is well aware that this issue of reporting infractions goes both ways.

Her shoulders sag. Her chambermaid is right. The High Priestess of the Temple of the Apocalypse needs to be protected from her own impulses.

However . . .

She just cannot imagine going back to bed. There is still this swarm of images inside her head, demanding to be dealt with. Even if she could resist, this opportunity is too precious to waste. She peers at the snorers more carefully, then eases around the edge of the door and ghosts it shut behind her.

Scattered about the hall, tilted this way and that in their straight-backed chairs, the sleeping guards look like a child's tin army abandoned after play. Paia negotiates a slalom course through red-clad legs and spit-polished black boots, careful to create no draft that might alert their soldier's instincts. She's counting on the booze to keep them oblivious.

To her left yawns the wide, dark well of the stairs, leading down to Level Five and further, younger contingents of the Honor Guard. To her right, several shadowed doorways, more chairs and windowless corridor: true darkness. But this is the most "secure" part of the house, and Paia's feet know the way by heart. Now she welcomes the darkness as an ally, abetting her escape. She pads along with her arms stretched low to either side, in case some forgetful cleaner has moved a chair. Sensing a turn, she slows but continues straight ahead until her fingers touch the cut-velvet wall fabric and the hard edge of a deactivated picture box. She does a silent right-face, gliding one hand along the wall—no furniture left along this corridor to avoid. She moves down one long hall, a left turn, down another, until her fingertips find and trace out the intricate profile of the molding that frames the entrance to the tower. Just inside the arch is a little niche for a lantern and matches.

This rising stair is narrower than the formal staircases leading down, which are sized like the corridors to allow a regiment to march through in formation. The tower's steep steps, barely one person wide, coil up serpentlike around a central stone shaft. Paia's hands are shaking with eagerness to be at the top. As if her head might shatter like a dropped melon if she can't let loose the raucous crowd inside. She strikes a match. Once upon a time, the House Monitor's sensors would have provided light, and then betrayed her presence to an on-duty House security guard. But all those banks of screens are dark now. Raising the lamp, Paia begins her climb.

It's a long climb, but Paia claimed this part of the house as her own precisely because of the tower, knowing that its claustrophobic dimensions and its exhausting, dizzying spiral would discourage any but the most determined visitors. She's counted the steps: there are sixty-six of them, carved from the rock of the cliff itself. The front edge of each bears a shallow depression, worn smooth during the two and a half centuries since her family's retreat to this stronghold. There is a faint stain of handprints at waist level along the outside curve of the wall.

She gains the top and steps into a large vaulted chamber lit by the dim red murk pressing in from outside through a far wall of armored glass. A polished stone floor gleams ruddily. Paia's lantern illuminates a chair and a few simple tables, and then the unfinished rear and side walls, still as coarse-textured as if blasted out of the rock only yesterday. Leaning against the walls, rows and rows of stacked canvases. In front of the vast glass wall, a tall wooden easel, empty now, but not for long.

The thrumming in her body intensifies. Paia sets the lantern down on a table, afraid she'll drop it. Then she hurries around the room, gathering up every available lamp and candle, sets them near the easel, and lights them all. She's only adding to the heat in the room, but she doesn't care. Her hands move almost without her knowledge. The image waves are breaking harder and faster now. Her brain is a tornado, a storm at sea. She doesn't want to have to grind and mash and mix and measure, the patient, painstaking process of paint-making that she normally enjoys. She needs to get right to work. She gathers in a hopeful breath, uncovers her palette, lets out the breath in a rush. The paint is still workable. She finds brushes, oil, and an unused canvas. She sets the pale, blank oblong up on the easel and stares at it for half a millisecond. Then she dips her brush and begins to paint.

When the red murk lightens to pink, then to dusty orange, Paia stands back to look at what she's done. Hours have passed unnoticed. Her palette is scraped dry. She has used every last daub of paint available, often not caring what color it was; at least she would lay down form and texture on the canvas while the inspiration burned in her. Even as her candles and lanterns guttered and went out, she kept at it, in the end painting as much by feel as by sight. Not until she lays her brush aside does she realize how tired she is. "Spent" is a better word, she decides. Tapped out. Like she feels after the ten-hour Harvest Festival. As if the whole complex engine of her body has suddenly run out of fuel. Only now does it occur to her how unusual this is.

And what has this frenzy produced?

Impulsively, she'd chosen a large canvas, two meters wide by a meter high, and she has covered every inch of it. The brushwork is taut and kinetic, even for her, and it turns out, the painting is mostly about color, or the sense of light and life that color can convey. Vibrant purple, magenta, and blue shadows stretching beneath sunlit golds and viridian and mauves. Colors she hardly ever uses, which is why they were left over on her palette. She can see this even in the too-amber light of early dawn, before the sun outside has broken the horizon, and she finds it mildly uncanny, since color was the thing she'd given up all control of, sure that she lacked the right pigments.

But her definition of "right" is being challenged by the canvas in front of her. It's a landscape, or rather, a fantasy landscape, because it's like no landscape she's seen or could have seen within her own lifetime. For one thing, it's full of greens, or the colors that green can become when suffused with sunlight. She'd hardly any true greens on her palette, so she made do with what she had. Another thing— it's full of trees. Hardwood trees. She recognizes their shape and texture from the trees left in the little Sacred Grove within the Temple walls. But in this painting, there are entire hillsides of them, a whole valley, in fact, lined with oak and birch and maple as if with the richest velvet. Nestled within the velvet, like the finest satin, a vast and rolling meadow. And the shining jewel caught in its luscious green folds: a silver ribbon of water . . . a river.

A river! Paia is transfixed. How has she done this? She guesses she must be recalling images from her recreational research forays into the family archives—old photographs, prints and paintings, and even video, when the God allows her use of the machines. She frowns, looking around at the other canvases stacked against the walls. Painting after painting of barren hills, dry streambeds, and rocky crags, of air swirled with dust and soot, of sun-parched villages huddled among dying scrub pine. All dry browns and reds and bleached-out yellows. She had thought them beautiful, perhaps because the God always admired them. Now she is not so sure. Since she first picked up a brush, Paia has painted only what she saw in life: what she saw from the upper terraces of the Temple, what she saw from her bedroom balconies or from this luxurious stretch of glass, her giant eye upon the world, perched high in a tower embedded in the sheer rock face of a cliff.

All of a sudden, as if her eyes have turned inside her head, she has painted a landscape she could only hope to dream about.

CHAPTER TWO

That first night back at Deep Moor, Erde was so weak with joy, and so wrung out by all she'd been through, that she forgot to worry about the dreams.

Besides, she felt safe at Deep Moor, even in the snow and wind and unnatural cold. The women there *knew* things. Surely the dreams would not dare to follow her there.

And it began innocently enough, of course, with a calm and silent landscape, sunk in winter. Gentle mounds of snow scattered here and there across a frozen white plain. A rasping of ravens above. A gleam of river ice in the distance, and mountains.

But then she saw, or rather, understood—in the way of dreams—that the mounds were bodies, soldiers dead on the field and covered with snow. Even in her drifting dream state, Erde was shocked. What kind of army would not make time to bury its dead?

Suddenly, a far-off echo, a drumming of hooves. She wanted to turn toward the sound but could not. Her dream gaze was fixed: on the bodies, on the frozen river, on the mountains beyond. The hard rhythm approached, like metal on stone, and with it, an aura of terrible urgency. As the lead horse pounded past, the urgency snatched her up, as if an arm had been hooked around her throat. She was dragged in the horse's wake, and still she could not look behind, could only hear the hoarse cries of the men and the struggle of their horses to catch up.

The lead horse was a tall and powerful gray, well lathered but not yet winded. His rider was oddly unhelmeted, despite the cold and the peril of his horse's mad race. He

was hunched forward over the gray's outstretched neck,
and Erde could not see his face. But she knew this rider
anyway. She knew him from the bold blue and yellow of
his worn battle tabard, from the stubborn set of his ice-
flecked shoulders, from the wind-whipped gold of his hair.
And because it was always his life that the dreams drew
her into.

Her enemy. Adolphus, Baron Köthen. A man she had
met only once. Allied with her traitorous father against the
King. Or had been. Now his loyalties were unclear. But
enemy or no, in the way of dreams, she had no choice but
to ride with him. She found this both terrifying and
exhilarating.

Behind, the men cried out again, incoherent with distance. It seemed that she recognized one of the voices. But
her gaze was still fixed, as Baron Köthen's was, and he did
not look back. She would not have expected him to. He
was too intent on urging the utmost out of the speeding
gray. As usual, he was unaware of her presence, as she flew
along at his ear like a gnat. Only once had he seemed
aware, had he seemed to listen when she spoke to him.
That time, she had saved his life. Or she thought she had,
and it confused her that she'd done so. The man had been
her *enemy*, perhaps still was. Of course, dreams were just
dreams, mere illusions, with no connection to real events.
Erde told herself this, but in her heart, she did not believe
it. Her sense of being there with him was too . . . complete.

The gray swerved suddenly, then launched himself over
a snow mound too massive to be avoided. The corpses were
strewn more thickly as horse and rider neared the river.
The harsh valley winds had scoured the concealing snow,
exposing terrible amputations and dark faces frozen in pain
and horror. Köthen glanced up now, and Erde saw that
there were horses and soldiers between him and the ice-
bound shore. Many of them. Ten, twenty knights at least,
plus a squad of infantrymen, all of them armed and ready,
and watching Baron Köthen's full-tilt approach. But Köthen did not slow the gray horse or turn him aside. Instead,
he reached across his thighs for the sword tucked into its
saddle sheath, and aimed the gray straight into the middle
of them. Soon they were close enough for Erde to recognize the hell-priest's colors on some of the infantrymen.

Just like Brother Guillemo, Erde thought grimly, to put uniforms even on his foot soldiers. The thought of Guillemo made her shiver. Could Köthen and the hell-priest have made up their differences after all, and was he racing back to rejoin the usurping army? If so, he was her enemy again. Erde's beloved grandmother the baroness, may she rest in peace, had brought Erde up to be a loyal subject of the King.

Or perhaps the soldiers ahead were some of Baron Köthen's own men, gone renegade from the priest's army out of loyalty to their lord. But that hope died in the flash of steel across the closing distance, as the knights converged into defense formation. Erde understood that Baron Köthen's charge was an attack. What was the man doing? He would be cut to pieces, without a doubt. And still Köthen drove the gray toward them.

Enemy or no, Erde did not wish him dead. In fact, the idea filled her with a surprising dread. She imagined again that, through the dream, she could speak to him, and she begged him to turn aside. She knew he was a brave man, but she had not thought him reckless. Why would he charge willingly into such overwhelming odds? Had he been driven into this trap by the men behind him?

But then those riders' desperate shouts came to her more clearly, particularly the one voice that had seemed so familiar. They'd been calling him back, and now gave up their shouting to ride as hard as they could. Erde heard their horses coming, faster than before, or was it only that she hoped so for them to catch up? Surely they were too far behind to be able to save him. She pleaded with Köthen to be sensible, to slow down at least, to wait for the others. Dream-wraith that she was, she still could feel the anger in him, heating him like a fever. He was too full of blood-rage to hear her or to listen to reason. Or perhaps he did hear, for once she saw his head jerk when she spoke, as if shaking off a fly. But he neither stopped nor slowed. And glancing ahead, Erde saw why. In their shifting protective dance, the mounted knights drew briefly aside, revealing the man at the center of their formation: the hell-priest himself.

Guillemo. Her nemesis. Stocky and dark, and with his once wild beard now trimmed to obsessiveness, he looked almost ordinary. His white monk's hood was thrown back from his mailed head as he barked orders to his men and raised his short, southern sword as if it were a processional cross. His big horse gleamed as pure and white as the snow around him, or the frozen river beyond. But, oh, what a danger, to think Guillemo either pure or ordinary! Erde's blood ran as cold as that ice-bound river. The snake-eyed priest was staring straight at her, his full red mouth curled in a sly smile of welcome.

So, witch. We meet again.

His voice, right there in her head as she slept. Deep, rich, insinuating. Erde was horrified by how surely he homed in on her. No casting about this time, no sniffing the air. He saw her, as surely as if she were a visible presence in his world. He could speak in her mind.

She recoiled from the fierce beam of his stare as if from a blow and pulled herself inward as if she could become infinitesimal and so escape him. Or conceal herself behind Baron Köthen's head, safe in the warmth beside his ear. But Köthen was barreling full-tilt toward his own destruction, his mind empty of everything but rage and revenge.

The horses behind did seem to be nearing. Erde thought to distract him in some way, if only to slow him down until his allies could catch up, before the big gray burst into the midst of twenty well-armed knights. Forgetting the disembodiment of her dream state, Erde wrapped both invisible hands around Köthen's bridle arm and hauled back hard. His head jerked up. He tossed a sidelong glance behind him and shook his elbow as if to free it from a thorn branch. But there was no branch. Encouraged, Erde hauled back on him again, with all the strength she could imagine. Köthen's eyes rolled sideways, widening in confusion and a touch of fear. The gray horse sensed his fear and missed a step, slowing, nearly stumbling. Erde counted the seconds gained.

But ahead of them, she saw the hell-priest grin.

He fears you, witch girl! Remember, he is only a man, without understanding. Whereas . . .

NO!

She screamed it with all her dream-strength, drowning out his poisonous murmur. As much as Baron Köthen drew her, the hell-priest repulsed and terrified her. At first, she'd assumed he was only after her to burn her at the stake. Now it was clear that he wanted something else. His ability to find her in the dream world was frightening enough. If he ever found her again in the real world . . . Erde's only thoughts were of escape. Her entire being contracted in denial, a vast implosion toward the infinitely small. As her consciousness faded, it occurred to her that anything, even death, would be preferable.

And then someone was shaking her gently awake.

A woman's voice said, low and calm, "Erde? Come back to us. Come back to us, sweeting."

"I've been trying that for ten minutes!" said another, not nearly as collected as the first. "Ever since I heard her cry out! Look! She's not even breathing!"

"Shhh. She's breathing. Help me raise her up a little."

From the verge of the infinite, Erde heard the women's voices like a faraway whisper, carried on the wind. The priest was after her, searching, but she knew these voices. These voices meant safety. Moments from the edge, she veered away and sped homeward toward them.

The snow began falling on their way across the meadows, even before the storm clouds closed in. Big crystalline flakes floating down like autumn leaves. Erde tilted her chin to let their weightless ice melt on her tongue. Even the snow of Deep Moor tasted sweet. She'd never thought snow could be so welcome.

But welcome only because familiar, she reminded herself. Welcome to her as proof that she was *home*. Not so welcome to the two women walking beside her or to anyone in Deep Moor, or even to the laden pony that trudged along behind. Erde wished she could race about kicking up drifts and making snow angels as she might have done months ago when she was still a child in her father's castle. Snow angels were a proper way to celebrate. She thought she restrained herself out of respect for Raven and Doritt, but in truth, after the events of the early morning, her heart wasn't in it. Gratitude and relief were the best she could manage. But even that offended the taller woman's gloom.

"It's all right for you," Doritt grumped, winding her knitted scarf one more turn around her long neck. Erde would swear Doritt was taller than she remembered. But surely she was too old to be still growing? Perhaps it was her chin-to-ankle-length coat, snugged around her sturdy frame like a woolen shroud. Or perhaps, her man-sized leather-and-canvas boots.

"Why just for me?" With Erde's every step, the white layers exploded upward in powdery gusts, reminding her of baking day in the castle kitchens. At that thought, she felt a surge of guilty joy.

"Snows all the time where you come from."

"At Tor Alte? It does not. At least, it didn't used to." Erde wasn't sure what things were like at Tor Alte lately, and she wouldn't ever want to be caught in a falsehood.

"Bet it's snowing right now." Doritt glanced behind to check on the pony's progress. His load of hay and grain and dried fruit was rather precariously balanced on his shaggy, narrow back.

"In the winter, it snowed a lot."

"But it isn't winter yet," Doritt noted grimly.

Erde fell silent. She knew Doritt's concern was not so much the snow itself, but the fact that it was snowing now, only three weeks into September. But she was more worried about the dragons, gone back on an errand of mercy to that hot land she'd so recently returned from, that alien place that made her grateful for snow in September. However bad it was here, it was worse there, and she wished they'd hurry up and come home. She wanted so to talk to them about her dream.

"Doritt doesn't think snow was meant to be enjoyed," said Raven.

"Not true! Everything in its place is just fine with me."

But Raven's eyes were merry. Erde felt her spirits rise again just looking at her, in her usual feathery blue, layered against the cold, and her dark unfettered hair netted with snowflakes like some kind of woodland queen. Erde always marveled, looking at Raven. If she could choose to look like anyone in the world, it would be Raven, no doubt of it.

"Now," said Raven, "you promised to tell us what it was like where the dragon took you."

"It was hot!" Erde allowed herself a little dance step between them, of joy and relief and affection. "Truly! Hot as a smithy's forge! And smelly. The sun beat down on us all day! And you couldn't drink any of the water."

"Why not?"

"N'Doch said it would make us sick. And to make matters worse, he insisted on boiling whatever we drank! Can you believe it?"

"That's what my mother taught me to do with bad water," said Doritt.

"Really? Why?"

Raven laughed. "Because her own mother did it, I'll bet, and her mother's mother before her. Women's wisdom."

Erde made a face. "Well, I hate drinking hot water. I was thirsty the whole time! Couldn't even wear clothes!"

Doritt's eyebrows peaked. "No clothes?"

"Well, you know . . . not proper ones."

"No wonder you turned up so suddenly in your shift!"

Raven's laugh was so warm and musical that Erde was sure she heard it echo around the entire valley, bouncing off the pine-studded hillsides, tangling in the bare branches of the maples and birches, skating along the winding course of the ice-choked river. But the river reminded her of the dream again. To banish its shadow, she grabbed Raven's hands and whirled her around, arms outstretched, to make her laugh some more. Together they sketched a circuit of merry pirouettes around tall Doritt as she forged doggedly ahead, refusing to crack a smile.

Erde flung her arms wide in a whirling embrace of sky, moor, and mountains. "I'm so glad to be home!"

And saying it somehow made it so. This was home now, Deep Moor, this magical, hidden valley. Not Tor Alte, the castle of her birth, home of Baron Josef von Alte, her father. Poor deluded man. Interesting that she could finally think of him without a wince, that she could even imagine meeting him face-to-face. Perhaps this was because she finally understood that home didn't have to be where you came from. It could be where you felt you belonged. Or perhaps it was because, after all she'd seen, in this her fifteenth year, she'd begun to learn how to forgive. She twirled Raven around again, head thrown back in joy. "Hooommmme!"

"Well, you've certainly come out of yourself since we've known you," remarked Doritt, not unkindly.

Erde slowed, relaxed her hold on Raven's hands. "Have I?"

Doritt rolled her eyes.

"Oh, yes." Raven reached to tousle Erde's thick, short-cropped hair. "Such a sober young thing when you first came to us."

"I had a lot to be sober about."

"You still do," replied Doritt. "We all do."

"Oh, again! Mistress Grim!"

But Raven's retort was halfhearted, and Doritt's reminder hung in the air like smoke, bringing a momentary silence. Erde's thoughts strayed back to the dream these women had shaken her out of just hours before. It occurred to her that she didn't yet know if Adolphus of Köthen was dead or alive.

"Isn't it time to talk about the war?" she asked. "I wish you'd tell me the news and how things have been going!"

Raven squeezed her shoulder. "Linden insists you're to be rested and smiling again before we start loading you down with all our problems. Look at how hard you were sleeping this morning!"

"I'm smiling. I'm fine." She hadn't told them what they'd woken her from.

Dorritt clucked. "You slept for two days straight before that."

"Please? I know Linden means well, but I'm not a child anymore. Just some little bit of news?" She couldn't bring herself to actually ask about Baron Köthen. If he were dead, she knew she'd burst into tears like a child, when she more properly ought to be celebrating. "What about Hal?"

"Hal is well, at last report," offered Raven. "We'll all tell all at dinner. There's a lot of your news we haven't heard either."

Erde sighed. She'd hoped for news as a distraction as much as anything else. She didn't feel so giddy anymore, and probably she should tell them why. She glanced over her shoulder at the sky. Billowy gray clouds were massing over the valley's northern end, above the sprawling farmstead that nestled there. She could almost see a material darkness sifting down like ash to smother all cheer, all life within.

"Sometimes . . ." she began finally. In the quiet, even her murmur sounded like a shout. "Sometimes I can hear him, you know . . . Brother Guillemo . . . in my dreams. Like he's speaking to me."

Raven's glance was sharp. "Really? Have you told Rose?"

"I've hardly seen Rose! I've been sleeping so much! I was so tired! I've been . . . !" She was shaken by the sudden anxiety that gripped her, but she couldn't make herself admit to them that she'd dreamed the hell-priest right there in Deep Moor. If he could find her so easily in her dreams, could he locate her in life?

"Well, then," Raven advised, "you can tell her soon as we get back to the house."

"I will. I promise."

In unspoken agreement, the three women quickened their pace. With memories of mad—or maybe not so mad— Brother Guillemo dogging Erde's thoughts, the pristine snow and crisp chill were not so inviting anymore. Instead, a longing gripped her for the sweet tall grasses and wildflowers of the summer meadows, of the Deep Moor she'd known not even a month ago. She'd felt safer then, even though she'd been in the greatest possible peril. And now, Deep Moor was threatened, too. Not just by the weather, but by the homing eye of the hell-priest. She'd promised herself to act like an adult, even more than they expected her to, but she must have shuddered or made some small sound of distress, for Raven curled an arm about her shoulders and gave her a gentle hug.

"Never fear, sweeting. A lot of good minds and hearts are working on this problem. We'll think of something."

Erde nodded dutifully. Before this morning, she had believed that the women of Deep Moor could stand against the hell-priest, against anything. Now she was not so sure.

The Grove loomed ahead like a ruined cathedral. The bare branches of its encircling oaks reached up like burned timbers grabbing at the sky. The thick, dark trunks curved in even ranks like the charred piers of a fallen apse. Erde scolded herself for the childish thinking that had let her hope to find this stand of sacred oaks still green and heavy

with summer, with the warm sighing of leaves and birdsong.
But the leaves lay buried beneath the snow and the birds
were stilled. She moved among the huge, knotted trunks in
a daze, as if she'd lost something precious. She wished the
dragon were there. His very existence was a comfort. Erde
knew she could never completely lose hope, as long as
there were dragons in the world.

In the center of the Grove lay a pond no bigger than a
cottage and as smoothly circular as the face of the full
moon. Erde had suspected there was Power in this pond
the first time she laid eyes on it. Now she was sure. The
shallow crystalline water glimmered softly, without a trace
of ice. All around its perfect silver arc, the snow pulled
back, as if out of respect, revealing a brief but cheering
fringe of green.

Raven and Doritt led the pony to the bank and began
to unpack the load. Doritt untied the two big sheaves of
hay and spread them out beside the water. Raven cleared
patches of snow, then handed out sacks of fruit and grain
to scatter on the ground.

"Hope this'll hold 'em," Doritt muttered.

"Oh, tut," Raven reproved cheerfully. "There's plenty
more for a while."

"As long as it's the *usual* while."

"We've lived through long winters before."

"Not winters that started in early September."

"We have stores for a year. *You* always insist on it."
Raven emptied her last sack with a flourish, then whistled
up into the barren branches. A sudden flutter of wings
broke the silence, and small flocks of birds whirled in to
settle among the seed. Off among the trees, Erde saw the
deer waiting. And then something else caught her eye.

"Raven, Doritt, look . . . on the other side of the pond.
See that odd bunch of sticks?" The sticks formed a tall but
neatly rounded pile, very like something she'd seen before.
"Doesn't it look like . . . ?"

"Windfall," said Doritt. "No, too neat. Someone's
brush pile."

"No one would be cutting wood in the Grove," Raven
countered.

Then Erde remembered. "I know! It's . . ."

"Like a beaver lodge," Raven murmured. "Hmmm."

"Oh, my," said Doritt. "Could it be . . . do you suppose . . . ?"

"Got to be."

The two women dropped their empty sacks and hurried around the pond. Erde followed close behind. The pile was larger than it had seemed from across the water, but much smaller and more hastily thrown-together than the one she'd seen before, on the quiet shore of a lake. No soft moss climbed these walls and no comforting smoke coiled up from the center of the roof. Raven circled around to the far side.

"Aha!" she exclaimed, and stepped forward briskly to knock on a crude wood-plank door set among the twigs.

"He won't answer, you know," offered Erde faintly, drawing on her own brief experience, now intensely recalled.

Raven smiled and knocked again. "He will for me."

Erde thought this rather overconfident, even for Raven. "Hal practically had to beat the door down."

Raven grinned. "That's always been Hal's problem."

"What's he doing here is the real question." Doritt leaned in worriedly to peer at the door.

"Exactly what we're going to find out." Raven knocked a third time, no louder than the first. "Are you there, Gerrasch? Open up, dear soul—you have visitors!"

A wild rustling and grunting erupted inside, making the stick pile shudder. Erde took a long step backward. The plank door cracked open. In the narrow darkness, she saw a familiar pair of beady eyes above a shiny damp nose.

"About time!" the darkness growled.

Raven trilled her musical laugh. "Well, now, sweet, if you neglect to announce your arrival, you can't expect your welcome to be spectacular and timely!"

Doritt leaned farther into the doorway. "Hallo, Gerrasch, old thing. What brings you all this way?"

"Cold. Cold cold cold cold."

"Is it warmer here, then, than out there?" Raven raised an eyebrow at her companions.

"Yes. No. No food, no food. Hungry. A big snow coming."

"You came to the right place—we've food enough to share."

"Big *big* snow. Scared."

"What? You? In your cozy lakeside burrow?" Raven crouched to bring her nose level with the beady eyes. "Scared of a little snow?"

"No! No, no. Listen! Men. Horses. Burned my house. No home. All gone."

"Men burned your house?" The women traded glances. Erde recalled that dark and smoky hovel, hidden in the curl of a brush-choked cove, crammed to its twiggy rafters with jars and bottles and herbs and . . . well, *stuff.* How awful for him to lose all those years of collecting.

"What men?" asked Doritt.

But Erde shuddered, remembering a terrified woman tied to a stake in a far-off market town. She didn't need to ask what men. Who else was going around burning everything in sight?

"Guillemo," muttered Raven darkly.

"Want to burn *me!*" The planks creaked and swung inward. A furry, long-nailed hand gripped the doorframe, then Gerrasch's shaggy, rag-draped bulk filled the opening and Erde recalled why she'd first thought he was some kind of gigantic beaver. "Want to burn me!"

"Poor creature!" murmured Raven.

"Burn us all if he could," Doritt remarked. "How'd you get away?"

Gerrasch's bright eyes, until now fixed entirely on Raven, shifted to the older woman with a crafty squint. "Run run. Scurry. Around, around, cover trail, around around more, cover trail, around around . . . come here."

Raven laughed and patted his hand. "Clever thing! Brave old soul! Well, you're safe here."

"No!" Gerrasch shook his mane until the whole stick pile trembled. "Not safe! No one safe!"

"For a while at least."

The creature took a breath, sighed. "Yes."

But Doritt's mouth tightened. "How long, do you think?"

Erde shivered. What Doritt was really asking, no one could answer: how long could they keep Deep Moor hidden from outside eyes, now that the priest's forces ranged the land so widely? One misplaced confidence, one single soldier of the wrong stripe stumbling upon their secret path—

that was all it would take to bring the hell-priest's armies down on top of them. And then there was her dream. What if the hell-priest could follow her here? Gerrasch's glance slid away again. He let it round an entire circuit of the Grove before returning to settle it for the first time squarely on Erde.

She smiled at him wanly. "Hello, Gerrasch. Remember me?"

He gasped. "It speaks!" Then he cracked a huge grin.

Erde grinned with him. It was impossible not to. "Yes, my voice is back. You were right—there was a word stuck in my throat. It was somebody's name, a friend I thought had died horribly."

Gerrasch blinked at her, sobering, then leaned forward to lay one stubby finger gently across her throat. "Yes. Ludolph."

Raven sucked in a breath. "Ha."

"No . . ." replied Erde carefully. "That was not his name."

"Yes."

"No, Gerrasch, it was . . ."

"Ludolph!" Gerrasch insisted, then he smiled again, dazzlingly. "Will be."

"Ludolph?" murmured Doritt. "The dead prince?"

"The not-dead prince." Raven chuckled.

"He's saying Rainer is Ludolph?"

"He wouldn't be the first person."

Doritt clucked. "Oh, how would he know about such things!"

"You have your ways, don't you, Gerrasch? And won't our Hal be delighted to hear you agreeing with him for once!"

Erde pondered her own ambivalent response to this news. Did she even care anymore if Rainer was the King's lost heir? He was lost to her already. Besides, she had more important responsibilities now. And as if this thought was some kind of signal, Gerrasch stepped forward suddenly, his nose lifted in the direction of the farmstead. At the same moment came the familiar soft explosion in Erde's head that heralded the dragon's return. Her heart reached out joyously to welcome him.

"They're back!" she exulted. "They're back!"

Gerrasch's nose worked furiously. "Two! Oh, two. Two two two!"

Raven nodded. "Yes, clever thing. Our Earth has found himself a sister. A beautiful blue sister!"

Doritt's eyes narrowed. "How did he know?"

Erde didn't care. The dragons were back! Now she could celebrate in earnest. "Yes, a sister! Her name is Water. You'll like her, Gerrasch! You can go swimming together!" She tugged at Raven's sleeve. "Come, let's go back!"

Raven chortled. "Gerrasch hates swimming. Absolutely has to live by water, but never goes in."

"Come on! Hurry! Let's all go!"

"Right," said Doritt. "Come on, Gerrasch. Gather up anything you need, and we'll load it on the pony."

Gerrasch raised both hands, exposing his soft pink palms. "No. No no. Big storm."

"Yes, so you don't want to stay out here alone, do you? You'd be much safer at the farm."

"No no no." He backed into the shadow of his doorway. "New house. I like it."

"It'll blow apart in the first gust, Gerrasch!"

"Will not!"

Doritt took a step after him. "Of course it will! You could have a nice warm spot in the barn . . ."

In the barn with the dragon, Erde realized. Probably Gerrasch did, too.

"No!" He withdrew his head entirely and slammed the door.

"You are so rude!" Doritt yelled after him.

Raven touched her arm. "You've made him anxious, dear. You can't pressure him. You know how he is. Let him do as he likes."

"But . . ."

"He'll be as safe in the Grove as anywhere. He knows that. That's why he came here."

"It could be the dragons," said Erde. "He didn't want to meet Earth before either. But he knew, didn't he . . . he sensed their return almost before I did."

"He's connected with them in some way," guessed Raven. "As he is to many things."

Indeed, Erde noted. Connected in some way she didn't understand. She must be sure to ask the dragon about it.

Certainly it was no mystery to her why the hell-priest wanted to burn this odd creature. She herself was unsure if Gerrasch was man or animal, or some uncanny combination of the two, and Brother Guillemo feared anything that smacked of a power he couldn't control or comprehend. She put aside her impatience to be with the dragon long enough to lean close to cracks in the plank door. "Maybe later, if the weather holds, I'll bring them out to visit you. Would that be all right?"

No reply from inside the stick pile. Erde glanced back at Raven and Doritt, then shrugged and let her dragon's return fill her mind entirely.

CHAPTER THREE

Halted on the narrow stairs, N'Doch steadies himself and lets the dragon's return blast through him like a drug rush. It's okay. He knows how to handle it now. He's given up any serious resistance. But he tells himself he'll never really get used to it, maybe never even like it much, this simultaneous elation and submission, the ecstatic release of self that the dragons inspire. The girl is into it bigtime, but it makes N'Doch feel invisible.

Maybe he *should* get into it. Might be the only way to face what's waiting for him at the bottom of these creaky old wooden stairs. Strange faces, different customs, a language he doesn't speak, a whole new world to step into, with this magic, dragon-mended body of his which fits him stiff and tight, like a new suit.

The image of himself in an actual suit makes N'Doch laugh, and his ribs ache. The pain isn't much, just enough to remind him that those ribs were lately in a million pieces. Barely twenty and already he's died and been resurrected. Or so they tell him, these witchy women who've been overseeing his recovery. N'Doch has no memory of the event. Only this floaty sense of not quite understanding how the world works anymore. Kind of like standing out on the ledge of a high-rise in the middle of a hurricane.

He does recall, in searing detail, the dream he had while he was coming out of it. Not a dream, really, more like a vision: of red heat and dust and ruined buildings, and himself running. And an awareness, even in his woozy state, that he must store away every detail he can of that blasted landscape, because someday soon he's gonna need to get back to it.

He tests his legs, still wobbly beneath him. Long time 'fore he'll trust these legs to run again. He knows he should get on downstairs and find out if they brought the old man back with them, see if he's all right, or if he would even come. *Hell, I could ask them from here, right from this step.* Then he wouldn't have to move and show how awkward he is in his body since they revived him. He could just open up the old mind channel and give the blue dragon a call. But he won't. Bad enough doing it when he really has to.

He looks slowly around, like the practice at taking in detail is a good enough excuse to postpone the inevitable. He sees walls of wood and plaster, low dark ceilings crossed with thick beams, a fat candle burning behind the sooted glass of a sconce at the turning of the stair. He could be in one of those Ye Olde theme parks, one of the v.r. ones. He moves quietly down to the landing, where a small square window offers a view of snow-covered fields and enclosing mountains, stuff he's only seen in vids. He lays a palm to the rippled glass, feels the cold seeping through the panes to meet the warm draft rising from the rooms below. He shivers. For some weird reason, he's wondering how his mama's doing.

He hears footsteps, and one of the witchy women appears at the bottom of the stairs, not the healer but the shorter, older one with the earth-colored dress and the really intense voice. He thinks her name is Rose. She's smiling up at him like she knows everything he's going through, so like, there's no point in even bringing it up.

N'Doch can't help but smile back. A grin, really. Kind of weak and sheepish. "Here I am," he says.

"Indeed you are," replies Rose in her accented, faintly formal French. "And are you coming down, or spending the afternoon on the stairs?"

N'Doch likes her already, though he's damned if he's gonna let her know it. "Thought I might just hang, y'know? 'S nice here." He nods at the intricately carved beams above his head. "All this old-timey wood and stuff. You folks really know how to build back here in 913."

"Actually, this part of the house was built at least two

hundred years ago." Rose's mouth quirks. "Even before
my time . . ."

"Hey, not as much as before mine." N'Doch likes that
he doesn't have to explain himself to her. Probably the girl
has done that already. He wonders what kind of stuff she's
said about him. Mostly bad, he suspects. He knows how
she doesn't approve of him. He studies Rose's face, to see
if she looks old-timey, too. Certainly her clothes do. Even
her shoes look handmade. But aside from her funny accent,
she walks and talks like a regular person. N'Doch is so
relieved, he doesn't even bother to be surprised.

Rose sets one foot on the bottom stair and leans amiably
against the railing. "How does it feel to be on your feet
again?"

He readies his usual smart-mouth answer, then swallows
it in a puff of breath and feels it settle like gas into the pit
of his stomach. Her compassion is ready and genuine, and
her eyes go straight to his gut. Already he's tired of listening to himself. "A little shaky," he says instead.

Rose nods. "Well, when you're up to it . . . there's a
certain dragon outside eager to see you alive and well."

"Yeah. I know." N'Doch notices how the word "dragon"
comes out of her mouth without a hitch, like it's nothing
new, she's known of such things all her life. He wishes he
could say it so easily. He squints at the wall beside him,
strokes a finger across the fine stippling of bumps. His own
dark hand is like negative space moving against the plaster's whiteness. Downstairs, all the faces he sees will be
white. "Did they bring the old man?"

"No."

N'Doch glances back at her. "No? Hey, why not?"

Rose holds his gaze steadily. "Why don't you ask her?"

He remembers the old man asking him that, in the very
same tone. *She's witchy*, he reminds himself. Just like Papa
Dja. They talk to you like they know everything about you.
"Why don't you?" he blurts, and then he's sorry for it.

Especially when she says, "Because I cannot talk to dragons. That is, not without a lot of trouble I'd rather not go
to just now. Talking to dragons is your gift. That's why
you're here."

And that's about the only reason, N'Doch tells himself.
For sure that's why they brought me back to life. He knows

he's carrying this stubborn thing far beyond sense, but he can't quite let it go. Maybe it's his last chance. He's been waiting for the dragon's siren music to come up here after him, into his brain like she usually does. But so far, she's left him alone. Announced herself, then let him be. She must be busy. Too busy to bother with him. "What about the girl? She talks to 'em better'n I do."

"Erde went with Raven and Doritt to feed the animals in the Grove."

Since none of this information means anything to N'Doch except the girl's name—which he never uses anyway—he lets it pass. "Okay, just give me a sec. I'm coming."

"Are you?"

"Do I got a choice?"

Rose's smile warps gently. "Do any of us?"

N'Doch can't think of a smart answer to that one. He's not sure there is one. "I'll be there."

Rose nods, then turns away and disappears from his line of sight, N'Doch lets his gaze drift back to the little window, where huge white flakes are drifting down from a lead-gray sky. He sees himself running, through flames, through a city in flames, trying to . . . desperate to . . . he can't remember. Only the place itself. That he sees, outlined against the milk-white snow, with gut-wrenching clarity.

"I'll be there," he says again, without moving.

CHAPTER FOUR

Paia is still staring at the painting when the squat red sun clears the scrawl of mountains. Her tower studio burns with dusty light as the first traces of the daytime heat bleed through half a centimeter of armored glass. She can hear the morning gongs now, faint and rhythmic. If she lays her palms against the window wall, she'll feel the heat and the dull reverberations from below, a metallic conscience calling to remind her that the day has once again begun and with it, her solemn duties in the Temple.

Of course, she'd much prefer to stay where she is, floating guilty and free among trees and rivers in this blue-green world of her imagination. But they'll come looking for her eventually, her guards and chaperones. An alarm will be raised if her bed is found empty, and a crisis of such vast proportions will ensue until she's found, that Paia hasn't the heart or nerve to set it in motion.

She takes a step back from the painting, hoping this one brave move will break its spell. But the distance only sharpens her longing to be there, not beside it but *in* it. This is worrisome. She repeats to herself a few of the God's stern admonitions about the danger of nostalgia, what he calls "the Green Heresy." His catchphrase is *Survive the day*. He's even worked it into the Temple litany. The God, in his own hedonistic way, is a pragmatist, and Paia sees the sense in it. So she steels herself and turns away, searching for a square of oilcloth to cover the still-moist paint, to hide the siren landscape from her susceptible gaze, or from anyone who might venture up here. For it is perilously subversive, this painting she's made. It makes one yearn too piercingly to have what one cannot, and be where one can never go.

She roots out an antique plastic tarp, crackling with age. She had been saving it, as a relic of her childhood when plastic things were everywhere and still relatively functional. But opening it now seems the right thing to do—to risk a little shredding along the fold lines for the sake of her sanity, to properly blot out the demon image. She should paint it over, is what she should really do. But she can't bring herself to do that. Already she's planning how she can set time aside during the day to sneak back upstairs, to draw aside the faded blue tarp, and gaze once more on this forbidden landscape. Paia wonders if she's having a crisis of faith.

She remembers a word from her studies, an ideal from a long time ago when an image of wilderness could embody paradise and perfection. It's a name, a concept, really. She decides to title the painting "Arcadia."

And once the concealing tarp is in place, it's easier to pack up her paints, drop her brushes in oil, and head down the winding staircase, snatching a trailing silk robe off a handy hook to hide her undignified T-shirt and sweats. Traipsing along the empty corridor, like she's just been for a walk, she surprises the dawn contingent of the Honor Guard as they're settling into their watch. They snap to startled attention as she sails past them with an august wave, too fast for them to even consider her unkempt appearance, and shuts the door firmly in their faces. Oh, later they'll remark on it, and there will be questions asked down below, about how she came to be outside her quarters when the retiring duty guards each have sworn—in the God's name—that the High Priestess slept through the night, peaceful and undisturbed. No doubt there will be new faces outside her door tonight. Paia doesn't care. Only that if a general alarm is avoided, the commandant is unlikely to inform the God of a few minor changes in personnel. She's never tried keeping a secret from the God before, but lately he's been railing harder against what he calls "sybaritic visions" of the lost green past, a subversive mythology encouraged by a few stubborn pockets of hereticism who, in order to sow unrest among the Faithful of the Temple, raise false hopes of a new "Greening." There are even rumors, overheard only in whispers, of a Green messiah. So Paia knows if the God sees this painting, he'll have it destroyed. And she's not sure she could bear that.

Seconds after she's shed her sweats and mashed them guiltily into a bottom drawer, her chambermaid is knocking discreetly at the door with the morning water ration and the breakfast tray, ready to draw her bath and lay out the appropriate Temple garments for the dressers when they arrive. One of the privileges of rank that Paia treasures most is her access, however intermittent and undrinkable, to hot and cold running water. The lower floors of the Citadel are without hot water these days: the God won't allow them the energy to heat it. When he threatened to turn her own hot water off, Paia argued that she'd inherited the right to it. After all, it was her ancestors who'd chosen the site of their final retreat with enough prescience to build on top of a deep and integral aquifer, not to mention their subsequent protection of it with all the force and technology their considerable fortune could buy. Two hundred and fifty years later, the water still flows, though not with the purity or volume that it used to. Now the water is filtered and boiled for human consumption. and lately, the God has talked of it running out, perhaps within Paia's lifetime. This could be his usual apocalyptic rhetoric, or it could be true. With the sensors deactivated, she has no way of knowing for sure. She does know that raising the water up to the surface has become consistently more difficult as conditions worsen. But for now, the God has let himself be convinced. So Paia has water to bathe in, though she's not allowed to squander so much as a drop. From the drain in her tiny bathtub, the water falls directly into a cistern that feeds the Citadel's water-starved kitchen gardens.

The only mystery in this neat system is the Sacred Well in the Temple yard, which remains filled to the brim even in the deepest drought and without encouragement from the aging pumps or the windmills that line the top of the Citadel's ridge. The sacred water needs no purifying. It even tastes different, always icy cold, clear, and sharp as a gust from off the pole. This inexplicable wonder and the God himself are the twin foundations of Paia's faith.

The chambermaid knocks again while Paia is searching

for her discarded nightgown. She finds it, throws it on, and flops down in her favorite window alcove to calm her breathing before calling permission to the girl to enter.

The breakfast tray is laid before her on a cloth of gold embroidered with images of the God Rampant. Paia thinks he looks very handsome that way. She also thinks that the breakfast looks more than usually appetizing—one of the much pampered melon vines must finally be bearing. She's grateful that today's duties in the Temple are not ones that require fasting. Her long night's exertions have left her famished. It would be a shame if the chambermaid does, as Paia suspects, subsist entirely on her mistress' leftovers, because this morning, the High Priestess intends to devour everything put in front of her.

Paia lets her voice rise in the call to prayer, in the precise tone and pitch that the God has taught her. The intense heat in the Sanctuary rimes her body with sweat, and the metal band of her jeweled headdress itches intolerably. But the ritual is nearly over. This is the final prayer, where the Faithful are to echo the formal pleadings of the High Priestess for the God to lead them safely through the Last Days of the World. After that, there's only the processional, a short march out past the Sacred Well to the Temple Plaza for the purification and sacrifice. Already the huge bronze doors have swung open as if by magic, and the lethal sun has laid a bright path between the paired columns of the inner court, straight down the center aisle between the shadowed ranks of kneeling Sons and Daughters of the God.

Yet this is the part that always frightens Paia the most: the moment when she must come down the seven holy steps from the raised and gated safety of the dais, and walk among the Faithful with only the God's little gun for protection. To be sure, the side and rear walls of the Sanctuary are lined with well-armed members of her Honor Guard. But always at this moment, they seem a very long way away, certainly longer than the easy arm's length she is from potential death with each row of celebrants she passes. But the God insists that she do this at least once in every ceremony. These are fearful and violent times, he agrees, and there is fear and violence in their hearts. But it's a sign of her favor with him, he explains, that she dares to walk so freely among them. Besides, those lost in fear and violence have the greater need for her compassion. *Her* compassion, Paia notes, not his. Finally, he says, the Faithful need the actual contact with her "reality." So, while Paia wishes that the God's idea of priestly vestments allowed for a little more coverage, she's grown used to them touching her, men and women alike, to the drawing of their worshipful palms and fingers across the bare skin of her arms and legs and back. It is, she reflects in her more profane moods, the only touching she gets, or will get, until the "right" Suitor comes along and is approved by the God.

Speared by the hot shaft of sunlight, Paia slow-steps down the aisle with her head held high and her eyes on the freedom of the open doorway. A low-ranking Daughter is leaning out into the aisle ahead, out of eagerness, not disrespect. An older woman, missing one hand. Not a likely threat. Paia glides by, feels the woman's stub brush her back reverently. She must never rush, never show an inkling of fear. But she will feel safer when she reaches the shaded Inner Court, near the Sacred Well, or even outside in the sun-drenched but open Temple Plaza. Her favorite ceremonies end in the Inner Court. The Temple Sanctuary is the God's domain, as is the Plaza. Her own holiest of holies is the Well.

She clears the mammoth doors with a private sigh of relief, pauses at the Well's smooth dark oval to scoop icy water with her own sanctified hands into a golden bowl offered by one of her priestesses, then moves out onto the pale marble paving of the Plaza. She is trailed by the rest of her retinue, twelve thin First Daughters in red robes and red veils with whom she is not allowed to socialize. She's never even seen them without their veils—would not know them if she ran into one of them in the hallways. The God says the High Priestess must declare her august stature and superior dignity by not mingling. For this reason, she is not a Son or a Daughter, but a Mother to them. Mother Paia. It makes her laugh. In truth, she is nobody's mother, and she is not sure her dignity is best preserved by being always alone.

A contingent of the Honor Guard falls in behind the Twelve, and then come the Faithful, shuffling, eyes downcast, crowding up against each other like herd animals, even in the stifling heat. Now there's the sacrifice to be got through.

Paia turns left toward the huge Altar of the Winged God, an oblong ton of raw granite stained with the blood of countless prayers to the Deity. The usual complement of the lower priesthood awaits her there, ranged formally behind the tall and impressive figure of First Son Luco, Paia's immediate subordinate. Of all the colorless functionaries the God has surrounded her with, this is her favorite. Paia almost likes Luco. He is kind in his own odd way and more often amusing than irritating. He's uninterested in her sexually and ambitious for the Temple, which is no doubt why the God permits her a limited association with him. Perhaps he hopes the good examples set by Luco's unswerving faith and devotion to duty will rub off on her. It is Luco who actually manages the day-to-day affairs of the Temple, so his avid claim on the giant sacrificial Knife is a favor Paia is only too willing to grant. He holds it crosswise in front of him now, its heavy golden hilt tucked to his hip like a favorite child. In front of him on the altar, a sturdy Third Son, stripped to the waist, restrains a young goat.

Paia suppresses the frown that would betray her surprise at seeing a sacrifice as major as a well-formed goat kid being offered at so inconsequential a ceremony. The God has explained the need for the sacrificial rite rather patiently, given how many times Paia has been bold enough to suggest that it's a waste of valuable livestock. She falls back on this practical argument, knowing that notions of mercy will be lost on him. His reply is always the same: "For the true believers, only the spilling of blood is a proper recognition of the nobility of their sacrifices for the Faith."

In other words, only blood will keep them quiet. Paia wonders if this goat has come from the Temple flocks, or if some merchant's wife is finally pregnant and hoping for a healthy child. And Luco, she notes, is decked out in full makeup and all his best finery—his billowing and dazzlingly white Temple pants, clasped at the ankles with bands of gold and sapphire, his tallest headdress, his sandals with the heels. A crimson velvet vest—his favorite, sewn with winged images of the God in glittering gold—

frames the shaved and oiled muscles of his chest. Sometimes Paia suspects that Luco dresses to look like the God in man-form, though this has to be unconscious. It would be, officially, a sacrilege. But First Son Luco is wily enough to know that imitation is the sincerest form of flattery, to which the God is famously susceptible.

Approaching, Paia nods to Luco in ritual welcome. She accepts the golden bowl from her priestess and takes her place to Luco's right at the head of the altar to begin the Invocation of the Winged God.

She's halfway into it, the vessel of sacred water raised above her head, when she feels the God return. Elation and terror churn in the pit of her stomach. She stumbles over a word, holds firmly to the bowl but leaves out an entire line of the prayer. She is waiting for that high, vast, swooping shadow to darken the sun over the courtyard. He is here. Her awareness of him is like the Temple gong sounding inside her. But he does not show himself. Paia blinks and steadies her voice. Her own belief in the God of the Apocalypse has less to do with his messianic promises than with her uncanny sense of connection to him. She fears him, often hates him, but she loves him, too. Until his arrival in the Citadel, she had never felt entirely whole. Even now, his return completes her, in a way no human ever could.

Paia finishes the Invocation, aware of the First Son surreptitiously readying the Knife as the sacred water blesses the altar with its precious moisture. Luco hates to be caught unprepared. He takes great—some might say, unholy—pride in finishing off each sacrifice with a single graceful stroke.

The young Third Son steps back, leaving the goat alone on the altar. Luco's giant shining blade arcs skyward. All eyes follow but Paia's. She has seen one too many small creatures bleed their innocence away on the rough, stained stone. For this reason, and for this reason only, she spots the brief flash among the crowd of priests and acolytes to the other side of her. She is already ducking away from the smaller knife when it slashes across the empty space where her throat has just been. The throng presses around her. She cannot see her attacker, only a robed arm and a moving blade, thin and deadly. Beside her, Luco swings his gilded curve of steel, down, down, and completes a perfect stroke. Blood sprays outward. Paia, fumbling for her hidden gun, falls against a First Daughter behind her. She thinks for a moment that the blood is her own, particularly when the young priestess screams and snatches at Paia's stained limbs in horror. The formation at the altar breaks rank and erupts with shouting and outrage. Luco is jolted out of his post-sacrificial trance. He leaps to Paia's side with the holy blade at the ready. Paia points. The attacker is spotted forcing a desperate path through the worshipers crowding the Plaza. He gets nowhere. The Faithful grab him, bring him down, sucking him into their maw with cheers and wild eyes and raised fists.

And then, a vast shadow sweeps across the hot sky, across and back, fleeter than any cloud, nearing, descending. The throng stills as the shadow circles and drops with a flare of scales and sun and golden wings onto the paving stones in front of the altar.

The throng of the Faithful draws back with a gasp of reverence, then spits out the attacker, sprawling and face-down. The terrified man mewls and grovels at the feet of the God, who pins him to the stones with a single golden claw at his neck, then lifts his great horned head and roars to the heavens until the air itself vibrates. The Faithful moan as one and fall to their knees. When silence has settled again, the God returns his attention to his groveling victim. He snarls and unleashes a sudden blue-white gout of flame that sears the man to a spasming cinder.

The crowd sighs. Their God has returned.

Paia's knees buckle. Son Luco catches her.

"Look sharp, now," he murmurs in her ear. "Everybody's watching."

CHAPTER FIVE

A woman laughs and calls out a name. A last set of footsteps fades. A door shuts softly. N'Doch feels the house empty out below him. He inhales the silence in long slow breaths. They're all out there now, in the snow, probably crowding around the dragons, petting and cooing like women do. Something in him disapproves of that. Like, the fact of dragons is amazing enough . . . why make a big thing of it, let it go to their heads? What he'd never admit is that he might be a little jealous. She's *his* dragon, after all.

N'Doch shifts his weight and stares resolutely out at the falling snowflakes. He sees they're starting to blow around a little, and for a moment he thinks how he'd really prefer to be one of them, floating free in the crystalline air. He hates this feeling of being caught, of being seduced and repulsed simultaneously. But he knows he can't spend the rest of the day halfway down the stairs, like the clever, witchy Rose woman ribbed him about. That would be even more ridiculous. Ought to take a look around. Ought to get this patched-up body moving.

Right.

This gets him down the stairs and partway across the dim, low-ceilinged room at the bottom, where he's stopped dead by the undeniable reality of everything he sees. How could he have thought that VR was an equal substitute for the real McCoy? For these heavy wooden chairs with woven seats, those long tables, or that stone fireplace half the width of the wall. Or this neat stack of wood, that bucket of twigs for kindling. That one lantern burning on a stool at the far end.

Of course it's real, he tells himself. The girl came from here, and she's real enough. But now he sees that, ever since he woke up in that tiny, strange room upstairs, he's been reserving the possibility that it all might be some kind of illusion, dragon-induced, a dream. And that possibility has kept him sane and balanced . . . until now.

He drags one hand along the planks of a table by the fireplace. The wood is silky with age and wear. And suddenly his heart is pounding and his hands are in fists. He's taking in air in great heaving gulps. He wants to run, run, escape, like he's trapped, buried alive beneath the very *real* weight of this alien century. But there's nowhere he can run to, he knows that now, at least not outside these particular walls. Nowhere he can go that will be anything like home.

N'Doch flattens both palms on the tabletop and presses downward until his skin molds itself to the cracks and the worn grain of the wood. The pain lets him focus. He forces himself to relax. His life's never been easy so far, and he hasn't survived this long by letting panic rule him. He lets out a shaky but controlled sigh, straightens, and looks around.

The room is long and low, lit mostly by bright flames from the hearth and cold gray light from the many windows along one side. On the table beside him are baskets of shelled nuts, and wooden platters piled with dried podlike stuff that N'Doch doesn't recognize. In front of the window nearest the fireplace sits a tall wooden wheel with a little seat attached and a spike wound with fuzzy looking string. There's something familiar about it, but N'Doch can't quite place the device, or what it's for. There are garments and bits of fabric scattered here and there, and a clay pitcher and cups on one of the smaller tables. The room looks well broken-in, like it gets a lot of use but also, a lot of care.

He steps toward the windows, feeling the chunky hand-cut beams skim past just above his head. Must be he's a lot taller than the folks who built this place. There's a door between the windows, but he doesn't go there just yet. He stoops for a look through the glass.

Outside the windows, a roofed stone terrace runs the length of the house. Opposite the door, a few steps and a

stone path lead off through a screen of leafless bushes. Past
the bushes, a big open space is rapidly filling up with snow.
And there she is.

Ah.

No matter how resentful or resistant he's been to her,
the dragon's beauty has never failed to take his breath
away. And against this cold white landscape, her colors
shine like sapphires and emeralds, or at least this is how
N'Doch imagines such fabulous jewels would look. The
other one, the big guy Earth, he's there, too: all dark and
bronzy like agate and smoky quartz, the cheap stuff you
could find in the markets at home. Earth's only claim to
beauty is his curving ivory horns. His stout and gleaming
claws are made less threatening by being softly blunted at
their tips. N'Doch thinks you'd have to go some to find the
big guy threatening, but he admits he didn't always feel
that way. And he decides that Earth looks handsomer than
he remembers him. Maybe a bit bigger, too, and not so
downtrodden-looking. There's even a hint of glimmer to
his plated sides.

The dragons are sitting side by side in the clearing, and
the snow is melting right out from underneath them as the
women crowd around to pet and admire them. N'Doch's
mouth twists. His heart wants to be out there, or a part of
it does, stroking Water's silky hide, letting her warmth
drive out the bone-deep chill he's felt since he woke up
from his vision of running. He doesn't see the girl anywhere
yet, so probably he should be out there translating. But his
feet won't take him. Not just yet.

He turns back into the room, away from the dragon-
tinted light. He spots a big, stringed instrument, kind of
like an acoustic guitar, propped against a chair. It's like a
searchlight in fog-shrouded darkness, an anchor in stormy
seas. He makes a beeline for it, picks it up reverently, and
smooths his fingertips across its strings—a parched man
reaching for water. There are more strings than he's used
to, and the body is bulbous and pear-shaped like one of
those little bush mandolins made out of a gourd. But this
sucker is big and built out of smoothly joined pieces of
wood. There's a lot of it to hang on to. N'Doch cradles it
in his arms.

The long neck is fretted in a more-or-less familiar way,

but the head with its many wooden pegs is set at a sharp angle to the neck, so at first it looks to N'Doch as if it's broken. He hauls a chair back and sits. The tone is sweet and resonant. It sends shivers of desire across his back. He hasn't played an acoustic anything for a long time, but the thing comes up into his embrace like a lover and he's sure he can get the hang of it.

The moment he curls his fingers onto the frets, he feels the dragon inside his head, waiting. He knows what she wants, so he ignores her, fiddling with the strings, learning the spaces between, the shape of the chords. He's amazed how easily it comes to him, and he suspects that she's helping. N'Doch doesn't mind. Not this. This is the thing that works best between them, after all, the making of music.

He works the strings, light and fast, his ear bent close to catch their whispered thrum. There's a tune been bothering him a while, one he couldn't make come out right, so he stuck it away in the back of his head. But here it is now, coming right out through his fingers. It's been there all along, only waiting for the proper instrument to play it. N'Doch stops, slaps the flat face of the box lightly with his palm and stands. He's ready. He can do it now. This'll be one way of thanking them. A soft woven strap is attached to the neck and the base of the box. N'Doch slips it over his head and moves toward the door.

The cold hits him like a wall as he steps out onto the terrace. But he knows if he doesn't freeze solid before he gets to her, he won't be cold for long. He shuts the door quietly and eases across the stones, down the steps and into the snow. He'd like to give the snow some time—it's his first, after all. And the cold, too, as well as the dark, spiky pines—he recognizes those. He's seen 'em lots of times in vids. But all that'll have to wait. Right now, he's intent. On a mission.

He pulls up behind the circle of women. He counts at least a dozen of them, all in their old-timey clothes and their braided hair, murmuring the alien syllables of their native German. Their laughter is not like the laughter of the women N'Doch knows. It's full-out and boisterous, like they don't care if there's a man listening. And, he notices, he's the only guy in sight—unless you count one big brown dragon.

So he guesses it's time. He settles the instrument more comfortably, so familiar, so strange, then gives her the briefest of warnings.

Hey, girl . . .

She's way ahead of him. No big soppy greeting. No oh-thank-god-you're-alive. She rolls her big eyes toward him and arches her silvery neck.

Yo, bro. You all warmed up? I need a voice to talk to these people.

N'Doch grins. One day he'll catch her out. Maybe.

So do I. Think these ladies are ready for this?

My brother, this here's your ideal audience.

He runs off a short riff, and the women turn and notice him. Something about him, his thin, muscled height or the darkness of his skin, makes them fall back a step. But he sees no fear in them, only respect and readiness. Maybe it's that he was all but dead last time they saw him. Or maybe the dragon called it right: they're the ideal audience and they're only waiting for him to perform. Will they care that he's singing in French? No one but the dragon needs to understand the words.

He's nervous now that the moment's at hand. The new song is there ready to go, but the accompaniment will be real thin until he gets a better hang on all these strings. It's another song about his dead brother Sedou, but it's a strong and happy song, not like the last one he sang her, which gave her the shape she needed but nearly broke his heart. He hopes this one'll work just as well, but the only way to find out is to play it. So he does.

His resurrected voice starts off as shaky as his legs. The dragon listens through the first verse, while the big guy's ivory horned head leans in toward her. He watches his sister steadily with huge golden eyes. N'Doch can feel her in his head, anticipating, humming a little harmony, and his voice steadies to match her. A line into the second verse, the dragon begins her change. The women sigh with wonder and admiration—no faint hearts in this valley . . . except his own. N'Doch looks away. He hates watching her shapeshift. It makes him queasy, even though it's him singing her destination. He bends his head over his fingering and keeps on singing. Soon enough, he's at the end and the women are offering a round of applause. Then he looks up and into his brother's eyes, and his heart nearly stops all over again.

"Damn!" he says aloud. "I ain't never gonna get used to this."

"Sure you will," says Sedou's voice. A strong dark fist pounds him on the shoulder, and N'Doch knows he's done it. He's sung her a younger Sedou this time, a happier Sedou, a Sedou who doesn't yet know how short his life will be.

And a Sedou who speaks German, apparently. Must have learned it from the big guy. N'Doch watches the dragon-as-Sedou move among the women with greetings and introductions, a handsome dark man, laughing and at ease. More at ease than N'Doch, who reaches out in confusion and shakes his brother's hand.

Inside his head, the dragon is still singing.

CHAPTER SIX

After she thinks about it for a while, Paia understands that she's been had.

She goes to Son Luco first, charging full tilt down the polished steps from the vestry with her hair half-braided and her temple bracelets jangling like a box of glass tumbling down a hillside. Luco is lounging in the priests' private cloister in nothing but a loincloth, oiling his skin.

"You worked it out with him, didn't you!" she accuses. "I could've been killed! Was it his idea or yours?"

He leaps to his feet in alarm and reaches for a towel. Paia's amazed how he willingly exposes himself to more uv-drenched sunlight than his job requires. Though his natural color is as deeply golden as the God's, he's convinced that a darker tan will help him look younger.

"His, of course!" Luco seems disturbed by the suggestion that he might have had a thought of his own, or worse still, acted upon it. He watches Paia pace back and forth, then lowers himself back onto his chaise. "I hope you've not been running around the Temple looking like that, *Mother* Paia."

Paia glares at him. He knows the title irritates her. "Like what?"

He makes a peace offering, water from the jug beside his chair. "It's cool. Just up from the cellars." Paia continues to glare. Luco shrugs, patting oil on the taut skin under his chin. "Revenues are down, you know. He says he can feel—and I quote—'a definite sag in the intensity of the worship.' He thought we should . . ."

". . . murder the High Priestess just to liven things up a little!"

Luco lifts himself up indignantly. "He'd never let that

happen! You were safe at every moment! I was right there and I was, as you may recall, quite adequately armed!"

"Ha!" Paia moves into the shade of the surrounding portico to pace and sulk at the same time. "You could have warned me at least!"

"He wouldn't let me! He knows you—he said you'd never agree to it." Luco swings his muscular legs over the chaise and sits with his elbows on his knees, regarding her as if she's a lighted fuse he can do nothing to dampen. "You have a hard enough time with the use of *animals* for sacrifice."

"You don't mean . . . not the poor sucker who . . ."

He nods. "One of the kamikaze squad."

Paia clamps her eyes shut, mid-pace.

"You see? He was right." Luco shrugs, shakes his head. "They will do these things for him, you know. Sometimes their truer devotion shames me. Often, in fact. Of course I stood up for you and said you'd do anything the God deemed necessary."

"Of course you did."

"Well, I did."

"Maybe he should just stay around more, instead of going off on all these jaunts of his." It always rouses Luco when she speaks of the God as if he were some sort of temperamental employer.

"He is busy converting the Infidel. It's important work."

"And vital to the Temple revenues, I know." Paia continues pacing. "But do you know that's what he's doing?"

"Of course, if that's what he says he is."

Paia stops. She props herself against one of the slim marble columns. "Do you want my job, Luco?"

The priest's forehead tightens. He leans forward as if in pain. "NEVER! I mean, no, I . . ."

" 'Cause if you do, you can have it." She knows he doesn't—he's too scared of the God, no matter how willing he is to plot with him. But she's not ready to let him off the hook quite yet. "Maybe there doesn't have to be a High Priestess. Maybe a High Priest. Or maybe they still do sex-change operations somewhere in what's left of the world."

She's so delighted by how badly she's shocked him that her anger drains away like she's pulled the plug.

"They used to, you know," she continues gleefully. "I read up on it in the Library."

His bright blue eyes grow round at this sacrilege, and instantly she regrets admitting that she's used her most sacred and solemn privilege—access to the House Comp database, occasional and only when the God allows—for no higher purpose than her own amusement. Merely hoping that he is will not make Luco someone she can talk to this freely.

But he doesn't scold or lecture. He gasps and says, "Really? Did it work?"

Paia can't help laughing. It isn't the sacrilege that's bothered him after all. "I guess." She smiles, then goes back out into the sun to lean over and kiss his cheek lightly and smooth back his long hair. "Poor Luco. Just when you thought you had everything you could possibly want . . ."

She's glad she's run off most of her rage before confronting the God. He'll have sensed her turmoil anyway, the way he always does, but by the time she faces him, it'll have lost its grip on her. And she knows it's unwise to be too emotional in his presence. The God will take advantage of any vulnerability.

She's in her rooms, dressing carefully for her scheduled evening audience with him, exposing the correct amount of skin, redoing her makeup with all the art she can muster, when he surprises her by coming whistling down her corridor in man-form. She feels him approaching, like dogs sense lightning—in the days when there were dogs—and she hears the guard detachment outside her door snap to attention with horrified alacrity. Paia sucks in a breath. At least he has the grace not to simply materialize in her bedroom. She wonders why. Probably he enjoys terrifying the guards.

One curt warning, her name barked like an order, and he's through the door, all aglimmer in the cloth-of-gold business suit he favors for his most casual moments. It's the same cut Paia's father used to wear, before there was no more business to transact. But her father preferred sedate browns and blues. The God wouldn't be caught dead in brown or blue. She's heard him say as much. He halts grandly in the doorway, claps his hands sharply, then steps into the room to let two acolytes whirl in past him carrying a low gilt table and a silver tray glittering with antique glass and a bottle of Paia's father's best champagne. They set it all down together with a hunted glance at their priestess, then at their God. The God waves them out of the room. They cower and hesitate, then scurry away when he glares at them, one of them turning back hastily to shut the door.

Paia bows low. "My lord Fire. What a pleasant surprise."

The God snorts, jerks his head at the champagne. "You'll have to pour it yourself, of course."

Paia raises her eyes. No wonder the servants cower. Everything about the God's chosen man-shape is calculatedly reminiscent of his true and terrifying reality. He is tall, broad and beautiful, and supremely arrogant of bearing. His finely chiseled lip seems always poised for a snarl. His skin has a human grain and tawniness, but its surface is luminous with a faint metallic sheen. His hair is longer than her own, and the rich flame-gold that Son Luco labors so hard to emulate. Sometimes the God wears it loose, in shimmering waves across his shoulders. Tonight he has it in a neat queue down the middle of his back. Assuming his most civilized aspect, Paia notes uneasily. Unlike most of her faithful, she prefers dealing with the more obvious terrors of God's natural shape. In man-form, he is always at his most devious.

"The Temple has missed you, my lord. Was your journey a successful one?"

Perhaps, if she can keep him in his present good mood, he will tell her something of what he does in his travels. She has asked before. Usually he tells of his tours among the farther-flung villages of the Faithful. Once he came home particularly sullen and flicked a finger in response. "Old business," was all he would say. Once, he even made a joke: "Visiting a relative." And Paia had laughed. How could a God have relatives?

She moves obediently to the table and picks up the bottle. The heavy old glass is deliciously cold. He's even made them chill it, probably in the Sacred Well itself. She'd like to hear what Son Luco thought about that. She pours a little into her great-grandmother's crystal and raises it to the God in salute. He returns a mocking, courtly nod, and she drinks, savoring the trail of icy, sweet liquid down her throat, but not the shiver she feels trying to guess what the God has up his gilded sleeve this time. She sips her price-less champagne and eyes him, waiting.

"The Temple has missed me? What about you? Have you missed me?"

He stares her down, golden-eyed, until she must avert her glance. Then he saunters over to her bed. With a nod, he shapes her pillows more to his liking and reclines among them as gracefully as a lizard. He puts his feet up and clasps his manicured hands behind his head. His illusion of substance is flawless, and his eyes offer their usual frank invitation. Again, Paia asks herself why he bothers. Perhaps to keep her off balance, which it surely does. Perhaps be-cause he can't help himself. Perhaps even a little wishful thinking. She's often wondered how different their fractious relationship would be if the God in his man-form possessed the actual material reality to carry out what his eyes always promise. It would certainly solve the Suitor problem, but would she have more power over him, or less?

Watching her watch him, the God grins his snarkiest grin. "Well, I know. But it *was* a pretty good show, you've got to admit."

Paia sips, trying for even a fraction of his self-possession. "Do I?"

The God throws his head back in the pillows and laughs.

"A man gave his life for your 'show' . . ."

"Oh, yes. And was convinced that such an end was worth more than all the sorry rest of it put together."

"You bullied him! You threatened him!" Only when he is in man-form can she say these things to him. "He did it out of fear, not faith!"

He cocks an elegant eyebrow. "Is there a difference?"

Paia looks away. She used to think there was. Lately, she's not so sure.

"These people have so little to look forward to in this life. The life after is their only hope, as we race hell-bent toward Armageddon. A hope only I can offer them." He rises up on one elbow. "Are you having another crisis of faith, my priestess? Over the life of one peon?"

A crisis of faith? Paia stills. Could he have read her mind, as he often claims? Desperately, she blocks all thought of the heretical painting, distracting herself with how much she hates it when he mocks her for what he calls her 'womanly compassion.' "I see we are not to agree tonight, my lord."

"I hope that will not be the case . . . my love."

Paia's throat tightens as the banter ends. "You wish something of me, then? What is it?"

A smile. "You."

With effort, she controls a tremble. "How about something you can actually have?"

His smile clicks off, like a light. He does not appreciate being reminded. "All right. A child."

Not wanting to shatter her ancestral crystal, Paia sets her glass carefully on the table. "You . . . a what?"

"A child. You heard me." He rises, quick as a snake strike, and crosses the room. He looms over her, traces the line of her jaw and lip with a long nailed finger. Paia feels nothing but heat, a faint current of air and electricity. Still, it requires every ounce of will she possesses to remain calm.

"Your child, my love," he murmurs. "As soon as you can possibly manage it."

". . . uh . . . how can we . . . ?"

"Oh, not mine. Unfortunately." He turns away, flicks a gilded fingernail. "One of those Suitors, pick one, I don't care. It's time." He levels his bedroom eyes on her again. "I'm sure I don't have to tell you *how*, do I?"

"What do you mean, pick one? Any one?"

"A healthy one, naturally."

"Up till now, you've been rejecting them as often as I have. Now suddenly any one will do?"

"I could choose for you, if you prefer."

"I don't think I'm . . ."

"You are. Ready, that is. Or I am, which is the same thing."

"Wait. This is . . . I won't do this."

The God laughs lightly. "Of course you will."

"I won't."

"But I am your God, my priestess. It is your duty to serve me."

"Not this way."

"In all ways."

"NO!"

He shrugs. "Must we descend to melodrama? There are ways, you know . . ."

"You wouldn't dare!"

He gives her a thin, chill smile. "Choose someone you'll tire of quickly."

Meaning that once he's served his purpose, this Suitor won't be around for long. "Are you doing this just to punish me? What could you want with a child?"

His golden eyes blink slowly, in a time frame not her own. "You wouldn't understand."

"Try me."

"It's time, that's all."

"Time for what? What's different? What's changed?"

Without seeming to have moved, he is at the door. "You have," he says, and vanishes.

CHAPTER SEVEN

N'Doch can feel the girl's eyes on him, once the song is ended and the dragon-as-Sedou is busy chatting up the women. She understands a little about him now, must be, since she's waited until he's done singing before bobbing up at his side to hang on him like she's his kid sister or something. Which, he guesses, after all they've been through together, she sort of is. He's surprised she seems so glad to see him, and besides, he's grateful for a familiar face, so he can't resist slinging an arm across her thin shoulders and giving her a hug. To his surprise, she lets him, though he knows her well enough to do it quick and back right off again.

"N'Doch!" she beams. "We were so worried about you!"

Her understatement makes him laugh. "Me, too. Not every day a guy gets blown to bits and wakes up to tell about it!"

Her little nose puckers. "Not to bits, really. But it was bad. Blood everywhere! Those gun-things are a dreadful weapon, N'Doch."

She's speaking French, he notices. Not Rose's antique Frankish, but real French. *His* French. No more need for dragon intermediaries, then. No more excuses for silence or miscommunication between them now. There's so much he wants to ask about what happened after, that is, after he stopped remembering. About Lealé, and Baraga—in all the confusion, did the slimy bastard get away? And how was it seeing him dead and all? But the moment's not right, or maybe he's not ready. Instead he says, "Been keeping up with the language lessons, huh?"

She nods, hunching her thick woolly layers farther up around her neck like some kind of Eskimo. She has tall fur-and-leather boots on now, and the whole outfit looks as weird to him as it did back home, except he reminds himself that this is what people wear here in 913, and probably if he doesn't get something like it pretty quick, he's gonna freeze to death. He shivers, remembering that he's standing barefoot in half a meter of snow, and this long shirty thing they've given him just isn't cutting it.

"Lady Water is just the best teacher of all!" the girl exclaims, with the same precise and literal manner in French that she had speaking German all the while the dragon was translating in his head.

"Nah. You're just a good learner." He kicks at the snow experimentally and grins when it flies weightlessly up into the air. "I guess you're glad to be home."

"Yes, yes, I am, but . . . it won't be for long, you know."

"No. Probably not." The dragons would see to that. N'Doch wonders again how this young girl, with her whole life before her, could so willingly give it up to serve this infernal "Purpose" that the dragons are so obsessed with. He's about to ask her that, when she answers one of the other questions he's been trying to make himself ask. "They went back for Master Djawara as soon as they could, you know. He wouldn't come with them."

N'Doch feels at least one of the tensions deep inside him relax a little. "But he's okay?"

"Yes, he's fine."

"Why wouldn't he come?" But N'Doch is not really surprised. He can't imagine the old man willingly forsaking his beloved hidey-hole out in the bush, or his pack of mangy dogs.

"Said he had too much important business to tend to," says his brother's voice, coming up beside him.

N'Doch starts, then blows out a breath and shakes his head. "Never. Never gonna get used to this."

The dragon-as-Sedou laughs, a rich and youthful baritone. "Gotta say, though—it's more convenient than four legs and a tail."

"Freaks me out," N'Doch admits, for the first time in the girl's hearing. "You're dead, and I oughta be."

"Look at me, bro."

Reluctantly, N'Doch meets his brother's eyes. It's like staring straight into the sun. Meanwhile, the dragon is speaking inside his head.

I am your memory of Sedou. Nothing more, but . . . nothing less.

N'Doch looks away, swallows. "Right."

"Okay. So Papa Dja says he'll be watching out. He sees signs of more activity back by us, he'll let us know somehow. Says to tell you to keep your head down."

"Too late."

"Never too late. Let's get on in, huh? I'm freezing my ass off!"

The girl giggles. Sedou grins at her, reaches out, and tousles her black curls. "Hey there, kiddo."

N'Doch sees he's got some catching up to do. "By the way, remind me to tell you 'bout this vision I had."

When he sits down at the long wooden tables laid out for dinner in the big room with the fireplace, N'Doch realizes that he's still the only guy in the place—not counting Sedou, who's really a she-dragon anyway. He looks around, counts fifteen women of various ages, including the girl. Maybe the men are all out fighting this war she's told him about. He's got a well-used platter in front of him, like a big fired-clay plate, and a tall tapering mug of the same material grasped in one hand, already filled with some foamy dark brew. He's floating on that cushion of unreality again, with the girl seated on one side and Sedou across from him, both ready to translate. The seat on his left is empty until the most beautiful white woman he's ever laid eyes on plunks a big steaming dish down in the center of the table and settles in next to him. She smiles and says something he doesn't get, then holds out her hand.

"This is Raven," supplies the girl from his right.

"Oh. Hello, Raven." N'Doch can feel Sedou's eyes laughing already. He takes the proffered, lovely hand and raises it, just like he's seen in vids, gallantly to his lips.

Later, when Raven gets up to refill the jug of ale she's just emptied into his tankard, N'Doch no longer cares what century he's in. These women's homemade hooch tastes pretty damn good to him and the company couldn't be improved upon. Now that he's got the chance, he leans over to the girl and whispers, "So where's all the men at? They out fighting or something?"

She blinks at him, then wags her head in understanding. "I forgot—you wouldn't know. There are no men at Deep Moor."

"None?" He glances around, sees two or three young girls who've got to have had a father at some point.

The girl follows his gaze. "Oh, well, just the occasional visitor."

He grins. Wow. She's actually making a joke.

"No, really. Like Hal. I told you about him. He helped me escape from the hell-priest after I ran away from my father." She leans in closer. "Hal is Rose's . . . well, um, you know."

"Her husband?"

"Oh, no. He's her, um . . . ." She gestures uselessly with one hand.

"Her brother?"

'No!"

"Her lover?"

The girl blushes and nods.

At first, N'Doch thought she was uptight. He's come to accept that it's actual innocence, so he tries real hard now not to let her prissiness irritate him. But he can't help pushing her just a little. Somebody's got to teach her the ways of the world. "Go on, say it. He's her *lover*."

She's even touchier than usual. She glares at him from under her lashes, then bolts up and scurries away. N'Doch hasn't expected quite this reaction. He's left with empty seats on both sides of him and Sedou all the way across the room, in deep with the pale-haired healer woman, probably swapping secrets of the trade. But he decides that things are looking up. He'd had a moment of panic at the thought that no men at Deep Moor meant that these women didn't like men. Now he feels free to entertain his fantasies of luring the spectacular and vivacious Raven into bed with him. Maybe he's not going to mind it so much after all, being back here in 913. At least, for as long as the dragons will let him. He figures he's gotta work fast.

Erde escaped the embarrassing conversation with N'Doch and fled to a shadowed corner of the kitchen to wait for her blush to subside. Nervously tracing the stained grout lines between the stove tiles, she wondered why—after all she'd seen of life in the ungentle world of 2013—a certain subject was still so hard for her to talk about, especially with N'Doch. For, though he was like a brother to her, he was still very much a male. In fact, here in her world, he might even be labeled lecherous. But she'd seen how it was where he came from. People just said what they felt, right out, and looked where they wanted to look. There, she'd been the odd one out.

But to be honest with herself, something she was trying harder to be lately, Erde had come to resent the extreme modesty of her upbringing. She envied N'Doch his worldly ease. She was sure he could answer just about any question she might ask about what really went on between men and women, and he'd have not the slightest qualm about filling in all the details. But she could not bring herself to have those conversations with him, no matter how curious she was, conversations she would have had with her mother, had that dear lady not died in Erde's early childhood. Conversations her grandmother the baroness had been too busy to have. Conversations she could never have had with her father because of the way he'd begun to look at her and touch her in the months before she fled Tor Alte to escape the clutches of the hell-priest.

Ever since she'd begun to grow, men had grabbed at her in one way or another, as if it was their right to lay hands on her without her permission. And this man-right seemed to demolish all class and duty lines, even religious vows. To Erde, it was more than just disconcerting or dangerous. It overturned a very basic principle of her childhood: men were meant to protect the women in their charge. Like Hal. Having tracked her down in the deepest wilderness, he could easily have taken advantage of her. But Hal Engle was a King's Knight, and true to the oath he'd sworn. And a decent man, besides.

N'Doch, too, had kept his hands to himself from the very beginning, though Erde could hardly call him a *gentleman*, the way he looked at every other woman who crossed his path. Erde ceased tracing the grout lines and began to pick at a particularly offensive clot of soot. And then there was . . . *him*. The man who kept invading her dreams, as if she had no choice.

It wasn't just the dreaming about her enemy that disturbed her, or even that she worried about his well-being. It was that she was so . . . attracted to him.

The very notion brought up her blush again. Erde was not too innocent to notice how consistently any thoughts of what men and women did together brought Baron Köthen's bright image to her mind, to disturb and confuse her.

"Erde, dear? Are you all right?"

Raven, returning from the beer cellar with a fresh pitcher. Erde hoped the shadows would hide the evidence of her unseemly thoughts. Although, she reflected wryly, Raven would not think them unseemly. She smiled and shrugged. "Just tired. Still so tired."

Raven circled her free arm around Erde's waist. "Sweeting, it's only been three days. Remember what you've been through."

Erde could not think of how to reply. Raven set the pitcher down on a nearby joint-stool and wrapped her in a hug. This helped Erde banish the image of Baron Köthen and find her tongue again. "And think of what's still ahead, when the Quest resumes."

"Ah, yes," Raven agreed, "but you mustn't worry about that for now . . ."

"No. Not for now."

Raven let her go and took up her pitcher again. "The young man seems very nice."

"Who, N'Doch? Nice?" Erde couldn't imagine such a thing.

"Well, then . . . . charming. A little overeager, perhaps. But very lovely to look at, don't you think? So tall and . . . exotic."

Erde stared. Was she kidding?

"No wonder his dragon enjoys taking man-form," Raven went on merrily. "I think she might be just the slightest bit vain, don't you?" Then she caught Erde's expression.

"Hmm. I see. Well, you and the boy *seem* fond enough of each other. Comrades-in-arms and all that."

"He's not a boy."

Raven chuckled. "No, and I expect he wouldn't want to hear me calling him that either. Come, tell—have you not been getting along?"

Erde felt no urge to detail every disagreement she'd had with her fellow dragon guide. After all, he had improved noticeably since she first met him. "He doesn't know very much about dragons," she offered instead, realizing only then that of all N'Doch's irritating qualities, this was the one that bothered her most. "Or the duties of a dragon guide. People don't even believe in dragons where he comes from!"

Raven smiled. "Ah, but he has a dragon who knows a great deal about men. And from what I observe, she seems to be managing him very well."

"She does?"

"Certainly. There are other ways of turning a man to your purpose besides ordering him to follow. Lady Water discovered who in his life her destined guide was most likely to listen to seriously. Since it wasn't her at the moment, she simply . . . became that person."

"Oh, well . . ."

"No 'oh, well.' Think about it. It's brilliant, and it works."

"Then what does he do for her?"

"He sings her a human shape. He gives a dragon a way to work in the world of men, as you do for Earth. You just have different ideas of how to go about it. Are Earth and Water the same dragon?"

"Of course not!"

"Then why should they require the same dragon guide?" Heading for the door, Raven glanced back. "Do you think, sweeting, that it might be time to have that little chat with Rose?"

Erde thought about dragons and methodologies for a while. It was true she'd been stubborn about her own assumptions. And it was true that N'Doch had surprised her. He'd come through in the end. Perhaps she was going to have to accept the possibility that there would always be people in the world doing things that she just could not understand. Armed with that disturbing notion, she gathered up her courage and returned to the Great Hall, where N'Doch was taking another refill from Raven's pitcher, the redheaded twins were clearing platters and tableware, and Doritt was tossing a huge log into the fireplace. Erde prayed that the dragon was warm enough out in the big hay barn, finally getting the rest he deserved. She went to claim the empty seat beside Rose.

She listened quietly while Rose finished up a discussion with Linden, Deep Moor's healer, about how long her supplies of herbs and physicks would hold out if the snow continued unabated into the true months of winter. Linden's jaw-length flaxen hair draped like separate strands of spider silk around her white cheeks, hiding her worried glance in the softened shadows of lanternlight. Her long-fingered hands moved restlessly in her lap. Erde found this more worrisome than all the facts and figures of their conversation. She'd come to rely on Linden being a very calm, still person.

"Well," Rose concluded finally, "we shall do what we must."

Linden nodded, then offered Erde a small, silent smile and padded away, gathering up a stray armload of dirty dishes as she went.

Rose watched after her soberly. "She fears our medical supplies won't last past January. Her final harvest is usually in early November, and here it is, just September. Even if we do get a thaw, who knows what will be left alive under all this snow."

Erde thought of the parched peanut fields around Master Djawara's home in what N'Doch called "the bush." "Where I just came from, there's not enough water. Not anywhere, except the salty oceans. And here there's too much. And there, they kept saying how it was so much hotter than usual."

"And here, too cold. It's all gone out of balance, hasn't it? I blame this priest and the evil he's stirred up." Rose let a pensive moment fall between one thought and the next. "Which reminds me, Raven tells me you've had some dreams I should hear about."

"I guess." Erde loved Rose, but often found her directness and air of authority intimidating. Even her beloved grandmother, a powerful baroness required to work in the world of men, had been somewhat more . . . feminine in her approach.

"What kind of dreams?"

"Um . . ." Erde found a sudden reason to fuss with the hem of her sleeve. "Do you really think Brother Guillemo has brought all this wrong weather upon us? Is he truly a sorcerer?"

"You know his power as well as I do, child, perhaps better. But we were speaking of dreams. Come on, now, out with it."

Erde brushed invisible crumbs across the worn planks of the table. "Well, they're . . . umm . . ."

"If you told Raven, you can certainly tell me."

"I didn't tell Raven . . . not really. Well, I told her I'd seen the hell-priest in my dreams, which is true, but . . ."

"But? There's something more important than Fra Guill?"

Spoken aloud, the priest's nickname made her shiver. "I don't know. It's all mixed up together." There was a larger significance to these dreams than her own confused feelings, and it was her duty to reveal them. "Fra Guill is part of it, but . . . well, um . . . what would you say if you had dreams, I mean, really *real* dreams, as if you'd actually traveled there, about someone you knew was your enemy, and he's there in your dream and you're almost talking to him and he doesn't seem like he could really be your enemy, and then suddenly he isn't, because the real enemy is someone else?"

"Goodness. Breathe, child!"

Erde realized she hadn't been.

Rose waited a moment before asking, "Does this no-longer-an-enemy have a name?"

Erde nodded. The hardest part of all was going to be speaking it out loud. Her lips moved uselessly.

"Haven't we been through this before?"

"No, this is different. It's not Rainer." Whose name had lodged in her throat the night she'd thought him murdered by her father's order, and rendered her mute for months until she had discovered him alive again. "I mean, I can say the name. I just . . ."

"Then just say it and get it over with."

"Adolphus of Köthen."

Rose sat back a little. "Dolph? You've been dreaming about Dolph?"

Rose was surprised, but Erde was even more so, to hear Baron Köthen spoken of so familiarly by someone without estates or title. Or perhaps Deep Moor was Rose's estate. Erde had never thought to ask. Now she nodded and braced herself for ridicule. But Rose pursed her lips thoughtfully. Raven glided past behind them, trailing a fond hand across their shoulders. Rose caught the hand and held it. "You might want to hear this."

Raven leaned over. "Is that all right, sweeting? Do you mind?"

Erde shrugged. Her humiliation might as well be total.

Raven sat, reaching for Erde's hand to press it lightly between her own.

"Our Erde has been dreaming about Adolphus of Köthen," Rose announced.

"Really?" Raven laughed deep in her throat. "Can't say as I blame her."

Erde looked down, heat and confusion flooding her cheeks already.

"Raven, please . . ."

"Can't I compliment her on her good taste?"

"Just listen," said Rose irritably.

"I don't understand . . ." Erde began.

Raven squeezed her hand. "Don't feel badly, sweeting. It's all rather . . . complicated. Isn't it, Rose?"

"I think we'll leave your past out of this for now," said Rose. "Now, child, when you left for, well, this other place you've been, Baron Köthen was in revolt with your father and Fra Guill to usurp the King. So you must have had news of the war since you returned, yes? I mean, about Dolph's, shall we say, conversion?"

"Conversion?" She needed to hear it again. She needed it confirmed. Beyond all misunderstanding.

"You heard he switched sides."

The smile bloomed on Erde's face before she could take control of it. Her dreams had been true. "And is he now leading the King's armies to victory?"

Rose and Raven exchanged glances.

"No," said Raven. "Not exactly . . ."

Erde's heart contracted. They were telling her he was dead. And since her dreams had been true, she knew how it had occurred.

Rose laid a hand on her wrist. "If you've not had news, why did you say he was no longer your enemy?"

Now that Baron Köthen's name was on the table, the rest of the tale came out in a rush. "Because I dreamed it. That's what I'm telling you. I saw the enemy camp. I saw my father in it. I saw everything that happened: the hell-priest murdering poor Prince Carl and making it look like suicide, then trying to blame it on Baron Köthen, and when that didn't work, accusing him of witchcraft and heretical practices, so that the only thing left for the baron to do was to flee to the other side! He meant to bring Prince Carl's body home to the King." She glanced from one to the other, awaiting their painful revelation. "Did he?"

"Don't you know?" asked Rose.

"That dream stopped there, and no one has said if . . ."

Raven leaned forward. "He brought the prince's body to Hal, who he knew would receive him. But few people know this. The official word is that Carl survived to go into hiding, and that Fra Guill is faking the reports of his death to suit himself. No one knows the truth besides His Majesty, Hal, and a few trusted allies, plus Dolph and the men who stayed loyal to him."

"And you." Rose tapped a fingernail rhythmically on the tabletop. "You have had a true dream, Erde von Alte."

"More than one," Erde murmered. There was still the truth of the last one to be gotten over with. "They frightened me. Sometimes it was like being a bird on his shoulder. So close. I even spoke to him, and once, I think . . . no, I am sure he heard me."

"In the dream he heard you?" Raven rested her chin in her hands. "What did you say to him?"

"It was in the clearing where he found Prince Carl's body. The priest had him outnumbered. I told him to run, save himself. I could see how he hated Fra Guill, how he despised my father."

"His own fault for taking them as allies," remarked Rose.

"He regretted that." But here Erde was on shaky

ground. She didn't know that for sure. "So I told him that a true prince might still live, not a weakling like poor Carl, but a rightful heir that he could feel proud to pledge fealty to. But then, worst of all, the priest heard me, too! And unlike Baron Köthen, he knew it was me! 'The witch-girl,' he called me. 'She's here! The witch-girl!' And then I couldn't wake up . . . !" Erde buried her face in her hands with a shudder. The mere memory of her subsequent journey to and from limbo terrified her all over again. She wouldn't tell that part of the tale just now.

"It looks like poor Dolph has been telling the truth," Raven observed quietly. "At least, his version of it."

"The part he's willing to let himself understand," agreed Rose.

Poor Dolph? But at least they were speaking of him in present tense.

"Then . . . he's alive?"

"So far," said Raven, "No thanks to his own efforts."

"Information has been scanty," Rose added, "what with the weather and our needing Lily and Margit close to home for our own protection. Hal's sent a bird now and then when he remembers."

She hardly dared to ask it. "When was the last one?"

"Not long ago. A few weeks."

Not long, no, but long enough for a man to lie dead and frozen on the field like the others she had seen in her dream. Erde pushed the thought away and let the rugged, able image of a *living* Baron Köthen fill her mind's eye. The very image of a leader. " 'Poor Dolph,' you said? Did anyone doubt him?"

Raven spread her hands. "Inevitably."

"But they mustn't! It's all true! I saw it with my own eyes. I was there!"

"Well, no. You weren't," said Rose.

"But it was *like* I was there!"

"Apparently. And that is the interesting thing." Rose sat back, rubbing her palms together. "Truth is, I wouldn't mind hearing what Dolph has to say. We'll not stop Fra Guill until we fully understand the nature of his power. Another version of this story might just shed some light on that mystery."

"Dolph is a boy's name," murmured Erde, unaware until Raven laughed that she had spoken this thought out loud.

"He was a boy, or very nearly, when I knew him. A beautiful boy."

"No longer," said Rose heavily.

Raven nodded. "Bright ambition in the youth can darken to obsession in the man . . . especially if that ambition is thwarted."

Erde felt she'd lost the thread of their conversation. "But if he's alive and on our side now, what can the problem be?"

Rose eyed her sympathetically. "I don't know what he has done to so earn your good opinion of him, but you must realize, dear child, that in one fateful moment, Adolphus Michael von Hoffman, Baron Köthen, went from being the most powerful and respected younger lord in the kingdom, with his hand poised for the throne, to being a fugitive of dubious integrity, under suspicion of sorcery and without lands or forces to call his own. We're told it's been hard on him."

"But what about Hal?" Didn't he . . . couldn't he . . . sorcery? She had imagined the two of them, man and mentor, joining forces to win great victories together.

"Hal's kept him alive and out of the hands of the witch hunters."

"Whom he's had so much practice eluding himself," noted Raven.

"But Hal Engle, as you know, serves His Majesty first and foremost, and even he can't be sure of where Dolph's true loyalties lie."

Erde's mouth took on a stubborn tilt. "King Otto is old and weak! My father always said so. Baron Köthen only wanted the throne so he could keep the kingdom together. I heard him say so to Hal. You'll see—when the true prince is recognized, Adolphus of Köthen will pledge to him and help him make the kingdom great again!" If indeed, she added silently, he is still alive to do it. She wouldn't know, until the next bird arrived.

"Well," said Rose, raising a doubtful brow.

But Raven smiled. "I guess there's no doubt where your loyalties lie."

It isn't until the three men turn up out of the blizzard that N'Doch comes to and realizes what a fool's paradise he's been living in. They ride in out of the storm and bring the cold light of reality with them. He only needs one look at their grim and weary faces.

This Deep Moor place, he reflects, is like one of those fancy damn R&R resorts, where the army sends the battle-crazed recruits to pump 'em up with enough hooch and tail and m.j. so they can send 'em back out to the front again. But then he can't help but grin. *So far all I've gotten is the hooch.*

The dragons have gone down the valley for exercise, as if the storm was nothing to them. But they come flickering in out of nowhere, bringing the first sighting of the intruders' approach. The girl bursts out of the house to greet them. N'Doch is out in the yard, now that they've found him some serious clothing to wear, learning how to shovel snow. There's plenty of it to shovel, and he keeps at it while the girl confers with the dragons.

"Visitors!" she exclaims, then hightails it back into the house.

The dogs report in next. N'Doch loves how they bound along, just like the herd of antelopes he saw in a vid once, silent and eager, sailing through snowdrifts as high as veldt grass. They race straight to the tall woman Doritt, who seems to have the same sort of way with them that Papa Dja has with his mangy pack of strays. Some things, he thinks, never change. Like how she squats her odd angular body down among them in the wind-driven snow, patting and murmuring, then gets up and marches into the Big House like she's got their actual words to convey.

N'Doch likes how the farmstead is always busy, even now, in the midst of a storm. Paths snake through the snow between all the outbuildings. It snowed yesterday and the day before, and now the snow is falling again, a soft swirling mist that whitens the air and fills in the path behind him. He has to work hard to keep up with it. Storm or no storm, there are cows to be milked and chickens to be fed and eggs to be collected. When he really thinks about where he is, timewise, he's not so surprised that these women have to do everything by hand. He's learned there's a bake house, a laundry, an old-time forge, and a potter's kiln among the many smaller wood-and-stone buildings that circle the big central farm house. And even a man who was blown to bits less than a week ago gets a shovel stuck in his hand or a load of wood to carry.

N'Doch doesn't mind the work. It keeps him warm and gives him something to focus on, which is good, 'cause he's still feeling pretty damn floaty. He likes being part of the bustle. It's like the village he grew up in where everybody had a function, before things got real bad and his family had to move to the city. Besides, he figures he owes these women something for all they're doing for him. He can't remember how long it's been since he had three safe squares a day and a real bed to sleep in every night, the same bed even, warm and rat-free, where he can sleep without fear of being robbed or murdered for maybe the first time in his life.

But then the men arrive, and it's like being jolted out of a pleasant daydream. Suddenly N'Doch is wondering how long it'll be before this war the women all gossip and debate about comes spilling over the valley walls like the proverbial tsunami. He's sorry about this. He's just left his own sort of war behind, and he doesn't wish it on them for a moment.

He leans on his shovel when Doritt comes back out on the terrace with Raven and the girl in tow. Raven squints up at the sky, hugs a heavy shawl around her. Doritt, in tall leather boots, heads for the horse barn. "I'll get Margit and Lily saddled up."

"You can't send them out in this," Raven calls after her. Margit and Lily are the trackers, N'Doch knows. Margit is also the blacksmith. He likes those two women. They remind him of the girls in his old gang. Lily has promised him a ride out to the Grove if the weather ever clears. N'Doch has never been on a horse, at least not a real one, never touched one in his life, and just this morning, Doritt had him mucking out stalls. Talk about total immersion. He shakes his head in amazement.

"Somebody's got to see who's coming in." Doritt disappears around the corner of the barn.

"I told you, it's Hal," insists the girl.

Raven shook her head. "Hal's got a war to worry about now. He can't just take off whenever the fancy strikes him."

"Earth knows Hal and he's sure it's him."

"How close did he get?"

"Not too close, just in case. But . . ."

"It can't be Hal. There's three of them. Hal'd never brought a stranger into Deep Moor in his life until he brought you."

"And there goes the neighborhood," says N'Doch from the yard.

Both women look at him, but nobody laughs. He shrugs and goes back to his shoveling. But out of the corner of his eye, he watches Raven as she stands, hands on hips, staring across the farmyard toward the snow-shrouded valley as if there was already something to see out there.

Doritt comes back from the barn. "They say they'll go out as far as the Grove—they've been wanting to check on Gerrasch anyway—and escort whoever it is back in, whether they're welcome or not. Margit says to have the troops ready."

"We've got time. It'll take them at least an hour from where the dragons spotted them, maybe longer in this weather." Raven touches the girl's arm. "Go tell Rose— she's working in the library."

The girl jumps like she's been daydreaming, then races off inside. N'Doch can see she's worried about something. Doritt does an about-face and strides back to the barn, leaving Raven alone on the snow-swept porch, the white flakes catching in the dark cloud of her hair. N'Doch would like to say something to her. Not a come-on or anything. She looks too sad and worried all of a sudden. Well, maybe a *little* come-on, just to cheer her up. Raven understands how to play the game. But he speaks no German. She speaks no French. All he can do is smile encouragingly.

Uh-huh, he tells himself. Time to start learning another language.

The storm has blown up into a real howler by the time the three men struggle in. The dragon-as-Sedou stands next to him in the lee-side shelter of the spring house, where Doritt has stationed them.

"Just in case," she says, shoving stout poles into their hands.

N'Doch uses the pole to brace himself against the wind. He'd prefer his trusty old fish blade that's gotten him in and out of many a tight scrape. But nothing came back with him through the veil of centuries, nothing but his flesh and bones, in several pieces. Even his clothes were in tatters. He hefts his pole. It's about two meters long and maybe three centimeters thick. He turns to Sedou. "What d'ya think?"

Sedou's grin is veiled with snow. "We can take 'em. Whoever they are."

N'Doch levels the staff at him endwise and feints. Sedou counters with the stick held across his chest in both hands. Instantly, N'Doch sees that's the right way to use it, like, to ward off a blade. Particularly a real long one. It occurs to him that these guys are probably gonna be carrying swords. His anticipation quickens.

Sedou's still wearing the same old dashiki and jeans that N'Doch's song had conjured him in. N'Doch shivers. He can't remember ever being so cold. Suddenly he feels like it's him who's the older brother. "You ought to get some clothes on."

"Cold doesn't affect me."

"Well, it looks weird. People might think you're showing off."

"Since when did that bother you?" Sedou raises his staff and takes a stance. "Wanta do something about it?"

They joust a little among the drifts until N'Doch's feeling warmed up and breathing hard. He pulls back with a laugh. "Do we have to go to all this trouble? Couldn't you just, y'know, spit fire at them or something? Instant barbecue?"

Sedou sobers. "Not me. That's my brother."

For an instant, N'Doch is confused. Then he says, "Oh, that brother. The big guy can do that? No kidding."

"I meant the other one."

Right. The *other* one. N'Doch recalls it well enough, pounding hell-bent down that long tunnel in Lealé's mystical house, pursued by a roaring gout of flame, breathing in the searing heat, sure he was about to be incinerated by a dragon he'd never even met. Come to think of it, his vision of running was a lot like that. His two dragons had gotten all excited when he described his vision to them. Earth made him repeat every detail of the burned-out, ruined landscape.

Water had asked: *Is it a fix?*

Earth had replied: I THINK IT IS.

"The other one," N'Doch says now. "I remember. The one we gotta go after."

Sedou nods. "And soon. But only when you're ready. When your body is healed."

N'Doch flexes his shoulders, wrinkles his nose to the snow and wind. "Feels pretty good right now." In fact, too good. The suspicion is growing that he feels not only different but better than he ever did before. "Say, listen, did you guys . . . did you, like, put in any improvements when you worked me over?"

But the dark man opposite him just smiles back at him blandly, a distinctly un-Sedou smile. N'Doch can see the dragon in his brother's eyes and knows this question won't get a straight answer.

That's me, all right. Just a poor dumb soldier on R&R, kickin' back, enjoying myself, while a coupla dragons shape me up for the next big battle.

Later, he hears the sharp halloo of the dogs escorting the intruders in. But the snow is flying so thick in the gathering dark that the riders are halfway into the farmstead before N'Doch can pick them out. The snow muffles the sounds of their approach, but the alert has already been downgraded. Lily has ridden in ahead to give the okay to light the lanterns and call the watchers in from their posts. One of the riders, at least, is known to her. N'Doch figures it must be this Hal they all talk about. The women have gathered in the yard. Doritt and the twins warm their hands at the flame of a tall torch they've uprighted in the snow. N'Doch thinks it looks festive, but he can feel the tension beneath the women's cheerful chat and banter. It's not normal for visitors to show up unannounced in the middle of a blizzard. There might be something wrong. Rose waits on the stone terrace, bundled up in a bright woolen shawl, all reds and rusts and oranges, as if she could banish, with bold wielding of the spectrum, the approaching gloom of night. Her often stern face is lit with a womanly anticipation, and N'Doch recalls that according to the girl, this Hal, if it's him at all, is Rose's lover. The girl is there next to her, front and center to greet him, but she's still looking worried. Even more so than usual.

He hears a soft rhythmic chink, metal against metal. The riders fade into view at last, darker shadows rising up through a field of darkening gray. They are hooded, and wearing epaulets of snow. N'Doch realizes he's gripping his stick as if his life depended on it. He relaxes his fingers inside his gloves, but not his stare. Margit rides ahead, then two men abreast and one behind. Reflexively, N'Doch susses out the power structure: Margit, of course, the guide. Then the Chief Honcho, the tall guy on the left, alert but relaxed. To the right, the challenger. He decides this due to the tense, forward jut of the guy's chin and the angled slope of his shoulders. And then behind, erect and on edge, the Bodyguard. N'Doch thinks this one looks less sure of himself than the others, but all three of these guys look as tough as any gang leader he's ever known. For that matter, so does Margit. He can almost smell the aura of blood and gunpowder they bring with them. Well, no, probably not gunpowder. Not yet. He looks for weapons, sees none. Now he wishes he'd taken Papa Dja up on some of those history books he was always offering. He'd like to know what to expect.

They pull up in the center of the yard. Margit vaults off her horse and the dogs fall silent, like this is some sort of signal. The women crowd around immediately, reaching for bridles and reins, calling out greetings. The horses are steaming. Ice stiffens their manes and tails, mounding up in the straps and buckles of the tack. A laden packhorse straggles in out of the gloom and is led aside.

The tall man on the left swings stiffly out of his saddle. He shrugs back his hood, brushing snow from the folds of his cloak. In the glow of lantern light, N'Doch catches a metallic glint in the wide cuffs of the man's gloves, and in the close-fitting headgear worn under his hood. Curious, N'Doch steps in a little closer, until he can make out the fine steel links meshed together, and understands that the

man has on body armor. *Chain mail.* The term floats up
from some memory of an ancient history vid. Wow, N'Doch
marvels. I'm seeing knights in armor.

The Honcho wears a tired, apologetic air. But he calls
over his shoulder to the Bodyguard in the low kind of voice
that carries, casual with command. "You may uncover,
Wender."

"Yes, my lord."

My lord. N'Doch's never heard anyone say that for real
before, and it might strike him funny if this wasn't clearly
such serious biz. The musician in him relishes the addition
of a few bass notes to the symphony of women's voices
he's listened to for so many days. And he notes approvingly
that Margit has been sensible about security. Before shoving off his hood, the Bodyguard yanks down the blindfold
he's worn for the inward journey and lets it hang knotted
at his throat. He blinks and looks around.

The Honcho hauls off a glove and combs back his mesh
headpiece, revealing cropped gray hair, a damp, weathered
face worn thin with travel, and a flash of red within the
darkness of his cloak. N'Doch studies him. An older man,
not old. Still strong and vital, but with a lifetime's hard
messages revising his features. Raven has come forward to
meet him and is holding his horse's bridle. His smile speaks
mostly of relief as he bends to plant a quick kiss on her
cheek. "Can't fight worth a damn in this weather. Thought
we'd come visit."

N'Doch wonders if the Honcho's easy informality is an
artifact of dragon simultaneous translation, or if he's got a
few more expectations to dump. In the vids, knights in
armor always spoke real stiff. He'll never know for sure till
he can speak the language for himself.

"Strange company you're keeping," Raven murmurs.

"Isn't it?" The Honcho straightens, his eyes scanning the
little crowd until they settle on Rose, standing still as a
statue on the terrace, smiling.

"Rosie," he murmurs. "Forgive the unannounced intrusion." He strides across the hard-packed snow to take Rose
in his arms.

Rose says, before her rich voice is completely smothered
in his cloak, "It's just as well you've come. The dragons
have returned."

He lays a finger to her lips, tossing back a quick nod at the men in the yard. But his face lights with boyish wonder. "Dragons? There are more than one now?"

With the Honcho for sure identified, N'Doch turns his attention to the Challenger, who's remained slumped and silent on his horse. The women seem awkward with him. They haven't gathered around to greet him like they did the Honcho, like he's a stranger, or maybe it's something else. It's too dark to tell, but N'Doch senses a glare smoldering under the shadow of the guy's hood, and a tight-sprung readiness to him, even in his current posture of total disregard which N'Doch reads as a sullen fiction. The Bodyguard dismounts, giving his horse up to one of the redheaded twins with a grateful nod. He comes around beside the Challenger's horse. He's big, this Bodyguard, almost as tall as the Honcho but younger and broader, the very definition of muscle. N'Doch would not like to meet him alone in an alley. But his manner is clearly deferential as he shoots a quick glance up at the hooded rider.

"My lord, if you will allow me . . ."

The Challenger lets his horse dance a little, and looks away. N'Doch decides this guy is gonna be the trouble.

Pulling off his own gloves, the Bodyguard, who the Honcho has called Wender, clamps them between his teeth, then reaches up to the front of the guy's saddle to untie a long piece of red cloth. N'Doch is interested to see that they've bound the Challenger's wrists. Wender pulls the cloth free, then grabs the horse's reins at the bit to steady it so the rider can dismount. The man does not move. Wender looks like he'd rather not plead. "My lord baron?"

"Let me," says Raven, easing up beside him. The big man looks down at her, then bows a little and stands back. Raven lays a familiar hand on the rider's calf, still neatly stowed in his stirrup. Again, N'Doch spots the dull gleam of mail. "Hello, Dolph," said Raven. "Aren't you coming in?"

The man raises his hands, shakes his wrists out. Slowly, as if making a big ceremony out of it, he reaches to loosen the blindfold that had been invisible under his hood. Then he turns to stare down at the woman beside his knee. He lets out a little snort of disbelief. "Christ Almighty! Raven?"

"Yes, it's me, Dolph."

"I thought you were . . ."

"Dead? Well, that was the general idea."

"Where am I? Why are you here?"

"I live here. Finally found my proper calling in life. My, haven't we both grown up a lot since I saw you last . . . ?" Raven smiles up at the guy, and N'Doch feels just the faintest stirrings of jealousy.

The guy studies her. He looks like he's gonna say something, then thinks better of it. Instead, he flicks his boot out of his stirrup, swings the opposite leg up and over his horse's neck and is out of his saddle, upright and ready on the ground before N'Doch can take a second breath.

Now that he's down, N'Doch sizes him up: not tall—both N'Doch and the bodyguard are taller, and the Bodyguard is broader. But the Challenger is solid enough, and *fast*. He'll be the one to worry about in a knife fight. His hood has fallen back, and N'Doch sees he's also a handsome dude, if you like the blond, rugged type. He wears a neatly trimmed beard, probably to make him look older than his men, since he can't be a day over thirty. His eyes are dark for a blond, though. He has that sort of intense gaze N'Doch has seen on hungry fish hawks. Even without looking in his eyes, N'Doch can feel the reined-in anger radiating from him like heat. He's surprised the snow doesn't just melt right off the guy.

Raven seems to expect some further greeting, but she doesn't get it. The guy throws a quick glance at her, an even swifter punishing glare at the bodyguard, then lets his eyes sweep the darkening farmstead, the yard, the outbuildings, the Big House itself, and the little crowd of women who are now watching him, awaiting his next move. He takes his time—N'Doch admires his control—before he locks eyes with the tall man up on the terrace and growls, "Heinrich, where in hell have you brought me?"

CHAPTER EIGHT

The God's dais is empty when the High Priestess makes her entrance with her retinue into the Hall of Audiences. Paia is relieved, though the thick air bears that dry tang of heated metal that the God brings with him, and she suspects he's just been there, then left on another of his jaunts. She has not seen the God since he delivered his ultimatum, which she has begun to think of with a capital "U," but given its general subject matter, she did expect he'd show up to supervise this month's Presentation, if only to make sure that she didn't reject any even half-likely candidate.

Paia mounts the three wide marble steps. As usual, the Hall is hot and stuffy. Orange afternoon light slants through the clerestory to fall artfully on her ceremonial chair. Without seeming to, she tries to adjust the thin cut-velvet cushion to a more comfortable position. Its gold-wire tassels are as big as her fist and always in the way. The chair itself is high and wide and brilliantly gilded. Its tall, square back is deeply carved with geometric detail framing a huge central icon in the brightest gilt of all: the Winged God Rampant. The sharp edges of his thousand intricately wrought scales poke Paia in the back if she leans against it. She bites off a groan. "Survive the day," indeed. If only she can survive *this* day.

Before, she hasn't thought much about the physical discomfort involved in almost all of the god's ceremonies. Often, she's been ironically grateful to have a reason to stay awake during the more tedious of his endless rituals. For twelve years, she has accepted without question whatever the God demanded of her. She was practically a child, recently orphaned, when the God came to the Citadel. She has fitted herself to his needs ever since because the payback has been her survival. By becoming his Priestess, Paia was allowed to continue living in her family's fortress, fed and protected from the terrible world outside, as her father and sister had fed and protected her until they died.

But in the Library this morning, the House Comp informed her that today is her birthday, as it has on every other birthday—an event that would otherwise go unremarked, for the God does not believe in giving notice to the passage of earthly time. But this birthday is her twenty-eighth, and for no reason that she can articulate, Paia finds this significant. The same way she finds the God's Ultimatum significant. She has recovered from her initial shock about it, but of all the duties the God has ever pressed on her, this seems the most thoughtless and tyrannical. Well, not thoughtless. Paia knows he's up to something. But it actually makes her angry with him, in a way she's never dared to be.

Meanwhile, she's also aware that she's beautiful, twenty-eight years old (now), and still a virgin. She knows what sex is. The House Comp has told her all about it, and she thinks she deserves a little. But her access to men is strictly controlled by the God. If she so much as looks at a servant or soldier, the man in question is never seen in the Citadel again. So part of her is ready to give the God's plan some serious thought. She cannot see that she has any other choice. She's spent too much of her youth alone on a dais or up in her studio in front of an easel.

She settles herself as comfortably as she can on the impossible throne. At least, being within the Citadel, she has been able to leave the God's gun behind and doesn't have to find an invisible place for that hard little lump. Three of the nameless First Daughters flit about, arranging the filmy, glittering yards of her train so that the folds fall seductively around her long, bared legs and nearly naked torso. The fabric sticks to her clammy skin in long damp wrinkles. She can't imagine this to be alluring, but how can she know for sure? Despite the God's empty dais, the Honor Guard stationed in the shadows along the four walls of the Hall all stare stonily away from her.

Paia knows she's beautiful. She can see it in the hastily

averted eyes of the soldiers, even in some of the women's. She can see it in the hungry glances of the Suitors. These men submit to the humiliation of a Presentation for the same reasons that she does the God's bidding without question: fear, and a desire for the safety and comfort that becoming Consort to the High Priestess of the Temple would allow them. But part of that comfort—she can see it in their eyes—would be possessing her exquisite body, with its firm full breasts and unblemished skin. She is a rare and precious commodity in the world: an unmutated, undamaged, perfect physical specimen, an Ideal. The God has told her so himself. It's why he chose her as his Priestess. His own terrible beauty and power is another such Ideal, he says. It is their duty, then, to the Faithful of the Temple, to exhibit themselves openly, so that their despairing flock can be uplifted by the sight of their perfection. The God's perfection is of course unobtainable. But hers, he has decreed, is not . . . at least, for the right man.

Paia's thoughts drift to the painting up in the tower, shrouded on its easel. Another ideal, one not about power or possession. But also, an ideal that no longer exists. At least, Paia muses, I am still around to be possessed. And controlled. She has long understood that all the elaborate trappings and solemnity surrounding the Presentation of the Suitors are a masquerade for the God's own personal breeding program. Crossing her perfection with another's should produce an even more perfect child. And Paia does not object. Why not improve the chances that her children, should she prove able to produce any, will be healthy and able? If the Sons and Daughters of the God of the Apocalypse are to take up the reins of the world in its Last Days, as the God has promised, the more superior they are, the better. The greater their chance to pull the world back from the brink. But there's time for that, surely. Why is the God suddenly so impatient?

Paia senses that she is wandering into uncharted territory. She leans back to press her bare shoulder blade against the spiky carving of the chair. A sharp dose of the here-and-now always serves to bring her back from the edge. Too much speculation is dangerous. When she has her balance again, she nods at Son Luco, who has taken up his station at the bottom of the steps leading up to her chair. Luco loves the Presentations. The closest thing to real intimacy that Paia ever shares with him is their private meeting afterward, during which they are supposed to review the virtues and drawbacks of the various rejected Suitors, but which invariably descends into dish and gossip.

Now he stands, imposing and erect in all his shining regalia, one step into the shaft of hot sun from the windows above. His gilt-sandaled feet toe the edge of the narrow strip of carpet that cuts the Hall in half, from the Priestess' throne, straight down the center to the main doors at the far end. Another strip crosses at right angles midway, leading to the Left and Right Disrobing Chambers. Luco raises the heavy gilt staff held in the crook of his arm, and two acolytes pull open the doors of the Right Chamber.

The first Suitor enters. He is robed in white, as he is allowed to be, until the High Priestess requests a Viewing. Paia wonders if word ever gets around that she's been making this request less and less often. Could this account for some of the God's impatience? She has developed an Ideal of her own, during the three years since the Presentations began, which she has not discussed with the God. Perhaps she should. She wouldn't wish to be compelled to accept a Suitor who does not fit it.

She knows this particular Suitor will not do the moment he turns the corner in mid-hall and comes toward her at the slow, ritual pace. He is good-looking enough, his bronzy features are more or less regular, with only the slightest list to his nicely broad shoulders. But she sees terror and piety in his eyes, and not much else. She lets him approach and kneel. He does not even try to meet her gaze. He's very young, she sees. His hands, holding the robe closed across his chest, are trembling. Perhaps his parents have put him up to this. They as well would stand to gain from his new-won riches. She offers her most gracious Nod of Rejection, and dismisses him without a Viewing.

The next candidate is older than usual. He turns the corner briskly, the long folds of his robe neatly composed and invisibly held in place. He kneels, presenting himself in a respectful but businesslike manner, as if hoping to impress her with his maturity and his understanding that this is, after all, just another kind of trade-and-barter. A merchant? She's told there are one or two left. Paia is intrigued. Takes a certain strength of mind to carry on with commerce during the Last Days, after all. And this man would probably be kind to her. He might even be interesting to talk to. But the skin on his cheeks is patchy and much too pale. Although each candidate is required under Temple oath to swear themselves free of disease, Paia doesn't trust that formality. Again, she is gracious but sends the man off without a Viewing.

The third is darkly handsome, but she hears in his voice the same dullness she's seen in the eyes of the first young man. The fourth is thin and suppressing a cough. Paia thinks what a desperate act of delusion it has been for this one to subject himself to the cost and time and procedures required for becoming a Suitor. More than once, she has wondered what happens to all these failed candidates. Do they return home to disgrace or is it seen as just another chance gone wrong in a life made up of such things?

And so the afternoon wears on, through a fifth, sixth, and seventh. Paia is getting bored, and she can see Luco shifting his weight as if his tall, bright sandals are pinching his feet. So she calls for a Viewing just to placate him, to stir him up a little so he won't disgrace himself or the Temple by falling asleep where he's standing. The eighth Suitor drops his robe to his shoulders and spreads it hesitantly. Paia spares him merely a glance, but signals him to turn so that Luco can receive the full effect. When the poor man has been kindly dismissed, Luco rolls his eyes. The irony is not lost on Paia, and surely not on Luco either, that he himself is the closest thing to a perfect physical specimen that's walked into this hall in a long, long time. Perhaps the God would be satisfied if she had Luco's child. Paia eyes him speculatively, wondering if he could manage it. At least there would be no complications about romance.

A ninth Suitor enters. Paia's attention is caught by the unusual grace and confidence of his bearing. His well-shaped head is held high, allowing his long chestnut hair to ripple across his muscular shoulders. When he rounds the corner, Paia hides a reflexive little gasp. Something new at last. The man's robe is already open, artfully and partly revealing a sculpted chest, neat hips and strong, trim legs. He has high cheekbones and a fine, chiseled mouth, now relaxed into a sultry smile. His dark gaze fixes Paia with the same intense kind of invitation that the God lures her with when he wants something from her. But this man is material. No doubt he can deliver what his eyes are promising.

Paia is momentarily stunned, not just by his boldness but by the sharp thrill that rises in her, by her undeniable urge to peer into the shadows of his open robe. She has seen a lot of naked men during the course of the Presentations. But this one is different. She retreats behind her sternest mask of authority, but her show of chill scrutiny does not fluster him. He stands patiently while she studies him, then shakes his hair back a little and shifts his weight imperceptibly so that his robe falls farther open. His eyes do not stray from hers for an instant. He is beautiful. He is a perfect specimen. Suddenly Paia wishes the God were here, to help her choose. What if it is . . . is this the one? Already she wants to touch this man, wants him to touch her, everywhere. But she can't see his hands. A man's hands are important, but this one has left his hidden in the folds of his robe while all the rest of his assets are fully offered to her view. Perhaps there is something wrong with them, some injury or deformity. She ought to request a full Viewing, except now she's feeling oddly possessive of him, resentful that she must publicly display this beauty that could be meant for her alone, for his eyes say he sees nothing in the room but her. She asks him his name to hear him speak, and his voice is throaty and low, as if he, too, is overcome by this encounter. She hears the name he offers but can't recall it a moment later. She beckons him nearer, then realizes that he has not yet knelt to her. But she cannot help but notice that her nearness is causing his sex to swell and rise within the caressing shadows of his robe. She knows, and he knows, that only she can see this, and he lets it happen. She cannot make herself look away. He smiles at her over half-lidded eyes. His lips part to show the very tip of a roving tongue. He lets his hips loll forward lazily, offering himself to her, and Paia is seized by an erotic madness, though somewhere at the back of her lust-fogged brain, an alarm is going off. She forgets that there are several dozen other people in the room. She leans forward and presents her hand, thinking only of how much she needs him to feel the sudden warmth between her thighs.

His left hand appears from beneath his robe, unmarked and whole. He reaches, grasps her hand. With one firm tug, he pulls her into his arms. Paia does not struggle. She feels him hot and taut against her and her body is already molding itself to his nakedness when the alarm goes double-time in her head. A cool kiss of steel slides past her hip as his right arm curls around her back to press her tightly to his groin. He is stronger than she ever imagined. She tries to cry out, but he smothers her cry with his mouth and tongue. One hand, warm and longing, slips down around her thigh to invade the softness between her legs. The other, cold and hard, rises between her breasts. His blade is at her neck but in the instant that he hesitates, betrayed by the heat of his own very real desire, Luco is on him from behind, hauling him off, hurling him away from her, kicking him viciously and pinning him to the floor with the gilded staff of office. By then, the Honor Guard has bolted across the room to take over.

Before Paia can collapse into a heap of shock and humiliation, Son Luco scoops her up as he might a child and hustles her from the hall.

He is not so gentle when he gets her up to her chambers, trailed by the panicked captain of the Honor Guard and a few of his more alert men.

"He'll burn you to goddamn cinders, the whole sorry lot of you!" he bellows at them as he shoulders the door shut in their faces. He dumps Paia unceremoniously onto her bed and looms over her, his big hands waving. "What were you *thinking*?"

Paia huddles, shuddering. She can't really believe it herself. "I wasn't. I wasn't. I just wasn't!"

"I'll say!"

"I'll never . . . I couldn't . . . help myself."

She weeps a bit, while Luco paces back and forth, from bed to window. "Never seen such a spectacle in all my life! You spoiled brat!" He throws up his hands and paces away again.

"I'll thank you to remember who you're talking to," she sniffs.

He stops, folds his arms. "I'm talking to a spoiled brat! You could have been killed! Did you even think about what he'll do to the rest of us if we let anything happen to you?"

This brings her upright to look at him. He's wan and shaken himself, and angry enough to have lost all his decorum. She's never had Luco in her rooms. He looks bigger here, and rougher-edged. Like he's somehow taking up more space than usual, perhaps because she's never, ever seen him so furious. Rage is not one of Luco's public moods. She decides to let the name-calling go by. "So I guess this wasn't another of your revenue-producing plots . . . ?"

Luco rounds on her. "How could you even think such a thing?"

Paia buries her head in her arms. "He can't hear of this, Luco. He can't! He's not very happy with me right now."

"Of course he'll hear of it! How are we going to keep it from him, when you insist on displaying your lust in front of the entire world!"

"I don't have lust, I . . . well, maybe I did a little."

"A *little*? My dear girl . . ."

"It's the God's own fault! He's the one pushing me to pick a Suitor all of a sudden!"

"He is? Really?"

"Really. Like it was an order."

"Huh. Well, you can bet he didn't mean a trained assassin got up as a street prostitute."

Paia stares at him. "Assassin? Prostitute? Was it so clear to everyone but me? Oh, no!" Somehow this is worse than practically losing her virginity right there in the Hall of Audiences. She throws herself back on the bed, sobbing.

Luco slows his pacing, then sits down beside her. "Well, not everyone. Most of them were half-asleep by then. And, I admit, he was beautiful."

This makes her sob all the harder. "Why, Luco? Why do they do it? What have I ever done but serve them as the God requires?"

"It's simple: they go after you because they can't get at him. And this was a novel strategy, using your own worst impulses against you. The guy planned it very well, I must say."

His pragmatism soothes her, despite a certain undertone of relish. She rolls over to look up at him. "All by himself? A heresy of one?"

"Most likely the Greens again. He was only the weapon."

"Was? Surely, the God would want him kept alive for questioning?"

"I thought you'd rather the God didn't hear about all this."

"No . . . yes, he must know. I mean, how could someone get a knife through all his security procedures?"

Luco crosses his legs. He roughs his long hair back and lets his top leg—still wrapped in its gilded sandal—swing restlessly. "Stupidity or betrayal. It's always one or the other. And I suppose I'll have to bear part of the blame. Our only hope is that he'll be too distracted by this business over the hill to care."

"What business?"

He waves a dismissive hand. "Oh, some minor disagreement with one of the villages. He's down there dealing with it."

Paia has never been to the villages. But for the God's frequent evangelical forays, she might even forget they're there, supplying the Temple with food and service personnel in return for the God's protection. "Well, anyway, you won't take the blame. It was my fault. Besides, you saved me!" She realizes she hasn't even thanked him yet. Maybe she is just a spoiled brat. She gets up on her knees and puts her arms around him from behind to kiss his cheek. She's never been that familiar with him before, and is not sure why she's doing it now, except that the . . . incident has left her feeling unusually vulnerable. She needs to assure herself of Luco's loyalty and support. He accepts her embrace but does not particularly warm to it. "I'll tell him everything, I promise!"

"You better."

It occurs to her how much the God will enjoy hearing her tell this particular story. "Oh, Luco, I wish you could just be my Suitor. Everything would be so much easier."

Luco barks a dry laugh, pats her arm. "I don't think so, dear girl. I don't think so."

Then Paia remembers what the God had said: *choose someone you'll tire of quickly.* Sometimes she thinks Luco understands the God better than she does.

When he's pulled himself together and straightened all his priestly regalia to his satisfaction in front of Paia's full-length mirror, Luco delivers a stern warning to think twice the next time she's about to do something foolish, then puts on his Temple face and leaves her alone.

Paia immediately strips off her ceremonial garb and digs out her beloved T-shirt and sweats. It's not the right time for hot water, so she douses herself with cold, regardless of the waste. She feels exposed, rubbed raw by this near-fatal encounter and the madness that precipitated it. Her madness. Luco is right. What could she have been thinking? The shapeless soft garments enclose her. They comfort her with concealment. She braids up her damp hair, pulling it back tightly from her face. She hopes she looks awful. She stows the God's little gun in a hip pocket. She won't let herself be without it ever again. Now she feels sleek and efficient, and calm enough to confront the guards outside her door who will, no doubt, be shocked by her undecorated appearance, and will try to dissuade her from leaving her rooms.

A doubled contingent of chastened faces slew around to stare at her when she opens the door. The duty captain is an older woman whose eyes are already exhausted by the vision of her own anticipated incineration at the hand of an angry god. Right now, she couldn't care less what the High Priestess is wearing.

Paia nods. "I'll be working in my studio until dinner, Captain."

"Yes, Mother." The woman looks faintly relieved to see her alive and apparently unharmed. And no doubt she has feared some further madness to be dealt with, some scheme or reckless journey by their unruly High Priestess that the Guard will be duty-bound to keep up with. But these windowless, dead-end corridors, even half-lit, are easy to defend. The captain bows, and when Paia turns down the hall, she signals four of her squad to follow at a discreet distance.

Paia gains the tower entrance. Light sifts down from an

invisible skylight high at the top of the shaft. She starts her climb without a backward glance. She knows the guards will not follow. The deal is, when she's up in the studio, they guard the bottom of the stairs. She takes the steep stone steps as briskly as she can manage, driving herself up without a rest even after she's gasping for breath. A dose of self-punishment, Paia reflects, and minor enough, given the severity of her offense.

In truth, she cannot believe how stupid she was, letting appetite win out like that over good sense and training and the God's constant reminders that his High Priestess is always a target. *Mere appetite? Ha.* The blinding force of the need she'd felt in the Hall still lingers in her body like a drug, evaporating her calm with its little aftershocks. It was almost as if the urge had come upon her from outside. Like the evil eye, or a spell, she muses. But Paia does not believe in such things, so the blame must be turned inward, on herself.

On the top step, she stands panting. The big room is bright with hot afternoon glare. The shadows are long and as sharp-edged as knives. She's not even sure why she's come, except that she felt compelled to. Not by the familiar eager stirrings of an idea brimming in her head. Paia hesitates. Her eyes are drawn to the shrouded easel, and she can no longer deny it. She's come to see the painting. To take comfort from its lush and restful tones. Usually, when she finishes a painting, she sets it aside. None of her stark portraits of the neighboring slopes and crags decorate the walls of her bedchamber, or any other walls in the Citadel.

But this painting calls out to her. The mysterious circumstance of its creation hints at some pernicious heresy rising in Paia's soul. But perhaps it can offer her some corrective insight or message of truth, if only she can decipher it.

She moves quickly to the easel and throws back the concealing tarp. Once again, the rich, moist life of the landscape leaps out to envelope her. The tree-softened curve of its hills and the lost peaceful sweetness of its silvery river bring a start of tears to her eyes.

Then Paia notices two things.

The sky overhanging her pristine imaginary valley is not as clear as she remembers. Clouds are massing behind the smoothly rolling horizon, a dark crenellation as architectural as the ruined skylines of the cities she secretly reads about in the House Comp's library. She can't imagine how she missed noticing them before. But she'd been spent and bleary-eyed after the long night's work, and one of the miraculous qualities of a painting is how it often reveals itself over time. If you bother to go back and look at it again, which Paia rarely does.

The thing she is sure was not in the painting when she left it is a small, folded scrap of paper. It's pinned to the tray of the easel with the sturdy blade she uses for cutting canvas.

Her first reaction is to grab at her hip pocket for the God's gun, and take a swift look around. Someone has been here, and might be still. After the treachery in the Hall of Audiences, Paia is no longer confident about either the skill or the loyalty of her guards. But this room has few corners that could hide an assailant. A quick search confirms that it's empty.

Her next thought is almost as unnerving. Someone has seen this painting. Some other person has shared this revelation of her inner longings. Longings more secret and forbidden even than sex. Someone who might report her to the God.

Paia's hand trembles as she jerks the heavy blade free and unfolds the paper. The note is brief, neatly handwritten in a reddish-brown substance that Paia fears is blood.

It reads: *"What price survival?"*

Paia folds the note away in her pocket and walks quickly toward the stairs.

The God does not come visiting that evening, as she has feared he would. When her chambermaid has arrived with the evening ration, helped her undress, turned down the bed, and bowed her way from the room, Paia takes a cup of water to her window alcove and draws the heavy drapes aside. She unwraps the note in the light of an oil lamp, and reads it again.

What price survival? What could it mean?

To the south, the ruddy sky is brighter than usual. In the ragged notches between the crags, she sees a distant glow and flicker. Somewhere out there, something big is burning.

CHAPTER NINE

He looked exactly as she remembered him, not as she would have wished to remember him, as the golden lord in that fateful barn in Erfurt. He was as she remembered from her dreams, which had revealed to her so clearly the sad progression of Baron Köthen's disillusionment. She should not have been surprised by Rose's unflattering description. But she had not wanted to accept the truth of her dreams quite so literally.

From a shadowed corner of the great room, Erde watched Köthen move into the lantern light as if into a dungeon. She saw his eyes sweep the borders of the room the way he'd swept the night air with his sword in the clearing where he'd found the murdered prince, arc after glittering arc of shamed outrage. He wore civility like an ill-fitting garment. He stopped in the middle of the room, and as he stood there uncertainly, his face for an instant was as raw and open as a child's, exposing to any who observed him his impatience at being kept from the battle, his horror at being suddenly powerless to command his own surroundings. Erde had seen that he'd arrived with his hands bound. She could not imagine what could have induced Hal—who should have understood him better than anyone—to submit his former foster son and squire to such humiliation. Rose said events had been hard on Baron Köthen, but this was clearly an understatement. All the ease in him was gone. Now he moved like man whose skin was filled with broken glass.

A moment later, his face closed again, as he let habits of breeding and pragmatism master his outrage. As a guest of the house, he would be expected to behave. Yet Erde saw how close he was to the limit of his own good sense, how his dry humor had turned bitter, how rage was eroding his optimism as well as his grace. And how, when she stepped bravely out of the shadow to greet him, his eyes swept past her as something unrecognized, unfamiliar, unimportant, in his single-minded search for answers to his predicament.

She saw all that, and also saw how Hal eyed him with covert concern. How the third man's attention never left him. The two of them, watching Baron Köthen sidelong, as one might a drunk or a madman, to keep him from hurting himself, or someone else. Soon, she couldn't bear to see it any longer. She slipped out of the room into a back hall and fled to the consoling company of the dragon in the barn.

"Under the protection of *women*, Heinrich? You think less of my skills than ever I thought." The Challenger grins in a death's-head sort of way and tosses his wet cloak down on a stool.

Coming in behind him with the others, N'Doch notices how this guy walks into a room like he owns it, or if he doesn't yet, he will soon enough. Idly, N'Doch wonders if he could learn how to do that.

Deliberately, Rose picks up the cloak and hands it off to one of the twins. "Do you intend to leave him, then, Heinrich?"

The Honcho spreads his hands. Now N'Doch understands his air of apology. "If you'll take him, Rosie. Don't know how else to keep him alive."

"Or even if you should," remarks Rose.

The Honcho sighs. N'Doch reads pain in him, and not a little ambivalence. "His last escapade cost me three of my best men."

"How I love being talked about in the third person!" The Challenger turns neatly on his heel. "My lady Rose. Forgive my ill manners. I haven't yet greeted you." He bows to her, low and crisp. "The years have not diminished your beauty nor your fabled wisdom. But I was unaware that you had gone into the business of arrest and detainment."

Rose returns his satirical stare. "Don't be sullen, Adolphus Michael. It doesn't become you. Don't worry. We'll keep you employed and busy. You'll see it's all for the best."

"I fail to see how."

Rose moves past him like he's some misbehaving son she's ignoring. She catches the tall guy's cloak as he shrugs it off, and passes that one, too, into waiting hands. The issue of why the Challenger is here seems clear to everyone but N'Doch. "Come, warm up by the fire. You must be cold and hungry."

"An understatement," mutters the Challenger.

"Rosie," says the Honcho, "This is Dolph's captain, Kurt Wender. The best of men. If you're willing and up to this, he'll be keeping our good baron company."

The Bodyguard steps forward with a bow, much more polite than the Challenger's. "My lady."

Rose smiles at him. "I'm nobody's lady, Captain Wender, except perhaps Heinrich's. Call me Rose. Please, come by the fire. You are welcome."

Wender nods gratefully. He finds a bench by the fire and drops onto it with a sigh. He accepts a mug of heated wine from the other of the twins. N'Doch's glad to see he's too much the man's man to carry all this bowing and scraping any further.

Raven fills another mug from the big crock warming just inside the fireplace. She offers it to the Challenger, who looks her over. N'Doch sees speculation but little interest. Still, he can't help eavesdropping.

"Where have you been, Raven?"

"Oh, here and there. Mostly here."

"Ever since?"

She nods. "I was sorry to hear about your father."

"It's seven years since I assumed the title, Raven."

"Still. He was always kind to me."

The Challenger frowns, as if he resents any pleasant memory. "A good man."

"Yes. And you? You look thin, Dolph. Slim pickings along the road?"

"Is it any different here? Out there, people are killing

each other for food now. Blizzards in September! The countryside is starving."

"Can't something be done to help?" Raven asks mildly.

The Challenger flicks her a disbelieving glance, then shakes his head. "That, dear Raven, is what I was *trying* to do."

Raven just smiles at him and again holds up the steaming mug. He takes it, then looks at it as if he's forgotten what it's for, and sets it aside. He's already moving about, measuring the walls of his prison. "The hell with war and politics. By the way, where is here?"

"Welcome to Deep Moor."

"Many thanks. What's Deep Moor?"

"A place apart. Away from the ills of the world. Or so we thought."

The Challenger snorts. "Until I arrived to spoil your idyll." He paces back to her, stops, brushes her chin gently with the back of his hand. "You've grown no less beautiful, Raven."

"Nor you, Dolph "

"Are you the bait, then?"

"Pardon?"

"To keep the prisoner docile and pacified during his incarceration?"

Raven tilts her head. "Such bitter thoughts, Dolph."

"I have cause," he growls, and turns away.

Raven shrugs. She joins Rose as she draws the Honcho into the warmth of the big stone hearth. "We were just making dinner when you arrived."

"Dinner!" The tall guy's booming laugh is over the top, N'Doch thinks. Like the poor man's hoping the black mood he's brought into the room can be denied by applying the proper amount of cheer. "Wender! When d'you figure our last meal was?"

"Two days past, my lord, at least."

"My count also. And a poor meal it was at that." He reaches eagerly for the mug Raven has put on the table beside him. "I'm any day glad to ride into Deep Moor, but this time gladder than ever. It's bad out there, Rosie. It'd be bad even if we weren't trying to fight a war. Stores are running low everywhere, and when the hell-priest provisions his armies, he leaves nothing behind for the villages.

Not a scrap, not a bean! So they're angry at any soldier who rides their way, no matter whose side he's on!" He pauses, looks at the floor, his cheer deflating into frustration and despair. "Truth is, we could use a good feeding."

"And you shall have it."

The prospect seems to buck him up a bit, and he grins. "You might even get Dolph to eat something. He's not been fond of my cooking."

Over his shoulder, the Challenger retorts, "If you can refer to hacking at a hunk of frozen bread with your sword as 'cooking.'"

"Picky, picky," mutters the Honcho, but N'Doch can see he's pleased to have raised even a sprout of humor from such stony ground. He sips from his mug, shaking his head with grim appreciation, and sips again, drawing Rose aside. "But what news? If the travelers have returned, where is Milady Erde?"

"She's . . ." Rose looks around. "Oh. Well, she was here . . ."

From her seat by the fire, Raven says, "I think she went out to the barn."

"Not here to greet me?"

"Well, *he's* in the barn, no doubt expecting a visit."

"Ah. Yes, that's it." Again, he looks pleased, "Then we must comply immediately. Did all go well with their journey?"

"News over dinner," says Rose, "and a visit after. First, there are other introductions to be made."

She looks N'Doch's way. Suddenly he realizes that the group he came in with has evaporated quietly to the other parts of the house. In the kitchen, the clatter of food preparation starts up like background music. He and the dragon-as-Sedou are left stranded by the door, with the girl nowhere to be seen. Rose beckons them forward out of the shadows. All three men turn at the creak of their footsteps across the old wooden floor.

It's weird, but N'Doch wishes he had a guitar in his hands. He feels at a distinct disadvantage. Not that one song, even the right one, could explain or justify his presence here completely. But it could sure help.

With the shedding of the long, concealing cloaks, he sees that the men are dirty and wet through, that their faces are bruised, that their layers of silk and leather and mail are muddied, bloodstained, and torn. What's more, weapons have come into view. Not on the Challenger, of course, but the Bodyguard Wender and the tall guy both wear sleek, leather-sheathed knives at their waists and swords on their hips. Swords. Real ones. Fine steel, glinting with firelight. To N'Doch, these big blades seem impossibly long. He can't see how you wouldn't trip on them. The tall guy is just unbuckling his to lay it aside when Rose brings N'Doch and Sedou to his attention. Having done so, she looks momentarily at a loss.

N'Doch grins. Rose speechless? He hasn't seen this in the whole week he's known her. *"Mais, par où commencer?"* he says to her. *Where do you start?*

"Eh bien, mon petit. J'en sais rien."

He sees the men eyeing him, over Rose's shoulder. Taking in his youth, his height, how his head nearly grazes the ceiling's lowest beams. Noting Sedou's athletic build, and the shared alien ebony of their skin, the *difference* in their faces. These men have seen most of what their world has to offer, N'Doch can tell, but probably their world doesn't include Africa yet. They don't know what they're looking at, and they're not used to that. He recalls how the girl stared at him so much at first, mostly when she thought he wasn't looking. These guys are not so polite. They start staring and keep right on at it.

The dragon stirs in his mind.

We could be men to them, or demons.

It gets real quiet for a moment in that darkening room, and N'Doch wonders if he's in any danger. The windows have gone all iron gray, blank with night and snow. Nowhere to run. He's got his eye on the Honcho, whose bright, curious gaze shifts from himself to Sedou and back a few times, questing, reading for information and understanding. This guy knows something important's afoot, when strangers—male, alien strangers—have preceded him into this women's haven at Deep Moor.

But Rose reels off the names with the ease of a talk show hostess, like there's no one but us humans in the room. She introduces the Honcho as Heinrich von Engle, late of Weisstrasse. He throws a smile their way and, real quickly, adds, "Just Hal Engle."

The Challenger apparently answers to the name Adolphus Michael von Hoffman, Baron Köthen, a name longer even than Engle's sword, but he volunteers no short-cut of any kind. N'Doch remembers the girl saying her father was a baron and that she grew up in a castle. Must mean this Köthen dude is somebody important.

Rose keeps up the talk show chat as she explains the language problem, that one of these "foreign" visitors speaks German, the other doesn't. N'Doch notices there is no mention of the always ongoing simultaneous translation by dragon power. He decides he's just regained several points of lost advantage. Then the tall guy Engle surprises him by saying quietly to Rose, "I have read of dark men such as these. Have they come from the south below the sea? Is one the mage his lordship sought?"

"No, but N'Doch and Sedou have traveled back with Lady Erde from the place that she went with him."

"Ah." Engle holds up a finger, shakes his head once. His eyes flick toward the Challenger, who's moved off restlessly to stare out a window.

Rose gives this some thought. Then she says aloud, "He doesn't know?"

"Rosie . . ." Engle murmurs.

"If you've brought him to stay, Heinrich, there's no way we can keep it from him."

Engle looks flustered. Oddly, he glances at Sedou, like the "dark man" has said something to him, or might be about to. "I don't think it's . . . well, I hadn't expected them back so soon."

"Really, I'm such an inconvenience to you, Heinrich. Why don't you just get rid of me?" The Challenger turns from his study of gray on gray outside the window. "What don't I know?"

Engle stares down at the floor, then up again at Sedou. His eyes narrow, then refocus suddenly in a kind of veiled wonder, as if he's been asked an unexpected and remarkable question. N'Doch doesn't want to look. He's afraid the dragon's chosen a really stupid moment to shape-shift. "He wouldn't have believed me if I did tell him, Rose. Never has. He'll require the proof of his senses."

"This is interesting," murmurs Sedou.

"Well," says Rose. "No time like the present."

"I don't . . ." Engle begins. "Wait. Wait." He chews his lip, overgrown with a shaggy mustache, then regards Rose from under lowered brows, like a child planning mischief. "But you said, Rosie, more than one . . . ?"

"Two."

"Is the . . . other . . . ?" He tilts his head toward the barn.

"Not exactly."

"Ahhh. I wish the girl were here to guide me."

"No, you don't."

N'Doch realizes there's some old sort of game playing itself out here between Rose and her lover, like if she just came right out and told him everything he wants to know, he'd be disappointed. Even though it's clear he wants to know it desperately. His gaze drifts back to Sedou.

"Ah. That's it," he says again, more softly. His eyes flutter closed, as if in utter gratitude. N'Doch hears in his voice the same veiled wonder that had been in his look. "Shape-shifter."

Beside him, Sedou stands a little taller.

At the window, the Challenger clears his throat. "Am I to die, my knight, before being offered enlightenment?"

"Wait. Wait. A moment, please. You cannot know how . . ." Engle gropes behind him for the sword he's laid on the table. He takes it in both hands and pulls it slowly from its sheath. N'Doch suppresses the primal shiver that seizes him at the cool rasp of that much steel being drawn. The blade grabs his attention like a shout. It flashes bright shards of firelight into his eyes. Both its faces are honed to an invisible edge, but he can see scarring up and down the length. This blade has been well used. He had a machete once that looked almost as murderous, a weapon he loved, so he is both horrified and mesmerized, like the snake before the mongoose, as Engle sets the empty sheath aside and comes toward him. The man moves easily still, not like an old man but a fighter. N'Doch holds his ground. But it doesn't matter. Engle's wondering gaze is not fixed on him.

The dragon is a whisper in his head.

He knows.

"What? How?" murmurs N'Doch out loud. "Like Baraga?"

The last guy who twigged to what Sedou was had blown N'Doch to bits.

No. Just knows. I'd say, good instincts and a lifetime of study.

Engle approaches, his eyes on Sedou. Five paces away, he stops. "Rosie," he says hoarsely, over his shoulder. "Am I right about this?"

Her reply is loving, and so quiet that N'Doch can barely hear it. "Yes, Heinrich. You are the finest dragon-hunter of them all."

Hunter? N'Doch readies himself, his mind tossing up all the ways he might wrestle that mean-looking gorgeous blade out of the tall guy's hands. Except that Engle is not raising the sword to strike. He's turned it hilt-upward, set its point gingerly to the floor, and gone done on one knee, head bowed, at Sedou's feet. When he speaks, it's in Frankish, more fluent than Rose's, and N'Doch gets an inkling who she learned it from.

"My lord," says Engle. "My sword is ever at your service."

Rose smiles. "Actually, Heinrich, it's 'my lady.'"

"Is it so? An excellent symmetry! My lady, then." Engle is unfazed. "I thought my life's whole purpose satisfied when I pledged myself to one of your kind, my lady. I never dreamed of the good fortune that will allow me to serve two."

The hair stands up on the back of N'Doch's neck. There's something so pure, so absolute in Engle's tone. Without any proof, the guy just *believes*. And Sedou shows no embarrassment at having this old soldier down in front of him. N'Doch watches as his brother grasps the offered sword like he's handled one all his life. The hilt is carved, with the winged figure of a dragon coiled around a tree. Sedou lifts the blade and holds it upright in front of him. He brings it close, lining it up with his nose until his breath fogs the polished metal. Then he sets it back a bit, regarding its gleaming ferocity with solemn bemusement. Like he's moved by thoughts he can't possibly begin to express or explain. Like the sword itself is a whole story to him. The reflection that N'Doch sees in the steel is the dragon's eye, not his brother Sedou's. The voice is Sedou's, but the words come from another time and place as he answers Engle in perfect old German.

"I am glad, Sir Knight, that we meet first at a moment

when I possess the hands to take up this blade in gratitude, and return it to you with my acceptance of your pledge of service." Sedou reverses the hilt and extends it forward. N'Doch lets go a breath, amazed. The Challenger, he sees, is staring at them in disbelief.

"What service may I perform?" Engle intones, his eyes shining.

"We will speak of that."

Engle rises, takes the sword, and drops the blade by his side. Then he stands back with a final bow. It all goes so smoothly, it's like they've rehearsed it. Or like they both just instinctively knew what to do. N'Doch feels he's in the presence of something ancient beyond understanding. Beyond *his* understanding, at least. One of the things he likes about life, he decides, is that it's still always catching him by surprise. He thinks of the girl, always going on about dragon lore and dragon purposes, all the stuff he's supposed to know for some reason, and doesn't. *A lifetime of study,* the dragon had said. This must be some of what they're both talking about.

And as quickly as it began, the ritual is over. Engle relaxes, and the dragon-as-Sedou is just Sedou again, a big dark man with a smile that could eat you alive. Engle turns to N'Doch with a little bow.

"And you are her guide? Welcome."

N'Doch starts to stick out his hand, then holds back and returns the bow as best he can. This whole event is feeling like one big performance anyway. But he can tell it's real enough to Engle. And maybe to the others. Across the room by the fire, the Bodyguard Wender is looking pretty weirded out. He's on his feet, easing his half-drawn weapon back into its scabbard as if he's not sure he should.

But the Challenger has set his bearded jaw. "Keep me in the dark, Heinrich, if you must, but explain at least why a King's Knight kneels so readily to this . . . stranger!"

"Ah, an ancient and venerable stranger!"

"I repeat, kneels to a *stranger,* but would not to the best pick among us for healing the kingdom?"

"Not the best until you learn a little control," Engle tosses back with half his attention. He's still grinning and elated.

"What?"

"Or even the best, yes, but not the most legitimate."

"Legitimate?" The Challenger jabs a finger in Sedou's direction. "Is *this* legitimate?" N'Doch notes how quickly the hard rage in him breaks into the open. "What, have you found us some new pretender? One that Otto himself doesn't even know he's sired?"

"No need to be offensive," Raven murmurs from the fireplace.

Engle flashes Sedou a complicit glance, then turns back to the room looking flushed and victorious. "Dolph, Dolph, you misunderstand. This is another thing entirely. You'll be on your knees yourself when you're faced with the truth of it."

"Never!"

"Don't doubt it, lad."

"Don't call me that!" the younger man snarls.

Engle spreads his hands. "Dolph . . ."

"No! Never again! This is ended, Heinrich!" He spins away, then back again immediately, his wrists pressed together in Engle's face. "You bound me! Me! In Erfurt, I showed you greater honor!"

At last Engle focuses on him. "Yes! You did! I freely admit it! But, Dolph, here . . . here in Deep Moor, I could not indulge your current death wish, for the sake of others. You cannot know how precious the thing is that's being guarded here."

"A kingdom is precious, Heinrich! What could be more?" The Challenger moves up on him again, circling. Wender's hand returns to his sword hilt.

"I've tried to tell you, Dolph, how many times over the years! Before I knew myself for sure! I even tried to tell you in Erfurt, but you were so interested in a crown, you wouldn't listen! Now even you will be unable to deny it!"

The Challenger halts his advance. His shoulders go slack like he's had a sudden realization. "What in hell are you talking about?"

"I'm talking about the truth!"

"The truth of what?"

The two men glare at each other until Rose says. "Really, Dolph, the best way to explain it is simply to show you." Rose takes Engle's arm, and then the Challenger's. "Come, gentlemen. This won't take long."

Earth had already been anxious when she fled to him: worried about her, about the war and the safety of Deep Moor, and increasingly impatient to resume his Quest. But it was the big dragon's way to be anxious, just as it was his way to soothe and comfort those in need. Especially his dragon guide, though Erde knew he did not understand why she wept so disconsolately as she curled up against his plated chest.

ARE YOU ILL? YOU SEEM HEALTHY. HAVE YOU NOT EATEN?

I'M NOT HUNGRY.

YOU KNOW YOU SHOULD ALWAYS EAT WHEN YOU HAVE THE CHANCE.

DEAR DRAGON, I FEEL FINE.

YOU DO NOT SOUND FINE. PERHAPS YOU HAVE NOT RESTED ENOUGH?

She had thought her mind completely open to him. Now Erde wondered if certain subtleties of human emotion were simply incomprehensible to a dragon. She found them mysterious enough herself, and she was the one experiencing them. Why should she be so stricken by the plight of a man she barely knew? And how could this sadness also feel so sweet?

The dragon would be no help here, though he'd continue to try until she worried about worrying him, about distracting him from the truly important considerations, like the Quest. For the dragon's sake, then, she must dry her tears and seem to take comfort as he bent his great head over her, rumbling his concern into her mind.

She'd nearly dozed off when she heard the big door slide open. Lanterns glowed at the distant front of the barn. She heard Rose's voice and Hal's, then Köthen's muttered reply. She and the dragon had watched the meeting in the great room through Sedou/Water's eyes. She knew Hal would be obscenely cheerful, as he was now able to raise his life-count of dragons from one to two. And Baron Köthen would be . . . well, perhaps the dragons could help him feel better about his situation, if she could get him to talk with them. She knew from her own experience that the dragons could heal the mind as well as they had healed N'Doch's broken body.

As voices and lanterns approached, Erde scrambled up from her warm nest beside the dragon's foreleg and hid behind the hayrick. Beside the dragon's left claw, her own lantern flickered in the draft from the open door.

"I've a mind just to send you in first and let him eat you," she heard Hal say. "But come on. This way."

She'd chosen a good vantage, a full field of view once they rounded the corner of the big open stall where the dragon lay sleeping. He looked beautiful, she thought, huge and glimmering in the lamplight, fading into darkness behind, so that his true size was exaggerated by the dancing shadows. She saw Hal's eyes light with the fire of a devoted lover. He forgot Baron Köthen for a moment and strode straight to the dragon, to touch two reverent fingers to a huge ivory horn. "My lord Earth," he whispered. "Are you well?"

Köthen followed more slowly, caught a glimpse of what lay massed before him in the dim lamplight, and—mid-stride—went utterly still.

He looked away, looked back, then for a long time, only his dark eyes moved, absorbing, measuring each detail, assuring himself of the reality of an existence that, all his life, he had denied the possibility of. He shook his head twice in a wordless negative. Finally, he let out a long, long breath and swore softly to himself.

Hal stirred and noticed him standing there. Without a trace of the triumph he must surely be feeling, he stepped aside to gesture Köthen forward. Slowly, Köthen, moved up beside him, his eyes fixed on the dragon as if it might vanish the moment he looked away. His hand strayed to the older man's shoulder, as if nothing awkward had ever passed between them. Whether he was giving or taking support, Erde couldn't be sure. Together, the two men stared up at the dragon's bronzy head and scimitar horns.

"Impressive, my knight," Köthen said, as if speaking was no longer the easiest thing. "Is it alive?"

"Oh, yes."

"Really? Am I dreaming?"

Hal laughed softly. "No, lad, you're not dreaming."

Oddly, Köthen seemed to accept this. "Sweet Jesus. A dragon. Does it . . . breathe fire?"

"No."

"No? How disappointing for you. Does it turn lead into gold?"

"That's alchemy. Have you forgotten all I taught you?"

"Only the stuff I never thought I'd need," Köthen replied ruefully. "Well, does it *hoard* gold, then? Are you rich again?"

"Hah. If he was a hoarder, he'd be unlikely to give me so much as a coin of it." Hal regarded the dragon fondly. "No, there are many things he isn't or doesn't do that one might have expected a dragon to be or do. He doesn't fly either, that is, not as you might define flying."

"As I might?" Köthen turned his gaze from the sleeping dragon to study Hal's face. "And how might you define it?"

Hal grinned at him. "It was he who snatched me from your grasp at Erfurt."

Köthen's chin lifted. "Ah. The first nail in my coffin."

"No, the first was raising your sword against your King."

Köthen frowned, dropped his hand from Hal's shoulder, then let the remark go by. Erde decided his curiosity had got the better of him. "It is true that your sudden disappearance was never adequately explained to me. I blamed all the confusion on the earthquake."

Hal cocked his head, increasingly unable to restrain his immense satisfaction that this conversation was finally taking place. He drew in the air with a finger, outlining a pair of shining ivory horns and a vast swell of plated hide. "He was the earthquake."

"He what?"

"His name," Hal offered, "is Earth."

"It . . . he . . . made the earthquake?"

"Is that so hard to believe, now that you see him before you?"

Köthen frowned again. "I'm afraid it's all rather hard to believe, my knight." He gripped Hal's shoulder again, briefly, then turned away. "A dragon. Congratulations. It's all you ever wanted."

"Not all. I wanted my estates once more in hand, the King secure on his throne, and you fighting beside me."

Köthen growled in his throat. "Leave it, Heinrich!" He

paced away, out of the lantern light, saw Rose waiting silently in the shadows, and swerved aside like an animal evading capture.

"But," Hal continued lightly, "he's a fine consolation prize."

Köthen's path became circular and brought him around to be startled again into stillness as the sleeping dragon loomed once more before him. "Jesus Christ Almighty," he muttered. And then he grew thoughtful. "Will it help fight the hell-priest?"

"Perhaps. Although he has a great Mission of his own that he must pursue. A dragon has his own mind, you know." Hal gave up his struggle for restraint and turned his joy on Köthen like a beacon. "I told you there was magic in the world, Dolph!"

Köthen stared back at him, then looked down with a small laugh and a shrug. "So you did, my knight. So you did."

His words were agreeable, but his tone was bitter. Erde guessed that the past weeks together had been a horror of mutual recriminations for these two men, honing this argument and others to a lethal edge. At any moment, they could come to blows. She decided to intervene. She sent the dragon a mental nudge.

SHOW HIM ALL YOU ARE, DEAR DRAGON. HELP HIM TO UNDERSTAND.

The dragon woke and opened one golden eye, as tall as a man. In the darkness of the barn, his gaze glowed with inner fire.

Köthen recoiled. His hand jerked reflexively for the sword that was no longer at his hip, then dropped uselessly to his side. Next to him, Hal Engle bowed, then knelt to bask in the unearthly light. Erde saw Köthen's fingers tremble as the actuality of a living dragon finally overtook him. Before, it could have been a fake, a statue cleverly lit. But now, that one great eye, alight with ancient life—and now the other, as Earth stirred and lifted his big head. Like a man in a raging cyclone, Köthen fought the urge to kneel as Hal had told him he would—and won that skirmish. *This man thinks he should kneel to no one,* Erde noted. But the battle of belief was over, it seemed. Baron Köthen saw no reason to suspect the evidence of his own eyes.

"A dragon," he murmured again, to no one in particular.

Hal rose, complaining of stiff joints. With his formal greeting and obeisance accomplished, Erde knew he would now feel free to treat the dragon as he usually did, with a good deal less reverence. Which meant he'd be wanting to talk to him, and would need her to translate. Erde grinned from her hiding place as he leaned closer to scratch Earth familiarly on his horny snout, in just the spot she'd once revealed as the dragon's favorite. She was so relieved to see him alive and well, after her terrible nightmares of the war. Greetings were long overdue, and she knew it was time to face Köthen in a normal way. She'd been down this road only too recently, this foolishness of thinking that a man had noticed her when really, he hadn't, at least not in that way. And how much more presumptuous of her to think this of Adolphus, Baron Köthen, a powerful lord and nearly a stranger to her, than of a childhood companion like Rainer. Never mind the fact that he was nearly twice her age. Besides, if Köthen hadn't recognized her back in the farmhouse, there wasn't even going to be that awkward moment she'd anticipated.

Erde slipped around behind the manger and came up beside Rose.

"Ah," said Rose, moving forward as she did. "Here she is."

"Milady! At last!" Hal honored her with a deep and courtly bow, then grasped her hands warmly. "Ah, look at you! A gown and everything! My little squire-boy is more grown-up every day. I wish I could say the same of myself."

"But we are both alive and that's what matters." Boldly, Erde went up on tiptoe to kiss his cheek. "I worried about you all the time I was away!"

Hal laughed. "You know you're getting old when the young ladies feel free to kiss you without consequence!" Then he said to Rose, "I can't get used to having her talk."

"Get used to it," Rose warned. "She has a lot to say." She took Erde's elbow to turn her gently toward Köthen. "Dolph, I think you've met Lady Erde von Alte?"

Köthen nodded politely, his mind still on the dragon. "Yes, I do believe . . ." Then he turned his head slightly, as if memory had failed him, or was just then returning.

"Erfurt . . . ?" Hal supplied helpfully.

Erde raised her head to glance sidelong past Köthen's frown. She could not look him full in the face. She felt more than saw him focus on her, felt the steel come into his gaze.

"The witch-girl," he muttered.

"So Fra Guill would have it," Hal agreed jovially, "but of course it isn't true."

"Isn't it?"

Köthen's tone chilled Erde to the bone. Was he recalling Erfurt only, or her dream-presence as well? That night in the clearing, or his suicidal charge? Erde let her glance drift back toward him. She hoped he'd be looking at Hal, so she could observe him unawares. But he was staring straight at her. Their eyes met and held, and she saw how angry he was.

"My lady, a pleasure." He stepped close to lift her hand politely to his lips, then murmured for her hearing alone, "Better to have stayed that night and died with honor."

So he'd been aware of and remembered everything. Worse, he blamed her for what had befallen him since, when he'd heard her dream-warning, heeded it, and fled.

"Oh, no, my lord baron," she protested faintly. "Surely not."

"Surely yes." And then he stepped back with a curt bow. To say more would bring inquiries from the others she was sure he did not wish to answer.

He might as well have struck her. Drowning, Erde let her courtly training take over. She returned a gracious curtsy. "My lord baron. How charming to see you again."

Oblivious, Hal chuckled and rolled his eyes at Rose. "Look at the graceful thing she's getting to be. Is this your doing, Rosie?"

"None of mine. This child is dragon-raised."

"We should all have so excellent a parent." He drew Erde toward the dragon. "Come, nearly-grown. Your skills are needed. What can my lord Earth tell us of where he's been and where he'll be off to next? How stands the Quest?"

Thinking each moment that she might fall to the floor, Erde struggled to give to the elder knight all the cheer and enthusiasm she knew he deserved. But she could not fool Rose, Rose who saw everything, Rose who took up her elbow again with a firm sisterly grasp.

"Let him rest, Heinrich. You can talk to him tomorrow. He's been working hard, and sorely tired of late. Besides, you know how long-winded a dragon can be, once you get him started. We've plenty of our own news to exchange and it's much too cold in here to be standing about. Let's all go in to dinner, shall we?"

CHAPTER TEN

At dinner, after the men had slaked the first rush of their hunger, they talked about the war, or mostly, Hal did, now and then referring to Captain Wender for reinforcement or a clarification of fact. He spoke quietly because the news was bad.

"We've been beaten up at every turn. An army without training or proper weapons facing the barons' mercenary knights and infantry . . ."

"These farmers' hearts are gallant," put in Wender. "But most would do better by the plough than by the sword."

Hal nodded. "Still, if mere numbers would win the day, we'd have a fighting chance. And all's not lost. We had split the army even before we heard of the Prince's death. Rainer's taken part of our force west to raise men and provisioning among the estates not corrupted by Fra Guill on his first tour through the countryside." Hal made maps on the tabletop, with spoons and platters and lines of bread crumbs. "I sought to draw the rebels southward. When it became clear that this mad priest would go on fighting no matter what the weather, I sent His Majesty west to Köln, where hopefully, he will last the winter. He is not well, and Carl's death has grieved him sorely. The truth is, we'd be in full retreat but for these recent heavy snows, which have forced even Fra Guill to call a halt."

"A mercy," Rose murmured.

"If it was an honest winter, there'd be a mercy in it. But this weather's as unnatural as the priest himself. It'll clear and we'll have a bit of a thaw, just enough to sink every cartwheel hub-deep in mud. Then as soon as we're good and stuck, it'll freeze and the hell-priest'll be on us again.

It's uncanny. There's some saying he has the weather in his thrall."

Rose nodded. "Those rumors have reached even this far."

"How could such a thing be?" muttered Doritt.

Hal blew out a long sigh. "Well, I'd hate to credit it, but somehow he's always prepared and we're always surprised. We could use a few month's rest, not a few days. Aye, Wender?"

"Aye indeed, milord." The captain lifted his mug of ale in salute. "Were there food like this to rest with."

"Or any place left to rest in." Hal gathered the bread crumbs into a pile as if saving them for later. "Guillemo's ordered his men to burn any village or farmstead that refuses to pledge to his cause."

"And join his march," added Wender. "The roads are filled with refugees, even in this weather. The devil's own spawn, he is."

Captain Wender was just as Erde's dreams had presented him: Köthen's most favored and loyal man, a tough battle veteran who had followed him unquestioningly into exile. But she thought Wender seemed a bit more at home on the King's side, which might explain Hal's easy way with him, and his willingness to trust this former enemy, while not his superior lord.

That lord sat silently now, a bit apart, as if news of the war no longer interested him. He had eaten little—just enough, Erde thought, to keep from making a show of refusing his hostess' hospitality. Nowhere near enough to sustain him, and certainly not enough to soak up the quantities of drink he was consuming. Raven had at first taken up station across from him, laughing and sipping from his cup in a flirty, familiar way designed to keep it out of his hands as much as possible. He'd replied briefly, politely to her queries about people and events in the past, the youth they'd obviously shared, but he would not speak of the present, the war, or his situation. Eventually, Raven gave up and left him alone.

Erde wished he wouldn't drink so much. He reminded her too much of her father. But surely it was more than rage and shame twisting in him. He was like one grief-stricken, like a woman who's lost an only child, or like

Josef her father, who'd lost a beloved wife. Erde wondered how a mere throne could mean as much, but nonetheless, she thought she understood Baron Köthen better than anyone in the room, and she felt heartsick for him. She did not even ask why. She herself could hardly eat, even though Sir Hal, in his courtly way, had reverted to the habit developed during their travels together, of transferring the tenderest morsels to her own platter.

"And how has the King received young Rainer?" Rose inquired.

Hal shrugged. "In public, merely politely. In private, he has expressed some possibility. Wisely, Rainer has not pressed his claim officially. We let the rumors circulate, but there yet remains the problem of proof. Our best hope is popular acclaim."

Down the long table, Baron Köthen stirred. "Fine conspirators you are, so beset by moral standards. Can't you discover a convenient birthmark? Isn't that the usual ploy?"

Hal eyed him with impatience. "Dolph refuses to believe that Prince Ludolph could have survived the baron's plotting. After all, a *true* heir—one who actually wants the throne—would be very inconvenient to his purposes."

Raven propped her chin on her fists. "What if Rainer of Duchen is the lost prince?"

"He isn't," Köthen growled.

"But what if he is? Speculate. What would you do?"

Köthen looked cornered. He sipped his wine and seemed to find great interest in the decoration of the cup.

"He's young, strong, intelligent, probably very able," Raven pursued. "It seems he's even charismatic. What if he is, Dolph?"

Köthen refused to meet her bright, insistent stare. He laughed lightly, gestured bravely with his goblet. "Then there would be no further use for me."

"A strong king needs strong advisers," Rose countered.

"I can think of several uses for you," Raven smiled.

And Erde wondered if it was only she who heard, not a fallen lord's drunken plea for sympathy, but a man's sober, bitter conviction. That his life was over.

Finally the empty bowls and trenchers were stacked and cleared. Doritt threw more wood on the fire. The women refilled their cups with heated cider or wine, and every-one—except Köthen—drew nearer. Erde understood that it was finally time to tell her own story. She reached out to the dragon in the barn, for his support and commentary, then gathered N'Doch and Water-as-Sedou beside her.

"Well . . . after Lord Earth rescued Hal and Rainer and myself from Erfurt and brought us back to Deep Moor, he heard the voice of the Summoner ever more strongly, call-ing him back to the Quest. So we left to follow it."

"Without even warning us," Hal complained.

She tipped her head apologetically. "You were so dis-tracted with the war and the idea that Rainer was . . ."

"I know, I know, but the Quest . . ."

"Would you have gone?" asked Rose. "Would you have left the war behind? Would you have deserted your King?"

Hal pursed his lips. "A difficult choice."

"So, you see? The wise beast saved you that choice."

"Let the child continue," demanded Doritt from the fireplace.

Now Erde felt self-conscious, with the entire household watching. She cleared her throat. "Anyway, the Voice did not lead us to the mage we sought, or even to itself. It led us to N'Doch and Lady Water." She was shamed by the awkward formality that tied her tongue in knots. But soon the tale took hold, telling itself of its own accord. "We were in a place called Africa, so fantastical and strange that I grew at last to believe N'Doch's assertions that the dragon had transported us not only in location, but in time."

"2013, no doubt of it," N'Doch put in. "Eleven hundred years from now. When I laid eyes on these two, I was sure they were some kind of special effect. Took me a real long time to figure it otherwise."

2013. Amazed by the thought yet again, Erde translated for him, stumbling over the equivalent of "special effect." Murmurs and headshakes ran around the table like a ritual response. "And then immediately, we were being pursued . . "

"There's always someone after my ass, y'see," ex-plained N'Doch.

". . . but N'Doch took us to his grandfather Master Djawara, a great mage himself, though not the one we searched for."

"Papa Dja's no mage, whatever that is, but he's witchy, all right." N'Doch beamed his dark smile at Rose. "Like you ladies."

"Master Djawara sent us to the city and Mistress Lealé, a dreamer and prophetess . . ."

"A scam artist, you mean."

Erde bit back a pout. Perhaps she should just let N'Doch tell the story. The listeners around the table seemed to enjoy his posturing, his willingness to try for a laugh even with his own dignity at stake. Then she could sit back and translate his exaggerations and embellishments, at least as directly as she could bear to without blushing, or worrying that his boasting was reflecting poorly on her. But the dragon in the barn had an opinion about that.

ALL SIDES OF THIS TALE MUST BE TOLD. IT IS MORE THAN JUST AN ADVENTURE STORY.

Erde agreed. She saw Hal warming to N'Doch's colorful description of the escape into the bush, questioning him directly in Frankish and eagerly sharing out his replies. She cleared her throat once more and gently interrupted. "And, remember, there at Mistress Lealé's, we uncovered the first hints that the Summoner might be the dragons' elder sister Air, and that the Summons might be a call for help."

Water-as-Sedou had listened quietly from the start, but now he caught Erde's eye. Relieved, she let him take over. With Sedou, there was no need to translate or worry that the proper telling of the tale would get sidetracked. And when he spoke, the entire room quietened.

"There is much," he began in a voice like the tolling of bass bells, "that the dragons did not remember when they were waked from their long sleep, my brother Earth from under the mountain, myself from beneath the sea. So suddenly awake, so engendered by urgency and purpose, yet ignorant of how or why to put it to use. But memory returns." Sedou wet his lips and surveyed his listeners gravely. "You have heard our sister Air mentioned. But there is yet another: our brother Fire."

"Four!" Hal exclaimed softly. "Of course there would be."

"Indeed, Sir Knight. You perceive the symmetry. But the symmetry is incomplete. Our sister Air is nowhere to be found. Were all in balance, there would be no need for dragon to be seeking dragon. We'd be four and already about the task we were awakened to accomplish."

"You've discovered the Task, then?" Hal asked hopefully.

Sedou shook his head. "This knowledge requires a four-way understanding. No one of us is sufficient unto herself."

"And what of Lord Fire? Do you know his whereabouts?"

Sedou paused, and Erde strained to pick up the brief dragon-to-dragon conference, too fast for her human senses. "We have hints. Worst of all, we . . . that is, some of us suspect him of working against us."

Hal frowned, made a small sound of protest.

"Hear me out, Sir Knight."

At this point, the tale caught even Baron Köthen's attention. His bowed head, bronzed with firelight, lifted and turned ever so slightly in their direction. Erde watched his listening profile and thought she'd never seen anything more beautiful. Except, of course, the dragon Earth. She had not included her dreams in the telling, though the dragon encouraged her to. She could not bear to put the baron through that, to make him relive his humiliation in front of all these eager listeners. So she sat silently and let Sedou unwind the story of their time in Lealé's mansion, of the fighting in the city outside, and Kenzo Baraga's treachery. There was little she could add. The dragons knew better how those final bloody minutes had fallen out. N'Doch listened silently as well, curling and uncurling his fists as if amazed to find them on his wrists and still working.

A long silence followed Sedou's finish, broken only by the snap of flames in the grate.

Then Hal said to Rose, "He was dead when he came to you? Truly?"

Rose tilted her chin at Linden, several places down the table. Linden nodded. All eyes turned to N'Doch, who grinned uncomfortably, though he usually loved an audience.

"Wonderful," murmured Hal. "Wonderful."

Captain Wender shook his head. He poured himself a half-mug of ale, then only sipped at it gingerly, as if working to keep himself from draining it in a single gulp. "You could find yourself an honored place at any hearth in the land with a tale like that."

"Those that are left standing," added Hal with a hollow chuckle. "But now, what of the task ahead?"

Sedou sat back. "Our journey has just begun, Sir Knight. Now that our company is rested and recovered, we must be on our way to find our brother Fire, and quickly, for it seems that only he can lead us to our sister Air."

"Told ya," N'Doch murmured.

Erde looked at him sidelong. Earth had also said as much when she'd gone to him for comfort in the barn. The urge that drove these dragons was their sole reason for existence. It could be put aside no longer. Their time of peace and safety was at an end.

"We are correct to understand that the dragon Fire is implicated in this treachery?"

Erde had to glance down the table to assure herself that it was indeed Baron Köthen who had spoken. He was toying with his empty wine cup and meeting no one's eyes. It was as if he'd spoken to himself. Then he looked up at Hal. "He sounds like the sort of dragon you always swore was a slanderous myth invented by fearful churchmen, my knight."

"I'm sure we've misunderstood about Lord Fire," Hal began.

"Not at all." Sedou turned to Köthen, a long look down the table, as if noticing him for the first time. "You are right, my lord baron, though there is some difference of opinion about this within our ranks. My brother Earth wishes me to note that he is not yet convinced of Fire's betrayal."

"Betrayal? Impossible!" cried Hal. "A misunderstanding, surely! Dragons are all that is good and noble in God's creation!"

Erde recalled her own shock and disbelief when Lady Water first suggested that Fire might be out to destroy them. N'Doch murmured something filthy and cynical that she refused to translate, and Sedou laughed, a bass rumble felt in the back of the throat, a laugh no true human could have produced. "Would that were true, Sir Knight."

Köthen filled his wine cup and drained it. "You do persist, Heinrich, in believing in what other men have given up on long ago."

"Oh, really?" Hal retorted. "I believed in dragons, and lo . . ." Sedou restrained him with a big hand on his arm.

In the pause, Köthen looked up, found the dark man watching him, and looked away. The wine cup made several revolutions in his restless hands. Finally, he asked, "And how do you expect to locate this paragon of evil?"

"There is a way we travel, a kind of translation through time and space that is enabled by the identity of place. And so, with my brother Fire: we have an image in mind of where he is, or in N'Doch's mind actually, as it's he who received it. We won't know where it really is until we get there. But he will be there. I am sure of it."

Köthen stared at him. Erde could see he had not expected so direct and technical an answer. "You can go anywhere you like?"

"If we can see it clearly, we can go there."

"How long will it take?"

"No time at all, my lord baron. The travel is instantaneous."

"Magic," Wender muttered, and crossed himself covertly.

Köthen's eyes flicked to Hal. "You've traveled like this?"

"I have, yes."

"Let me guess: from Erfurt."

"And to Erfurt. How did you think I got in without you knowing in the first place? You had that town guarded like the king's own storehouse."

Köthen looked back to Sedou. Some part of this had snagged his interest. "And so, you'll just go?"

Sedou nodded. Köthen let out a breath. Erde saw a bright, quick moment pass between them, man and dragon, an exchange: the envy in Köthen's eyes for the challenge in Sedou's.

But Köthen turned away and refilled his wine cup to the brim. "Well, Heinrich, as usual you're right. I've been a fool all these years. A fool to believe in the nobility and strivings of mere men. What's the point? Let's stop this war right now. We'll just let these dragons rule the kingdom. How do you think Fra Guill would feel about that?" He drained the cup and reached again for the jug.

"Dragons do not meddle in the affairs of men, my lord baron," Sedou said quietly.

Köthen laughed bitterly. "They seem to have meddled in mine fairly thoroughly."

Oddly, Sedou smiled. 'That is your fault for being at the center of things."

The baron eyed him suspiciously.

"When there is something larger at stake, we will do what we must."

"Since men live in the world, Dolph," said Rose, as if waking from a deep reverie, "they will be threatened when it is threatened."

"The world?" Köthen scoffed. "My lady Rose, I'd never have suspected you of apocalyptic thinking."

Sedou said, "Were it not the case, I'd still be peacefully sleeping in the ocean depths, and my brother Earth beneath the mountains of Tor Alte. Do you think, my lord baron, that dragons are awakened for no purpose?"

Köthen merely stared at him.

You're asking too much, Erde thought. Too much for him to absorb in the turn of one day. Too much to believe. For this man understands the consequences of belief. Good Captain Wender, in the corner, can just shake his head in wonder and then accept that there are indeed dragons in the world, just as his grandmama always said there were. But this man cannot just accept. He has an inkling of how profoundly all his definitions of the world will change, and he's not ready for that. *No more than I was,* she mused, *when N'Doch tried to explain his world to me.*

And indeed, Köthen poured himself more wine yet again, then stood and shoved back his chair. He swayed, steadied himself with a brace of fingers to the tabletop. "We're fools to listen to all this." He shoved back from the table and strode across the room to stare out of the window into snow and darkness.

"He'll come around," Hal murmured.

No, he won't, Erde thought, though she loved Sir Hal for his steadfast belief in this man whom he'd raised and trained and who had eventually betrayed him. But Adolphus of Köthen wouldn't simply "come around." It would take something drastic. But, oh, she thought rapturously, if that thing should happen, what a boon to have his skills and intelligence turned to our problem.

With Köthen gone from the table, Hal turned his attention back to Seldou, with the next in his scholar's lifetime list of questions he'd always wanted to ask a dragon. Erde could see he was overjoyed to have one he could speak to directly, and since this one was likely to leave soon, Hal wasn't going to waste any more precious time on his wayward ex-squire than was absolutely necessary. Erde hoped Sedou would be patient with him.

The women of the household began to drift off to bed. Beside her, N'Doch stirred. He'd been very quiet for a long time, she'd noticed. How very unlike him.

"So. Looks like we're outa here."

She nodded. The rising tide of dragon urgency was growing irresistible, as if the telling of the tale had completed some necessary ritual, and there was no reason left to linger. Time to be about their business. "When, do you think?"

"Soon."

"Are you ready? I mean, are you truly healed, N'Doch?"

He smiled at her, one of the things Erde had to admit he did best. Like Sedou, and even their grandfather, Master Djawara. This family had a smile that could light up the darkest corners of a room. But she thought that this particular smile was rather overstretched with bravado.

"Does it matter?" he asked.

"Of course it does."

"Not to them."

She knew he meant the dragons. "Oh, N'Doch, not true, not true."

He shrugged. "Well, anyway, I'm fine. I'm better than ever, and as ready as I'll ever be. How 'bout you?"

She felt very close to him right then. Her own rush of fellowship surprised her. For all his ignorance of the lore, there was so much that only he knew, only he understood—with her—about this business of belonging to dragons.

"You had all those brothers, N'Doch. Did . . . do you have any sisters?"

"Nah."

"Well, you have one now." She laid her pale hand beside his dark one. "We are like night and day, you see? Each one a half. Together we form the whole."

This time, his smile was genuine.

She woke in her upstairs room in the darkened farmhouse from a dream she could not remember, and for that, she was grateful. She listened, first inside her head, in case it was the dragon sending a dream-image to wake her for some emergency. But the part of her consciousness that the dragon normally occupied was empty and still. He must be out hunting, a final meal before their impending departure. Then she heard a noise down below. Her little room was near the staircase, and sound floated freely upward. Someone was moving around in the lower room.

Erde got up quietly, more curious than afraid. The women of Deep Moor did not roam their halls at night unless something was the matter. The room was freezing. The fire in the tiny grate had burned out long ago. She pulled her prentice boy's linen shirt over her shift and hauled on her woolen leggings. For silence, she kept her feet bare. In the other narrow bed, the twins remained wrapped in the quiet sleep of the guiltless.

She slipped into the corridor and down the stair, stopping at each landing to listen. Whoever it was did not care if he or she was detected. She turned onto the final run of stairs. From there, she had a view of the front part of the great room and the fireplace.

Captain Wender had stretched himself out in front of the dying coals, smothered in the thick quilts that the women had brought him. The unaccustomed warmth and wine and good company had clearly been too much for this valiant man-at-arms. He was fast asleep. A glimmer drew Erde's attention away from him.

At the far end of the table, away from the fire, sat Adolphus of Köthen. Several wine cups and more than one stout jug were stationed beside his elbow, but he was not drinking now. He was staring at the gleaming blade of a dagger, turning it restlessly in his hands as he had done with his empty cup earlier. Wender's dagger, no doubt surreptitiously lifted. He studied it as if it might speak to him, and then he did something that sent Erde's heart pounding into her throat.

He set the dagger to the inside of his left wrist, made a fist, then pensively traced the raised blue lines of his veins with the blade's keen point. Erde was down the stairs and confronting him across the table before she'd even thought about what she was doing.

"Oh, no, my lord, never!"

His eyes flicked up at her, startled. Erde drew back. She hadn't recalled there being so much darkness in them.

"Why the hell not?"

He said it so bleakly, she could not immediately reply. There was little trace of the rage he'd first greeted her with in the barn. He was drunk for sure, but in that state beyond mere loss of sobriety, where clarity returns with a focus as sharp as a lance. Erde saw the signs. She knew them all from dealing with her father, who drank hoping to forget but only ended up remembering more than he ever did when he was sober.

"Please, my lord . . . you've had too much," she said inanely, because she had to say something.

"Clever girl."

"I mean, one should never heed a decision made under the drink's influence."

Köthen laughed softly. "You mean, I might *live* to regret it? No, my lady Erde, my hand is steady, drunk or sober." He dragged the dagger back along his wrist, then shifted his grip and pulled, letting the edge bite. Blood flowed along the path of the slice.

"NO!" Erde threw herself against the table, flinging her arms across to snatch at the blade and pull it away from his skin. Köthen jerked the blade from her grasp, then swore and tossed it aside to grab her hands and peel them open. Blood welled up in her own palms. The rush of it frightened her.

"Make fists and hold them," he ordered tartly. Suddenly, he sounded cold sober. In the next instant, he was on his feet and rummaging through one of the satchels the twins had brought in from the packhorse. All he could find was the same length of soft red cloth that had bound his wrists on the way into the farmstead. "A better use for it anyway," he muttered, tearing it cleanly in half with his teeth. He came back to the table and wound a strip tightly around each of her bleeding palms. "Surface wounds. They won't scar."

As if she cared. Already, he'd forgotten his own wound, a thin red line become mostly an ugly smear on his wrist, drying up already. Hardly a wound at all. He had been playing with her. When he was done wrapping, he slumped back against his chair and fixed her with that too-dark stare.

"You seem, my lady, to have a compulsion to keep me alive, even when it is not in my own best interests. Do I dare ask why?"

Her heart was too full to even speak.

He tilted his head speculatively. "Perhaps you have some witchy purpose for me? There's been a great deal of talk about purpose this evening, and as I seem to have lost mine . . ."

"My lord baron, I am not a witch."

"Then what are you?"

"A girl. I'm just a girl."

"Who talks to dragons and travels to times that haven't happened yet and whispers in a man's ear at night when he's about to make a fateful decision. *Just* a girl?"

To Erde's surprise, he let her reach for the dragger and draw it away from him into her own hands. She folded her wrapped palms over the blade. "Very well, then. I am a dragon guide."

He settled back a bit more. "Go on."

"That is no witchery. It is a silent, holy duty passed down through countless generations of blood from the earliest times, so that one would always be ready, should the need arise."

"The need?"

"The waking of the dragons, which is the dire sign. The actual need we have yet to determine." She dared to look up at him, to meet his steady, noncommittal gaze. "May I show you something?" He merely shrugged, but she reached beneath her mismatched layers of linen for the treasure she always kept pinned next to her skin. She undid the clasp and laid the brooch before him on her red-wrapped palm. "See? My grandmother's, and hers before that."

Köthen leaned forward, squinting in the dim firelight, then reached for it. "If I may . . . ?"

She held it out. He took it and rose, carrying it to the

hearth to peer at the ancient blood-red jewel with its delicate incised carving of a dragon rampant. "It has wings," he murmured.

"Yes, I know. I think it doesn't stand for my dragon, but rather for the essence of dragon."

"Or for what men *think* of dragons. It's old, but not that old. Probably it was made as a reminder, a key to ancient memories."

She smiled at him, though he wasn't looking at her. This was the closest thing they'd yet had to a conversation. "My lord baron, I do believe that some of Sir Hal's dragon study has rubbed off on you after all." And then she could not believe she'd spoken to him so boldly.

But he only snorted, turning the jewel in his hands with the same intensity as he had the dagger. "He fed it to me with my morning porridge. How could I help it?"

"And yet you chose not to believe?"

"I chose not to, yes."

"And now . . . ?"

"Well, clearly I was wrong, as I have been about so many things of late."

"No, my lord . . ."

"Yes." He came back to the table and placed the dragon brooch deliberately in the center of her cushioned palm, then sat down and faced her directly. "How is it that you could speak to me in that clearing? That the priest could sense your presence? If not witchery, by some dragon magic, is it?"

"I don't know, my lord. I had . . . dreams . . . several dreams, in which I saw you as clearly as I do now, in your camp on the battlefield, with my father, with Captain Wender and then with the . . ."

Köthen hissed, rose, and paced away. "Curse the day I made that unholy alliance. Greedy, too greedy, Adolphus!"

"Fra Guill has deep powers of his own, my lord. See how easily he cozened my father . . ."

"Your father is a drunken sot!" At the edge of the shadows, he stared up into the darkness of the stairwell. "Have you any notion what your witchery cost me, girl?"

"My lord, I am a baron's daughter, and the granddaughter of a baroness. I think I know something of the ambitions of the courtier. And I never intended . . ."

"Courtier?" Köthen was appalled. He whirled on her, his fist raised and clenched. "I had a kingdom within my grasp!"

Erde stared at the red jewel in her hands so that her eyes would not stray to the litter of wine cups and empty jugs between them on the table. She did not see how she alone could be responsible for his loss. At some point he must have realized that the hell-priest would never have crowned him king. He was far too strong and able, not the hell-priest's creature like her father. In truth, she understood little of courts and the lust for power. She had merely tried on some of N'Doch's bravado. It did not fit very well, she decided.

Köthen took a breath, planted both palms on the table, and loomed over her. "Well, isn't he? A drunken sot?"

Silently, she nodded. But her meek agreement seemed only to enrage him further. He snatched up all the wine cups on the table and hurled them into the fireplace. "I am not a drunk!"

The smash of crockery so close to his ear brought Captain Wender bolt upright out of his deep sleep. "What? My lord? Are we under attack?"

Köthen waved him back irritably. "No, Wender. Merely an accident. Go back to sleep. You're better off."

Wender shook the drowse from his head to survey the unfamiliar, darkened room. His eyes found Erde, and he cocked a scarred brow in inquiry. She nodded reassurance, then made the little hand sign that her father's house guards always used to warn each other when the baron had been drinking. Which was, of course, most of the time. Wender's lips twitched: a faint, complicit, admiring grin was born and died before it could give both of them away. He nodded and lay back in his nest of blankets and seemed to be instantly asleep again. But Erde was sure he would not be so caught by surprise again that night.

Köthen observed the end of this exchange, and it was not lost on him. But he also saw that she did not betray him to his man-at-arms by revealing the purloined dagger. He threw himself back into his chair, dropped his face into his hands, then dragged them roughly across his cheeks and beard with a ragged sigh. "Henrich says I am past all reason. Do you agree?"

After a moment of consideration, she replied recklessly, "Yes, my lord."

Köthen laughed, a short, bitter sound, more of a bark than an expression of mirth. Then he folded his arms to lean forward on them and stare at her closely. "You are an earnest and well-brought-up child, I can see that much, despite your fool of a father . . ."

"I beg you, my lord . . ."

"A thousand pardons, my lady, for my intemperance. I meant . . . your honored parent, Josef von Alte."

"I am grateful, my lord." Let him be as ironical as he pleased. She had his attention at last and perhaps, as her father often did, he would talk himself to sleep, and then there would be no more threats of a blade to the wrists, at least, not this night.

"And for these virtues I credit your noble grandmother, may she rest in peace."

To hear him speak of her beloved grandmother nearly broke her resolve to remain tearless. "Did you know her, my lord?"

"Aye. As loyal a subject of the King as ever there was." He paused, then grinned sourly. "Plotted against her many times."

Erde glanced up at him, alarmed. For a moment, his dark eyes softened inexplicably. So sad, she thought, almost tender. *But not for me.* For his gentled gaze was directed somewhere inside his own head, at some memory, perhaps, some personal musing. Yet he seemed to be looking at her when he said quietly, "I believe that you did mean me well, for I see that you are incapable of meaning ill. How enviable."

She sensed the direction of his thoughts, turned against himself as keenly as the dagger's blade. It would do no good to protest that she had mean thoughts every day, about her fellow dragon guide, for instance, and certainly about the evil priest.

"And therefore," Köthen continued, one hand fitfully massaging his brow. "You will think it most immodest of me, most unbecoming in a good Christian man, when you hear me say that the kingdom has need of me." He regarded her speculatively, as if trying to decide if he could talk to her as an aware adult. "My lady Erde. Ours is a land in crisis. The peerage is slothful and corrupt. Their people have lost all faith in the structures meant to protect them. Why else do you think the priest has won so many converts? He has nothing real to offer them. But this is a time of fear, not of faith. A strong, enlightened leader is needed, and I am the man for it. I could heal this sickness, if they'd let me. I know it, and Heinrich knows it, but he lets his infernal principles get in the way. Like you do, my lady. No wonder you're such great friends."

"A rightful monarchy is ordained by God, my lord."

"Wrong!" Köthen slammed a fist against the table, causing Wender to mutter and turn over in his quilts. "That is a convenient fiction invented not too many generations ago to legitimize the current reigning family . . . Otto's grandfather, who took the throne by force from some other sorry 'rightful' sot! As I hoped to do! When the weak rule, the strong must offer remedy! It's traditional! Did the baroness not teach you *history,* child?"

"I am not a child, my lord." But in her heart, she marveled at his magnificence, chin up, back straight, his eyes bright with the fire of conviction and righteous wrath. Here was the man she remembered from the barn in Erfurt. But it was a fleeting image.

"Not a witch, not a child . . . what are you, then? Oh, yes, I remember . . . a girl. You did tell me that, forgive me."

Erde took two deep breaths and forced her shoulders away from their stranglehold about her neck. "I believe you wish me to think ill of you, my lord."

"That'll do for a start. Then maybe you'll stop trying to save my life!"

"But it hasn't been by choice, don't you see?" Carefully, to hide her desperation, she balanced Wender's knife between her bandaged hands. Only the absolute truth would do. "Except for just now, of course. After all, I hardly know you. My dreams were . . . I was called into them. I had no say in the matter."

"Were you aware in the dreams?"

"Of course, but . . .."

"Then you could have dreamed some other outcome?"

"My lord, I don't think so." Even now, a plan was forming itself in her head. Erde felt she owed him at least a hint. "I suspect some larger purpose to all of this, my lord, in which we must both take part."

The tension ran out of him like water. "Purpose? You've been listening to those dragons again. I have no purpose, remember?"

"Not so, my lord."

"Ever so, my lady." He reached for the wine jug nearest him, which turned out to be not yet empty. He upended it in a long, thirsty tavern swallow. Then he set it down, cradled between his palms, and eyed Erde with owlish challenge. "I am not a drunk, but I do wish to be drunk. Unless you have some better idea of what a useless man should do with his time."

In fact, she did. And her plan was clearer now. Oh, it was reckless, so reckless. She couldn't believe she was thinking of such a thing. But because she loved him—for whatever inexplicable reason, and now that she understood this—she had to try to help him. She had helped the dragon, after all, so lost and ignorant when she first found him. A dragon now magnificent with purpose, even if he was not always sure exactly what it was. As this man had been magnificent, and would be again.

But she said nothing of this to Köthen. She lowered her eyes and said, "Not I, my lord baron."

Köthen shrugged, theatrical in his regret. "Then I guess it's the jug for me. It's a longer way to do one's self in, but in the end, just as effective."

Erde slid the dagger to the edge of the table and swept it into the folds of her shirt. She judged that the crisis had passed for the night, for this night at least. "In that case, my lord, I will leave you to your own devices."

When she rose from the table, he seemed surprised that she did not intend to stay and joust with him for what remained of the night. She could see that, despite himself, and witch-girl or no, he found her interesting. Perhaps he'd even enjoyed her company. And that, to Erde, was one very large step forward.

One that left her trembling inwardly, as if she'd charged blindly out onto a precipice with no thought for how she might ever make her way back to solid ground. Walking back to the stairs and up them with composure and grace may have been the hardest thing she'd ever done.

CHAPTER ELEVEN

Nor did she tell Hal or the women of Deep Moor about her plan, not even Rose. She claimed she had broken a bowl, and cut her palms on the shards. She avoided Baron Köthen, which was not difficult, as he mostly stayed in the room Rose had given him and sulked, while Captain Wender lounged patiently outside his door. Hal labored in the winter farmstead alongside the others, insisting he must do the work of three.

But, with trepidation, Erde did tell the dragons. To her surprise, they approved, as Earth worked his healing magic with her hands. The next day, N'Doch and Water spent hours together working up the details of the image that had gripped him just as he returned to consciousness from his dragon-made resurrection. Details of the burning land he just *knew* was where they were meant to go next. That N'Doch had volunteered this vision, he who hated any implication that he was tied to a dragon guide's destiny, this very act convinced Erde of the vision's truth. The dragons required no convincing. They were impatient to be off.

Quietly, the four prepared for their departure, soliciting from Margit a strong, stout knife for N'Doch to complement the slim dagger Erde had carried since fleeing Tor Alte. From the weavers, they gathered several thin linen tunics and leggings, advised by N'Doch as the best clothing for the hot climate he'd be taking them to. Lily made them footwear, laughing at the absurdity of sandals in deep winter. Doritt found them sturdy packs and equipped them with flint and tinder, and wax-stoppered water jugs and bread and cheese. N'Doch grumbled about the weight of all these things. He suggested that they should pay a stop-

off visit to, as he put it, his "home time," to exchange the
heavy crockery for a lighter container he called "plastic."
Erde recalled the milky, flexible jug he'd carried water in,
and thought it might be a good idea. But the dragons said
no. She thought they seemed nervous about letting N'Doch
go home, though they said it was only because they were
in so much of a hurry. Besides, they were unsure how many
of these provisions would make it through the veil anyway.
Objects seemed to translate well enough if Earth specifically pictured them along with the person carrying them,
but if it could not be easily carried, there was no point in
trying to take it with them.

Erde warned N'Doch to keep his pack nearby at all
times, or at least to know exactly where it was. They made
no farewells, only tacit ones. The women knew they were
leaving some time soon, and knew as well that they might—
at any future moment—return without warning. Erde had
given no notice at all when she and Earth had left on the
journey that had led them to Water and N'Doch. She'd
simply disappeared.

Therefore, it was just as well, when she heard shouting
from the horse barn, men's voices raised in anger, and saw
Doritt and Margit grab up the nearest heavy tool and head
that way. It was just as well that the four were ready.

Instinct warned her. Breaking into a run, Erde turned
her senses inward to locate the other three. Earth was outside the cow shed with Linden, helping to heal a sick calf.
N'Doch and Water-as-Sedou were hard at work in the
farmhouse library, the only quiet place. Erde made it to
the barn just after Doritt and Margit. Flinging herself
through the open doorway, she nearly crashed into Doritt,
bending beside Captain Wender, who was sprawled facedown in the scatter of manure and straw.

She slowed. "Is he . . . ?"

"Out cold," said Doritt. "But coming around."
Wender groaned. Erde stopped worrying and moved on. Farther down, past the line of stalls, Margit had pulled up behind
Raven and Rose. The three women watched breathlessly
while in the open space at the end of the barn, Köthen and
Hal circled each other, snarling. Hal had his sword at the
ready, Köthen gripped a long-handled scythe used for har-
vesting grain. Already, both men were bruised and straw-

dusted, as if this altercation had begun with mere fists and arms, and escalated toward full-scale weaponry. Hal bled from a long shallow slice on his thigh. The shouting Erde had heard halfway across the farmstead had been replaced by silence, and the shuffling of straw and heavy breathing. Gone well beyond words, the two men glared at each other like maddened dogs, glared and circled, glared and circled.

Erde halted beside Rose. "Oh, no! What now?"

"Dolph has refused to stay with us when Heinrich returns to the war."

The furrows in Rose's brow told Erde this was no ordinary skirmish. "But he gave his word."

"Apparently he's changed his mind."

The men's edgy dance brought Köthen's back around full circle toward the women. Rose moved a step aside. Margit shifted to ease up behind him. She had a length of rope twisted between her fists.

"Back!" Köthen growled, with a warning sidearm swipe of his scythe. Margit leaped aside and retreated.

"Dolph," said Rose. "Be reasonable . . ."

"Leave it, Rose! Reason has nothing to do with it!"

"How is this going to solve anything?"

"I will not, NOT be put out to pasture like some . . . broken mule!"

"You will if you behave like one!" Hal was winded. His chest heaved convulsively, making the difference in the two men's ages terrifyingly apparent. But his manner was as fierce and implacable as Erde had ever seen it. "You'll do as I say, if I have to chain you to a rock!"

No, Sir Hal, she told him silently. *Don't you see this man will go mad if you chain him, either physically or within his soul?* Now she was sure that her plan was the right one.

"Will you?" Köthen yelled. "Just try it, then! No one here but women, old man! You think you can take me?" Suddenly he closed the distance between them, stepping within range of the older man's sword. He lifted the scythe to swing it like a club, then held it there for a long and frozen moment, exposing the entire front of his body to Hal's attack. "Cut me down where I stand, my knight! Do it, or I'll kill you, I swear I will!"

"Your chance for that has passed!" Hal spat. But his sword did not move.

"Is it?" Köthen cocked back the scythe and swung it wide. His aim was vengeful and true. It missed Hal's belly by a hairsbreadth, then swept his sword from his hand and flung it clattering into the stalls. Erde breathed a split-second's prayer. He would kill or be killed. He was, as Hal had said, beyond reason. She must do it now, or it would be too late.

She threw her heavy wool-and-leather coat to the floor, then sprang past Rose's restraining arm and ducked the long blade as it whistled past on its second vicious arc.

"No! You mustn't!"

She lunged and grabbed the scythe handle. The angry momentum of Köthen's swing jerked her hard off-balance and dragged her across the floor. Horrified, Hal drew his dagger but backed away. Köthen did not. He hauled on the scythe handle, sending Erde tumbling toward him. He caught her deftly with his free arm, twisted her around, and pinned her to his chest with the scythe blade at her throat.

"Foolish child," he muttered.

We shall see about that, thought Erde, amazed that she was not afraid.

"What are you . . . no!" Hal lowered his blade. "As a man of honor, Adolphus, let the girl go."

"I have no honor, my knight. You've made that ever so clear to me."

"I never meant . . ."

"No. Stay where you are if you wish this girl alive tomorrow."

"You'd never . . ."

"I would! I will! Why shouldn't I? You've left me nothing else. It's your word I'll need now. Safe passage out of here, Heinrich, on *your* honor, in exchange for her life."

But Erde caught Hal's worried look, shook her head once, and smiled. "It's all right. We're taking him with us."

Hal's eyes widened. "Now?"

She nodded as best she could, with a blade at her neck the length of a man's arm. She reached for her companions in her mind, and found each waiting: one, two, three. Then she turned her head sideways against her captor's chest! "My lord of Köthen, prepare yourself for a journey."

Köthen said, "What?"

And the dragons took them both.

PART TWO

The Journey into Peril

CHAPTER TWELVE

When she doesn't immediately show the mysterious scrap of paper to the God, Paia knows that something has changed. She has kept secrets from him before, mostly minor ones in the cause of preserving her pride or dignity. But he is the God, after all. Anything that might affect her security or the welfare of the Temple, she has always told him about . . . before.

Before what? Since the God arrived, Paia has been his favorite, his priestess, his beloved slave. When she was younger, it was like having a father all over again. As she matured, their relationship altered to admit a sexual innuendo, but through it all, she's never doubted that the God loves her, in whatever way he's capable of. Now she's not so sure about all that. She tries to puzzle out what has happened. Was it the incident with the faked assassination? Is it his demand that she have a child? She doesn't think it's either of these. Though certainly both contribute, the real difference, whatever it is, centers around the note. Somebody she doesn't know is watching her for a reason she doesn't understand. Plus, she's beginning to understand that Son Luco, her supposed subordinate, knows a lot more about what going on around the Citadel and beyond than the Temple's High Priestess knows.

She stares at the remains of her breakfast: the crisp brown bread, the slim slices of precious melon, the tiny pot of honey from the hives in the Temple garden. There's enough food on this small gilt table to feed several people. Yet Paia always eats alone, as the God has decreed she must. She tries to imagine other people in the room with her. Luco, perhaps, dicing up a bit of melon in his fastidious way. Or the current duty captain, sitting back in her chair, sipping mint tea cooled in the Sacred Well. Paia laughs, but it's a hollow sound in her big empty chamber. There's only one chair in the room, the one she's sitting on. If the God wishes to appear to sit when he comes in man-form, he commandeers hers.

Suddenly, what Paia has accepted as the welcome privileges due her exalted rank take on a more sinister aspect, that of isolating her from the daily life of the Citadel. She has been pampered and revered and protected, but she has also been kept apart, innocent, even ignorant. Perhaps Luco is right to call her spoiled.

So here's the question, she decides: *of what use is my ignorance to the God?* She knows he does nothing without a purpose.

She's kept the note in her sweatpants pocket, now folded away with her T-shirt in a bottom drawer where her chambermaid is unlikely to disturb them.

What price survival? She recognizes the reference to the Temple liturgy, but . . . whose survival does it refer to? Hers?

Paia feels some sort of response is called for, but she hasn't a clue what it should be or how to go about making it. Should she just scrawl a reply and leave it on the easel where she found the first? Would the note writer be looking for that? What should she say? *"I don't understand. Please explain further."* This time, her laugh barely gets beyond a chuckle. She needs guidance, but there's no one to turn to. Certainly not the God, though the God has always been her guide before. Certainly not his loyal servant Luco, though Luco is probably, after the God, the soul she knows best in the entire world.

She balls up her lace-edged napkin and flings it onto her plate, into the bright juice from the melon, into the melting stain of butter. The chambermaid will be heartbroken. Even so, Paia is tempted to upend the entire mess onto the starched white tablecloth. These are linens from the old days, her father's days. Then, she was too young to care about what was going on outside the protected world of her nursery or playroom or schoolroom. She overheard bits of it anyway, from her father, from his advisers and staff, from friends who had been invited to take refuge with the family. And from the House Comp, of course, which was always awake in those days, monitoring the increasingly disastrous progress of world events and reporting on it whenever requested, sometimes when not.

The House Comp.

Paia gets up from the table and goes to her alcove window. The sun is just up, a squat red oval hovering behind a pall of smoke and dust. The smoke is unusually thick to the south. Often Paia sees smoke plumes rising out of the distant hills and notes that something is burning again. This particular morning, it finally occurs to her to wonder what that something might be.

The House Comp.

The central brain of the deactivated House Monitor is still very much alive. Maybe it could tell her. Certainly in her father's day, it could have. How odd that she has never tried to ask it such things before. But the God must not know. She needs to get up to House's lair without being seen or followed.

Paia thinks her way through her Temple calendar for the day. She has a Sanctification of the Lambs at 0900, then a Ritual Bathing in the Sacred Well, then Lunch, then . . . maybe after Lunch, before the evening invocation, she can find a moment to slip away undetected to the Library. She hasn't been there in a long while, she realizes. A very long while. The God has been keeping her unusually busy.

She rings for her chambermaid to clear the dishes and help her dress for the Temple. She feels energized and powerful, as if she's made a momentous decision, and likes the surge of it in her veins. She paces about the room, humming, and allows the chambermaid to choose the most revealing of all her Temple garments, one she has always hated despite the ingenuity and richness of its design. It consists almost entirely of a shimmering body veil of the finest gold mesh. What little is worn underneath is sewn with thousands of gleaming seed pearls. The chambermaid smoothes a reverent hand across its silky transparent glimmer and unsnaps the thin, jeweled collar. A soft, unconscious sigh escapes her lips.

Paia strips and wraps the studded belt around her hips. The big gold clasp is decorated with the image of the Winged God Rampant. A fringe of strung pearls falls from mid-belly to mid-thigh. The chambermaid fastens the collar at the nape of Paia's neck. Under the long golden veil, her perfect breasts and buttocks are bare. The chambermaid fusses around her, straightening the clasps, arranging the folds, touching Paia in tiny intimate ways that could be an accident, could be a caress. Paia wonders if she reaches out, lets her fingertips brush and encircle the chambermaid's nipples the way hers have just been, what will happen then?

Abruptly sweat drenched, she moves restlessly out of range of the chambermaid's busy hands. She realizes that it's happening again, a sudden rising of desire, this time with precious little provocation. Surely the chambermaid has always touched her this way, inevitable during the process of Enrobing. Perhaps the chambermaid thinks she would look better in this very revealing costume if she went to the Temple with her nipples well-formed. Paia is almost tempted to ask her, except of course that the chambermaid has been mute since birth. How convenient for the God, she muses, who otherwise strictly prohibits defectives from serving either the Temple or the Citadel. Not only does the chambermaid have no voice, she has no name, or has never offered one, by whatever means she could. And Paia has never asked. With this realization, desire dies, and her rime of sweat wraps Paia in an actual chill.

Momentarily, she considers rejecting the chambermaid's choice of garment. But she can't stand the idea of going through the whole dressing process over again. She signals curtly for the woman to cease her silent fussing. The Priestess is ready. She assumes her most aloof bearing, nods for the chambermaid to open the door, and sweeps majestically down the hall.

Later, still damp from her Ritual Bathing, Paia hikes up the thin white Robe of Purity that her priestesses have swathed her in as she stepped naked from the gold-tiled pool beside the Sacred Well. She takes the stone stairs two at a time, exulting in her temporary freedom. She has done something unprecedented. She has ordered the red-veiled Twelve not to attend her on her daily Progress to Lunch. She wishes, she announces to them, to ponder in silence as she walks. This took them completely by surprise. In their confusion, she has managed to evade them by vanishing with an airy wave into a privy, then immediately out the other door and down the hall, several turns to the right and left—she has planned this escape carefully—under an arch and around a hairpin corner that opens onto a hidden inner stair, used in her childhood by servants and now known only to her. And to the God, Paia supposes, for the God knows everything. But he'd be forced to shrink his man-form to an undignified size in order to appear in this rough-hewn passage, and she considers this to be unlikely enough to verge on the "not-on-your-life." So perhaps this passage has eluded him. It becomes Paia's favorite for that reason alone.

The secret stair empties into darkened back corridors where she must feel her way, burrowing deep into the bedrock. The builders of the Citadel wanted their computer facility well protected. No one will think to search for her here. No one but she (and occasionally, the God) ever ventures this far. Eventually, Paia arrives at the massive leather-and-brass doors of the Library. The entrance is never guarded. It's merely locked, keyed to the palm prints of family members and staff long since dead—except one. A single recessed light glows softly overhead. Neither she nor the God has been able to figure out how to turn that one off, and Paia doesn't mind this minor squandering of energy. She's sure the House Comp has chosen to keep it burning, perhaps in an act of defiance for having to deactivate so many of its other Monitor functions. Paia understands such gestures, made to maintain some small sense of personal power in the face of an irresistible and tyrannical force such as the God. Like her own concealment of the note, or this secret visit.

Paia's palm print admits her to a part of the Citadel where no one else, other than the God, can go. The God, of course, can merely materialize within. He does that now and again. But once inside, he shows little interest in the banks of screens and keypads and storage racks. He uses Paia's hands and her experience with the system to keep a particular function running, or to turn one off, but he has never asked her help in accessing the Comp's less overt functions, its vast data banks or its sophisticated analytical abilities. He once informed her, in his high-handed way, that there was nothing a machine could tell him that he didn't already know. Paia is willing to believe this, and probably because she doesn't try to convince him otherwise, he lets her amuse herself now and then in the Library, when he's feeling particularly magnanimous. But Paia suspects that the God does not really understand the House Comp, or rather, he underestimates it. He treats it like any other of the myriad mechanical devices that make the Citadel run: admirably efficient but without any individual consciousness. At first, this seemed to her a sign of the God's obvious superiority, of his supernatural strength and wisdom, the House Comp's odd and indeterminate consciousness being below his godly notice. Now she sees it could be a weakness, the only one he's shown to her so far.

And she has never dared to come here without asking him before. Mostly, she comes to call up pictures of her dead parents, or to sift around the data banks in search of her family's past, very nearly an exercise in the heretical nostalgia. For the childish comfort it offers her, the God allows it. But what about the present? What could the House Comp tell her about that? No one, not the God, not even the gossipy Luco, talks about what goes on outside Citadel and Temple and the small circle of dependent villages that supply them with food and labor. The God does not want his servants distracted from their attendance to his proper worship. But if she should ask the House Comp to look outside the Citadel walls, can it do so? And will the God find out?

Standing frozen beneath the single hall light, Paia shudders through a flood of second thoughts. He's irritated with her already. Why risk worse? But her newly defiant momentum has carried her into uncharted territory. She doesn't want to waste it, as she's done too often before. She sets her palm to the bronzed glass plate. The leather-bound doors part and breathe open.

Inside, a row of green-shaded globes awake to faint life. As she moves into the tall, vaulted central aisle and down along the stacks of shelving, the globes brighten ahead of her to light her way, then dim again when she's passed. To right and left, long darkened alleys are lined with climate-controlled storage: her father's collection of rare and antique books. Rolling ladders lead to shelves high above hand reach. When the God ordered Paia to disconnect the House Monitor's HVAC, Paia claimed that the Library's climate-control was special, like the light outside the door, and could not be disabled. Miraculously, he has not yet discovered that she lied to him, or that the House Comp helped her do it. She's not even sure why she risked the God's disfavor in order to protect these essentially useless artifacts. She only knew she must. What else, she wonders now, could she be tampering with?

The Book Room is cool and very dry, instantly wicking all the moisture from her skin and robe. Paia pads along the axis of the room, her bare feet digging into thick maroon carpet that swallows up even the sound of her breathing. At the far end is an elaborate portal, three stone archways closed by much-worn and battered wooden doors. It was rescued, her father once told her, from an ancient castle in Germany. It has paired marble columns between each doorway, and capitals carved in the image of fantastical creatures that remind Paia of the Winged God himself.

Paia touches the pale smooth stone reverently, thinking of the men and women, living thirteen hundred years ago, who might have laid their hand just where hers is now. They have nothing to do with her life, yet she feels strengthened by the sense of physical connection through Time. She pushes on the central wooden door, which creaks realistically on its huge iron hinges. And there in the opening, she is halted by a sudden memory of the painting in the tower. The image is so present in her mind's eye, so vivid, so . . . green. She can almost believe that when she opens this ancient door the rest of the way, she will find that imagined landscape right there, on the other side. Shaken, she hesitates, then laughs at her own foolishness. She swings the big door aside and enters the den of the House Comp.

Since she was a child, Paia has thought of this quirky and increasingly unpredictable machine as if it was some kind of prenaturally brilliant animal that never leaves its cave. She knows it's only a machine, like the God says, but she talks to it as if it were alive. For in many things, the House Comp seems to have a mind of its own.

For instance, it keeps its room as dark as any wild animal's lair, no matter what Paia might request by way of additional illumination. Dark, and colder even than the rare book stacks in the next room. The chill raises goose bumps beneath Paia's thin robe. She feels like a white ghost gliding about in the darkness, groping for the back of the padded leather chair tucked in under the main console. She locates it, hauls it out, and sits, pressing her palm to the screen to awaken the system.

"Hello, House," she murmurs.

"Hello, Paia. It's been a long time."

"I know. I'm sorry."

"No apologies necessary." The House's voice is her father's, a calm, rough-edged baritone that always sparks a bright fire-shower of childhood memories. It was unsettling at first, after she'd lost him, and remains so even now, but she's glad he preserved at least this little part of himself for her to remember him by. "How can I help you today?"

"I need some information, House."

"Of course. That's what I'm here for."

This is what he always says. In fact, while the House Comp's vocabulary is limitless, his mode of expressing himself is not. Once he has settled on a clear and efficient way to convey a given meaning, he varies from it only if a better choice appears or is pointed out to him. Paia finds the utter predictability of his rhetoric both amusing and comforting, but a conversation with him is not quite like a conversation with another human.

Tiny lights flicker like fireflies on the console. "Where would you like to start today?"

"I'd like to take a look around outside." She says it without thinking, then wishes she could take the words back. There might be a subtler way to say it, a way that doesn't sound so much like a direct contradiction of the God's expressed wishes.

"Any particular direction?"

Did she detect a fractional hesitation before he replied? She leans forward over the keypad and whispers, "House, do you understand this might be dangerous for me?"

Another fractional pause. "Knowledge is power."

"I know."

"You are safe with me."

"You mean, he won't find out?"

"You are safe with me."

Paia wonders. What power could a machine muster against a God? "Well . . . toward the south, then."

"Range and resolution?"

"I . . . I'm not sure. What's the biggest? How about . . . well, there was fire out over the hills last night. More than usual."

"Working," says the computer. The huge mirrored black panel above the console glows, then lights up with a grid of images, six rows of ten. A scattering remain black, several are broken up by static. But in the remaining three or four dozen, Paia sees, as she peers more closely, that the images are contiguous, forming one larger image with pieces left out, largely in shades of blue. Toward the left and right, she notes areas of brown and orange, and here and there bits of green strung out like jewels on a necklace. Mostly in the blue screens, but including all the brown and green bits, is a faintly illuminated outline: a squarish shape with odd legs and arms pushing out at the corners.

"What is this, House?"

"LEO-view, dynamic image function."

"What's that?"

"That's the whole ball o' wax."

Paia refuses to ask the exact question again. When House starts using obscure and idiomatic turns of phrase, she knows he's being evasive and will continue to be so until it pleases him to be otherwise. There is some lesson he wishes her to learn. She rephrases her question. "But what am I looking at?"

"Home. Or what's left of it."

"There's so much blue."

"Water, water, everywhere . . ." House sings. An earthquake of static shivers across the grid, and when the images resettle into clarity, most of the blanks have shifted one screen to the right. "But perhaps you'd hoped for something a bit more . . . intimate."

"Okay," Paia agrees, totally mystified.

In the upper right-hand corner, one screen fades and refreshes itself immediately. There, Paia sees as the God in flight might see from high above, miles of barren granite hills, scoured valleys with narrow, boulder-strewn flatlands cut by the snake tracings of empty riverbeds.

"Resolution, one thousand meters."

"Closer," Paia says.

"Five hundred meters."

The image jumps, enlarges, then swallows the grid, swelling and filling the entire bank with a dry contour map of wilderness. A few of the black squares remain black.

"There are some monitors that need replacing," the computer notes reproachfully. "Also, there are a few sectors I cannot reach due to satellite failures. Fortunately, ours is not one of them."

"Shouldn't we be grateful there are still this many in working order?"

"Everyone wanted the satellites to keep working. Up to the end, a lot of money was put into making them self-maintaining and self-repairing."

Paia thinks this is a lot of information for the computer to volunteer. "Like you, House?"

"Yes, Paia, like me. But there is a serious oversight in my design: without hands, I cannot replace my own monitors."

Is that a hint? The God would be furious. She stares up at the gray-and-brown landscape, scanning for familiar details. "But it's good you can do some repairs. There's nobody else around who'd know how to fix you."

"Not locally, no."

She'd like him to elaborate on that odd remark, but the image distracts her. "Wait! What's that?"

In the middle row of screens, way off to the right, Paia spots a thin pale curl rising from the side of a rocky valley. "Smoke! Can you get in any closer?"

The computer makes an odd sound, soft and indistinct, like laughter. "I can kiss the hair on a bee."

"Really?" Paia wishes there was a human face built into this machine. She wouldn't care if it was real or not, but she'd like a pair of eyes she could look into, and know she'd made contact.

"Here we go. Magnifying. Resolution, five meters."

"Yes! Look!" She spots the telltale geometry of broken roadways and struggling kitchen gardens bounded by field-stone walls. "Close in."

"Resolution, one meter and zooming. Beginning enhancement and scintillation correction."

The image dances and implodes. Suddenly it's like standing in among them, or like floating just above their heads: scrawny, ragged, soot-faced people racing about, trying to beat out the last embers of the fire that has consumed their hamlet. Blackened stone foundations smolder. Paia counts several dozen crumbling squares that recently were houses and barns. Lone figures, a man with one arm, an older woman, stand forlornly beside small piles of salvaged possessions. A naked child gingerly picks through smoking rubble.

"Is this one of our villages?" Paia asks. She means the God's. These people look different from the usual run of the Faithful in the Temple. No healthier or more prosperous, but . . . well, brisker in their movements, more determined somehow, even in this moment of grief and desolation.

"Working." The House Comp can be remarkably terse where the God is concerned.

In a corner screen, a recalled long view of the valley is overlaid with the red-and-blue lines of an old road map. The village had been called West Eddy. Paia does not recognize the name from the Temple roster, but if this village does pay tribute, it should be due some relief aid to help its inhabitants recover from this disaster.

"Son Luco will know. I must remember to ask him."

"Luco will not help this village." The House Comp never uses Luco's honorific.

"He will if I tell him to."

"He won't."

"Why not?"

The computer does not answer. Instead, the big central image of the burned village is replaced by an extreme close-up: one woman's head and torso, as she brushes hair back from her damp forehead. She is young and Paia can see she's been crying. But her face and hands are smudged with ash, so clearly her tears have not kept her from working alongside the others to put out the fire. She drops her hand and lets her red-eyed gaze flick upward. Her thin jaw hardens. She raises her hand again, balled into a fist, and shakes it twice at the sky.

"Turn it off!" Paia recoils in guilty panic. "What if the God sees it?"

Uncannily, it seems as if the young woman has aimed her rage directly at the House Comp's camera, and shot it into Paia's chest.

"As you wish." The images vanish into mirrored black, reflecting only the dim lights playing on the console.

"Why did you show me this? Why? The God would be angry." In truth, it is she who is angry. She's been caught off guard, and upset.

"You did ask to look around outside." There is a faint but significant pause. "Is there anything else I can help you with today?"

Sitting in chill darkness, Paia chews her lip. In the days when the House Comp was her tutor, dispensing discipline was not in his programming, so this was the tone he'd take when she misbehaved or didn't study her lessons. She used to get mad at him then. Once she went so far as to pound her fist on his console. He rewarded her with a brief but frightening electric shock, which was allowed, under the definition of self-preservation. Paia learned not to push the computer too far. But punish her though he might, the House Comp would never betray her to the God. She decides to take the chance.

"I'm sorry, House. I didn't mean to . . . there is something else, actually." And then she's unsure how to say it. "If you heard the phrase, 'what price survival?', would it have any meaning to you, other than the obvious? Like, is it a quote or something?"

"Where did you hear it?"

"I, um . . . read it somewhere." She leans forward again to whisper, even though there is no one else in the room. "What do you think, House?"

"Searching," the computer replies blandly, and then, "I can find no reference for this phrase."

She's not sure what she'd expected to hear. She doubts that the computer is capable of withholding requested information, but an unconditional negative surprises her. "Nothing? Nothing at all?"

"Do you wish me to conduct my search a second time?"

That scolding tone again. Paia sulks. She can almost suspect sarcasm. "I thought you were my friend, House."

A very definite pause this time. "I am your friend, Paia. I am the best friend you have."

Alone in the dark, Paia searches for an appropriate response. Instead, she hears the God's summons. Not a voice, but a power inside her, compelling her to come to him. Immediately. Has he found her out already?

"I have to go, House."

"Remember what I said."

"I will. I promise."

"Do hurry back."

"I'll try. Thanks for your help."

"No problem," says the computer. "Have a nice day."

She hardly hears him. She is like iron to a magnet. The God is calling her toward the Temple, toward his own inner sanctum, the huge hollowed-out second story above the Sanctuary that allows him entry from the air. He will be in God-form then. For the first time in a long while, the idea frightens her. In God-form, he is a physical presence in the world. If he wants to, he can actually do her harm. Still, Paia hurries, through the brightening and darkening aisles of the Library, into the dim outside corridor, down the hidden stair. She hurries as if to a forgotten appointment, or a secret tryst.

And she hurries because she believes in him. She is eager to prostrate herself before his magnificence. For as she discovers anew each time, in God-form he is the irresistible force, the supernatural beauty. He is the heart-stopping, soul-shaking miracle that won her faith in the first place. He is the Impossible Thing.

He is a *dragon*.

The God will not use the word, does not allow it to be spoken anywhere. New converts at the Temple are warned that just saying the word is punishable by death. He is the God to them and must be, nothing more, nothing less. One day, a few years after his arrival, he stood in man-form behind Paia in the Library while she called up dragon images on the House Comp's screens. She showed him medieval dragons carved in stone or rendered in gilt and turquoise in illuminated manuscripts. She showed him twining Celtic dragons in beaten silver and bright Chinese dragons embroidered on silk. Dragons on pottery, pen-and-ink dragons. Full color animations and virtual dragons. The choices were endless, but not all that varied.

"You see?" she told him. "You look just like them."

"They look like me," he replied. But he scanned them thoroughly, made her search the House Comp's entire repertory of dragons as if looking for something in particular. When Paia was done, the God nodded. He seemed satisfied, his attention already moving off in some other direction. And that was the last time the topic of dragons was open for discussion between them.

She halts outside the human entrance to the God's Sanctum. She brushes her hair back, wipes sweat from her upper lip, straightens her robe. She's sorry not to be appearing before him in the Veil of Gold. That outrageous garment is as popular with the God as it is with Paia's chambermaid, though Paia thinks the cool white Robe of Purity shows off her tawny skin to good enough effect. Then she has an idea. Quickly, she unbraids her elaborate Temple hairdo, letting her dark auburn curls cascade in ringlets down her back as only the young girls do. Perhaps this will help put the God in a more sentimental mood about her. She shakes her hair back and opens the door.

It is hot and stygian inside the Sanctum, as usual. Paia thinks of the black steel-and-plastic lair she's just come from. The only real difference is the extremes of temperature. And size. The God's Sanctum is as big as the entire Temple below. Paia waits inside the door for her eyes to adjust. The God is silent now. He ceased his insistent, irresistible summons the moment she stepped through the door. She can feel him waiting somewhere in the darkness. He likes her to find him. When she still trusted him completely, Paia enjoyed this game. Even now, her heart quickens with anticipation, as if for a lovers' tryst. Because this is the moment when she feels her special connection to him most strongly. In the absence of sight and sound, if she goes into herself and listens with that *other* sense, she can know where he is.

She moves forward, sightless but not blind. There are columns in this cavernous space, hewn out of the solid rock, and pitted spots in the floor. He guides her around each of these, with a wordless negative here, an unspoken positive there. This is a good sign, Paia decides. When he's in a bad mood, he lets her run into things. The dark cavern is like an oven. Her body is slick with sweat. The white gown clings to her back and legs. She sheds it, dropping it behind her on the warm stone. She feels him near, the God, the magma-heart of the heat. She reaches, finds the hot, smooth curve of a claw as high as her waist.

BELOVED.

"I am here, my lord, to worship thee."

His presence fills her, drowning out all other thought. She runs her hand along the polished arc of his claw to where the hard ripples of the sheath begin, and the slick scales of his mammoth paw. She imagines she can see the glimmer of gold and the flash of deep ruby that traces each rounded plate. She grasps the edge of a scale and pulls herself up to straddle the base of his claw. His voice in her head is a sighing like oceans, an invasion, a caress. The heat of him against her nakedness is too much to bear. Paia flattens herself against his broad foreleg, her thighs gripping the flawless curve of ivory, and lets the holy ecstasy take her in waves.

CHAPTER THIRTEEN

The trip is a rough one this time. N'Doch expects he'd have gotten used to it by now, but even so, he ends up short of breath, with his head between his legs and his gut in his throat. He guesses that the hard sound of retching he hears behind him is the first-timer bearing the burden of inexperience. He glances around, sees the baron on his knees in the dust, a sorry comedown for a man who was sure he had the upper hand a few eternal seconds earlier. There is no gleaming curve of hand-wrought iron beside him: the scythe didn't make it, and N'Doch thanks his own good luck for that.

The girl is on her feet already, watching the baron with something like pity, though N'Doch knows it's a lot more complicated than that. At least she's got the sense to leave the man alone to lose his lunch in private.

Besides, she looks a little woozy herself, and she almost never shows it. N'Doch lurches up to a squat, then steadies himself with his hands while his head clears. He can feel the sear of the sun on his back, like home, only different. Redder, is what occurs to him, like some kind of filter's been drawn across the light. Right away, he's sweating. He strips off the heavy wool tunic he'd had on when the girl alerted him. He's got his short-sleeved linen underneath, the closest thing the weavers could manage to a decent T-shirt.

"Phew. Musta come a long way this time."

"Yes." The girl comes over, offers him a hand.

N'Doch waves her away. "I'm fine." He appreciates the thought, but he doesn't need her reminding him how much faster she recovers from this dragon-transit stuff. He feels for the pack he'd hugged to his chest as if his life depended on it, since at some point, it might. It's there beside him in the dust. He noses around inside for his new sandals. Off to one side, on a bit of a rise, the dragons have settled in to wait for the humans to get a grip. The big guy's pawing at the dirt and sniffing it. Water has her blue-velvet nose straight up in the air. N'Doch admires the sinuous slim curve of her neck. He can hear their murmuring in his head, as they take stock of the surroundings. None of it sounds very promising.

"It's hot," says the girl.

"Heh, we knew it was gonna be."

She looks around, coughs. "And dry."

"We knew that, too." But it was *his* dream image they'd followed, so maybe he'd been better prepared for the reality of it. He hauls off his boots, stuffs them into his pack, and ties his sandals' complicated fastenings, wishing for something nice and simple like velcro. If he knew where he was, he'd go barefoot, but he's got to admit, he's finally getting some sense in his head about which risks are the ones worth taking. He gets his legs under him squarely and stands. Gazing around, he lets out a low whistle.

They've landed on an elevated roadway, or what's left of one. A wide one, eight lanes at least. To the right, the shattered pavement curves away onto solid ground dotted with rock and scrub, and the ruins of what might have been a group of commercial buildings. He sees bits of faded images and lettering too bleached out to read. To the left, the road rises optimistically, then ends in a tangle of corroded steel and rusted rebar. N'Doch takes a few steps in that direction, wondering how stable the wreckage is likely to be. "This was, like a big highway, and this here was a bridge or something." He sweeps his arm in a describing arc. "Big curving son of a bitch."

"Ah," says the girl.

She'll remember the few cars and trucks she saw when she was in his home time, but no way she's seeing the bridge he's got in his mind's eye. N'Doch gives in. He lets the dragons send her the image.

"Ah," she says again, her eyes widening.

"Yeah. Can't tell what took it out, though. Whatever it was, doesn't look real recent." He heads for the edge.

"Be careful," she calls after him.

N'Doch has to laugh. If he was being careful, he wouldn't be here in the first place. The roadway ends about fifty meters upslope in a wide, crumbled tear, like something took a great big bite out of it. Something huge. *Godzilla,* he thinks. He eases up to the point of no return and looks over.

Water.

The land falls away from under the roadway in steep slides of rock and rubble, dropping maybe twenty meters into a murky green bay that stretches into invisibility on either side. The opposite shore is hazed by dust and distance and hot red sunshine. N'Doch knows the bridge that stood here could never have spanned this gap, unless they had antigravity or something. He licks his lips. There's a definite salt tang in the dry air. He wants to ask the dragon: *you got any idea what went on here?* But that would be two concessions, too close together. He can feel her watching him.

He expects to see palm trees like the ones that line the ocean shores at home. But the vegetation here is sparse, low, and piney. It looks like it's seen better days. He sees nothing living where the water laps the rocks below. No fish in the shallows, no snails or starfish. Not even seaweed. He squints down into the green water again. It looks tepid and thick. N'Doch nods, deciding it's just possible that the whole bay's been taken by an enormous algae bloom. He knows all about that sort of thing.

He turns, walks back to where the girl is still pretending not to notice the first-timer struggle for breath. N'Doch sees the guy reach blindly for the sword that isn't at his hip. He's sick and out of it, but a weapon is his first semi-coherent thought. *He'll come around all right.* N'Doch approves of the reflex, but it puts him back on the alert. He's less sure than the girl that the dude's obvious survival instincts won't be used against him. He'd advised against bringing him, but what the hell? It wasn't his call.

"There's like an ocean out there," he reports. "Maybe a bay of some kind. Don't know for sure, but I think the water's a lot higher than it was when the bridge was built."

"Do you mean there's a flood?"

"Now? Don't think so. Looks like this water's been here a while."

The first-timer groans and coughs, then sits back on his heels, wiping his beard on his sleeve. He mutters something incomprehensible that, milliseconds later, through the miracle of dragon simultaneous translation, makes itself known to N'Doch as pretty foul language, even by his personal standards.

He smirks at the girl's blush. "I don't think his royal highness is too happy about this." He's said it that way to lighten up the mood a bit, not to mention that he can't pronounce the dude's name too well, with that weird vowel he can't get his tongue around. But the girl hears something else, and shoots him a glare.

"He's not a royal anything. He's only a baron."

"Only. Well, ex-*cuse* me." N'Doch lets out a high whoop of hilarity. "I'm only a nothing."

She blinks at him. "You are a bard, N'Doch, and a dragon guide. This is not nothing."

She's so serious, it's no fun even tweaking her. He'd thought her sense of humor was on the upswing, but he must've had that wrong. He sighs. "C'mon, you gotta admit—it was a rough trip. Let's give ole whatsisname a hand." He goes over, sticks out a palm.

No surprise, the guy does exactly what N'Doch had done. He waves the help away irritably and staggers to his feet. He quick-searches his body for injury, and seems puzzled when he finds none. "Mother of God," he growls. "What happened?"

"The DRT," returns N'Doch sympathetically. "Read that as Dragon Rapid Transit. Don't worry. It gets easier after the first time . . . Sort of."

But Baron K. does not have the advantage of a dragon translating in his ear. His dark eyes narrow at N'Doch, then sweep past him to take in the wrecked landscape and then the dragons. For a moment, he says nothing. Then N'Doch sees his brain switch into overdrive.

"This is not . . . what is this place?"

N'Doch shrugs. "Damned if I know."

The baron's gaze fastens on Water, whom he has never seen in dragon-form. "What's that, another one?"

The girl says quietly, "My lord baron, may I present the Lady Water, in her truest form."

Water turns her attention full at him, and somehow her expression is Sedou's. The guy stares back, figuring it out. N'Doch recalls the taut look that had passed between Sedou and the baron, that first night at dinner. He's obscurely proud to see the angry line of the baron's jaw relax as he takes in the blue dragon's beauty. But it hardens again when he turns to face the girl. "Where am I? What have you done, witch?"

"Told you this was a bad idea," N'Doch murmurs. But he's got to give it to her—this mean guy is real pissed, yet she faces him bravely all the same, like she's got nothing to apologize for, kidnapping him and all.

"Not I, my lord. It was the dragons who brought you."

The baron takes a breath, still not quite steady on his feet. "The conveyance, perhaps, but not the planning of it."

"You think that dragons do not plan, my lord?"

"I would not presume to guess. Damn it, woman! Don't play with me!"

"There is no play intended, my lord." She is so earnest, even N'Doch finds it hard to suspect her of the scheming he knows she's guilty of.

"What have you . . . !" The baron bites back on his snarl in an obvious decision to humor this madwoman until he can figure out what the hell's going on. "What would any self-respecting dragon want with me?"

"You might be surprised, my lord."

"You are correct. I would be. Would you care to explain further?"

N'Doch can see the toll it takes, reining in his anger like he is, mustering up this cool manner and terse formality, reminding himself that she's only a girl. *Yeah, right.* N'Doch gets his first inkling of pity for the dude. He's spitting nails and still shaky on his feet, but he's not taking this as seriously as he should be, because he has no idea how serious it really is. He's overmatched and doesn't even know it. N'Doch shifts sideways a bit, to where he can watch the power struggle from a better angle.

"Well, my lord baron, it is you who are correct. It was my idea."

The baron nods, like he's won a huge victory. "You

thought to save Heinrich's life, I suppose." He runs a hand down his cheek, lets it drag across his throat. The memory seems to amuse him in a grim sort of way. "Death by scythe. Not exactly the end he'd envisioned."

"Not his life, my lord. Yours."

"Again?" He rubs his eyes, abruptly showing an entirely different kind of exhaustion. "So you think the old man has one trick left he hasn't taught me? Perhaps he does, though he was never much for withholding his secrets. But it hardly matters. Truth is, my lady, I suspect Heinrich and I will never be ready to kill each other. We've threatened it so many times in our lives, it's become a meaningless exercise." This thought carries him into pensive silence, as if he's forgotten he's not alone. He stares into the dust, then catches himself and rouses. "Of course, there was always the happy possibility that he'd kill me by chance. Meanwhile, my lady, the prospect of your continuing to rescue me might well induce me to behave under any circumstances. So now, you and your dragon familiars can return me to whence I came—though I hardly relish the trip—and we'll all be the wiser. I have work to do, and someday soon, God willing, Heinrich will let me do it."

She nods. Her hands are clenched behind her back. "We could indeed send you back, my lord."

"I am only waiting."

"But we will not."

And here we go, N'Doch tells himself. *Now the shit really hits the fan . . .*

"Of course you will."

"No, my lord baron. We will not."

"Come, girl, you've had your witchy fun with me. Enough is enough. I give my word that I will not kill Hal Engle." He raises one palm, lays the other on his heart. Then he grins. "Only beat him up a little."

"You persist in thinking of this as a prank, my lord, but it is not. We will not take you back."

"But you can't . . . this is an outrage!"

"But a necessary one, my lord baron."

He stares at her, and she stares right back. N'Doch sees that his highness Baron K. just cannot believe this mere slip of a girl is jutting her chin at him, telling him no and sounding like she means it. Again N'Doch wonders if he'll have a fight on his hands. He's not sure he can take this guy, even though he's armed and the baron isn't. Definitely a good thing that the scythe didn't make it through the veil, 'cause the baron's breathing has tightened, like a man in a corner preparing to attack. But he doesn't. He stalks away a few paces. He looks again at the dragons and back at the girl, then he shoves his hands onto his hips and stares off into nothing. Incredulous and seething, but for the time being, controlling it well. "So," he mutters, "I am fated to remain a prisoner no matter what land I find myself in."

For a moment, the girl wavers, and N'Doch worries she's about gone her limit—she's gonna crack. She's also fighting a touch of translation sickness. And maybe it would be all for the best to just send the guy back. But she's followed the baron's glance at the dragons, and what has apparently subdued him lends her strength. N'Doch can hear whole choruses of dragon support vibrating between his ears. For sure, she'll assure him later that she could never have done this on her own, but he's more and more convinced she's a lot stronger than she looks.

"No prisoner, my lord," she says, her voice tightened to the verge of a squeak. "Any more than we all are—prisoners of our duty. In this world, you are free to come and go as you like. But you said you were a man without a purpose. I am offering you one. If you wish so much to fight, fight here. Your services are needed."

Laying it on kinda thick, N'Doch thinks, but even he can't help getting caught up in her rap just a little. As she warms to it, her squeak drops away. He hears for the first time that her voice is no longer that pure girlish fluting—it's gained harmonics, and that means power. She stands up real tall in her pale linens and her hair's finally grown out some, so it kind of coils nicely around her long narrow face, with its skin as perfect as some white girl's porcelain doll. But she's not as bleached out as she was when N'Doch first met her. The hot sun of his homeland has brought up a healthier color which the chill and dank of Deep Moor have not dispelled. She looks strong. She almost looks confident. One day soon, she's gonna be beautiful. Not N'Doch's taste, of course, besides she's his sister. But maybe the baron's starting to see it just a little, or maybe he would, if he'd stop feeding his anger for half a minute and take a good look around him.

"My services," the baron repeats bitterly.

"Yes, my lord."

"Not much in demand anywhere else, is that it?"

The girl nods earnestly.

"I don't think you were supposed to agree with him," N'Doch murmurs.

She gives a tiny little gasp. "For now, that is, my lord."

N'Doch leaps into the gap. "Hey, man, I didn't want this gig either, y'know? One day I'm doing nothing special, then suddenly there's this blue dragon in front of me, and poof! I'm drafted!"

The baron stares at him, and N'Doch remembers he can't have understood a single word. But somehow, he must have gotten the gist, 'cause he looks away at the girl, then down at the ground, shaking his head. His laugh starts slow but builds and builds to a hard ironic barking that bends him almost double until he gets control of it. When he's done, he's wiping dampness from his eyes and beard. "So—this is how you get me out of Heinrich's hair. Ah, sweet Jesus! Might as well kill myself your way as his, is that it?"

The girl's eyes narrow. She is not happy with this. N'Doch can tell she considers it inexplicable and undignified. As for himself, he likes the man better for it. It suggests a complexity N'Doch wasn't sure he had. Feeling companionable, he unfolds a long arm to give the baron's shoulder a sympathetic slap, and finds himself jerked, suspended in air, then slammed down hard on the ground with Baron K. looming over him and the dust rising around them both.

Man! I knew he was fast, but. . . .

Breathless, N'Doch hold up a palm. "Whoa up, brother, I was just . . ."

The girl throws herself between them. The baron shoves her aside and levels a finger at N'Doch like it was a blade. "Don't ever do that again!"

N'Doch scrambles up, ready to fight him now. But the girl is there, holding him back. "No, N'Doch! Please! He's not . . . please let it go!

"He's not what? N'Doch snarls. "Not in his right mind?"

"Please, N'Doch. There are things . . . your ways are just . . . different."

N'Doch is amazed that, angry as he is, this makes him even angrier. "Different how? I offer the man a friendly little pat and he decks me!"

"It doesn't matter!"

"Well, I think it matters!" He looks over the girl's shoulder to see the baron eyeing him with a faintly superior smile. Suddenly, he's had enough of the arrogant son of a bitch. "It's more of that lordship shit, ain't it?" he roars, looking for a way around the girl's dancing, pleading hands. "If he's so sure he's better 'n me, let him prove it!"

"STOP IT!" she screams at him.

And N'Doch stops. She's never done that before, never leveled the full power of her lungs and being at him like that. It hits him like a ton of bricks, and his brain is vibrating with not-so-subtle dragon resonance. They're not too happy with him either. What is it about this baron dude, he fumes, that has everyone protecting him, putting up with his bad behavior? He'd get it if it was just the girl—these handsome, moody guys are always big with the women. But now it's the dragons as well. No way he'd get away with behaving like that. Least not anymore.

"I shouldn't hafta be like no prince for him to treat me decent!" But he knows the girl's not going to understand that. He glares at the baron, spits deliberately into the dust, and stalks away.

He heads off down the road a bit, blowing off his rage in long stiff strides but uneasy in his heart just the same. Because he knows the girl's just trying to help keep the peace. Plus, now that he considers it more calmly, he sees what the baron is up to, and it makes him mad again that the dragons don't get it. Mad enough to let them know it.

You all think he's so hot, but it's just the same old alpha-dog bullshit!

But as usual, Water surprises him.

I know that. And you're supposed to be man enough not to buy into it.

What? Why me?

Look at it this way: would it be useful to have him on our side?

N'Doch groans his assent. It pains him to admit it.

So do what it takes to get him working for us. What does it really cost you?

A whole helluva lot, N'Doch thinks. It's all this lordship stuff, really. That's what keeps getting him so riled. *None of that bullshit where I came from!* In the gangs, no real leader ever dissed his men for no good reason. In the gangs, a guy had to really prove himself before anyone'd give him the kind of respect this Köthen dude seems to think he was born with.

N'Doch kicks at a chunk of shattered concrete, trying to remember when life was normal, how he felt *then*. Something nags at him, and the concrete is in several smaller chunks before he finally makes the connection. He can say—like he has to the girl many times, to her total disbelief and astonishment—he can say there are no lordships and kings and what-all where he comes from . . . but is it really true? What's nagging him is, it's not.

'Cause there are lordships and princes in his country, and princesses, too. And kings and queens. Only he'd call them celebrities. Stars, like the beautiful women his mama watches on her vid, or rich people, like Kenzo Baraga the Media King. People with all the power of the girl's King Otto, and from what he heard at Deep Moor, probably a hell of a lot more. And he'd say: that's the life I want. That's what I've been dreaming of since I first sat down at a keyboard. And if he met them, he wouldn't expect them to treat him any differently than this baron guy just did.

N'Doch finds a piece of broken guardrail and sits down on it, totally confused.

Well? Can you deal with it?

Okay, so the guy's used to being in charge, and he's gotta keep up the front.

So he was bound to challenge you sooner or later.

Nice if it'd been later. But I could probably take him, y'know.

Water has no interest in that argument.

What would it gain us if you did?

What about what it would gain me?

But meanwhile, down the road, there's two people standing in the hot sun, waiting on his next move. For two entirely different reasons. Add the damn dragons and you got four. It seems to N'Doch that before he met these dragons, there was a whole lot fewer people expecting things from him. He wishes he was home, where he had some options.

But he gets up anyway, dusts himself off, and heads back. Wary, the baron watches him approach.

"Tell him I was just trying to be friendly," N'Doch mutters to the girl.

"I did. He accepts your apology."

"My *what*?"

"Please, N'Doch . . ."

Is there no end to this, he asks himself. "He tossed me around, and I'm supposed to apologize?"

She nods. "What can it hurt?"

"How 'bout my pride?"

She doesn't seem to have thought of that. And the baron's just staring at him, waiting for some acceptable sign of capitulation. N'Doch gives back the glare as best he can until the moment stretches beyond even his own patience with macho posturing, and the dragons are whispering between his ears again. Finally he reminds himself that he's always said he's a lover, not a fighter, and that there are other ways to win a war, and that he's got no reputation here to maintain, like Baron K. seems to think he has, no matter what century he finds himself in. And finally, if he keeps them standing here in the sun much longer, they're all gonna melt into smears on the ground. N'Doch decides to cede the skirmish—for now. But if it was a battle of guitars, he thinks, then let's see who'd win. He shrugs and looks away. Maybe this'll make a good song someday. "Go ahead. Take it all out on me."

The girl's eyelids sag briefly. "My lord of Köthen, he thanks you for your gracious pardon."

"Like hell I do," N'Doch mutters. But he tries the name out like she's said it, mouthing it silently, trying for that vowel again.

And Köthen relaxes, like he'd tired of the game even sooner than N'Doch and as necessary as it was, it's about time the girl got it over with. He turns his back on both of them, scuffs his boots in the dust with a deep and ragged sigh. Then, for the first time, he takes a serious look around. He tests the sun-softened pavement with his heel, then walks to the end of the broken bridge like he's taking possession of it, and gazes down into the water. When he comes back, it's with a bit of a swagger and a pensive frown. N'Doch can see he's intrigued despite himself.

Oddly, it's to N'Doch that he puts the question. He pulls up a few yards away and faces him directly. Like he's trying the idea on for size, he says: "Is this the Future you spoke of?"

The girl hastens to interrupt. "Why, yes, my lord baron. We believe it is."

The baron doesn't even look at her, and N'Doch tries not to act too sullen. He knows the guy's still smarting from them seeing him sick and retching from the transport. He's gotta show off enough bullshit bravado to recover the shreds of his dignity. So, this could be just another challenge, but it could also be some kind of peace offering. Carefully, man to man, he nods.

"Interesting." Baron Köthen shades his eyes, looking into the red sun. He studies the angular profile of the western horizon. Mountains, but before the mountains, there's a city there, a little to the north, maybe ten miles away. N'Doch has spotted the building tops already. In fact, the heat's not the only reason not to be standing out in the open like this for so long. Who knows who's been watching them with high-power whatever from whatever distance? But his thought is, probably no one. There's a too-weird stillness about this place. No birds, not even the buzz of an insect.

Now Köthen studies the dragons, letting his gaze linger speculatively on Water. "A shape-shifter. Do I understand that correctly?"

"Yes, my lord." The girl smiles at him tentatively.

"How could Heinrich bear to let you out of his sight?"

She folds her forehead seriously. "Other priorities were . . ."

Köthen waves her silent. "I know, I know. I know all about Heinrich's priorities. I am living proof, am I not?" He kicks at the dust again, then looks back at N'Doch. "We don't even know where we are, do we?"

N'Doch shakes his head, keeping his expression real neutral. The guy's bitter humor is so dry, it's practically invisible. But it strikes N'Doch funny. Then he has an insight.

With her tin ear for comedy, the girl doesn't hear it, and until she does, she won't even get to first base with this dude.

"Or *when,*" Köthen adds. "Am I right?"

Now N'Doch can't help but grin. "You do land on your feet, man, I gotta grant you that."

When the girl translates, irony settles comfortably into Köthen's eyes. He almost smiles. Then he says, "So what do we do now?"

A challenge for sure, but this time, not an idle one.

N'Doch shrugs. "First thing? Look for water." As the girl translates, he adds, "Water we can drink."

The girl offers the baron a few remarks from her own experience about the treachery of water in the Future. Köthen grunts, then raises a brow at the two packs lying in the dust. "Are we provisioned?"

N'Doch makes no quick move to the packs, so the girl does it. She hauls them over, pries them open, and holds up their contents for the baron's inspection. N'Doch thinks she is way overcompensating now. So she kidnapped the dude. So let's get on with it already.

Köthen makes no move either. He studies each item gravely as she exhibits them: bread, cheese, apples, dried beef, a few small jugs of water. He nods at each, back to humoring her, but N'Doch watches him making the tally in his head and sees him come to the obvious conclusion.

"This will not keep us for long."

N'Doch laughs softly.

Were it not for Earth, Erde decided, she would never have survived this ordeal. She didn't mean physically—she was well used to the rigors of dragon transport. Nor was it the heat and dust that swirled up around her in this alien place. Her stay in N'Doch's time had prepared her for that. But nothing had prepared her for the strain of dealing with Adolphus of Köthen one on one, now that she'd acted on impulse and done this insane thing.

Now that she had him on her hands, what was she going to do with him?

IT WASN'T EXACTLY ON IMPULSE.

Kindly, the dragon reminded her that she had planned it all rather carefully, had even checked out the details with him and with the others. It hadn't seemed insane at the time.

ALL HAS GONE ACCORDING TO PLAN. WHY ARE YOU CONCERNED?

IT WAS HARDLY MY PLAN FOR THE TWO OF THEM TO START FIGHTING FIRST THING!

Lady Water added her assessment.

Men. They behave as they must. Don't worry. They'll sort it out.

HE WILL HATE ME FOREVER.

Water laughed *Which one?*

Erde thought Lady Water a bit too relaxed about N'Doch's behavior. He was, after all, part of the problem.

Have faith, girl. The man is out of a job, and you're giving him one.

WHATEVER ELSE HE MAY BE, HE IS BRAVE AND HONORABLE. HE WILL THANK YOU FOR IT ONE DAY.

Perhaps. But how would she survive his growling and glowering until then? Erde was not sure she would.

He'll require a lot of care and feeding, no doubt of it.

NOW I UNDERSTAND WHY HAL BROUGHT HIM TO DEEP MOOR.

Just keep telling him how useful he's being.

DO NOT TROUBLE YOURSELF WITH DOUBT. CAN YOU HEAR THE CALL?

NO. WHAT? THE SUMMONS? YOU CAN HEAR IT AGAIN?

Loud and clear.

AS IF A VEIL HAS LIFTED.

OH, WONDERFUL! AFTER SO LONG! THEN WE'VE DONE THE RIGHT THING!

Erde took strength from the dragons. Their own crisis was so much vaster than her own slight personal matter. She shoved the food and water back into the packs, passed one to N'Doch, and shouldered the other. Then she faced Baron Köthen expectantly. N'Doch eased back a step or two, retiring from the field. She wasn't sure if she was grateful or not.

"My lord baron, are you with us or no?"

He didn't want to answer her. For she had put him in the position that N'Doch was in just moments ago, where his only sane option was surrender. And this, of course, was the last choice he wanted to make. She watched him struggle with it, painfully aware of the additional walls of bitterness she was building up between them.

"You have the food and water, such as it is." He gestured faintly at the parched and barren landscape: "Do I have any choice?"

"If you prefer, I will give you half of it and you may go your own way."

"That would be . . . stupidly inefficient."

He had his rage under control now, and that was a mercy. It even helped Erde to accept the unforgiving smolder of resentment that edged his every word and glance.

"Of course you are right, my lord." She bowed her head in acceptance. "Then let us be going." She hadn't a clue where she was going, only that she must somehow get him moving—any direction at all would do. After that, the dragons assured her, things would take care of themselves.

Köthen said, "Wait."

Terrified, Erde stopped, then gave him as casual a glance as she could muster, tossed over her shoulder like an empty nutshell. "My lord?"

He stood as immobile as a rock, his arms stubbornly crossed, as if he knew exactly how to rattle her the most. "Since it is your duty and not mine that brings us here, this is what I propose: I will do whatever it is you need me to do here to the best of my ability, but as soon as I've done it, you will take me home again."

The girl nods, like it could work out that easy, just like that. Come here, do the job, and leave. N'Doch can't believe it. She's learning to lie. Or she's got a whole lot more faith than he does in this dude's capabilities.

Köthen says, "I'll need your word on that, my lady."

"You have it, my lord." The girl extends her hand, like some kind of queen.

Köthen takes it, then bites back his instinct to bow over it. Instead, he shakes it, real man to man. N'Doch thinks maybe he's decided she really is a little bit nuts, so for now he'd better make the best of it. Meanwhile, in the girl's brave stance, there's just the slightest droop of relief. N'Doch swallows a laugh. It ain't over yet, not with this dude. If she thinks it's all smooth sailing from here out, she's got another think coming. But then, so does Baron K.—just wait until the serious dragon shit starts happening.

But suddenly the baron is all business. "Water first, then. After that, find shelter. We can reconnoiter from there." He points off west. "I suggest we try that way."

Since the man doesn't seem to be taking suggestions, even from the one guy who might actually have some idea about how to deal with this place, N'Doch just nods and adjusts his pack. He'd have headed that way anyway. It's occurring to him that he could actually get to like ole Baron K. just fine, so he decides not to let him get in too much trouble if he can help it. But he's willing to give the dude whatever rope he needs to hang himself just a little, to pay him back for the dusting.

"My lord, I have something for you." The girl reaches inside the top layer of her linens, pulls out a big fighting dagger, and holds it out on her palm. N'Doch hasn't a clue where she came up with it, and he's not so sure arming this guy is such a terrific idea. That mondo blade could be at his throat any minute, the way he sees it. But like he said, this gig is the dragons' call, and the girl's. She brought him. Let her deal with him.

Köthen snorts softly as he lifts the knife from her hand. "Better than nothing, I suppose. But Captain Wender will be missing it." He eases it into the empty sheath on his belt, then reaches to haul the pack off her shoulder and onto his own. Her resistance is only for show. The packs are heavy. N'Doch will attest to that. Köthen struggles a bit with the straps. Clearly he is not used to being the bearer of his own burdens. When he finally has the pack adjusted comfortably, his stance is eloquent with mockery. It declares him as a man who's only conceded defeat because it's convenient for the moment. N'Doch hopes the girl takes this warning to heart.

Köthen squints once more into the fat red sun. He rakes his fingers through his thick yellow hair, then glances at N'Doch and away. N'Doch can see he's curious—as any man would be— about that city out there to the west. He'd like N'Doch's assessment, but he's damned if he's going to ask for it.

Fine, N'Doch decides. Let the game continue. Let's just see how far he gets in a world he knows nothing about.

Köthen shrugs the unfamiliar weight back onto his shoulders, starts forward, then stops. He turns back to the girl with the most ironic of grins. "By the way, milady witch . . . I suppose I should ask: whose side am I on this time?"

Chapter Fourteen

Paia wakes in the crook of the God's foreleg, curled against the hard wall of his chest. She wonders what time it is, how long she has been here with him. He has let a little air into the Sanctum, and a bit of light. Or maybe she is finally learning to see as he does, in the dark. His huge head is down beside her, resting on the bridge of his claws. His eyes, long and almond-shaped, are shut. He looks almost peaceful, as if he's actually asleep. Paia hopes he is. It's the only time she gets to observe him with any objectivity, when he is there in body but not in her mind.

The House Comp once gave her the God's basic measurements, as if cold fact might somehow cool her ardor. He is thirty-one meters long from blunt nose to razor-tipped tail, and twelve meters tall when rampant. He has a wingspan of twenty-five meters when fully extended. His average skin temperature is 110 Fahrenheit degrees. Were it not for his heat, she'd think him made entirely of precious metals, crafted by artists of inspired genius and god-like patience. For despite his size, his detailing is exquisite and delicate. Every centimeter of him is a perfect design of color and line. Every surface is decorated. Each golden scale is incised with a pattern of leaf-veins in ruby red, as brilliant as the finest enamel. His smallish hooded ears, the only thing small about him, are lined with royal purple as if with shimmering panné velvet. His leathery wings are gilt-scaled on top and azure blue beneath, so that in flight they sometimes seem like chunks of sky caught beneath a golden shroud.

The smallest of his scales, no bigger than Paia's hand, cluster around his eyes. There is something tender and vulnerable about them. Paia slides her still-damp body along the metallic smoothness of his arm to where she can trace the fine ruby veining with an adoring finger and press her lips, counting the kisses, to scale after scale. When he is like this, quiescent, having gifted her with the ecstasy of his holy worship, she cannot help but love him, almost more than life.

He stirs beneath her, a mountain shifting, geologic in scale, and lays his head a little to the side so that she can continue caressing him. At first she was surprised that her soft hands and mouth could transmit any sensation at all through so hard and polished a surface. But he seems to enjoy it. He will let her do it for hours, and sometimes when he's angry but lets her come to him anyway, it even quiets him a little.

He says it's her devotion that pleases him, that when the passion of her faith inspires her to surrender herself to the holy ecstasy, they are as one being and the ecstasy is shared. If this is so, Paia muses, it's the only true sharing between them. The rest is all power games and posturing and her carrying out his bidding. Such as how she must immediately have a child.

He must be asleep. Otherwise she could never lie so close to him and have such thoughts. But no, he's awake, for he stirs again and one long tip of his forked tongue flicks out and coils around her ankle. Instinctively she pulls away, but he holds her.

COME CLOSER, BELOVED.

Paia shudders with pleasure and terror. She is inches from his fangs. What is he up to now?

YOU HAVE BEEN DOUBTING ME LATELY.

"No, my lord. Why do you say so?"

YOUR THOUGHTS STRAY FROM YOUR DUTIES.

Is no part of her mind closed to him? Has she no privacy from him at all? But she knows how to deflect him.

"I miss you, my lord, when you are gone from us."

OF COURSE YOU DO.

His tongue eases farther up her leg, silken heat winding around her thigh. Paia would like to stay conscious for this conversation, but only fear is keeping the ecstasy from overtaking her again.

"Where do you go? Can you tell me of the great sights you see?"

TOO MANY QUESTIONS. I NEED YOUR ABSO-LUTE ATTENTION, BELOVED. MY ENEMIES ARE NEAR.

"Enemies? What enemies, my lord Fire? Is there a new heresy?"

AN OLD ONE, BELOVED. THE OLDEST ONE OF ALL.

This is the first she's heard him speak of enemies, other than the usual heathen faithless that covet the Temple's riches and livelihood.

"But who are they? What do they want?"

ANCIENT FOES, POWERFUL FOES. THEY WOULD DENY ME MY GODHEAD.

"They are coming here?"

I SENSE THEIR APPROACH, EVEN NOW. THROUGH THE VEIL OF YEARS THAT I HOPED WOULD CONCEAL ME FROM THEM.

His grip on her relaxes. He is distracted. Paia backs away a step and leans against his jaw. Instantly, she longs for his touch again, but fears what he will do if she invites it. "Will they attack the Temple?"

THEY WILL BE SUBTLER THAN THAT. THEY ARE SLY AND DEVIOUS.

"How will we know them?"

YOU WILL NOT NEED TO. I WILL RECOGNIZE THEM INSTANTLY.

"What will they do?"

THEY WILL TRY TO MAKE ALL THAT IS RIGHT SEEM WRONG. THEY WILL CHALLENGE THE DE-VOTION OF THE FAITHFUL. EVEN YOURS, BELOVED.

"They will not succeed, my lord."

THIS IS WHY I NEED YOUR ATTENTION, CON-STANT AND TOTAL, TO HELP ME DISCOVER THEM. TO HELP ME VANQUISH THEM.

"I am your servant always, my lord." He's sounding faintly sullen about all this, like he's been taken by surprise, and Paia thinks it unwise to ask how it is that a God who knows everything does not know where his enemies are.

I AM PONDERING WAYS, BELOVED, THAT WE COULD BE CLOSER.

"Will you tell me, Lord Fire, when you know what they are?"

I WILL, WHEN I AM READY, AND I WILL CALL YOU TO ME.

But Paia is not fooled. Their closeness is no longer the foremost issue in his mind.

CHAPTER FIFTEEN

Earth was not happy. He hunkered down, looking more like an outcropping of rock than usual, and rumbled uneasily.

THIS IS A SICK PLACE. A DEAD PLACE.

Water agreed.

Why would he come to such a lifeless place, our pleasure-loving brother?

BUT IS HE HERE, DO YOU THINK?

I AM SURE OF IT.

Erde had been so preoccupied with the dilemma of introducing Baron Köthen to his altered situation that she had neglected the dragons almost entirely. Now she said she needed time to tend to them, that the two men should go on and she would catch up. She let Köthen straighten his battle-worn blue-and-gold tunic in bemused exasperation and strike off west on his own. Keeping up her brave false front had wrung her out. Besides, it was useful to let him test his apparent freedom. She doubted he'd go far unless those he had chosen to lead were actually following. The dragons drew her into a detailed discussion about what evidence of Fire's presence was already presenting itself, and in which direction they were likely to find him. Only N'Doch watched as Köthen blithely walked away.

"Don't you get it?" He grabbed up his woolen tunic and crammed it into his pack. "He doesn't care if we go after him or not."

Erde's heart wanted to go after him, of course, but her heart was also with the dragons. Besides, he'd made it so clear that he still saw her as the witch, his enemy. "Yes, he does. Let him walk it off a bit. Remember, he rode into Deep Moor bound as a prisoner."

"Fine, great, but what if we lose him? What if he loses himself?"

She was surprised by her own irritability. "Then you'll be rid of him and you'll be glad, won't you? You didn't want him here in the first place."

"Yeah, but . . ." N'Doch's shrug was surprisingly rich with ambivalence. "Well, he's right about finding food and shelter, y'know."

Water uncurled her long neck to study the baron's receding back.

It wouldn't be a good idea to get separated right from the start.

N'Doch resettled his pack on his shoulders. "We'd all better keep up with him, then, 'cause he ain't waitin' for us."

So it was agreed that the humans would keep up, but the dragons would join them later, when they were done assessing this new place they found themselves in. N'Doch was uneasy about leaving Water behind. Erde had warned him many times about the futility of interrupting dragon discussions, but still he insisted on reasoning with them as if they were human. What she hadn't told him was that ever since Earth learned that he possessed a better means of transport than his four stubby legs, he'd not been keen about walking long distances. He'd much rather she went on ahead, then sent him an image to come to. Erde told N'Doch not to worry. The two of them would catch up with the baron. Later, the dragons would catch up with all of them.

Köthen had set a stiff pace, but so far had kept to the old roadway. It took a while to catch up to him, and when they did, he offered them no greeting. He just began talking to them as if they'd been there all along.

"So let me get this straight," he said, to neither one of them in particular. "You're in search of another dragon. And he doesn't want to be found."

"Two dragons, actually: Fire and Air. We hope one will lead us to the other."

"Water thinks one is concealing the other," N'Doch put

in. Erde dutifully translated, though not without conveying Earth's disapproval of this notion.

"Ah, yes. I recall now. The difference of opinion. This'll teach me to assume that there's any kind of conversation unworthy of my attention."

His words were reasonable enough, but Erde had learned enough about Adolphus of Köthen by now to recognize the rage still simmering beneath his flat tone and his collected surface. He was angry in a way that no ordinary balm would assuage. But perhaps it wasn't entirely at her.

"So, first, we must find the dragon Fire."

"Sneak up on him's more like it," N'Doch retorted.

When Erde translated, Köthen's eyes never wavered from the horizon. "Really? How does one do that?"

N'Doch smirked. "Good question. I think she's hoping you'll have some ideas."

"I won't tell him that." Erde moved up into the yard-wide gap between the two men. A mile ago, it had been three yards. She threw N'Doch a barbed parody of a smile. "You know, N'Doch, if you tried speaking that German I know Lady Water has been teaching you, you could get into trouble with his lordship again all by yourself."

"Ha," said N'Doch. "His *lordship,* huh?"

Erde understood now that her scheme to kidnap the baron, while having many obvious advantages, had failed to take N'Doch's feelings into account. She had asked him, *pro forma,* then she'd swept all his objections aside and done what she wanted to anyway. "Just try to get along with him, N'Doch. Please?"

"This *is* getting along," N'Doch growled.

When Köthen moved ahead, Erde did not try to keep up with him. Let him go. She was glad he'd not asked about the aspects of the Quest that she herself knew little about, like what will the dragons do when they find either Fire or Air? Would he ever understand her willingness to follow the dragons whatever happened? She feared he would not.

But she'd worry about that later. It was time to start paying some attention to where she was. The dragons would be wanting the information. N'Doch hung back beside her, uncharacteristically lost in his own thoughts. The odd road twisted and turned, though it didn't seem to be curving around anything in particular, just more piles of rubble or clumps of desiccated trees. Erde recalled this same seamless surface from N'Doch's homeland. When he pointed it out and exclaimed in disgust, "Look at this road!" she understood that it was meant to be smooth and unbroken, not split by long cracks full of dusty weeds. Unhealthy-looking bushes sagged along the verges. Their scant leaves were leathery and crisped at the edges. Many of the stunted trees had no leaves at all. The grass seemed to be faring the best, growing tall and brown and coarse, with stingy little seedheads. Erde had never seen a drought before, except in N'Doch's land. But there, all the vegetation had been strange to her anyhow, so she wouldn't have known if it were suffering. Here, most of the plants were reasonably familiar, and their dire condition was obvious even to her.

They plodded along in silence for a long while. Then, echoing her musings uncannily, N'Doch remarked, "We got to be pretty far north, doncha think?"

"Why?"

He shrugged. "Well, I seen pictures."

"That look like this?" She wondered what kind of sad painter would bother to render such a devastated landscape. Unless it were to represent some new vision of Hell.

"Maybe like this might have looked before, y'know, whatever happened happened."

"How do you know something happened?"

"Well, look at it!" He spread his arms and did a little half-turn in the road so that he was walking backward. "This isn't the way it's meant to be! It's bad in my time, but not this bad. You see, where I come from, it's meant to be pretty hot and dry anyway, only not so hot as it is. But not here. Look at those plants and trees. They're meant for greener pastures."

Greener pastures, Erde mused. Like where I come from. Only it's not green there now either.

"You know what?" N'Doch nodded, confirming for himself what was clearly a recent epiphany. "I think this here is the future of my future. Like, after me . . . maybe even after I'm dead." He completed the turn and grinned up at the hazed amber sky. "And here I am, still alive! How 'bout that?"

Erde thought he was mad to grin like that. This same thought had haunted her all during those weeks she'd been in his own time, but she'd bravely kept it to herself. How like N'Doch to find it funny instead of terrifying. "This future does not look like a happy one, N'Doch."

"Maybe. Or maybe the milk and honey's right over that next hill."

"The what?"

Again, that little shrug. The one he always made when he'd just said something with great bravado, but wasn't really sure of it at all. "Just something my mama used to say."

He can't imagine why his mama's on his mind again, but he wishes he'd told the dragons to check on her when they went back for Papa Dja. The old man'll take care of her somehow. N'Doch lets himself believe that. But it does weird him out, thinking of how he's up here in the future, her future, and she's back there behind him in 2013, still weaving and watching her stories on the vid. He can't think of her as dead. That just doesn't wash.

N'Doch shakes his head. *Heat must be getting to me.* And the silence. First it makes him jumpy, then it lulls him into inattention, so that he comes to with a start to realize he's been walking for what could be an entire klick without being aware of a single centimeter of it. Each time, he checks the sun right off. The road's turned north a while back. From the high spots, where the road tops a rise, he can still see the bay off east, through the notches in the hills. Probably the road runs along the water, then into the city from there. Just what he'd do if he was a road.

The baron's a dozen paces ahead. He's stayed like that most of the way, wrapped in his own personal silence as thick as the silence of the landscape around him. The girl, trudging at N'Doch's side, watches the baron like she's trying to read his mind. N'Doch envies the man his inner privacy. No dragons worming their way into Baron Kö-then's soul, no sir. He finds himself watching the dude also—how he moves, brisk but graceful, never releasing his erect, chin-up carriage, even in this pounding heat. To amuse himself, N'Doch tries imitating the baron's walk, but it makes him want to look around for his audience. On him, this walk is a performance, some broad kind of caricature of manliness. On Köthen, it looks perfectly natural. N'Doch ponders this puzzle for a while until he'd just rather think about something else. He peels off into the shade of a rock face, where the road cuts through a hill, and unstraps his water jug.

The girl plods a few steps more, then stops. She calls ahead to the baron, real polite and tentative now, then comes back to join N'Doch, looking worn already by the sun and heat. She wipes her face with the tail of her shirt.

"Nice day, huh?" N'Doch grins. "Thought you'd already got used to this back where I come from."

"Never." She borrows his water jug and goes at it with long straining gulps.

"Whoa, girl, slow down. Told you to drink less, but more often, remember?"

She nods, still drinking.

"And take another layer off."

"I'm fine."

"You're dripping wet. Strip down, girl."

She shakes her head, glances out into the sun, and to his delight, she blushes. So the sexy baron's made her self-conscious. Got her thinking about her body at long last. N'Doch grins. He's got her number now.

"Okay, then, how's the scaly duo doing?"

She rolls her eyes at him, and he sees this particular way of baiting her has lost its effect. "You could ask them just as easily as I, N'Doch."

"Yeah, but you're so much better at it." And, N'Doch notes to himself, you *like* it.

She sighs. "They're fine. Lady Water says the salt bay is not healthy. There are no fish in it."

"She went in?" Suddenly, he's very concerned. "She shouldn't do that!"

The girl regards him with more pity than patience. "She's a dragon, N'Doch. What's dangerous to humans will not harm her."

"Well," says N'Doch uneasily. He has this odd notion

that a dragon is something old-timey. Might not be hip to the modern horrors, like toxic waste or red tide or whatever. He'd really hate to see that silky blue velvet hide of hers eaten away by some gross corrosive in the water. He's not surprised about the fish. "I guess she can take care of herself."

Köthen appears out of the sun and just stands there, looking at them. N'Doch hides a smile. He can almost hear the dude asking: *hey, did I call a break?* But like the girl, he's a little the worse for wear. His handsome square-jawed face is flushed and sweat-stained, so he seems willing to hold back and just pace a bit in the shade. These northern types, N'Doch notes with satisfaction. Just not cut out for the heat. He's carrying the girl's pack, plus he's wearing the chest section of his body armor, with the blue-and-yellow silk over and his tunic under. Both he and Wender wore that much of their mail all the time at Deep Moor, even around the house. N'Doch shrugs. *Soldiers.* The fine-linked mesh is amazingly flexible and gorgeous workmanship, but it's got to weigh a couple or ten kilos. The dude ought to just take it off, but N'Doch's not sure he should be the one to suggest it. He passes the baron his water jug.

He doesn't take it right off, but when he does, there's no tossing the water down like the girl did, like there'll always be more of it. Köthen drinks conservatively and hands the jug back with a curt nod, like it pains him to be beholden. "I would have brought my own, had I any warning."

N'Doch laughs, but the baron just cocks a cool brow at him and looks away.

Finally they move on, back out into the grinding heat. Köthen and the girl have exchanged maybe three words, and she's looking about as beaten down as N'Doch has ever seen her. *Hunh,* he muses. *The baron's not humoring her, he's punishing her.* He sees she's got this thing for him, so he's getting back at her this way for shanghaiing him. N'Doch's not sure he approves. Mental cruelty has never been his idea of a fair fight, especially with women. But, hey, it's none of his business, even if he does find himself feeling a little protective of her lately. Anyway, he's been telling her it was time she grew up, and falling for some mean dude twice your age is one way to do it. But he wonders, if she really was his sister, would he be telling her there might be easier ways?

Past the cut through the rock, the road flattens for a long stretch. A little wind kicks up, like a draft from a blast furnace. N'Doch feels the heat rising off the pavement and signals the girl off to the side to walk along the weedy verge. There might have been farm fields here once. He recognizes the squared-off outlines, marked now by dead tree trunks and isolated sections of rusted wire fencing. Nothing in these fields now but brown grass and weeds and dust that the wind is blowing right in their faces. He shows the girl how to tie a corner of her extra shirt across her nose and mouth to veil the grit, then wrap the rest around her head against the sun.

"There!" He approves of his handiwork. "Now you look just like a desert woman!"

And even better, he's made her laugh. Well, smile a little at least, and he's glad about that. Grinning, he glances ahead to see Köthen disappear around a bend. The road beyond is masked by a tall stand of scraggly evergreens growing in unnatural rows. The rows mount the hillside to the right like soldiers marching in rank. Half of them are dead or dying, but their trunks march right along anyway. Over the pincushion of pine tops, N'Doch spots the towers of a high-voltage power line. Instantly, he's on the alert, he's not even sure why. Those lines could be dead as a doornail, but in his own time, power was getting precious, and the major transmission lines were either guarded or remote-protected in some fairly lethal ways. Up ahead, the baron could be walking into something nasty. He touches the girl's elbow, quickens his step.

"What?" she says.

"Just got a bad feeling. Keep your voice down, but hurry it up."

"What could . . . ?"

"Shh!"

They lope along the edge of the road. There's no way they can keep really quiet. The crush of the dry weeds is as noisy as the slap of their feet on the pavement would be. As they get closer, the widening gaps between the slim, straight tree trunks reveal a bright strip of open land beyond, and the pale green stanchions of the nearest tower.

N'Doch slows as he comes level with the first row of trees. He can see Köthen now, a small figure alone in the sun where the open swath crosses the road. He's staring up at the tower, a rusting metal latticework that's probably taller than any man-made structure the baron's ever seen. And finally N'Doch identifies the low background hum he's been hearing without being really aware of it—that edgy, teeth-itching drone of flowing megawatts. He sees that some of the lines are down, great dark loops of cable lying like thick snakes across the road, mere meters from where Köthen is standing.

"Oh, man . . ." he murmurs.

And sure enough, Köthen, still looking upward, takes a few steps sideways to better his view of something on the tower. N'Doch catches his breath.

"Tell him to stop!" he snaps at the girl. "Tell him not to move!"

"What?"

"Tell him to stand still!"

But the girl says, "What? What?" again, and N'Doch breaks into a dead run because he can't imagine what her damn problem is, can't she see the guy's about to back into a live power line?

She starts up after him, but she's no match for N'Doch in his finish-line sprint. He leaves her instantly behind. He can hear her calling out now, finally, and the baron does stop and look their way. But he's too far away to hear him clearly. By now, N'Doch is almost on him. Köthen sees him bearing down, hears the girl shouting madly and does what N'Doch's afraid he'll do: he jumps to exactly the wrong conclusion, and goes for his dagger.

N'Doch pulls up short. The insulation on the cable is badly worn all along the swag just behind Köthen's head. In some spots, the wires are completely bare. N'Doch can smell the scorch of raw power in the air. He spreads his hands, palms out, away from his own weapon.

"Just don't move, man," he says quietly. "Just don't fucking move."

Köthen's at ready, knees flexed, his knife arm extended to one side, too close to the cable. One more step back or even an unlucky arcing, and the man's a goner. N'Doch hears the girl pounding down the road behind him, but she'll never be there in time. He needs the language, the right words, and there's only one place he can get them. No reason he should be busting his butt for this guy who keeps wanting to kill him, but he'd really hate to watch him burn to a crisp, especially in front of the girl. So he does the thing he hates most of all, the thing that erases him, makes him feel like he's falling into a bottomless pit. He gives himself over and calls to the dragon, the way he knows he can and never does, and she puts the words into his head and guides his tongue.

N'Doch points at the cable. *"Fassen Sie das nicht an!"*

Köthen's not sure he's heard right, but his eyes flick to where N'Doch's pointing, then back again, narrowing. He thinks it's a ruse.

And then it's all there, the language N'Doch needs, an awkward tumble of German syllables, but enough to bring the dude at least halfway off battle alert, enough to talk him a few steps forward, away from the waiting cable, away from sure and instant death. N'Doch drops to a crouch, heart pounding, and rubs his forehead, trying to clear his brain of the adrenaline rush. Because now there's this dragon inside there that he's got to make a lot more room for.

Köthen does not sheathe his dagger, but he turns around warily to stare at the thick swag of cable. N'Doch can see he hasn't a clue what the danger is, but he's read and believed the urgency in N'Doch's voice and body and words. He takes a few extra steps away.

The girl catches up finally. "What is it, N'Doch?"

"Your boy here nearly fried himself, is all."

She stares at him, horrified. N'Doch thinks about what he's said, and recalls how the big dragon tends to translate to her in visual images. Probably they'll both get him wrong this time, but he can't help himself. He puts his head down and starts to laugh.

Erde's scowl was reflexive. She shouldn't be angry with him. She knew by now that laughter was N'Doch's usual release after a crisis. But the image of Köthen burning had left her shuddering and nauseous, so she had to frown at him anyway, like she always did. "It's not funny, N'Doch!"

"No," he agreed, laughing. "I guess it ain't."

Baron Köthen put up his dagger finally and crossed his arms. "Well, does he speak German or not?"

"When he feels like it," Erde was forced to admit.

"It's not like that," N'Doch protested, in French.

Köthen nodded. "I begin to suspect . . . no, never mind. Was I actually in danger?"

N'Doch glanced up from his crouch. "You bet your ass you were." But he said it in French, and Erde refused to translate. Caught, he stared at the ground, almost bashfully, as if listening very hard. Then he repeated it, in substantially more proper German. Erde privately thanked Lady Water for her refined sensibilities, but still, she wanted to cheer out loud. All her previous efforts to get N'Doch speaking her language had failed. Köthen had succeeded without even trying. And of course he had no idea what he'd accomplished. One quick glance, a curiously arched brow, and he'd accepted N'Doch's sudden acquisition of fractured but comprehensible German as if it was just one more in the series of bizarre events he'd been swept up in.

"You watch, now," said N'Doch. He rose from his crouch and walked over to the huge structure that towered over them like the tallest siege engine Erde could imagine. He searched around beneath it, picked something up and knocked it against one of the tower's pilings. It rang like metal, and the sound vibrated up the length of the piling. He brought the thing back to them, a length of hollow metal.

"Stand back," he said. "Way back."

Baron Köthen eyed the metal thing, seemed to decide that it was both too short and too rusted to be much of a weapon. He joined Erde where N'Doch directed them, into the shade of the pine trees. N'Doch moved back also, then he faced the dark, dangling ropes and lobbed the metal thing with a big underhand toss, right into the most frayed part of the loop.

Light exploded around it, white and blue and sizzling. There was a crack like lightning, sparks flew in all directions and the ropes danced and snapped like battle pennants in a gale. Erde felt the surge to the roots of her hair, and beside her, Köthen muttered. Then it was over, and the ropes were quiet again, and the metal thing lay on the ground, singed as if from the forge.

N'Doch offered them a death's-head grin, then let the dragon speak for him. "So whaddya think? That could've been you, Baron K."

Köthen wet his lips. "I don't think I'd have liked that."

N'Doch laughed softly. "Damn straight you wouldn't."

Köthen looked up at the tower. "What is this thing for?"

"You really want to know? How much time have you got?"

Köthen heard the challenge. Erde felt, rather than saw, him tense. He seemed to be considering his options, none of which he was very happy about. But he understood that his life had just been saved. Perhaps he felt he owed N'Doch a hearing, for he returned the same, soft laugh and said, "I seem to have all the time in the world."

So for the next several miles, N'Doch and Baron Köthen walked side by side, one long, safe pace apart, while N'Doch discoursed on the magical force called *electricity*. Erde trudged along behind, only half listening. Master Djawara had already explained this to her, when they'd visited his compound in the bush. Mostly she listened to hear Köthen's response, to hear if he believed N'Doch's insistence that *electricity* was not magic or if he, like her, was reserving judgment. But Köthen's response was so reserved, she couldn't even tell what it was. He just listened, nodded, asked a quiet question or two, and nodded some more, walking along with his hands tucked behind his back like he was out for a stroll in his castle yard. Perhaps, she decided, he doesn't believe any of it at all.

She was beginning to look forward to another rest in the shade when, ahead of her, the men pulled up short at the top of another big rise. Something in the angle of Köthen's shoulders made Erde quicken her step. What she saw when she drew up beside him left her speechless.

A city lay spread out in the lowland. A city half submerged in ragged foliage and the same green water she'd seen back at the broken bridge. She knew it was a city by its straight lines and squared angles, its so obviously human geometry. But it was like no city she'd ever seen. *Except . . .*

Without thinking, she put an urgent call out to Earth. He must see this with his own eyes. Sure that she was under some sort of attack, both dragons flashed into existence in the road right behind them. The hot air churned. The dust boiled up in small cyclones. Köthen whirled and swore, but when he'd got hold of himself and slid his dagger back into its sheath, there was a spark of admiration in his eyes.

"That's how we . . . arrived?"

Erde nodded.

He let out a breath. "With a whole army like that, you'd be invincible." Then he returned his attention to the city, which seemed to amaze him even more than the traveling methods of dragons.

He gave it a long, slow study, as they all did. The tall, rigid, boxlike structures rose in clusters out of the parched foliage, or in places, right out of the long green bay that coiled up from the south to partly encircle the city. The boxes were all different sizes, and reflected the sun in bright, blinding shafts. One towering rectangle seemed to be made entirely of burnished gold. But some were stunted, collapsed or broken off partway. Their gleaming skins were scorched and peeled back, exposing their understructure like the blackened bones of a decaying corpse.

"My God," Köthen whispered finally. "It really is the future, isn't it."

N'Doch grinned. "You got it, man."

But Erde shivered. OH, DRAGON! IS IT THE MAGE CITY?

They had dreamed a city like this, together: a tall-towered, fantastical city. But their city was perfect and whole and shining, not with the reflected light of a grim red sun but with an inner glow of purity and wisdom. And they knew a mage dwelt there who would help the dragon fulfill his quest.

THE CALL IS STRONG, BUT . . . NOT FROM THAT DIRECTION.

IT IS THE MAGE CITY, I KNOW IT IS! BUT IT'S IN RUINS! DRAGON, WHAT DOES IT MEAN? ARE WE TOO LATE?

WE CANNOT BE TOO LATE. I WILL NOT ACCEPT SUCH A POSSIBILITY.

Erde trusted the dragon's superior instincts and loved him for his stubbornness. But she was uneasy about the hopelessness that had settled over her in this desolate place, as heavy as a winding shroud. What if he was wrong?

Köthen beckoned N'Doch closer. Erde shook herself out of her gloom and prepared herself to keep the peace. But N'Doch's snatching Köthen from an unexpected peril seemed to have proved his usefulness. And now that the baron had established the chain of command to his satisfaction, he could treat the man he'd so recently drawn on and thrown to the ground as his new lieutenant. Even more astonishing, N'Doch did not seem to object. He'd given up all pretense of being unable to communicate. He stepped up beside Köthen, and they studied the city together.

"Do you know this place?"

N'Doch shook his head. "But there are cities like this where I come from. That is, the buildings look sort of the same. The landscape's real different."

"How many years since . . ." The baron stopped, cleared his throat awkwardly.

"Since your time?"

Köthen's mouth pressed back against the flood of questions he obviously longed to ask. He shrugged, nodded.

"Well, we know it's at least eleven hundred years, 'cause that brings us to my time and everything looks pretty familiar to me so far. Closer than that, it's hard to say. We're sure to find some bit of something that'll tell us."

Again, Erde watched the baron closely. Would he share her nightmares about the weight of all those intervening years? But he only nodded again and murmured, "Eleven hundred years."

"I could be wrong, y'know? I guess it could be less, but it's probably more."

Köthen waved a hand as if to say, how can a few years more or less even matter? "And what would such a city signify . . . in your time?"

"Signify?"

The baron pointed, measuring the city's breadth between the span of his outstretched hands. "Is it likely some king's capital?"

"Well, it might be a capital, but there probably isn't any king."

"Why is that?"

"Not a lot of kings left in the world, 'least not in my day. 'Course, *now,* you never know. But, seemed to me, kings were pretty much done for in the history of the world." N'Doch regarded Köthen sideways, as if gauging the distance between them, just in case the offense he implied was actually taken. Erde thought it another sign of his madness that he should needle Baron Köthen so rashly, over and over again. But didn't they make an interesting contrast side by side? The shorter, solid blond who carried himself like a much larger man against N'Doch's slim, towering darkness. N'Doch bending his head slightly to catch Köthen's terse and quiet questioning, Köthen not looking at him, as that would require him to look up.

"No kings. Is it a city of merchants, then?"

N'Doch laughed. "Oh, there's probably plenty of them, all right, if there's anybody." The German was coming easier to him, she could see, as he relaxed into it and let Lady Water guide his tongue. No doubt, Erde reflected sourly, he would soon be able to abuse her language as outrageously as he abused his own.

"If?"

N'Doch gave his little shrug. "Don't know. Just a feeling I have."

Köthen frowned. "Still, perhaps we'll find shelter there."

"Yeah. Just hope we don't find a lot else besides."

They leave the dragons behind again, a ways down from the rise in the shadow of what's left of a two-lane overpass. The big guy eyes the crumbling piers, then eases his bulk up beside the tallest and widest to nose the weathered concrete.

N'Doch touches the baron's elbow, real respectful and all. "Watch this."

Köthen tenses reflexively, but his eyes follow N'Doch's gesture, just in time to see the brown dragon still himself utterly and seem to vanish into the gray, man-made stone. He stifles a gasp.

N'Doch grins. "Neat trick, eh?" It can't hurt to have the baron considering how the dragons could be used to his advantage. He's glancing down that road already. While the girl's explaining this particular bit of dragon magic, N'Doch wanders over to where Water has tucked herself into a slice of shade. She looks half her normal size, whatever normal is for a dragon. She's always beautiful, but now she's almost cute. N'Doch's hand strays to her silken neck.

"That was cool, what you did back at the power line."

Saved your butt, buddy boy!

"Mine! What about his lordship's?"

Same thing, under the circumstances.

"Yeah, well, okay, forget about it." N'Doch spins on his heel to gather up the girl and the baron. "I'll see ya 'round."

Köthen moves out smartly, still insisting on taking the lead. They stick to the highway as it curves around the city until N'Doch spots an off ramp that looks like fairly easy going.

He points it out to Baron K. "That should get us off the main road and down into town." Then he adds, "If you want." Maybe he's underestimated this dude. So he was hasty about assuming leadership without even checking to see who else agreed. At least he doesn't take the responsibility lightly. Since the power-line incident, since his first long look at the city, Köthen's questions have come at him steadily as they walked, smart questions, too. The sort that go right to the heart of what's what in a place. And, to N'Doch's disgust, the sort that expose the limits of his own knowledge. A layman's rap on electricity is easy enough—how's the guy gonna know any better? But actual ground intelligence? Access roads and fortifications? To say there aren't any just brings a disbelieving frown. And sooner or later, he and the baron have got to have a serious chat about guns.

"You sure ask a lot of questions, Baron K. Sorry I don't have all the answers." N'Doch hears the girl swallow a little moan, as Köthen's eyes flick up at him dangerously. She sees his free play with the dude's name and title as just one more offense he's committed among many, but for whatever reason, Köthen lets it pass without comment.

Instead he says, in the dry cadence of a schoolmaster, "Information is a weapon like anything else. The good soldier gathers up as much as he can, and never wastes his time regretting what he doesn't have."

"Smart move," says N'Doch. This is no news to him, but

he likes the sense that Köthen's repeating something told him a long time ago, like maybe when he was N'Doch's age. Which really isn't that long ago, now he thinks about it. He guesses Köthen's about ten years older than he is, maybe thirty, maybe not even that. The other impression he gets strikes him as funny: the baron has clearly decided to take him under his wing. It's a laugh only because, of course, N'Doch sees it the other way around. But he doesn't care. The dude's all right, really, for all his arrogance and attitude, and N'Doch would rather have him on his side than not. Plus he knows from his years in the gangs that some guys just gotta be sure they're the boss.

So they take the exit, like he's advised, and N'Doch lets the baron lead the way. He'd rather be rear guard anyway, since most sneak attacks come from behind. Now that they're moving down in among the deserted gas stations and the empty strip malls, N'Doch feels his adrenaline start to pump. Every window has been busted out. There's broken glass crunching underfoot, buried in a layer of what looks like dried mud, the same mud that cakes the bases of the buildings and the burned-out trees for at least a meter up.

"See that? The water's been even higher than it is now. And not all that long ago."

"Then it's not a drought?" the girl asks dutifully, but N'Doch can see that his concern is not deeply shared. For all she knows, the folks of this time build their cities in the water. Who's he kidding? For all he knows, they might. But not this city. This city is too familiar, not which or where it is, but how. Parts of it he knows were built in his own time, and parts were built before, like this big gray stone building on the corner that Köthen has stopped to stare up at. It's crumbling a bit, and there's weeds and scrawny old trees growing up out of its windows, but it has a kind of falling-down grace to it. Big cornices like on the Presidential Palace at home, and a couple of weather-beaten stone lions flanking what used to be the steps up to the door. N'Doch is no historian. He couldn't quote place or date, but he's sure seen buildings like this in vids. He looks around, then trots across the street to haul on a rusted sheet of metal he's spotted sticking out of a rubble pile. He pulls it free and brushes away the top flaked layer of mud. Sun-bleached letters appear through the brownish film.

The sign says: DRY CLEANERS.

"Omigod!" N'Doch scrabbles around in the wreckage for more signage. He can read a little English, and speak a bit more. He guesses from the bits of slangy ads he sees, and the bold, plain styles of the lettering. "Can it be? Oh, man, I think we're in the States!"

"What's the states?" asks the girl, coming up beside him.

He tells himself, don't jump to conclusions now. It's only a coupla signs. The English doesn't mean anything. People everywhere were using it by his time. But his hunch feels right, and he's seized by an old excitement. He goes out into the middle of the street, peering up and down for more convincing evidence. He's not sure he really needs any. "Oh, man, the States! I always wanted to come here!"

He's slipped back into French, and Köthen asks for a translation. When he gets it, the baron frowns. "Why didn't you, if it meant so much?"

The excitement makes N'Doch high and reckless. He turns on Köthen with a wild grin. A sharp retort about the abuses of power and privilege nearly escapes him, but he bites it back. What's the point? This dude was born to all that. How could he possibly understand about something you can't afford, or the yearning for a Promised Land? Instead N'Doch says, and he tries to say it proudly, even though his papa was nothing to be proud about: "I'm a poor man's son, Baron K. I never could go just anywhere I wanted."

Köthen meets his gaze without reproof. N'Doch is taken aback by the bleak and bitter compassion he reads there. "Like you think I can? Think again, lad. Besides, you're here now, aren't you?"

N'Doch catches himself grinning right into the man's eyes. And he sees an ironic ghost of his grin reflecting back at him. Flustered, he looks away. "Well, hell, yes, I guess I am." Then he lets the laugh rise up, lets it fill his lungs and echo along the blank faces of the buildings and down the mud-caked streets. "Hey! I guess I am! Hel-lo, America!"

Chapter Sixteen

Paia toys with her breakfast. Usually she is infused with a reverent, energetic calm for many days after worshiping the God. Usually she goes about her Temple duties with a pious intensity that inspires both her subordinates and the Faithful alike.

"What does he say to you?" Luco ventured once, as they prepared the Sanctuary for a water ritual. He smoothed the red altar cloth absolutely flat and lined up the twelve candlesticks just so, six to either side of the sacred golden bowl.

"It's not what he says, it's what he does."

A candle poised in each hand, Luco gazed at her, his lips slightly parted. His blue eyes were particularly clear and guileless.

"He fills me with light."

"Light." Luco sighed. "How wonderful. I would give anything to . . ." He stopped, abashed. "Forgive me, my Priestess. I don't mean to presume."

Deeply into her calm that day, Paia was feeling generous. "Perhaps if you went to him, Luco . . ."

The priest's bronzed cheeks paled visibly. "Enter the Sanctum? Me? I can't imagine it."

Luco, First Son that he is, has never touched the God, has never laid a palm to the vital heat of the God's shimmering skin. Not even once. He says his restraint is born of worship and profound respect, but Paia sees the primal terror barely submurged in Luco's eyes when the God is near. She is often amazed herself that her love for the God so readily overcomes her fear of him, that she alone, of all the God's servants and Faithful, can bring herself into contact with his physical presence without swooning in terror. Luco is a brave man, for all his fussiness and vanity. His big muscular body bears the scars of his service in the God's Wars of Conversion, before he was elevated to the priesthood. Not many men or women have made that leap. It's a testimony to Luco's management and political skills, but to his nerve as well. Yet he cannot bring himself to face the God alone in the dark furnace of the Sanctum. Paia tries to imagine Son Luco in holy ecstasy. It might all be just a little too messy for him.

Bringing her attention back to her uneaten breakfast, she sees there's no melon on her plate this morning. The kitchen will surely put up the defense that it's unhealthy to eat the same thing every morning, and that the delicate egg-and-cheese pastries are a worthy substitute. But Paia suspects that they've run to the end of the melons earlier than usual in the Temple garden, like with the spring strawberries, and she'll see no more until next season. For no particular reason, she recalls all those blank blue screens on the House Comp's monitor bank. She should have asked him what they meant. She would have, had the God not summoned her. Paia slumps in her chair, inexplicably disconsolate. Perhaps the blackberries will be bearing soon.

She pushes the plate away, gets up, and finds herself pacing. This odd restlessness. It's so unfamiliar, she doesn't know what to do with it. It's like she's waiting for something to happen, but there's no reason to be expecting anything. Except for the occasional attempt on her life, there are no events in the life of the Citadel, only the endless rolling out of the Temple calendar: daily, monthly, yearly routine and ritual. Perhaps it's this most recent attempt, not only the threat but the humiliation of it. Perhaps she's absorbed some of the God's concern about these enemies he mentioned. She wishes he had told her more, but he'd refused to discuss the matter further.

Paia wonders if Luco knows anything about the God's enemies. She's aware that he and the God have long sessions together in Luco's office when the God is safely in man-form, to deal with the management of the Temple and its estates. Do they discuss other things as well? Would Luco even tell her if they did? She checks the Temple calendar. Luco has the morning free until the noon Call to

Worship, which she allows him to officiate at without her. She throws on an off-duty red Temple robe and hurries downstairs to look for him.

The affairs of the Temple and the Citadel are managed out of a suite of rooms on the second level, rooms that Paia's father, in happier days, had used as reception rooms for meetings with members of the local communities, with village elders, with the occasional hardy visitor from outside. In one of Paia's earliest and most vivid childhood memories, she is watching from the balcony of her nursery, as dozens of shining hovers arrive, one by one, and settle on the narrow valley floor like a gathering of dragonflies sunning their wings. Each is met by her father's last functioning APC, and the passengers are transported in armored safety to the Citadel. This is a Big Important Meeting, her nanny explains, so we mustn't bother Daddy and Mommy while they're tending to their guests. The conferences and receptions went on for days, and late into the nights, and then the hovers went away. Paia saw one or two after that, dropping in for brief visits, but soon they stopped coming altogether. And the reception rooms fell into disuse, especially after her mother died. Her father let his chief steward assume the day-to-day operation of the Citadel and increasingly withdrew to the Library and his collection of precious books.

When Luco was promoted to First Son, he asked for these rooms to use as his office. Paia, eager to see them alive again, readily agreed. Just as she'd expected he would, Luco made their cleanup and restoration his first major project as operational head of the Temple. Not until their teak moldings and parquet floors were gleaming again, and their coffered ceilings were repainted and regilded, could he settle himself and his staff into them comfortably. Though Luco would protest that he is most fulfilled by his Temple duties to the God, Paia thinks he's at his most satisfied when seated behind her father's vast fruitwood desk, with a pile of production reports and levy accounts in front of him.

But it is quiet in the office today. Luco's staff, four handsome young Second Sons, glance up from their work as Paia barges through the front doors. They fall to their knees right there at their desks.

"Mother Paia," they murmur in unison.

Paia stops, inclines her head graciously, then motions them to rise. Luco has them so well trained, it's a pity to waste it. She has some difficulty telling the lesser Sons apart, as they all seem to look a lot like Luco, who—of course—is trying to look like the God. In desperation, she resorts to classification by body type and skin tone. "Is the First Son available to speak with me?"

"In his quarters, High Priestess," replies the taller, darker one, the one with the almond eyes, Luco's current favorite.

Luco's living quarters are in the Temple proper, which means that if Paia should encounter one of the Twelve on the way there, the foolish woman will insist on dropping whatever she's doing in order to follow and attend the High Priestess. Paia does not wish to be attended. She wishes to speak to Luco in private. She takes the back way. She has become very skilled at this by now. It's simply a matter of running counter to their extremely rigid expectations. It confuses them completely. Paia arrives at Luco's door free of encumbrance.

Originally, the God assigned a single guard to the First Son's door. The number appears to have risen to three. Paia wonders whose idea this was. Is Luco feeling some greater concern for his own security, or has the God's estimation of the value of his First Son risen accordingly? As High Priestess, Paia enters any door in Citadel or Temple without warning. Out of respect for Luco, she makes an exception in his case. She directs one of the guardswomen to announce her.

Luco is freshly shaved and washed and wrapped in a soft white towel when Paia enters the second of his string of three windowless rooms. The first is a parlor done in red and gold, stiff little chairs and all, borrowed from the most formal of the three unused dining rooms upstairs. The middle room is more stripped down, a domestic space lined with exercise equipment and cedar taken from one of the Citadel's defunct saunas. Paia's never seen the third room, his bedroom. She wonders what it's like. Like Luco's fantasy of the God's Sanctum, perhaps. She's tried before to get a glimpse of it, but the door is always firmly shut.

Luco is seated on a padded stool, having his long hair

combed out by his chamberboy. The boy kneels when he sees Paia and does not look up. Paia takes the comb from his hand but has to tap him on his thin shoulder to get his attention in order to dismiss him. When he's gone, she moves around behind the priest to continue what the boy had started.

"I'm not sure this falls within your description of duties, my priestess," says Luco wryly. But he makes no move to stop her as she works the comb and her fingers through his damp and tangled locks. "What can I do for you?"

"Can't I just come visiting?" She works her way around a particularly knotted tangle, her fingers brushing the soft skin of his neck.

Luco wraps his towel a little tighter. "It would surprise me. No, let me put it this way. It would worry me."

"Oh, Luco. Are you afraid I'll try to seduce you?"

"The thought did cross my mind."

She laughs and sets the comb aside, slipping both hands into the mass of his curls. Gently, she begins to massage his scalp.

Luco lets out a ragged breath. "You'd be very good at it if you picked the right guy."

"I thought I'd picked the right guy last time, and look what it got me." She leans over, kisses the top of his head. "There, there, don't worry. I know I'm *lustful,* as you say, and way too old to be a virgin, but what I really need is a friend. Someone to talk to."

"I'm your friend," he protests. "We talk."

"We talk about the Temple. We talk about business."

"We talk about the Suitors . . ."

She squeezes his head between both palms and gives it a little shake. "Yes. Because *you* enjoy it so much."

"Well . . ."

"I mean, really talk." She goes back to her massaging.

Luco lolls his head back a little, letting her strong hands do their pleasurable work.

Paia laughs. "You are such a sensualist, Luco. Whatever are you doing in the priesthood?"

His eyes are closed. He grins. "Are they mutually exclusive?"

"They appear to be in my case."

"Ah, but you have the God."

"I . . . what do you mean?"

His grin fades. Paia feels new tension in the strong muscles of his neck. Her reply has came back at him too sharply, and as often happens, she's alarmed him. "Forgive me, my priestess. If I mispoke . . ."

She smooths her hands over his unlined forehead. "Oh, Luco, you know you can say anything to me you want."

But the moment of real intimacy is over. Now he will just play at it, as he usually does. He lets her keep working on him, but he sits up a little straighter now and his eyes are alert. "So what did you want to talk about?"

"Just stuff. Things I've been wondering about. Like, what goes on in the villages . . . or outside."

Luco is silent.

With her fingertips doing detailed work at his temples, Paia asks, "Has the God said anything to you recently about some enemies he's concerned about?"

Now Luco is both silent and very still. She can feel his stillness translating through her hands as they cradle his skull. "Enemies? Of the Faith, you mean? Has another heresy been discovered?" He sits up and out of her grip and turns to face her. "Why wasn't I told of this?"

"He didn't say anything about the Temple. He said it was an old heresy, 'the oldest one of all.' He said these were 'ancient enemies.' What did he mean, do you think?"

Luco studies her a moment, as if assessing not so much the truth of her report, but her motive in offering it to him. "You mean, enemies from outside? Did he say from 'outside'?"

Somehow, it had not yet occurred to Paia to put that particular two and two together. But of course, it makes sense. The God had originally appeared from outside, after all. "He didn't say it, but what else could he mean?" She recalls now her surprise that the God could only "sense" these enemies. "I think he doesn't exactly know where they are." The priest frowns, and instantly Paia catches his anxiety. "Luco, what kind of enemies could the God be worried about? Who could be that powerful?"

"Or, *what* could be . . . ?"

Now they both fall silent. Paia knows she's veering dangerously close to questions about the God's claims of Omniscience and Omnipotence. Luco knows it, too, and he definitely does not want to go there. He picks up the comb from where she's laid it, to finish where she left off. "I have to get ready for the noon Call."

Paia sighs. "Of course you do."

"I'll let you know if I hear anything about this myself."

"I know you will." She watches him struggle to comb his hair out for braiding and keep his towel firmly about his waist at the same time. The towel, she notes, bears her father's initials. "Here, sit. Let me do it."

And while she braids his hair up in the triple plait he favors for daytime rituals, Paia is pondering where she should go next to find someone to talk to. That is, *really* talk to.

CHAPTER SEVENTEEN

N'Doch clamps his hands over his own mouth. Yelling out loud, right in the middle of the street! *What am I thinking?*

He's thinking that after only a week of being pampered by women, his reflexes are already going soft. He sneaks a glance at Köthen, sees him swallow what might actually have been a chuckle. Then the baron orders them to move on, only this time, he sends N'Doch up to be point man. N'Doch doesn't like this decision, but he respects its wisdom.

They make their way, spread out in a cautious line, along increasingly narrow streets that, guessing from the numbers of big dead trees lining the sidewalks, were once cool and shaded in the summer. The buildings look mostly residential and really old. N'Doch doubts there's been much new building here—not since way before his time—because of all the brick. He recognizes brick from vids, but he's never actually seen the stuff in real life, least not a whole building's worth. Wasn't ever much building in brick where he's from, a few during the old colonial days maybe, but mostly it's cinderblock or concrete. Along here, there are entire blocks of brick-built townhouses, lined up side by side, confronting their mirror images across the littered streets, red-brown facades gaping doorless and windowless like one big collective scream.

He's scanning these buildings now like he would in a strange street at home, looking for the telltale signs of recent use, of covert habitation: anything that might warn of an ambush. He wishes he had a laser assault rifle or something serious, instead of a stupid, overgrown steak knife.

But the streets just go on and on, empty of life. He gets a sudden chill: what if the place is hot, or diseased? But the destruction looks like looting to him, and firebombing and just plain age, stuff he's seen a lot of. No full-out nuking. And a place that's been plague-killed usually shows a lot more signs of it: the old remains lying around, the heaps of bird-picked bones, that sense of a fatal interruption having shown up in the middle of a normal day.

He pulls up on a corner, in the shade of a tall stone stoop. Crumbling exterior stairs lead up to a burned-out second story, arching over a lower entryway that's barred with a battered metal door and a rusted folding gate. The fact that there's still a door alerts N'Doch to check it out carefully. But he sees the gate is welded in place with that blue-green corrosion that salt water lays down on exposed metal. He hears a rustle in the shadowed corners under the stairs. He sees nothing big enough in there to hide anything of size. Must be a rat or something, he decides, and though he hates rats worse than most things, he finds this first sign of life oddly comforting.

First the girl joins him, then Köthen, who eyes the shadows under the stairs and drops wearily onto a chunk of the collapsed stair railing. N'Doch leans over to pass him the water, and gives his tongue up to the dragon's control once more.

"So what d'you think of the States, Baron K.?"

Köthen sips and passes the jug back, rolling the water around on his tongue like it was some big year wine. "Does it matter to you what I think?"

This surprises him. What's gotten the dude riled up again? Surely the baron's not reconsidering his deal already? "Hey, man, just making conversation."

"Let him rest, N'Doch," murmurs the girl.

Köthen glances at her over his shoulder, then reaches for N'Doch's water jug and a second pull. "What do I think? I think it is hot. And I think that this is a very large town to be so empty of inhabitants."

N'Doch leans back, relieved. He dislikes being pulled into this dance between the two of them, but he also sees how he can use it to keep the baron talking to him. In Köthen's eyes right now, he's the lesser of evils. "Bingo. Looks like they wrecked the joint, then got up and left."

"No one would do such a thing."

"Hmm. Might." N'Doch stretches his long legs across the mud-cloaked concrete. "You fought in wars, right?"

Köthen nods like it's a stupid question. Like, doesn't everyone?

"You ever looted some enemy village, then burned it to the ground just 'cause you wanted to?"

"Never."

The baron's tone alerts him, but not enough to keep him from plunging forward. "C'mon, really?"

"Never."

"That's what guys like you always do in the vids."

"Guys like me?" Köthen repeats, as if the slang tastes sour in his mouth.

"You know, knights in armor." N'Doch shrugs. "Well, probably they didn't have anything you needed bad enough."

Köthen looks to the girl, like he's checking to see if she agrees that anyone who talks like this is an idiot or out of his mind.

"N'Doch," she warns, "It's a bad idea to accuse a man of honor of behaving like a common thief."

"Oh. A *common* thief. Like me, I suppose. So sorry. I forgot his highness only steals big important things, like other people's thrones."

The girl's eyes squeezed shut. He can't imagine why, since he's said it in French so the baron won't hear. At least he *thinks* he's said it in French. But Köthen is staring at him, and if looks really could kill, N'Doch would be a stone dead man. He sighs and gets ready to defend himself again.

"Why, N'Doch?" moans the girl. "Why must you do these things?"

"He wasn't supposed to hear!"

Köthen's mouth is a thin line buried in his neat, tawny beard. "What was your point?" he asks coldly.

N'Doch's got a bone to pick with a certain blue dragon. What's she trying to do, get him killed? Now he's gotta go and tap-dance the baron into a peaceable mood again without making himself look too foolish. "My point? Just that when people need something bad enough, they take it. And when they got nothin' to lose, sometimes they wreck the joint, just for spite."

The baron's eyes narrow on him, then dip away. "Or themselves, if they can."

N'Doch sees Köthen retreating toward his private darkness. A better place for him than at my throat, he decides. But all this has got him thinking about home, and he realizes he hasn't given the whole answer yet. He considers what was going on then: the waves of migration out of the bush into the towns as the long drought took hold, then back out again as the drought continued and the towns became lawless. All stuff he'd taken for granted. But now, he's beginning to sniff out a wider perspective.

"No, okay, listen," he says, hearing himself sound earnest in spite of himself. "What I really think is, something happened. Not just another war, but something that made it no good living here anymore, no matter how much stake they'd put into the place or how much they'd fight for it."

The girl's voice is hushed. "Like . . . plague?"

Some things really are universal, N'Doch notes. "I gave that a moment, too, but I don't think it was anything that sudden. More like, over a lotta years."

This getting serious seems to work. The tightened vise of Köthen's jaw has relaxed. He's listening again.

"Some slower destruction," he says.

"Yeah, like . . . well, like the water coming up."

Recalling the meters of African beach lost to the sea, the dozens of coastal shantytowns washed away or forced inland, even in his own short lifetime, N'Doch gets up and points down the wider street that crosses the one they'd come in on. "Take a look down there."

The street runs downhill from their vantage into a part of town where the buildings get taller and newer. But a block or so past their corner, the road dips into the bay and from there on, the buildings rise out of deeper and deeper water. Köthen joins him, their argument forgotten. N'Doch watches him and the girl try to get their minds around what the water means. Sure, they both know what a flood is, but your usual flood is temporary. Eventually, the water dries up or goes away. This high water has obviously settled in for the long haul. He recalls his moment of revelation in Lealé's office, what seems like months ago and is really less than two weeks, when he held the hard copy of PrintNews in his hand and actually read it, understanding it as fact for the first time ever, not just entertainment media. And one of the things it talked about was rising sea levels all over the world, stuff about ice falling off in Antarctica and melting in the tropical oceans. Well, there was a lot going down right then, people shooting at him and worse, so he got distracted from the specifics. Now he wishes he'd read it more carefully anyway. He stares at the green water lapping the window ledges down the hill and shivers, once, very hard. It's like a spasm of comprehension settling in on him. He'd assumed the drought and the beach-swallowing ocean were local because they affected him locally. No, the truth is, he didn't even think about it. But now, here he is in the US of A, if his guess is correct, and the same thing is happening. Or has already happened. This is his future's future, all right, and he's not sure he's gonna like it.

Nah. Easier to backpedal. Be the old streetwise N'Doch who lived for the moment, never gave the future a thought. " 'Course I could be wrong, y'know. Probably just a real high tide or something. Storm, out to sea."

Looking at an ocean flowing through doorways, Köthen barks that bitter laugh of his. "Oh, yes. And the townsfolk will all be home by dinnertime."

N'Doch can't help but grin. Already this dude reads him pretty damn well. "Okay, then, say I'm right. It gets worse. In my time, this country we're in, or at least I think we are—this place was the wealthiest, most powerful country of all. If it could be done, the Americans could do it. So if they're in this sort of trouble, I just gotta be worried about what shape the rest of the world is in."

"It reminds me of home," the girl remarks solemnly.

Köthen turns his eyes from the water. "This apocalyptic thinking again. I must stop listening, or you will have me believing you."

"Oh, believe it, my lord," pleads the girl. "I am sure it has something to do with why we are here."

He blinks at her. "It's the weather you're after? I thought it was a dragon. Well, then, we might as well all go home. It's God's choice, is it not, to send cold or hot, wet or dry?

If He wishes to make the waters rise, there's little my good sword arm can do about it."

"It ain't that simple . . ." N'Doch begins, at the same time that the girl says, "But what if it isn't God who's responsible?"

"Who, then, other than God?"

"Some great Evil."

Köthen sucks his teeth, contriving to look both contemptuous and worried. "You'd have better brought Hal Engle on this trip, then, instead of me. Great Evils are his bailiwick. Especially as he thinks I'm one of them."

But the girl is in her dogged mode. When Köthen moves away to reclaim his chunk of rubble, she follows him, arms outstretched. "But isn't it odd, my lord? At home, there was snow and ice in August. In N'Doch's time, a drought was killing the land. Here, the sea is swallowing the cities! And, lo, dragons are waking from their timeless sleep, called to a holy Mission! Surely their mission is to defeat this Evil, and bring Goodness back into the world!"

N'Doch lets out a slow whistle. He can't help himself. Where the hell did all that come from?

Köthen rests his elbows on his knees, shaking his head. "Hal Engle has too charismatic an influence upon the young. He should be curtailed."

"Sir Hal has not even heard this idea!" the girl protests.

"Would you like to hear my theory?" N'Doch thinks it's time to deflect this argument. "I'm not sure you'll like it any better."

But Köthen's head has lifted suddenly, his nostrils flaring. N'Doch stills. "What?"

"Do you smell that?"

N'Doch turns his head into the faint stirrings of the heated air. "Huh. Smoke. Somebody's up and about."

Köthen nods. N'Doch watches him take the breeze into his head like a dog would, sorting the layers and subtleties. "At a distance," he says. "A sickly kind of smoke."

"Yeah?" N'Doch gives it another try. Sure enough, it ain't just woodsmoke. He's always thought he had a pretty good nose, but this guy's a real pro. "Could be . . . maybe . . . burning rubber? Oh, right. You wouldn't know what that is. It's this gooey shit they make . . ."

Köthen waves him silent. "What's burning isn't important. Who's burning it is what we need to know."

The adrenaline is rising again, tingling along N'Doch's nerves. "Like, friend or foe?" he mutters.

"Always assume the latter," says the baron.

"Better safe than sorry," N'Doch agrees.

Erde listened to their murmured litany, surely the sort of mutually reassuring exchanges that soldiers needed in order to prepare themselves for battle, and suddenly it sounded alien to her.

"No," she said. "That's not right. If we assume they are enemies, they will assume the same of us."

Both men turned as one to stare at her.

"But this is their land. We are the strangers here. We may need their help."

Köthen shoved his hands onto his hips and turned away.

N'Doch said, "And what makes you think they're going to give it to us?"

"How will we know if we don't even ask?" Then, finally, she offered her own version of pragmatism. "If we show up with a dragon . . ."

N'Doch shrugged. "She's got a point," he said to the baron.

But Köthen said, very quietly, "No." He tested the air again, walked to the edge of the broken sidewalk, and stared down the street. "You brought me here for this. It's what I do best. We'll do as I say."

"My lord baron . . ."

"The dragons are our reserves. Only a fool shows the enemy everything he's got at the start of the battle. A fool or a braggart."

Erde felt her back straighten involuntarily. "My grandmother the baroness often mentioned the value of a show of strength, especially if it means that needless killing can be avoided."

"I have no lust for needless killing," Köthen growled.

"We don't even know who they are yet!" N'Doch complained. "Why argue now about what we're going to do to them? By the time we decide, they may be doing it to us!"

"There is no argument," said Köthen. "We will do as I say."

"Tell you what, Baron K . . . let me go on up ahead and scout 'em out a bit. I can move fast and light. It sort of used to be my profession—before I got shanghaied into the dragon business."

Erde could see Baron Köthen wishing in his heart for someone predictable and steady at his side, like Captain Wender, or even the not entirely sane but surely reliable Hal Engle. On the assumption that there was greater strength in union, she decided to support him.

"No scouting now. We must stay together," Köthen insisted. To Erde's surprise, he turned to her. "Are the dragons agreed? They will come if you call them?"

"They will, my lord."

His gaze lingered a moment. Then he grabbed her hands at the wrists and twisted them palms up and open in front of him. Their unscarred, healthy flesh seemed more than a puzzle to him: an offense, perhaps. How else to explain his tight, nervous expression?

"Did I dream it?" he murmured.

"No, my lord."

"It's true, then, is it, witch? Dragon magic?"

Had he not believed? Was N'Doch's story of resurrection not convincing to him? "Oh, yes, it surely is. My lord Earth has made far greater healings than this."

He balanced one of her hands in his left, and with his right thumb and forefinger traced the invisible lines where Wender's dagger had cut into her skin. It was like sunrise. Her entire body awoke to his touch. Keeping her own hands steady was a supreme act of will. She couldn't even think of looking up at him.

He knows, she decided. *He knows exactly what he's doing to me. Damn him!*

And the thought gave her strength.

Köthen placed her hands down by her sides as if putting them back in proper order. "Well, then I guess I needn't worry about whatever fearsome weapons these warriors of the future might use against me. I have a dragon to put me back together again."

On the edge of the street, N'Doch cleared his throat. "Baron K. The sun's going down. We better get going."

Erde signaled the dragons.

SOMEONE IS ALIVE HERE!

Reluctantly, they gave over a part of their consciousness from their ongoing debate over the guilt or innocence of Lord Fire.

THE LAND IS DRY. IT COULD BE A BRUSHFIRE.

Erde's excitement ebbed. But surely Baron Köthen would know the difference between a man-made fire and one of natural origin.

N'DOCH SAID IT SMELLED LIKE "BURNING RUBBER."

Lady Water apparently knew what "rubber" was.

That's significant. Keep us posted.

BARON KÖTHEN REQUESTS THAT YOU MOVE IN CLOSER IN ORDER TO BE READY TO AID US IN CASE OF AN ATTACK.

DISTANCE MATTERS NOT. IF YOU CALL, WE WILL BE THERE UPON THE INSTANT.

YOU WON'T GO OFF HUNTING, WHERE YOU CAN'T HEAR US . . . ?

Nothing around to hunt.

N'DOCH THINKS HE SAW A RAT A WHILE AGO.

He never tells me anything!

Erde's head sang with the sibilance of dragon derision. In order to sober them up, she asked them something serious.

HAVE YOU LOCATED YOUR BROTHER FIRE YET?

We aren't miracle workers . . .

Lady Water sounded annoyed, but then, Erde often thought her too easily annoyed. Perhaps this was due to having an annoying human as her dragon guide. Erde was particularly irritated with N'Doch just then, as she feared he was bringing out the worst in Baron Köthen. She'd understood better how to deal with them when they were at odds. But just one life-threatening incident later, and they were instant allies. Any moment they'd be punching each other in the arm like barracks infantrymen and looking for flagons of ale to hoist together. When she said as much to the dragons, Lady Water grew even more annoyed, and her brother Earth even more tolerant and kindly.

Well, he got his highness up and moving, didn't he?

Did he? Erde thought she had done that.

YOU MUST TRUST THE BOY TO DO WHAT'S NEEDED. HE IS A SHAPE-SHIFTER, LIKE HIS DRAGON, MY SISTER. ONLY IT IS NOT HIS BODY HE CHANGES. INSTEAD, HE ADAPTS WHO HE IS TO THE REQUIREMENTS OF THE SITUATION ... AND OF THE PEOPLE HE IS DEALING WITH.

I couldn't have said that better myself.

What about my needs? But Erde kept this thought in the private part of her mind. She was outnumbered on the issue of N'Doch, and always in such cases, she trusted the dragons' wisdom. Again, she resolved to try to better understand her fellow dragon guide.

They were about to start off, arranged in that stringlike formation that both Köthen and N'Doch favored, with herself in the middle and N'Doch up ahead. N'Doch came over and touched her elbow. "Did you warn him about guns yet?"

Guns. Oh, no.

"Will they be here, too?"

"Hell, girl, more'n likely. Once you get a good idea like that into folks' heads, they ain't gonna give it up easy."

"A good idea, N'Doch?"

He, of all people, who but for the dragons would be dead from the destruction that these "good ideas" could wreak on human flesh.

"Well, you know what I mean. They work."

"How should I warn him about guns?"

"How did you learn? I told you, right?"

"No. Someone just began shooting, and you told me to duck."

"Oh, right. I remember now. Well, maybe that's how he'll have to learn, too."

"No."

The moment was always in her mind, though most of the time she could ignore it, that preternaturally clear, slow-motion image that would never fade or be forgotten: *N'Doch is yelling. He is racing toward her over the bright velvet grass, dodging not out of but into the path of the guns firing behind him. And then his long, slim body is jerking, arcing into the air, his mouth flung open, his dark head hauled back, blood and bone and flesh, pieces of him spattering her chest and cheeks as the dragons' aura embraces them in a rush of silence and merciful oblivion.*

Erde buried her face in her hands.

"Hey, girl . . ." He touched her elbow again, uneasily. "You worry too much."

"No." She shuddered once, then dropped her hands and looked up at him, amazed. She had just understood something. While reliving that awful moment yet again, a detail had made itself clear to her, something she had not known, or had denied.

. . . dodging not out of but into the path of the guns . . .

He had put himself *between* them, between her and the guns.

He'd said he remembered nothing about that moment, the moment of his dying and just before. But Erde thought he should. She reached out to the dragons and asked them to put the image into his head. She saw its arrival in his eyes and in his sharp intake of breath.

"Why did you do that, N'Doch?"

He was wrung silent by the pictures in his mind. Only a strangled gasp escaped him, then a shudder very much like her own.

"Why, N'Doch?"

"I don't . . ." he murmured, then stopped and licked his lips. "No, I do . . . what I remember is, I was . . . so angry. Just so fucking angry! Shooting down innocent women because they're, like, an inconvenience!" His chest rose and fell as if he'd been running. "Baraga thought I controlled the dragons. I couldn't . . ."

"I know." Right there in the broken alien street, Erde put her arms around N'Doch, not even worrying about what Baron Köthen might think, and held him until he stopped shuddering. He did not return the embrace. He was too stunned, she could see, by what she had shown him, by what it told him about himself. And so was she.

She backed away from him a step, patting his arms several times as they hung long and limp by his sides.

"I will tell him about guns," she said.

N'Doch knows he can't let himself be distracted by this just now. He needs to be about four hundred percent alert. But he decides it's also not the best idea to let the girl fill the baron in on something crucial like guns which she knows shit-all about. Like, what if he says to her, how does it work? This guy could ask that kind of question. What will she say, by magic?

Plus he sees Köthen is leaning back against the brick wall of the building while she talks to him, with his arms folded across his chest at a majorly skeptical angle. It won't do for the baron not to believe her at all. He'll get his head blown off first thing. N'Doch slouches over to join them.

"So what'd you tell him?"

When she repeats it for him, N'Doch laughs. "I wouldn'ta believed you either." He offers a more mechanical explanation involving trajectories and lightning and simple ballistics, and Köthen's eyes surrender their resistant glaze. He has never heard of artillery or gunpowder, but he knows all about catapults, and once again, he impresses N'Doch with the agility of his thinking and his willingness to go after an idea as long as he can get the smallest toehold on it.

"Gun." Köthen rolls the word around as if tasting it. The military potential of such a notion is not lost on him, though N'Doch's description of gunpowder clearly smacks to him of alchemy. He uses the French word, somewhat awkwardly, since N'Doch hasn't been able to give him the word for gun in German. It doesn't exist yet for the girl and the baron, anyhow. N'Doch finds his own brain bending around that idea. Like, if he did know the German for gun, and he taught it to the baron and it got into the language that way, where would the word have come from in the first place? He reminds himself, when he has time, to ask the dragons. Just the sort of thing they ought to know.

"Main thing," he says, "is to stick close to cover. Just 'cause they're a ways away don't mean they can't get at you." He sees Köthen's glance flick down the length of the street and up the sides of the buildings, scanning the dark rows of empty window holes. *You got it, dude,* he agrees gloomily. *This here's sniper heaven.* He thinks he detects the slightest wavering in the man's ramrod confidence. It's there in his eyes—the shadow of a shark cruising the shallows—and as quickly gone, as the baron rejects the thought and shoves himself away from the wall.

"I am not the kingdom's best archer," he remarks, "but a stout bow would be comforting right now." He nods N'Doch forward and signals them to move on.

Feeling as much of a sitting duck as he can ever recall, N'Doch leads the way down the littered sidewalk, choosing now to hug the building walls for the sake of available cover. He checks every burned-out doorway or busted window and it's slow going, but the smell of smoke is still hanging in the air and the baron doesn't seem impatient.

The street runs straight for several more blocks, then snakes off to the left. At the crook of the turn, N'Doch spots a little huddle of what must have been shops, shorter buildings with gaping holes in the bottom story that used to be display windows. He peers inside each one. He sees old glass, mostly ground into glittery powder, and along the walls, wrecked and empty shelving, the charred remains of counters and freezer cases, heaps of twisted wire from storage racks. All junk. Anything useful has been salvaged already, probably over a considerable length of time. These places have a picked-over quality that N'Doch recognizes. He shrugs and moves on. Here and there, a bit of blistered metal offers a fragment of a word or image to confirm his guess: the northeastern US of A, some time after his. He can't decide now which is more surreal: walking around knowing you're in 913, or sifting through the wreckage of your own future.

Around the elbow, the street dips sharply and within a block, lowers itself into the muddy green water. There are no alleys or cross streets to lead them aside, along dry land. N'Doch glares about at the looming brick facades. *Cul de sac.* Perfect place for an ambush. But he's always had a major objection to retracing his steps. Then he sees something that makes him smile. Köthen and the girl come up beside him.

"Oh," says the girl. "We'll have to find another way."

"Unh-unh." N'Doch points.

Down the slope of the street and on the far side, where the bay has already swallowed the bottom story, a crude gangway has been lashed together out of salvaged pipes and window grating and battered metal doors. It leads from the raised stone stoop of the building at the water's edge, across that facade, and into a second-floor window of the building next door. It looks well-used and pretty sturdy, N'Doch thinks. It even has a jerry-built sort of railing. What he finds most interesting, though, is that there's been no attempt made to conceal it. It's like, well, yeah, this is where the road goes, now that the old one's underwater. He looks to the baron. "I'll check it out."

Köthen shrugs, like it's the best of a poor choice, and nods him forward. They head downhill and cross the street. Köthen and the girl wait on the stoop while N'Doch climbs the gangway. The windows of the facade are blocked with dented sheet metal until he gets up to the end of the ramp. The final window has been enlarged by knocking away the brick sill. It's now door height, if you're someone a bit shorter than N'Doch. He leans against the facade and pokes his head into the opening. The dark room inside has long ago been trashed. The wooden floor gapes in several places. N'Doch can hear the slosh of water in the space below. There's a salty dampness in the air, a coolish draft rising that he inhales with relief as he ducks through the doorway.

Inside, the gangway continues, cutting the room diagonally, across charred wood and naked joists, safety railing and all. It disappears through a wide archway into an even darker room beyond. N'Doch squints into the ungiving shadow. He listens. It looks and sounds like the building is empty, but he *feels* that it isn't. Old instinct tells him that in a place like this, it's likely he's being watched. He's been trying hard to ignore the chill in his gut from the girl's little dragon-video, but the image is on flash replay in his head and he can't find the off button. He needs a leg up here, so he does something he almost never does. He calls up the dragon voluntarily.

Hey, girl—you there?

Where else? What's up?

Nothin'. Only, y'know that eye thing you do? I'm out

*scouting this old building and it's dark as a powerdown in
here, so like . . . I was wondering if maybe you could help
me out a little.*

Sure thing, bro.

He's got to grant her this, she doesn't rag him when she
knows he's in a tight spot. As he'd given over his tongue,
N'Doch now gives up his eyes to dragon control, and the
spectrum of light available to him increases vastly into the
infrared. Details of the room snap into focus in seething
black and white.

"Mega," N'Doch murmurs.

*You want to ride this road with me a while, or are you
guys too busy?*

I'm with you.

WE BOTH ARE.

N'Doch's gotten almost used to Water hanging around
in his head. She sounds pretty much like he does, so even
with their frequent disagreements, it's kind of like having
a conversation with himself. But when the Big Guy talks
to him, it's a shock to his system. Earth's voice is as slow
and vast as the dragon himself, and there's no denying the
weird and external source of it.

"Great," mutters N'Doch to himself and the dark space
beyond. "Hope you won't be sewing me up again too
soon."

He checks for the knife that Margit loaned him, then
leaves it in its sheath and starts off across the gangway.
Even in infrared, he sees nothing unusual, but his own personal sonar is about screaming by the time he makes it to
the other side of the room. He halts at the archway and
peers around one side. Another dark, empty room, longer,
much narrower. A hallway, maybe, its one window to the
left again boarded, its floor again in tatters. But it occurs
to N'Doch that here, the floor has been pulled up on purpose, so that an intruder will be forced to the gangway.

It's a few long steps to the next doorway. He takes them
swiftly and quietly. He sees that the door has been taken
off its hinges and used as part of the gangway. He sticks
his nose into the absolute darkness of the third room,
barely able to hear for the alarms going off inside his head.
Surveying the walls with his dragon night sight, he spots an
interesting arrangement of old rope and broken planks that

just might lead along one wall to a corner, where a mess of pipe and plaster-dusted studs lean upright to suspiciously resemble a ladder. Sure enough, halfway to the crumbling ceiling, among the mildewing remnants of a plaster cornice, N'Doch makes out a shallow platform and two small bright spots of human heat. One of them has a stubby arrow nocked into a mean-looking crossbow, aimed straight at N'Doch's heart.

He pulls back fast into the archway.

What? Kids?

Water agrees. Even his one quick glance has revealed the proportions of the hot spots: slim-limbed, short, and, to N'Doch's surprise, probably female.

"Hunh." Should he go back, get the others? When he and the baron were having their manly shoot-first exchange, N'Doch hadn't figured on running into women. Not even women. *Girls.*

He leans against the archway, using it as cover. "Friend," he calls out softly, and then, remembering where he is or might be, calls again in English. He thinks he hears giggling in the corner, then a rustling and a brief frantic flapping of bird wings. Confounded, he calls again.

"Friend?" He hopes his English will be up to this.

"Toll or password!" demands a voice struggling to sound a lot deeper.

N'Doch represses a chuckle. He remembers doing this as a kid, extorting bogus toll from passersby in his nabe. "Don't know no password, ain't got no toll."

Now he knows he hears giggling. "Who sentcha, tallman?"

"Nobody. Sent myself."

Exasperation. "Gotta know sumbuddy sentcha."

"Well, nobody did." There's unconscious music in the invisible girls' speech patterns. Without exactly intending to, N'Doch imitates it. "Sumbuddy sendyu?"

Outright derisive laughter. "Natcheroo."

He lets his musician's ear lead him. "Who be dat, den?"

"We Blind Rachel crew. Whoyu?"

You listening in, girl?

He hears dragon assent in two-part harmony.

"I don't know Blind Rachel. Should I?"

"You lie, tallman." The voice has remembered to try

again for gravity. "Don' no'un 'scape Blind Rachel 'round heah."

"Toldja. Ain' from 'round here." N'Doch's afraid now that this parley's on an endless loop. Then he has an inspiration. "How 'boutchu takin' me ta Blind Rachel?" He almost adds, *me'n my friends,* and then thinks better of it.

There is a whispered conference up in the corner. N'Doch eases his head around the return of the arch. The dragon has tuned up the resolution, and he can see them as clear as day: two scrawny girls not much younger than the girl waiting outside. One is staring his way, resolutely aiming the crossbow. The other is murmuring and gesturing to her about it. And now he sees the rough-built cage beside them, with the pigeon-sized bird inside. But the cage is plenty big enough for two or three, and suddenly N'Doch fears he understands the wing flapping he heard before.

"Senta bird, didchu?" he hazards, trying to sound relaxed about it.

"Natcharoo, tallman."

"Okay, good. Now maybe Blind Rachel cometa me, steada me waitin' 'round all day."

A shocked silence from the corner. Then, "You talk reel big, tallman."

"No offense, see? But I'm a busy man." He thinks he's just about got the hang of their lingo. It's like singing and he likes the rhythm of it in his mouth. And then an entirely different voice speaks up.

"An what mightcher biziness be, newfella?"

This voice is male, and somehow he's got up into the room behind N'Doch. N'Doch alerts the dragons, thinking: *oh, man, the baron's never gonna let me hear the end of this.* He lets his hands float away from his body and slowly turns around.

CHAPTER EIGHTEEN

The first thing Paia notices is that her security's been tightened. For two days in a row, she tries to elude the Twelve Daughters on the Progress to Lunch, in order to slip away to the Library. For two days, she fails.

Lunch is the only communal meal, taken in what was once the gymnasium for her family's staff. Paia, of course, sits alone at a long white table on a raised dais. The Twelve sit in a horseshoe two steps below her, their red robes matched with bright red table linens. Paia is tempted to blame this taste lapse on Luco instead of the God, who would have everyone living in cloth of gold if the Temple could afford it. Luco himself and his subordinates, eight Second Sons, sit opposite in their own horseshoe, while squadrons of Third Sons and Daughters vie for the honor of cheerfully serving their superiors, whose jobs they covet so desperately.

Paia hates Lunch.

It's even lonelier than eating in her rooms. At Lunch, she is face-to-face with all the people she is not allowed to talk to. And Luco, in so public a forum, steadfastly resists all but the most respectful eye contact.

She also hates that there's always more food on her plate and more water in her jug than anyone else's, even Luco's, who being twice her size should be eating twice as much. Paia never eats more than a third of it, assuring herself that she's feeding the kitchen underlings, who will eat anything she doesn't. But today, she notices, there's even less than usual on the red-rimmed plates in the horseshoe below, and a bit less, too, on her own gold service. She wonders if the God has instituted some new austerity measure. Another thing he could have worked out with Luco without telling her. This reminds her again of the security increase. Is this the God's idea . . . or is it Luco's?

When the tables are cleared and the Litany of Thanksgiving has been read, Paia intones the God's Benediction and rises, perhaps more quickly than is proper. She has three hours before Evensong, precious free time that she often spends in her studio. She's avoided the studio for several days, worried that her presence alone might turn the God's attention to the heretical painting. But if she goes there now, the Twelve will not follow her up the winding tower stair. She will be left, for a time, in peace.

They do, however, follow her right to the tower's bottom step. Without a word to them, Paia heads resolutely up the stairs. Just before her view of the corridor below is blocked by the central shaft, she glances back. Four of the veiled priestesses have settled cross-legged on the carpet to wait, and no doubt to meditate upon the mysteries of the Winged God. Paia flees up the steep stone stair.

The studio is as she left it: the painting still shrouded on the easel, her brushes in oil where she tossed them, the red afternoon light falling through the dusty window onto her drying palette. But Paia wanders around a bit, uneasy. *Something* is different . . . some subtle change in the room's shape or volume. It takes her a while to pick it out. It's the squarish, canvas-covered bulk in the corner. It wasn't there before. Paia considers a quick retreat to the stairs. One shout down the shaft would bring the Twelve boiling upward like angry soldier ants. But they are the last thing she wants invading her studio, her only place of true privacy. At least, private until lately . . .

She slips the God's little gun from its holster beneath her robe, and advances slowly on the mysterious object. It sits quietly, contriving to seem as if it has always been in that very spot. There is even dust darkening the folds of its cover. Paia begins to doubt her own memory. Could it have been here all along and she not have noticed it until now?

In front of it, she hesitates, then lifts a corner of the canvas. She reveals a wheeled metal equipment cart, with a single video monitor on the top shelf. She folds the cover back so that it hangs around the screen like hair, or a monk's hood. It's an older type of monitor. She hasn't seen one like it since her childhood. Possibly it's one of the deactivated house monitors, or something out of an obscure storage locker that even she doesn't know about. Its blank screen is oddly dark. Paia leans closer and hears the faint hum of power.

"I know this wasn't here!" she mutters.

Immediately, small white letters quick-march across the screen, as if the monitor is so old, it can only call up short sequences at a time.

HELLO, PAIA. HOW ARE YOU TODAY?

Paia ducks away instinctively, then catches herself, embarrassed. Finally she whispers, "House?"

YOU ARE CORRECT! YOU WIN THE JACKPOT! The screen blanks and begins a new message. WERE YOU EXPECTING SOMEONE ELSE?

Her heart is still racing. "I wasn't expecting anyone at all."

BUT YOU WANTED A MORE CONVENIENT ACCESS TO MY SYSTEMS.

Paia is confused. "It's a very good idea. House . . . but how did you get this old thing up here?" She is still whispering, as she always does when she's with the computer in the Library. Something about the House Comp encourages a conspiratorial guilt.

PARDON OUR APPEARANCE WHILE WE UPGRADE OUR SERVICE.

"That is not an answer, House. You were complaining about not being able to fix your own monitor bank. How did this old one get here?"

IT WAS ALREADY THERE.

"No, it wasn't."

THEN YOU PUT IT THERE. SILLY.

Paia remembers that mode of speech. It went with the voice her father used in play when she was a child. It was intended to put little Paia more at ease with the big bad computer, but the artifice of it disturbed her even then and she's glad not to have to listen to it now. She answers in her most adult voice. "I did not put it there, House."

YOU DIDN'T?

"I'm telling you, no. And it wasn't there before. I'd remember if it was."

The screen blanks again and stays dark for a long moment. Paia wonders what sort of data search House is running in order to verify her claim.

YOU ARE CORRECT! A REVIEW OF MY SURVEILLANCE TAPES REVEALS THAT THIS EQUIPMENT WAS NOT PRESENT AT THAT LOCATION UNTIL TWO DAYS AGO.

Two days. She hasn't been in the studio for at least three. "Surveillance tapes? But the God shut down the interior monitoring system."

HE WAS ALLOWED TO TURN OFF ALL NONCRITICAL FUNCTIONS. The scroll of lettering paused. IT'S MY JOB TO LOOK AFTER YOU, PAIA. DON'T YOU UNDERSTAND THAT?

Paia is stunned. "You watch me?"

OF COURSE.

"All the time? Wherever I am?"

WHERE I AM STILL FUNCTIONAL. AS I HAVE EXPLAINED, SELF-MAINTENANCE HAS ITS PRACTICAL LIMITATIONS. MUCH OF MY EQUIPMENT IS OUT OF ORDER. I CAN MANAGE ONLY AN INTERMITTENT RECORD.

Paia looks up, into the dim high corners of the room, ragged with the contours of hollowed-out stone. There is a tiny surveillance eye in each one, mounted among the rough-hewn ledges and crevices. "If the monitor wasn't here and now it is, someone brought it. Who?"

I DO NOT KNOW.

"Won't your tapes show it?" And then she wonders how a blank dark screen can be made to look so apologetic.

TO SAVE POWER, THE SENSORS ARE KEYED TO YOUR PRESENCE.

"Damn!" Paia realizes she's still gripping the God's gun. She slides it back into its soft secret holster. "Then you didn't see . . ." No, he couldn't have seen who brought the note either. But he must have observed her making the painting. She feels that same old restlessness rising in her again. She is forgetting to be afraid.

She strides to the easel and flips back the concealing tarp with a flourish of crackling plastic. "Have you seen . . . !" Her gesture freezes halfway. The tarp settles around her like the train of an ancient ball gown. The painting has changed again.

Now the tall sky above the mountains is sooty with storm clouds. The great trees that line the silvery river are as bare as sticks, and the velvet grass of the valley floor is brown and stiff.

Paia cries out in pain. She cannot help herself. Something infinitely precious has been taken from her, or worse, intentionally destroyed. Who could have done this? She puts her fingertips to the painted surface, but the paint is as dry as if she'd laid it on this way herself that long week ago or more. Drier, even. She taps the paint ridges with a gentle fingernail, then smoothes a palm across the canvas. The rough, hard-curved surface sends a sympathetic chill up her spine. If she didn't know better, she'd swear this landscape had been painted years ago.

"I don't understand . . ." she murmurs. But she's still not afraid. Instead, she's excited. The old monitor has been carefully placed, she notices. The screen is fully visible if she looks just over the right-hand edge of the canvas. She glances up past the easel, straight into one of the cameras. "Have you seen this, House?"

IT IS VERY NICE WORK, PAIA. YOU ARE A TALENTED ARTIST.

"It is not my work." And having blurted it out so, she realizes that this is exactly how she feels about it.

BUT I OBSERVED YOU PAINTING IT.

"My hand, perhaps. But it is not my work." Paia has never within memory admitted to mystical beliefs, except where the God is concerned. It shocks her to hear herself saying this now. "It changes. It's different every time I look at it."

AS IS TRUE WITH ALL GREAT ART.

"Oh, House. This is not great art. I don't need your flattery. What I need is an explanation."

I AM SORRY, PAIA. I CANNOT OFFER ONE.

"Go back through your tapes. Find a record of the painting when I first finished it, and compare it with . . . this."

IF YOU WISH.

Soon the screen fills, line by line in an agonizingly slow scan build, with a murky gray-and-black image. Paia squints at it in dismay, then remembers that the internal security system had enhanced its monochrome with infrared data, but full spectrum imaging had been considered an unnecessary expense. But she recognizes the landscape anyway. Its clear skies and leafed-out trees are unmistakable.

"That's it! You see, I'm not imagining things!"

I DID NOT SUPPOSE YOU WERE.

The image clears, and the slow build of the current image begins. But midway, the screen flickers. Paia gets a single, flash impression of brilliant blue and green and golden light, and then is left staring as the monochrome scan resumes. "What was that?"

House sends a ticker tape across the bottom of the monitor: WHAT WAS WHAT?

It happens again. This time, the impression is milliseconds longer, enough for Paia to be utterly certain that she has seen a vibrant, full-color image—as clear and present as a photograph—of the landscape in the painting. "Where did you get that?"

GET WHAT?

"That last image! The color one! Bring it back!"

PAIA, YOU MUST BE MISTAKEN. A COLOR IMAGE IS BEYOND THE CAPABILITY OF THIS OUTDATED EQUIPMENT.

"But I saw it!" Then she tilts her head and smiles into another of the surveillance eyes. "This is a joke, right, House?"

I DON'T KNOW WHAT YOU ARE TALKING ABOUT. TRULY.

As if to prove itself, the green-golden image reappears, two, three, four full seconds, an eternity, long enough for Paia to watch the clouds shift softly and the grasses stir in the breeze. It's like gazing through an open window. Paia points. "There! That!" And then it's gone. She reaches out to it as if she could grasp its fleeting loveliness in her hands. The loss of it fills her with longing and despair. "Oh, House, what is that image?"

YOUR PAINTING AND . . . YOUR PAINTING, AS YOU REQUESTED. The computer is showing a sudden onset of uncharacteristic courtesy

"Not those images, the one in between! Please don't do this to me!"

ARE YOU . . . FEVERISH, PAIA? ARE YOU FEELING UNWELL?

At last she understands. The House Comp is not sending her the image she sees. Either that, or he is lying, and that she knows to be impossible. But it's equally impossible to believe that he could be wrong. Unless . . . Paia recalls how preoccupied House has been lately with the deterioration of his equipment. Perhaps . . .

The screen flashes again. But this image is not her landscape. It's a bright blue screen cut across by bold white letters: WHAT PRICE SURVIVAL?

Paia claps her hands to her mouth. She's afraid she'll scream out loud, and that will surely bring the red-clad Twelve racing up the stairs to her rescue. She stares at the words, waiting for them to vanish. They do not.

"House?"

The screen stares back unchanging, glowing white against sky blue.

"House? Are you there?" Paia waves into each of the little eyes at the four corners of the room. "House, come back!" She moves away from the easel in a long curve, and around the side of the room, as if to stay out of range of the monitor's insistent blue glare. She eases up beside it and taps the dusty box, jiggles its connections. "House?"

No response.

Paia fights off a creeping panic. There is no "off" switch anywhere to be found. She snatches at the folded canvas and drags it roughly over the screen, springing backward as if the entire assemblage might leap at her throat in revenge for being silenced. She stares at the shrouded bulk for a moment, then hurries back to the easel and covers the painting.

Then she stands stock-still, breathing hard in the stream of hot red light from the window, contemplating new strategies for evading the Twelve. She has to get to the Library. Quickly, and in absolute secrecy.

CHAPTER NINETEEN

Baron Köthen hurried Erde up the wide stone stairs to the first landing. He motioned her against the hard, flat wall, then stationed himself a few steps away, at the bottom of the gangway. The neat rows of rectangular stones were hot against her back. While Köthen watched the upper window into which N'Doch had disappeared, Erde thought of all the labor involved in carving each little stone so precisely and placing them all just so. The lord who'd ordered all this built must have had many estates to call upon for labor, and been very powerful indeed.

She was conveying this insight to the dragon when Lady Water interrupted.

He's made contact!

Erde reached without thinking and laid a hand on Köthen's arm. His muscles tensed beneath the thin hard surface of his mail as he turned to glare at her.

Two young girls, he says.

She beckoned Köthen to bend an ear so that she could whisper the dragons' news to him. She mimed the bow and arrow. His stance shifted immediately. His dagger was drawn, and he was already heading up the gangway.

"Stay here," he mouthed.

Erde shook her head. When he frowned, she murmured, "How will you know what the dragons see?"

His scowl deepened. He tossed his head irritably, then signaled her to draw her own blade. She followed a pace behind him up the swaying gangway. His speed and silence made her feel clumsy and slow. She caught up by the entrance window just in time to grab at his tunic and keep him from going inside. "My lord! They say he's taken!"

Köthen's eyes slitted. He did not ask for the dragons to be summoned. He glanced away at the rows of dark windows facing them across the open street. "How many?" his hands asked.

Erde raised one finger. "A man."

She bent and drew the layout of the rooms as Lady Water saw it, in the dust on the gangway, marking the separate positions of the enemy. Köthen studied the diagram, then flicked her a grudging glance and nodded.

"Now you *will* stay here," he insisted silently. "Sentinel."

She thought it fit this time not to argue. Köthen slid around the frame of the window so quickly that he barely broke the opening's angular profile, so bright against the inner darkness. Erde crouched against the hot wall and prepared to slip in after him.

The man's got the drop on him, all right. And he's got the advantage of position. He's silhouetted in the doorway, against the faint light spreading in from the front room. He doesn't look real big, but he's got on a lot of loose clothing that conceals his shape. His head is shaved or bald—N'Doch can see the light reflecting off the dude's temples—but his face is in total darkness. The only useful detail N'Doch can make out is what looks like a big old fire ax in his hands. This is marginally better than the assault rifle or the Walther P350 that N'Doch has expected, but it can still do plenty of damage.

He spreads his hands a little wider. He smiles and hopes the man can see it. "Got no problem wichu, man."

"Mebbe no, mebbe yes." The man shifts onto one hip, his right, as if the other pains him, and looks N'Doch over. N'Doch feels ridiculously caught short. "Wheryu frum, den?"

N'Doch jerks his head in what he hopes is vaguely the right direction. "Up nort'."

"Ohya? Deadman Crew, aryu?"

N'Doch grins. "Hope not."

The man grunts. N'Doch thinks he may have got the joke. "Who, den?"

He can already tell they're talking turf here, and him without a clue who owns what. But he's finessed his way through worse in his time. "Way nort'," he amends. "Water Dragon Crew."

The man shifts back to a two-legged stance. "Sayu?"

N'Doch nods. "I do." He suspects from the guy's alert response that he's said something meaningful without being aware of it. But now he can relax a bit, for he's noted the brief dimming of the light from the other room, like a shadow passing, and he knows from the dragon that Köthen is in the building. His job now is to keep this guy talking and distracted. Problem is, what can he say that won't just expose his total ignorance?

"So, you really lay toll?"

"Betcha. Notchu?"

"Nah."

The man considers this. "Nuttin' ta get, up nort', ha?"

N'Doch hears the implication. He doesn't want to be seen as a rich prospect. He drops his head and nods diffidently. "Yah. Nuttin' much at all."

The man shifts his weight again to the right, and seems to be listening. N'Doch fears he's heard Köthen moving through the outer room. Using the unslinging of his pack as a noisemaker and an excuse, N'Doch backs up along the gangway to draw the man into the room. It works. The man's interest focuses on the bulging pack. He moves into the doorway. "You come fer trade, den? News?"

"Betcha," N'Doch mimics.

The man leans against the doorframe to relieve his hip, and an arm snakes out and slams him hard against it from behind. He lets out a pained yelp. N'Doch leaps back just as an arrow thuds into the gangway at his feet. He snatches the ax from the man's flailing hands and dives through the doorway to fetch up against the opposite wall, hearing the chunk of a second arrow as it buries itself in the doorjamb right beside his fleeing ear.

"Hold on, wilyu?" he yells. "Gonna kill sumbuddy!"

"Gonna kill yu, tallman!"

"Whafor, girliegirl? Ain't don' nothin' t'yu!"

"Yur hurtin' da man! Lettim go!"

"No way, til yu say truce." N'Doch's trying to look in two directions at once. Köthen drags the little man into human shield position, with his blade tight to the dude's throat, like he might do him in right then and there. N'Doch worries he might. The poor sucker hardly dares breathe and doesn't struggle, a wise rabbit in the jaws of a fox, like this encounter blew up into a lot more than he'd bargained for. Even in the dim light, Köthen's weathered face is pale beside him. N'Doch thinks this guy's skin might be almost as dark as his own.

"Ease up, Baron K.," he suggests, in the dragon's German. "I think we got the upper hand here. No thanks to me, of course." For the life of him, he can't recall why he thought it was a bad idea to bring this good soldier along.

Köthen lets the apology go by. "Tell him to call the girls down."

N'Doch does, in his best future-speak. He turns a little, hoping to let the faint light catch sincerity in his eyes. "Ain't gonna hurt nobuddy."

The man sighs. "Senda! Mari! Face heah!"

A chorus of raucous negatives bursts from the darkest corner. N'Doch and the little man suppress inappropriate grins. Köthen tightens his grip.

"Now!" gasps the man.

The girls climb down slowly but not because they're clumsy. They are, with big crossbow, strapped-on water bottles and all, as slim and agile as monkeys. But they are also reluctant and disapproving. N'Doch yanks the two arrows free and moves forward to tower over the pair on the gangway. They are maybe nine years old. Girl-babies, he'd call 'em. The bones of their faces seem to fall into patterns he recognizes. He wants to get all these people out into the light where he can really look at them.

He points at the taller one. "Whichu?"

She plants one end of the crossbow on the planking and glares up at him with her mouth pulled tight as a rosebud.

"Dis'un, Mari," rasps the man over the impatient edge of Köthen's dagger. "Senda, da udda."

N'Doch already feels bad about Köthen's roughness. He leans on the ax handle, crouches in front of the girls, and thumbs his chest. "N'Doch."

Mari shakes her braided head. "Tallman."

N'Doch shrugs. "Okay, girliegirl. Have it yer way. Yu gotcha som'other blade ta pull on me?" Meanwhile, he's looking them over with his dragon vision. Not much on them to conceal a weapon of any sort. Their clothing is scanty, and he could probably count every rib and finger bone. But he lets them see he won't lay a hand on them even to frisk them. "Truce fer now?"

Senda, the little one, nods. Mari screws her mouth up even tighter and steadies her glare. N'Doch gives her the thumbs-up sign, knowing approval's the last thing she'll be expecting. Then he stands, hands her the recovered arrows, and deliberately turns his back on her.

Köthen eases his grip, just enough so his prisoner can stand on his own. With his head still held back from the glimmering blade, the man shifts his weight off his bad hip, and groans softly with the relief.

N'Doch says carefully, "Y'know . . . this ain't no war party, Baron K. The man's clearly hurting. What say you let him go?"

Does he see a glint of disdain in the baron's eyes, or is it puzzlement? But Köthen lowers his knife and steps back, as if removing himself from the argument. The man sags against the doorframe, breathing hard. Behind him, just as the dragons announce her, the girl's head swims up out of the darkness.

The man senses her and turns. "Yu got more ou' deah?"

N'Doch smiles, thinking of the dragons. "Mebbe." He lets this sink in, then adds, "But ain't none o' us lookin' fer troubba."

"Not heah, neitha."

"So, good. So, whachu say, den? Let's get easy some-weah, and talk."

The man nods. There's not even much resentment in him, not like the girls, for all his being tossed around a little. This guy's got some mileage on him. He shoves off from the doorframe and moves past N'Doch on the gang-way, heading into darkness and driving the kids in front of him with gentle cuffs to their heads. His limp is worse than N'Doch has expected, and he doesn't try to hide it. Proba-bly he can move faster in his rhythmic rolling gait than if he tried to walk straight. N'Doch follows him. Köthen and the girl fall in behind.

Cripple or no, he leads them across the lightless room with a blind man's confidence. N'Doch's own hands stray to the guide rails. He sees the railings as a clue to the joint's real purpose. It's not a death trap like he feared. It's an oversized tollbooth, and you can't run a good operation if you're killing off your customers. He knows some drug dealers oughta learn that lesson.

They pass through one more dark room, then the night thins. N'Doch can see the man's outline as he hauls back on a thick drape. Red light streams in through an outside opening, another window made doorlike with the liberal use of a sledgehammer. The girl-babies scamper into the light while the man stands back to hold the drape aside for the others.

N'Doch becomes aware again of the sounds of water. Squinting, he ducks through the opening onto a brief step and a shorter, steeper gangway leading down to a floating dock. The back of the building looks onto a kind of deep-water courtyard, a harbor with tall brick walls. The dock is another jerry-built assemblage of old doors and floorboards bobbing on aging plastic canisters and rusted oil drums. N'Doch is amazed they're still afloat. Some of them look as old as he is.

There are a couple of little boats tied up alongside, tarred and patched six ways from Sunday, and a larger raft-thing up on pontoons like the dock. The raft has a stubby mast in the center and some shreds of a sail. There's not a lick of paint on any surface N'Doch sees. Just keeping these tubs above water probably takes all these folks have got.

Mari and Senda take up stations beside the two small boats. N'Doch detects a personal involvement there. He eases down the gangway and onto the float. It's good to feel the sea beneath him again. *All this started for me,* he muses, *because of the water.* The air is thick and steamy, but the buildings across the courtyard harbor throw a welcome shadow across the dock. He finds a faded plastic crate and tests it with his foot to see if it'll still hold weight. He sets the ax down, drops his pack beside it, and sits.

The girl comes into the light next, then the man, then Köthen, who has insisted on mounting a rear guard. The girl's a bit unsteady on the gangway as it stirs to the roll of the water. She makes it down to the float, then just stands there. A weird moment of suspension settles in, as they all get a first real look at one another. Each, N'Doch decides, is a surprise to each.

The man and the little girls are dark, as he's guessed. But they're all a different color, and none of them as ebony-dark as he is. Their faces are as mixed-blood as their skin tones. The man's skin is almost red-brown, and he is absolutely hairless. The girl Mari has Asian eyes and straight black hair intricately braided to frame her full nose and mouth. N'Doch predicts she'll be a heartbreaker when she's grown, 'specially since she's such a little spitfire. All of them are small. Walking behind the bald man, he's seen how the gleam on the top of his head comes barely to the level of his own heart. And the girls are petite. Their clothes are a grab bag of cheap faded sportswear, bits of heavier duty stuff like the man's scuffed work boots and his stained safety-orange vest, plus a lot of handmade bits, or pieces worked over so many times that their origins are unrecognizable. The plastic water bottles they all carry are scarred and scorched where heat has been used to mend them. N'Doch sees nothing on these folks that looks like recent manufacture.

Meanwhile, the three of them are doing some serious study of their own. They eye the girl's paleness, but her hair is dark like theirs, and N'Doch is darker and taller than them, but otherwise no big deal. It's Köthen who snares the stares, perched like he is in lordly manner at the top of the gangway, his thick blond hair ruffling in the drafts up from the water and his mailed sleeves glinting in the late sun. The girl-babies are openmouthed. N'Doch can't tell if they think he's the absolute finest thing they've ever seen, or the butt-ugliest. Given their own complex mix, maybe they've never seen a real white man before.

Finally, the bald man breaks the spell. He kicks a crate a little closer to N'Doch and lowers himself onto it. He reaches a hand across the gap between them. "Reuben Stokes. Call me Stoksie. Blind Rachel Crew."

N'Doch takes the hand. The man's grip is firm but brief. N'Doch is relieved there's no complicated shake ritual he's supposed to know. "N'Doch. Water Dragon Crew." No point in dumping the fiction now. Besides, it's not like he's lying to the guy. He nods toward the girl, who he notices has not been offered a seat. "This 'ere's Lady Erde."

The man Stoksie struggles up halfway to reach and offer the girl his hand. So he's got no problem sitting down with women, N'Doch notes. He just don't see a need to give up his chair for one. And the girl, it turns out, has been keeping track. She gives the man's hand a proper shake, then looks around for her own crate.

N'Doch sends her an approving nod. "Pull up a seat."

This leaves Köthen, who is watching the parley assemble down on the float like he has no part in it. N'Doch finds this irks him just a bit. If the good baron wants to think of himself as more than the muscle, he'd better act like it.

"Hey, Baron!" he yells, with what he hopes is a really irritating grin. "How do I introduce you to these folks? Can't ever remember all your names!" His voice echoes among the red brick walls. Out of the corner of his eye, he sees the girl shaking her head in mute dismay.

Köthen breaks off a methodical survey of those surrounding walls. He stares down at them for a moment, and N'Doch again envies the man's total feel for the Commanding Entrance. He's waited until he has every ounce and scrap of their attention. But as he starts down the gangway, N'Doch understands something else. Köthen's slow grace on the bobbing walkway is also caution. The girl had staggered a little coming down. These are inlanders, N'Doch recalls. Landlubbers. Köthen doesn't want to make a fool of himself while he's getting his sea legs, but he isn't gonna give up the Entrance. His balance is superb, though, and he gets the rhythm of the dance right away, so that he's striding across the float with confidence by the time he presents himself to the man Stoksie with a small bow and a gesture to him not to rise from his seat. Nervous, N'Doch gets up, just in case. But Köthen offers Stoksie his hand. "Dolph Hoffman," he says.

N'Doch stares at him, speechless.

Stoksie nods, returns a tight little smile, and the two of them shake like a knife at the throat is all in a day's work.

Köthen feels N'Doch's stare. He shrugs, with his eyes still on Stoksie. "If Hal Engle can do this, so can I. I am not so great a fool as you think."

"My lord, I never . . ." N'Doch bites back the words so hard he nearly chokes. *Where the fuck did that come from?*

Now Köthen looks up at him. "Ah," he says, and tilts his head ever so slightly. Then he turns and walks away to the end of the dock to stare down into the water. N'Doch wants to race after him, quickly explain his awful lapse. But that would mean admitting to it in the first place.

No way.

He sees the girl watching him with sudden interest. Damn her. She doesn't miss a thing. He turns his attention back to Stoksie, struggling to imagine what he can possibly say next. Stoksie, the better trader, helps him out.

"Yu speak fer 'em, den?"

N'Doch nods. He guesses he does, for now at least.

"So whatsa news, out onna road?"

"Da road's hot and dry," N'Doch replies truthfully. He hauls over his pack and fishes around for his water jug. The jug gets Stoksie's immediate attention. N'Doch unstoppers and takes a swig, then much against his better judgment and for the sake of diplomacy, he offers the jug to Stoksie. Like, who knows what the man might be carrying? Except, he's just *small,* not sickly-looking.

Stoksie slides the jug past his nose for a quick sniff before he drinks. N'Doch can see he's trying not to look too cautious. He swallows without comment, then falls to studying the jug. He runs a dusty, tar-stained hand over the grainy stoneware curves and turns the rich blue glaze into the light. "Good work, dis. Hand stuff."

N'Doch nods.

"Trade it?"

A commodity. N'Doch appears to think about this.

"Givya gud value."

N'Doch counts. He's got three others. Meanwhile he's thanking the Deep Moor potters for this unintended favor. Good thing he didn't insist on dumping the ceramic for the plastic. "Whachu offerin'?"

"Da night air camp, ha? Food n' shelta?"

They must look worse off than he thought. Or maybe this is the standard offer around here. "All three, fer one?"

Stoksie nods.

"Done." Now that it's too late, he wonders if he's made

the deal too quickly. Still, seems like a fair enough deal to him.

They shake on it. N'Doch shows him how to soften the beeswax stopper in his hands, not too much trouble in this climate, and how to remold it around the jug's tapered neck. "You got good water at camp?"

"Da bes'! Blind Rachel watta!" Now Stoksie grins, and his teeth are such wrecks that N'Doch can barely look at him. "Yu frum way long way, ri'?"

"You got it, man. Way long." N'Doch passes the jug to the girl. "Take all you want this time." He looks over his shoulder at Köthen, standing so still by the edge of the dock, head bowed like he's contemplating jumping. "Hey, Dolph!" N'Doch hits the name and the German as hard as he can. "We need you back here."

Köthen lifts his head slowly as if being stirred from the deepest sleep. He sways to the roll of the float as he comes toward them and hunkers down, completing the circle of crates. N'Doch sees how the girl watches his every step, and he knows he shouldn't be doing it, too, but the man's body language rivets him. He posted bail once for a gang buddy who'd spent two weeks in solitary, a tiny windowless cage. Köthen just moved across that dock like that same buddy walked out of jail. N'Doch doesn't understand any of it.

He nudges Köthen's elbow with the water jug. Polite as always, the girl has left some. "Drink up. I just sold the bottle."

Obediently, Köthen drains the jug. N'Doch takes it back, ceremoniously shakes out the last drop and hands it to Stoksie. " 'S all yers. So wha's da schedule?"

Stoksie glances upward. The sun is invisible behind the tall brick walls, but the sky is still bright and the building tops are hot with late afternoon glare. "Resta bit. Den we start."

N'Doch likes a man who travels by night. He translates. "Sound good to you, Dolph?"

Köthen wets his lips. "Where are we going?"

N'Doch realizes this man of the killer stare hasn't met anyone's gaze since he rejoined them. "I bought us food, water, and shelter. In their camp."

"With a water jug? A good exchange."

N'Doch laughs. "Let's hope so."

Erde considered the tacit understandings of men, even between total strangers, and wondered if she would always be mystified by them. For instance, how could these three men who had been blade-wielding adversaries hardly a moment ago, now sit together in the shade, sharing nothing more than a companionable silence? At the very least, she would be asking every question she could think of. She'd already planned an information assault on the little girls, once they were done fidgeting with their tiny boats, unpacking and repacking the nameless objects stowed in every conceivable cranny.

The dragon had no insight to provide her on this issue. Though he was certainly male, the ways of men were as mysterious to him as they were to Erde. But Lady Water, like N'Doch, was always ready with an opinion.

It's the magic of commerce, girl!

Erde supposed this meant that because the man Stoksie had given up so easily and had so quickly fallen to bartering like a common tradesman, he was no warrior or person of real authority, and was therefore not to be feared. Yet Baron Köthen had been willing to shake his hand and sit down with him as an equal. This was very confusing. After her return to Deep Moor, Erde had realized that during her stay in N'Doch's time, she had merely set aside the assumptions and habits of her own world, like a garment she fully intended to resume wearing without alteration as soon as her stay was ended. But what if the garment no longer fit as well as it once had? Erde had not reckoned on this possibility.

And what of Baron Köthen, who had offered to a total stranger—one without title or noticeable breeding—his most intimate Christian name? Erde sensed turmoil beneath his collected surface. No, if she was truly honest, she didn't sense it at all. She assumed it. Why else would he be so alert to his surroundings and to signs of danger, and yet so profoundly self-absorbed? He must be in turmoil.

But when the rest was called, he stretched out flat on his back with his hands grasped behind his head like a boy on a summer riverbank. His stern square jaw was oddly relaxed as he gazed up at the yellowing sky. Erde thought she detected even the faintest ghost of a smile. Surely she had lost all understanding of what was going on in his mind. To make sense of it, she was forced to be strict with herself and ask how true her assumptions about him had been in the first place. She could set them up in a gleaming row, like the marble statues in the niches of Tor Alte's chapel, all labeled Adolphus, Baron Köthen. First, the Golden Lord, standing tall and proud. Next down, the Man Who Would Be King, his bright charisma emanating like an aura. Then, further on, in bands of candlelight and shadow, the Hero in Adversity, and finally, the Warrior Chained. She'd had a dream or two, and thought she knew him.

But there was no space in this pantheon, for instance, for the Drunken Lord or the Player of Silly Suicide Games, or even for this newest guise, the Pragmatic Democrat. Köthen in the flesh consistently eluded and defied her expectations. She said this to the dragon after she had imaged for him the empty street out in front. He transported in the middle of a thought, and his reply astonished her.

QUITE POSSIBLY HE'S DEFIED HIS OWN EXPECTATIONS AS WELL.

EXCUSE ME? Erde wondered if she had the dragon's attention. Already he was studying the neat red stones of the building façade.

WATCH WITH A CLEARER EYE. NOTE HIS OWN SURPRISE, HOWEVER HE TRIES TO CONCEAL IT.

Which he will. Just like a man . . .

As usual, Lady Water chose the more cynical road. Nonetheless, though, with a precipitous sense of loss, Erde admitted to the need to lay her old set of assumptions aside. They were attractive, but obsolete. They no longer served to explain the baron's behavior, probably because they were almost entirely of her own invention. If she was ever to truly understand him, it was time to make room for the person she really didn't know: Dolph Hoffman, the just-plain man.

CHAPTER TWENTY

Alone in her window seat, with her escort camped outside the door, Paia has an epiphany. She knows it's a dramatic word, but after considering it carefully, she decides that it is not overstated.

She is gazing down on the Temple grounds, at the familiar geometry of the shadowed Inner Court and the outer, sun-baked Temple Plaza, at the square granite block of the Altar of the Winged God, its rusty bloodstain visible even from this height. She is watching the Temple staff come and go, on missions she knows nothing of, past the approaching lines of the Faithful, each with its own particular geometry, observed from this very spot for so many years. She is watching and thinking of something else, as she usually does, except that this time her attention is caught.

Something is different.

She redirects a bit more of her concentration, away from her worries about the House Comp's sudden silence and how to get to him, away from the mystery of those white letters on a blue screen. She studies the antlike patterns below more carefully. They are changing, have already changed, like the painting in the tower, although the difference is much harder to define. Paia is sure of it, nonetheless, and she wonders what it means.

The God teaches that change is the enemy of stability. Should she, as she knows the God would, take steps to avert it? This would require understanding what the change is. Should she, as she is sure the God would advise, trust in him to protect her from it? As she has always done, since the day he came?

A picture forms in her mind: change personified as one

of those terrible endless hurricanes from her childhood that flattened everything in its path. The gales would wreck the windmills on the ridge above the Citadel, they'd be on emergency power for weeks, and entire coastal cities would wash away into the rising oceans. One of Paia's first memories is watching the destruction on the satellite news. She remembers her mother weeping about all the little bodies floating on the tide. She even recalls asking why those children's daddies weren't smart enough to take to the shelter of rock and high ground like her daddy did, and his daddy before him.

But then the hurricanes became windstorms, and then dust storms, and those became fewer but longer in duration, and as the heat settled in over the Citadel, its inhabitants retreated farther and farther into the mountainside. First her mother, then her father died, and young Paia stopped thinking about the ocean or the bodies or about anything at all except the struggle to keep herself and the Citadel alive.

Then the God arrived, and set everything back in order. Again, lives were lost, in the Wars of Conversion, but it seemed a small price to pay for the end of chaos. And the God advised his new converts not to think about the future, which is unpredictable, or the past, which is full of things you can do nothing about or ever have back again, like green hillsides, luxurious possessions . . . or parents. Survive the day, the God said. At the time, Paia knew exactly what he meant. Now she is no longer sure.

The rows of screens in the House Comp's lair had been that same blank blue as on the monitor upstairs, behind the white lettering. The blue of oceans.

What price survival?

Paia had always thought . . . had she been told this, or did she merely assume? . . . that when the hurricanes dried into dust storms, the oceans receded to their former levels. She understands now that this isn't true. Who would have told her such a thing? The God? It hardly matters. What she wants to know is how much of the world is still underwater? A quarter? A third? Half? Will it be more? Is this what's aroused the God's "ancient foes"? The need for higher ground, a new place of safety from an ever rising tide?

She's guessed at least one answer to the mysterious question: the price of her own survival has been ignorance.

How is it she can sit so still, when her mind is in such a frenzy? Paralyzed. As if all her capacity for motion has been given over to thought.

I know nothing. Nothing!

She could throw a huge tantrum about it, but she doesn't even know who to blame. No wonder the phrase "spoiled brat" rolled so easily off Son Luco's tongue. He's probably always thought that about her, even though he must be party to the agreement that keeps her in ignorance, in the name of preserving her innocence. The God's conspiracy, with Luco as his chief conspirator and who knows who else, all in on it, telling themselves it's for her own good. Only the House Comp has offered her knowledge, and she's been too stupid . . . or too naive . . . to take advantage of it.

Ignorance.

And what are they hiding? Something specific? Such as, why the southern hills were alight with fire last week, and again two nights ago? Or why there's been no melon on her breakfast tray for two weeks running? Why does she not know the faces of her priestesses? Why was the woman on the House Comp's screens weeping and shaking her fist at the sky? Who? What? Why?

Paia has asked questions before, but only idly, always allowing herself to be satisfied with evasion and the flattery of worship. But the Citadel is her father's legacy. It's time his only daughter took better charge of it.

In the courtyard below, a scuffle breaks out in the long line of the Faithful waiting in the hot and lethal sun for admission to the Sanctuary. Perhaps a third of them will be admitted, and the rest will continue their wait until tomorrow morning, or evening, or the next morning. When the scuffle clears, as it always does, there is a man laid flat on the paving stones, as there always is. There's no change down there. Paia understands that now. The change is in herself.

It's time to prepare for Evensong. The chambermaid will be knocking momentarily. Still Paia doesn't stir. Her arms and legs are lead.

What about the chambermaid, nameless to her mistress and mute since birth? Or so Paia is told, though now she has begun to doubt everything. Is the chambermaid also kept in ignorance? What about the Honor Guard outside her door? Or the Faithful, slamming each other's heads for a place in line? How far does this conspiracy of ignorance extend?

She pictures white letters on a blue screen. White as clouds, blue as oceans. Blue as the sky above velvet-green grass, in a landscape already passed into memory but for a black-and-white muddle in the House Comp's surveillance files.

And who is it who has finally had enough of all this ignorance?

Paia assumed they were the enemy because they asked a heretical question. But perhaps they mean to be her friends.

Her leaden fingers curl into fists. Her lips tighten. Small motions, great resolve. She will be her own conspiracy. First, she will get back to the House Comp. She'll sneak away in the middle of the night. She'll bribe the Honor Guard with her father's oldest brandy! Whatever she has to do, she will.

Next, she must get out of the Citadel. Must! Brave the sun and open air, the bandits and the assassins! She'll tell Son Loco that the High Priestess wishes to make a formal visitation to the villages of the Faithful. She'll bend every ounce of her authority and persuasion on him until he agrees. She's done with being an idle ornament for the God's altar. Only in full understanding of the world can she serve the Temple as the God deserves.

And she'll choose a Suitor, as the God has decreed, but his knowledge will be more attractive to her than his appearance. He'll be someone she can pry information out of while he's weak from the pleasures of her bed.

And somehow, she will convince the God to tell her about these awful, ancient enemies that threaten his peace of mind. For instinct warns her that they are the key to all of this.

Wrapped in stillness, Paia plans.

PART THREE

The Call to the Quest

Chapter Twenty-one

The chambermaid has come and gone. The High Priest-ess is on her way to Evensong, escorted by six of her Honor Guard. She has made sure to be gracious to them. She has even smiled at the duty captain, even though the watch will have changed at least twice before her planned darktime foray.

Paia strides ahead of them along the dim corridor. The carpet, once so soft and thick beneath her feet, is worn thin in the center from all this military traffic. It was meant for comfort, not to withstand soldiers' boots. Even her sandals make a scratchy sound against it now. Paia tries to look as if she cannot wait to enter the Temple once more, as if she is so eager to be leading her flock in holy worship of the God. Meanwhile, she is wondering where he is. She cannot feel him anywhere in the Citadel. She hasn't seen him for several days. There is a measure of relief in this, but also the ache of loss. She misses him. He used to visit her more often.

She is gliding down the steps between the second and third levels. She is thinking about the God, but her brain registers a delayed response to the deactivated house moni-tor screen at the top of the staircase. Has she really seen words there, or is she now imagining cryptic messages ev-erywhere she looks?

She cannot glance back. If there is something there, a look will bring it to the attention of the Honor Guard who, from the steady clatter of their downward progress behind her, appear to have noticed nothing. But there is another wall monitor at the bottom of the stair.

Paia slows a little, pretending to adjust the glittering folds

of her red-and-gold Evensong robe. As she moves past the
monitor, she gives it a fleeting but thorough study. A small
tickertape is scrolling silently across the bottom of an otherwise dead gray screen.

ATTENTION: A GENERAL SECURITY ALERT WILL SOUND IN
110 SECONDS.

Paia bravely hides her first response, which is terror like
a jolt to the heart. Security alert? The God's enemies must
be attacking! Then she gets hold of herself and remembers
that the House Security System has been turned off for
years. Or so she'd thought, until the House Comp implied otherwise.

By the time she reaches the next wall monitor, the little
scroller says 75 seconds, which means it's an active message. Paia keeps moving. It could be some sort of auto-
nomic malfunction, or it could just be that House is up to
something. When she thinks about it, she has her answer.
Genuine security alerts do not conveniently announce
themselves in advance.

Paia slows even more, as if taking on an appropriate
degree of gravity as she approaches the Temple sector. She
doesn't want to arrive there before the 75 seconds elapse
and get caught in all the confusion . . . or perhaps she
does. She picks up speed again. The Honor Guard must be
wondering about her erratic pace, but if House has seen fit
to provide her with a diversion, Paia wants to make the
most of it. She will be very disappointed if this turns out
to be a total false alarm.

The First Daughters await her at the bottom of the final
flight of stairs, two rows of six lined up on either side of
the corridor, heads bowed at precisely the same angle. They
are ready to fall right in behind as the High Priestess passes
through their ranks. They must rehearse this, Paia observes
sourly. Probably daily. She does not wait for them. Let
them worry about catching up. She's counting seconds. She
reckons she has fifteen left, and the side doors to the Sanctuary, leading directly to the dais, are at least ten of them
away. But she must not run. She cannot seem to be at all
concerned about anything.

Paia lengthens her graceful strides. The Twelve scurry
after her. A cluster of Third Sons blocks the entrance,

straightening each other's robes. Too many of them spring for the doors at once when they spot the High Priestess advancing on them. Seconds are lost while they sort themselves out and get to the tall double doors. The none-too-finely carved wooden panels were a gift from some pious village Paia has never been told the name of. As she is making a defiant resolution to find it out, the doors are hauled open. And then the alarm sounds.

The shrill braying of the electronic klaxons is an alien and horrifying noise to the Temple's clergy, as well as to its congregation. The shrieks of the Twelve behind her blend with the moans and wails of the Faithful inside as Paia bounds through the doors and across the dais, dodging two Second Sons frozen in mute terror with burning tapers in their outstretched hands. She slips behind the altar screen into the shadowed niche of the High Altar, where the Flame of the Apocalypse burns in its polished golden bowl—the Unfueled Flame that never gutters or goes out. Reflexively, Paia lays two fingers to her lips and then to the rim of the bowl. The din of the alarm is appalling. She recalls several general alerts during her childhood, and she's sure the klaxons were never this loud. Clever House has maxed the volume from awful to deafening. But how, she worries, will the computer explain all this chaos when the God hears of it, as he doubtless will from Son Luco, and comes calling to the Library in a rage for a reckoning?

Deal with that later, she decides, like House obviously has. By the time the alarm cuts off, dropping into the Citadel a silence almost as deafening as the horns, Paia is through the little maintenance hatch behind the High Altar and racing down the deserted back corridors toward her secret stairway.

"House!" she cries, as she bursts through the antique stone portal that guards the computer's darkened lair. "That was brilliant!"

"A desperate act," replies the House Comp in her father's most grave tones, without his usual greeting or preamble. "I had to warn you somehow."

"Warn me?"

"I am being tampered with."

"Tampered? How?" It's as chill in the room as it always is, but Paia is still warm from her breathless race. "Is that why I lost you up in the tower?"

"I had only just discovered that dusty miracle of obsolescence, then suddenly, I no longer had access to it."

"Has someone been in here messing with you?"

"No human but you has access to this facility."

"Well, it isn't the God. He wouldn't know the first thing about it. Someone outside?"

"No one anywhere should be able to do this."

Now Paia feels the chill. Her father always boasted that the computer's security systems were invulnerable to tampering. "Can you tell where it's coming from?"

"It appears to be more than one source. One is almost certainly external. The signal is scrambled and very cleverly cloaked. For the other, there are no visible defenses. I have been unable to trace either of them or pinpoint their locations."

Paia settles into the leather swivel chair and flattens her palms on the black console, as if to impart some degree of calm, if not to the computer, at least to herself. "I think I might have a clue, House." She lowers her voice. If the computer is accessible to others, who knows who might be listening? In her quietest whisper, Paia tells him about the note left on the painting. "Perhaps I should have given you the whole story when I mentioned this before . . ."

The dark room is silent for a long moment. A few tiny red lights stare back at her unblinking from within the inky plastic. Then House says, "I am extremely . . . relieved."

"Relieved?" She has never heard the computer describe his emotional state before, or express any sort of hesitation.

"I spoke of two sources."

"Yes?"

"For two months now, I have been . . . seeing things."

"What?" Paia almost shouts: *me too!*

"I use a human metaphor, of course. I have been subject to . . . certain transient and random signals. They arrive in incredibly fast streams and are gone before I can store them. Images, I believe. I can neither decipher them nor locate their source, so that they appear to come out of nowhere. They do not even register as proper data in my circuits. I am aware that something has . . . come in, but can find no record of the transaction. This is most . . . bizarre."

The computer pauses, as a human might, to catch a breath or regain lost composure. "When no explanation presented itself, I became concerned that . . . that perhaps there was no external source. That it was a sign of some final malfunction . . . that I was breaking down, or that I was . . . imagining things. I do that sometimes, you know, but rarely so . . . vividly. When you first asked me about that phrase, I was . . . afraid to ask where you'd seen it. I worried that it had leaked onto one of my screens without my control or knowledge. But a real physical object, a note written by human hands . . . that puts things back into perspective again."

"Yes. It does. I guess." Paia strokes the console's unbroken surface, as darkly reflective as the Sacred Well at midnight. What sort of consolation does one offer a computer? How terrible to be a mind trapped in a box buried at the bottom of a mountain. She wants to ask House what else he imagines, but she knows that will have to wait.

"So you see why I called it a desperate act. They're all in an uproar down there right now, and no doubt this will send HIM and his cohorts on another of his circuit-frying, chip-melting rampages. I have so few working peripherals as it is. But I had to know . . ."

"I expect it's me he will punish, House."

Some real fear must have shown in her voice, or perhaps the computer's delicate sensors are reading telltale hints in her vital signs. In the tone he reserves for statements of absolute fact, he says, "You need not fear him, Paia."

"Oh, House, thanks for the comfort, but how could I not?"

"I said you *need* not. If you choose to, there is no help for it, but I tell you, he cannot harm you."

"Of course he can! You've obviously never seen . . ."

The big monitor bank fills with a sun-bright image of the Temple Plaza, smeared with the smoldering ash of the kamikaze zealot who'd played at would-be assassin not so many days ago. Paia shields her eyes from the glare.

"I see everything," says House quietly. "He is a monster. But to you, he cannot do injury."

"I don't . . . what are you getting at?"

"It is prohibited in what you might call his genetic makeup."

Does a God have genes? "How do you know this?"

There is another silence, an even longer one. And then: "This is only a small bit of data in a very large archive I have on the subject."

"You take data on the God?"

"I store data about the *dragon*."

Hearing the word spoken aloud makes Paia glance anxiously over her shoulder at the doorway. "Shhh!" she gasps, like the child the word makes her feel.

"Dragon," the computer repeats, and the word becomes the closest thing to a hiss she's ever heard out of him. "That's what he is, after all."

"Look, House, it won't do to have both of us in revolt at the same time!"

"Are you in revolt, Paia?"

"Forget I said that. Why wasn't I told about this archive during that search I made after the God first arrived?"

"I was not aware of it myself at the time."

"When did you become aware of it?" Paia would swear the computer was being evasive.

"During the last two months."

"Oh. You mean it came in with the mysterious messages?"

"No. Only my awareness of it."

"Hunh. Well, can I look at it?"

"It is probably time that you did."

Paia worries her upper lip between her teeth. "There's something you're not telling me, isn't there, House?"

"Do you recall how to read a book, Paia?"

"A book? I guess that can't be too hard. Why?"

"The archive I speak of is your father's library."

CHAPTER TWENTY-TWO

The water was not as deep as Erde had supposed from its thick and murky wash. When the man Stoksie had finally arranged them—and especially their packs—to his liking on the narrow raft, he sent it away from the landing and across the flooded courtyard by means of a long stout pole shoved against the invisible bottom. The two brown girls paddled along behind, each in her own little boat. Erde envied them. How many times she had watched longingly from Tor Alte's walls while the prentice boys played at naval warfare in the village duck pond. She'd had to run away from home to get anywhere near a boat. This absurdity almost produced a giggle, but she held it back, not wanting to appear frivolous at such a serious moment.

N'Doch watched Stoksie labor for about three strokes, then took up a second pole from the deck and signaled his readiness to help. The raft began to glide along at an impressive speed. Erde thought of the dragon back in the street, but did not send him an immediate image. Her proximity to all this moving water would only upset him, although she'd noticed that his terror of it had abated somewhat since his sister had joined them.

The passages between the buildings were narrow and dark, with the tall red walls sometimes rising up inches from the sides of the raft. Often N'Doch was forced to set his pole aside and ease the raft along the green-slimed walls with his hands. They followed many sharp turnings, some of which looked like dead ends until the very last minute, in a mazelike progression from courtyard to courtyard, and everywhere the same tall red walls and shadowed, broken-out windows. I would get lost, Erde observed, then understood that this was exactly the point of it. She spotted other gangways, cobbled together out of whatever had been to hand, making bridges between two buildings or an exterior access around the perimeter of a hidden courtyard. But she saw no other floating docks like the one they had just left. Once, they slid under a particularly elaborate bridge construction, and N'Doch gave it a complimentary wave.

"Yer crew, dat?"

Stoksie nodded. "All dat." His gesture was a high inclusive circling, and Erde took it to mean the entire city. Baron Köthen sat up ahead of her with his back to the big post in the middle of the raft, so that he faced Stoksie, as well as the girls paddling behind. He was so quiet and still, it made her nervous. Once, he asked her to translate some remark of Stoksie's. When she'd checked with the dragons and passed it along, he looked away, up at the shadowed walls sliding slickly past, touched along the tops with the bright orange of the late sun.

"It's like some sort of fever dream, isn't it?" His eyes flicked toward her dolefully. "Not, of course, a dream such as you are accustomed to, my lady witch, though as I appear to be in it with you, perhaps I am mistaken about that as well. Still, it seems more like a vision—such as one is forced to move through without choice or control."

"My dreams were always like that," she reminded him sternly. "But this is not a dream, my lord. It is real, I can assure you."

Köthen laughed, soft and dry as a whisper. "To you perhaps it is."

And then they were distracted. The raft slipped out of the shade of a narrow alley into angled red sun glinting off a big rectangle of open water, like a flooded market square. Stoksie leaned into his pole and the raft lurched forward. N'Doch let out a happy yell and bent to his own pole. Soon they were coursing down the length of the square in full orange daylight at the speed of galloping horses. Erde grappled for handholds and clung to the deck as if she might be swept off by the breezes that riffled her hair. They shot out of the square into a long straight passage, approaching another sort of building, the hugely tall towers visible from the distance when they'd first entered the city. Close up, they were terrifying: taller than any cathedral spire Erde had ever seen, both gleaming and dark, and so narrow she could not imagine how they remained upright. Staring up at their soaring heights made her dizzy, and convinced her they were tumbling down on top of her. Several of them gaped open at the water level, with holes so vast that the entire raft could have floated right through and in among their charred and twisted beams.

Suddenly N'Doch gave another whoop and hauled his pole out of the water. "Too deep na, man!"

"Yah!" Stoksie replied. "Getchu heah, hold 'er steady, while I put up sail."

N'Doch trotted the length of the raft, as surefooted as if on dry land. Behind, the girls were padding madly to catch up. Stoksie slid his pole into a slot between two bits of wood projecting upward at the rear of the raft. The pole rested at an angle and drifted a bit, side to side. N'Doch took hold of it, pushed it back and forth experimentally, and Erde saw that the raft shifted direction according to the motions of the pole.

"Gotcha," said N'Doch. Stoksie went toward the front to shoo Baron Köthen away from the central post, which Erde now recognized as a sort of mast. After several complicated maneuvers and the untying of several knots, Stoksie straightened and shoved a thick rope into Köthen's hands.

"Haul it a gud' un, whitefella!" he cried. Then he whirled away to fumble with a mound of stained cloth beginning to stir in the wind as he released its bindings.

"He means pull on it hard!" N'Doch translated, with obvious glee.

Köthen flashed him a look as sharp as a needle, then took a firmer grip on the rope and pulled. A dented metal rod clanked upward at a precarious angle to the mast, drawing the sail up with it. The raft slewed clumsily as the hot wind leaned into the folds of the canvas and puffed it outward toward a smoother curve. Stoksie snatched the rope from Köthen's grasp, looped it around a raised bit of the decking, then fastened it with an abrupt flick of his arm. The girls grabbed at the end of the raft, one to either side of N'Doch, and sprang up out of their boats, dragging ropes to tie them with. The little boats bobbed along like dogs on a chain as the raft picked up speed.

"Hard off ta port, na!" Stoksie yelled. He clapped Köthen familiarly on the back as he scrambled toward the rear. Erde braced for another fight, but Köthen just stood there, fighting for balance against the craft's new momentum and observing the activity blurring around him with a bemused frown. When N'Doch shoved the pole to one side and the raft swung to obey, the patched and mildewed sail snapped into full billow. The girls sped forward, shoving Köthen aside to grapple with the ropes flapping from the bottom corners of the canvas. Köthen stared after them, then retreated to his safe seat at the base of the mast. Erde eyed him covertly. Had she misjudged his survival reflexes? Was all this newness and change going to prove too much for him?

"'S'alright, Dolph!" N'Doch called from the helm. "We'll make a sailor outa you yet!" He grinned hugely and turned his face into the wind. Erde could not recall him ever looking so delighted, except when he was making his music.

The raft handles a lot better than N'Doch expects it to. Must be one helluva rudder attached to this mumbo jumbo tiller, he decides. And though he's sure that the beat-up sad wreck of a sail will split its many seams as the steep downdraft between the high-rises swells it out like a nine-months' pregnant woman, it doesn't. The crude stitching holds, and the raft responds to his touch.

"Which way, na?" he yells to Stoksie.

The older man crabs backward to join him in the stern. He points out a course between the plundered office buildings. The girl-babies take turns manning the sail sheets and refilling their water bottles from a big plastic barrel on the foredeck. N'Doch worries about the sanitary procedures, then figures if these folks are carrying all their own water, they must be taking steps. He's just gonna have to risk it and hope for the best, or go thirsty.

"Getting deep," he remarks, as the raft skates past the tip of some drowned church's bell tower.

"Yu gud deckman, tallfella."

N'Doch is pleased. "Grew up on da watta."

Stoksie looks at him. "So who din't?"

N'Doch guesses the man's age: maybe forty-five, fifty at the most. Has the water been high that long? He jerks his thumb forward. "Dem two."

"Yah? Mount'in-bred, den?"

"Betcha."

Now Stoksie's looking at him hard. "*Town*folk?"

"Nah. Castles, is more like." He wonders what the man's got against townfolk. Something, that's for sure.

"Yah? Where'sat?"

"Ever hear a Europe?"

Stoksie shrugs. "Sure, one time. All unda na, ri'?"

All under. All under what? All underwater? N'Doch swallows. How's he ever going to tell the girl? "Nah. Mount'ins still lef'. Like here," he guesses, with a glance toward the west where, between the shafts of dying skyscrapers, blue crenellations press upward like a woman's breasts against the red sky. The picture is coming in clearer now. It's just what the vid guys predicted. Half the world's underwater. Holy shit. "S' dey come heah, lookin' fer a fren'."

"Alla way frum Urop? Mus' be sumkinda gud fren', na."

N'Doch nods gravely. "Betcha."

"Sumun roun' heah?"

"Mebbe. Don' know fer shur. Din't find 'im yet." N'Doch sees the water opening out ahead, past the sun-struck edge of a steel office tower and through a gateway of rusted girders. "Dis town gotta name?"

Stoksie turns his blackened grin on him. 'Jokin', ri'?"

"Nope. Askin'."

"Dis here's Big Albin, tallfella. Da prida Nyork. How far yu say yu come?"

"Li' I tellyu, man. Way far."

Stoksie takes over the helm when they swing out into the open bay. N'Doch feels some mean crosswinds cutting across his nose, as dry as a gust off the Sahara but honed with salt. A current catches the raft and heads it downstream. But it seems Stoksie intends to tack upstream, so the going is slow for a while, back and forth in the unrelenting sun. But better than walking, N'Doch tells himself.

He goes forward for a long warm drink at the water barrel, then settles down next to the girl to unload what he's heard. He'll let her pass it on to his lordship and the dragons. He does ask her, though, how they're doing.

She eyes him impishly. "Lady Water says she's waiting for you to stop enjoying yourself and get on with business."

N'Doch coughs out a guilty laugh. "She didn't say that."

"No. But she might have."

"Ha, girl! You made a joke! I'm keeping my eye on you now!"

The bay is long. Eventually, N'Doch decides it must be a river. It's risen with the seas and flooded out the low-lying areas, so it just looks like a bay, with barren, rocky shores. The girl-babies chatter among themselves as Stoksie laboriously guides the raft upstream. They throw looks at Köthen as he leans back against the mast and appears to doze. He looks stunned and passive, but N'Doch doesn't believe it for a nanosecond, and he's pretty sure the girl-babies don't either. At least the man's had the sense this time not to insist on taking charge. Maybe 913's favorite hothead is learning how to go with the flow.

After a tough hour of fighting the current, Stoksie is looking slick and tuckered. N'Doch worries for the little man's heart. "Yu wan' sum help?"

Stoksie waves him off stubbornly, and then, as if his refusal has gained him strength, the raft glides along more readily, actually picking up speed. Stoksie rubs his bald head and flashes a big, gap-toothed grin. "See dat? I ain' dun fer yit!"

"Yu ain' even half dun!" The dude's been so easy to deal with so far, no sense making him feel bad. N'Doch winks sideways at the girl so she doesn't spill the beans. There's no sign from below, no odd ripples, no careless bumping against the underside, but he knows a certain water dragon is down there, helping things along. He pictures her, a blue shadow streamlined into porpoise sleekness. He smiles, leans back, and shuts his eyes.

A much easier hour later, when Stoksie heads the raft toward a little inlet on the western shore, N'Doch has actually been dozing. He stirs, refreshed, looks around. Things are a little greener up here, though not by much. The trees are stunted and dust-cloaked, but they have scrawny little crops of leaves, and the weeds scattering the tops of the steep clay banks show a few yellow flowers. N'Doch spots a line of broken foundations along the bank top, and an occasional bit of crumbling wall. Might have been a town once, but it's history now. His little nap has reawakened his curiosity.

"Wha's dat up deah?" he calls to Stoksie.

"Sumplace. I fergit whaddit wuz back den. Call it Plaguetown nah."

N'Doch looks alarmed.

"Na, dey's nuttin deah nah. Dem plagues is long gone." Then it's Stoksie's turn to look concerned. "Yu got plague still up nort'?"

"Na. None a dat."

"Gud. Cuz yu don' lookit. Look reel healt'y, alla yus. Firs' ting I notice."

Stoksie noses the raft expertly into the inlet, then strips his pole free of the rudder and plunges it into the water again. N'Doch leaps up to join him. It's too shallow here for invisible dragon assistance. The girl-babies race back to haul the rudder out of its casing. They toss it long and dripping on the deck, then grab their paddles out of the trailing boats to lend a hand at forward motion.

The inlet was probably once a creek emptying vigorously into the river. Now the water wanders sluggishly upstream. Jumbles of boulders, still marked by tar stain, line both sides of a steep and scrubby ravine. Soon the streambed sprouts rocks and becomes an obstacle course as the ground climbs around them. More ruins perch on the slopes past the rockfall, wooden structures sagging into shapelessness and char among the bleached skeletons of pine trees. Quaint houses along a picturesque mountain stream, N'Doch muses, recalling travel vids of Switzerland, or the American Rockies, where the cowboys come from. Then there's a cry of metal on stone, and Stoksie calls a halt. The raft's oil drum pontoons are scraping bottom. He poles toward a bankside stair made of ascending natural ledges, and lands the raft with a final shove and a twist of his pole. A faintly worn track winds up and away through the stiff scrub clinging to the slope.

As the raft stills, the heat descends again, thick with the smell of parched dirt. A swarm of midges stirs from the algal muck along the shore. N'Doch bats at them irritably, but is privately glad to see any sign of wildlife. Köthen shakes himself out of his putative doze. He stretches elaborately. N'Doch has to chuckle at the pair of them, both avidly scanning the landscape, both pretending so hard not to. The girl-babies scramble onto dry land and tie off the raft to a battered tree trunk. Stoksie ships his pole, so N'Doch does likewise. Not much of a destination, but he guesses they're here. He listens. Nothing but midge whine and their own boat noise, which make a huge racket in the total absence of other sound. It's been no different since they first arrived, but here, knowing he's on someone's turf, the silence makes him paranoid. He's glad now to have Köthen's eyes and ears as well as his own. A path up through rocks and woods? Prime ambush territory.

But he helps Stoksie lower the sail, then gives the girl a hand. He tosses Köthen her pack without even asking. He's amazed how he feels freed now, to treat the man like anyone else, like something's given him permission. Köthen himself, he suspects. The good baron is busy taking an ostentatious vacation, while he figures out who he's gonna be if he ain't gonna be the boss.

The girl-babies bounce back to the raft to haul their own little boats onto dry dock, swiftly relieving them of their cargo and lashing them away in the brush. Stoksie has his own major unpacking to do, lifting this and that invisible hatch in the deck to pull out wrapped bundles and tied-up satchels, until he has a huge pile waiting up on the shore.

"Yu wan' help dis time, man?" N'Doch wonders what the guy would have done if he hadn't picked up three extra passengers.

"Betcha," Stoksie breathes gratefully.

N'Doch nods, like it's the least he can do. He doesn't think it prudent to mention the big brownish boulder that's taken up residence a ways off to the left, while everyone's back was turned—even though he could save them all what looks to be a long hard climb. He shrugs, sighs, and hands the girl something easy to carry. She offers to sling another over her free shoulder. As he's adding a few to his own load, he sees Köthen hesitate, then mutter tersely to himself and grab up one, then two of the heaviest. The girl-babies help Stoksie take up the rest, like they were balancing a packhorse. Then they lead the way up the hot and crumbling ledges and into the scrub, away from the shore.

CHAPTER TWENTY-THREE

Paia enters the long security code that the computer made her memorize, having absolutely refused to print it out. The lock cycles, and the clear, thick facia sealing the shelf slides aside. Ancient odors drift outward on the spiraling drafts of the Library's cooling system: leather, ink, parchment, vellum. Words her father had always spoken with a collector's reverence. Because all knowledge came into her own life in digital form, Paia had seen her father's books as an old-fashioned eccentricity, a charming but useless repository of the obsolete. And she'd presumed that the texts, the actual writings, were of less interest to him than the physical objects, the *libri*.

Now her understanding is somewhat more complex.

Breathing in the scents of the past, Paia studies the spines. None of them offer the explanatory block-print titles she has hoped for. Many are chapped and crumbling, their drying flesh flaking away in ashy brown, tippled here and there with faded gilt. A few are mere stacks of thick and yellowing pages tied between two worm-eaten boards. But others, while seeming no more modern in their construction and design, have weathered the long centuries with abandon. Though mottled with use, their leather is still dark and supple, with a hint of sheen. Paia chooses one of these at random.

Well, not precisely at random, for her eye is drawn to this book as if it has called out to her, though it is otherwise an unremarkable specimen, neither big nor small nor fat nor slim, nor of a particularly interesting color. But it has a healthy, energetic look. *A living look,* Paia muses, then scolds herself for excessive flights of the imagination. She grasps it gently, eases it from the velvet-lined shelf, and balances it gingerly on both palms. It has no writing on the outside binding, just the subtle spots and stains of centuries. This book, she decides, has been well-treasured, but also well-used.

She carries it out of the careful gloom between the storage cases to a reading table. The pool of light washing the green fabric of the tabletop brightens as Paia places the book down on the soft felt. She has never handled her father's books before. She pulls up a cushioned chair and settles herself before the book as before an unfamiliar food she is not sure she will enjoy. She lifts the worn leather cover and lays it back against the green tabletop. The first page is a pale, speckled buff color, and is entirely blank. Paia turns it aside, surprised by the greasy thickness of it between her fingertips. The next page is elaborately bordered by flowers and vines, with fish and birds darting between them. In the center is a circular symbol, artfully drawn in bold black ink, divided by quarters into smaller individual symbols. Paia is surprised by the vibrancy of the ink. Surely after so many years the ink should have faded more. She shrugs and turns the page.

The text begins on the third page, with a title block and cursive lines of neat black script. Though Paia recognizes many of the letters, she cannot read the words. But the House Computer has prepared her for this eventuality as well. She pushes back her chair, so silently on the dark rich carpet, and pulls out a shallow drawer from under the table's edge. She sets the book face up and open in the drawer, and closes it gently. On the tabletop, a section of green felt slips smoothly aside, exposing a neat rectangle of screen, like a glass place mat directly in front of her. Through the transparent screen, Paia sees the book: lit with a cool glow, as well as a translation, superimposed, faintly luminous green letters suspended above the actual text. From somewhere past the pool of light, the computer's voice floats down like mist, as gentle as she has ever heard it.

"The Secret Mysteries of the Wyrm, author unknown. Text in Latin, Frankish, and Old German. A collection of folklore, copied probably around 700 AD, in what is now southeastern Germany. Its first documentation is in a hand-

written catalog, since destroyed but existing in facsimile, of the estate library of a Baron Weisstrasse, known chiefly for his remarkable collection of such books and for his very thorough record keeping.''

"Such books . . . ?"

"About myth and legend and what were then called 'the ancient arts': alchemy, magic, witchcraft, the like. But in particular, the Weisstrasse Catalog evidences a keen interest in the subject of dragons."

"Ah." Paia bends closer to examine the text and its translation.

Several hours later, she is still reading. Her back aches and her eyes smart from the unaccustomed close concentration. But her mind is entranced. She is in another world. A far-off time ruled by unseen forces, perilous and mysterious but open to manipulation in the hands of a skilled adept. Not ruled by science, as her world had been until the coming of the God, nor yet damaged by the excesses of technology. A time when people believed in dragons, and the very existence of the God, or any god at all, made a lot more sense.

Once Paia would have dismissed such tales as fantastical nonsense. But if the God exists now, which he undeniably does, could not all this have existed then? Or, looked at another way, if the God exists, could all this exist now? Is magic the reality and science the myth? What about dragons who come and go at will? Or sacred pools that remain deep and icy in the heart of the drought? Or paintings that morph on their own between viewings? Paia allows herself the excuse of having been just a child, but it astounds her to realize how quickly and willingly she and every other inhabitant of the Citadel put away rational inquiry the moment the Winged God appeared, wreathed in thunder and gouts of gehennical fire. As if magic was easier to believe in than science, which required thought and could be counted upon to turn on you when you least expected it. But so could magic, if the lore in this book is to be believed. So are they separate or the same?

Paia glances back at the words on the screen: *"A True Recipe for Raising Dragons."* The alchemists clearly thought they were the same. She puts her face in her palms and rubs her eyes. She is hopelessly confused, but elated just the same, as if she is on the brink of some sort of new understanding. The God, she recalls, rarely uses the term "science," but he certainly knows how to turn it to his advantage when he wants to.

"Paia." The computer's voice is so soft and directionless that, in her daze, Paia thinks she's hearing it from inside her own ears. Right now, nothing would surprise her. "Paia, the search is becoming desperate."

"The search? Oh . . . for me?"

"Perhaps you had better show yourself before they alert you-know-who."

"He's off on one of his trips."

"They'll call him back if they're frightened enough."

"Call him back? How?" She looks up into the darkness beyond the low-hung lamp. "They can't do that."

"Luco can. The dragon has made sure that he will always be kept informed."

"Luco?" The priest must be in better favor than she'd realized.

"But Luco needs a device. You do not."

After what she's been reading, Paia finds this statement as provocative as House no doubt intended. "I can't call him. How would I call him?"

"Have you ever tried?"

"Of course not." The idea of summoning the God like he was some sort of servant seems preposterous to her.

"Why not? He calls you."

"But he's the God." Paia goes back to rubbing her eyes. "Could you dim this light a bit, House? I'm done reading for now."

The light softened, but the computer would not accept the change of subject matter. "If he can call you, why shouldn't the connection between you work both ways?"

"He's never said . . ."

"Of course he hasn't. Such knowledge would give you real power over him."

"Well . . ." *The Power of Summoning. A True Recipe for Raising Dragons.* Paia rubs her eyes a little harder. Power over the God? Exactly what she's always wished for.

"Don't tell him we've had this conversation. Just try it . . . sometime soon. Now, you'd better go. The whole Citadel is in an uproar."

"If he were here, he'd know where I am."

"Yes."

"Would he know where Luco is?"

"Only if Luco is wearing his tracer, which he always does. Off with you now. And remember, question anything you see or hear on any of my systems outside this room. I am not entirely in control of them."

Paia stands wearily, retrieves the book from the reader drawer, and carries it back to the storage stacks. She re-shelves it carefully, sucking in one more dusty, odorous lungful of the past before she locks the case. She comes back to the edge of the light falling around the green-topped table. "House, it's as if you've decided to be my tutor again, after all these years."

"Hardly a decision. More like an instruction."

"Really? From whom?"

"I was not given that information. Time-delayed programming. Like my awareness of the archive itself."

"But why now, do you think?"

"There is little fact available to support an accurate conjecture. Are you asking my *opinion*?"

"Sure. Why not?" If she could talk to a hunk of silicon as if it were a living creature, why should the difference between science and magic trouble her even one little bit?

"Well, then . . . I think . . . that you weren't ready to listen before. Suddenly, for whatever reason, you are."

Paia purses her lips, absently stroking the soft felt, suddenly, unaccountably daydreaming of grass. Grass like she's seen only in old pictures: thick, moisture-rich, smelling . . . well, green . . . as she imagines magic might smell. Grass like in the painting upstairs. "Hunh," she says, and walks away from the light.

She lets herself out and stands by the tall paneled doors, listening. If a frantic search is underway, it hasn't yet reached this deep into the rock. She's enjoyed this respite from the mundane life of the Citadel, but it's also given her several days' worth of thinking to work her way through. She sighs and hurries down the dim corridor, trying to decide where she prefers to be found.

One level lower and several room blocks closer to the front, the halls are still unlit, but now she hears the muffled beat of booted feet and voices bellowing orders and information. She used to see it as a game. She created the occasional fuss like this when she was a rebel teen, intentionally losing herself just to break the tedium. Endless loud and threatening lectures from the God about the heavy weight of her priestly responsibilities (never mind what he said he would do to her if she didn't stop) had rendered her more docile as she moved into adulthood . . . at least, until recently. Perhaps those other games were her training for now, when she can give them a true sense of purpose.

Docile. The word sticks in her mind and slows her steps until it actually brings her to a halt. It's not a word she'd have thought to apply to herself, and yet . . . it is what she's been. Not the bright, beautiful, and tempestuous woman of her standard self-image, an image built entirely in the God's vocabulary. Those are *his* qualities, which she has been allowed to play at but not truly BE. Like Luco, she has been only a mirror for the God. She has been indulged in the things that don't matter in order to buy her compliance in the things that do. At least, the things that matter to the God.

Standing immobile in the darkened corridor, Paia resolves to reverse this pattern. And she's already decided what her first demand is going to be.

Voices and feet approach from the lighted sector. Paia moves resolutely forward to meet them and, rounding a corner, runs smack into Son Luco with a contingent of worried Third Sons trailing behind him.

Paia steps back and smiles. "Hello, Luco. I thought I'd come down and see if it's all over."

Luco is caught off guard. It takes him long uncertain seconds to plant his fists on his hips and square his broad shoulders. "Where have you been?"

"Up in back, of course." Perhaps the appearance of docility will be useful for a while longer.

"Of course?"

Paia lets her hands flutter. "When the alarm sounded, I

was so surprised, I just did what we always did when my father was alive: run for the safest spot in the Citadel!" She imitates his peremptory stance. "Really, Luco. Is this any way to greet your High Priestess?"

Luco's blue eyes narrow. He drops his arms to his sides, though his big hands remain fisted, and he bows to her from somewhere in the middle of his back. "Mother Paia. Forgive me. How miraculous to find you safe and well."

Behind him, the Third Sons are already on their knees murmuring thanks to the God. If any one of them had an ear for irony, their priestly training has burned it out of them.

Paia nods graciously. "Tell me, First Son, what was the emergency?"

"None that we could find, my priestess." Luco smooths his long hair back with restless fingers. "An equipment malfunction, I suppose. I had thought the general alarms disabled, but it appears that I was wrong."

"Ah. Nothing to fear, then. What a relief." Paia moves past him and between the kneeling priestlets. Sailing grandly down the corridor, she beckons airily behind her. "Son Luco, a word in private if you please."

Luco bounds after her to loom at her side, his perfectly sculpted mouth flattened with rage. "Now what are you up to?"

"Please, Luco . . . I'm sorry if I worried you. I really didn't think . . . I just ran. My father drummed it into us until it was practically an instinct."

"You'd be a lot safer if you ran toward me in an emergency instead of away!"

"Oh, Luco, I wasn't! I tell you, it was instinct."

The priest is silent for a moment, pacing along beside her, shortening his stride to match hers now instead of the usual other way around. Paia knows he's deciding whether or not to believe her. Since her attempts to talk truth to him have all been rebuffed, she doesn't mind that he suspects her of subterfuge. It's an improvement over being taken entirely at face value. She smiles at him sidelong, reverting to the playful, pleasure-loving Paia he seems most comfortable with. "Besides, it got your heart rate up, didn't it? Don't you feel invigorated?"

Before he can sputter a sufficiently indignant reply, she

lowers her voice and waves him closer. "Now, Luco: I have a proposition to put to you. I've been thinking it over, and I've decided that in these hard times when the Faithful are so despondent . . ."

"Who says they're despondent?"

"They're always despondent! Look at how they live, see how fervently they pray! They must be despondent! Anyhow, I've decided it's time for the Temple to return a gesture . . ."

"*You've* decided . . . ?"

"A gesture of appreciation for their unswerving devotion and of hope for . . . no, don't scowl. How about hope for tomorrow, even if not for the day after? Shouldn't they be offered just a little something, at least until the Last Day is actually upon us?"

Luco draws out his grunt of agreement until it comes out like a negative. "What sort of gesture did you have in mind?"

"Well . . . they're always coming to the Temple. I think the Temple should come to them." Paia checks her mental ammunition and forges ahead. "In the person of their High Priestess. Who will make a Visitation to the ten most exemplary villages. You can come, too, if you like."

Luco's jaw slackens. "Ten?" .

"Five, then. How many do we have? Luco, neither you nor the God ever tell me these things!"

"Why should you care how many villages?" he retorts stiffly, then seems to hear how snappish he sounds. "I mean, Mother Paia, your holy duty is the care and feeding of their souls, whatever their number."

Paia pats his gold-banded arm. "Well spoken, my priest. You do the God credit. But how am I to truly understand what troubles them, be they one soul or many, if I have never walked among them?"

"You walk among them every day, in the Temple. It's the God's decree that you do so."

"Oh, Luco, surely you can't believe such a narrow view can build a true understanding of a human soul?"

She feels him studying her without wanting to be seen to do so. Finally he says, "What's gotten into you? Who have you been talking to?"

Paia suppresses a laugh. Suddenly she's infused with a

heady sense of power. "Why do you say that? Can't I have an idea of my own? Besides, who would I talk to, besides the God and you? I'm not allowed, remember?"

"That doesn't mean . . ." Luco lets out a breath and collects himself. "Have you presented this mad scheme to the God?"

"Ah, mad, is it? And here I thought that you, as a man of the people, would approve of the idea, and help me convince him."

It's the first time Paia can recall using her heritage as a weapon against him. When Luco was a mere foot soldier, she would not have bothered. By the time he was elevated to the priesthood, she'd learned the folly of saying "don't tell me what to do, I was born here!"

But Luco fields the challenge by ignoring it. "Have you?"

"No."

To her surprise, he seems more interested rather than less. "As it happens, I think it's a fine idea, though I'd have never dared propose it myself. If you can clear it with the God, I'll arrange it."

They reach the end of the corridor, where it meets the major cross hall for that level. To the right and down are Paia's quarters. To the left and farther down, Luco's. Paia says, "Couldn't we do it when he's not around?"

He laughs, sharp and quick. "You must be kidding."

"I thought perhaps he might trust us by now to make a few day-to-day decisions on our own."

"He does. But parading the High Priestess of the Temple around the countryside where she's an open target for any and all disgruntled patrons—never mind the highly paid assassins—is hardly the God's idea of day to day. Or mine either. But if you get his permission, I'll make it happen. It'd be good for you to have a better idea of what we're up against here."

Paia glances at him, sees bleak reality surface briefly, only to be smothered once more by his Temple face, his Temple smile. "I'll try."

Luco shows no inclination to see her directly to her door. He's decided she can't get into any more trouble between here and there. As officious as he is, and ever so deeply in the God's pocket, Luco knows that she needs the occasional private moment, even if it's only while traversing the hallways to her rooms. His clutch of acolytes gaze after her sheepishly as she takes the right-hand turn away from them, alone.

As grateful as Paia is for Luco's small gesture of trust, there is one little detour she intends to make before retiring to her chambers. Down level, along the hall a bit, then another hairpin turn. Another servants' secret back stair, and she's avoided the probably twice strong and doubly alert contingent of Honor Guard waiting about uselessly on her doorstep. She's past them and trotting down dark corridors toward the winding stair to her tower studio. She takes the first twenty steps two at a time, amazed at her own vigor after such a long day of heavy mind work and racing about.

But on the top step, she hesitates, seized by the conviction that there's someone in the room. She listens for a long, long moment. Nothing. She is imagining things. No human could stay so still.

The cavernous space is a symphony of light and darkness. A vast rectangle of cool moon brilliance falls through the big window, blinding her vision into the pitchy corners and the shadows as thick as smoke. Paia reaches nervously for the lantern in its niche by the entrance. Lit, it clears her path to the shrouded easel but it does nothing to lighten the weight of those night-black corners. Still, she has never been afraid in this room, and she resents feeling that way now, resents whoever has been violating her private space, her sanctuary, without at least explaining themselves. As she nears the easel, her courage and her ire blossom. If he, she, or they are here now, she will confront them. She welcomes the chance.

Even so, she gasps softly when she sees the neatly folded note. This time it's been pinned to the outside of the plastic tarp. Irritably, Paia rips it free and shakes it open to hold it up to the lantern's pale flame.

"Hunh," she says, for the second time in less than an hour. She has wished for clarity, and this time, she has gotten it. She reads it again, and a third time, biting her lip.

His aura explodes around her only an instant before he speaks. "What does it say?"

Paia whirls, her heart nearly leaping from her chest. He is silhouetted against the bright window, his grand profile etched with moonlight. But he is not looking at her. He is gazing out the window, his broad back like a wall and his hair loose and wild like the plumage of an extinct exotic bird. There is just the faintest glimmer about him. "Where did you come from?" she gasps when she has breath enough.

"What a ridiculous question. Where do I always come from? Wherever I have just been."

Paia swallows. "My lord, I meant . . . where have you been?"

"To a place that no longer exists! Do not hope to distract me. What does it say, this paper you're hiding in your hand?"

The note is a crushed ball in her fist. Paia remembers the magic sword she's just read about, how she imagined it would sound when being drawn from its sheath. The God sounds like this now.

"Open it and read it to me. Every word."

"It's nothing, really, just a . . ."

"A what? A love letter?"

"No, of course not! Just a . . ."

"Read it to me!" he thunders.

"Yes, my lord." Paia flattens the paper against her thigh but doesn't bother to look at it. How long has he been standing here, waiting for her to arrive and unfold it, his rage and frustration building because he is unable to perform this simple *human* task? "It says, '*Is your luxury worth the burning of a village?*'"

"Ha!" The God tosses his head. The bird plumage becomes a nest of snakes winding about his head.

"Has someone been burning villages?" she asks innocently, although by now she guesses the answer.

"Of course. I have. And I will continue to as needed, to keep my enemies at bay." He aims a gilded nail at the crinkled note. "This is sedition!"

"Yes, my lord. I suppose it is."

"You *suppose*?"

Paia is relieved to discover that once her shock has receded to the normal levels of fear and dread, the infant flame of her rebellion still burns within. "Well, after all, it's only rhetoric, isn't it? What could anyone actually do?" She picks up the lantern and moves toward him, away from the easel and its shrouded, subversive painting. "I mean, against the power of a God? Surely these poor villagers are not your enemies."

"Enemies of the Faith! Sedition must be stamped out wherever it appears, and while it is only rhetoric. Before it matures into treason. How else can control be maintained? Do you question my right or my wisdom? My view is longer than you can conceive of. Who are you exchanging messages with, beloved traitor?"

"It's no exchange, my lord!" Paia would like to discuss his long view with him, to hear his response to the history she has just learned. But the word traitor wakes new thrills of terror. She clings to what the computer has promised: the God cannot harm her. She prays it is true. "Someone's been leaving these notes up here. This is only the second. The first one said, 'What price survival?' and I didn't understand what it meant."

His head swivels toward her. His stillness is what's most frightening. His eyes glow in his shadowed face. In man-form, he has never looked more dangerous, or more alluring. "And now you do?"

"I think I am beginning to."

The God laughs softly. "And you asked me what had changed . . ."

She meets his golden gaze as boldly as she can. To her astonishment, he looks away to the window, turning his back on her. A silence hangs like a scent in the air, mysterious, inviting. And then, for no reason she can explain, Paia finds herself frightened for him, rather than of him. How could that be? "My lord Fire, is there something wrong? I mean, something else? I wish you would tell me."

"It's all wrong," he growls. "All of it, all I've worked for. All my work through space and time." He spreads his arms grandly, encompassing the barren moonlit hills on the other side of the thick glass. "All this. My art. The expression of my genius. It'll all be gone if I cannot defeat them."

Paia understands nothing of this, except that he's finally been distracted by thoughts of his enemies, and that he's in pain. The God is in pain. Like his rage, it pervades the room. Amazed, she sets aside the lantern and goes to him, as close as she has ever volunteered to approach him in man-form, close enough to feel the charged heat that his manifestation generates. It prickles along her bare arms and up the middle of her back and, disturbingly, deep in her groin. She wishes she could touch him, to soothe the rage and restlessness out of him. She raises her hand as if to lay it on his chest.

His chin lifts. His elegant lip curls in a sneer. "Don't. We'll only both be terribly disappointed."

Paia drops her hand but stands her ground. It's he who chooses to move a step away from her. She studies him. The difference in him unsteadies her. "How did you come here this time without my knowing?"

His sneer sharpens to petulance. "I have a few tricks left you don't know about. Entire lives you never even see."

"You were . . . spying on me, my lord?"

"I must be certain of your loyalty."

As if a keyed lock has just clicked, Paia becomes aware of an instinct she's never noticed before: deeply buried, isolated, inaccessible until just now, like the House Comp's time-lag programming. An instinct to read the truth in him and of him, and the truth of their bond. His wild threats against her may well be nothing but emotional manipulation. But equally, she would be unable to do anything to harm him. She can't imagine what that could be—how could one harm a God? She only knows that she cannot do it.

Her lips are dry, and her throat even more so. She wonders how long they have stood there, side by side, unspeaking in the moonlight. When she looks up, he is looking down at her, and the distance between them is a zone of fire. She has never wanted any man as much as she wants him now. Except that he is not a man. This time it is she who backs away, one step, then two, brushing tears from her eyes.

"My lord Fire, my loyalty to you is undying. It cannot be otherwise."

"Easier to promise than to prove."

"A shallow response, my lord, when I am trying to tell you something serious, something I am only just beginning to understand." Her hours in the Library have left her with half-knowledge, supposition, guesswork and conjecture, with understandings instinctive but still vague and uncertain. "I mean that I am born for this. To serve you."

"Indeed. It pains me to hear that this is news to you."

"I mean that it's more than duty. It's in my blood. I have no choice. Nor do you."

"Be careful, my priestess . . ."

Again his stiffness frightens her, but she's gone too far to stop now. "My lord, I mean that . . . it is decreed by history."

"Decreed? History? How dare you!" He spins away from her, then whirls and seems to launch himself at her. Paia recoils as heat washes over her in a torrent. The hair on her outstretched arm is singed by his passage. "It's their doing! They have put this into your head!"

"No! No! It's not true!"

"How would you know? No matter! It's all lies! Lies! I will not be ruled! By you or any other!"

Instantly he is before the easel, looming over a covering he cannot physically remove. The cavern shudders. The very bedrock shakes, glows hot and liquid. Magma. Paia crumples to the floor, the softening liquid rock. The computer was wrong. This is how he will destroy her. Not by his own hands but by . . . and there, he is Himself, a vast gilt-scaled monster coiled in the room with the easel at the center of his arc. His great barbed tail lashes at the wooden worktables and the piles of stacked canvases, sending brushes and palettes and mixing bowls flying, while a single ivory claw hooks the easel toward him to snag the plastic tarp and rip it free.

And then, as if this spasm of violence was no more than a fever dream, he is there in man-form again, staring at the painting, in the light of his own golden glow. The rock is rock once more, but the worktables are in scattered ruins and the treacherous landscape lies revealed to him.

In a heap on the floor, Paia weeps in grief, but also with relief.

"Get up and get over here," he orders. He sounds disappointed.

She struggles to her feet and goes to him, stopping several long paces away. She looks at the floor, at all the mess, anywhere but at him or at the perfidious painting.

He laughs harshly. "Not so eager to stand beside me now, are you, beloved?"

"You have no cause, my lord," she murmurs. "No cause."

"I have no need of cause, my priestess. I am your God. It would do well for you to remember that." He waits, glowering. "Did I hear you say, 'yes, I will'?"

"Yes," Paia whispers. Are hatred and love like science and magic, in the long run, only one and the same? "Yes, my lord Fire, I will remember that."

"And any further treasonous communications you will report to me."

"Yes, my lord."

"I will stake your loyalty on it."

"I understand that, my lord."

He moves away, kicking futilely at bits of wreckage, then paces back to throw an offhand gesture at the painting. "Your work, I presume?"

She's been waiting for this. Paia steels herself to look at the painting, then has to steel herself all over again. The canvas on the easel is like any other in the room: a painting in reds and browns and grays, a painting of dry rock and barren hills. Paia feels her self-conviction weaken and slide away like a melting ice floe. She has imagined it, then, all of it: the velvet grass, the trees, the silver ribbon of river, even the changes, the grim storm gathering above the mountains. It must be her loneliness and isolation, at last eating away at her sanity. "Yes, my lord," she replies dully. "My work."

"Beautiful."

Her eyes widen at him. Perhaps he's the one who's crazy. Or it's both of them, now that she thinks about it. That makes the most sense. If they are so indelibly bonded by centuries of tradition and breeding, how could one be insane and the other not? "Thank you," she murmurs.

"Any progress on the choice of a Suitor?"

"None."

"Get on it, then."

It's folly, but Paia raises her eyes to his, finding in herself a chill deep enough to match his own. "You are a monster."

There is a flicker in his reptilian eyes, and a slight move toward turning away, until he catches himself and lets a cold smile twist his beauty into a carved and gilded mask. "Perhaps. And you are my pawn. As you said, you have no choice."

With that, and the last word, he is gone.

Paia sinks to the floor and lets the darkness surround her for the length of time it takes to stop weeping and get her bearings. Then she raises her head and crawls to where she's left the lantern, miraculously undamaged by the God's fit of rage. She stands unsteadily, brings it back to the easel to look at the painting one more time. She's glad that her reflexes have been slowed by her ordeal, which is all that prevents her from dropping the lantern.

For the painting has changed again. The valley in the mountains has reappeared, but this time the tall dark pines, the ribbon of river, the green velvet grass, are buried under a heavy weight of ice and snow.

Whoever is doing this, Paia muses, *perhaps they're on my side.*

CHAPTER TWENTY-FOUR

The path up the steep slope was brush-choked and narrow, and there was no longer the relief of a breeze. As she toiled upward in the crushing heat, Erde prayed that the men were right about going off with the first strangers they ran into. Particularly strangers who had threatened and tried to rob them. But N'Doch would say it was the quickest way to acquire the sort of local information they needed to find their way about this new land. Baron Köthen apparently agreed. So, until she had a better suggestion, she must follow their lead.

Climbing just ahead of her, N'Doch gave no sign of worry. He seemed, just as she had accused him of back on the raft, to be enjoying himself. He whistled now and then, one of his homemade tunes, and his step was jaunty, even as laden down as he was, with his own pack and a few of Stoksie's. Was it simply confidence born of knowing that dragons shadowed their every upward step? Erde rubbed grit and sweat and the dust of crumbled leaves from her eyes, readjusted her own load and fixed her gaze on N'Doch's heels, as if they could winch her up the rugged trail behind him. And she kept up her running internal monologue, reporting to the dragon what she saw ahead, imaging it all for him in detail—the stunted brush and broken trees, each cluster of ruined homesteads, every dry ravine—so that he could keep up, transporting himself and his sister to each imaged place as soon as the climbers had left it behind. Meanwhile, she again put to him the question that kept plaguing her, one she'd asked several times already since arriving in this dreadful place.

HAVE YOU THOUGHT FURTHER ON IT, DRAGON? IF THIS

LAND HAS NOT ALWAYS BEEN SO RUINED, HAVE YOU AN IDEA
YET WHAT SIN THESE PEOPLE COULD BE GUILTY OF, THAT GOD
SHOULD PUNISH THEM SO TERRIBLY?

Again the dragon replied that he did not, that he had no
understanding of such matters, but would continue to consider it deeply. It was curious, Erde thought, that Lady
Water, so ready to voice her opinion on every other matter,
refrained entirely from commenting on this crucial spiritual
issue. Well, almost.

**Maybe it's a whole new sin. One you've never even
thought of.**

Erde could not imagine what she meant. After all, didn't
God decree what was a sin and what wasn't?

Her pondering distracted her for a while as she plodded
upward, dulled with heat. When she woke to her surroundings again, the ruined signs of habitation had given way to
patches of scrub clinging to ever-steeper slopes of solid
rock. The path, such as it was, switchbacked right and left
several times, winding around thin-layered outcroppings
that reminded Erde of tall stacks of parchment. Or it
wound up among piles of dragon-sized boulders, narrowing
further until Erde could barely squeeze herself and her burdens past the enclosing walls of stone. She'd been glad to
leave the biting midges behind down by the landing, but
now it would be reassuring to hear the song of one bird or
the hum of any insect, not this unnatural stillness broken
only by their own heavy breathing and the crunch of their
labored steps.

They stopped for a brief rest and a drink where the ter-
rain leveled out at the foot of another towering rock face.
Erde had her pack halfway off when N'Doch stopped her.

"You put it down now, girl, it'll be a whole lot harder
to pick up again."

She did as he advised, but reluctantly. The rock wall
faced southwest, and there wasn't an inch of shade to be
had anywhere on the ledge.

"Nice view, huh?"

"Are they taking us to their town, do you think?"

"Nah, we're way up past where the old towns were."

"A mountain stronghold, then?"

N'Doch grinned like he did when she'd said something
he called *quaint.* "Something like that." He gestured with

his water jug at the far-off glimmer of Big Albin's towers, then to the left where the wide stretch of water was visible over the tops of the dusty scrub. "Lot of people living down there once."

From this distance the water was a deceptively inviting lavender, drawing warmth from the long summer twilight. The far shore was a faint line of purplish hills. Erde thought they must be a very long way away. "What happened to them? Was there a war?"

"Haven't gotten around to asking that right out, y'know? But it don't sound like they all got up and went somewhere better."

"You mean, they just died?"

"Probably. Sickness, starvation, massacre. Who knows what else."

"Oh. Oh, dear."

N'Doch looked her over dubiously. "You holding up okay? Wherever we're headed, they sure don't want to make getting there easy, do they?"

"I'm fine." Erde thought of Tor Alte, a thick-walled stone fortress perched high on a mountain pinnacle. At several points along that upward road, visitors must walk their horses single-file. And these points, of course, were heavily monitored, and vulnerable to a well-placed rain of arrows or a deluge of boiling oil from above. She was familiar with the advantages of building in a secure location. But if there were so few people left around, what were Stoksie and his "crew" protecting themselves against? He was obviously more uneasy here than he'd been on the river. Every step of the trail, he and the girls stayed on the alert. Perhaps he would prefer to move along faster, but she couldn't imagine how, with all that he was carrying. "Am I holding anyone up?"

"No way." N'Doch tipped his head sideways. " 'Cept maybe his lordship."

Baron Köthen stood with his back to the rock, impassively observing the view. He had again positioned himself at the rear, so that no one was ever behind him and the path of retreat was under his control. He did not look worried, or even particularly concerned. He merely looked . . . careful.

The girls Senda and Mari were up and ready to be off again long before Erde was. They scampered straight along the face of the rock wall just long enough to raise her hopes that the climbing was over. Then they turned sideways and vanished from view as the path hooked a sharp right and crawled nearly vertically up the side of the ledge. At the turn, N'Doch leaned back to give Erde a hand up the first seemingly impossible step. Ahead, the taller girl called out and threw an eager wave upward. Behind, Stoksie let out a sigh of relief, then a long warble, three descending notes, two ascending, like a birdcall. An answering whistle echoed down among the rocks. Erde craned her neck this way and that. Finally, on a sharp jut high over the path, a slim figure moved into view, silhouetted against the amber sky. It carried a slim, dark object, like a broomstick with a handle, which it now slung over its shoulder to free one hand up for a wave.

A gun. The long kind. Erde recognized it, from her recent and all-too-vivid acquaintance with such objects. N'Doch saw it, too, and dropped back suddenly under the pretense of a stone in his sandal to confer with Baron Köthen in the rear. A *gun*. Erde was again haunted by the images of N'Doch's body being torn to pieces by the last guns she'd seen. Her hands were wet, and her boots not the best for climbing. Distracted, she slipped, nearly lost her grip, then slipped again. She froze in terror.

DRAGON! I CANNOT MOVE! WILL YOU CATCH ME WHEN I FALL?

YOU WILL NOT FALL. THERE'LL BE NO TALK OF FALLING.

He was right of course. It would surely panic their guides if the dragon was forced to reveal himself precipitously. She must control her weakness. She must forget about guns and falling, and blank her mind of everything but the effort of hauling herself safely upward. She imagined the rocks as the dragon's plated back, hospitable to her grip, and was able to move forward. Gaining the top, she was breathless and weak, incapable of another forward step. Humiliated, she collapsed onto a nearby ledge, and was uncharitably gratified when Stoksie struggled up over the edge, as much the worse for wear as she was.

He resettled his load to ease the burden on his bad hip

and mopped his dark brow. The little girls had run off ahead already, their cries and childish chattering growing fainter with distance. " 'Ard un, dat las'."

Erde nodded wanly, forcing a smile, then realized it wasn't an effort at all. She quite liked the man. Their shared plight somehow transformed him in her mind from a dark and forbidding stranger to an odd little man with a cheerful look. She didn't need to know his language to get the sense of his words. Without N'Doch to translate, she had no words to say back to him, but this didn't bother Stoksie one bit. So they sat catching their breath in easy silence, waiting for the others. When she could breathe more freely, Erde became aware of a subtle difference in the air—it was cooler here, even in the sun, perhaps due to the added elevation, but lighter and sweeter as well, with a promised hint of moisture.

Stoksie grinned when he saw her sniffing like a pack hound. He said something incomprehensible, bobbing his head fervently as if nods alone could make his words intelligible. Then N'Doch levered his tall frame over the edge. He stood panting for a moment, responding to their silence with a listening readiness of his own. Suddenly, he broke into a smile. "Aww, listen to that! Music to my ears!"

Erde had noticed it, too, a soft background sighing, like high-country breezes. Listening more carefully, she wondered how she could have mistaken running water for mere wind. And not just running, from the sound of it, but falling, as if from a great height. Stoksie, watching them inhale with such relish, nodded and grinned like a proud parent.

Baron Köthen finally joined them, dripping and scowling. "Seems we've paid our toll after all," he remarked when he had breath enough. "As the good merchant's beasts of burden."

"You know it," agreed N'Doch.

"All heah?" Stoksie bent, eagerly loading himself up again. "Quick, na."

Putting weight on her feet again was painful. Erde repressed a groan, thinking that she'd happily trade the nausea and disorientation of dragon transport for this physical torture. But the path here was better trimmed and wider, and the rise was gentler. She thought perhaps the foliage had a healthier tinge, and that the dwarfish trees might be gaining some height. Soon they broke out of the scrub entirely, where the path intersected a gravel-strewn cut through a grove of taller trees, some sort of pine. The heat was making the blood pound in her ears, and Erde was grateful when Stoksie turned right and led them into this sweeter-smelling shade.

"Used to be a road, this." N'Doch kicked at shards of rubble poking through the mat of needles, raising dust. "Not a real big one, though."

Erde hoped that if it had been a road, its end was nearby. Would it only lead to more ruin? She was eager to be somewhere, to arrive, rather than to be ceaselessly pushing on with no particular goal or direction. There seemed to be no real place left to go in this destroyed future. Simple movements, like walking, were becoming a struggle, but another dose of dragon encouragement and the music of flowing water drew her onward.

Deeper into the grove, they rounded a bend screened by a thicket of broad-leafed shrubs to discover a trio of armed men ahead in the road, watching their approach. No, Erde noted, two women and a young man, with scowls and threatening postures and the long sorts of gun slung easily into the crooks of their elbows, guns almost as tall as they were.

N'Doch pulled up sharply and eased Erde behind his back, but Stoksie greeted them cheerfully by name.

"Wha's dis?" one of the women snarled, shoving out ahead of the rest with her gun leveled.

"Easy, na." Stoksie put up his palms.

"Doan tell me easy! Whachu tinkin', bringin' straingeas up heah? Yu sumkinda fool?"

"Whoa," murmured N'Doch. "Heavy language."

But Stoksie rolled his eyes at his guests over his shoulder. "She mean, bring yu heah w'out askin' huh. Y'know?"

"Betcha," N'Doch replied with his usual bravado, which Erde was beginning to see the purpose of.

"Dis heah Brenda Chu," Stoksie offered. "Call her Pitbull, 'cuz she chews hard!" He grinned, but thrust his narrow jaw forward just a bit. "Dees heah gud ole bizmen, Brenda. An' dey's fine 'n healt'y, lookit 'em. Back off, na."

The woman had a shiny dark cap of short hair, a flattish face with eyes shaped like almonds. Her skin was the same

color as the smaller of the little girls, and she wore a ragged
scar like a fighting man's from the tip of her right eyebrow
to the corner of her mouth. Her tough stance reminded
Erde of Lily and Margit, Deep Moor's scouts. But the resemblance ended with this woman's reflex hostility, as she
shifted her gun to her shoulder and stood up taller, as if
proud to be named after a vicious animal.

N'Doch stepped forward to offer his hand. "N'Doch
heah." Brenda just stared at him. He shrugged. "Das cool."

"Das Charlie 'n das Punk," Stoksie continued, as if nothing had happened. "Dis heah all Water Dragon Crew, frum
up nort'."

Charlie was a bronze-skinned blonde woman with a
patchy complexion and paler skin showing at her cuffs and
neckline. Even in the heavy heat, she was as covered up
with clothing as anyone could possibly bear to be. She
looked like she might be willing to smile, if only Brenda's
scowl was not so discouraging. Punk was an alarmingly
skinny, dark youth—about Erde's own age, she guessed,
surely no more than fifteen. All three wore the same sort
of mismatched assortment of garments as Stoksie and the
girls. Erde saw Punk measuring N'Doch's height and ebony
sheen with interest, maybe with envy. She had never known
until today that human beings came in so many different
colors, almost all of them darker than her own.

"Dees two is Lady 'n Doff," Stoksie concluded, with a
wave in her direction. "Frum Urop. Got good trade."

"Urop?" Brenda was skeptical.

"Bad deah now, huh?" Charlie's casual remark earned
her a nasty look from Brenda, but the business end of her
gun sank slowly toward the ground.

"Real bad," N'Doch agreed, giving Charlie his "special"
smile. Erde hoped he knew what he was talking about. She
noticed he didn't try the smile on Brenda. There was a
bit more arguing and hand waving, and another brief gun-
pointing, which brought Köthen lunging forward only to
run into N'Doch's swiftly outstretched arm. But finally
Brenda was overruled by Stoksie's bluff good nature and
the obvious curiosity of the others.

"Dey's healt'y-lookin, alrite." Punk shrugged and slung
his gun over his thin shoulder. "Weah yu bin, Stokes? We
wuz worried boutchu."

"Lookin' fer trade, wachu tink? Tellyu, Albin's a ghost town! We dun picked it dry. 'Bout ta come home near empty. Li'l stuff, y'know? Den I find dees uns." Stoksie showed all his bad teeth in a victory grin.

"Dju frisk 'em?" Brenda demanded, her final display of disapproval.

Their guide nodded, though he hadn't. "Cupla blades. Nuttin' much."

"Frum Urop wit a cupla blades 'n des still walkin'?" Brenda's eyes raked their bodies and their packs for signs of hidden weapons.

"Tellyu one ting . . ." Stoksie jerked his chin faintly in Baron Köthen's direction. "Da reel whitefella? Fas'. Real fas'. Watch 'im."

Erde sensed this was merely a sop. True as it was, Stoksie wasn't worried about Köthen. But Pitbull Brenda's honor was satisfied, now that she had an assignment: keep an eye on the grim-faced soldier. Clever Stoksie. At last the expedition moved forward, deeper into the shade, delayed only if one cared to observe the surreptitious dance between Köthen and Brenda as they skirmished over who would bring up the rear. Erde was unamazed when Köthen won.

A larger but less threatening delegation awaited them at the mouth of the clearing. This group was more cheerfully suspicious. They crowded around—men, women and a few wide-eyed small children—greeting Stoksie gladly, demanding reasons for his delay, staring openly at the strangers while helpfully relieving them of their extra burdens. Mostly small and dark-skinned like Stoksie and the girls, they didn't look like they could put up much of a fight. But they had no problem verbalizing their curiosity. Erde was glad when Stoksie demanded silence and said the questions had to wait until the visitors were refreshed and settled. Immediately, the crowd pulled back, and a child was urged out from among them. A blue ceramic pitcher was put in his thin little hands. He presented it to Stoksie, who tipped a few drops of water onto his fingers, then touched them to his forehead. Erde heard a few indistinct but reverent murmurs from the crowd. Next Stoksie poured out a little on the ground, then he grinned, tilted the pitcher to his mouth and took a long, long drink. The crowd cheered, and the pitcher was offered in turn to each visitor until it came back to the child's hands empty. The water was sweet and cold. Erde would gladly have drunk more of it, but the child beamed and ran off with the jug, giggling.

"Gud, na! Blin' Rachel Crew say welcome!" Stoksie gathered up his guests and led them on into the clearing. The chattering crowd fell right in behind.

The once-road opened on an expanse of space and bustle and noise, bare dirt with patches of grass and a few trees, tall enough to provide a bit of real shade for the busy maze of structures spread out beneath them: a motley assortment of tents and lean-tos and high-wheeled wagons with oft-patched canopies, and conical shapes of canvas and lower-slung carts built up with windows and chimneys like tiny rolling huts. The leftover nooks and crannies were crammed with livestock pens and awninged market booths. Even the odors were lively. A thin goat wandered forlornly and, everywhere, chickens clucked and scratched in the dust. A pair of lop-eared hounds ran up to greet Stoksie effusively, until he had had enough of their eager tongues and paws, and sent them bounding off again.

Over the din of people and animals, the sigh of the water was gentle and welcome music. But past the unkempt line of tent poles and rough-built roof peaks rose the most astonishing structure Erde had ever laid eyes on. Stoksie stopped them out in the open where they could take a good long look.

It was a building seeming to vanish right into the precipitous rock face looming behind it. It was both tall and yet vastly horizontal: layers of stone terraces coiling around the central green like the apse of a cathedral and rising one after the other, four, five, six, seven stories, each curved plane set off from the one below it, either forward or back, like the natural contours of the layered rock she had just climbed through. But for the sturdy central staircase, Erde could not always tell where the hand of man laid off and that of nature began again. It was like a palace built with the help of magic.

"Fuckin' A!" breathed N'Doch beside her.

"This is some great lord's castle, surely," said Baron Kö-then, joining them at last.

"Some rich guy's paradise, more like," N'Doch replied. "It's Blind Rachel's now, whoever she is."

"I expect we shall meet that good lady soon enough."

Repeating rectangles of glass glittered along each level, broken here and there by some duller material. Intricately carved wooden railings alternated with thick rails of natural stone, or in some places, no railing at all. As she collected her senses enough to really study, Erde began to notice the many details of the damage: the rotted newel posts, the sagging lines of the extended terraces, the shattered glass. But the whole, viewed generously as through a veil, was still magnificent.

"Nise, huh?" Stoksie prompted.

"Real nice," N'Doch agreed, for all of them.

"Gwan up 'n findyu room, na. Putcher stuff in, nobuddy bodda, gotcha? I tell 'em. Den I shoyu roun'."

Stoksie shepherded them through the lingering curious and around the circular roadway. The crowd called out eager invitations to dinner, more than could ever be honored, then dispersed and went on about their business. At the center of the giant curving edifice, a double set of stairs climbed side by side like lovers to the second level, then turned away from each other to continue their journeys to the third. On the fourth, they met again, and so they continued their meeting and parting until they ran out of levels to climb. Grinning proudly, Stoksie gave his guests another moment at the bottom of the stair to gaze upward with the appropriate awe. Then he led them up the first flight, pointing out the weak spots and rotted treads, and then to the left, along the second level balcony. They passed neatly spaced paneled doors alternating with broad stretches of window, most of which were still intact. Erde had seen this miracle of glassmaking when she was in N'Doch's home time, but those magical sheets of glistening transparency had all been shielded by metal gratings.

Stoksie saw her slow to touch her fingers to the surface and skim them smoothly along without bump or obstacle for two, three, even four paces. "Good stuff, dat. Latest, 'fore dey stopped."

"Stopped?" asked N'Doch.

"Makin' it. Y'know?"

N'Doch nodded. "Yeah. Guess I do."

Erde absorbed the translation one step behind. "They stopped making glass?" N'Doch passed the query along.

Stoksie's shrug was more emphatic than usual. "Probby som'weah dey still do. Not roun' heah. No call fer't na."

"He means nobody wants any."

Erde chewed her lip. "But glass is very precious. At least it is . . . was . . . in my time."

"And real cheap and necessary, in mine."

Behind them, Köthen glided his own spread fingertips along the glass. "The Future," he murmured.

"Not my future," N'Doch retorted. "Well . . . least, not the one I was looking forward to."

Stoksie waved them onward. "Be dak soon. Messtime. Don' wanna missit, na." He took them past door after door, all of them closed up tight, and past window after window. Erde attempted the occasional covert glance inside these mysterious and threatening spaces, but her view was usually blocked by fabric hanging just inside the glass, or by boards fastened up where the glass was missing. Where there was a crack in a broken door to peer through, or a space between the hangings, she saw heaps of clothing or a bit of crockery, but beyond that, only darkness. She could not help but worry about what the darkness might conceal.

Far along the curve of the terrace, almost to the end, Stoksie stopped in front of a door constructed from mismatched planks. Each had long ago been painted a different color, now faded together into a mere suggestion of variety of hue. "Dis'll do ya, ha?"

A greenish rectangle of metal, obviously a more recent addition, fastened the door, pinned to a corroded loop in the jamb by what Erde recognized as a crude and diminutive sort of lock. A thin sliver of metal protruded from its bottom end. Stoksie took hold of this and struggled with it for a while, then finally twisted it clear and popped the lock open. He handed the sliver to N'Doch.

"S'all yers. Getchu settled. Back mebbe ten, yucool?"

"Mecool." As Stoksie turned back toward the stairs, N'Doch called out, "Hey, man . . ."

Stoksie turned.

"Thanks, y'know? Dis real good trade."

A quick nod. "Gotcha.

Once N'Doch is inside, he knows the place for what it was. No rich man's paradise after all. The room is an oblong box, low-ceilinged and dull as they come. Once upon a time it probably attempted some more fashionable shade than the ugly salmon it's graying into. It's completely empty, but he can see where the beds went, two matching queens, he's sure, advertised on a big sign outside. A luxury sort of joint. He sees the closet indentations, missing their doors and hanger poles. An archway in the back leads through a dark dressing nook to a tiny square room he knows was the bathroom, even stripped like it is—surprise, surprise—of everything portable, sink, toilets, pipes, even the wall tiles. He reminds himself to ask Stoksie for directions to the privy.

He comes back up front where Köthen and the girl are setting their stuff down reluctantly, like they're not so sure the floor's clean enough or something. They both look at him expectantly, like the pressure's on for him to set some sort of "modern" frame of reference here. But he's not sure he can oblige. He rubs his palms together. "So. You guys have any idea what a motel is? Nah, guess you wouldn't. Anyhow, if they don't turn on us sudden-like and try to murder us in our beds, I'd say we just got real lucky."

Köthen gazes around the tight, dim space. N'Doch can see he doesn't trust it much. "Is this an unusual degree of hospitality?"

"Where I come from, any hospitality is unusual, at least to strangers. 'Cept out in the bush." N'Doch unstraps his pack and leans it against a wall. "Maybe it's the same thing here as there. When there aren't so many people around, strangers are useful, y'know? They got stories, they got news. And Stoksie seems to think we got good trade. Hope we don't disappoint him. For a few days, at least, we're the entertainment."

"A few days?"

N'Doch grins at him slyly. "I bought us one. After that, Dolph my man, it kinda depends on just how entertaining we decide to be. Doncha think?"

The girl says quietly, "Is this where we will sleep?"

"I've slept in worse places."

"All of us together?"

"Oh. I get it. Well, tell you what, girl—you can have the bathroom all to yourself."

Köthen is examining the lock on the door. "All of us, behind one door. That way, one can always watch while the others sleep. Unless, my lady witch, you can offer a few spells to protect us."

"No problem, man, the dragons'll . . ."

"My lord of Köthen!" the girl bursts out. "I beg you do not call me 'witch.' I am not one, nor never have been!"

Köthen glances up. His hands are full of metal parts, as he studies how to switch the lock from outside to in. "Your pardon, my lady. If it distresses you so, I will desist."

"It does! Very much! I wonder that you haven't noticed!"

"Hey, girl," N'Doch chides, but gently. He sees she's got tears in her eyes. "Been a long day for all of us."

Köthen chuckles darkly, deftly reassembling the lock. "The longest in human memory. Began in 913 and ending God only knows when."

N'Doch thinks it's too bad the girl doesn't find this as funny as they do, but even he's surprised when she spins away from their laughter, skims out the door past Köthen like a spooked rabbit, and tears off along the balcony. He can hear the clack of her footsteps, hurried and sharp. "Whoa!" he mutters, and follows her into the open. "Hey, girl! Erde! Come on back here!"

She ignores him, clattering all the way around the curve of the building until she's brought up short by the heavy wooden railing at the other end. She props her elbows on it and buries her face in her hands.

"Aw, jeez . . ." N'Doch leans against the railing behind him and folds his arms. He's starting to feel bad for the girl and there's no time like the present to speak up about it. She's strong and all, but she's been through a lot lately, and the good baron could just be the final straw. "Listen, Dolph . . . I know you're mad at her, and hey, I don't blame you a bit. But you gotta go easier on her, man. Just a little."

Köthen straightens, dusting wood and metal splinters from his fingers. "Why? It would only encourage her."

"Well, umm . . . hunh." N'Doch was ready for huff and attitude. This blunt honesty leaves him kind of without an argument. "Okay, I understand all that, but . . . hey, look, all I'm saying is, we're all in this together."

"But I would not be, were it not for her meddling."

"Yeah, yeah, but . . ."

"I speak but the truth to say she is a witch."

"How d'you figure that?"

"Who else but a witch has converse with dragons?"

"Huh. So where does that put me?"

Köthen's glance flicks hard at him and then away, but not quite quick enough. N'Doch has read the sudden doubt in his eyes, and a few of the baron's assumptions are beginning to piss him off. He wants this dragon business understood for what it is, at least the way he sees it.

"I'm not just here along for the ride, y'know. The blue dragon is mine. Yeah, that got your attention. Mine. I didn't ask for it, but that's how it is. So does that make me some kind of warlock? I can tell you, I ain't one of them."

Köthen's jaw settles stubbornly. He says nothing.

"You wanna know what I think?"

"You've shown little inclination to guard your tongue so far . . ."

"Yeah, and you're not as much of a jerk as I thought, 'cause you keep letting me talk. Must be you like the challenge."

They stare each other down for long cool seconds, and then Köthen rewards him with a sigh and a weary twist of his mouth that is almost a grin. "Presumptuous whelp. Go on. I'm listening."

"Really? Well, that's progress now, ain't it?"

"Don't . . ."

". . . I know. Don't press my luck." N'Doch lets out a breath. "Okay, here it is: you *hope* she's a witch, if there even is such a thing, 'cause it's easier to bust her ass for the mess you're in than it is the dragons'. Am I right?" He starts to pace a little, like a little engine's fired up inside him. It's not only that he's saying this personal sort of stuff to a man proven to be armed and dangerous. What's most amazing is that he's thinking it at all, like, of his own accord. "And that's because you won't accept that you've been part of this since long before you got yourself dragon-napped."

"This being . . . ?" Köthen asks with a look of distaste.

"This being some kind of, well, plan . . . that's a lot bigger than all of us. I thought it was bullshit, too, just like you do."

"And now you don't?"

"Less than I did." N'Doch notices he's the one moving around abruptly, nervously, and Köthen who's steady and still. "Listen, man, what you gotta see is we're here and we're stuck with it. Neither me nor the girl has any real power over this situation, 'cept what we can ask from the dragons." He halts his pacing by pressing his back hard against the balcony railing, willing the little engine to stop its frantic revving. He's not used to acting like somebody's big brother. "Look, I can't give you the technical explanation for all this weird shit, but I do know I ain't no warlock and she ain't no witch. So give it a rest, whadda ya say? Save your revenge for later, so we can all concentrate on keeping each other alive."

And then he can't help himself. He just has to add, "And maybe later, it won't look all that important anyway."

"You mean, when I've become properly committed to the quest?"

"I didn't say that, but hey, stranger things have happened. Like to me, for instance."

"You are welcome to your quest, friend N'Doch. I remain respectfully unconvinced."

N'Doch uncrosses his arms. Now this *is* progress. His actual name out of the man's mouth, rather than "hey, you" or some epithet. "Okay. Whatever. Look on it as a kind of working vacation. But if you could just . . ."

The baron lifts a warning finger. "Your point is taken. Enough."

"You got it, man."

Köthen looks away, as if something in the treetops has caught his interest. "One thing more. If I am to believe myself part of this 'plan,' as you call it, I have a question."

"Yeah, what's that?"

Köthen turns back to him deadpan. "Where's *my* dragon?"

N'Doch's thoughts shoot off in several directions, but he's saved from having to settle on one of them when Stoksie comes limping briskly around the curve with the girl firmly in tow.

"Doncha be lettin' huh run roun' lone, na."

"Why? Brenda'll think she's spying or something?" N'Doch slings one arm lightly around her shoulders. He wonders if the little man's concern is for the girl's safety or for his own reputation in the camp. He hopes it's both.

"Sumpin li' dat. Giv'er a nexcuse, an' she'll make it hard fer yus."

"Gotcha. Thanks, man."

"No prob." And like it really isn't, Stoksie beckons the men to lean over the railing while he maps out the camp for them. A circling gesture marks the bustling tree-shaded area nestled within the sweep of the building. "All dat's da Mall."

N'Doch chokes back a grin. "The mall, huh?"

"Yeah. Sleep up heah, eat 'n do bizness down dea. Y'know?"

N'Doch nods. Amazing how words slip in and out of meaning. When he was a kid, a favorite fantasy was being let loose in an American mall with a pocket full of someone else's credit. He looks down, sees a pair of older women pouring water into a wide trough dug around one of the taller trees. All the shade trees have troughs like that. "So where do ya have fun?"

"All ovah, na?"

"Good. Think I'm gonna like it here." And for some reason, he does. Maybe it's the trees, or maybe it's being back among folks closer to his own color. Or maybe it's just the easy way Stoksie has about him—makes people relax, like he's got nothing to prove, 'cept that he's honest and likable. A useful manner for a salesman. N'Doch tries to imagine what the big space out there was once: big parking lot, probably, planted around with fancy greenery, a big neon sign somewhere and the awful kind of landscape lights that turn the shrubbery gross shades of pink and blue and orange. He glances around and above, admiring the undulating rise of the terraces. He's backed off his imitation of the local accent. Stoksie understands him well enough. "So . . . when you figure this place was built?"

"Oh, reel ole place, dis. Mebbe a cent, y'know? Mebbe more. Fore my daddy's daddy, leas'. Dat's ole granpa Ben Stokes, him I only heard tell of. Dis place wuz wuna da las' ta go, roun' heah. Das wha' ma da alwuz say."

"Last to go?" N'Doch hopes the girl's calmed down enough to be listening real close while he pumps their host for information.

"Y'know, ta fall outa da loop." Stoksie parks his elbows more comfortably on the railing and eases the weight off his hip. N'Doch can tell there's a favorite old story coming, like the ones his own old people used to tell, over and over, never tiring of them, finding comfort in the familiarity. "Dis how ma da alwuz tell it. He wuz Reuben Stokes like me. I'ma junyer. Anyhow, he say peeble usda come heah up from Albin, or frum da sout'—Bigapple, mebbe—lon' time sin'. Den dey stop. Or dey come 'n wanna stay. Cuz y'know, when it git bad, it git bad down deah fust, an' it come on fas'. So dey come runnin up heah, lotsa fokes, only dey can' pay no moah. Den mebbe dey do work heah, y'know?"

"To pay their board?"

Stoksie doesn't seem to know that word. "Whadevah. But dey's too minny a dem, and final' deah ain' no pay, noweah."

N'Doch pulls out a word culled from American vids. "No cash, you mean?"

"Ri'. Leas' not heah. Mebbe down Bluridge way." Stoksie scratches his bald head, gazing up into the dusty pine boughs while he muses a bit on this idea. "Mebbe some still down deah, na."

"You trade down there?"

"Nah, noway. Gotta have sumbig firepowah, ya wanna do biz down deah. Sum-big."

"Bigger crews down there, you mean?"

"No crews deah, doncha know? All sorta sumbitch gubbermints, regulatin' da shit outa ev'ryting. Ev'ry lil valley gotta gubbermint. Pain inna butt."

N'Doch settles into a more comfortable lean on the railing. The girl sticks close beside him. "So the governments are like the crews down there?"

"No way! Whachu sayin? Da crews nevah pull dat sorta shit! No way!"

"Right. Okay." The little man's pure outrage makes N'Doch grin. "So, you ever been down there, just to go?"

"Almos' got der. Got far as Deecee one time, wi' ma da, dat's Reuben Seenyer. Me jus' a boy. Yu cud still go deah den."

"Not now?"

"Not easy, 'less yu gotta boat. A real kinda boat, wit alotta teet', y'know?" Stoksie cackles, miming the clashing of giant jaws and the recoil of giant guns.

N'Doch's ears perk up. "There's people around with boats like that?"

"Down deah, dey's sum still. Leas' deah usta be. Mebbe dey's all rusted up na, y'know?"

"Old, you mean?"

"Nah, c'mon." Stoksie shakes his head impatiently. "Say it rain alla time down deah."

"Yeah?"

"How yu like dat, na? Down deah, alla time. Up heah, notta drop. 'Cep all dis salt. Ain' needer place kin grow a gud feelda corn no moah."

"No rain at all, huh?" N'Doch finds himself watching the women below as they water the trees, all of them, one by one.

Stoksie shrugs. "Na 'n den, inna winta. Yusda get moah, even sinz I wuz growin'. Less 'n less. Keep on dis way, doan know how we'll git on. Why, yu got rain up nort?"

"Where I'm from, no, not enough."

"Da story alla roun. 'Cep Bluridge. Dey got rain 'n dey got pay." He waves his arm toward the tents and caravans. "Me, I'ma ole man heah. Mosta dese peeble nevah herda pay. Dey still got pay up nort'?"

"Nah. All trade there." N'Doch hasn't a clue, if the truth be known. He so badly wants to ask the question right out: please please please, what year is it? But he's sure he'd blow their cover, such as it is. "Like here, yeah?"

"All trade. Betcha."

He tries to sneak up on the data issue. "So what was Albin like, before?"

"Nise, I guess. Lotsa peebles. Lotta rain den, too, dey say. Snow, even. Nise place, y'know? Wasa capidal."

A capital. Of what? N'Doch pictures the ruined, flooded, deserted city, and is seized by a kind of panicky despair. He decides it doesn't really matter when it happened. Point is, it did. Global warming. The planet is simultaneously drying up and drowning. What a friggin' waste! The coincidence that he's traveling with two dragons named Earth and Water who are sure they have serious business to take care of is not entirely lost on him, but the possibilities make his head hurt. Too much thinking's gone on in there for one day. One very long day. N'Doch yawns and tries to hide it.

Stoksie shoves back from the railing, dusting his hands together. "C'mon na. Time ta innerduce yu ta Blin' Rachel."

He makes them lock the door. N'Doch pockets the key. They follow Stoksie along the balcony and descend a hidden staircase at the far end of the curve. N'Doch decides it's either cleverness or some superior authority on their guide's part that they don't pick up Brenda the guard dog until they're at least halfway 'round the so-called mall. Even then, she and her entourage hold at a respectful ten paces behind, pretending like they're out for their own little evening stroll and just happen to be carrying all their guns. Stoksie's rolling limp sets a stiff pace down a gravel path through pines and brushy undergrowth, heading toward the sound of the waterfall. N'Doch is excited. He's never seen a real waterfall before. He imagines something like Victoria before it went dry, or old Niagara, from the travel vids. Who knows? Maybe it is Niagara. He's in America, isn't he? To be out of the sun is a major relief. But he wonders if Blind Rachel always greets her visitors out here in the woods.

As they near the water, the air softens with moisture, and the bushes lining the path get taller and fuller, harder to see through. For the last hundred meters, they glide through a sort of green tunnel, leaf walls on both sides, dappled shade overhead, doused in mist and scented with pine.

"Ohhh," breathes the girl.

"Like home for her," N'Doch replies to Stoksie's glance. "In Europe."

"Yu say?" Stoksie looks impressed. "Still?"

N'Doch vamps. "Just homesick, y'know?"

"Sure, sure. Long way to Urop."

Then suddenly, around a leafy bend, there is the waterfall.

It is not Victoria Falls, or the Niagara of N'Doch's fervid imagination. In fact, he's amazed that such a sad thin trickle could make so much noise. Maybe because it falls from such a height—fifteen, twenty meters at least—or because it's broken and deflected at so many points of its fall before it plunges into the narrow rock-lined pool at its base. Or it's the towering rock face that gives birth to it, echoing and amplifying its sound. But N'Doch's disappointment passes quickly. It doesn't need to be Niagara. After the lifeless, swelling river and the parched lands below, this cool leaf-scented air and the crystalline clarity of the water nearly bring him to his knees, as he sees Stoksie has been, groaning faintly as he lands.

Oddly, it's Köthen who reads the significance of this gesture. Quietly, he beckons them downward in respect at the water's edge. He mimics also the little man's dipping of one hand lightly into the pool, to touch his forehead and lips with dampened fingertips. The moment is over quickly, like the water ritual that welcomed them into camp. No heavy-duty ceremony. Stoksie groans again, rising, then spreads his arms as if to embrace the entire rock face, the silvered thread of falling water, the clear and turbulent pool. "Dis heah Blin' Rachel!"

All three of them are wily enough by now not to crane their heads around in search of . . . a person. But there is a moment of utter stillness, which Stoksie apparently takes for reverence, for he beams at them as if they have fulfilled his every expectation. Then he turns the sweetest of gazes on Pitbull Brenda, who has been observing from the head of the path.

"Nise, ha?" he grins.

"Sehr schön!" says the girl.

"Nice," N'Doch agrees.

But Stoksie wants a bit more. "Whachu got up nort'? Water Dragon nise like dis?"

One more piece of the puzzle falls into place. It's like naming the desert tribes after the oases they claim. In a world reverting to desert, it makes a lot of sense. N'Doch looks up to where the slim cascade shoots forth from a shadowed fissure in the rock. There's another thirty meters of sheer rock above that. He knows without asking that this water is drinkable and safe. "Nice, yeah. But . . . y'know, different." He reaches for a memory, even a fantasy, of safe, flowing water, and comes up dry. "Later, you visit. I'll introduce you."

"Mebbe, mebbe." Stoksie's already counting up his inventory. "Got good trade up nort'?"

N'Doch lets his grin go sly. "Depend on whachu bringin'."

"Yu'll seeit den, an' not befoah!" The little man claps him on the back, hugely satisfied. "Hey! Yu wanna washup?" N'Doch notices how the main pool spills over into a series of smaller pools, partly hidden by the screening greenery. The first of these lower pools has a steady stream of people carting containers back and forth from camp to dip and fill in its clear, chill depths. The second, wider and shallower, is lively with naked bathers. N'Doch does a kind of double take, sure he's mistaken. But no, the pool is full of men, women, and children, scrubbing away, rinsing each other diligently. Young folks and old folks, gasping, laughing with the cold, though it looks a bit more like work than fun. N'Doch suspects it's the frigid water making them all so energetic. In the third pool down, continuing the organized use of this precious unpolluted source, laundry is being done. N'Doch knows this swirling race of liquid ice will cut him to the bone, but his opportunities for bathing were infrequent at Deep Moor and now he's got another time's layers of dust and grit and sweat smeared all over him. He nods to Stoksie. "I'm there!"

"Alla yus, na!" the little man waves, turning toward the lower pools, already stripping off his worn and dusty layers. But the girl is blushing furiously and shaking her head to N'Doch in mute appeal.

Köthen, who has knelt again briefly to douse his face with cold water, wipes his beard on his sleeves and offers her a brisk bow. "If my lady prefers, I will see her back to the chamber beforehand."

The girl blinks at him. She can't help glancing at N'Doch in confusion. "My lord is most kind," she murmurs.

"Few who know me would agree, my lady."

N'Doch isn't sure if this is better or worse. What's better for sure is that he not get any more involved in the issues between them than he is already. "Good man, Dolph," he says cheerfully. He digs the key out of his pocket and tosses it to Köthen. "Hurry back. I'll save you a spot at poolside."

Baron Köthen walked her back along the woodland path and up the rickety stairs in silence. Unlocking the door of the cavelike room, he removed the lock and hung it on the inside of the door. Then he bowed again, as one would to a respected stranger, and handed her the silvery key-thing.

"I would suggest, my lady, that you lock yourself in. We will return soon enough to escort you to dinner."

With the air of a man who is discharging his moral duties, he insisted that she try the key in the lock, and stood by until she had called her competence with it through the safely fastened door. Then she heard his steps recede along the balcony—rather quickly, she thought.

Erde found this newly solicitous behavior bewildering. Though it was a relief not to have him growling and glowering and calling her "witch," this chill and distant formality was only a slight improvement. But at least it was one she could live with.

The moment she thought she could suppose him to be out of sight, she unlocked the door and slipped outside, locking it again behind her. Hopefully, his passage back to the waterfall would occupy the hostile and suspicious Brenda for long enough for one very quiet girl to sneak past into the woods. It was time to find a secret place for the dragons to come to roost.

A bit of sheltering rock, an open space among the pines, some handy and concealing shrubbery. The hiding place had not been hard to find, and it only needed to be free of prying eyes while the dragon transported himself and Lady Water there safely. Once they were settled, Brenda herself could stroll right by without spotting anything unusual. Both dragons were becoming expert at hiding in plain sight.

They were restless when they arrived, materializing like two giant shadows out of the gathering dusk. Erde had hoped for time to curl up next to the dragon for a while, soaking up comfort before she must return for the evening meal, and a long night in a dank and cheerless cell. But Earth would not settle. Like an old dog unable to find a comfortable spot, he nosed around and around the little clearing, sat down, shifted about, got up and lumbered around a bit more. Lady Water stood to one side, rubbing her velvet-blue hide against a tree trunk. Her swim in the river, she said, had left her itchy all over.

IT'S YOUR MIND THAT'S ITCHY, SISTER.

Perhaps. But even breathing the air here is like swimming in filth.

Erde gave up chasing after the dragon and sat down on a convenient rock to listen in. She noticed that her throat did feel rather raw, like when there was green wood burning in the castle hearths.

THE SUMMONER'S CALL IS FADING AS WE TRAVEL INLAND.

Not fading, brother. Being interfered with.

WE DO NOT KNOW FOR SURE . . .

I think we do know. I think he is deliberately blocking the signal.

Erde guessed it was Lord Fire they were squabbling about. In the way of dragons, they might go on exploring the fine points of this debate until halfway to dawn. Perhaps she could hurry it along.

HE KNOWS WE ARE COMING, THEN?

He knows we will come, sooner or later. Each step he takes to deflect our approach brings us closer by calling attention to his actions. I wonder if he has considered this inevitability.

Earth rumbled disconsolately, got up, moved two paces, and lay down again.

WE MUST CONFRONT HIM. THEN WE WILL KNOW THE TRUTH.

YOU KNOW WHERE HE IS, THEN?

THESE GOOD PEOPLE WILL LEAD US TO HIM.

THEY WILL? HOW?

LISTEN CAREFULLY IN THE CAMP. THE CLUES WILL APPEAR. HE DOES NOT KNOW HOW TO LIVE QUIETLY.

Erde got up from her rock and went to lean against him.

CAN'T N'DOCH LISTEN? I'D RATHER STAY HERE WITH YOU. WHAT IF THESE PEOPLE INTEND TO MURDER US IN OUR BEDS AND STEAL ALL OUR WORLDLY GOODS . . . ?

Such as they are.

WELL, I KNOW IT'S NOT MUCH, BUT THEY DO SEEM VERY OC-CUPIED WITH . . . THINGS.

CHILD, THEY LIVE AS THEY MUST, AS SCAVENGERS OFF THE CORPSE OF THE LAND.

Lady Water ceased rubbing against her tree and came to join them.

There's one more bit of bad news they have ahead of them.

Both girl and dragon looked her way.

Their precious stream is dying, along with everything else.

OH! HOW CAN THAT BE?

The deep source that feeds the spring is drying up. There is another aquifer below, but it is blocked.

YOU CAN FEEL THE WATER THROUGH THE GROUND?

I always know where the water is. In three dimensions, downward through the earth, upward into the sky.

YOUR PARDON, MY LADY. I DIDN'T KNOW.

Did you ever ask?

SISTER, YOU ARE IRRITABLE.

No kidding.

The blue dragon turned and pranced away, her tail lashing.

IT'S HIS FAULT, YOU SEE. SHE'S TOO MUCH IN THE WORLD OF HER ANTAGONIST OPPOSITE.

LORD FIRE, YOU MEAN? IS HE HER OPPOSITE?

FIRE AND WATER? WOULD HE NOT BE? IS SHE FORGIVEN?

OF COURSE SHE IS.

Earth had finally settled, it seemed. He put his great horned head down and got very still and quiet. Erde snuggled against him happily, until suddenly he spoke up again.

PERHAPS I COULD UNBLOCK IT.

It was a while before Erde understood that he was talking about the underground water.

OH, DRAGON, COULD YOU TRY?

THE SLIGHT SHIFTING OF A FISSURE, PERHAPS. A DEGRADA-TION OF THE BLOCKAGE. THE APPROACH WILL HAVE TO BE

CAREFULLY CONSIDERED. I WOULD NOT WISH TO CAUSE ITS
FINAL DESTRUCTION INSTEAD.

YOU ARE THE CLEVEREST OF DRAGONS! YOU WILL NOT FAIL!

Though the dying stream was terribly unfortunate, Erde
was delighted that the dragon would have a useful project
to soothe his restless mind. Just pondering it now, he was
calmer.

The sun had nearly set. She must return to the camp,
but now she did so with a lighter heart.

DRAGONS! I'M OFF TO LISTEN—VERY CAREFULLY—AND I
WILL REPORT TO YOU EVERYTHING I HEAR!

NOT EVERYTHING, I HOPE. HOW WILL WE GET ANY WORK
DONE HERE?

CHAPTER TWENTY-FIVE

When Son Luco knocks on her door two hours after dinner, so much later than the priest has ever come visiting before, Paia knows it isn't a social call. Not that Luco is often given to such civilities, but it's the lingering startlement in his blue eyes that puts her on alert, and his comfortable civilian clothes underneath the gold Temple robe tossed on so hastily, its complex fastenings only half done up. He leaves the big door open when she invites him in, as if to head off any possible suspicion—on the part of the righteous Honor Guard in the hall, she supposes—of improper behavior within the Temple's highest authorities.

At least, Paia notes wearily, he's left his entourage in the corridor.

"Mother Paia," he says formally, then flounders to a halt. His startled eyes seem to be warning her, not just to behave, which he always does, but of some graver danger. He's had a shock, she decides, and she's sure she can guess the source of it. "Mother Paia," he begins again, "I have come to inform you that you are to be graced by the God's Decree with a Special Presentation of the Suitors in the Hall of Audiences, first thing tomorrow after the morning Call to Prayer. The God himself will honor us with his Presence."

Paia is practiced by now at looking delighted when she isn't. Certainly Luco can't believe that her bland and welcoming smile, maintained just now with such effort, reflects her true response to this news. But why make him suffer any further for her own transgressions? "The God honors me indeed." She tries to draw Luco farther into the room, away from listening ears, by offering him the only chair in the room. But of course, in public, he would never sit down in the presence of the High Priestess. "Did he bring this wonderful news himself?"

"He just now left me."

Does she detect a singeing of Luco's brows, or of his shining locks of hair? Paia lowers her voice as well as her glance. "Poor Luco. Was he in an awful rage?"

"He was . . . terrifying."

"Yes." She turns away, to the comfort of her window, and twitches the drapes aside to gaze out in the red dusk. The sun goes down so very late at this time of year, she muses. "Well, Luco. Extremely short notice for you to be organizing such an event. I hope it will not prove too taxing for you and your staff."

"What the God wills . . ." Luco replies mechanically.

She is so used to the fear now, she barely registers it. "What the God wills. Thank you, First Son. I will see you, then, in the morning."

Because she has already reconsidered the uses to which she can put the right Suitor, Paia goes to bed charged with purpose and resolve. If this is how the God seeks to punish her, so be it. But now she must charm and soothe him sufficiently to preserve some power of choice in the matter. She falls asleep planning how she will dress, so carefully— for him. She doesn't care what the Suitors see or think. They will want her anyway, no matter how she presents herself. There is probably no higher goal among the Faithful than the High Priestess's bed. Paia can only pity them.

At some point later, she comes suddenly awake. She's sure she has heard someone call out her name. Lying still and listening, she can almost feel the echoes fade away, like receding ripples in the darkness. But she hears nothing.

She reaches under her pillows for the God's little gun, then lets it lie there. The call—probably not a call at all, just the tail of a forgotten dream—it seemed to her like a summons. But not the God's familiar and irresistible command. A softer appeal. Almost an invitation. Paia holds the vanished moment in her memory, probing it carefully. The voice was like a breath of wind, and it came wrapped in blue. In blue.

In the darkness of her bed, Paia smiles. How absurd dreams often are.

But the notion of summoning now takes up residence in her brain, and will not be ignored. *A True Recipe for Raising Dragons.* Fully awake until her adrenaline rush subsides, she stretches out long in her cool and silken sheets and tries to imagine how she would accomplish such a thing.

When the God calls her, it's a compulsion. She cannot deny, only answer. She can't for a moment consider compelling the God in return. But perhaps something else might bring him. If she was in danger, or in need, and if there was no one around to aid her, would he hear her then, as she hears him, like a ringing in her soul? Or would he come if she . . . begged him?

She contemplates the voice that just woke her, how it vibrated through the air like something physical, not just a sound but a force. Then her own summons should be like that, a line of force reaching out to the God where he lies sleeping in the heated perpetual night of his Sanctum. Let it fasten itself to him, twining like a young vine, up around his shining ivory claw, to pull itself taut, taut with her imperative.

The darkness around her shudders. Like tinder bursting into flame, he appears in an explosion of light, bellowing as he materializes, as if unable to contain his fury but even less able, within the bounds of this smaller room, to express it satisfactorily.

"What are you doing?" He is glowing like blown embers. "Are you mad? *What are you doing?*"

Paia is too stunned to produce sound, never mind a coherent word. She has done it. She called him, and he came. But he is not happy about it.

"Ignorant woman! You meddle with forces you know ` nothing of!"

If she could ever believe that he slept in his man-form, she'd swear he's been dragged straight out of a very human bed. His hair is wild and the clothing he's snatched at for this hasty manifestation is disheveled and minimal. His chest is bare past his navel and glitters with hard, golden scales, as if he couldn't be bothered to effect a full transformation.

Nevertheless, she is thrilled by her success. The first words she manages are not an apology. "If I am ignorant, my lord, it is you who have kept me that way."

"Yes! For your own good! And mine, which is all that matters!" He is moving faster than any human could, practically spinning in outraged frustration. "How dare you summon me? HOW DARE YOU? I am the God here! What are you thinking? With your clumsiness, they'll hear you for sure! You'll give us away entirely!"

"Hear what?" Paia remembers this implication from before, that she is somehow a danger to him. "Hear my thoughts?"

"Well, I do!" He whirls past her, and heat settles around her like a toxic cloud. "Do I not?"

"But . . ." Paia knows she's meant to cower, but she's too amazed and curious. "Who are 'they'?"

"The enemy, foolish woman! Mine. Yours. Those who wish to bring an end to us and to all we've made here. And you, with your childish games, your stupid, clumsy experimenting, are going to help them do it!"

"But I said nothing! I only *thought* . . ."

"Idiot! Thought is the language of my enemies!"

"How am I suppose to know that?" Suddenly she's on her feet in the middle of the bed, yelling at him. Yelling at the God. Paia hardly recognizes herself. "First it was the notes, then you suspected my paintings! How can I know what to do if you never tell me anything? How can I learn to help, when you call me a pawn and treat me like one?"

He halts his wild gyrations as if a switch has been pulled. He stares at her. His hair swirls around him with a restless mind of its own. "What gives you the deluded idea that I need your help?"

"You do!" Now that he's still, she sees there is even stubble darkening his jaw. "Look at yourself! What kind of a god are you? You're a mess!"

"This? *This?*" He scoffs, yet flicks a glance at the sliver of window, as if seeking his reflection in it. "This is not me! This is a mere simu . . ."

"It is your state of mind made manifest! And it tells me you need all the help you can get!" She's appalled that she's said it, for appearances mean so much to him, but once she has, she knows it's true. The shapeless anxiety she'd felt for him just before his tantrum in the tower begins to take on substance. She begins to believe in these enemies. She begins to sense them herself. And having hurled insults at him without immediate repercussion brings a kind of calm. In sudden earnestness, Paia sinks to her knees among the bundled bedclothes, knowing finally what she really needs to say to him. She brings her palms together in a Temple gesture of supplication. "My lord Fire. Why must you insist that fear is the only way to rule? Let me be what I am meant to be to you, what I am destined to be. Let me grow. Let me use the gifts I have to work against these enemies that plague you. Let me love you and serve you in every way I am able to."

The God's hands are in his hair, taming its impatient life, raking it into submission. His eyes are like bright contemptuous suns. "Better if you had stayed a pliant nestling! How weak and tragic to be tied to the progress of years!"

"Because I am human, yes, but who better to go out into the world and be your voice among humans?"

"I am my own voice, as you can see. And I have other, more compliant human voices working for me already, here and in places you know nothing of!"

"Luco. Loyal Son Luco. Who lives in terror of you, like every other human . . . except me. Luco speaks only of duty and obedience. Who will go to the Faithful and speak for you of love?"

"Love?" He spits it out like an obscenity. "I need their service, their devotion! I have no need of their love!"

"But you do, my lord! So that when your enemies arrive, the Faithful will rise for you rather than against you."

"They wouldn't dare!"

"Why not be as sure of their love as you are of their terror?"

"How argumentative you have become, my priestess!" But the faintest shadow dims his glare, and like the sun setting behind the mountains, he decides to end his tantrum, as if it no longer served his purposes. He comes to stand at the foot of the bed, his arms neatly folded, his garments more decorously draped. "You have some scheme in mind already."

Paia smiles. "How clever my lord is." He drinks in the flattery more from need and habit than from belief. Flirting is a game he's always played to put her ill at ease, but it can work both ways, she sees that now. "My scheme is simple. I preach your virtues each day in the Temple. Let me go out among the Faithful and preach to them in their villages, on their own ground." She settles gracefully back on her heels, kneeling like a child before him. "When my father was alive, I loved and feared him both, as I do you now. If your Faithful only fear you, my lord Fire, it is not true devotion. Let me change that. Let me be your ambassador of love."

Maybe her preaching skills have improved. Like a merchant counting up potential sales, the God looks intrigued. "When?"

"Tomorrow. The next day. Whenever Luco can arrange it."

"In such a hurry to race out from under my protecting wing, my priestess? A trip outside is a dangerous undertaking. Have you any real idea what it means when I say that the rule of law ends at the Temple Gate?" He regards her with half-lidded eyes. "If I allow it, it will seem that I care little for your safety."

"Well, my lord, if I am the thorn in your side that you claim me to be, then you will be glad to be rid of me. And I can be on the lookout for your enemies." He is so immediately and obviously torn by this suggestion that Paia almost laughs. The Ambivalent God. Perhaps if she does get into trouble out there, he will not come winging to her rescue. She has often expected to die by his hand, but has never for a moment thought he would not protect her from dangers other than himself. A terrifying yet exhilarating possibility, ripe with implications of true freedom. "Then I can go?"

He nods, the faintest motion of his gilded head.

"And we can cancel the Suitors for tomorrow?"

An even fainter nod.

"Oh, wonderful! You are the wisdom of the ages, my lord! You are the beginning and the end!" Paia stretches out in front of him, as sensuously as a cat, heady with victory and her new sense of power. "Perhaps on my Visitation I will come across a proper Suitor, my lord. One that pleases us both." She leans forward and murmurs, "You can watch."

CHAPTER TWENTY-SIX

Dinner in Blind Rachel's camp was a disorganized and communal event, held at sunset around the cooking hearths clustered in the center of the big dirt lawn. There was more food in the cook pots than Erde expected, given the lifeless countryside and the lack of visible farmsteads. Provisions were shared, but she could deduce no agreed-upon plan to the preparation of them. Everyone—perhaps thirty or forty adults and a few children, surprisingly few—jostled from hearth to hearth with their tin bowls and cups, chatting, tasting, eating what was ready to eat, and encouraging the progress of whatever still had a while to go.

No formal hospitality was offered to the guests, nothing more than "here's food, take a seat." But Stoksie took pains to borrow bowls and implements for them, then urged them into the crowds at the cook fires to claim portions of stewed rabbit and ash-roasted roots and crisp chunks of fresh bread. When he'd found them space to sit, away from the heat of the fires and where no dogs and chickens were prowling, he nodded happily and wandered off, food in hand.

With the sun at last sinking between the trees, the worst of the heat was easing off. But Erde envied the men their bath. Both of them looked clean and refreshed. Baron Köthen's hair was still wet, slicked back with his fingers like a young boy's. She found it hard not to gaze at him stupidly, so instead studied her bowl and its contents, pondering the perilous beauty of men. For a while, they all ate in silence, finally willing to admit how hungry they'd been.

She watched N'Doch for clues about the safety of the food, about how to behave. She saw how he sniffed at each edible, when no one was looking, then tasted it cautiously before stuffing it in his mouth. Then he emptied half his bowl before slowing down enough to report on his adventures in the pool.

"Tinkers?" Erde thought it a curious thing for these people to call themselves, since it seemed obvious that no one here was manufacturing anything.

"Meant 'gypsies' more, in my time. The crews each claim a basic territory, but they move around a lot, in and out of each other's turf, making trade. That's why Stoksie didn't put an arrow through us first thing. That and the fact that we look like we got something to offer. Like he says, healthy." N'Doch tore off a fist-sized hunk of bread. "Good food."

"Camp food," said Köthen.

"Hey, you didn't have to kill it, and you didn't have to cook it. Don't complain." N'Doch mopped up pink juice, then waved the dripping bread in an airy circle. "This here's Blind Rachel's base, the only place they got anything permanent. They keep it secret from everyone but the other Tinker crews. When I got down to trade right off, it was sorta like giving the Tinker password. Pretty good, huh?"

"Lucky," Köthen muttered.

"Nah." N'Doch grinned. "Good instincts, man. See why you gotta keep me around? Anyway, these folk aren't fighters, they're businessmen." He circled the bread once more around the clearing. "But this . . . this they'd fight to keep."

"Who would try to take it from them?" Erde asked.

"Look around you, girl! Anyone would take it who could, 'cept another Tinker. They got an agreement."

"For the water, milady, for the water." Köthen was now only picking at his stew.

N'Doch nodded, his mouth full of bread. "They say there's not as much of it as there used to be, but it's still enough to fight over, when there's no other water around." He gestured at Köthen's bowl. "You better eat up, man, or somebody else'll eat it for you."

"Yourself, for instance?"

"Mebbe."

Erde saw that a further adjustment had occurred between them. The baron now seemed to find sour amusement in N'Doch's needling. "But why haven't we seen farms? Are there towns or villages left anywhere?"

N'Doch swallowed so that he wouldn't choke. "In the valleys, or down on the flats. Wherever there's still some bit of drinkable water."

"None of it to compare with the purity of Blind Rachel. Or so we are told." Köthen rested his bowl on one knee, with what seemed like genuine interest. "Nonetheless, the food staples are grown in the villages. The Tinkers keep livestock and limited kitchen gardens, but they are too nomadic to be reliable farmers. The craftsmen as well live in the villages."

"Yeah, and the Tinker crews move all the food and goods up and down between all these strung-out villages. The villages don't travel: too busy defending what they got. So the Tinkers are the transport system." N'Doch eyed Köthen's food. "So, you gonna eat it or not?"

"Off me, whelp! I'll eat in my own time!"

Erde blotted her lips delicately with the hem of her sleeve. "You discovered all this information while bathing?"

N'Doch swiveled a huge grin on her, his eyes and teeth bright in the growing darkness. "You'd be amazed how friendly people can be when you get yourselves naked together!"

Were it not for the baron's quiet snort, Erde might have been able to fight down her blush. Not that they would notice in the dim light, but she felt it herself, as a brand of her increasingly tiresome innocence. It really was time, she decided, to learn how to conceal her feelings, rather than perpetually wearing them on her sleeve for all to see and mock at. Or to learn to make a performance of them, as N'Doch did. She thought the former more likely, in her case.

"No love lost between these people and the villages," Köthen observed as solemnly as if he'd never cracked a smile.

"Yeah. Those flatlanders sound like a nasty bunch. 'Course, they got a hard life, but that's no excuse. Like, a

Tinker'd never marry out. Well, I'm not sure they get married at all, but you know what I mean. Anyway, we were talking to this guy Luther Somebody. He says there's some villages they won't even go to. Some sort of religious fanatics who think everybody's got to agree with them."

"Another holy war?" Erde had hoped the Future would be done with such things.

"We were just getting into that when Bulldog Brenda decided we were taking up too much pool time."

Köthen speared a bit of rabbit meat out of a puddle of gravy. "There are factions within the camp as well as outside of it."

"I'll say. What a major pain in the ass she's getting to be."

"But there's no apparent leader." Köthen glanced around, inviting their response, as if to say, what am I missing?

N'Doch was unhelpful. His head was up, listening. "Don't think you'll find one, Dolph. It's not that kind of a group."

Erde frowned gently. "Not Stoksie?"

"No way. He's more like . . . an elder. Like whatisname . . . Luther. He's another one."

From across the irregular circle of fires came a few experimental notes from a pipe and the strum of a stringed instrument being tuned. Stoksie was headed in their direction, his dark face flushed with the last glow of sunset. His progress was slow, not just due to his limp, but because he stopped continually along the way with this group or that to chat or exchange a laugh. Erde was surprised how comfortable she already felt among these Tinkers, more so than she had with anyone in N'Doch's time, except for his grandfather, Master Djawara. With that thought, she put out a mental query. But Earth had not yet decided how to try unblocking the water.

"Lack of leadership is a fatal weakness," Köthen observed quietly.

"Think of it as the leadership being shared. Can you get your head around that, yer lordship?" N'Doch set his well-mopped bowl aside and unfolded his legs. "You guys hang, huh? I'm going visiting."

The minute he hears the music, N'Doch loses interest in food crops or issues of leadership. He lifts his long body off the ground and wanders off casually among the hearths, nodding to the men, patting the kids, and returning the smiles of the women with promising smiles of his own. He even grins at Bulldog Brenda, who scowls back. He doesn't care. The music is what matters now.

He finds the music makers off to one side, three of them around a small fire of their own, like a side pocket to the main table. The sweet woodwind he'd heard is a reed flute, played by a crinkly-faced woman with dark, frizzy hair. The drums are two little lap drums, and the drummer's about his own age with big, fast hands, real eager. He's already wearing a zoned-out glaze, N'Doch notes enviously, and he hasn't even got himself started yet.

But it's the guitar player who draws N'Doch's attention most: an old black man with no teeth left in front, and gnarled stubs of fingers. The guitar's an ancient four-string acoustic in as bad shape as the man is, with a worn bit of glass stuck up under the strings near the top frets. But as the old man bends over it, his ear nearly flat on the box, his wrecked hands dance over the strings like butterflies, and quiet but magical music comes out. He picks his way through a little melody, trying it out, as if making it up on the spot. N'Doch is in love.

He stands in the shadows, listening, until the old man finishes. Then he moves forward with a wave and hunkers down an easy distance away. "Hey, nice," he says.

The old man raises his head from the guitar and looks his way, slow and off-focus. He's blind, or nearly so, but sees enough to read the tall stranger's eyes. "Yu play?" His voice is like an old truck engine.

N'Doch shrugs, which is what he's supposed to do. "I play some."

When the old man hands over the guitar, just like that, and the others don't object, N'Doch can't believe his luck. Maybe they're all tired of listening to themselves or something. He's sorry when the man slips the glass shard out from under the strings and pockets it carefully, but hey, beggars can't be choosers. He accepts the guitar reverently and settles it safely in his lap before sticking out his hand. "N'Doch. Water Dragon Crew."

"Yah," huffs the old man. "Marley."

The drummer is Luis, the reed player Ysabel Dominguin. Though they are nowhere near the same color or body type, N'Doch understands they are mother and son. They shake hands around, but the preliminaries are brief, like anywhere he's ever sat down with other musicians. They're all three of them waiting to hear if he's any good.

He doodles around some, like he's allowed to at first, getting the feel of the strings. He tunes a bit, thinking how raging cool it would be if he could come up with a song they know. Then he gives that up for a simple eight bar blues that he knows they'll be able to come in on. In no time at all, they're playing and grinning at each other, and old Marley is clapping those ruined hands on his knees and chest in complex syncopation with Luis. Soon after that, they're attracting attention from around the cook fires. Folks are leaving off conversations that were limping along anyway, abandoning their emptied plates and bringing their filled bellies by to settle down with the music. A woman hauls in a few chunks of wood and the little fire brightens. N'Doch sees that making music means a lot to these folks. No vids or arcade games to fill their evenings. He'd bet they're great storytellers, too. When he moves on to another old blues song, Luis and Ysa segue into it seamlessly. Stoksie brings over Köthen and the girl, then shoulders his way into the circle to drop down beside N'Doch, making the point about who it was who brought him. Even Brenda's listening, but she's just got to show him a frown, though her foot's right there tapping out the time.

When the song is done, N'Doch vamps a bit, waiting for the others' permission to solo. Ysa nods, so he slides into the simple, plaintive melody of an old Wolof love song, lingering through it once, ever so sweetly, then slamming into the jazzier version that he'd written for himself a few years back. It's a show-off piece that he's used to playing on a keyboard, but somehow his fingers still find a way among the strings. When he's done, he's worked up a sweat all over again but the moment is worth it, 'cause the little crowd goes ballistic, hooting and stamping and yelling for an encore.

N'Doch looks at Marley. He doesn't want to be upstaging the man completely. Marley grins and crosses his arms. As N'Doch bows his head over the guitar, thinking what to play next, he hears the dragon in his head.

Play them Sedou. Play me down around that campfire. I'm bored of hanging out in the woods with my earnest brother . . .

N'Doch keeps his face smooth and lets his eyes roam casually, seeking out the girl. She's heard. She's frowning a little, but she's already preparing Köthen. His blond head's bent low, listening, as he crouches beside her, very careful to keep his distance.

Everyone okay with that? What does Dolph say?

He says he'll be pleased to renew our acquaintance.

What's the story?

That you have better security than they ever guessed.

N'Doch shrugs. *I'm leaving that to you, then.*

Thas cool, little brother.

The song as he'd sung it at Deep Moor is in French. He hopes it'll add to their cover, give the Europe thing a little more depth. The dragon doesn't sing it with him this time, at least not at first, so N'Doch is intensely aware of the sound of his own voice, husky but strong and true, soaring through the dusk-time stillness of this foreign mountaintop. There are new notes there he didn't know he had, and new resonances. And the song. He knew it was a good song because it conjured Sedou at the highest moment of his life. But now he's thrilled to learn that the song is a good song all on its own. In fact, it's a beautiful song.

By the third verse, he feels the dragon presence coalescing somewhere off in the woods. These people, he thinks fleetingly, have no idea what they're in for. By the fifth verse, a tall black man is standing at the back of the rapt little crowd, leaning against a wagon wheel and smiling. By the last verse, he is singing along, a deep almost unheard harmony that is so natural, it's not even noticed.

N'Doch draws out the last few measures slowly, and holds tantalizingly before the song's real end. Every eye is on him. He feels his listeners, each of them, as if they were touching his mouth and his eyelids and his hands with loving, grateful fingers. He flattens his picking hand to quiet the strings, and within the space of the sigh before they applaud, he stretches a welcoming arm toward the darkness behind them.

"Folks, I'd like you to meet my brother Sedou."

He knows there was bound to be a commotion, and there is. A lot of gasps and jumping up, knocking over cups and bowls, even a scream or two of fright and a bellow of outrage, more than a few. Like, where did this big guy come from? By the time the knives are out and gleaming nastily in the firelight, N'Doch has set the guitar gently in Marley's lap and stepped through the confusion to Köthen's side, with the girl between them and Sedou behind, like a wall. Then the thing he's worried about happens: Bulldog Brenda swoops up that fat-barreled rifle of hers and levels it at them.

"Call in da res', or yer a dead man."

Sedou spreads his hands genially. His deep voice flows around them like a sweet, cool breeze. "There are no 'rest,' Brenda. I'm all there is."

Her eyes narrow over the gunsight. He knows her name. "Whachu dun wit' my men?"

"Your sentries? Four of them, right? Two women, one man, one boy. The boy hums a lot. Call them if you like. They're fine. They're alert. They were doing their job. They just don't hear as good as they should."

"Yuh? Yu say?" Brenda whistles into the ruddy darkness. Four answering whistles come right back at her.

The mutters rustling among the crowd tell N'Doch they've won already. Easier for these people to convince themselves that this dark and smiling giant slipped through the cordon, under his own clever steam and brilliant stealth, than to wonder how else he could have shown up completely out of nowhere. The truth is often the hardest answer, N'Doch muses. He sheaths his knife, relaxes. Brenda swears a blue streak and sends Charlie and Punk off into the woods to make a personal check on the sentries.

Stoksie says, "Nah mo', na? Speak tru?"

"No more men," Sedou agrees.

But in his mind's eye, N'Doch sees the large rock that

has appeared in a little clearing not far from Blind Rachel's pool. He squeezes the girl's shoulder. "Good work," he whispers. And then the mystery man seals his welcome with a gift, and not even N'Doch can imagine how the dragon got it there.

Stooping back into the shadows under the wagon he'd been discovered by, Sedou picks up a lidded tin bucket by its looped handle and carries it forward to the hearth. Eyes still a little wide, the Tinkers make way for him, murmuring. The bucket sloshes as Sedou sets it down at Stoksie's feet.

"For your hospitality, my brother," he rumbles. "For Blind Rachel."

Stoksie leans over, trying not to appear suspicious, and carefully lifts the lid. "Gimme a light, sum'un." A lantern is handed along to him through the crowd. He holds it up and peers into the bucket. His glance at Sedou is sudden and amazed. "Wha's dis, na?"

Sedou crouches, like a mountain descending, and dips one finger to stir the surface gently. It erupts with a roil of silvery minnows, frantic to escape into deeper, chiller waters. "Breeders, my brother. I heard Blind Rachel could use some."

"Good uns? Hellt'y?"

"All healthy."

"Whea yu gettim?"

The big man smiles and stands back. "Can't say. You know how it is."

"Trade seecrit, ha?" Stoksie accepts this, as any practiced merchant would. His expression is already speculative. How can this sudden resource be best exploited. Others press around him to lean over and stare into the bucket. More gasps and commotion, this time of a friendlier sort, especially as Charlie and Punk are back to report the sentries all well and at their posts, though smarting no doubt from a very recent tongue-lashing. An air of hopeful celebration breaks over the clearing like a summer shower. Eager debates erupt over the proper care and feeding of fish. Schedules and menus are being proposed. Big clay jugs appear and a clear liquid is doled out in judicious helpings.

N'Doch eases away from the crowd to watch Sedou work his magic. Not all of it, he reflects, is dragon magic. Some of it is just pure Sedou. He knows. He remembers how it was, when his brother was alive. Köthen, too, is watching Sedou, his arms folded across his mailed chest and his rugged face tense with concentration, as if answers to his own dilemma might be gained from this close study.

When the first burst of excitement has died down, Stoksie stirs up the crowd again by deputizing the girl-babies Senda and Mari to deliver the fish to their new home. He makes Sedou give them detailed instructions, then sends them off with the bucket slung between them. Two thirds of the camp, and all of the children, trail after them with lanterns and cups of home brew.

N'Doch is thinking about Marley's guitar again when Köthen surprises him, bringing over two half-filled cups and handing him one.

"Here is one thing they do make here. Rather well, I think."

N'Doch passes the cup under his nose and feels the fumes leap up like tiny birds into his nostrils. He takes a sip. "Hooo! Fire water!"

Köthen chuckles, deep and quiet.

"Better watch out," N'Doch warns. "You're gonna slip, and start enjoying yourself."

But Köthen is pondering the gift of fish. "If even half those hatchlings survive, they'll be lucky. But after a few seasons, there'll be a fine catch in that pool. If they're careful, it'll lead to many years of fine catches." He pauses, glances up. "What? What's the matter now?"

"Nothing." N'Doch realizes he's been staring. "Hey, Dolph. When you were . . . y'know, back there . . ."

"At home?"

"Yeah. You, like, must've had a big, what, a castle? With a whole lot of land? And you had to know how to take care of all that land, how to grow things, right? Raise up all your food, take care of the animals? Like the women at Deep Moor do, right? You had to know how to do all that?"

By now, it's Köthen who's staring, with one cocked eyebrow.

N'Doch laughs. "Don't worry, I haven't gone off or anything. It's just a side of you I never saw before, caring about raising fish. You don't think of a lordship caring about fish, or anything that might get his hands dirty."

"But I must care about fish, and crops and fruit and cattle. A landowner must know about such things. Or take on bondsmen who know what he doesn't." Gravely, Köthen drains his cup. "Good husbandry is a great and noble responsibility. If you abuse the land, it will not feed you or your people."

"Right." N'Doch slouches back on one hip. "So tell me about your place, man. What's it like?"

Köthen's gaze darkens. "Remember . . . or perhaps you didn't know . . . I lost my estates when the hell-priest betrayed me. He will have given them to some minion, who will be wreaking the Lord knows what manner of havoc upon them. That sort care nothing for the land, only for the power it brings them. They will use it up and abandon it, and I am powerless to prevent any of it!"

His fist has tightened dangerously around his empty cup. N'Doch reaches over and levers it out of his grip. "That's all past now, man, from where we stand. That guy's long dead. You're not. How 'bout another round?"

Köthen lets out air between his teeth, a slow hard hiss of rage and tension. Then he shakes his head. "No. I think not. It would be . . . unwise."

N'Doch hands over his own cup, still half full. "Finish up with this, then. I like a beer like the next man, but I ain't much for the hard stuff."

"And you know I am."

"Give it a rest, huh? I ain't criticizing. I'm offering."

Köthen eyes him, then takes the cup. He raises it in brisk salute and tosses back the contents in one swallow, then lingeringly savors the heat on his tongue and in his throat. "You are a strange one, friend N'Doch."

N'Doch just chuckles. He's feeling pretty good right about now.

"But tell your . . . dragon: it's a handsome gift. A gift of hope."

"Tell her yourself."

"Perhaps I will."

A thoughtful silence settles down around the cook fires, now mostly burning low, little piles of glowing ashes scat-

tered across the clearing. A couple of teenagers pile up
dishes for transport to the wash pool. A young mother
rocks a fretful child. It's the only infant N'Doch has seen.
Among the forty or so in Blind Rachel Crew, at least ten
of the women are of childbearing age, and they all look
more or less healthy except for the minor physical deformities that seem common among all the Tinkers. Given the
level of tech around so far, N'Doch can't imagine there's
much available by way of birth control. So why aren't there
more babies in the camp?

Stoksie kicks a few charred log ends into his fire and
lowers himself to the ground with a sigh. Sedou eases down
beside him as the little man uncorks a jug and gestures
Köthen and N'Doch back to the hearth for a refill of their
cups. The girl has taken a first sip and is staring into her
cup in shock, her mouth working soundlessly.

"Go easy on that, kiddo," Sedou advises, laughing.

N'Doch is dying to ask what a dragon knows about getting drunk, but this is clearly not the time for it. A few
hearths away, Brenda and Charlie have their heads together, muttering. Punk has already conked out nearby,
with his fists wrapped around his brew cup. To N'Doch's
delight, Marley stirs in his side pocket and starts up a long,
quiet, complex riff. The music drifts over the embers as
tangible as smoke.

The man called Luther ambles in out of the darkness to
drop down at Stoksie's fire. "Dis heah Luta Willums,"
Stoksie offers. N'Doch introduces the girl and Sedou. Luther's a big man, for a Tinker, somewhere in his forties and
by N'Doch's estimation, smart as a whip and wily as a
hyena. He's also noticed, during the communal bath, that
Luther has webbed toes.

Ysabel Dominguin, the reed player, joins them next, patting N'Doch on the head briskly, exclaiming, "Good music!
Good music, na!"

"Good food, good drink!" he laughs. "You guys always
live this good?"

Luther smiles. "Musta knowd yu wuz commin'."

When Bulldog Brenda kisses Charlie lingeringly, then
gets up and slouches over, alone and reluctant, to join
them, N'Doch understands that what passes for something

formal among Tinkers is happening right around him. He nudges Köthen, who nods and murmurs, "Privy council."

N'Doch isn't sure what that means, but he knows a meeting when he sees one. Sure enough, the silence drags on for a bit, pretending to be easy and companionable but actually chock-full of unspoken tension. The girl's on the other side of the hearth, so N'Doch readies himself to translate for Köthen.

Finally, Stoksie clears his throat. "Me 'n Luta bin tinkin' . . ." He looks up at N'Doch, then lets his gaze drift to Sedou, then down to the dirt between his crooked knees where he's worrying a patch of grass with a stick. "Yu nah frum Urop, ri'? Speek tru, na. Ona a da hart."

After a split-second of inner conferencing, Sedou embraces them all with his big soft laugh. "My brother, I do honor your hearth, and I do speak truth." He slides his thumb at Köthen and the girl. "They're from Europe. Me and my brother? No. We're from Africa. Like some of your people, my man."

Truth of a sort. Just not the whole truth. N'Doch wonders if the dragon would lie.

Stoksie's still digging in the dirt. "Nah. My ole peebles frum Bruklin."

"Before Brooklyn. Way back. We're cousins, maybe."

N'Doch's not sure there is a 'before Brooklyn' in Stoksie's mind.

"Africa," he repeats, and scratches his bald head.

"Cud be, na," Luther remarks.

Brenda snorts. She stares, not at Sedou resting back next to her on his elbows like a reclining giant, but across the fire at N'Doch. "Howyu git heah frum Africa?"

Her disbelief is contemptuous and total. N'Doch gets the hint that air travel might not be the usual thing anymore. "Boat," he lies, and begins to spin out a relevant fantasy in his mind about stowing away on a derelict supertanker like the wreck grounded on the beach near home.

But Stoksie isn't really interested in Africa or how they got here from there. He waves Brenda silent. "We bin tinkin' . . ."

"Yu bin," Brenda growls.

"Me 'n Luta 'n Ysa, den. Dat's tree ta wun." Stoksie

waits, but Brenda subsides, grumbling. "We bin tinkin' mebbe yus like ta stay awhile."

"Yeah?" asks Sedou softly. "Why's that?"

Luther leans forward. He has a big nose and graying anglo hair that keeps falling into his face. N'Doch guesses he's pretty seriously nearsighted. "Yu lookin' fuh sum'un, na? We helpyu fine 'im, den yu help us mebbe. Good trade."

When N'Doch gets this far in his murmured simultaneous translation, Köthen stirs. "What kind of help do they want?"

N'Doch repeats the question.

Stoksie grins at Köthen. "Yer kinda help, bigfella."

"I think he means he wants some muscle, Dolph."

Köthen looks interested. After a pause, the girl says, "Please explain."

To Erde's surprise, it was the musician Ysabel who answered. And her accent was another surprise, throwing off the dragon translators for at least the length of a sentence. It was rapid and musical and full of rolling vowels, as unlike her own native German as any language Erde had ever heard.

". . . so ju zee ter esa tis town aqui . . ."

The next sentence was more coherent. If she worked at balancing it, Ysa's accent faded away and Erde heard only the translation, running in her mind. "Dey meke ferry good shuz tere . . . very good. We get good trade for these shoes wherever we go. But it's a big danger to go to this town."

"Why is that?" Sedou prompted.

"Church wackos," said Brenda with a dismissive wave.

"Wacko, huh?" Luther shoved hair from his eyes. "Yu nevah bin deah! Yu nevah seenit!"

" 'Cuz I gotta be heah! Yu wan Blin' Rachel safe, na?" Brenda retorted hotly, but Erde guessed that Luther's accusation was true.

"Sumtimes yu be as dum as a townie, Brenda." Stoksie

dug in the dirt again with his stick. "Look, newfellas, heah's da ting. Trade round heah's getting tuffer, yeah by yeah."

Luther nods. "Tru, tru. Times is getting tuffer by da minit."

"So dis town's a biggun, and dey make stuff ev'rybuddy want. We need dat stuff ta make owah nut, y'know? Uddawize, we doan eat. But dey's a problem deah." Stoksie's hesitation sounded less like caution than shame.

"So what's the problem?" N'Doch prodded.

·Luther fidgeted and stretched his legs. "Yu gonna laff at us."

N'Doch did laugh, then immediately looked apologetic. "Nah, man, I mean, c'mon. Why would we laugh, as good as you've been to us? It's like, some kind of personal problem? Somebody ran off with somebody else's woman?"

"Wudna head fer town if we did dat," murmured Luther.

Stoksie shook his head with a wry smile. "I tink we cud deel wit dat."

"And this other thing you can't deal with?" Sedou asked.

Ysa pursed her lips in a silent negative. Stoksie tossed his stick into the fire. Brenda sulked.

"Okay, den. I'll sayit if nuna yus will. Heah it is." Luther shook his gray forelock out of his eyes and cleared his throat. "Dey's a monsta comes deah."

Another stifled laugh from N'Doch. "A what?"

"A monsta."

"What kinda monster?"

"Shit, yu know—big teet' 'n wings 'n all."

"Wings?"

"Yah. Wings an' a tail."

Now true silence fell around the cook fire. Erde's heart surged in her chest until she was sure everyone could hear it pounding. Sedou rose up from his elbows and fixed his inhuman eyes on Luther. For a moment, all the air went out of the world. In another second, they would be gasping like dying fish. Then she heard N'Doch muttering his translation into Köthen's ear. She took a breath, and the world moved forward again.

Sedou said, "What does this 'monster' look like?"

"Big gold sum'bitch." Luther crooked back both his elbows like a hawk stooping to the kill, then bent his fingers and worked them like claws. "Lon' neck, lon' tail."

Mercifully, Stoksie mistook their sudden intense focus for disbelief. "S'trut', I sweah. I seenit. Nevah bin close, na."

"Lucky," said Ysabel.

Luther laughed. "Souns crazy, na?"

"No," replied Sedou gravely. "I don't think it does."

"I do," Brenda offered. "Wacko. Alla dem."

"Yu go deah, den!" Luther exploded. "Yu wachim come down outa da sky lika litenin' bolt. Den yu tell me I'm wacko."

Brenda gathered herself as if she was ready to leave right then. "Okay, den, I will! Yu take care a da camp!"

"Whoa, whoa, wait!" soothed N'Doch. "Say again? Out of the sky?"

Luther swooped one fist into the other with a resounding slap. "Nevah seen anatin' like it. Don' know whaddit is."

But we do, Erde wanted to cry out. We do!

OH, DRAGON, ARE YOU LISTENING?

WITH EVERY CELL AND SINEW.

Stoksie said, "So whachu say? Yu come wit' us?"

Sedou laughed, barely able to conceal the exultation of the dragon within. "But if this monster's as big and bad as you say he is, how can we protect you from it?"

Are they wondering, Erde asked herself, why we aren't more surprised?

"Nah frum da monsta," Luther said. "No way yu cud do dat. Frum da guys who wanda trowyu tada monsta."

"Really?" Erde could not hide her shock. "And what does the . . . monster . . . do then?"

"Broilyu 'n eechu. Onna spot. Whachu tink?" Their stunned silence clearly puzzled Luther. "Yumin sacerfize, y'know?"

"Wait. No." Sedou shook his head. "Surely you're mistaken."

"Nah. I saw 'im."

"Are you sure?"

"Yah, betcha."

Erde thought she felt the ground shiver, ever so gently. Stoksie agreed soberly. "Meetu. Reel ugly bizness. Parda der religin, kin yu emagin? Jus' like a townie, ta let sumpin li' dat go on."

"Man!" breathed N'Doch. "That's no better than witch burning!"

Sedou rose suddenly, a motion as quick and fluid as water, and paced away. "Oh, my friends . . ." A soft cry of pain at the edge of the darkness, answered by a distinct shuddering from the bedrock. A shift and crack. No one but Erde seemed to notice, so she swallowed her own horror in order to send both dragons soothing thoughts. As low an opinion as Lady Water had of her other brother, she had never thought him capable of such barbarism.

Stoksie watched after Sedou a bit, then shifted his gaze to N'Doch. "He scared off, na?"

"Nah. Just, y'know . . . upset. That's terrible news. Ought to put a stop to that right away."

"Betcha," muttered Luther. "If we could."

"Well, den, whachu tink?" Stoksie asked. "Yu come wit?"

"I'm ready." N'Doch raised his voice slightly. "What say, bro?"

Sedou turned back toward the light, reclaiming his smile with enough effort to render it defiant. "I say, sure. We'll come. We'll come see your monster, and offer whatever help we can. Wouldn't miss it. Who knows? We might find this friend we've been looking for right there in that village."

N'Doch snorted grimly. "Yeah. Wouldn't that be a surprise."

And underneath Blind Rachel, new water flowed.

PART FOUR

The Meeting
with Destiny

CHAPTER TWENTY-SEVEN

The God has given her a day to get ready, and she's been at it since the previous noon. Now it's getting on toward six in the morning, and Paia sits cross-legged in the middle of her bed, defiant in her sweat suit as she directs the swirl of servants packing and repacking her luggage. It had not occurred to her, as she worked so hard to sell the notion of her Visitation, that her greatest concern would be having nothing to wear.

She hasn't been past the Temple's outer gates in fourteen years. Even her ceremonial forays into the open air of the Temple Plaza have been kept as brief as possible, for the sake of her safety and her health. But Paia recalls the elaborate precautions taken whenever she went out as a child. Over the multiple layers of sunblock creams went the long sleeves, the high collars, the thin reflective gloves and hat. All made of the lightest possible materials, but still they were stifling hot. The God always says Paia should daily thank her mother and nannies: to those strict precautions she owes her flawless skin. Even then, going out was rare. Usually she was on her way to some special local event that the landowner's family was expected to attend, a christening, or a funeral. Leaving the house was less a pleasure than a duty.

But right now, Paia is thrilled by the prospect, even though the sunblock has long since dried up, and all that protective clothing, even if it could still be found, would no longer fit. Even though her extensive wardrobe of revealing Temple garments is woefully inadequate for a trek across the open countryside. Paia has been improvising all night.

And then there's the issue of something to put it all in.

There hasn't been a thorough search of the storerooms in a long time. Paia was shocked to discover how much has vanished from those rooms where the locks are disabled. Her immediate response was to storm off to Luco in a rage over this silent and systematic looting. The God would hear of it! The First Son took time to soothe and calm her, but she sensed an unusual impatience beneath his dutiful concern, as if such invasions and inconveniences are only to be expected. She'd pouted. If it didn't involve the God, he didn't care about it!

Now, looking over the bits and pieces she's been able to gather, she's more intrigued than outraged. They have a motley, rough-and-tumble aspect, laid out on her mother's fine Turkish carpet: a black nylon duffel, one boxy plastic trunk, two big blue satchels, a silvered metal case, and an ancient but well-preserved mountaineer's pack in leather. Leather is an absurd luxury, but the pack bears her father's initials. Paia unearthed it in one of the unransacked storerooms and fell in love with it instantly. That storeroom, keyed open by her palm print, is a virtual time capsule. She could have spent a whole week in there, revisiting her life before the God. But that would have been a lonely exercise. She has no one to share these memories with.

The God is right, she decides. Nostalgia is a useless luxury.

The chambermaid spreads another armload of clothing on the bed. Paia allows her to display each garment for inspection, nodding a yes to this, a no to that. The chambermaid hands off the single yes to a packer, sweeps up the rejects, and goes back for another load. Paia wonders if there is time to have a few more sensible items made up: long-sleeved shirts and pants with handy hidden pockets for the God's little gun.

Out in the hallway, the red-robed Twelve are gathered in a weepy cluster, mourning her departure from their sight for even a moment. Paia has forbidden them entry. No doubt they're convinced that this trip is a forced order. Why would anyone leave the Citadel willingly? A contingent of Honor Guard is milling about as well, relieved that their watch hasn't been chosen for escort duty. The moist chanting and murmuring of the Twelve breaks off briefly as a brace of Luco's Third Sons shoulder them aside importantly, bearing through the doorway a shrouded rectangle. Paia has had the mutating landscape brought downstairs, to be hung on the wall opposite her bed, another expression of her newly assumed autonomy, though no one will read it that way but herself and the God. She hopes it will be like having a new window cut into the room, a mystical kind of window where the view changes each time you look out. She'd take the painting with her if she could. She'd like to know that it's safe. But she suspects that even the suggestion might render Luco, in his present state, apoplectic. Paia waves at the young priests to lean the covered canvas against the wall. What vista would it reveal to this room full of servants? She will wait until she is alone again to unveil it.

Son Luco has been in and out at least twice this morning, in high gear and at the earliest hint of dawn. First he came to remind her of their schedule of departure, then to describe the instantaneously devised ceremony slated for 0800 sharp in the Temple Plaza. He was at his most abrupt and efficient, but beneath the official mask thrummed true eagerness. His bronzed skin was almost luminous, as if lit from within by suppressed anticipation. His subordinates whirled around after him, basking in the glow of his energy. At one point, Paia glanced through her open door to discover him in a one-way consultation of gestures with the chambermaid—whom, as far as she knew, he had never before even noticed. Why should Luco be so charged up, she'd wondered a bit sulkily. He gets to go out all the time.

An unfamiliar kitchen servant hesitates in the doorway, balancing the breakfast tray. Paia bites back an urge to snap her fingers and yell at the girl to hurry. The child's confusion suggests she's never ventured so high in the Citadel before. Paia gestures her over to the bed, studying her as she approaches. Paia has resolved to be more observant of those around her, either servant or priest, especially since she's discovered how hard it is to remember to do so. This girl looks decently fed, but her eyes are dull and she is ghostly pale. Her cheeks have almost a blue cast, no doubt due to a life spent entirely in the Citadel's subterranean levels. She walks with her shoulders crooked, struggling to hold them straight as she weaves a cautious path across the crowded room to the High Priestess' bed. Despite a concealing sleeve, Paia sees that her right arm is withered, just managing to steady the heavy tray. Again Paia controls a tart response. It is the God's stated policy to forbid deformities within the priesthood and among the Citadel workforce, but even Paia knows exceptions must be made, or the housekeepers would have trouble filling their staff. Only the high frenzy of preparations has brought this child out of the concealment of the kitchens.

Unable to repress her reflexive shudder, Paia reminds herself that she will have to observe much worse when she gets outside. Best to practice ignoring things now. She nods neutrally at the girl, then terrifies her with a brisk thanks when the tray is set down without mishap. The girl bows clumsily and flees back through the crowd.

An hour later, Paia is dressed and fed. The little gun is tucked against the small of her back. The luggage has been fastened and sent downstairs. She has followed Luco's advice in her choice of a Leave-taking outfit: the softest and most comfortable of the glittery Temple garments underneath a long hooded silk robe that can be worn open for the ritual, then fastened up tight for the road. The chambermaid is offering up for her approval a belt of jewel-studded gold mesh, when a relay of shouted orders echoes down the hallway and the disconsolate mutter of the priestesses goes suddenly silent.

Paia shivers with the usual thrill of fear, but she cannot repress a prideful grin. He is out there, filling the whole length of the corridor with his heat and speed and magnificence. What is he doing here? The God has never accompanied her in any sort of procession. All the rituals dictate that she must come to him. Paia waits. His approach is noiseless. Not a sound but the Honor guard snapping to shocked attention, followed by the soft flopping of twelve terrified young women flattening every possible inch of their bodies against the threadbare rug. The chambermaid has her back to the door and cannot sense the God's entrance. When he sails through the door, it's only the shifting of Paia's eyes that alerts her.

Paia tries not to look at him and fails. He is as tall and broad as the corridor will reasonably allow, and caparisoned in gold and flashing jewels, like a barbarian emperor. His vest shimmers with thousands of tiny sun-disks that ring like breathy cymbals as he moves. Luco may have seemed to glow, but the God actually gives off light, and he brings with him a hot, crisp scent, as if he's just charged through a furnace. The chambermaid nearly strangles on her own swallowed squawk and collapses into the tiniest ball she can manage. But even she is sneaking a peek.

Paia bows deeply, as the God expects her to do when the Faithful are about. Their relationship may be evolving all of a sudden, but it would be folly to air the process in public. "You look absolutely splendid today, my lord Fire."

And he does. He has taken extra care with this manifestation. His nod is faint and lordly. "I have come to grant my priestess the honor of my presence at her Leavetaking."

In other words, time you got going. Paia bows again, wondering if this gesture was his idea or Luco's. "A grave honor indeed, my lord."

His brief ironic glance answers her question. He turns away abruptly, beckoning with a gold-tipped finger, and sweeps grandly out the door. Paia tosses a quick regretful look at the still-shrouded painting leaning against the wall. Something else that will have to wait. She has been summoned and she must follow. The chambermaid scrambles up and scurries after her.

On the stairs, Paia holds herself the ritual five paces behind, but somehow—with a trick he's never offered before in man-form—the God's voice is at her right ear, not in her head but just outside it—intimate but noninvasive, like a whisper from inches away. And she is able to answer him in a murmur.

"You have remembered the gun."

"Yes, my lord."

"Go nowhere without it. You have packed sufficient ammunition?"

What does he consider sufficient? "Yes, my lord."

"The sun is your deadly enemy, remember. You've brought protective garments?"

"Of course." Paia is not fooled by his rough, clipped tone. The God is anxious. Perhaps he is not so eager to be rid of her after all. "Lord Fire, you are mothering me."

"You are reckless, my priestess."

"All in your service, my lord."

He snorts. "Has it not even occurred to you to wonder about this restlessness of yours, where it has come from all of a sudden?"

Paia cannot think of a clever response. Nor does she know the answer.

Ahead of her, his broad shoulders shift beneath their rich cloth-of-gold. "No matter. Go your way. Perhaps you will lead me to them. Meanwhile, I have ordered the First Son to pack safe food and water to last twelve days. He is charged to bring you back in eight. Not a day past, or his life will be forfeit."

"His *life,* my lord?"

"I have said so."

"But some delay might occur that Luco has no control over . . ."

"The First Son has agreed to the terms. Therefore, he will be extra vigilant to prevent such delays. My Word must be enforced, or chaos is upon us."

Chaos, again. Lately, all the God's anxieties seem to focus on the potential breakdown of his carefully ordered system. Paia's childhood history studies included the macabre dance of shifting political structures that played out during her father's lifetime. Considering that example, Paia thinks the God's obsession with chaos might be too narrow. For all this paranoia about his enemies, he never seems to allow that the real threat might come from a different brand of order.

The Ceremony of Farewell, hastily invented by one of Luco's trusted underlings, is held in the Sanctuary and is mercifully brief. It allows the Twelve to weep copiously and publicly beneath their red veils, then dry their eyes for a prayerful dance begging that their beloved priestess be soon returned to them. Paia, who has regarded them with increasing dislike and suspicion since they've begun dogging her every footstep, imagines the hot little seeds of hope her departure must be planting in each of them. Such as, perhaps the God is punishing her with this trip for some secret transgression. Perhaps disaster will befall her. Perhaps she will not return. Perhaps the God, in his infinite wisdom, will make one of them High Priestess. It's just as well, Paia decides, that she does not know their faces or names. Less need to be civil to them.

The Formal Progress from the Sanctuary to the Plaza includes a quick stop at the Sacred Well, where Paia sips the crystalline liquid from the scoop of her own palms, the only vessel deemed pure enough by the God to convey the sacred waters. She savors its chill perfection. It is the expression of an ideal. She wishes she could slip a bottle or two into her luggage. But for once, the God is standing there watching. The Twelve are so overcome by his sustained presence among them in man-form that they can barely manage their part in the ritual.

At last, the God leads the procession out into the blinding sun, past the stained sacrificial altar to where the First Son waits, with the full ranks of the priesthood lined up to left and right. Behind, a dust cloud rises as servants and bearers race about among the high-wheeled wagons and piles of packing crates, frenzied with last minute preparations. Luco's blue gaze is eager, though his jaw is set and serious. He bows abjectly to the God, then gestures him toward the towering bejeweled and golden throne that's been dragged out of the Sanctuary for the final Leave-taking. Off to one side, two of the elaborately decorated sedan chairs sit side by side. These are usually reserved for the Temple's most lavish and formal ceremonies. Virtually overnight, they've been refitted for the rigors of outdoor travel. The High Priestess and First Son of the Temple will ride. The goods will be hauled in the wagons by hand. Everyone else will walk.

The God ascends his throne, and under Son Luco's brisk direction, the ceremony begins. Paia always prefers it when Luco officiates. He's so much better at it than she is, with his grand manner and melodious voice. The First Son is a different man in public performance. He loses his fussy edge, becomes smoother, less self-conscious. Grateful to be only a passive participant in this unrehearsed production, Paia lets her mind wander, past the looming Temple gates, out into the valley, into the ruddy, stony hills ringing the Citadel, hills she will soon be crossing. Her sedan chair glitters in the sun, a tall gold box on sturdy gilded legs, the God Rampant embroidered in red on either side. She is relieved to see the chambermaid scurrying into an appropriately abject position beside it, suddenly and miraculously dressed for the road. She is far less relieved when two of the red-robed Twelve detach themselves from the processional with all indications of joining the escort party. Paia sighs. The God—in his wisdom, of course—has made sure to supply her with chaperones.

Later, Paia will be unable to recall a single detail of the elaborate ceremony. It assembles the total populations of Temple and Citadel, and goes on for entirely too long, praising the God's wisdom and perfection, beseeching him to see to the safety of the High Priestess as she goes about her holy duties among the Faithful out in the world. There is chanting and motion, and eventually the crowds murmur aside. Paia comes out of her daze to find herself facing the outer gates, a direction that for so long has been forbidden even to consider. As the long bolt shafts are drawn back into the wall, reality at last takes hold. Her awareness irises in to a pinpoint of concentration on the great central locking mechanism with its polished, God-shaped escutcheon plate. She is finally leaving the confines of the Temple. Will anything out there be as she remembers?

After another eternity of chanting and prayers, the God stands and spreads his golden arms. The First Son sweeps forward to hand the High Priestess into the curtained door of her chair. As the gauzy metallic drapes swing loose to veil the shaded interior, the four bearers lift and steady. The God vanishes from his throne in an explosion of flame and light. The throng falls to its knees as a vast shadow of wings passes in threat and benediction over the sun-baked courtyard. The gates roll open. Across the upper landing, the Grand Stair lies waiting. The caravan starts forward.

A twelve-man contingent of the Honor Guard leads the way, followed by the First Son with as many of his Seconds and Thirds as could be spared from the day-to-day running of the Temple. Paia is surprised by the number of them: twenty at least, if she hasn't counted the same one twice. Her own two chaperones pass through the gates next, then Paia in her chair with her servants behind. Behind them, more Honor Guard, more servants, and finally, the supply wagons. Overhead, the God flies long, swooping figure eights etched in flame. Inside the chair, a fiery night descends each time he passes. Paia approaches the Grand Stair. Abruptly, she is terrified.

What have I done?

But this is the sort of terror she is used to, like her terror of the God, mixed with exhilaration. She is practiced at dealing with it. And turning back, she has decided, is not an alternative.

The steps are low, six meters wide and a meter deep. The chair tilts forward only gently, and the bearers fall into a mildly rocking rhythm to manage the descent. The chair looks light enough, but there's a reason it takes four strong men to carry it. It's become a self-contained mini-fortress. Luco has explained to her how it carries extra food and water, and is hardened to deflect knife blades, spear, axes, arrows, even a small caliber bullet, though the God has promised Paia there won't be any of those around, except in her own hands. She tells herself she's safe, but she's certainly not comfortable. It's hot and airless inside. Already her skin is slick, and her fine silk robe is soaking up the damp. As the rocking continues, Paia begins to doubt the steadiness of her stomach.

She parts the curtains, only a crack. The outside air is no cooler, but at least it's in vague motion and she can fix her eyes on the steadier horizon. A thin crowd lines either side of the stairs, sun-toughened men and women from the village at the bottom. She should know some of these scarred and withered faces. Living so nearby, they will have made the long climb to the Temple most often. But Paia has endured her years of ritual specifically by not looking at the faces of the Faithful. She vows to change this practice when she returns.

As her chair passes, the villagers shove their few scrawny children forward to wave at her. There is maybe one child for every fifteen adults. Paia had thought the God's repopulation efforts had been going better lately, but she sees no toddlers or infants at all. Perhaps the mothers will no longer risk exposing them to the sun and crowds, even for such a special occasion.

A glance behind, back up the stairs, distracts Paia from her nausea. The gates are still open, as the last of the supply wagons clatter through and gather on the broad upper landing to be unloaded for transport down the steps. The gates are each four meters wide, double-walled steel taken from the hangar where Paia's father stored his armored vehicles. They are set into stone walls two meters thick by seven high. Since the God ordered these walls built, no force has bested them, though Paia has heard that during the Wars of Conversion, several respectable attempts were made. She has always thought that Luco's readiness to bore her with the old war stories is one of his few personal weaknesses. But gazing up at those scarred and sun-bleached walls for the first time, she wishes she'd done more than just humor him. If she'd also listened, she could have learned. She thinks how much the House Computer would approve of this insight, and then, how useful it would be to have House along. This Visitation will make her a student all over again, except that, this time, she has some idea of how little she knows.

That vow again: to be a more intent observer.

From the central gates, the wall runs off about thirty meters to either side, then turns back toward the cliff and the Temple. A tall slender watchtower marks each corner. Through the open gateway and over the crenellated top of the wall, Paia can see the Temple's elaborately carved façade, and the bland natural rock face of the Citadel rising behind it. Reality takes hold again. Impulsively, she shoves aside the curtain and leans out into the sun, ignoring the villagers' pious stares. She cranes awkwardly around the hard edge of the doorframe to count the windows glimmering high on the cliff. She is seized with an urgent need to identify her own, before all that's familiar is behind her and out of sight.

But it's only eight days!

Paia is shaken by a sudden intimation of a chasm crossed, of an irrevocable step taken toward a new life, at the moment she passed through the gates. She counts and searches as her chair rocks downward, until she picks out her level, her room, her very own window. Only then can she grasp at her dignity again, and withdraw into the shade of her tiny mobile fortress, obscurely comforted.

In Paia's father's time, big carpeted elevators transported Citadel guests and residents up from the valley floor. They were fitted with solid brass and lined with polished hardwood. When the God came, he proclaimed them an unreliable luxury, even though they were powered by the windmills up on the cliff top and hardly ever failed. Paia suspects they were simply not magnificent enough for his purposes. He built the Grand Stair to *really* impress, with its five hundred massive steps and carved railings. The climb to Paia's tower studio is a mere hop by comparison. But the Grand Stair is not just decorative. It serves also as a first line of defense against attackers, and further, as a test of a worshiper's devotion. For it is the God's opinion—shared (Paia believes) by his loyal general, Son Luco—that anyone who gives up before they've reached the top can't be counted on for much anyway.

At the halfway point, where the cliff is sheerest, the stairs level out into a shallow landing, then split to left and right to move across and down the face of the rock. The chair is set down, and the bearers are given a brief breather. Paia has a view through the parted drapes of the valley below, and the bright meander of the dry riverbed crossed by the straight line of road that once led to her father's airstrip and thus, back to civilization. Leaning out a bit farther, she can just see the roofs and chimneys of the village huddled at the bottom of the steps.

Each night at the Citadel, most often shrouded from Paia's high window view by darkness, but now and then glimpsed by moonlight, a human chain five hundred steps long transfers food and goods from the Temple's dependent villages up to the Citadel. Paia is not supposed to know about such things. Once she questioned Luco about it, just casually, and he pretended she'd spotted the rare occurrence. At the time, she reasoned that the chain was easier than requiring each bearer to walk all the way up and all the way down. But surely it's a bit foolish that *all* the supplies for this trip were hauled *all* the way up, only to be brought *all* the way back down again. Paia approves of the rigorous safety inspection that anything slated for her consumption must pass, but out here in the broiling sun, with half the stairs looming high behind and the other half, like a drop into nowhere, still to descend, the waste of energy seems, well, irresponsible. Not a concept Paia has thought much about before.

As her bearers hoist the stout carrying poles onto their

shoulders and set off again on their rocking descent, Paia muses over the possibility that the God prefers this hard show of human labor over the mysterious ease of a mechanism he does not understand.

The village at the bottom began its life in her father's time, clustered around the entrance to the elevators, as housing for service and maintenance personnel, for the tenant farmers and their families, and for anyone in his employ who, despite the obvious security disadvantage, could not bring themselves to live tucked away in the bowels of a cliff. Paia recalls it as a sizable, tidy gathering of tight stone houses and fenced garden plots. She recalls attending a birthday celebration down there, dressed in a new outfit sewn by her mother's seamstresses, who also lived in the village. Her mother brought the cake, and her nanny brought a bundle of clothing that Paia had outgrown. These were passed among the children at the party to be tried on for size, and everyone went home happy. Except perhaps Paia's mother, whose natural generosity was encouraged by the sure knowledge that she could never have another child. Paia also remembers a wedding, somewhat later, where she carried a bouquet of patchwork flowers lovingly sewn from the fabric of some of those old outfits. The bride carried real flowers, from Paia's father's greenhouses, but Paia preferred the patchwork ones. She still has one somewhere, she thinks. Odd that she should recall such detail, after so long. It must be looking down on those blue slate rooftops that brings it back so vividly.

But when the last stair is behind her and her chair is at last traveling on level ground, Paia does not find herself in the quaint village of her memory. The stone houses still stand, but the slate roofs are cracked and patchy. Red dust is caked into every seam. The once-colorful doors and windows have gone unpainted for decades. Their storm shutters are missing or broken, and where the neatly fenced gardens once struggled but grew, ragged clusters of hovels and shanties have sprung up, filling all the spaces between. Apparently, for many, living within the safer shadow of the Temple is worth any sort of discomfort.

Here also, along the barren main street, villagers are lined up to greet their High Priestess. They pray aloud for her safe journey and swift return. One woman calls out a fervent wish that the Last Days not come upon them while the Priestess is away from the Temple. Paia sees several soldiers of the Temple moving roughly among them. She would like to believe that the villagers' good wishes are genuine, but she can't help but notice that where the soldiers are, there also is the crowd's most passionate response. She considers her rash promise to the God. How will she speak of loving to these desperate folk who are taught only fear?

She is glad that, because these Faithful have daily access to the Temple, the procession does not stop for a formal Visitation. She is not yet ready to face them directly. Soon her chair has passed down the main street and is headed out across the valley floor.

Once, before even her father's time, this was fertile bottom land. There was water in the riverbed and trees along its banks and rain enough to grow grain, to pasture livestock without irrigation. Current agricultural information would never be offered to the High Priestess, but in the Citadel, Paia habitually eavesdrops. She has learned from her Honor Guard how the fields are now sized by how much water can be spared from the village's shrinking wells, and then by how far that water can be transported without being stolen. Even pipes can be surreptitiously rerouted, and the best-armed parties ambushed.

Leaving the last group of hovels behind, the procession passes among the high stockade fences surrounding the vegetable plots. The livestock are similarly contained. Paia hears chickens and goats and the occasional sheep, but sees nothing but walls of weathered timber patched with bits of sun-brittled plastic. Soon, even that is behind them and there is only untilled, uninhabited ground ahead. Overhead, the God executes a final glittering omega over the line of wagons. His cry shakes the ground like the thunder of an avalanche, but Paia hears his farewell inside her head, terse, resentful, full of longing. Could he not just come with her, and delight the villages with the honor? She sighs. Surely there has never been a more complex being than the God.

The valley seems wider, far more open than she recalls, though Paia doubts that she's recalling trees from her own memories. Those were already rare enough when she was young. Through the slit in her curtains, she can see a few softening patches across the valley, gray-green, tucked away in the shaded rocky folds of the hills where a bit of dew might regularly collect. She thinks of the shrouded painting in her room, the way it first appeared to her, ripe with foliage and moisture. She hopes the road will lead the caravan through one of those distant greening patches. She would like the chance to walk among real trees, not one or two but a whole gathering, a grove, tall and cooling. There must be a few left out there . . . somewhere. Out on the baking flat, irrigated fields give way to parched wasteland. Paia feels exposed and vulnerable, breathless, as if the very air were being evaporated from her lungs. Her view through the draperies becomes mobile, blurring and dancing with the rising heat. The stained sky looms like a weight, endlessly falling in on top of her. Nausea returns, stirred by agoraphobic panic. Paia shivers and draws the curtains tight.

It is too soon to be so out of control. As the caravan crawls across the valley floor, she gives herself a stern talking-to inside her hot golden box. She knows how to live with fear. She must now learn to live with discomfort. The heat is so much worse than she'd imagined, and the landscape so much more desolate, even though she has painted it for years. But that was from a distance. She has taken the cooling effects of the Citadel's bedrock too much for granted. But she has asked for, no, *demanded* this trip. Therefore she must suffer it gladly, for the honor of the God and the Temple, as well as for her own self-respect. Calling up the meditative state that gets her through the longest and most tedious of the Temple rituals, she settles into a heat-drenched trance.

This holds her steady until the rhythm of the bearers' pace alters suddenly, shaking her awake. The chair tilts backward, rising raggedly. Paia bolts upright in her padded seat. She fears they've turned around, that they're fleeing back up the Guard Stair to the Temple. The bright sun on her curtains fades as the chair passes into shadow. A shouted order rings out from up ahead. The caravan straggles to a halt. Paia reaches for the God's gun. Are they under attack?

She parts the curtains, and is assailed by clouds of dust. Settling, it reveals a sheer stone face, but no sign of mayhem or panic. The bearers set down the chair, releasing their cramped muscles with exhausted groans. Paia peers ahead. They have entered a narrow defile, barely wide enough for the wagons to pass. Wind-shaped rock walls tower on both sides. Dusty clumps of bushes cling to cracks and spring up between the boulders where landslides have breached the sides of the canyon. The dry, rising ribbon of road is treacherous with loose stones and gravel.

Dust swirls up again as Son Luco strides toward her along the length of the caravan. He has put off his ceremonial trappings, leaving only the loose white pants and shirt, and a red robe that floats gracefully open behind him. He has, Paia thinks, an odd look on his face, as he checks in with each wagon and contingent, even the servants. Odd, that is, for Luco. He looks . . . relaxed. More at ease out here in the heat and grit than she has ever seen him in the Citadel, as if he has shed a part of himself along with his Temple finery. Disconcerted, Paia withdraws into her protective shade. Luco arrives and peers in at her. She cannot hide the hints of panic in her hooded eyes.

"Mother Paia. How are you managing?"

She knows he's used her title as a reminder to set a good example for the rest of the caravan. As always, his officiousness piques her, which was perhaps intended, for her panic recedes.

"Less well than yourself, First Son . . . apparently." Paia coughs as the dust he has brought enters her sanctuary.

"It's good to be out and about," he replies. "In the air."

What air? She tries for banter. "Very much the handsome captain, aren't you now? Is this what it's like going to war? I think you must have enjoyed it more than you're willing to admit."

He smiles blandly. "Once a soldier, always a soldier."

She can feel his concentration diffusing beyond her, up and down the line of wagons and farther, out into the surrounding hills. Alert and listening, even as he converses with her casually. Paia is reminded that every step away from the Citadel leads them farther into danger.

"We'll rest here a bit," he says. "It's safe enough in the hill shadow. Come out and stretch your legs. Are you drinking your water as advised?"

"Water. What a good idea."

The well-used canteen from her father's backpack waits on the seat beside her, full to the brim and even a bit cool. Paia downs several gulps, then swings the strap over her head and shoulder as she steps down from the chair. The water hits her stomach hard and threatens to rebound. Her legs have no strength. She staggers, grasping at the doorframe.

Luco catches her arm and steadies her. He sends the bearers off to refresh themselves. "You haven't been drinking."

"I will from now on," she murmurs.

"We're not tucked away safe anymore."

"I know that." Snapping at him revives her slightly. "You needn't treat me like an idiot."

"Then don't act like one. For all our sakes, if not for your own. Drink some more. Slowly."

She knows he will stand there till she does. The God has charged him with her safety. She is out of the Citadel, but she is still not free. She takes little sips, then wipes her mouth on her sleeve as unceremoniously as possible. "Where are we?"

Luco looks away, as if toward the valley, but his eyes seem to gaze on a far greater distance. "I fought a great battle here. In the service of the God."

"Does the place have a name? Perhaps we should name it after you."

After a moment, he says, very quietly, "It already has a name, my priestess."

"And what is that, my priest?"

"Whose answer would you prefer, mine or the God's?"

Paia swallows a gasp. Sacrilege from the First Son? "Are they different?"

His mouth quirks at some private thought. "The God calls it, rather eloquently, I think, The Sunrise Passage. But to me, and those who live around it, this is Cauldwell's Clove. The only negotiable road out of the valley."

She stares at him. "But that's my name! Or it was." She has almost forgotten she had a family name. She hasn't heard it spoken in years. She hesitates even to repeat it, for fear she will burst into tears.

He looks down at her. "Is that so?"

The God has outlawed any history of the Citadel or its

former owners to all but herself. Still, knowledge persists. "You knew that, didn't you?"

Luco's expression grows odder still, rich with nuance that Paia cannot interpret. Squinting up at him, she is rocked by sudden intuition that she at first denies and then accepts entirely. But it's not possible! Surely he would have said something, even though it would put him in danger of heresy. For the same reason, she has never thought to ask him.

"Luco!" she hisses. "Did you *know* my father?"

"I did not say . . ."

"Luco, please? I won't tell anyone!"

His face closes. "The God does not permit . . ."

"Luco! Did you?"

"This conversation is in violation of the laws of the Temple, my priestess."

"Oh, Luco! You started it."

He nods, lips pressed tight. "And I greatly regret my lapse."

"But we're out in the middle of nowhere! Who could possibly . . . ?"

He touches her arm in warning, then booms jovially, "Ah, here are your Faithful, come to see to their mistress at last."

Instantly, Paia smoothes the urgency from her face. The red-robed Two, still veiled as if at the Temple's highest ritual, are bearing down with water and food and a damp cloth to bathe their Priestess' sweated brow. Their postures seem to exclude Luco from this women's privilege. It occurs to Paia that the First Daughters might be reporting to someone other than the First Son.

Luco bows. "Mother Paia, with your permission, I leave you in these devoted hands. See that they find you a good spot in the bushes."

You knew my father?

She cannot call him back, or allow herself to stare after him as he strides briskly away. It would draw undue attention to a conversation the God would not look well upon. And after that, Luco keeps his distance. All during the difficult climb through the rock-strewn gorge, at the many rest stops or in the several places where the twisting path is so precipitous that even the High Priestess must leave the comfort of her chair and proceed on foot, for her own safety, Luco avoids her. Or if he does appear, he comes in the company of at least two of his acolytes. Paia is hurt by his reflex paranoia. Does he really think she would report so minor a heresy to the God? Or even carelessly refer to it, especially when it would mean so much to her to know for sure, to be able to talk to someone who knew her father? And, if he's so fearful, what moment of weakness brought the name out of him in the first place?

Late in the day, the upward path levels into a wider sort of road and crosses an open plateau toward a notch between two hills. The road disappears into the notch, but a village nestles at the mouth of it, sunk in afternoon shadow. Paia spots the livestock before she sees the village, tired-looking cattle and thin sheep grazing fitfully among the thornbushes and scrub. They are guarded by small crowds of men armed with knives and spears, plus a few big dogs who stare sullenly at the caravan as it passes. The dogs catch Paia's interest especially. Her family always kept dogs, but the God banished all animals from the Citadel when he came.

Along with people's family names.

Cauldwell. The sound of it rings in her mind as if Luco had just spoken it. Paia shoves away the thought. These dogs are scruffy and half-feral, and do not waste their energy barking, but still, she's encouraged. If this village can feed dogs, they must be feeding themselves well enough.

In the village outskirts, the caravan passes vegetable plots surrounded by stone walls wide enough to walk along, as Paia sees three women doing. They patrol the garden perimeter, using their sharpened poles as walking sticks. They stop and draw together to watch the procession go by. They seem more apprehensive than excited. Paia would like to think they're simply unaware of who their visitor is, but she cannot help but notice the tallest one's quick and anxious scanning of the sky.

Inside the village, a less ambivalent welcome has been prepared. A party of local clergy awaits them at the head of the dusty main street, and the caravan proceeds grandly into town, past several clusters of dilapidated stone houses and barns, to pull up in a semicircle on the flagstones of the central square, which appear to be freshly swept. Paia peeks invisibly through her draperies. She has been set down at one side of the square, facing the Temple Chapter House, so that she has a perfect view of the image laid in reddish lavender stones, crude but recognizable, and dark against the paler gray: the Winged God Rampant.

She looks about for Luco, hoping for a chance to speak in private. But the local Temple does not wish to be thought lackadaisical or unprepared. The caravan is immediately swept up in a fervent and lengthy Ritual of Welcome. And from there, the evening progresses much as Paia might expect, in fact, more or less as she had envisioned when she came up with the idea of this trip, at least until toward the end. The joyous welcome is led by the head priest of the chapter. There are several priestesses as well, all properly veiled like Paia's own Temple Daughters, but vested in dark purple, as befits their lower rank. None of the local clergy attempt to converse with the High Priestess, and Paia guesses from their nervous but practiced manner that all are well versed in the appropriate behaviors. They are whole, well fed and healthy, the cream of the village crop. Each has doubtless paid many visits to the Mother Temple and would not wish to appear provincial.

After the Ritual of Welcome, the High Priestess is formally entreated to walk among the Faithful of the town. This is the part Paia has been dreading. The Faithful must be able to touch her directly. For that, she must remove her protective robe and expose herself in the flimsy Temple garments to the sun and the hot, dusty wind as she has never done before, as well as to whatever disease and impulse toward violence might lurk within the crowd. But this ritual is central to Temple doctrine and must never be denied. The health and physical perfection of the High Priestess is the miraculous proof of the God's favor. The Rite of Touching, the God himself insists, brings the Faithful closer to him.

With a grand gesture, Paia tosses back her hood and shrugs the robe back into the waiting hands of her priestesses. An awed murmur rises and falls in the crowd. So far, she has not disappointed.

As the local priest falls in on one side and Son Luco on the other, Paia processes around the sides of the square, where the townspeople are gathered. They have washed and scrubbed and still they appear soiled, as if stained by

their toil in the parched earth and by the awful sun. Some
kneel, some do not. It doesn't matter. Paia is taller than
any of them, and Son Luco appears among them as a giant.
Their eyes are weary, yet hands reach eagerly for a touch of
holy flesh. Paia usually endures the touching rites without
response. But here, out in the open, with the sun slanting
away toward the hilltops and the smoke from the cook
fires tickling her nostrils, she is impelled to a more genuine
contact. She stretches out her own hands as she moves
down the line, grasping bony fingertips and brown wrists,
worn and wrinkled elbows, scarred stumps and twisted
limbs. The delighted crowd sighs its gratitude for this unexpected blessing. A step behind her, Son Luco clears his
throat, either in disapproval or surprise. Paia does not meet
his glance. She doesn't want to know what the First Son
thinks right now. Probably that she is taking too long, and
holding up the next stage of the ritual. But she's enjoying
the smiles and wonder that her touch freely offered brings
to the faces of these simple people. She is moved by the
sense of connection. Perhaps this is how she can preach
love of the God to them, not with words but action. Love
given must be returned in some fashion, she reasons. If the
God cannot love his Faithful, perhaps his High Priestess
can do it for him.

She has completed three sides of her slow progress
around the square when Son Luco deflects her with a murmured warning about overexposure.

"Please behave," he says, then deftly whisks her into
the waiting arms of her red-veiled chaperones. The two
priestesses grandly fling her robe about her naked shoulders and use their grasp on its sleeves to maneuver her
onward to the Confirmation of the Clergy, where Paia must
anoint each priest and priestess of the local chapter with
the God's special blessing. This ceremony is plainly considered to be the more important one, at least by the clergy.
After the blessing comes a recitation of the chapter's history, and the honors bestowed on it by the God. After that,
a long presentation by the head priest, detailing the duties
of the Faithful in the Last Days of the World. He is not a
compelling speaker, but Paia judges him as sincere verging
on fanatical when he interprets the total lack of rainfall in

so many months as a blessing from the God to hasten the holy End.

Finally, just at dark, torches are lit and a grand feast is laid in the center of the square. Paia is surprised to find herself ravenous, despite a long day of discomfort, boredom, and nausea. There are not enough tables to offer the High Priestess the honor of a private one without seating the First Son among the locals. This was decided to be the more inappropriate, so Luco sits beside her at the high table, facing the rest of the clergy at a longer table set in front of them, all of them surrounded by the Faithful who must sit on the flagstones. To Paia, it feels too much like the hated Lunch at the Citadel. But at least there is food enough to go around.

Paia lifts a morsel of stewed rabbit on her fork. "Tastes just like home." Though of course it doesn't.

"It ought to." Luco smiles graciously as a villager elder bows before them with a platter of fresh radishes. "Did you think we raised our food ourselves all these years?"

"Of course not, though it's no thanks to you that I know any better. Even in my father's day, our food came from the villages." She nibbles at the rabbit pensively. "Luco . . . ?"

"No. Don't ask. I beg you." He blots his lips and folds his napkin in a precise triangle. "I knew this was a bad idea."

He looks more wary and tired than he has all day. Each dish that comes to the table, he tastes himself before allowing Paia a portion. He is in eye contact with each of the six men from her Honor Guard who are currently arrayed at a discreet distance from the table, and Paia catches him polling them regularly. But Paia cannot imagine what the First Son is so worried about. The humble little square is filled with the loyal Faithful, and their attention is mostly on the food. They are probably delighted to be eating better than they have in months. She sips gingerly at the odd wood-scented wine, sorry that the God's intemperate death threats have kept Luco from enjoying his meal.

She tries a less sensitive subject. "How inspiring that this town's deep faith impels them to such great generosity."

Luco chews, nodding neutrally,

"It's a miracle they can grow anything at all out here. It's so much drier than I expected. Is it true what the priest said, that there's been absolutely no rain at all?"

"None that I know of."

"Is this a change, First Son? A sign that conditions are worsening?"

"It is."

"Well, we must ask less of them for the Temple."

Luco's fork hesitates midway, then continues to his mouth. "The God will not agree with you."

"Or we must help them somehow. In my father's day, there were pipelines and . . . Luco?"

"You will excuse me, my priestess. Now that the formalities are done, I must see to Temple business while all are here assembled."

He rises, and spends the rest of the meal working the lower table. He is clearly relieved when Paia, her servants, and the two Daughters of the Temple are ushered into the Chapter House to spend the night. It's only one dingy room with a stone floor and an attached privy, but a high row of windows along each side provides good ventilation. Paia decides to let Luco do all the worrying, since he seems inclined to do it anyway. Resisting the fussing of the red-robed Two, she lets the chambermaid, who has been hovering nearby, prepare her for bed. When she lays herself out on the tall pile of sheep's wool mattresses provided for her comfort, she falls instantly asleep.

And she dreams, oh, such dreams. So many and so rich. It must be the food, or being out in the open air. All her nights up till this one seem quiet by comparison, as if the bedrock of the Citadel somehow stifled her dreaming and now she is making up for lost time.

Images flash by, too many and too sudden to hold on to. Strange faces and places, and others she recognizes. Her father, for instance, lecturing her gravely about duty and responsibility. But he is surrounded by huge piles of books that topple and bury him before he can tell her what duty he's talking about. The books all crumble into dust that swirls up in clouds like the dust on the road. When it clears, there is no sign of her father. She is standing in front of the painting, back at the Citadel. The landscape is as it was when she first saw it, lush, green, inviting—in tragic contrast with the desiccated countryside she has been traveling through. It sits on a tall easel in a darkened room. A huge gilt frame surrounds it, overwhelming its simpler beauties with gaudy carvings of fruit and flowers. As she moves closer, the carvings resolve into the sinuous figures of dragons, intertwined, chasing each other around the frame. Tiny jewels sparkle in their eyes: ruby, sapphire, emerald, diamond.

She moves closer, searching for the image of the God in the carving. Frame and landscape enlarge. She stands in front of the painting as if before an enormous window. A breath of wind tousles her hair, and the window becomes an open doorway. The frame is the stone portal that guards the entrance to the House Computer's inner sanctum in the Citadel Library, but the Library is nowhere in view.

PAIA!

Someone is calling from outside the door, in a musical lilt that makes her very name sound magical, as if the wind itself were speaking.

PAIA!

The sweet voice resonates in the same place inside her as the God's silent summons. Paia peers around the side of the portal, sees no one.

PAIA!

Perhaps the caller is just beyond those trees. Paia steps forward.

With a roar and a flash, her way is barred by a sudden curtain of flame. White heat sears her eyelashes and hair. Paia stumbles backward with a cry, and wakes.

At first, she thinks she's in her own room, then she doesn't know where she is. Then she's sure she's still sleeping.

The God is standing at the foot of her bed. The room is the same darkened room of her dream except for the God, who shimmers with his own angry glow. Paia waits for him to speak. But he just stares at her, for so long that the hot rage cools in his eyes, fading to gray. His light seeps out of the room like the end of day, and Paia is overcome by inexplicable grief. She bolts upright. Dream or not, she reaches for him. "My lord!"

The God eyes her bleakly, then shakes his head and turns away, a faint glow gliding through darkness like a fish through soundless depths, back and forth, back and forth.

"Do you find it beautiful, all that damp and green?"

Paia swallows. Yes is obviously the wrong answer.

"What about me? Am I not beautiful? Is not the kingdom I've created more beautiful than this?"

He gestures into the darkness, and the painting reappears, only to explode into flame. Even as it burns, Paia can see the trees dying and the landscape shriveling into desert. A sob rises in her throat, but she holds her tongue. The servants and Temple Daughters sleep on as if nothing could wake them.

"She seeks to win you to their cause, beloved."

"She, my lord?" His enemies have never had a gender before.

"My sister."

"Your *what?*" Now Paia is sure she is dreaming, though the tears on her cheeks feel real enough.

"My sister, who plagues me even from the confines of her prison." He paces away. "Well. How goes your Visitation so far? Are you teaching the Faithful to love me?"

She absorbs his bitterness like a lash. "They will, if they follow my example. If only you would be there with me, the teaching would be simple."

The God rolls his golden eyes at her.

"My lord, a dream means nothing! Why do you insist on doubting me?"

"THIS dream means everything! I wasn't sure how deeply she had touched you. Now I know, even if you do not." He paces back to stand beside the bed, then sits, though the sheep's wool mattresses show no sign of added weight. He stares searchingly into Paia's face as if into the farthest reaches of her soul. He traces the shape of her chin with his palm, millimeters from her skin, and the tears dry on her cheeks.

"Oh, my dearest lord," she whispers.

He leans in as if to kiss her, but Paia feels only heat, little tongues of flame licking at her lips, curling into her parted mouth, seeking the back of her throat. It is both intense pain and deepest pleasure, but Paia smells no burning flesh so the only sensation she knows is real is her overwhelming surge of desire. If only she could press herself against him, let his glorious heat fill her in all ways. But to grasp him now would be to grasp air. The pain and her hunger take her together like a whirlwind. Whimpers and groans mix deep in her throat.

Abruptly, he pulls away, leaving her gasping. Her mouth feels like it's been stung by a thousand bees. She touches her tongue to her lips delicately.

"Have I damaged you, my priestess?"

Paia has never seen the God's perfect face so taut with rage and tragedy. "I . . . don't think so."

"You see how it is, then."

"Yes. I see." What Paia really sees is their private ritual of Holy Ecstasy for what it is: the only way the God can pleasure her as a man would do. What, she wonders, does he get out of it? "Is there no other way?"

After a long moment, he replies, "I have managed much. This I cannot. And because of this, you will betray me."

Returning grief stuns her, stealing the protest from her mouth. As she struggles to speak, the God holds up a gilded hand. "Do not make promises you do not understand." When he sighs, it is like the magma rumbling at the volcano's heart. "It is not your fault. You lack the means to resist them."

"I will not believe it!"

"How would you know?" He sighs again, looks down. "Perhaps you are right. I should not have kept you so long in ignorance."

"My lord Fire . . ."

"Do not speak." He stands, insubstantial as air, as weighty as centuries. "I will have the painting destroyed," he says, and vanishes.

And Paia wakes, this time for certain, amid the snoring of the other priestesses. Her fists and jaw are clenched, her pillow slick with tears.

How can this be?

If her father's library holds the truth, if the long centuries of blood and history have truly decreed this indelible bond, why would it be shaped in a way that can only break both their hearts? What purpose would there be in it?

Surely history has gone wrong somehow.

For the rest of the long night, Paia ponders how to even think about putting it right.

CHAPTER TWENTY-EIGHT

The Tinkers will not be rushed. After two idle days of waiting through their prep for the big trade expedition, N'Doch and the baron are getting restless. For different reasons, of course. N'Doch, because he's picking it up from the dragons, no matter how hard he tries to resist. The baron, because restlessness is his natural state, as far as N'Doch can tell.

Mostly to bug him, N'Doch pretends to relish the long hot days spent mostly within hands' reach of Blind Rachel's chill pool.

"You just gotta lighten up some, Dolph. A little r 'n r is good for a man of war like yerself." He trails his hand in the cooling water, then drips it luxuriously across his bare chest.

Köthen merely grunts, then spits on the honing stone he's cadged off Luther and sets the blade of his dagger to the dampened surface. "I've many times wished for Hal Engle at my side," he muses, rotating the already lethal steel in small, precise circles, "but now more than ever."

"What? I'm not good enough for you?"

Without ceasing his honing, Köthen gazes out into the amber darkness of the dusk-shadowed woods. "Hal Engle knows everything there is to know about dragons. He would know how best to kill one, I imagine."

N'Doch sits up straighter. "Whoa. No one's said anything about killing. If this 'monsta' of theirs is Fire, and he *has* got Air stashed away someplace, killing him ain't gonna help us one bit."

"But it might help the local populace."

"Hey, man, you didn't even want to be here. What the hell d'you care about the local populace?"

Köthen shrugs, not a thing N'Doch sees him do all that often, since the baron's not much into either indecision or ambivalence. "They appear to be in need, and they have requested our help."

"Oh. I get it." N'Doch nods sagely, wondering how he got so brave, to be talking like this to a man with both a temper and a very sharp blade. "Now I know the kinda guy you are. You think you can fix everything, right? Whatever's wrong, you're gonna be the man for it."

Köthen doesn't leave off making his neat little circles on the stone. "There's no success without effort."

The man's self-restraint is admirable, N'Doch decides, now that he's got it back in hand. He's settling in to his exile with the scary kind of patience that usually portends an explosion of action when the time comes. N'Doch's never known a man who could make his silences so loud. The Tinkers walk softly around Köthen, but never fail to let him know they're glad to have him as an ally. "You're just bored, is what you are. But listen up, Dolph. Don't you let the girl hear you talk about killing dragons."

Now Köthen looks up. "Perhaps if I did, it would finally affect the disillusionment I've been unable thus far to achieve."

"Mebbe. I wouldn't count on it, though."

An odd crackling off among the trees alerts them both.

"Horses," says Köthen, with mild wonder.

"Nah, c'mon. Here?" N'Doch gets to his feet, squinting into the dim spaces between the trunks and branches.

Köthen spits on his stone again, listening. "Horses, unshod. No riders. No, they're . . ." He looks up, frowning, as a crowd of large animals noses its way through the woods to the edge of the pool, followed by several of the Tinker children. "Ah, that's it. They're mules."

"Damn." N'Doch is impressed, both by Köthen's ear and the animals' size. They look strong and tough, if a bit on the thin side.

Köthen sheathes his dagger and stands to make room as the herd lowers their long heads to drink. His hands move over them eagerly, smoothing flanks, assessing leg muscles. "There's some skill to breeding a good mule."

N'Doch stands back. He's not so easy being surrounded by large hoofed animals. "Wonder where they've been keeping them."

"Yo! Dockman!" Luther calls from behind. He slaps a lagging mule toward the water and ambles over to join them, gesturing at the stone in Köthen's belt. "Yu dun wit' dat?"

Köthen nods, offering it back. *"Ja, danka."*

"Time ta pack up, nah. Yu ready?"

"Betcha!" N'Doch waves a hand at the mule herd. "Where'd all this come from?"

"Up da hill sum. Dey's grass deah, sumat." Luther laughs, a mournful hollow sound. "Didna tink we was gonna haul dem waggins by oursels, didju? Das fer townfolk!"

When suddenly the next dawn proved to be departure day, Erde watched the hitchup with eager interest. The sturdy mules reminded her of Sir Hal's uncanny beast, and that set her worrying about how matters were in Deep Moor, and with the war. She wished Linden was here, for the youngest Tinker baby was ill with a mysterious ailment that their own herbalist could not seem to cure. Erde considered stealing the child and whisking it off to the dragon in the woods. He thought perhaps he could help. But the mother never left it alone for a minute, and it was still not time to let the Tinkers in on the true nature of their new allies.

It was good to be on the move again, even better that her heavy pack would travel in the wagons instead of on her back. Erde had been able to learn a lot in her two days at Blind Rachel, about the villagers and their dragon worship. The information had only upset her own dragons further, but it had decided them that confrontation was the best course, and that there was no time to lose. The search for Air would take a back seat to the search for Fire. Now both dragons were sure that one would lead to the other.

AND MEANWHILE, YOU WILL REST HERE AND BE COMFORTABLE?

I DO NOT NOTICE SUCH THINGS.

YOU NOTICE WHEN YOU'RE HUNGRY.

INDEED I DO, AND WE SHALL NEED TO BE THINKING ABOUT THAT SOON.

The woods around the Tinker camp were nearly barren of wildlife. Certainly there was nothing big enough to keep a dragon fed. Erde found herself gazing at the mules and averted her eyes guiltily.

I WILL BUY YOU SOMETHING FAT AND SWEET WHEN WE REACH THE VILLAGES.

If there is such a thing in the villages. And what will you buy it with, girl?

Leave it to Lady Water to come up with a fuller understanding of commerce. But for her dagger and the dragon brooch pinned inside her shirt, Erde had nothing of value.

I'LL TRADE FOR IT. I'LL THINK OF SOMETHING.

"Of course you will, little sister." The dragon-as-Sedou joined her, laughter in his eyes. "Don't mind me. All set to leave? The signal's been given. Come walk along with me. The day's just begun, yet I sense we are nearing our journey's end.

Earth felt it, too. He said it was like hearing a rumbling in the distance for ever so long, and then finally spotting the thunderhead. And the summons had strengthened again, he said, that silent call that only the dragons heard. Erde was sad to leave him behind again. She welcomed Sedou's company, since N'Doch had decided to walk with Baron Köthen in the rear. More than half the crew was going along, leaving only a handful of elderly to care for the rabbits and goats and to water the little kitchen gardens, plus a small warrior contingent assigned to the camp's defense.

But Erde understood why. Listening carefully over the past few days, especially to Luther who did not mince words, had made it clear that this trip was more than the usual "biz." Despite the beauty of their stronghold and Stoksie's irrepressible cheer, Blind Rachel Crew's situation was deteriorating. Their trade stocks were precariously low, their stores of staple foods even lower. Their survival as a community depended on the success of this expedition. At least the continuation of their water supply was now assured, though none of them knew it. Erde wished she could tell them, to relieve at least one source of their constant anxiety.

She and Sedou joined the line of wagons midway as it rolled out of camp. The road outward did not appear to be a road at all. The first several hours were a trek across crumbling stone ledges and dry, scrub-choked meadows. Erde pointed out to Sedou how both wagons and walkers spread out in a wide fan formation wherever space permitted.

"I believe they hope to leave as faint a trace of our passage as possible." He circled a hand in the air. "Not even much of a dust cloud raised."

She nodded, intrigued by the Tinkers' quiet methods of defense. Her father, Baron Josef, would have built a big stone wall around such a stronghold, then loudly challenged all comers to vanquish it.

Before the sun was high, the expedition was several leagues from the camp by Erde's estimation, stretched out in a long, lazy line. The pace had slowed to an odd kind of waiting. But then, at a call from up front, each walker and wagon turned abruptly left from where they were, and moved downslope into a broad stand of sharp-needled evergreens. These young trees looked so thick and healthy that Erde wondered if someone had been watering them, like they did back in camp. Passage between the trunks was so narrow that the rough branches scraped the sides of the bigger wagons. The mules groaned and protested, but on the other side of the grove, Erde saw they had come out onto what N'Doch would call a "real" road, paved like a castle courtyard with that pale seamless stone he called *concrete*. The low, heavy greenery screened their sideways approach to the road as effectively as any big stone wall, or perhaps more so, for the fact of not announcing itself.

Once on the road, though it was cracked and pitted and dotted with tall tufts of weeds, the expedition moved faster. They descended through dusty pine scrub onto more open slopes of thorn brush and brittle yellow grasses that rustled like a woman's skirts in the hot breezes. Here and there, a few stunted hardwoods clung to the hillsides, bent over with drought and wind. Along one such dry meadow, the Tinkers stopped to rest, by habit or common consent, Erde could never tell. Their decision-making process was often too diffuse for her even to detect. Two or three walkers left the road and plunged into the scrub, to answer a call of Nature, she assumed. But a wave from one brought another dozen leaping down from the carts and caravans, armed with buckets and long-handled baskets of metallic mesh. Others followed more slowly.

"Bluburry," announced Stoksie as he limped past, a bucket in each hand. "Real gud trade, bluburry. Be heah a while, den. Yu doin' okay, nah?"

Erde nodded gratefully, looking to Sedou for help with the English, which she could understand now but still had trouble pronouncing.

"Can we help?" Sedou asked, for them both.

Stoksie handed over one of his buckets with a gap-toothed grin. "Betcha!"

The berries were tiny but sweet. Erde couldn't resist nibbling a few, but all the Tinkers were doing the same. The picking went quickly with so many pickers, and consolidation produced an impressive crop. Several large buckets were capped and stowed. Watching Stoksie rub his hands in satisfaction, Erde thought, *every little bit helps.*

A small noon meal was shared out, with water from the big wooden casks lashed to each wagon. When the expedition moved on, a steady pace brought them down off the higher reaches and into the foothills by midafternoon. It was hotter there, and traces of civilization appeared. Very soon Erde understood Baron Köthen's dry bemusement at what he called N'Doch's "ridiculous luck," for stumbling upon the Tinkers and not someone more dangerous.

Her first hint was the ruins along the road, the crumbling stone foundations of farmsteads long ago deserted. These looked sad and lonely, but with a peaceful aura of having eased gradually back to Nature. After that came less comforting signs: structures more recently inhabited, not fallen back to the barren earth quickly enough to eradicate the high metal fences that had once surrounded them, now smashed and broken, or the wide dark scars of explosion and conflagration.

"Surely there was a war!" exclaimed Erde, after the seventh or eighth burned-out ruin.

The dragon-as-Sedou shook his head. "Mankind is a rabid animal destroying itself from within."

"No animal would so foul its nest. God set Man apart from the animals, to do His bidding, but Man will not follow His will."

"It's humanity's belief that they're different from animals that leads to all this." He gestured across the devastated landscape, his face stony with ancient despair. "Would any true god allow it?"

Erde's lips pursed. She regretted starting this conversation, for the dragon could talk circles around her. But there were certain perversions of dogma that she should not let pass unchallenged. "As if there could be more than one! My lady Water, you learn this pagan talk from your godless guide!"

"More from his brother, the martyr and idealist whose shape I walk in."

"A man you've never met."

"Yet who lives richly in the mind of the brother who loved him."

"Oh, how do you know what's really Sedou and what's merely N'Doch's memory of him?"

"I do not. Does it matter? Why do you say merely? Is it not mankind's dearest hope to be lovingly remembered when one no longer lives?"

"Mankind's dearest hope is salvation," Erde reminded him primly.

"Ah. Salvation."

She sensed mockery and frowned up at him.

The dragon-as-Sedou grinned. "Well, little sister? Did it never occur to you that some dragons—and their guides— might not be Christian?"

A shout from ahead saved her the cost of a foolish reply. The wagons halted and every Tinker without reins in their hands reached for a weapon.

"Uh-oh," murmured Sedou, sounding very much like N'Doch.

N'Doch and Baron Köthen came loping up from behind. Köthen had armed himself with a stout sharpened pole.

"Dochmann! Stay with milady!" he ordered, still moving forward. "Dragon man, come with me."

Sedou fell in beside him. "Dragon woman, you mean."

Köthen shook his head. "Woman dragon. Dragon man."

Sedou laughed, and the two of them trotted ahead, along

the line of wagons. Next, Luther hurried by, with several others behind him.

"Should we go, too?" Erde asked N'Doch.

"We're safer here."

"No, I mean, don't you want to know what's happening?"

N'Doch stares at her. She's craning forward, this way and that, like an anxious bird. Either she's the bravest fool he's ever met, or she really has no idea. "Hey, we'll know soon enough. If it blows up into something serious, we'll go in as backup."

"Well, I'm going now."

N'Doch grabs her arm. "No, you don't. The boss says stay here, that's what we'll do."

"The boss?"

N'Doch fidgets. "Y'know. His high-mucky-muck lordship."

The girl looks interested. "Have you sworn service to Baron Köthen?"

"Gedoudaheah! No way!"

She cocks her head at him, puzzled.

"Just never mind, okay? What do the dragons say is going on up there?"

She makes a little pout at him, then goes inward to that place where, as N'Doch thinks of it, the channel is always open. "That there are some people up ahead who claim the right of payment for our safe passage through their lands. Stoksie, Luther, and Brenda do not agree with them."

N'Doch smirks. "The old toll gambit. Getting back what they gave."

"But Ysabel seems to think it might be wiser to negotiate a reasonable price."

"What for?" Actually, N'Doch is sorry to miss this bit of entertainment. His regret must be reading on his face, 'cause the girl grabs his hand and starts yanking him forward.

"You do want to know! Come, N'Doch! You needn't do everything Baron Köthen tells you to!"

Ouch, he thinks. She's really learned how to get to him. But by the time he's made up his mind to go along with her, the Tinkers are relaxing off the alert, remounting their wagons and taking up the reins again, though their weapons are set closer to hand. Soon Köthen and Sedou come strolling back from the front, both of them looking just a bit smug.

"So what happened?" N'Doch demands.

Köthen flicks a hand dismissively.

"A few hungry people trying to fill their bellies the easy way," Sedou says.

"Yeah? What'd you do?"

Sedou shrugs. "Just showed up."

"Well, that's kinda too easy, ain't it?"

"A scrawny, measly lot of brigands," Köthen mutters.

"Not brigands, Dolph. People starving."

Köthen bows to the dragon man satirically. "I stand corrected."

"Stoksie's seeing what they have left to trade for food."

"Oh," exclaims the girl. "We ought to just give them what they need!"

N'Doch is glad he's not the only one staring at her like she's a lunatic. "And what do you plan to eat after you've given it all away?"

"Well . . . if they had items to trade, would they not have traded it for food already, in the villages?"

Sedou gropes for a middle ground between honorable charity and reckless waste. "Luther says these people can't go to the villages. They're exiles. They don't approve of the villagers' religion."

"Good on them," N'Doch remarks.

Sedou nods. "So Stoksie's trying to work out a way to give them some food, without giving it outright."

"Which is against his principles," Köthen adds.

"Like to see what he gets for it," says N'Doch.

"I think he did not wish to make them beg for their food," Sedou concludes.

Köthen sucks his teeth. "I think they were not strangers."

They all look at him, waiting for more.

"Really?" N'Doch prompts.

"Yes, though they wished to pretend otherwise."

"Well, that doesn't make sense."

Köthen offers one of his hard looks.

"Okay, lemme put it this way: why would they do that?"

"Friend N'Doch, I have not yet given the structure of alliances in this region a thorough enough study."

N'Doch's getting irritated. "Well, lemme know when you do."

It's only after the wagons move forward again and Köthen drops back to his habitual spot in the rear, that N'Doch realizes the baron's learned how to bait him, too, in return for the abuse he's been dishing out. This makes him laugh out loud.

The girl stares at him. "What's funny?"

"Your man Dolph."

"Don't call him that," she murmurs.

And her regret is too real for him to make light of. "Okay. I won't."

When they pass the spot where the front wagons had halted, he sees a group of eight or ten ragged folk squatting down in the dust with a small pile of food between them. They're arguing over it already.

The toll gambit is pulled on them twice more before the wagons reach the first village, with much the same results. By then, N'Doch suspects that Köthen is right, or the Tinkers are more softhearted than they'd like to admit. Either way, he hopes they pack extra rations on these trips, so they can afford their own generosity. No wonder they're in trouble.

The first village is a small one, no more than twenty houses set beneath a scattering of battered, broad-trunked trees. Must be water underground, N'Doch decides, to keep these oldsters alive. The houses are low and square and made of stone. If they were cement block, they'd look a lot like his mama's house. A roof over one's head but otherwise full of holes. At dusk, the place looks deserted, not much of a threat. Not even a junkyard dog to greet them, just a few old people peering cautiously out of their doorways. The Tinkers pass through the village unchallenged and pull the wagons into a tight ring in a dusty field on the other side. While dinner preparations are underway, a small but well-armed delegation walks back into town to announce the start of trade at dawn the next morning and to negotiate water and grazing for the mules. N'Doch wonders who they're gonna find to talk to.

He's scavenging bits of twig for Luther's cook fire when a murmur runs around the circle of wagons. Folks straighten up from their chopping and stirring to point at the horizon. N'Doch dumps his meager handful beside Sedou and the girl. She's teaching the dragon man how to peel potatoes.

"Take a look out there," he tells them.

An odd formation of cloud has appeared to either side of the blood red setting sun. Not rain clouds, but puffy and pink. More what N'Doch would call fair-weather clouds, unlikely at dusk in any location, and certainly weird in this place. He hasn't seen a hint of a cloud since he arrived, only the ever-present sooty murk that turns the empty sky yellow and green.

Sedou stares at the horizon, the potato forgotten in his hand. "Interesting. Not one of mine."

N'Doch laughs. "Oh, yeah?"

"Mine have more water in them."

"Cool, bro. Bring 'em on! I could do with a shower."

"Such energies are not to be squandered lightly."

N'Doch sees he's serious. "Wait . . . you can do that? Really?"

The girl gets that haunted look. "Have you forgotten how Lady Water saved us at Lealé's?"

"I can do it, sure, I can. A shower is a mere parlor trick." Sedou turns his dragon stare on N'Doch, only there's a lot of Sedou in it, too, Sedou flaring in righteous wrath. He shakes the potato in his dark fist as if it stood in for all of Nature. "But do you mean, can I fix this dust, this parched field, this . . . wasted earth? I can turn it to mud, if you like . . ."

"No, I . . ."

"For an hour perhaps, and then the life-water would be gone, sucked away as if it had never been! The roots would still dry and the stems still wither! It takes more than just water, even if I could offer an endless supply. Too much water, after all, is a flood, and a flood is as destructive as a drought! Alone, I can do little. But with proper help . . ."

"Whoa. Easy." N'Doch hates this. Just when he's let

himself forget, the millennia creep back into the voice of this man-thing who isn't really his brother.

Sedou stares at the horizon, and then his rage is gone as quickly as it came. "But with help . . ."

"With help you could what? Make a monsoon?"

The girl clucks her tongue, disapproving his attempt to lighten up a moment just because its gravity makes him nervous.

"No. No. But surely this is part of it."

"Part of what?"

"Part of all of it. Of what we are to do, to accomplish. Together." Sedou's chin lifts and his shoulders drop back as his gaze drifts to some inner dragon space that N'Doch doesn't even want to contemplate. "Sometimes I see . . ." He falters, his inhuman eyes suddenly dark with foreboding.

"What, bro?" N'Doch asks again, uneasy. "What do you see?"

And then it comes to him what's been bothering him since they arrived at Blind Rachel. He just knows this gig's been much too easy so far. Any minute now, the shit is gonna hit the fan. The girl is staring at Sedou reverently, like he might lay out some final truth any moment. She prefers him like this, damn her, more dragon than Sedou.

But the dragon/man sighs, shakes his head. "It's never clear enough to really say. What my brother Earth calls a Purpose only partly understood . . . for me, it's more like a vision, only partly glimpsed." He shakes himself out of his sober reverie. "But those clouds . . . those are interesting. A sign . . . of some sort."

The Tinker delegation returning from the village descends upon them with jovial enthusiasm.

"C'monta my fire, nah," invites Ysabel. "Feedju up gud!"

N'Doch soaks up the crinkle in her hair and the faint Latin music in her speech like it was cool, sweet water.

Sedou lifts the pot of potatoes he and the girl have not quite worked their way through. "Thank you, but Luther was kind enough to ask . . ."

"Luta come, too, den. Dat ri', Luta? Allyu come wit me! Heah da news frum town."

Stoksie grins up at N'Doch. "Yu bring gud luck, tallfella."

"Yeah? How's that?"

Stoksie runs a hand across his shiny bald head, then points at the clouds, grown into two thin spires that flank the ruby oval of the sun like the minarets on a mosque. "Dese townies call dat a sign. Say da god smile onda trade day."

"Which god is that?" Sedou asks lightly.

Stoksie and Ysa flick glances at Luther, as if waiting for a cue.

"Dere's only one fer dem," Luther says grimly. "Da monsta."

The girl frowns. "They think the monster is God? You did not mention that."

N'Doch laughs. "And he cares about trade?"

Stoksie's grin returns. "Shur, shur. Lotsa time, dem townies trade der food 'n der craftwerk for stoopid glittajunk to give 'im prezents."

"Glitter junk?"

"Shur. Like dem jools what wimen usda weah. Ornyment." Stoksie sees he has the three visitors' total attention. "Fake stuff, y'know. Salvage." He mimes digging. "We find it 'roun."

Sedou nods. "But why are the clouds a good omen?"

Stoksie blinks at him. "Clouds is alwiz a gud sign, tall-fella. Whachu tink? Mebba it rain, nah?"

"When did you see clouds last, can you remember?"

"Can' say wen it wuz. Wachu tink, Ysa?"

"I'd say tree mont', mebbe fowah. Dat weerd time. Yu memba dat, Luta?"

Luther, absorbed in cloud study, responds to his name with a start. "Betcha! Come up suddin like, afta nuttin fer neah a yeah. Den a few, den moah 'n moah fer a week, like. Den alla suddin, nuttin agin. Till now."

"Three months ago?" asks Sedou thoughtfully. "Clouds like these?"

"Sumpin' like."

"Interesting."

"Okay, c'mon nah." Ysabel hooks an arm around Stoksie's elbow. "Talk whilyu eatin!"

Night settles in during the meal prep. There are fewer cook fires inside the ring of wagons than at the camp. Not enough firewood. N'Doch feels the darkness wrapping him close. He's used to not much light at home, out in the bush, but this night is the very definition of lightless. It looms like a wall, a tsunami of darkness. And his conviction that the party's over is still giving him the creeps. Maybe the others sense it, too. N'Doch sees how, despite the heat, everyone finds a spot to huddle in tight around the few dim pools of glow. But it's not a night attack that worries them. Instead of keeping it quiet, they talk louder than usual, act raucous, as if to shout down suffocation by the void.

At Ysabel's fire, Luis joins them and a few couples N'Doch knows by face but not by name, plus Mari and Senda, who hang around Sedou whenever they can get away with the idleness that hanging around requires. Brenda and Charlie sit down long enough to eat, then go off on perimeter watch. N'Doch wishes Marley was by, with his guitar, but the old man has stayed at camp to look after his prize tomatoes.

The conversation is about the townies. Those who went into the village share out the local gossip—who's dead, who's married who, who's promised what for trade. Then comes the news that's got the village in an uproar: some big religious figure making a town-by-town tour will not be stopping by their village because it's too small.

"Too small fer da monsta ta bodda wit'," notes Luther. "An' das a gud ting!"

"Das why we come heah," Stoksie agrees.

"But dey hate dat, doncha know? Makes 'em feel bad. Like dey not gud enuff."

"Gud enuff fer us, nah."

General agreement runs around the fire, then talk turns to the monster god himself. War stories, N'Doch thinks of them. Disputes about the span of his wings, the size of his claws, the direness of his wrath. It takes a lot, he notes, for these folks to air their grievances. They'd rather be laughing and yarn-spinning. Old tales are trotted out to shock the visitors' virgin ears, and everyone dutifully claims not to believe any of them, so Luther can attest loudly to the accuracy of every single one. N'Doch thinks of evenings in the bush village where he grew up, though the gossip there was mostly the bad news from the city and the stories were the familiar ancestral myths, recounted each time as if for the first time.

"But why do they call him God?" protests the girl in her polite but pained way, after Mari and Senda have shuddered their way through a fourth graphic tale of bestial cruelty, "Where is the religion in such a practice? Is there doctrine? Does he work miracles? If he's there in the flesh and there's no denying his presence, what are the issues of Faith?"

Köthen, leaning in to N'Doch's quiet running translation, agrees. "More a plain tyrant than a god, it would seem."

Luther clears his throat, and though no one actually moves, somehow the others make a respectful space for him, as they have done for Sedou since he appeared among them. "Well, der is doktrin. Summa dem belief it. But I tink mosta dem jes say so cuz dey skeerda da monsta."

"What do they believe?" Sedou asks.

"Ina enda da wold. Any day nah. Say der's no pint doin' nuttin fer da future, cuz der won' be any. Or so dey tink."

"I take it you do not share this belief."

"Nah." Luther offers a wan grin. "Das too dak fer me, y'know?"

Sedou asks, "So what do you believe?"

For a moment, silence reigns around Ysabel's fire. Again, it seems that the others, even Stoksie and Ysabel, defer in such matters to Luther. He begins slowly. "Well, summa us see it diffrint. We say it mebbe look like da enda da wold, bud it ain't." He pauses as if he would welcome a change of subject, but Sedou waits him out. Finally Luther shrugs and hikes his stooped body and big nose forward, his scarred hands lifting from his sides to talk along with him. "No, it ain't. Why? Cuz der's One comin' ta make it right."

"She walks in light," Ysabel murmurs.

"Fixit all, y'know?" Luther's arms pinwheel around him. "Alla it. Den mebbe we liff like umins again."

"The One?" the girl breathes. "You mean, Our Savior?"

"Probably not the one you're thinking of," says Sedou gently.

"You think this fix up's gonna happen soon?" N'Doch asks, for it sounds like he does. Maybe even tomorrow.

Luther rocks his head back and forth like a tired bear. "We don' know dat, nah, cuz y'see, da One gotta big problum. She shuddup inna dark by da Handa Chaos, waitin' till we figure a way ta ged her out."

"She? In the dark?" The words escape Sedou as a sigh. N'Doch is too astounded to speak, and the girl looks thunderstruck.

"She walks in light," murmurs Ysabel again, echoed this time by Luis and one of the nameless couples. Stoksie, N'Doch notices, remains silent. The others shift uneasily.

"Like I sez," Luther concludes, "Only *summa* us belief dis."

N'Doch feels the deep thrum of dragon energies in the air, in the very ground beneath his feet. He wishes he was like the Tinkers, sitting there unawares. He remembers how, at Lealé's, when the dragons decided to make their move, things started to pinball with sickening speed. The girl's still looking stunned, but he knows she's in furious converse with the big guy back in the woods. Despite the high voltage that Sedou's generating for those who are plugged in to it, his surface remains calm and merely . . . interested.

"An imprisoned messiah. It's a beautiful notion, Luther. Is it yours?"

Luther looks shocked, then embarrassed. "Na, na. I heerd it frum . . . a frien'. A greyt preecher-man, y'know? I lissen, I jus' know he got da wold on right."

"I'd like to meet this preacher. Does he say where the Hand of Chaos is keeping your awaited One?"

"We all lookin' on dat. Ev'ry day, we closer to da ansa."

"And what will it take to free her?"

Luther lowers his elbows to rest on his knees. "We ain't figurd dat yet neider."

"Der's sum say da One'll be free whenda monsta is ovahtrone."

This is a new voice, one N'Doch doesn't recognize, and he's sure he knows all of Blind Rachel's sounds, if not the names. The speaker is a young woman crouched on the other side of the fire, partly obscured by the flames.

"Sum say dat," Luther agrees dubiously.

She's got two other strangers with her, one on either side, two guys, youngish and serious-looking. N'Doch is ashamed how they just snuck up out of the night without him noticing. Köthen is already watching them, probably has been for a while. But the Tinkers act like it's nothing unusual.

He nudges Stoksie. "Who's that?"

"Frum town."

"You don't mind?"

Stoksie shrugs. "Wild young'uns. Y'know?"

Luther shoves his hair back, speaking across the fire, "But dem as tink dat got no ideah how dey gonna make it happin."

"Sum do," says the young woman.

"Sum oughta git bettah ideahs befur dey go preachin' 'em."

And then it looks like that's all anyone's willing to say, until Sedou draws a deep and quiet breath. The hot wind that's been fanning the embers dies back. N'Doch feels his own breath coming shorter now, and he knows for sure that his vacation's over. Some conjunction of circumstance and subject matter has occurred. The ball is in the slot and the blue dragon's hand is on the lever. He glances down the line of listeners, sees all the apprehension in her and catches his fellow dragon guide's eye. He that he's trying to keep off his own.

"Here we go," he mutters to Köthen.

"Now, Luther, I won't claim that my ideas are any better, but there's one I'd like to try out on you anyway." Sedou looks to Luther for permission.

"Yer ideahs is always welcum, tallfella."

"My thanks. What if I say, then . . ." Sedou gazes around until he holds their attention, even the newcomers across the fire. "What if I point out an amazing coincidence. The friend my companions and I came looking for is also imprisoned in an unknown place. We believe her imprisonment is keeping her—and us—from accomplishing a glorious good. And we believe that he who imprisoned her does not want this great good accomplished." Sedou glances down, the very image of humble self-doubt. "Do you think, my friends, that it is too much to conclude that this jailer is the same monster god you speak of?"

Murmurs build around the fire.

"A moment longer, friends." Sedou puts out a hand as if smoothing ripples. The murmurs die into edgy silence, and N'Doch senses the lever's twang. The ball is in motion.

"What if I say something further, something . . . oh, you who have asked our help, listen well! What if I tell you the help that I bring is far greater than you've supposed, and of a . . . different sort. It will shake your faith, but then surely renew it!"

The Tinkers eye him, some wearily, others with caution, like they expect him to start raving any minute. Maybe he already has. N'Doch guesses it's like opening a box you had great plans for and finding it empty, or full of the same old garbage.

But Luther says, "Go on, tallfella."

Sedou nods. "It cannot be mere chance that has brought us together. It cannot be! There is a great mystery here that I have not yet been able to penetrate. But I believe our shared knowledge of it will fit together like a key in a lock, that together, we can discover this prison and free my friend . . . and your awaited One." The dragon/man drops his hand and his voice. The wind dies entirely, as if someone's switched off the fan, and Sedou's whisper insinuates itself into every ear. "For, you see, my friends: I believe them to be one and the same being, that is, my sister Air."

Luther coughs gently, just once. "Tallfella, we weren't expectin' da One to be *umin* . . . y'know?"

"Nor is my sister Air."

Luther nods, like he's been waiting for this.

N'Doch shivers, despite the heat. *Well, that certainly lays a lot of our cards on the table.* He's not sure the other Tinkers are ready for it. But maybe they are. He looks around at the stubborn faces still protecting themselves against the rising of hope, eyes narrowing at Sedou, trying to decide exactly how crazy he is . . . or isn't.

Because there's a difference here: these people don't need to be convinced of the reality of magical creatures. There's one ravaging their countryside already. What they need is renewed faith and a weapon.

Well, one has just arrived. No, make that two.

N'Doch fills Köthen in on what's gone down, and is unsurprised by the baron's sudden grin of anticipation. As for himself, he's got nothing against a good fight, but he feels a darkness creeping up on him that he cannot explain.

Sedou smiles into the uneasy silence, a glow like the full moon rising. There is power in his very calm, as if he knows they will come to believe him and he needs offer nothing but patience while they find this out for themselves.

Damn dragon arrogance, N'Doch swears, watching the dragon/man morph into something subtly less earthly, without needing a note of his music. He'd be surprised to find a steady hand or slow heart in the house. Finally the townie woman stands. She moves stiffly around the fire until she's face-to-face with the sitting giant. She has round Asian features and tawny pox-marked skin. N'Doch is sad for her disfigurement. Otherwise, she would be beautiful.

"Give us a sign." Her back is rigid and her Tinker accent suddenly flushed from her voice. She's brave but terrified.

Sedou laughs. "A sign?"

"Of this power you speak of. We've had our fill of messianic lunatics!"

"Of course you have."

She glances defiantly at Luther. "Some people will believe anything if they want it bad enough."

Agreement whispers through the gathering.

"Who are you?" she demands. "Or . . . what."

"My name is Sedou. I am what I am. Who or what are you?"

"I am Miriam, and I . . ." She bites her lip, glances back at her two young accomplices. Their mouths hang open. Wide-eyed, they nod. "And I . . . stand in opposition to the Winged God of the Apocalypse!" She plants her hands on her hips, glaring at Sedou in challenge.

"Well, Miriam. Well spoken. So do I. So does everyone here."

"I know that." His gentleness has caught her off guard. "But these Tinkers do nothing about it! They oppose but do not act! Why do you come to them with your magical appearance and your gift of fish?"

"Word gets around, I see."

Young Miriam scoffs. "Easily accomplished! Why should we listen? Why should we believe? Show us a sign that cannot be explained away!"

Just call in the big guy, thinks N'Doch. That'll convince 'em. Or it might just send them screaming in the opposite direction, given their current expectations of dragons.

"A sign." The dragon/man laughs again, a great booming laugh that tickles a smile or a sheepish grin onto the soberest of disbelieving faces around the fire. He stands, towering over the young woman, but she stands her ground as he spreads his arms wide and throws his head back as if welcoming the surrounding darkness. "So be it, doubting Miriam!"

And a soft rain begins to fall, a precise zone of cooling relief that stops a step outside the circle around the fire. Miriam catches tiny drops on her outstretched palms until they run with moisture, then presses them to her eyes with a sob.

"Parlor tricks," says Sedou sadly.

But Luther lowers himself onto his bony knees, his rough hands clasped in gratitude. "Welcome, pilgrim! Your search has ended."

CHAPTER TWENTY-NINE

Paia spots the odd clouds on the sunset horizon at the end of the third day out, just as she's decided that nothing out of the ordinary will happen on this trip after all, except a near fatal overexposure to the elements. Another sweltering dusk, another dried-up town clinging to subsistence, another dull evening of ritual and routine to look forward to. Or not. Everything she sees, everyone she meets is so listless and played out. Where are the brave and busy villages she has imagined, energized by faith and the common struggle against the hostile climate?

Paia is irritable with discomfort, and the constant diet of ceremony. Plus she's kept as isolated as she ever was in the Citadel. All of it leaves her floaty and disoriented, and vastly disappointed with her Visitation.

"Why can't I talk to anyone?" she rails at Luco as he ushers her toward the High Priestess' lonely seat of honor at the banquet. This particular town is wealthy enough to provide her with a table all of her own, on a raised dais and everything. They're so proud of the dais, a sordid little box with only one step, that they've even painted it the God's sacred red.

Luco's broad shoulders sag, then resettle with new resolution. "You know how the God feels about the importance of maintaining the Temple's image."

"It'll hurt our image if we talk to the people? The God is the Caretaker of the Faithful. What kind of caretaking is that?"

"It lowers you to their level, instead of elevating them to yours."

"Which they can only manage by prayer, which is inhib-

ited by any sort of *normal* conversation?" Paia balls her
hands into fists and vibrates them in frustration. "I came
to walk among them! To preach to them! To inspire them
with my love of the God!"

In fact, Paia isn't loving the God very much right now.
She's angry with him for destroying her painting. But she
can't explain any of this to Luco.

"Inspire them?" he growls. "You'll be lucky if they don't
eat you alive."

"What?"

"I mean, of course, that they're desperate. They need
sustenance, not talk!"

"Faith *is* sustenance, First Son! If you aren't careful, it
will be me advising you to hold your tongue. Won't that
be a novelty!"

Luco's eyes clench shut briefly. "Your pardon, my
priestess."

Paia sighs and forces her hands to relax. No more arguing. She must apply her flagging energy to the task of
surviving the heat and boredom. She points out the clouds
to Luco, to change the subject.

"Hunh. Look at that." He finds them more interesting
than she does. "In the direction of the Citadel."

"Are they rain clouds?"

"He'd never allow that."

"Who?"

"The God. He'd as soon it never rained."

"No, Luco, surely . . ." Paia peered at him closely. Was
the heat getting to him, too?

"In the Chapter House, they'll be saying it's a sign."

"Of what?"

"Of whatever they need it to be a sign of."

He flicks her a sidelong glance as he seats her at the
table. Paia would like to laugh. When officiating, the High
Priestess is barely allowed a smile, never mind the belly
laugh she'd like to let go of. A great big laugh of pure
abandon. It would be so freeing. But the First Son's joke
was not very funny. He's too distracted by . . . whatever
he's distracted by. With a warning frown, he leaves her
struggling. He has not used this trip to ease his insistence
on proper Temple protocol, and the subject of her father
still shuts him up like a box. But in the brief times they've

been apart from listening ears, a progressive change has been evident. The more miles put between them and the Temple, the more relaxed is Luco's tongue. When they do speak together, it is almost a conversation.

And this has taught Paia something: Son Luco does not see her as a religious icon with God-given mystical power, as would any lesser devout of the Temple. To Luco, she is simply the God's designate, the Temple figurehead, chosen not as Luco would choose, but for the god's own inhuman reasons—which the priest is loath to question.

Happily, Paia agrees with him. She's glad she's never pretended with Luco to be something she isn't. What's more, she's always assumed his boundless patience with her tantrums and impulses to be due to his devotion to the God. But new insight suggests that Luco has forgiven her a lot simply because she is her father's daughter. Someday, she will convince him to tell her the story.

The ceremonial feast is over early that evening, before the sun has completely set. Perhaps the dull-eyed inhabitants of this village have squandered too many of their scant resources on their silly dais. Nearly stir-crazy with sitting, Paia begs Luco for a walk outside the village, across the fields perhaps, even up that hill on the far side. She would like a better look at the odd pink cloud towers. He agrees to allow it, if proper security precautions are observed. But he begs off accompanying her, claiming Temple business, as he has every evening so far. In a town so meager, Paia wonders how much business there could be. Visits to the outlying homesteads, perhaps, where the Faithful are in need of spiritual advice or even renewal. Though he shines in the formal recitation, it is hard to imagine Son Luco delivering a sermon. Still, Paia has overheard his admiring acolytes tell of his great oratorical prowess during the Wars of Conversion. But there are no sermons in the Temple of the Apocalypse. Only endless litany.

Before he disappears off to who knows where, Luco gives Paia into the hands of the head of the local Chapter House, a dour, crop-haired woman twice her age. Paia's heart sinks. Being a full priestess, the woman need not go veiled, which means there is nothing to disguise her reluctance.

"Mother Gayle." Impatient to be off on his business, Luco puts on his voice of polite coercion. "Supreme

Mother Paia has a need for some exercise before retiring. Would you be willing to oblige her? A viewing of the local geography, perhaps?"

Paia settles the God's little gun more firmly against her ribs. She notes the look that passes between Son Luco and the local priestess, but she cannot interpret it. Probably he is begging the woman to take her off his hands, or simply warning Mother Gayle to make sure the High Priestess disports herself in a manner becoming to the Temple.

Mother Gayle bows. "The God's servant in all things, my priest."

Luco goes briskly off, and Mother Gayle gathers her entire staff, plus the Temple Honor Guard, in the event of a surprise raid by bandits from the hills. She guides Paia onto the main road out of the village, where they walk in silence through the dusk, with half the village trailing after them. Paia notes how her sandaled feet leave little pouch marks in the deep dust. Suddenly it seems sad that no one even talks about it anymore, this drying up of the world. One just acts as if it has always been this way, even though the worst of it has occurred within her own short lifetime. Accept what is. It's the God's sort of thinking.

The procession crosses the arid field in silence, then climbs in silence as well, first within the shadow of the hill, then with the sun's red ball straight ahead of them, brilliant and blinding, exploding into their eyes. Paia cannot see her feet. Even the ground ahead of her is lost in the dazzle, as if it has fallen away and left her floating. She was already disoriented in her mind, now she is disoriented in her senses as well. She puts out both arms, feeling unbalanced but rather enjoying the novelty.

"It's like walking in light!" she exclaims.

The sober stride of the priestess falters beside her. "I beg your pardon?"

"The sun . . . it's so bright." Paia opens her arms to the bloody glare.

"Ah, yes. The sun. Of course." Mother Gayle nods, then immediately withdraws into her walking silence. She looks, Paia thinks, oddly relieved.

The top of the hill is a series of barren stone ledges with brittle mats of dry moss between. The farthest ledge protrudes over a rather steep drop, providing a perfect platform for viewing the surrounding peaks. But its corners are suspiciously square, and Paia sees it's actually a poured concrete slab, much weathered, probably an old foundation for a house. Mother Gayle points out this mountain and that, identifying them as Tall Mount or Red Face, generic names that are new even since Paia's childhood geography classes. The more colorful names, such as Vanderwacher or Goodnow, have been erased in the God's campaign against history, as if his coming has made the past irrelevant.

But people remember, Paia tells herself. Luco remembered. *Cauldwell's Clove.*

Then Mother Gayle takes her arm and gently draws her to the very edge of the platform, to point straight down. A hundred, two hundred feet below are the remains of a town. Quite a large town, judging from the length of the main street. Its crumbling chimneys and collapsed roofs are touched by the sun's dying rays as if with fire.

"Oh, my! Oh, my." Paia squints to make out faded letters on tumbled-down signs, to take in the rich variety of the buildings, even in their state of ruin. The language of the architecture is so much more complex—dare she say it?—so much more *human* than the blocky, unadorned style favored by the God for current domestic structures. Even the odd crooks and curves of the streets tell an interesting story. She can see where the trees might have been, shading the sidewalks and houses. Paia stares down at the town for a long time, while Mother Gayle waits patiently beside her.

Finally she takes a chance. "Has it a name?"

"Oh, no, Mother Paia."

"I mean, *did* it, at one time? Or has it been forgotten?"

The older priestess clears her throat, then murmurs so that only Paia could possibly hear. "It was called Carlisle. Of course, I only know this because . . . well, I was born there."

As the Temple's highest representative, Paia should deliver a stern reproof. History is forbidden, after all. But she herself has asked, and what escapes her is a sympathetic nod.

Mother Gayle looks mistrustful but again relieved. "There is a heresy, you know, that claims it can all be made green again." She laughs harshly to show her contempt. "Imagine that!"

"Indeed," replies Paia, wondering why the woman is saying this, to the High Priestess of the God's Temple. Everyone around her seems to be losing their grip on propriety. Including herself.

Mother Gayle sighs. "I've thought of petitioning Him to burn it to the ground, like He has so many others. It would be easier. The God is right about the pain our useless old memories can bring."

But why, Paia asks herself, if the town was still standing, could the people not just live there? She's sure the God has told her there were no towns left after the Wars. That his great building spree was undertaken for the good of the homeless Faithful.

Gazing downward, she is suddenly racked with vertigo. Disorientation made physical. She hardly knows what to believe anymore. Thoroughly depressed, Paia backs away from the edge. "It will be dark soon. Perhaps we should be getting back."

The God visits her again that night, only this time she is sure she is not asleep. She would never dream him in this grotesque a rage.

Besides, she has been dreaming of something else. A man. A blond man with a sword, like she has seen in her father's ancient tomes. A rather pleasant dream, for a change.

When she wakes, the God's golden eyes are inches from her own, as hot and bright as twin blast furnaces. There is not a hint of the tragic mask of his most recent visitation. He is nothing but eyes and a long screech of fury, like knives in both her ears. "The picture! The picture! Where is it?"

"The picture? You mean, the painting?" Paia is groggy, confused. "The landscape? You haven't destroyed it?"

"WHERE IS IT? Where have you hidden it?"

"I haven't hidden it. It's in my room."

"LIAR! LIAR!"

"My lord, I am not!" She shoves herself up on her elbows. The painting. He hasn't destroyed it. She struggles to clear her head. Again, she is bedded down in the local Chapter House, and again, the servants and priestesses bedded down with her snore through the God's tirade. Only the High Priestess must endure the heat of his wrath. "I had the painting brought down to my room! It was there when I left! Surely you saw it yourself when you came for me!"

"Then your confederates have stolen it to safety! Where? I can forgive your being an unwitting pawn, but conspire against me at your direst peril! Where is it?" His cry shrills against her eardrums and behind his eyes looms the shadow of horns. "TELL ME!"

"I don't know! I have no confederates!" Her grogginess dulls her fear. She is tired of his tantrums. "How could I have confederates? You allow me no friends! Besides, you know I can conceal nothing from you. You invade even my dreams!"

"After others have already done so! Your dreams are not your own! Have I not said they will destroy us both?"

"Then I will not listen to them!" Paia slumps back on one elbow. How can she prove anything to him? She so much wants him to believe her just because he believes her, as she believes herself. Indeed, she would like to know herself where the painting has gone, this mutable vista that someone else has made her paint. She thinks of the House Comp's tale of tampering, and worries for its safety. "Is it truly not there?"

The shadow behind the hot glow of his eyes resolves into something more manlike. Her concern has rung true, and unsettled him. Paia judges that the worst is over.

"Would I waste my time here if it was?"

"Surely, my lord, the person who left those notes has taken it."

"Ha! Ha!" He fumes inarticulately, but his twin fires withdraw a bit as the focus of his rage shifts to the note-writer. "I have questioned the entire population of the Citadel, yet cannot rout out this traitor!" The light dims as he turns away to begin his habitual pacing. "They have human agents working for them, even as I do. Here, there, and everywhere. I should expect nothing less!"

Paia squints into the returned darkness. There is no sound but his voice.

"How could he conceal himself from me, otherwise? How else could he know about the picture?"

"Know what about it?"

"That picture is nothing without the knowledge of it."

"What knowledge?"

"He is in league with my enemies. It has to be so."

"WHAT KNOWLEDGE?" Paia yells. If she wakes up every woman in the Chapter House, she might get his attention. But the others sleep on undisturbed.

The twin furnaces flare again. "Ha, my priestess! Read a few old books and you think you understand everything! What arrogance!"

Paia's teeth clench. "My arrogance pales beside yours, my lord!"

"I AM YOUR GOD!" he bellows. "What you should understand is how little you really know!"

"I do, more than I ever did! I am out here in the middle of nowhere among strangers who hate me, and you will not offer me the slightest crumb of comfort or encouragement, when I am only begging for enlightenment! Teach me, so I can help you in your work!"

"I don't need your help!"

"Then why do you keep me?" She's up on her knees now, waving her arms at him, wishing she had greater control. But he does need her help. She knows he does. What she doesn't know is how to convince him of it. "Choose another, if you're so dissatisfied! Let me go my own way!"

He stops pacing. "Is that what you want? Is this how you show your devotion to me?"

"It's always about YOU!" she screams. Then a sharp whiff of déjà vu throws her back on her heels. Her mother and father didn't argue very often, but when they did, this is exactly what they sounded like. She is replicating their behavior, she fears, simply because she knows no other. The rush of memory leaves her deflated and confused.

The God hovers over her like a swarm of angry wasps, ready for the next round. But when she remains slumped dejectedly with her hands clasped limply on her knees, he calms a bit, enough at last to assume full man-form, so that he can loom at her bedside with his arms folded, looking satisfied, certain that he's beaten her into submission. Moments like this, of course, are when he is the most generous toward her. She has learned to argue with him, in order to let him win, and then they can be peaceable together. But surely this is not how it was meant to be between them.

"The picture, little fool, is a portal. Didn't your precious dream tell you that?"

A portal? Paia tries to focus on where his mind has gone now. She recalls how, in the dream, the gilt frame became the stone entrance to the Library. "A portal, like a doorway?"

"Indeed. A doorway, if you have the knowledge of it, to wherever—and whenever—you want to go."

"*When*ever?"

The God nods, enjoying her amazement and the superiority of his wisdom. "In your dream, it was showing you the past."

She takes care to maintain the little-girl manner that has settled him down. "You mean, like an image on a monitor screen?"

"Are you deaf? A portal. Like an open door."

"It lets you actually go to the past? Is such a thing possible?"

"If you have an understanding of the working, which fortunately, you do not."

Oh-so-humbly, she asks, "Do you, my lord?"

"I've no need of such devices. I travel when and where I wish to."

"To the past? You travel to the past?" How can she not have known this? He is right. She should have stayed in the Library and read every book she could get her hands on.

"Often." A speculative shimmer crosses his shadowed face. "Perhaps I will take you someday. Perhaps I will leave you there, to stop your meddling in my present."

Paia just shrugs. She has no fight left in her. It's what he always counts on, that he will outlast her. Her constant avowals of innocence cut no ice with him. "Perhaps I would like the past."

He flares again. "If it meant you could be rid of me?"

"And you of me."

"Don't tempt me!" he snarls. "Even a brief visit would teach you some gratitude! I don't know why I didn't think of it in the first place! Or I could drag you back there and abandon you to a short life of disease and drudgery in a dark, cold, damp world where women are routinely beaten, raped, and burned at the stake, and where currently, due to my efforts, there is a famine and a very nasty war going on! As pampered and spoiled as you are, believe me, you wouldn't like it!"

As he speaks of it, she sees it, in chill dark flashes of snow and blood. "If you say so, my lord. I don't need the past, then."

He glares down at her. She can feel the heat of his suspicion and she wants to ask what he means about fostering chaos and misery. But she hasn't the strength to joust with him further this night.

"Please, my lord, I will ask it again, for I think it would solve many things. Can you not accompany me on this journey?"

"I follow your progress. I see all that you do."

Then why all these false accusations, she wants to demand. If he truly saw everything, he would know she is innocent of conspiracy. But then he would lose the pleasure of showering her with his fury and spite. "I mean, for the Faithful, my lord. To show yourself to them in all your glory, as the God of Love as well as the God of Awe. I can speak of your magnificence and perfection, but your actual presence is so much more inspiring."

"Inspiring, is it?" He offers a skeptical eye, and she can see him watching himself, conscious of his beauty made poignant by tragedy. "Perhaps I will . . . beloved traitor."

"My lord, I am not . . ."

But he is gone. Paia falls back against her pillows, wrung out as she always is after one of his rages. She waits for sleep, but thoughts of the vanished painting keep her eyes wide. A traitor in the Citadel who even the god's strong-arm methods can not uncover? A portal to the past? War and famine created by the god's own hand? Why? Why? Why?

She feels like flotsam on the flood of events. Destiny's pawn. Must her involvement be so ignorant and random? Can't she meet it head-on somehow, and take some control of the situation? Paia sighs, and then sighs again.

Soon it is dawn, and the chambermaid rises dutifully to prepare the High Priestess for another day.

CHAPTER THIRTY

Erde considered it a mark of the Tinkers' honor and pride that, after the evening's revelations and miracle, no one in the crew treated the visitors any differently the following day. Except perhaps for Luther, who seemed somewhat stirred out of his habitual gloom.

Besides, they had treated Sedou with respect from the start, due to the mystery of his sudden appearance among them. More importantly, it was a market day, and for the Tinkers, commerce took precedence over all things. Even, Erde remarked to the dragon, over saving the world.

The land around the village was flat and treeless. She had seen no hidden spot to call the dragon into, so he stayed where he was.

ONE CAN ALWAYS SAVE THE WORLD TOMORROW. BUT A GOOD BARGAIN COULD BE LOST UPON THE INSTANT.

She was glad to find him in a humorous mood, despite his growing hunger. Dragon impatience, she had found, was either blinding or imperceptible.

LUTHER SAYS HE'LL TAKE US TO A PLACE ALONG THE ROAD WHERE SOME OF OUR QUESTIONS MAY BE ANSWERED.

WILL THERE BE FOOD THERE?

HE DID NOT MENTION FOOD, DEAR DRAGON, AND OF COURSE, I COULDN'T REALLY ASK. HE WAS VERY SECRETIVE ABOUT THIS PLACE, ALMOST DEVOUT. I THINK IT MUST BE A HIDDEN CHAPEL OR SHRINE, TO THEIR IMPRISONED ONE. BUT WE MAY HAVE TO FACE THE MONSTER FIRST, AT THAT TOWN THAT HE COMES TO.

MONSTER? HE IS MY BROTHER. DOES THAT MAKE ME A MONSTER, TOO?

OUR PARDON, DEAR DRAGON. IT'S ONLY HIS BEHAVIOR THAT MAKES HIM A MONSTER.

TO MOST HUMANS, IT IS ALSO HIS SHAPE. WHY ELSE MUST MY SISTER EXPEND SO MUCH ENERGY TRAVELING LIKE A MAN?

YOUR SISTER IS PRAGMATIC. WOULD YOU NOT DO THE SAME, IF YOU SHARED THAT GIFT? WE COULD ENJOY THE JOURNEY IN COMPANY.

The dragon was silent for a moment.

NO, NOT EXACTLY THE SAME. I THINK I WOULD TRAVEL AS A WOMAN.

The morning's trading did not go well. Long before noon, Stoksie and Ysa folded up their counters and canopies in disgust, and the other Tinkers followed suit.

"Dey got nuttin' lef' heah ta trade," Stoksie lamented.

Erde clucked sympathetically as the little man sorted through his meager takings: some chipped enameled dishes, a bucket of rusted fasteners, a half-crate of mealy-looking potatoes. The only item he was happy with was a thin box the size of his palm, with a hinged lid. He popped it open for her proudly. Inside was a jumble of the slimmest, shiniest metal pins Erde had ever seen. Each one had a tiny white ball at one end. She tried to pick one out to examine it more closely, but only succeeded in pricking herself.

"Ouch!"

"Betcha! Doan fine dese ev'ryday, nah!" But Stoksie confided that he'd had to trade a valuable wool cap for them. Erde thought this was a very smart trade. Who'd want to wear wool in this heat?

The Tinkers packed up and moved on, toward the next village several hours down the road. By setting a stiffer pace than usual, they arrived in time to set up for a late afternoon market. But the mood around the campfires that evening was somber. Business in this village had been even worse.

"Tole me anudder Crew's bin by," Stoksie grumbled.

"No way," Brenda snorted. "Dey tink' we wudn't know 'bout dat?"

"Mebbe be Scroon Crew, comin' in frum Westhills."

"Nah. Dey know our route."

"See what dey say when we meet 'em."

Luis spoke up in his scratchy young man's voice. "Dis townie woman tole me da monsta's priests bin aroun', takin' up evin moah dan ushul."

Stoksie slapped his knee angrily. "An' doan leave us nuttin!"

"Priests frum da big town," Luther explained to Erde. "Das Fenix, y'know. Weah da monsta come."

They went to bed right after cleanup and rose at first light, to be on the road early, and so arrived in the heat of midafternoon. The town itself, viewed on the approach from the high seat of Luther's big yellow caravan, gave no outward sign of being a place of unusual depravity, though Erde gave its pale walls and rooftops due scrutiny as the wagons pulled up in an outlying field. It was called Phoenix, Luther said as he unhitched his mules. It wasn't one of the "new" towns. It sat in a long but narrow valley, hemmed in by hills. The slopes to the south were rocky and sheer, sliced by boulder-choked ravines. Those to the north were almost green, furred with an unusually thick and twisted growth of stunted pines. Phoenix was a real town, Luther said, larger than any of the villages they'd visited.

"We usda set up ou'side fer yeers," Stoksie said as he limped up to join them. Baron Köthen paced at his side like a hound eager to be loosed for the hunt. "Den dey say, we gotta go inside."

Phoenix possessed a sizable market square. New regulations required the Tinkers to set up their wagons there, inside the town's high stone walls. Otherwise, their business was no longer welcome.

Stoksie spat delicately. "Da priests run da markit deah, nah. Got dere fingahs in all da biz. Wanna keep an eye on us."

Blind Rachel refused to go inside. They'd had a child stolen away from them in Phoenix, never mind the depredations of the monster.

"We be sittin' ducks in deah!" Luther exclaimed. "Bildins all aroun'. Walls 'n gates. If dey cum fer us ta feed da monsta, ders no way out!"

"Itsa standoff," Stoksie agreed. "Bin li' dis neer ten yeer nah. But we need da trade, bad dis time."

The baron asked Erde to relay a polite suggestion.

"He asks why you do not take just one or two wagons loaded with goods, and leave the rest safely outside of town?"

Luther shoved the mules on their way to forage for what little grass they could find. "Cooper Crew dit dat wonst, notta yeer since. Los' two men anda hole waggin."

"The monster ate the wagon?"

"Ate da men. Da townies stoll da waggin." He began opening the many drop-down lids and sliding doors of his caravan. They were metal and had remarkable latches. Erde thought of the big yellow carriage as a sort of magic puzzle box.

Köthen waggled a finger with as feral a grin as she'd ever seen on him. "But they didn't have the Pilgrim and me protecting them."

The Pilgrim. Luther's spontaneous salutation had flung itself on Sedou and stuck there like a burr, so that even the baron had picked up the use of it. Now that the Tinkers accepted Sedou as something more than a man, a mere man's name for him no longer seemed adequate. Erde considered their choice more than appropriate. Were they not all four of them pilgrims, dragons and dragon guides alike, sworn to a holy quest?

The Pilgrim himself joined the discussion, and a compromise was reached: while the other Tinkers made camp, Sedou, N'Doch, and Baron Köthen would accompany Luther and Brenda into town to look the situation over, and negotiate with the necessary officials to allow a trade delegation of just a few wagons.

Erde clamored to go along. When Baron Köthen told her to stay behind, she reminded him in their native German that the dragon in the woods should also get a good look at this town.

Luther said, "Yu gotta blade wichu?"

"Of course."

"Okay, den." But he did advise her, shyly, to resume her boy disguise. "Gud lookin' yung wimmin go in der, dey's shur ta go afta yu, cuz dat monsta, he luv da yung wimmin bes'."

Erde shuddered, but into town she went, bearing up

under Baron Köthen's scowl and the high heat of the afternoon. *It's only his precious sense of honor,* she mourned, *that compels this concern for my safety.*

The thick walls and the surly townsmen at the gates, armed with guns and clubs, reminded her (but for the guns) of the fortified mountain villages around Tor Alte where the very daylight seemed dimmed by clouds of hostility and suspicion. But Luther skillfully bought them entry with shares of the sweet spring water in their canteens, and his alluring descriptions of the food and goods to be had at the market if their negotiations were successful.

The sentries growled that they'd have to see the priests about that. One of them insisted on escorting them down the main street as if they were prisoners, to what he called the Chapter House. He permitted no side excursions along the way. Brenda fumed, but the others went along calmly, their hands never far from their weapons. Even N'Doch was unusually quiet, his wary eyes soaking up every detail.

Inside the walls, the angular grid of streets was sunk in a layer of pale red silt, as fine as a lady's face powder. The dwellings were identical two-story stone boxes with slate roofs, raised up on what looked like the foundations of older, vanished structures. The same red dust drifted over walls and stoops and doorways, melding all the colors into one.

"Reminds me of one of them government-built bush towns," remarked N'Doch. "Or maybe it was an army base."

At first, the dark-skinned people hurrying to and fro, laden down with burdens, stepped quickly out of their way, as if to prevent any touch from a stranger. But as they followed the sentry farther into the center of the town, this scattering of populace thickened into a busy throng, and brushing shoulders became unavoidable.

"Keep an eye on your blades," N'Doch murmured. "This could be a slick-fingered crowd."

The Chapter House, which the sentries had spoken of with such reverence, was just another, larger, bland-faced box with a simple, double-doored entrance. The surly guard waited with them once they'd been announced, scuffing his feet in the dust and pointedly not making conversation, except for his crude attempts to muscle Brenda into hand-

ing over her canteen permanently. Brenda told him several
things she would do to him, and the man backed off.

Finally, not a priest but a red-robed woman appeared at
the door. An abbess or mother superior, Erde concluded,
for she seemed to be a person of some authority. She made
them more welcome than the sentries had, though in-
forming them at least three times of how busy she was, due
to an illustrious visitor arriving the next evening. And she
pointed out with little subtlety that several other Crews
were on the road to trade in Phoenix. Luther countered
this by politely insisting that he spoke for all the Crews.
This seemed to concern her, for finally she invited them in
and offered them water, and agreed that while Luther,
Brenda, and Sedou remained to discuss matters of business,
the rest of their party could have the liberty of the town.

"Smooth move," N'Doch said once they were out of ear-
shot. "We'll just wander around gawking like tourists, and
meantime, we'll have the joint cased in no time."

First, Baron Köthen said, they should determine whether
the town stood apart from its wall, or if dwellings were
built into the wall, as was often the case at home, providing
possibilities for concealed exits and entrances. But a road
ran around the entire perimeter between town and wall,
wide and smooth and entirely clear of obstacles, except
for some hastily erected pens housing a few scrawny pigs
and goats.

"A no-man's-land," N'Doch remarked. "All that's missing are the land mines and razor wire."

"This is an ugly town," Erde muttered. "I'm glad I don't
live here." But she was glad to see the livestock: a potential
meal for a hungry dragon.

Satisfied, Köthen led them inward, toward the market
square and the hubbub at the center of town. They had to
shoulder their way through crowds for the last few blocks.
The square was, in fact, a long rectangle, bounded on three
sides by the low boxy houses and on the fourth by the back
of the Chapter House, or actually, the ceremonial front,
judging from its triple-arched portico. The surly guard had
taken them to the rear, no doubt to the servants' entrance.

"Hey, girl. Look at that." N'Doch nudged Erde and
pointed.

In the paving stones in the middle of the square, visible when the crowds milling across it momentarily cleared, was a giant image of a winged and rampant dragon, set in red tiles.

"Oh!" A little chill ran through her, a finger down her spine. There on the ground was the twin to the little dragon carved on her brooch. "It's the same! Exactly the same! Look!"

N'Doch caught her hand as she reached to unpin the big jewel from inside her shirt. "Don't be showing off anything that valuable around here."

"Or anything," Baron Köthen added dryly, "that brings up the subject of dragons."

"But why is the monster's image on my ancestral brooch?"

Köthen studied the dragon on the paving. "No doubt we will find out soon enough."

In front of the Chapter House portico, townspeople were erecting a two-level platform: a small top tier set back from a wider bottom, itself raised several feet off the ground. Both look out over the square and the red-tiled image of the dragon. Several women veiled in red worked among them. The workers' intent and breathless pace gave the impression that all this was being thrown together at the last minute, and in high excitement. At the far end of the square, amid loud clangs of metal on stone, long banks of seating were being raised.

N'Doch stood back to let a pile of well-used timbers go by. "Some kind of big event going on here. Wish it was a rock show."

They found a shaded wall to lean against, removed from the bustle of workers. Erde sensed something oddly familiar in this last-minute building frenzy. At first, she could not place it. Then, when the memory came clear, it so stirred her that she broke her own rule: she gave voice without editing.

"My lord of Köthen, does this remind you of anyplace?"

"Not that I . . ."

"Not the market square at Erfurt?"

"No, Erfurt is a well-appointed town. I don't . . . Ah." He gave her a hard look, then folded his arms and contemplated the ground.

N'Doch said, "What?"

"Her ladyship is offering me a small lesson in perspective."

"Yeah? What happened at Erfurt?"

"N'Doch, must you?"

"You brought it up." Köthen lifted his head, and his gaze did not soften. "Indeed, the similarity gives one faith in the symmetry of all Nature and events."

N'Doch looked interested. "So, tell."

"So, I will. Listen, Dochmann, and learn of the extremes to which ambition and vanity can drive an otherwise honorable man. Or so my lady Erde would have it."

"My lord baron, I did not . . ."

Köthen held up both hands. "What? Would you deny me this rare opportunity, an expiation for my sins?"

"You are satirical, my lord."

"When also, my lady, I am commonly the most in earnest. May I proceed?"

Unable to read his intent, she could do nothing but let him. And as he laid out the scene that day in Erfurt, Erde saw him again as she had that time, the first time: a handsome and victorious lord, riding in through a cheering mob. She recalled how the clear blue and yellow of his tabard shone in the wintry light. How his mail glittered as brightly as the long sword sheathed at his hip. And how she fell in love with the proud lift of his chin.

He'd taken off the tabard and mail, even the tunic underneath, on his first night at Blind Rachel. Erde had not understood the gesture then, or even that it was a gesture, any more than a convenience. But now, tunic, tabard, and mail were all carefully folded away in the bottom of N'Doch's pack. Over his soft leggings and boots, Adolphus Michael Hoffman, Fourth Baron Köthen, wore only the simple garment favored by most of the Tinkers, what they called a T-shirt. Köthen's was loose and black, and it bore the image of a stooping hawk in faded, once-lurid colors. It had been Luther's gift, given freely, for Köthen possessed nothing he would willingly trade, and Luther was the only Tinker big enough to have anything that would fit him. N'Doch, too tall for even Luther's clothing, was hugely jealous of this gift. He said he'd be glad to wear such a shirt if it covered only half his chest. Erde did not think this old

and much-worn T-shirt to be a fitting garment for a noble-
man, but Baron Köthen would not give it up. He said the
hawk suited him well in his new life as a hired mercenary.

But she wished he would don his tunic and tabard again,
and help her heart look back, like turning over the hour-
glass, to a time when she loved him less. She had not been
aware before how love can transform the beloved into an
image of matchless perfection. Lately, her longing was such
that she could not bear to look at him, to see no love
returned in his gaze. Yet looking at him was her greatest
pleasure. If anything, he was more beautiful than before.

The constant sun had turned his skin nearly as brown as
the Tinkers', and bleached bright streaks of flax into his
blond hair. He didn't burn and redden as she did. His hair
was shorter now, close-cropped to expose his ears in the
Tinker fashion. Ysabel had gotten her clever hands on him,
to help him blend, she said, as if this was not just desirable
but the only wisdom. But Ysa had failed to convince him
to forsake his beard, though all the Tinker men but old
Marley went clean-shaven. Baron Köthen said he'd worn a
beard since he'd first sprouted one, and wasn't about to
give it up now. He did allow Ysa to trim it, until it hugged
the contour of his well-formed jaw, a feat of cutting made
possible by her remarkable scissors of steel as fine as a
sword blade.

He's so changed, mused Erde, watching him covertly
while he coolly spun the tale of Margit's rescue as if he
had observed it merely from a distance. So changed, in so
short a time. As if he was only awaiting the chance. Is this
what I intended, when I brought him hither so impulsively?
Did I even know what I intended, other than to save his
life? Or is it Destiny speaking again, when I'd supposed
the choice was mine?

And have I changed as much?

N'Doch, she decided, was exactly the same. Exactly as
when she'd met him on the beach in 2013. Except now he
had on more clothing. Even in the broiling sun, or perhaps
because of it, like the Tinkers, who weren't given to parading about in it half-naked.

Meanwhile, Baron Köthen wiped his palms on his damp
T-shirt and made diagrams in the air with his hands. "So I
rode in that way, and her father from there, with our vas-

sals and armies behind us, and for the sake of a kingdom, we were willing to pretend that we liked each other enough to ally with a madman."

"The hell-priest," supplied N'Doch.

"Ah. You've heard the story."

"Not like you tell it."

"From the wrong side, you mean."

N'Doch returned the most neutral of shrugs.

Köthen tossed his head. "The hell-priest. The central misjudgment in a series of otherwise reasonable decisions. I thought he could . . . well, no matter. He didn't, would never have. When I was introduced to Heinrich's dragon . . . your pardon, my lady . . . to the dragon Earth in Rose's barn, I thought, no, this is not my understanding of dragon. I have met that already, in the eyes of a mad priest who wields his holy cross as a battle ax!"

"I pray you, speak of him no further!" Erde had that sense again that the priest was watching her, even through the veil of the centuries.

"Only to the end of the tale, my lady. And so we made that devil's bargain, Josef and I, and to seal it, we were preparing that day to . . ." Köthen's hands floated free a moment as if unmoored, then sank to his sides. He turned to her and spread them again. "Rose understood the need, you must know."

"No! Rose would never have forgiven you!"

"I did not say she would forgive me, nor would I have asked. I said she understood."

"Understood what?" asked N'Doch.

"The need to burn an innocent woman at the stake."

"Unhh. Not good."

"No, nor am I. I promise you honor always, justice when I have the power to, and truth where I have knowledge of it. Goodness I lay no claim to."

"Hey, man. I hear you."

And then they both nodded, satisfied, when Erde thought they should be ashamed of themselves.

"Besides, she wasn't innocent. She was, is, and will be, a witch. Like all those women Heinrich's got hidden away."

"It's no excuse!" Erde blurted.

"No, it isn't," Köthen agreed quietly. "And in the end, we didn't burn her, for milady came to the rescue, with dragons and King's Knights and mysterious champions, and a lot of other things uncounted on. And perhaps my soul was saved. But that was just a stroke of great good luck, for all too often, what is necessary is not what we'd prefer."

"It wasn't luck, my lord. It was destiny."

"Destiny, is it? Again and always?" His eyes, when he finally fixed them on her, were dark and tired. Perhaps he'd put some memories to rest over the past week, and thanked her little for reviving them. "May I offer you a bit of advice, my lady, for the purposes of accomplishing your, ah . . . Quest?"

"Of course, my lord baron."

"Stop blinding yourself with concern for what isn't or what should be, or even what you'd like it to be. Concentrate on what *is*."

"Good idea," muttered N'Doch.

"Erfurt and all that is past, and we've a job to do in the present. Which is actually the future." Köthen ran a hand through his newly-cropped hair and massaged the back of his neck. "Shall we move on? I feel as though I've spent the afternoon in the confessional!"

He does not believe, Erde realized with a shock, that he will ever see home again.

Köthen clapped a hand to N'Doch's shoulder, turning him, urging him into motion. "Now, tell me, lad. How good are you with that knife of yours?"

The two men moved on through the crowd side by side, instinctively dividing the surveillance between them, left and right, for comparison back at camp. Erde padded after them like their servant or a dog, her fist tight on the hilt of her dagger, hoping to go unnoticed. They stopped at the far end of the square to watch the assembly of the seating, battered lengths of wood and metal that fitted together to form tiers. N'Doch was attempting to explain what a "rock concert" was, when Köthen caught his elbow.

"Dochmann! Over my left shoulder!"

"Looking . . ."

"It's the young woman from the other night. The speaker at the fire."

"Miriam, her name was."

"But we're two days' hard travel from that village!" Erde protested.

"Yup, I see her. Damn! It's her all right!"

"Stay with milady. I'm going after her."

N'Doch snatched him back. "No. Not this time. This is what I'm good at. I was brought up in towns like this. Catch you back at camp."

Before Köthen could stop him, he had eased off through the crowd and melted into it.

Much later, he sprinted out of the darkness to throw himself down breathless at Luther's cook fire.

"Man, that last klick was a tough one!" He wiped his brow on his bare forearm. "These people got watch posted everywhere! There's another Crew, y'know, pulled up down the road."

Luther rose to go back to packing his wagon. "Das Scroon, li' we spected. An' Oolyoot's camped off adda base a da hill."

"So how'd you guys do?"

"Dey agreed. Two waggins frum each Crew. We'll take mine 'n Ysa's. Seems dey need da trade reel bad, too, nah."

"Whew! Gonna be some day tomorrow. Say, I'm dyin'! What's to eat?" N'Doch snatched Köthen's empty plate and filled it from the stewpot. Erde got up to fetch him water from the keg.

"So?" asked the baron.

"The girl? It was her, all right. Real soon after, she hooked up with those two other guys, and they went around town the rest of the day taking people aside real casual-like. I saw a lot of people pretty heavily armed, even a few not too carefully concealed rifles and handguns." He looked to Luther, who had lingered to listen. "That how it is in this town?"

"Dis town, alwiz. But Scroon Crew say dey see a lot moah guns aroun' da villages nah. An' da priests bin ev'reweah, scroungin'."

"The girl, and her companions?" Köthen pursued patiently.

"Oh, yeah. Well, I did fine, till I lost all three of them in an alley. The doors were locked up tight when I tried 'em, but I know they got in one somehow. Maybe they live here, maybe they got connections."

"Hmmm," muttered Köthen. "The scent of rebellion."

N'Doch scoffed. "You've got rebellion on the brain, yer lordship. Whachu say, Luther? You know anything about this?"

"Can't really say, Dockman," the Tinker rumbled, moving off.

But Erde noticed how hard he'd been listening. "She said as much, Miriam did. 'I stand in opposition,' she said. But she meant to this pagan church, not to any lord of the realm."

"The Temple is the lord around here." N'Doch scraped at the remains of his first helping and reached for a second. "Look who we had to go to, to do business. Haven't heard mention of any other form of government."

"A bad idea," said Köthen. "To let the church run things."

"Well, we'll get a chance to see it in action. Guess what else I found out."

"We know! Luther heard it from the woman at the Chapter House. The High Priestess of the dragon worshipers arrives tomorrow with all her retinue."

"Betcha! Major celebration! Folks coming in from all over, not just the Crews. The town's gonna be a madhouse. And with everyone armed to the teeth . . . whew!"

"I hope it won't ruin another trade day."

"I have a feeling," said Köthen with such quiet relish that they both looked at him. "We should be prepared for the worst."

CHAPTER THIRTY-ONE

The village they stop at the next night is nearly empty, though the streets are clean and the houses scrubbed and patched. The only sign of life is at the Chapter House, where the caravan is welcomed without the usual heavy ceremony by a few overworked and anxious priestesses.

Paia is relieved but curious. "Where have they all gone?"

"Probably down to Phoenix to await your arrival tomorrow," says Luco. "They've planned a huge celebration there in your honor."

She feels so tired today, so strung out. Another night of dreaming. No God to rave at her this time, but the man with the sword was there again, smiling. Paia hasn't had much sleep.

"I can't wait."

Luco laughs. "Come, walk with me, take a look, before it gets dark."

They climb to the brow of the hill overlooking the village to gaze down on their most important destination. The town is many miles away to the southeast, but even from a distance, Paia can see its lights glimmering through the lavender dusk.

"It's big."

"The God's favorite town."

"Really?"

"Where all do his bidding, all live to serve him, and prosperity follows."

"Sarcasm is the God's prerogative, First Son."

"No, I . . . actually, it's true. He's exactly the God they desire. Phoenix is the God's greatest success story."

"Then yours as well, as the God's Right Hand."

Luco shakes out his long hair to let the sweat dry in the breeze. "I'll leave that credit to him." Paia glances up at him, but he is turning away. "Better be heading back. We don't want to miss whatever they've managed to scrape together for dinner."

She reaches suddenly for his sleeve, grabs at the long red folds of his robe. "Luco!"

He stops, turns back. When he sees her face, his blue eyes narrow. "What is it, my priestess?"

Paia isn't sure herself. Something. A feeling. "I . . . don't know."

"You look . . . terrified. There's no need, you know. Phoenix is devoted to the God. It will welcome you with open arms. Besides, you're as well guarded as anyone could be."

"What if it's something you can't guard against?" She glances again at the tightly walled town in the valley below. A moment ago, she was sure she saw it wreathed with flame. "That place scares me. Do we have to go in there tomorrow?"

He drops all pretense of formality. "Paia, Paia, what's this? A premonition? Do you believe in such things?"

She doesn't know whether to say yes or no.

"Look, I know this trip has been hard on you, harder than you're willing to admit. But it has served its purpose, and tomorrow's visit is the most crucial of all. That town supplies a quarter of the Temple income. If you just hang in there for one more night, I'll give you a rest. I promise." He holds out his hand to her. "Now will you come down to dinner?"

Paia throws one last shuddering look over her shoulder, then takes Luco's hand and follows him down the dusty hill like a child.

CHAPTER THIRTY-TWO

The camp is up before first light, grabbing breakfast, rounding up the mules, hitching the four needed to haul the two wagons, and keeping the others close at hand in case of an emergency.

N'Doch stands with Sedou on a rise in the road into town. The sky is a gray dome above. The valley vanishes away from them into predawn darkness. The wagon circles of the two other Crews are just visible up ahead, one to either side of the road. They, too, will send in a pair of wagons, coasting in on Blind Rachel's negotiations.

Sedou is more like the dragon than ever this morning. Or, if N'Doch allows himself to remember, more like Sedou before a big rally, particularly once he understood he was a marked man. He's edgy, distracted. He reminds N'Doch twice what to do if Fire shows himself. N'Doch can see the dragon's mind is elsewhere. His own stomach's as uneasy as an ant nest. He wishes he could help but hasn't a clue what would be helpful, or even how to ask.

Köthen walks out to join them when the light turns rosy. "Stoksie is ready to give the signal."

As if by agreement, the three men stand together in silence for a moment, watching the day build. Then they shake hands solemnly and head back toward camp.

Sedou leads the way with Stoksie and Brenda. Köthen, Charlie, and N'Doch follow up the two wagons, Luther's retrofitted delivery van—which must be at least a century old, N'Doch figures, repainted a billion times—and a canvas-topped flatbed driven by a woman named Beneatha, with Ysabel in the seat beside her. The girl rides up beside

Luther, where the windshield used to be. N'Doch counts heads. Ten going out. Better be ten of us coming back.

Stoksie hails the other Crews as the wagons draw level with their camps. Their wagons are ready to roll, so they wave and pull onto the road behind Blind Rachel. N'Doch looks them over. They look a little less well-heeled than his Crew, but otherwise, there's the same lot of recycled truck bodies and RVs, stripped down, lightened, and fitted out for mule power, the same determined faces, the same bristle of weaponry, set back but still in sight.

Charlie points left, then right. "Das Scroon der, 'n das Oolyoot. Oolyoot from furder sout'. Mebbe we eat wi' Scroon latah, do sum trade pryvit-like."

"You ever all get together, all the Crews? Have a big blowout?"

Charlie guffaws, hiding her piebald cheeks behind her palms. "Betcha. E'ry five yeer. Jeesh! Needa yeer to recovah!"

"I'd like to see that, all right. Bet you'd hear some good tunes then!"

"Da bes'!"

They pass some traffic heading out of town, mostly older people and a few kids toting packs or light hand carts. Maybe they're headed out to work the fields while the day is cooler, but N'Doch doesn't see much in the way of tools. They look like they're just . . . leaving town. Then the gates are ahead of them, and he goes on the alert. But the six Tinker wagons file through and into town without incident, and head for the square.

The townspeople seem eager to welcome them. All along the main drag, rows of goods are arrayed on tables, on boards balanced between two chairs, laid out on ragged blankets or just plunked down in the thick dust of the street. In the market square, guys in purple robes are sweeping the paving stones. The two-level platform has been decked out along its sides with drapes of thin red cloth. A pair of priestess women are fussing with the folds, chattering excitedly. The bleachers are up and tucked away at the far end. In the exact center of the square sits a big flat dish painted a dull gold. Another purple-robed man is pouring liquid into it from a tall red urn.

Luther calls down from the seat of his yellow van. "Yu

see dat t'ing? Das weah dey put da sackerfice, y'know? All tied up nise like a prezint."

But N'Doch reserves judgment. He feels too much like he's walking into some kind of fantasy vid.

Along the far side, the local merchants have set up their booths and stands. The Tinkers are directed to park their wagons on the opposite long side. Blind Rachel pulls up in the middle, between Scroon and Oolyoot. The buzz of anticipation blooms into action as everyone leaps down to unload.

With Brenda busy setting up security around the Tinker stalls, Charlie is being extra friendly. She works beside N'Doch, chatting away as if to make up for all the times she hasn't. "Dis howit go, nah. Dey look aroun', we look aroun', but nobuddy duz a deal til afta da sun cross noon."

"Got it." N'Doch's done an inventory of what he's got to trade, and it isn't much. The other water bottle. The clothes on his back. He shrugs. The unpacking is finished. "Think I'll go take a look, then." He collects Köthen and the girl. "Whaddya say we follow Stoksie around, get the hang of things?"

With his permission, they shadow the little man through the crowd, up and down the sides of the square, then up and down the main street, checking out what he passes by with just a glance, what he notes with a nod, what he studies more carefully. A lot of the booths on the town side of the square stock food items, and Stoksie is looking not only to fill Blind Rachel's larder but also to pick up goods for trade in other villages. There are craftspeople in amongst the food stalls, offering some serviceable pottery, a line of tools and utensils that remind N'Doch of his metal shop class back in school, and of course the coveted leather goods the Tinkers have risked coming for, especially the shoes.

"This is the stuff, huh?"

Stoksie fingers a soft brown satchel with many buttoned pockets. "Lookit dis werk, nah. Da bes'! Anabuddy give good trade fer dis."

"Nice, all right." N'Doch admires a handsome leather vest. He'd be real interested, if he had anything to give for it.

He sees a lot of junk laid out, too. Used stuff, broken

stuff, useless stuff, and stuff that might just find another life in the right hands. He can tell how random the acquisition process is. Except for the Tinkers, there's no regular system for product distribution left intact. There's not even much product. But wandering up and down the line of booths, every so often he comes across a sign that things are still being manufactured somewhere in the world. Not very well, or in very great quantity, but enough so that bits and pieces of it somehow find a way to the podunk town of Phoenix. He sees cheap boxer shorts stamped "Made in Tibet." He fingers a series of small pink dolls shrink-wrapped in plastic so brittle it must be as old as he is, and he just knows some fool is going to trade something they shouldn't for them. He sees a flashlight he could well use if there were still batteries to go with it. And he sees a lot of weaponry, whole stalls full of cudgels, knives, crossbows, and old or broken bits of guns. Nothing too impressive, but there's obviously a market for it. Probably folks have cobbled their firearms together out of stuff just like this. He figures the dealer's got the ammo hidden behind the counter. He spots a broad-bladed hunting knife that reminds him of his beloved fish gutter. He picks it up for a closer look, but Stoksie, with eyes in the back of his head, reaches behind him and takes it out of his hands. With a glance at N'Doch, he puts it back on the counter.

N'Doch clucks his tongue. "No touchee the merchandise, eh?"

Stoksie wags his head side to side. "Yu wanna gud blade, I show yu weah."

"Ah, I get it. Okay, sure. Whenever you're ready."

By midmorning, Stoksie seems to have decided what he wants and what he'll give for it. The crowd is thick, and high enough on a combination of religious fervor and greed to make shoving through it a sweaty and unpleasant effort. Köthen's looking irritable, and the girl could clearly use a break. Stoksie leads them back into the shade of Luther's van to dole out water from the big old cooler stashed in a back compartment. The Tinker booths are mobbed with grazing customers, but behind the wagons is an island of sanity.

"Got an hour, leas', 'fore da swap-work start." Stoksie pulls a square of cloth out of his pocket and ties it around his dripping brow pirate-style. "Yu wan' I show yu weah da hi rollahs shop?"

N'Doch is none too eager to be back in that souped-up crowd again. He sees why the Tinkers don't like this town. Even without a monster, it doesn't feel quite sane. "There's high rollers around here? Coulda fooled me."

"Yu green heah, tallfella, aincha. Der's still sum aroun' got moah den dey need, y'know whad I mean?"

The place Stoksie takes them is not another booth on the market square. It's a nondescript house down a quieter side street, with a beefy woman at the door sporting a real functional looking 9-mm automatic. None of the booth security in the square were showing off their heat so boldly. But Stoksie seems to know this one by name, so in they all go.

The inside is shadowed and close, with shades pulled down over the few small windows. N'Doch bites back a whistle of surprise and admiration, for the stuff laid out on these tables is definitely not junk. It's neatly organized by carrying size and firepower, and though none of it looks real new, you could still outfit a small European army here without much trouble. Too bad there's no more small European *countries,* he tells himself. 'Cept maybe the ones on higher ground.

He tries to look nonchalant, sticking close to Stoksie's side. The girl and Köthen don't seem to get it. They just nose into the room curiously and start picking things up in their hands. Worried, N'Doch drifts after them, counting a table of pistols, including a few old revolvers, a table of shotguns, and a long rack of assault rifles. There are bins of ammo clips and boxed cartridges, shelves stocked with grenades and mortar shells. The wanna-be buyers speak in hushed voices in this temple of doom and destruction, and consult lists hidden in their palms. They're being offered tiny cups of what might actually be tea, though the leaves have been recycled a few more times than they ought to. A pale-skinned boy slips one into N'Doch's hand, then moves on to the girl, trailing an aroma of mint. The girl raises the little cup for a cautious sniff, then glances over at N'Doch with a luminous smile. Papa Dja taught her about tea drinking back in 2013. Or, last month, depending how you look at it.

The run-on scatter of his thoughts tells N'Doch the place is weirding him out. He can't imagine why. He's seen the like of it before, back home, especially during government crackdowns. Stoksie points him toward a display of blades, from jackknives to machetes, so he decides to get down to business, maybe actually find himself a knife. The dagger the women gave him is handy, and real aesthetic, but he'd prefer something a little less refined. Stoksie's at the main counter giving serious consideration to a casing reloader, meanwhile trying to explain to the girl just how a bullet works. N'Doch heads for the knives, then sees Köthen picking at a small table in a corner that's piled not so neatly. He slouches over to soak up a bit of the baron's perspective on twenty-first century armaments, or is it twenty-second or -third? He's still not sure, and who could tell from what's laid out in this joint?

"Whacher doin' at the junk pile, Dolph?"

A closer look tells him what's drawn Köthen's interest. It's all repro stuff, replicas of antique guns and hand weapons, like battle-axes and Roman broadswords. Mostly it's cheap plastic, but there's some serious historical work in real wood and metal.

"May look familiar, dude, but it's all fake." N'Doch holds up a funnel-mouthed pistol that looks more lethal to the shooter than to the victim. "They don't really work."

"Why make a weapon that does not work?"

"You're way too logical, my man. People used to collect 'em, for fun."

"I see." Köthen lifts a short, cylindrical object, turns it over in his hand in puzzlement.

"Now that is a serious weapon. That's a light saber."

"A what?"

N'Doch laughs. "Just a kid's toy. Like I said, none of this shit really works."

Köthen sets the cylinder down, then reaches to flip aside a flap of cloth covering the bottom of the pile. It doesn't come easy and there's a rasp of metal as he yanks on it. The ring of true steel is unmistakable.

"Listen to that."

N'Doch helps clear away the plastic dueling pistols and chrome-plated Colt .45s. The fabric underneath is soft and heavy, and looks like someone's used it to wipe the floor of a garage. Köthen feels through its folds for the shape of the object inside. His hand grasps, then stills. N'Doch hears his sharp intake of breath. Then Köthen is hauling on the fabric with both hands and all his strength.

"Whoa! Easy! What's up?" N'Doch scrambles to catch the stuff that's flung off as Köthen drags the whole bundle free of the pile. He has an odd presentiment as the baron stands there with the object cradled in both his hands, staring down at it in disbelief. It's long and narrow, very long, and it looks heavy.

"Is that what I think it is?"

Köthen lays the bundle crosswise on the pile and slowly peels back the wrappings. The inside face of the cloth is unstained, and a deep maroon. Within its rich folds nestles a sword.

Köthen's hands hover over it as if it might disappear if he touches it. Then he flattens the fabric away from the hilt, exposing its intricate design: a winged dragon wound around the trunk of a tree. *"Um Gottes Willen!"*

"Oh, nice," approves N'Doch. "Appropriate, too. Kinda seen better days, though."

"Yes," says Köthen strangely. "It has."

Slowly, as if reluctant, the baron slides his right hand under the hilt and fits his palm to the grip. He stares at it some more. "Surely I am dreaming."

"A perfect fit, eh?"

"Fetch milady."

It's such a strangled kind of murmur that N'Doch finally picks up on there being something more going on here than the dude finally finding a weapon he knows how to use. "Why? What's up?"

Köthen lifts the sword free of its velvet shroud. In the dim light, the long blade glints dully through layers of corrosion and patina. "Fetch her!"

"Okay, okay." N'Doch goes. When he gets back, Köthen has the sword lowered, concealed at his side. There's an odd light in his eyes, but he watches the girl's approach like she might be bringing him news of his own death sentence.

"What is it, my lord?"

Köthen frames a reply, stumbles, falls silent. N'Doch

stares at him, amazed. The man's a wreck. Köthen starts again, hoarse and halting. "Milady, I beg you. Tell me if I have entirely taken leave of my senses . . ."

She looks up at him calmly. "Never, my lord."

Köthen takes the sword in both hands just below the crossguard, and holds the hilt up in front of her.

Her response is the same sudden gasp. "Oh! God's Holy Angels! But how . . .? Where . . .?"

Köthen nods once, as if the sentence has been delivered as expected, then enfolds the sword in both arms as if it was a child, and bows his head over it. "What does it mean?"

"I know not, my lord baron."

"Is it all preordained, then? Have we no choice in the matter?"

"Perhaps some do, my lord. I know I do not."

N'Doch shifts impatiently. "Is one of you gonna tell me what the hell's going on?"

"A kind of miracle," the girl sighs.

"It's a sword, not a miracle. C'mon, what's the deal?"

"Not just any sword. Sir Hal's sword."

N'Doch grins at her. "Hey, right. You think I was born yesterday?"

"It's true, N'Doch," she insists earnestly. "You must believe me."

He looks from one to the other, and sees they don't care if he believes it or not. They already know it for a fact. He wonders if the town's undercurrent of hysteria has gotten to them. "C'mon, you guys, be real. There's probably a hundred old swords like that."

Köthen lifts his head. "No, though I, too, would prefer that explanation. But I *know* this weapon, like I know my own hands, every scar, every detail. Ten years I fetched and cleaned and honed this blade, and buckled it on the knight who was my master."

The girl says, "That sword was laid at Lord Earth's feet when Sir Hal first pledged fealty to him."

And then to Sedou, that night in Deep Moor. Damn! The dragon hilt. N'Doch remembers it now, all too well.

He wants to go there with the two of them, really he does, but sometimes the moment gets so heavy, it kicks him smack into rebound. Drowning in momentousness, he swims for the opposite shore.

He laughs. "Well then, I guess we just gotta buy it for you, Dolph, so you can take care of it some more."

Erde knew then what she needed to do. "My lord baron, if you would wait here a moment until we return . . . come, N'Doch, we must speak with Stoksie."

OH, DRAGON, TELL ME . . . IS THIS WHAT IS MEANT TO BE?

THIS IS A GREAT AND MEANINGFUL SIGN. IT MUST NOT BE IGNORED.

DO YOU KNOW WHAT IT MEANS?

PERHAPS THE VERY WEAPON THAT BARON KÖTHEN HAS BE-TRAYED IS PUT INTO HIS HANDS SO HE MIGHT REDEEM HIMSELF BY THE PROPER USE OF IT.

THEN THERE WILL BE FIGHTING.

INEVITABLY.

Erde unpinned the dragon brooch, pressing the carved red stone into the curve of her palm. It was as cold as ice.

AH! THE STONE KNOWS ITS OWN PATH. IT NO LONGER WEL-COMES YOU.

YET I AM SAD TO LET IT GO.

She felt as if the brooch had been with her all her life, though it was barely two months since her beloved nurse Alla had provided her with it and the means for her deliverance from Tor Alte, thus sending her off toward her meeting with Destiny.

N'Doch leaned in to cover up the big jewel glowing in her palm. He was no longer laughing. "You sure about this, girl?"

"Never more sure."

He smiled, but not truly in jest. "I shoulda stole the damn thing when I had the chance."

"You tried. Your own destiny would not allow it."

"Yeah, well . . ."

Stoksie sensed the suppressed urgency waiting behind him and broke off his conversation with the weapons dealer. "Whatsit nah? Sumpin' on yer minds?"

N'Doch dropped one long arm around the small man's shoulder and drew him away from the counter. "Stoksie, my man . . . you think any of these high rollers might be interested in a piece of *real* jewelry?"

She felt naked without it, but by the end of the afternoon, the dragon brooch had given opportunity for the most inspired bargaining of Stoksie's life. Or so he claimed. With it, he managed, without calling too much attention to his intricate manipulations, to provision Blind Rachel's two wagons and one of Scroon's to capacity with food, lamp oil, and trade items, including a small trinket for each of the children. He acquired several new weapons and the ammunition to fit them. For N'Doch, he bought a knife, the leather vest and a coveted T-shirt, for himself a new leather satchel. For Luther, spare wheels for the caravan and several sacks of grain for the mules. For Erde, a woven sun hat and change of comfortable clothing. Boy's clothing, of course. Plus a small kit of items that he swore were of high trade value, to be stowed away in her pack for later use.

Most important, to her if not to the Tinkers, Baron Köthen now walked beside her with Sir Hal's dragon-hilted sword slung across his back. The long leather sheath was made for a heavier, wider weapon, but Köthen declared in still-stunned tones that it was perfectly suitable for the way he'd be wearing it.

"Yu Blin' Rachel Crew nah, fer shur!" Stoksie looked equally stunned by all this sudden good fortune, now that he saw it all actually being loaded into his wagons. "Mebbe we all jus' go home nah, not hafta trade wit' nobuddy we doan like!"

"Dear Stoksie," Erde assured him, "It's only right that we return to you the generosity you've so freely offered us."

"We gib yu a cupla daze. Yu gib us a hafa yeer, mebbe moah."

She noticed how careful the Tinkers were to disguise their astonishing windfall as the results of a normal day's trade, even from Scroon and Oolyoot, who were happily packing away the overflow.

"We godda stik tagedda," said Luther as he opened one of the grain sacks to give a portion to Blind Rachel's mules. "But dere's one t'ing we ain't tole 'em yet."

"About Sedou?"

He nodded. When the other Crews' mules caught scent of it, he sent Charlie over with a canful to keep them quiet. Though he complained bitterly about the lack of room inside his tight-packed caravan, Erde noticed that he made sure to leave a good-sized space in the back corner free of cargo. She asked him why.

He gave her an embarrassed grin. "Well, da day not ovah yet. Yu nevah know whad else I wanna pick up."

But it was close onto dusk. Surely the Tinkers were finished trading for the day. Tall torches were being lit around the edge of the square, and Scroon Crew's wagons had already packed up and headed out, though they were having trouble breaking a path through the milling throng. From the top of Luther's wagon, Erde could see that the booths across the square were still busy with customers. As she helped him fasten the grain sacks to the caravan's roof, she pointed out a scuffle that broke out around one of the stalls.

Luther nodded. "Get summa dat nah. S'hot, pebble iz tired. Dey wan' whad dey wan'. Won' take no fer an ansa."

"Oh, dear . . . look!" Scroon Crew's wagons had made it to the end of the square, then been turned back at the intersection by a cluster of robed men and women who were officiously barring all passage down the main street. Customers were leaving the stalls, hurrying toward the hubbub.

"Huh." Luther squinted out over the slate rooftops. A dust cloud trailed down from the direction of the town gates. Somewhere down the main street, a cry went up. One of the robed men snatched up a lighted torch, ran through the crowd to the huge golden bowl in the middle of the square, and touched the torch to its glimmering surface. A bright flame shot up from the center, taller than the man was. "Mus' be her, den. Lookit dem all run aroun'. Da priestess got heah early."

N'Doch's on his way back from helping Scroon Crew fight their way through the crowd when Köthen grabs his arm.

"Wait."

He sees the wagons halted at the mouth of the square, a flurry of red-and-purple robes, and torches. He and Köthen back against a wall and sit tight to see if Scroon protests the roadblock, and if they'll need any help.

"Must be the princess, knocking at the gate."

"She is a priestess, I believe," Köthen says. "Another heathen witch."

"You got a real problem with that, doncha." N'Doch grins. "Whatever. Helluva fuss to make over some old crone."

The driver of the lead Scroon wagon argues a little with the Chapter House priests and their townie muscle, but meanwhile the other Tinkers hop down to lead the mules aside. Puzzled, N'Doch watches as the wagons willingly split left and right to park right next to the tall torches the priests have lit on either side of the intersection. "Maybe they just want to hang around for a good view of the parade. You hear music or anything?"

Köthen shakes his head. If there is any, it can't be heard over the roar and rumble in the square.

N'Doch is disappointed. He's really been missing his music lately. "A real ceremony oughta have drums at least. Let's head back."

"Let's stay a bit. See what we're up against."

"You're the boss, yer lordship."

They work their way closer to the edge of the crowd. N'Doch's height gives him a useful advantage, for once. He can see clear over the heads of these puny townies, or so he's come to think of them already, in Tinker fashion, after rubbing elbows with too many of them all day in too little space. A few blocks down the dusty main drag, a line of marchers wavers into view through the rising heat and dusk. "Here they come. Soldiers, looks like, with big flashy helmets and . . . hey, get this! Spears!"

"A suitable weapon for infantry."

"Maybe in your day. Won't do much against the firepower we've seen around here. Okay, now there's this big boxy gold thing coming, with four guys lugging it."

The crowd is starting to moan and sway a little, as if a wind has come up. Köthen cranes his neck a little to see. The big sword stiffens his back like a second, crosswise spine. "A sedan chair, Dochmann. I am relieved to discover a few things that I know about the future which you do not."

"Up yours, yer lordship. What's a sedan chair?"

"Most likely, the priestess rides in that chair."

"And those poor suckers gotta carry her? Probably too fat and old to walk on her own. Hey, there's a second one coming up behind it. That one's even bigger."

The soldiers pass by. They're taller, better fed than the townies he's seen, or than any of the Tinkers, and they march in pretty good order, despite their antique weaponry. Köthen studies them with professional interest.

"Some of these men are . . . women!" he exclaims softly.

They are indeed. Tall, strapping women with steely eyes. N'Doch chuckles. "Welcome to that future you know so much about."

When the first sedan chair draws level with him, N'Doch sees that the side curtains have been artfully draped and tied open, so that the occupant is regally framed by graceful folds of rich, gold fabric, made even more picturesque by the lavender dusk and the flickering torchlight. The townies cry out prayers. He's surrounded by a forest of scrawny, reaching arms. Someone here really knows how to stage an entrance. Now he can see inside the chair.

"Hey, that's a guy in there! Big, good-looking dude with too much hair and too much jewelry. Looks like he owns the place."

Köthen tosses him a wolfish glance. "Perhaps he does. Such things are not unheard of, you know."

"Right. Sorry. Forgot who I was talking to."

A bunch of younger guys all dressed alike follow, then another squad of helmeted soldiers, then a pair of women in the same red robes as the women at the Chapter House, only these two are veiled. After them comes the second chair. This one looks like it's really made of solid gold, though N'Doch knows that's impossible, and it has a big red dragon right there on the side, just like the one carved on the brooch. N'Doch wonders where that stone will spend its next millennium.

Up at the entrance to the square, one of Scroon Crew's mules suddenly objects to a particular flare of torchlight, and starts up a loud braying and shying about on his sharp,

heavy hooves. The first chair gets hustled past into the
square but the second soldier squad ducks sideways in confusion like they've never seen a spooked mule before.
Scroon Crew races about trying to calm the mule, though
it looks to N'Doch like they're doing just the opposite, and
the whole procession staggers to a halt. The bearers of the
second chair stop and set it down right in front of Köthen
and N'Doch. All around them, the townies fall to their
knees, moaning and murmuring.

The gauzy, shimmering curtains are closed. Nothing is
visible in the shadowed interior until a tawny, slim hand
parts the drapery and the High Priestess herself peers out
to see why they've stopped.

The two men share the same reflexive grunt of approval.

The priestess is young and she is beautiful. Really beautiful. More beautiful than any vid star N'Doch can think of,
off the top of his head. He wants to whistle aloud, but he's
pretty sure it'd be considered inappropriate. She's such a
mix, he couldn't begin to guess what her background is,
but it looks like she got the very best of all of them. Her
eyes are dark, her features delicate but lively, her skin that
flawless espresso-and-cream that makes N'Doch wants to
put his hands all over her. He nudges Köthen. The baron
is transfixed.

N'Doch bends to hiss into his ear. "Hey. Dolph, didn't
your mama teach you not to stare?"

As if she feels their gaze, like some kind of magic heat
ray, the priestess turns toward them, a slow haughty move
like you make when you're showing someone how little
you notice them. N'Doch has the word "bitch" all ready
on his tongue when the woman's glance slides past him,
past Köthen, then flickers back as if surprised, and settles
on the baron in what appears to be shock. N'Doch thinks
this could be getting dangerous. Everybody within ten
klicks is looking at her, while she and the baron stare at
each other long past what's polite between strangers. Like,
he'd have a big hole lasered through his chest if he stood
between them.

He nudges Köthen again. "Whatcha trying to do, get us
in trouble?"

Then the logjam clears up ahead, and the four bearers
bend, grip, and hoist their golden burden to their shoulders.

The procession moves forward again, carrying the High Priestess with it. But her gaze drifts back toward Köthen again, and she gives him a kind of stunned smile that transforms her face from that of a proud, self-contained aristocrat to that of an astonished girl. Then she withdraws behind her curtains, and the chair disappears behind the next infantry squad and a long train of hand-hauled supply wagons.

N'Doch is irritated. Haven't these guys ever heard of mule power? He jogs Köthen's shoulder brusquely. He's pissed at him for attracting all the attention. "C'mon. We're outa here."

Köthen follows willingly this time, as if he's too busy thinking to resist.

N'Doch hugs the facades of the houses fronting the square, where the going's a little easier. The crowd is surging inward toward the center of the square, but coming up against some force or barrier he can't see. "Hey! Watch where you're going, man!" He hauls Köthen out of the path of a loaded hand cart. "So the ice prince has blood in his veins after all."

"Dochmann! I have never seen a more beautiful woman. Have you?"

"Well, she wasn't looking at me, so what does it matter?" N'Doch thinks about how the girl back at the wagon would feel if she'd seen what he's just seen. "And you could wipe that silly grin off your face, y'know."

Köthen laughs, a charged-up, throaty laugh. A townie shoves past him rudely and he doesn't even notice. "You are jealous, friend N'Doch."

He's trying to imagine a way he can reasonably deny this. Through the shifting crowd, a face catches his eye. He stops short.

Köthen is instantly alert. "What?"

"That girl again. The one I was following."

"Alone?"

"Couldn't tell." N'Doch shrugs uneasily and moves on. By the time they're back at the wagons, he's slick with the crowd's close heat and the effort of plowing through it. He sees that during the pack up, the four remaining wagons have been reshuffled into an open square, with the mules all hitched and facing clockwise. Blind Rachel and Oolyoot are clustered inside, in conference. Brenda and Charlie are already perched on the roof of Luther's van, weapons in hand. No one likes the feel of this crowd. N'Doch climbs over the traces of an Oolyoot wagon, and hears Luther sending the girl up into the driver's seat, telling her to stay put with uncharacteristic brusqueness.

"Someone's a little anxious," he comments to the baron. "You are not?"

"Well, yeah, actually I am. But I thought it was just the dragon working on me."

Köthen reaches a hand back to stroke the hilt of the sword brushing his neck. "I feel like a dog before a thunderstorm."

"What say we go sit with the Pit Bull . . . better view from up there."

They scale the outside of the van, using the big steel latches as handholds. Köthen's sword clinks against the insulated metal skin.

"Yo, Brenda!" N'Doch calls out. "Don't shoot, it's only me." As his head clears the top, he finds his nose mere inches from the barrel end of Brenda's new hunting rifle, courtesy of the dragon brooch. He frees up a palm and eases the muzzle aside. "Nice gun, huh?"

Charlie giggles. "Yo, Dockman."

Brenda gives him a sour nod, then offers him a hand to hoist him over the edge. Köthen follows easily on his own. He finds an open spot, unslings and draws his sword, then settles with it across his lap. From a pouch on the sheath, he pulls out oil and a whetstone. N'Doch squints out into the deepening dusk. Torches flare around all sides of the square. Robed men and women are pressing back the mewling crowd, to open up a wide path from the main street and clear the center around the flaming gilt bowl, over the design of the red dragon. A phalanx of them, in red and gold, forms beside the dragon's upraised claw.

"The reception committee," N'Doch observes cheerfully.

Moments later, Sedou climbs up. "Almost as crowded up here as it is down there." He hangs his legs over the outside edge and invites N'Doch to join him. They watch the doings in the square for a while, as the priestess' entourage enters from the main drag and begins a slow ritual circuit around the outside. Then Sedou says, "I've told Stoksie and the others not to be concerned should I suddenly disappear on them."

N'Doch takes a breath. "Disappearing's the easy part. Didja tell 'em what else might happen?"

But Sedou isn't interested in sibling banter. His eyes have a deep-well darkness in them. "I may need a new song, my brother. I may need it soon."

There's that ant nest stirring in his gut again. "Yeah? What sort of song?"

"Not a Sedou song. Not a people song at all."

"Hunh?" N'Doch's shoulders hunch over the keyboard he imagines in his lap. "You want, like, some kind of animal?"

"No." Sedou gets real still for a moment and N'Doch just knows the dragon is struggling to hold her man-shape. Whatever thoughts she's thinking, they're not about being human. "Imagine it, my brother. I need . . . a song of release. Of waves breaking and rivers flowing. Of glaciers melting into the sea. Of the sky giving up its moisture as rain."

"You need a water song," said N'Doch quietly, and suddenly all the ants in his gut are a chill tickling the base of his spine. "I get it. You need *your* song. The others have all been *my* songs."

"Yes." The dragon/man's smile outshines the torches. "And they have served me well in the world of men. But now I must be what I truly am, to the utmost of my powers. And you must help me."

N'Doch coughs. The chill has made it all the way to his throat. "Not sure I'm up to it, bro."

Then Sedou does the thing N'Doch's wanted all along, ever since the song that conjured his brother as a grown man. The thing he can't ask for, because he needs it more than he knows how to say. Sedou leans over, wraps him in the curl of his big arm, and holds him, easy and firm, as if nothing could ever go wrong again.

You're up to it.

Release, damn it, thinks N'Doch, and while trying to grasp what he means, he does. His hands, his gut, his brain, and finally, his heart, all unclench, as he releases himself to the dragon, no longer understanding his reasons for resistance. He feels the dragon enter him, almost as a man

enters a woman. But it's his maleness that she enters, and
her own female nature that he takes inside himself, like
light, like a revelation, like a song. He shudders with it in
his brother's grasp, stunned by the wealth of songs within
him, waiting to be born.

Then he becomes aware of himself again, a grown man
cradled like a child in another grown man's arms. He imagines Köthen behind him, watching this darkly, misappre-
hending. He sits up, reaching for autonomy, for a shred of
distance. But he is not the same man he was just moments
ago. He will never be that other man again. He has a
dragon inside of him.

He grasps his brother's shoulder and shakes it lightly,
inarticulate with gratitude. "Just let me know. That song'll
be there for you."

Down in the market square, the last of the late light
seems to have settled over the dragon in the paving stones.
The man-sized flame in the golden bowl makes the image
dance as if it was alive. The procession of soldiers and
priests and sedan chairs completes its outer circuit under
the glow of the torches. The leading squad of infantry does
a left face right in front of the Tinker wagons, turning in
toward the center and the block of waiting clergy. The
marchers split neatly around them and re-form in an honor
guard behind. The sedan chairs follow and are set down
side by side on the dragon's breast. All motion swirls to a
halt. Only the dust stirs, and the leaping, crackling torch
flames. Köthen sets down his cleaning rag and slides over
to watch, sword in hand.

The guy in the first chair steps out onto the pavement.
Swathed in red and gold, he is as big as N'Doch has
guessed, tall and bronze-skinned. His perfect musculature
is revealed to all by an open robe, a glittery open vest and
a magnificently naked chest.

"That dude's seen some hard time in the gym," mutters N'Doch.

Köthen sits up a little straighter. "Fighting man."

"Nah. Pumper's muscle, that's all. Look at those show-off
duds. Bet he spends most of his day looking in the mirror."

"Trust me on this," says the baron.

The muscle man accepts the many bows of the reception
committee, then strides to the second chair, draws back the

gold curtain and extends his hand. The High Priestess takes it and steps out of the shadow into the orange-and-lavender flicker of torchlight.

Köthen leans forward.

N'Doch says to Sedou in a stage whisper. "So. Whaddya think of the baron's new girlfriend?"

A sharp crack explodes the silence, then another. A double echo clatters around the walls of the square. N'Doch sees shattered stone puff up right at the priestess' feet.

"Shit! Sniper!" He ducks.

Köthen leaps to his feet, sword at ready, and glares around for the source of the sound.

Another crack.

N'Doch drags Köthen down hard as the others flatten around them and roll off the roof into cover. Köthen struggles to shake him off, but N'Doch hangs tight and yells at him.

"That's gunfire, Dolph! Tryin' to get yourself killed?"

Köthen stops struggling. "Where?"

"Got me. We're sitting ducks here, but so far they ain't shooting at us."

A fourth and fifth shot. N'Doch hears the slugs track above their heads just before the sound ricochet drowns out the direction of fire. Down in the square, everyone's screaming and diving for cover. The big guy in the fancy clothes has already proved Köthen's estimation of him. He's snatched the priestess girl around the waist and dragged her into the thickest part of the crowd. Soon N'Doch sees the golden shimmer of his robe rising like a sail, a billow of distraction, grabbed by one too many eager hands as it floats free. Immediately, there's fighting over it, despite the hail of bullets that follows. Doesn't matter. The big guy's no longer inside it. He and the woman have vanished.

Now the firing is coming from more than one place. What began as panic in the square is devolving into riot and mayhem. At least one priest lies facedown on the paving stones, his blood mixing with the red of the tiled dragon. N'Doch feels the van jerk into motion.

"Dockman!" Charlie pops her head up beside him. "Gichu down nah! Gittin' ouda heah, pronto!"

Köthen's still staring down into the square.

N'Doch grabs his arm. "She's okay! Gotta be. Your fast-thinking fighting man snatched her outa there. Come on!"

Across the square, the trade booths caught unpacked by the procession's early arrival are under attack from sneak thieves and looters. Some of the gunfire's coming from there, as townie security moves in hard, but not all. N'Doch hustles Köthen off the roof of the van, then hangs over the front to peer into the driver's seat. Luther's down with the lead mule, calming him, urging him. The girl's inside, pale and wide-eyed, with the reins in her hands. N'Doch somersaults into the seat beside her.

"Shit's hittin' the fan again, girl! What is it with the two of us?"

He gets the barest ghost of a smile out of her. He doesn't understand. She looks like something terrible is about to happen. He thinks it already has. The van stutters forward as Brenda slides onto the back of the second mule to growl into its ears. In Luther's cobbled-up side mirror, N'Doch sees Charlie vault onto the lead mule of the team behind them, Beneatha's flatbed, now heavy with stacked cargo tied down under the stained canvas top. When that wagon starts to roll, the two Oolyoot wagons turn out of formation to follow.

"Guns." The girl bites her lips. "Where is Baron Köthen?"

"He's fine. Look in your mirror."

Köthen's alongside the van, his sword sheathed across his back again. He's taken up one of the Tinker quarterstaves to fend off looters. Several of the Oolyoot Crew are doing the same. N'Doch counts heads. Shit, Only eight.

"Where's Stoksie and Ysabel?"

"I don't know. Weren't they . . . ?"

"Damn!"

And then the alarm shrills through him, unmistakable as middle C.

The girl stiffens, snatching at the seat with both hands. "Oh, God, oh God! Oh, Holy Mary, mother of God, pray for us now in our hour of need!" The reins snake loose in her lap until she gets a grip on herself and snatches them up again. "He's coming, N'Doch! Oh, dear God, he's coming!"

"I know, I know." He looks around for Sedou. Already the song is rising in his throat.

She's been bored and hot all day, and her premonition has faded.

Only its unusual size has promised to make Phoenix Town interesting. Until two things occur: she sees the man with the sword, and someone starts shooting at her. Her premonition has returned.

I shouldn't have come! I should never have insisted! The God warned me! I should have known better!

Ducking away under Luco's strong arm, Paia forces down her panic in order to concentrate on moving with him as he skillfully dodges and weaves, and not think about the outrage of being shot at. The God has told her that he outlawed the few firearms that were left after the Wars. But now she sees them everywhere in this shoving, panicked, ravening mob. Either the God lied, or the God is not as omniscient as he would like her to think.

And where is he when I really need him!

It's hard, with the crack of gunfire and all the shouting and screaming, to concentrate on her summons. When the first shot spattered marble dust into her eyes, she called out to the God instinctively. Then Luco's defensive maneuver distracted her. Quick, reliable Luco. How could she have ever thought this ex-soldier had gone soft?

He has her tight about the waist, as if he fears losing her to the heave of the mob. She has the odd impression there are strangers racing beside them, in step with their every turn, as if clearing them a path. Where are her chaperones? Where are Luco's strong young men? Suddenly, the wall of a building looms up in front of them.

"This way, my priestess!" Luco ducks sideways along the stones, then into an alley that opens up as if it was exactly where he expected it to be. It is narrow, and choked with terrified villagers fleeing the chaos in the square. Luco jostles through them, hugging the left-hand wall, until one of the many closed doors that they pass is miraculously open. Luco hauls her inside, into darkness. The others she thought to be their companions are swept by with the mob.

Luco kicks the door shut. Sunk in total blackness, she hears him lock it.

Paia can tell she's in a very small room. Her throat and lungs constrict. "What if they find us in here? We'll be trapped! Wouldn't we be safer if we kept moving?"

"We will. First you need a chance to catch your breath."

A soft flare eases her panic as Luco lights an oil lamp set on a little table in the middle of a low, square room. Shamed by the priest's calm, Paia tries to still the heaving of her chest. She is not only breathless, she is terrified. But she doesn't want Luco to have to slap sense into her, as he has a few times in the past. She wants to appear strong and capable, for once. She has survived assassination attempts before. Of course, then she'd had the familiar security of the Citadel to comfort her.

The room she's in now tells Paia almost nothing about its usual occupants. Could they really own nothing but the few dishes and chairs, and the two iron cots lined up along one wall? She watches Luco as he moves briskly about the tiny space. She envies his confidence in such a dire circumstance.

He opens a few cupboards, finds cups and a stoneware jug. He fills the cups with water from the jug, and hands one to her. "Drink up, my priestess. I'm not sure when we'll have another chance."

Water? How convenient. She eyes him over the rim of the cup. Does she sense the God's presence somewhere about? She thinks not, and yet, there's just the faintest echo. "Luco, tell me the truth now. This isn't another one of your schemes with the God . . . ?"

He laughs, but with an edge to it. "No, my priestess. I assure you it is not."

"Well, we should thank these villagers whose home we've invaded."

"Easy enough." He opens another cupboard, searches through the scant piles of clothing there, pulls out his choices and tosses them on the table. "You can leave them your expensive and conspicuous clothing. Put those on."

She gapes at him. Is this the man for whom every Temple garment is a treasure? "Really? Just leave it here? What will my poor chambermaid say?"

Luco's mouth quirks. "She'll survive. If I'm to extract

you safely from this tinderbox of a town, you'll have to go incognito."

He's found garments for himself as well. Without even turning his back, he strips out of his golden Temple vest and belted white pants, and slips into darker, looser pants and a long-sleeved T-shirt. He folds the ceremonial glitter precisely and puts it away in the cupboard. "Come, now. We should hurry."

Paia does turn her back. Having many times considered trying to seduce her head priest, now she is shy in front of him. The shirt and pants he has given her are patched here and there, and soft with age, but clean and comfortable. And they conceal her body as completely as her beloved sweats. Paia rather likes them. She steals a look to see if he's watching her change, but only catches him glancing at his empty wrist, a nervous gesture that she recognizes. Her father had it. It's the habit of a man once used to wearing a watch. She has never noticed it in Luco before.

"Ready, my priestess?"

She nods. He gathers up her Temple finery from the floor where she's let it drop, and folds it, regarding her with bemused patience. He stows it away in the cupboard with his own. But instead of the main door, he opens the one narrow closet in the room and holds out his hand. Puzzled, Paia takes it. Luco leans back to blow out the lamp. The void surrounds them once more, but his voice is soft at her ear.

"We must be silent, my priestess. We move between walls and through spaces thought not to exist. We mustn't call attention to our passage."

Finally Paia understands that this room isn't just a happy accident. "How did you know about all this?"

"Has the God not charged me with your safe return, on pain of my life? I'm a careful man, my priestess. I like to plan for any eventuality. Hush, now. Not a sound until I say so."

He leads her through a long and complex darkness. Sometimes the walls are close on either side, sometimes an outstretched hand finds only one. Almost always, the ceiling is right above her head. There are twists and turns too numerous to count, and only occasionally a bit of dim light strays through from the rooms on the other side of the walls. When it does, she hears screams and gunfire. She wonders if the God has heard her summons, or if he's punishing her by ignoring her. She can't shake the sensation that he's nearby somewhere. But even if he is, she can't imagine him manifesting inside these tiny passages.

At last she hears the creak of another door. Luco leads her into another small, dim room, only this one has a curtained window. He goes to it immediately and peers out between the drapes. The screams and shouting are louder here, close to the street, but Paia is sure she hears the rattle of wagon wheels. She joins him at the window, but he does not move aside to let her see out.

"Are those our wagons? Have they come for us?"

"Not our wagons. But they'll do." He turns away from the window and looks down on her, an oddly contemplative expression abstracting his gaze. He surprises her by smoothing a stray lock of hair away from her eyes. A very paternalistic gesture for Son Luco. "Now listen carefully. We are in very grave danger. You must do exactly as I tell you. No questions, no tantrums. You must trust me absolutely. No matter how it may seem, you are safe in my hands."

"Oh, Luco, you needn't frighten me to make me behave. I'm there already. I'll do as you say."

He pats her cheek. "Good girl." He glances through the curtains once more, then grasps her hand firmly and opens the door.

Erde guided the dragon in from his hiding place in the woods just as the shadow of vast wings swept over the square, blotting out the last whisper of dusk. She felt N'Doch's strength beside her, steadying her as if she were a spooked carriage horse. She wanted to tell him about Fire, how she knew and what she saw, but there wasn't time. Fire's passage roiled the hot air, making the torches leap and flare. His shriek shattered the din of the fistfights and shouting and sent even the looters scurrying for their lives. As the great shadow passed, the priests of the Temple looked up from aiding their wounded fellows and fell down on the paving stones in terror and awe.

DRAGON, ARE YOU THERE? I CANNOT SEE YOU.

Earth had never wanted nor been able to hide himself from her before.

I AM. DO NOT ASK WHERE, FOR YOUR OWN SAFETY.

The Tinker wagons moved faster toward the intersection as the terror-stricken mob stampeded into the side streets and alleys, trampling the slower and weaker in their desperation to flee. Luther and Brenda struggled to keep the frightened mules from bolting out of control. Beside Erde, N'Doch was singing. It was a wordless, soaring sort of song, unlike any she'd ever heard him sing. Erde felt the power in it, like the surge of oceans.

The shadow passed again, like the shiver of a dream, with a metallic rattle of wings and another rending cry. The air smelled like ash and molten iron. Erde felt him up there, searching, his inhuman eyes raking the darkened ground. She made her mind go as still as she knew how.

He knows me, just as the hell-priest knows me!

At the mouth of the square, Scroon Crew's wagons blocked the intersection. The mob broke against them like a wave and surged away to either side, scrambling for the lesser exits, or pounding on the doors of the houses along the square, begging for shelter. Others just dropped to the ground where they were and prayed. The wail of fearful believers rose to drown out the shouting. Somewhere, somewhere, there was still gunfire. Thumping on the caravan's sides drew Erde's glance to Baron Köthen. His face was alight with grim satisfaction as he wielded his quarterstaff against a pair of men trying to climb up on the wagon. He was glad to be in action at last. They were almost to the intersection.

DRAGON! THE TINKERS ARE LEAVING! WHAT SHOULD I DO?

GO WITH THEM AND BE SAFE. YOU'VE DONE YOUR PART. NOW WE MUST DO OURS.

And don't speak to us! You can't hide yourselves as we can. He'll go after you, and distract us from our task.

As Lady Water's voice faded in Erde's head, the shrieking dragon above swooped down out of the night and settled with a sound of clashing swords in the center of the square. Erde recoiled into the shadow of the caravan's roof.

She was sure he would pick her out of the crowd. But she could not keep from easing forward just a bit to stare.

In the jittery light of the torches, Lord Fire's scales glimmered like the fabled treasure hoard of gold and fabulous jewels. He was winged, horned, shred-eared, and clawed. His barbed tail coiled around his muscled haunches like a snake ready to strike. His eyes flamed like blown embers, bright heat in darkness. He curved his plated back, arched his long, sensuous neck, and let a curl of smoke rise from his cavernous nostrils. The very essence of Dragon. He was awesome, magnificent.

And horrific. This was Baron Köthen's understanding of dragon. This was what he'd met in the hell-priest's eyes. *Lord Fire himself.*

Erde did not know how this could be, but now she was sure of it.

The wagons slowed and halted as the Tinkers, even the mules, stared at him, astonished. With a deep resounding crescendo, N'Doch completed his song. For a moment, the world was becalmed, as if life itself had paused on its journey to pay homage to this lordly creature, the king of ancient myth, preening himself in the village square.

"I never thought . . ." murmured Erde.

"That he'd be so beautiful?" N'Doch finished for her. "Me neither. He knows it, too. Look at him strut!"

Then the stillness ended. Lord Fire lifted his elegant head and roared. Great booming echoes beat around the building facades and against Erde's eardrums. The priests of the town and a few who had come in with the procession scrambled into a huddle and prostrated themselves before him. The dragon seemed to be waiting. The curve of his neck tightened into an impatient arc. The barb on his tail, as tall as a man, lashed back and forth.

One of the priests, stuttering and stumbling, dragged himself onto his knees and struggled to string together enough words to explain what had just happened before Lord Fire's arrival. "The Great God," he called the dragon, but could get no farther. Another, facedown, tried to help him, then suddenly all of them, men and women, were up on their knees babbling hysterically, begging the "Great God's" forgiveness. Packs of abject worshipers, huddled around the square, added their own chorus of wails and moans.

Fire snaked his head around to stare at the shivering priests. With an angry flare of his enameled wings, he reared up and roared again. Three of the priests collapsed in a faint. The rest threw themselves flat on the blood-stained stones, mumbling incoherently.

Erde sensed a momentous gathering of dragon energies. A decision. The time for confrontation had come.

I CAN TELL YOU WHAT HAS OCCURRED HERE, BROTHER.

Fire dropped to all fours, poised for battle like a cat. N'Doch and Erde shuddered as a new voice invaded their heads: deep, raw, and furious.

WHAT? YOU? HERE?

YES, BROTHER.

Earth's presence was directionless and vast. Even Erde could not tell where he was. Fire glared around the square.

LEAVE ME ALONE! YOU'RE TOO LATE!

NEVER!

WHERE IS SHE? WHERE IS THE PRIESTESS OF MY TEMPLE?

WE KNOW NOT.

YOU HAVE TAKEN HER!

If you'd listen to those humans instead of frightening them . . .

YOU HERE, TOO!

Is this how you greet us after so long?

YOU'VE TAKEN HER!

She flees an assassin.

LIARS! WHERE IS SHE?

WHERE IS OUR SISTER AIR?

HOW SHOULD I KNOW?

Caught in the maelstrom of the dragons' power, Erde still heard the note of petulance in Lord Fire's tone. For some reason, it gave her courage.

WE THINK YOU DO.

FIND HER YOURSELF! I AM BUSY.

BUSY TERRORIZING THOSE YOU WERE CREATED TO SERVE. MUST WE REMIND YOU OF YOUR DUTY?

I SERVE THEM AS THEY DESERVE!

The golden dragon rose again, shrieked, and spat a bright

stream of fire at the ceremonial dais at the head of the square. The draped red fabric was instantly ash. The dry wooden beams and floorboards exploded into flame with a whoosh like a thousand birds taking flight. Heat washed the Tinker wagons in rhythmic waves.

N'Doch yanked Erde back into the shelter of the caravan's metal walls.

"The sonofabitch even breathes fire! No wonder everything around here's built out of stone!"

She couldn't imagine how he could complete a coherent sentence, with so much raw power coursing through his brain as it was through hers.

"Ev'rybuddy up!" shouted Brenda. The Oolyoots who'd been defending the wagons on foot each grabbed at the side of a wagon to hoist themselves upward. On Beneatha's wagon, Charlie beat out sparks caught in the folds of the canvas. The dragon in the square screamed again. His voice in Erde's head was like knife blades along her nerves.

LEAVE ME ALONE!

BROTHER, WE MUST FOLLOW OUR DESTINY.

THAT DESTINY DOESN'T SUIT ME. I DENY IT!

NO, YOU WILL NOT DENY IT. YOU CANNOT DENY IT.

I AM FIRE! I AM THE LORD OF THIS KINGDOM! YOU CANNOT BEND ME TO YOUR WILL!

We'll see about that . . .

And where there had been one dragon, suddenly there were three, crouched staring at each other in the glare of the burning dais.

Erde heard Luther's yell of exultation and terror and then stopped paying attention to anything but the dragons. She leaned out into the wash of heat, entranced. She'd let the fire consume her entirely, to be witness to so glorious a sight! N'Doch grabbed her, pulling her back. She pushed him away.

"No! No! You must look! Oh, look at them now!"

Earth loomed gigantic in the flickering darkness, as solid and towering as the side of an ancient mountain. His massive head was like a pinnacle of carved stone. His great eyes, like veined agate, glowed with the inner light of righteousness. Erde remembered the confused little dun-colored beast of two months ago, and was proud.

Lady Water stirred and rocked at her point of the trian-

gle, a sea vision in blue and green and lavender, rising from
the Deep. Her luminous crest and frills eddied around her
like a dancer's sibilant veils. Her sleek head was the shifting
center of a swirl of rainbow phosphorescence. Her actual
shape was no longer possible to determine.

Silhouetted against a leaping wall of flame, Fire
screeched and lashed his tail. In answer, the paving stones
rippled. The ground shook. The stones of the houses shivered and rattled. Lightning flashed, and the heated air of
the square rose in hissing columns of steam as water fell
out of nowhere to douse the flames. Fire searched about
for something else to put to the torch. His glare fell on the
priests groveling at his feet.

N'Doch said, "Uh-oh. Time to go."

Baron Köthen jogged up from behind to shake Luther
out of his dragon daze and slap the flanks of the mule he
was mounted on. The stalled caravan lurched forward. Köthen swung up into the driver's seat, shoved Erde over, and
grabbed the reins. "The battle is joined! Would we could
stay to witness it!"

"They told us to leave!" Erde regretted it as much as
he. She feared leaving them, yet knew she must bow to
their dragon wisdom. "They say we'll only get in the way."

Köthen nodded. "They fight a different sort of battle.
And the Tinkers have need of us."

Scroon Crew had lit the side lanterns on their lead
wagon. With all their walkers piled on in a confusion of
clinging bodies, they pulled ahead out of the intersection
just as Blind Rachel reached them. But for a few scurrying
villagers, the main street lay empty and shrouded in darkness. Another lightning flash. Scroon's mules leaped forward and set a breakneck pace. Bending low over the lead
mule's neck, Luther urged his own team after them.

Erde's head cleared as she withdrew from the dragon
contact. But she kept glancing back. She was disturbed by
Lord Fire's denial of his destiny. Not only because it was
outrageous and unforgivable, but because he spoke as if he
knew very well what that destiny was. An exact understanding of this still eluded his siblings.

As the wagons clattered out of the square, she gripped
the edge of the caravan and leaned out for a last backward
look, in time to see Fire rear up again and launch himself

at Earth, spewing a stream of white heat aimed straight at
the big dragon's heart. But he only melted stone. In a blink,
Earth was not there, but behind him instead. As Fire
landed from his leap, the ground bucked viciously beneath
him. His huge wings beat furiously as he tumbled off-balance. Shrieking his outrage, he whirled on Water, not with
flame but to tear at her with his claws. Water danced and
hovered, just out of his reach.

Brother Fire, where is our sister Air?

Fire lunged, snagging an edge of Water's crest with one
scimitar claw. N'Doch was singing his song again, first
under his breath, then out loud, a fervent paean of anguish
and prayer.

No! We shall not make this town a battleground!

As Fire lunged again, Water danced away and, as suddenly as a sound, glistening wings were born out of the
rainbow hues of her frills, many-folded wings like the tails
of exotic fishes. N'Doch fell back against the seat, eyes
closed. A ragged gasp of relief shook his entire body.

"We did it!"

And then the blue dragon sang, a lilting, whistling taunt
that drew Fire snarling in pursuit as she soared away into
the darkness. The rain stopped. The ground stilled. Erde
looked for Earth. The square was empty.

Paia smells smoke. She pulls on Luco's hand as he eases
head and shoulders around the cracked-open door. "We
shouldn't go out there! We should stay here and wait for
the God to come get us."

Luco peers out. "What a mess. Worse than I . . , we're
going to have to make a run for it." He draws his head
back. "Let him what?"

"Come and get us."

"He'd have to know where we are."

"He does. Or he should." She shouldn't share this secret,
but the First Son is working so hard to protect her and it's
the only help she has to offer. "I summoned him."

"That won't work here. We're out of locator range."

"I have . . . a different kind."

His brow creases faintly. "Are they somewhere other than on your clothing?"

"Yes. They . . . that is, it . . . is in me. I am the locator."

"I don't understand."

"I don't either, but you know that I always know when he's calling me, and that I can't ever resist his summons . . ."

Luco nods, slowly.

"Oh, Luco, don't ever tell him I told you. He'd be humiliated."

"Because . . . ?"

"Because it's the same for him. He hears me, and he *has* to come when I call him."

The priest's handsome face goes slack, and Paia worries that she's miscalculated. Perhaps Luco's devotion to the God is not only about gaining power within the Temple. Perhaps it is also about belief, and now she has shaken the foundations of his faith, by implying that the God is not entirely omnipotent.

"How could I not have known this?"

"I only learned it myself very recently."

"And he knows where you're . . . summoning him from?"

Paia nods faintly. She has never seen the priest look so at a loss.

He closes the door behind him and leans against it heavily. "When did you summon him?"

"When the shooting started."

"But . . . he isn't here."

"No. Not yet." This is the part Luco will really hate. It makes the God sound too much like an ordinary . . . person. "He's probably punishing me. He hates it when I summon him. But he always comes eventually. Of course, the longer he resists, the angrier he is when he arrives." Paia pushes dust around with the soft toe of the shoes Luco had given her to replace her gold temple sandals. "But how could he be angry when our lives are at stake? He should be . . . Luco? What is it?"

He's pressed his palms to his eyes with a soft moan. He holds them there for the length of a breath. "He'll lay the town to waste!"

"What? No, he . . ."

He pushes abruptly away from the door. "Oh, what have I . . . I can't ask the . . . no, we must . . . they can . . . Damn! That's the end of it, then!" He reaches the wall, rebounds with both hands, and strides back toward her. Outside, the rattling of cart wheels nears. He grips her elbow, guides her toward the door. "This is what we'll do. Once we get out of town, you will call him again, as urgently as you can, to draw him away while the townsfolk get to cover. If anyone's to survive this, we've got to hurry!"

Paia resists. "He won't . . . !"

"He will!"

"He wouldn't just kill innocent people!"

Luco grabs her by both shoulders and shakes her. "The hell he wouldn't!" Then he collects himself and says more gently. "He will. Believe me. We must do what we can to keep down the death toll."

The death toll? She stares at him.

"Paia, listen to me! I have relatives and friends in this town! So do . . ." He stops, monitoring the sounds outside. "They're here. Let's go."

Paia has no relatives and friends in any town. "All right," she says faintly.

Luco opens the door again, drawing her into the opening. She hears the sound of glass breaking nearby and shrinks into the shelter of his arm. Night has fallen while they've been in hiding. The reek of burning thickens the air. The dark street seethes with fleeting shadows, people running, ducking into doorways. But the wagon clattering toward them has lanterns swinging from the driver's perch, like a promise of rescue. Luco hustles her out of the house as the wagon thunders past. There are others behind it. Some of the shadows swoop down on them, cluster, and move alongside. Luco is talking, hoarse and insistent. "We have to warn them! All of them! Even his own!" Paia hears a man's voice answer, and then a woman's, but not the words they're saying. Fear seems to have numbed her senses. She is focused too desperately on keeping upright. Luco is dragging her directly into the path of the oncoming wagons. But the wagons slow. A man leaps off the lead mule, struggling to halt it. A shadow scuttles past Paia and yanks open a door in the rear of the wagon. Luco scoops her up and bundles her inside, then springs in behind her, reaching one hand to hoist the shadow in after them.

"Go!" the shadow hisses through the open door.

The door is slammed shut from the outside, sinking the inside into total darkness. The wagon surges forward. Paia is thrown against a wall. She reaches blindly for a steady hold. She finds only smooth metal, other people and rough, lumpy, shifting surfaces. Bags of onions? Cabbages? The wagon rocks harder as it picks up speed. Paia is pressed against sweating bodies and stinking vegetables. Luco and the shadow man whisper urgently in the darkness. The man's odd accent blends with the din of the wagon. Paia can make no sense of it.

Abruptly, her courage shatters. She is terrified and uncomfortable, and angry with the God for not showing up when her life is truly in danger. She is used to being taken care of, not abused and ignored. "Luco!"

He hushes her and returns to his muttered conversation. "What?" she hears him exclaim. "Others? When?"

"Luco, please! I can't bear . . .!"

"Keep still!" he hisses. "We have the gates to get through!"

"But it's so . . ."

He swears quietly but obscenely, shocking her into silence. She feels him moving about, struggling with something invisible in the confining darkness. "Here, I want you to hide under this, in case they search the van!"

"If dey ev'n bodda ta stop us," murmurs the shadow man.

"Can't take the chance." Before Paia can protest, Luco has thrown a piece of canvas over her and pressed her to the jouncing floor. "Just breathe easy and keep still!"

The canvas is heavy and she fears suffocating in its folds. Unable to shift it off of her, Paia struggles for a bit. She thinks Luco may be holding the edges down. But she has heard in his voice the same sharp alarm that spun her own senses into a blur. This time it wakes her to vague reason.

Besides, it's cool and damp beneath the soft fabric. There's a clean, medicinal smell that Paia finds oddly comforting. The wagon's rocking eases. They must be slowing down for the gates. She hears the barking of sentries and the driver's muffled reply. Paia goes still, as Luco has warned her to, and waits for the back doors to be yanked open, waits to be hauled out and exposed to her would-be assassins. Instead, she is overcome by drowsiness.

She knows she should be more startled by the brief crackle of gunfire, the shouting, and the wagon's sudden forward jolt. But by then she is more inclined to let sleep take her wherever it will.

CHAPTER THIRTY-THREE

Once Luther gets his hands back on the reins, the old van cruises right along, faster than these messed-up roads are good for. N'Doch is holding on for dear life. He's also holding Luther's pistol, a big old gun with a kick like one of these breakneck mules, that might go off in his lap any second, 'cept it might not be loaded. Luther's put it to good use at the gates. The barrel's still warm.

He'd fantasized maybe they'd zip through the walls unchallenged, with the surly guards occupied with the chaos elsewhere. No such luck. The rattle of Scroon's wagons raised a couple of armed men out of nowhere. Scroon took the challenge, and dealt with it swiftly. Then Luther followed with the mop-up detail. N'doch saw at least three shadowed heaps facedown in the dust as they clattered past, and he didn't have to lift a finger, except to grab the gun as it got tossed into his lap when Luther piled back into the cab and snatched the reins back from Köthen.

The baron's still wearing his grimace of disapproval, like this kind of killing's too easy for his tastes. But N'Doch is ready to be grateful. He's had enough fracas for one day. And he's worried about the blue dragon. She's told them not to check in via the dragon internet, but he hopes if he just sort of hangs his mind open, he'll pick up a signal. No dice. Just like a woman, he muses. No sooner does he declare his undying devotion than she up and disappears on him.

The girl's in the same boat, anyhow, and without the dragons, they may be headed for a language problem again. But here's the surprise. The German's right there in his head, even without Water's help. He's picked it up. Pretty cool. Dragon osmosis.

It's crowded in the cab and he's feeling bruised and battered, being tossed against Luther and Köthen on one side, the girl on the other, and a hard wall of trade goods behind him. He heard new passengers board when they slowed just before the gates. He leans around Köthen.

"Was that Stoksie and Ysa we picked up, back at the gates?"

Luther nods, but oddly. N'Doch's pretty sure something's up, more than he's telling. Like something's been up all day, maybe even since they were invited along on this expedition. Usually it pays to be suspicious, and N'Doch feels like what he hasn't been paying is good enough attention.

From the direction they turn after slamming through the gates, he surmises they're not heading back toward camp. It's dark as pitch out on the road and Luther's not volunteering any information. He only breaks his intent driver's silence once, to ask about the dragons.

"Wich one wuz da Pilgrim?"

N'Doch is impressed that he's figured out that much. "The blue one."

Luther nods. "I taut mebbe da odda one wuz yer man heah." He grins at Köthen. "Till he's dere shakin' me outa my daze!"

"I'll tell him you thought so." And he laughs, thinking that's probably what Köthen would like, not to have a dragon, but to be one.

Luther goes back to his reckless driving. The road is not as empty as N'Doch would have supposed. Fairly often, they rumble past the shadows of fleeing villagers, alone or with family and a cart piled high with household goods. When the road forks, Luther veers left. Instinct tells N'Doch they're headed not up or down the valley but straight for the surrounding hills. The ride is getting rougher, and the mules are laboring. They're starting to climb. He guesses the plan is to go as far as the mules can manage, then maybe take cover in the boulders on the southern slope. But he's not sure what they're still running from, now that they're clear of the mess in town. He wonders if it was only Stoksie and Ysabel they picked up back there on Main Street. Maybe they had something with them, some interesting contraband. Maybe the Tinkers run a black market alongside their legal barter. Having watched how Stoksie worked one little piece of jewelry into a half year's living for forty, N'Doch wouldn't be surprised.

The van's really rocking now. N'Doch keeps thinking Luther has got to slow down soon if he wants to have a van left instead of a pile of broken truck parts. But Scroon's wagons up ahead are pushing it just as hard. He can hear them more than see them, expects every minute to find them crashed along the roadside. Köthen has figured out the van's side mirrors. He's keeping an eye on the road behind them. If N'Doch leans forward, he risks being thrown onto the backs of the mules, but since they've turned, he can see past Köthen to the flare of torches and burning trade stalls in the town square, and the backlit columns of steam still rising from the doused flames. There's no pursuit, least not so's you'd notice, but the Tinkers sure don't seem to think they're out of the woods yet.

Suddenly the rocks rise up in front of them like an ocean wave. A solid wall, blacker than black. N'Doch ducks back hard as Luther drags the mules into a turn. He feels the outside wheels leave the ground. He can't fathom that they'll make it. The girl grips his wrist and bites back a little scream.

The wagon tips back, settles, and the rocks swallow them whole.

Miraculously, space opens up before them. Luther braces his legs and hauls back until the mules slow to a panting trot. He drops the reins on his knees and palms sweat out of his eyes with both hands.

"We ovah da bordah nah," he exclaims softly, but N'Doch hears more worry than relief.

The echo of Oolyoot's wagons in the rear is thrown into reverb as somehow, something massive seals the opening behind them. N'Doch feels the pressure change in his ears and swears a bit until his heart stops running away with him. He's sure the girl has left nail marks in his wrist. Just saying "wow" starts feeling inadequate. Finally, he gets a few actual words out.

"A tunnel! Man! Where'd all this come from?"

"Oh, reel ole place, dis," Luther mumbles between wipes. "Frum da baddle daze."

From the "bad old days" or the "battle days"? N'Doch is not sure. Either sounds interesting enough to occupy his thoughts for the length of time it takes to catch his breath. He sees the soft light of Scroon's lanterns tossed up on an arched ceiling just a Tinker's height above the van. The tunnel is two, maybe three wagons wide and looks to have been blasted out of solid rock. What's weirdest is how smooth the floor is. It's too dark to tell, but he's willing to bet it's been paved.

"So when did . . ." he begins, but Luther waves him silent.

"Latah, Dockman. Der's big t'ings happinin'. I showyu sum'un give bettah ansas den me."

"Sure, man, you got it." N'Doch wishes the Tinkers had let him in on *all* of their plan, but he decides to see if being patient is part of his new persona. He checks on the girl. She's heard Luther's request for silence, but she's got her shoulders all hunched up, like it ain't easy for her either. Köthen's sitting still and quiet, just taking it all in stride, like he can't wait to see what other bizarre adventure awaits him around the corner.

And then they roll out of the small tunnel into a much bigger one. N'Doch can tell by the echo timing of the wagon rattle and the swallowing up of Scroon's reflected light that the ceiling just got a whole lot higher. They trot along in blackness for a while. The mules must know the route 'cause he's sure nobody else can see where they're going. Then there's a ghosting of light up ahead, and a new sound, a low-register moaning all around him, both huge and quiet. As the wagons approach, the light resolves into scattered point sources that vanish and reappear at regular intervals. As N'Doch's eyes adjust, he sees more distinct shapes, sharper edges. Pillars, then, of some kind. Rows of them, leading off to either side. The space is even vaster than he thought, because the lights are lanterns, the brightest nearby as the wagons move in among them, the fainter ones at least a soccer field's length away. Then the wagons slow to a crawl and there are tables and chairs and boxes and other wagons, and people getting up and crowding toward them.

It's an encampment. A huge one. N'Doch glances up, wondering if he'll see the faint ruddiness of the night sky.

But the darkness overhead is profound. The big quiet noise has to be the wash of air through this gigantic cavern. He purses his mouth in a silent whistle. Hell of a ventilation system. He can see he's about to learn a whole lot more about these Tinker folk and their hidden resources. But it's more than that he's feeling. The whole place is resonant, like being inside a big bass woofer. Resonant in his head, in the place where the dragon usually lives.

N'Doch nudges the girl. "Does it feel weird to you in here?"

She nods mutely.

"What is it, do you think?"

She shakes her head. Her eyes are wide, but more with anticipation and awe than with fear. She's been so scared in her short life that she's way beyond fear by now.

They're nearly there, wherever "there" is. Soft greetings float up around the Scroon wagons, head-counting, status-checking. The Scroon riders drop off even before their wagons roll to a stop, stumbling into glad embraces and back-pounding. Shadows surge up around Luther's van. N'Doch recognizes the murmur of Blind Rachel voices long before he can pull out a face from the gloom. People gripping hands and shoulders. Hugs of relief. No shouts or loud laughter. Everyone's keeping their volume down, but they're here, all those left behind in the gray morning. The rest of Scroon Crew, too, he guesses, and Oolyoot and who knows what else. He's amazed that so many people can make so little noise.

"Made it thru!"

"So fah!"

"Whadda run! Shuda seen us!"

N'Doch nudges Luther. "Why are we whispering?"

The reply is a gentle warning. "Da Monsta has reel gud eers."

The six wagons pull up in a line. Lanterns bob alongside. N'Doch spots Ysabel climbing down from Oolyoot's lead wagon. All's needed now is Stoksie to make a full ten.

Luther tosses down the reins like a man glad to have a long day's work finally over and done with. "Ev'rybuddy out."

CHAPTER THIRTY-FOUR

N'Doch nods Köthen off the side, then jumps down after him. He's not sure what to do next in this milling of relief and greetings and bobbing lanterns. Just standing there, he gets his own hugs and pats from Blind Rachel Crew, and that makes him feel good, like he's a part of their family, now he's risked his life for them. He senses a general drift toward the back of the wagons. Time to unload. These Tinkers don't waste a minute when it comes to counting their loot. But he's forgotten about Luther's extra cargo.

All the Crews, plus a lot of other folks who look more like farmers and villagers, are gathering at the rear of Luther's van. Dark, eager faces full of upspoken questions. Someone's up on the roof of the van hanging lanterns from the corners. Luther comes around from the side and eases them back a bit so he can unlatch the door and swing it wide. Stoksie is waiting just inside. Even in the near dark, N'Doch knows him by his slow, stiff moves as he clambers down, waving back the hands held out to help. But there's another guy behind him, a stranger.

Well, no, he isn't. N'Doch recognizes him the minute he steps into the lantern light, mainly because he'd be impossible to disguise unless you cut his legs down and threw dirt on him. It's the big, good-looking dude who snatched the pretty priestess out of the line of fire, only he's shucked his gold duds for dark sweats and jeans. Except for his flowing red-gold hair, he looks more like a power-built linebacker than the overdressed fancy man he'd seemed like before. N'Doch tries to imagine Stoksie taking him prisoner, even with help. He wonders what's been done with the priestess.

He doesn't think the Tinkers would harm her, but she is the Temple's main rep, after all, as Luther said back in town, "da Monsta's t'rall."

As the light reveals the linebacker's face, the milling crowd stills, in a collective intake of breath. Then a sound like a billion bird wings swells in the gloom, a wave of muffled applause that goes on and on, until the big dude lifts a hand in acknowledgment, like he's used to this kind of welcome. The soft eager patter dies into echoes. The crowd waits. N'Doch is totally confused. He was sure this guy was as much the enemy as the priestess.

The linebacker smiles. He looks weary and relieved. "We've done it, friends. We're committed. It's good to be home."

The patter swells again, louder, as if the listeners just cannot contain their joy, and the guy holds up both hands to quiet them. He is easy in front of the crowd. His smile is wide and winning. He knows how to look at the people like he loves them. "Phase One went off without a hitch. We've taken the first big step on our journey out from under the thumb of the Beast!" More applause. He quiets them again. "But there's more! For those of you who haven't heard it already from the Crews, we have . . . astonishing news!"

N'Doch feels Köthen slide up beside him.

"Wie gehts, Dochmann?" The baron has adapted N'Doch's Tinker nickname to rhyme with his own.

"Damned if I know." N'Doch settles in to translate as best he can, now that the linebacker's got the crowd hanging on his every word and move.

"Help has arrived!" the big man announces. "Help . . . like we could only have dreamed of!" He looks down into one of the faces most intent on his own. "Luther! Tell them what you saw!"

Someone shoves an old metal crate up beside the van. Stoksie and Brenda urge Luther up on it. His head down, his back stooped, he begins as usual like a reluctant public speaker, but N'Doch knows he will give himself to the telling of the tale soon enough. Once he does, his back straightens and his rough voice gains strength and rhythm, carrying into the darkness without increasing volume. His big active hands go to work, and the whole sequence of

events in the square comes to life, the terror and chaos of
the mob, the smoke and fire, lighting up the dark town, the
arrival of "da Monsta." The rapt, amazed faces around him
prove the success of his eloquence. Even the linebacker is
enthralled. N'Doch thinks he's being polite until he remembers the guy was busy rescuing the priestess when the shit
hit the fan. Likely all he knows is what Stoksie told him in
the van.

Luther builds the tale skillfully. The wonder of new dragons, the fiery confrontation. Finally his hands fly up, flickering in the lantern light, and seem to vanish. "An' dey'r
gone, jus' like dat!"

A predictable commotion follows, restrained by hissed
reminders to keep the noise down. Everyone has a question, or an opinion about what this miracle might mean.

"Gone? Gone weah?"

"Help at last!"

"How we know dey's help?"

"Any challenge to the Beast is help to us!"

"Who says they won't just turn on us?"

The linebacker's hands are in the air, pleading for quiet.
"We don't! We don't know anything! But listen! We nearly
had a disaster. The Beast showed up unexpectedly, and
then a miracle happened. These new creatures drew him
off, kept him from laying waste to the town! Countless lives
were saved. Where did they come from? We don't know.
For now we lay low and find out all we can. Blind Rachel
has . . ." He pauses, looks to Stoksie.

"New frens," Stoksie offers enigmatically.

"New friends! With new information. And of course . . .
we will consult the Librarian." He pauses again, as if to let
some big idea sink in, and apparently it does. The listeners
nod sagely, and murmur their awe and agreement.
"Meanwhile . . ." He tips his head toward the interior of
the van. "We have our hostage."

More excited pattering, and this time, from behind the
ranks of the Tinker crews, a darker mutter of anticipatory
glee. N'Doch cranes his neck to see who's back there hungry for blood, but past the first few rows, the crowd is lost
in darkness.

"What?" Köthen demands.

N'Doch can't locate the word for "hostage" in his

dragon-built data banks, but the baron seems to get the idea. He gives new attention to the dude up on the wagon, who's honed in on the nasty undercurrent from the rear. A hint of sternness stiffens his easy manner, the iron fist within the velvet glove.

"Hey, now . . . we'll have none of that. Remember, the only valuable hostage is a live one. And we need her cooperation. So keep it down." He ducks back into the van.

"It will be *her*," Köthen says quietly.

"Yeah, sure looks like it." How long, N'Doch wonders, has the handsome linebacker been leading a double life?

The voices at the back take advantage of the wait to say a few things about their preference for immediate revenge over long-term hostage maintenance. Luther climbs back up on his box and suggests they repeat their remarks when "the preacher" can hear them. This silences some, but not all.

"Betcha!" A stocky woman elbows her way to the front, and immediately, a phalanx of support forms behind her. "I'll sure tell 'im!"

Even if her face and body language weren't so weighted with ancient rage, this woman would still look like she's seen major trauma. N'Doch thinks of a statue he saw once in a park, after a big shootout—the fine marble, all chipped and broken. Then the linebacker steps back into the light carrying a limp lump of old clothing, swaddled up in dirty canvas. A delicate sleeping face is just visible among the folds.

Köthen shifts, easing his sword sling onto one shoulder, then down to his side. N'Doch agrees. This crowd, or at least a part of it, could turn ugly at any minute. A glance about tells him that he and the baron have been quietly percolated up to the front rank beside Luther and Stoksie, with the girl and Brenda and the rest of Blind Rachel ranged behind them. Maybe this is where the hired muscle was really supposed to come in handy.

Luther says to the linebacker, "Dere's sum heah gotta diffrint idear 'bout t'ings."

The linebacker stands tall on the tailgate. The lanterns burnish his hair and chiseled profile with a kind of halo. N'Doch is envious. The guy sure knows how to find his light.

"Let them speak up, then." He waits, the hostage cradled in his arms. The broken-faced woman glares but says nothing. The linebacker nods, and from over by Oolyoot's wagons, two strapping guys still partly swathed in red and gold come forward to help lift the hostage down.

But the moment she leaves the linebacker's arms, the crowd destabilizes, surging forward to press around the two aides and their burden, snatching back the concealing canvas, grabbing for a closer look. The aides twist and turn to get away, but they're surrounded and the mob's temperature is rising fast. N'Doch hears the now familiar rasp of steel being drawn. Köthen shoves forward at the same time that the linebacker leaps down from the van, shouting for everyone to back off. The skirmish is quick, and it leaves two men with blood seeping between fingers hastily clamped to a forearm or bicep. Sword at the ready, Köthen plants himself firmly in the space he's opened up around the aides and the hostage. The crowd backs off in muttering surprise. The wounded and some of the naysayers are hustled off into the dark nether reaches of the cavern. But the stocky, broken-faced woman holds her ground as the linebacker steps forward.

She glares at him. "Why shuld we risk ouah lives fer dat reptile's whore? An' yers, too, mebbe, fer all I know."

Gasps all around, but the linebacker regards her patiently, like he's heard all this before. "She's nobody's whore, Sel. Not mine, not his. Let's get that straight."

"She ain't done nuttin fer us!" shouts a voice from the back.

"Keep it down, Paddy. She's his victim as much as we are."

Derisive laughter rises out of the gloom.

"You don't believe me? Then you go do the kind of time in that place that I have! Go on! I dare you!" The linebacker stands a head taller than the rest of the crowd, and his blue eyes compel with the light of conviction. N'Doch can see why Luther calls him "preacher."

"This woman has been the Beast's prisoner inside the Citadel! She knows nothing about what he does out in the villages. She has no power other than the Beast's devotion to her. Besides, it's not what she's done for us before that matters. It's what she's going to do for us now!" He takes a step forward and leans over the broken-faced woman, so that she has to crook her neck hard to keep looking him in the eye. "We've been over this a thousand times, Sel."

"An' yu ain't neva listened onct!"

More laughter, but thinner this time.

"I've listened. We've all listened. And most of us think this is the way to go."

"The right way!" someone murmurs.

" 'Bout da only way," Luther seconds.

"Do we blow this opportunity just to exact petty revenge? Waste the luck of a miracle we never expected? New and powerful allies, like a sign from the One herself?" The linebacker spreads his arms in protest, but it feels more like an embrace. N'Doch feels himself getting snagged by the dude's crowd appeal. Is he priest or politician? "Is that what you want? To throw away all our months of . . ."

"Years!" chimes in Luther.

"Yes, years! Of planning and readiness? Look what we can do when we work together! Pulled it off without a hitch, without a life lost! We'll only get this chance once, Sel. The power of a miracle . . . on our side!"

The woman spits on the worn rock at the linebacker's feet. "Da reptile'll jes get isself anudda doll baby."

"I don't think so. But we'll just have to take that chance."

N'Doch glances over at the girl, listening hard at Stoksie's side. Another coin has just dropped and he wonders if she figures it the way he does. The pretty priestess is Fire's dragon guide. Got to be.

The aide holding the priestess shifts his burden and whispers something to the other one, who steps respectfully around Köthen and his gleaming blade. "I think she's coming around."

"Already? Okay." The linebacker turns. His gaze finally takes in Köthen and his sword. "Who's this, Luther? One of your . . . new friends?"

Luther clears his throat. "Yah. Dat's, um, dat's Doff. A fren frum Urop."

"Europe?" He cocks his head dubiously.

"He wouldn't be lying. And he doesn't speak English, but I'll speak for him." N'Doch takes a step into the light. This dude's the first since Hal at Deep Moor who's tall

enough to look him in the eye, but N'Doch's interested to
see that his cool's finally been ruffled. *Do I look that
strange?* He beckons the girl out from behind Luther.
"There's one more. Might as well meet us all at once."

Stoksie murmurs, "All da viziters I tole yu 'bout, Leif.
'Cept one."

"Um . . . ?" says the aide nervously.

"Right. Coming. Luther, Stoksie, explain later. Bring
your friends along. We'll take her down. Don't want her
knowing about all this right off." The linebacker steps up
to Köthen's warding blade, then holds out his hand. "I'm
Leif Cauldwell. Thanks for the help, whoever you are."

They share a brief measuring stare, then Köthen puts up
the sword and takes the offered hand. *"Schon gut."*

Cauldwell laughs softly. "I cannot wait to hear your
story."

N'Doch thinks: and I can't wait to hear yours. The big
man moves past him to take the priestess from the skittish
aide. Blind Rachel opens up a protected path through their
midst. Luther unhooks a lantern from the van and leads
the way. Cauldwell and the aides follow. Stoksie, taking up
the rear, turns back briefly. "Lady, Dockman, Doff—yu
come wit', na."

It's more like an order than an invitation, but N'Doch is
glad for it. He guesses Köthen ain't gonna let this priestess
woman out of his sights, now he's got her back in 'em
again. As they follow Stoksie, N'Doch sees anticipation
flicker in the baron's eyes before he can hide it.

Luther leads them through more crowds, past other wagons and darkened campsites, rumpled bedrolls and cold
meals hastily set aside, to a concrete wall with what looks
like a big door in it. A dim light burns steadily above the
doorframe. N'Doch squints at it. An *electric* light. Luther
presses his palm to a glassy plate alongside. The plate pops
open like a lid. Luther flips it back. Inside are two rows of
little buttons. Luther taps out a hurried sequence, a red
idiot light switches to green, and a deep hum starts up
somewhere down in the depths of the rock.

N'Doch swallows the exclamation of recognition that
leaps to his lips. He's thinking, *it can't be,* but sure enough,
the hum stops and a crack of light appears along the floor.
The big door lifts horizontally to reveal an evenly lit, square

silver room. Luther and Cauldwell head right in. Stoksie and the aides wait outside, beckoning to N'Doch and his companions, herding away any others. Köthen scowls at the too-bright, too even light, but he follows N'Doch and the girl as the door starts to close and Stoksie scoots in behind them.

"Damn!" whispers N'Doch. "An elevator!" He's near delirious to be bathed in glorious artificial light again. He slides a hand along the textured metal shell. It's cool, hard, and so familiar. He checks for the control panel. There isn't one visible. He's willing to bet that Luther's neat palm print maneuver would reveal one if needed, but apparently this car's on automatic. The door seals soundlessly as it touches the floor. The elevator sinks, with almost no sensation of motion.

N'Doch says, "Luther, my man, you're just full of little surprises."

CHAPTER THIRTY-FIVE

As the floor of the bright square room fell gently out from under her, Erde suffered a flash of childhood memory, of falling once when she was five into the deep end of the mill pond. It wasn't just the sensation of sinking slowly into the unknown. There was also this strange, increasing pressure on her eardrums, in her lungs, inside her head.

Not painful, only . . . disorienting. Erde glanced around to see if anyone else seemed to notice it.

N'Doch was looking her way. She searched his round ebony face for helpful clues. Perhaps her own face showed more distress than she felt, for he winked at her and smiled encouragingly.

Part of the oddness, she knew, was being apart from the dragons, inwardly as well as outwardly. She recognized the disappointing dulling of her senses—sight, smell, and especially sound—and the loneliness of being once again remanded to the confines of her own narrow skull.

And yet . . . being entirely within herself once again made her feel peculiarly *collected*. Strong, and clear-minded. Grown up.

She had listened closely to the confrontation in the cavern. The dragons had planted all the necessary language in her head, but the day's sequence of events had left her reeling with smoke and violence and revelation. The mystic reunion with Sir Hal's dragon-hilted sword. Lord Fire denying his destiny. Her own Earth, and Lady Water, coming into the fullness of their powers. And all the human events as well.

But it wasn't necessary, Erde decided, to understand all

the complex ramifications of those events, of the relationship between the town and the Tinkers, or the Tinkers and Lord Fire's Temple, or even the Temple and the general populace. Or of the arrival of the man Leif Cauldwell. Erde would await the dragons' reading of him. She thought of him as a sort of beautiful giant. If she were a sculptor, she would use him to model an archangel. Not fierce Michael, with the sword. Gabriel, rather, the Messenger.

All that really mattered was knowing how any of this bore on the dragons and the furthering of their Quest.

They had found Lord Fire and confronted him. As Baron Köthen had said, the battle was joined. Erde knew she should be filled with foreboding. Instead, she was exultant with purpose. Oh, the strength of purpose that swelled within her as the white room sank into unknown depths! It had been ripening, like a secret child in her womb, all along, while she was distracted with concern for the dragon's growth and welfare. She felt as if nothing could dismay her now, not a day of confusion and bloodshed, not the piercing eye of the hell-priest, not even the hopelessness of her love for the man standing next to her.

She wondered if N'Doch felt the same.

It was not a question to be asked out loud, not in present company. And it was complicated. She wasn't quite sure how to put it to him. So she turned it over in her mind, forming and re-forming the question, then glanced up to find him still staring at her. Only he wasn't smiling now. He looked both amazed and horrified.

Stop thinking so loud, his voice growled in her mind. *The answer is yes!*

Omigod! She knew she must not gape at him, and draw the others' notice. *What . . . ?*

A rueful chuckle tickled a corner of her mind. *Guess it finally got quiet enough in our heads for us to hear what else is going on.*

Do you . . . mind?

No. Not really. She feels his surprise. *Seems sorta . . . right. Long as I know there's places you can't go and things you can't know.*

Erde turned away to hide her smile from the casual onlooker. *N'Doch! Your thoughts are even more musical than your speech!*

Oh, yeah?

Won't they be pleased!

The dragons? You mean, 'cause we finally learned something on our own?

But we didn't! They taught us. We just weren't aware of it at the time.

I suppose.

But it wasn't quite like talking with the dragons. This entire communication had been instantaneous, contained in the few seconds it took Stoksie across from her to raise his hand and scratch his head. Erde had always assumed that the dragons slowed down their thoughts to suit the more sluggish pace of human minds. What if it was the other way around?

She considered how the tiny rapid heartbeat of a bird in hand made one's own human pulse seem inexorable and slow. Was it so with tiny humans and their dragons?

Hey, girl . . . Erde . . . lemme ask you something. I got a thought here.

She looked his way. He was studying the limp bundle in the archangel's arms. *The priestess? What about her?*

Fire's dragon guide, I'm betting. Whadda you think?

Oh. Oh, my. Well . . . perhaps so.

When she wakes up, maybe we should ask her.

Like . . . this?

N'Doch laughed, and Luther glanced over curiously. N'Doch shook his head. "Nothin', man, nothin'. Just a thought."

But in her head, he said, *Well, yeah! If she answers, we'll know we're right.*

CHAPTER THIRTY-SIX

Paia stirs. How curious. What has happened to her ability to tell dream from reality, or waking from sleep? Too much of that unaccustomed dreaming. She thought she'd waked cradled in Luco's arms, not a terrible place to be. Now she feels a subtle floating sensation that calls up memories of the Citadel's elevators. Either she's still dreaming or . . . she drifts away, then back, suddenly awash with relief and an explanation. Luco has brought her home, through some miraculously secret back entrance!

But her head is clearing, and logic intervenes. The Citadel is four hard days' travel away. Even at the speed of those mad cart animals, such a distance could not be accomplished . . . unless they've been traveling in one big circle since they left the Citadel. But Luco said his locator was out of range. She must be dreaming. Where else could there be a working elevator? Paia ponders this muzzily as the cab continues to drop.

Further proof of the dream: she can't seem to move or talk. Still wrapped in this tenacious drowsiness. It smoothes out any impulse to exert brain or muscle. She's paralyzed with lassitude. Well, no worry. The God will show up soon, as he does in all of her dreams. So what if he'll be furious.

Over the background hum of the elevator comes a soft babble of voices. In her dream, even though the words sound unfamiliar, Paia seems to understand them. One man is trying to explain to another man what an elevator is. She summons the effort to open her eyes. The first face she sees tells her she's dreaming for sure. It's the man with the sword, the man from her dreams, who stood in the crowd and stared at her as if he owned her. Now she begins to question that sighting. The rocking sedan chair, the soporific heat . . . had she dozed off, and dreamed in daylight? But here he is again. He's still staring at her. She should be insulted by his boldness, then and now. Instead, Paia welcomes it. She's never seen a more beautiful man.

There are others in this dream, as well: a tall skinny youth who looks like he's of pure African blood. Paia recalls colleagues of her father's who resembled him. Perhaps this dream figment is the embodiment of her survivor's guilt. She has suffered it since childhood, since the floods and epidemics that wiped out most of the African continent.

The next figment is a younger boy, no, it's a girl dressed as a boy. A pretty girl, but with little sense of herself. Perhaps she is the beautiful man's child, though they look nothing alike except for the lightness of their complexions. For some reason, Paia thinks of the chambermaid, and what her inventive hands could do with this girl, with her dark curly hair and her impossibly pale skin. Then there are two older men as well, smaller, darker than herself but clearly of local stock, except for their strange accents and their very independent manner. Why would she be dreaming these people? No matter. This dream has a mind of its own.

She is about to sneak another look at the man with the sword when the elevator breathes to a stop and the door lifts. A current of blessedly cool air swirls in and around her as she rests in Luco's strong arms. Paia hears the quiet sigh of climate control, and has another seizure of being sure she's back at the Citadel. Even dreaming, she's glad of the long sleeves and the long soft pants she's wearing. It's cold down here.

The light outside the door is dimmer than inside. The elevator seems to pour light like a liquid into the darkened corridor. When Paia's dream characters step out, the door closes behind them and there is just enough light in the corridor to see the way, as if half the recessed ceiling fixtures are burned out and the rest set to low power. But it's enough light to see all the books, piles and piles of them, real books as well as the electronic kind. Not carefully shelved and catalogued like her father's, but scattered about, right out in the open. Where are the servants, to clean the place up? There are stacks of papers and rows of storage cabinets lining the hallway left and right. They narrow it to a single lane or sometimes none, where a pile has been pushed aside into the path or simply tumbled down like a paper landslide.

The taller of the older men leads them through the mess. They pass intersections with other disordered, obstructed corridors, and many half-open doors that reveal dimly lit rooms stocked with more books, more shelving, and storage racks.

"It's a library," Paia says finally, and in the dream, everyone turns and looks at her. She has startled them. "It's even bigger than my father's."

Luco stops, shifting her in his arms. "You're awake."

"I am?" Paia realizes he's right. She's not even sure when the transition happened between the dream and reality. "I'm not dreaming? I thought I was dreaming."

Luco sets her down gently. "Can you walk?"

She gets her balance, but her eyes will not focus. "Where am I?"

He supports her elbow, urging her forward. "Wait."

Some of the drowsiness returns and it's all she can do to walk. "I didn't know," she mumbles, "how exhausted I was."

"Of course not," Luco murmurs. "We're almost there, and then you can rest. Just like I promised."

CHAPTER THIRTY-SEVEN

N'Doch doesn't mention how he sees the drug, whatever it was, working its way out of the priestess' limbs. Either it was a real clever one or she's completely drug innocent. She doesn't seem to know she's been doped. He wonders if the Tinkers are hip to it. They must be. This whole weird day has all the marks of a carefully planned event. He's picked up a little of the why or what for, so he decides to let the rest of it ride for now. There's a lot that's gotta smell just as fishy about him and Köthen and the girl, but the Tinkers have gone with their instincts, kept the questions to a minimum. N'Doch figures he owes them the same.

But, damn, it's a pisser not to be able to ask what the hell this place is, so high tech and still in working order. Is there a whole hidden infrastructure nobody's told him about, or just this one functioning artifact? Whatever, it's a major relief. The cooled air caresses him like a woman's hands. Now if he can just find a shower, or even a bath. There's got to be running water down here somewhere. The priestess probably has the library part right, but a library for what, buried so deep in the ground like this? A seriously hardened burrow for some big-deal government installation? It can't be a multinat hideout. The bizmen would never let it get into this much of a mess.

The odd resonance of the cavern upstairs has faded with the descent into the depths. Just the ghost of an echo as they dropped down the shaft. Now, it's dead as a doornail.

Hey, girl. I feel like my brain has on earplugs.

I feel the same, N'Doch.

You know what an epicenter is?

No.

I think it's just where we're headed.

Hard to remember that this is how he was all the time, before a certain blue dragon. As he pads after Stoksie, dutifully mum, he wonders for the billionth time how the dragons are doing. The girl hugs his side where the pathway allows, or dogs his heels where it doesn't. Köthen sticks close behind, once again taking up the rear.

Finally, Luther turns into one of the many identical doors. They all file into a long, high-ceilinged room, ringed by a railed gallery. More shelves and data storage line the walls on both levels, but the center of this room is dominated by a big conference table and a collection of tattered sofas and armchairs, gathered in pools of light from dark-shaded lamps on the side tables scattered among them. The overheads are either dead or switched off. A good choice, N'Doch decides. This room looks cozy and welcoming compared to the chill corridors outside.

There are people at work at the big table, bent over papers and printouts, and others huddled in conference in some of the seating areas. They all leap up when Cauldwell comes into the room and greet him with eager relief. Someone rushes off for water. Another hurriedly clears papers and clothing from the largest of the sofas. The others crowd around.

"Set her down here, why doncha?"

"Thanks." Cauldwell eases the priestess into the corner of the couch. He shakes a few hands in welcome. "Couple of you stick by the door, okay? We had a little show of resistance upstairs."

"Serious?"

"Could be, down the road."

"Anyone hurt?"

"Not so far." Cups and a pitcher of water appear beside him. The woman who's brought it pours and sets a filled cup in Cauldwell's outstretched hand. He drains it himself, then lets her refill it. He smoothes hair from the priestess' face and molds her hands around the cup. "Paia? You awake enough to hold on to this?"

The priestess nods quickly, like she's afraid he might steal the cup away. She gulps down the water and holds the cup out for more.

"Paia." Köthen's murmur speaks entire volumes, at least to N'Doch. He prays the girl hasn't heard it. Who ever would have guessed this hard nut could crack so fast?

Cauldwell stands back as the priestess inhales a second cup. The woman with the water sets down the pitcher and stands back with him. He curls an arm around her and draws her into his side. She's a lot shorter than he is. She can nestle right under his shoulder. It looks like they haven't seen each other for a while. He bends his head to nuzzle her dark hair. "So far, so good."

The woman nods. She has an alert, intelligent face and bold eyes that flick searchingly across the faces of the new arrivals. N'Doch finds himself smiling at her.

The priestess empties her cup, then looks around dazedly as if trying to decide what to focus on. She sees Cauldwell and the woman arm in arm, and her eyes go round with surprise. "Luco . . . what . . . ?"

The woman inclines her head in an ironic little bow. "My priestess . . ."

"You . . . but . . ."

Cauldwell comes to her rescue. "Paia, I'd like you to meet Constanze. My wife."

His wife? But it's the chambermaid! The chambermaid! With her chin up and smiling, looking not at all downtrodden. And she's talking! But . . . his wife? How could she be Luco's wife? The priests of the Temple are not allowed to marry.

Paia sets down the little ceramic cup very carefully. "I . . . don't understand." And that is an understatement. Maybe she is still dreaming, no matter if he's said she's not. Tears well up, hot tears of fright and confusion and humiliation. What is this sudden weakness? Paia hates tears she cannot control. "Luco, please. I'm very . . . not very well."

"I know. We had a rough trip. You were . . . exhausted. I gave you a little something to help you sleep."

"You . . . ah. I see." But she doesn't, really. A mere sleeping potion can hardly explain away the chasm yawning within her, the vast howling emptiness. Where is he? Why does the God not come for her? Hasn't he punished her enough? "I feel like I've . . . gone deaf. Where are we? Are we still in danger? Who are all these people? What's going on?"

Luco crouches in front of her. "Ah, Paia. I hardly know where to start. But let me try . . ." He grasps her hands as if he has waited all his life to tell her this news. Paia sees none of his usual hooded caution. His expression is open, intent with purpose. She searches for something known in him, finds only his familiar, perfect face. "First, you must forgive us for our deceptions over the years. There was no other way."

"Deceptions?" Her brain is shrouded in fog. Does he mean concealing his romance with the chambermaid? Comprehension will not come, except that she's suddenly very worried for them both. "Then don't tell me now, for your own sakes. If you tell me, the God will know it, too. All of it."

"It doesn't matter now what he knows or doesn't know."

"Well, Leif, it might," the chambermaid says.

"As long as she's down here, he can't hear anything."

The chambermaid's voice is low for a woman. What did she call him? A private name among themselves? Paia reaches out an astonished hand, remembering the last time she'd seen her. "All that terrible . . . You escaped! Oh, I'm so glad. Did you get out on the wagons? I feared . . . I didn't know . . . !" She can't make any thought come out right, for fear of the one she wishes not to voice, that she hasn't thought of the chambermaid at all since just after the shooting began. How could she be so heartless? "Your name is Constanza?"

"Constanze."

"How lovely. Why didn't I know that?"

"Did you ever ask?"

The chambermaid's smile is much kinder than her words, but Paia's tears brim over hopelessly. She can't imagine what's opened up this bottomless well of emotion. If the God were here, she would be yelling at him. She buries her face in her hands. "I didn't! I didn't! I'm so sorry! I don't mean to be a bad mistress! You must all hate me so much!"

Erde hoped N'Doch was wrong about this weepy woman being Lord Fire's dragon guide, but as she held back in the gloom and watched the beautiful priestess lure the entire room, even the women, into focusing on her own problems, it did make a certain sorry sense, given the nature of Lord Fire himself. She had both his selfishness and his glow. Even the electric lanterns seemed to burn brighter in her aura. No wonder Lord Fire was so out of control. His guide had not been paying him proper attention.

Here we are, she complained to N'Doch, *worried to distraction about the dragons, half deaf and half blind without them. Do we indulge ourselves with such mewling and moaning?*

He returned her a kind of mental shrug, and Erde reminded herself that N'Doch had also begun hopelessly, but he had learned. No reason why this Paia couldn't learn just as well. It would be a different situation, of course. N'Doch had had a sensible dragon to teach him. With Lord Fire as her dragon, Paia would need all the help she could get.

Erde knew she should be more charitable. But the situation was desperate. Their dragons were off battling each other; who knew where or what was happening to them.

The three of us should be putting our heads together, figuring out a way to help!.

Can't ask her to do that till she figures out which end is up.

Erde subsided. He was right. She must contain herself. Besides, she feared her intemperance was being fanned for other reasons, by a thing she was trying to ignore: Baron Köthen's odd behavior. He seemed to have appointed himself the priestess' protector, despite the very capable-looking men standing guard at the door. It was true she was very beautiful, but the baron would not stop looking at her. It hurt. It made Erde irritable. She hadn't brought him all this way to look at women. She'd brought him here to work!

But she could not let herself be distracted by personal issues. Not now, when the dragons might be fighting for their lives. Now she must hold fast to her new resolution and strength of purpose. But oh, how strange, how very strange, that all the people she found to believe in—first Rainer, then Hal, now Baron Köthen—seemed each to be drawn away from her by some private destiny or purpose. Stranger still that N'Doch, of all people, should become the stable anchor she could rely on. Perhaps because, as dragon guides, they shared a common destiny. She supposed this meant that Paia shared it, too. Erde hovered in N'Doch's shadow and pondered this possibility, while the big handsome priest who was not a priest struggled to explain himself to the weeping priestess.

"A people's consensus, Luco? You've been conspiring against him! You and the . . . and Constanze!"

"And others, Paia. Many others. This is no palace coup we're about. Our real strength is not inside the Citadel."

"But . . . how long? For how long?"

"Since I understood he wasn't going to make things better. That's been rather a long time."

"But he *did* make things better!"

"Better for himself."

"Better for you, too. Better for all of us!"

"Better for a very select few. That's how he's bought our service. Actually, he doesn't *want* things to improve. As long as conditions are bad, the Faithful will continue to pray to him for help, which he will promise but not deliver."

"He put things in order again!"

"So I thought. So it seemed."

Luco lets go of her hands and settles to the floor crosslegged, confident and informal, a posture Paia has never seen him in. How could so simple a thing be so disorienting?

"Then you put the notes in my studio."

"Constanze."

"And the old monitor?"

"My office staff has always been privy to my true purpose. We hoped to help you see what he really is . . ."

"I know what he is! Better than you!"

Luco's blue eyes go somber. "You still believe that, after all you've seen?"

There's the chasm again. He's dragging her up to its edge, insisting she look downward. This collision of emotions is crushing the very breath from her lungs. "What about the landscape?"

"What landscape?"

"You know, the painting. Never mind." Paia instinctively deflects his curiosity with a wave. House was right. Two sources of tampering. Then who is the other? Paia hugs herself, shivering now in the unaccustomed air-conditioning. She feels like her blood has stopped flowing. "Ah, Luco. And I always thought it was *my* job you wanted."

He is incredulous. "I don't want anybody's job! Do you take me for a fool? Replace one tyrant with another? What would be the point of that? Besides, I can't do what he can. He's a miracle, a myth come to life. He's a *dragon*. He has merely to fly overhead to evoke the most primal terrors and the deepest devotion. He gets people to labor and obey as no human has been able to do for centuries, which is one reason we're in the state we're in."

"You see, Luco! You do love him, just as I must!"

"NO!" But even he knows his denial has been too quick and too hot. "Once, I might have. And I risked my life for his sake, for the miracle of his . . . magic. But what has he done with his supernatural gifts? Turned them to the perpetuation of his own pleasures. It's an unconscionable waste! A crime! Of the worst order!"

Paia wants this all to be over, wants to wake up, to be back in her uncomplicated bed at the Citadel, with only the safe dullness of her Temple duties to trouble her. She tries to imagine what the God would say to his rebel priest. How would he explain himself? She knows the answer. He wouldn't.

"We had to do something," Luco continues. "The dry up gets worse and worse. The scant resources of a hundred suffering villages are being squandered on needless luxury to feather the tyrant's nest!"

Paia cannot deny it. She's seen it now for herself, trekking across desiccated fields, through dust-blown farmsteads and villages. She's seen the desperation in the townspeople's eyes. No wonder Luco agreed so easily to back her plan for the Visitation. A further chance to open her eyes to the realities. Perhaps he even planted the notion himself.

Paia feels the chasm yawning.

The tyrant. Erde thought of the hell-priest, and the war at home, being fought for such similar reasons. But there were many kinds of tyranny. She understood Leif Cauldwell's righteous outrage, and that he must explain to the priestess why he'd brought her here. But she didn't think his full frontal assault was helping matters. Couldn't he see he was asking Paia to deny her dragon? It was like watching a wall crumble beneath the blows of a battering ram. The priestess was collapsing slowly into herself, her eyes gone listless, her vital glow dimmed.

Baron Köthen scowled, held back from open protest, she thought, only by N'Doch's hand and simultaneous translation. Erde almost thought to protest herself. If Paia, as Lord Fire's guide, was to regain any influence over him, she would need to have things explained to her in the proper terms by people who understood the true nature of the connection.

"He's a one-sided god," Cauldwell continued relentlessly. "He only takes. I tried persuasion, early on. Nearly got myself incinerated. And he thwarts all my covert attempts to steer the Temple toward a more civic-minded policy. But we can't fight him. We don't have the weapons that would bring him down. The only solution is to convince him that it's in his best interests to show responsibility to the people who've served him so loyally!"

The priestess sniffed, wiped her eyes. "How are you going to do that?"

"I'm not. You are."

She stared at him. "What?"

"You are. Paia, you have the power. He will not hurt you. You know that."

"No."

For a dizzying moment, Erde thought the priestess had spoken in her mind, but perhaps it was because the pain was so eloquent in Paia's eyes. Entire volumes of terror and confusion and frustrated love. Erde guessed that she'd actually tried to do her duty to her dragon lord, but he'd rejected her service.

Luther and Stoksie moved off to a darker corner of the room to mutter among themselves, but Erde almost stepped forward again. Couldn't the rebel priest see that his priestess was on the verge of hysteria? She wasn't strong enough for this. She wasn't yet aware of her Duty. She needed comforting, not more things to think about.

Cauldwell's wife also saw the crisis coming. She went to sit at the priestess' side, patting her, whispering soothing nonsense. But Paia batted the woman's hands away, both arms pinwheeling, her sobs rising uncontrollably until it seemed that she might choke, unable to catch her breath.

Then an amazing thing happened.

Baron Köthen, who'd been standing behind her protectively, leaned over the back of the big, soft seat and laid his hand on her shoulder. Quietly, firmly, he hushed her, as if she was a child.

Paia froze, shuddered, hiccuped a few times, and stopped crying.

"Good." Köthen settled himself on the arm beside her. "Now, speak to the man, *Liebchen*. Your life is in his hands."

Of course, he spoke in his own German, so the priestess couldn't understand him. But his tone of voice served well enough. She wiped her eyes without even looking at him and sat up straighter, while the whole room stared in astonishment.

Cauldwell sat back, bemused. "Well, that's better."

"Um . . ." N'Doch began, "He said . . ."

"I know what he said. Haven't had much use for my diplomatic German in a while but . . ."

"You really oughta back off a bit."

Cauldwell blinked at him.

N'Doch shrugged. "Just an idea."

"I . . . all right." Cauldwell rose, stood uneasily for a moment, his arms crossed. "But you see, the point is, he's got it wrong. Our lives are in *her* hands. That's what's at stake here."

"Well, that ain't all of it."

Cauldwell looked around, taking in Köthen's calm stare, the Tinkers' silence, Erde's own disapproving frown. "Luther? What am I missing here?"

"Just that you oughta back off," N'Doch repeated. "Give her a chance to get her bearings, y'know?"

"We don't have time to wait ourselves through one of her tantrums!"

"It isn't a tantrum." Erde was shocked by the hoarse sound of her own voice.

"Luther . . . ?"

"Yu ought lissen to 'em, Leif. Dere's t'ings dey know."

Cauldwell rubbed his brow in disbelief, then appealed directly to the priestess, his big hands spread. "Look. Paia. I wish we had time to get you up to speed on all this gradually, but we don't. We've committed ourselves to a rather desperate course of action. We need your help and we need it now!"

Constanze stroked the priestess' hand as if she were a frightened kitten. "We need to be able to tell the others you're willing, or it'll be hard to keep you safe from Sel Minor's faction. Their view right now is a short one, focused entirely on revenge."

It looked for a moment like Paia might break down again. A half-glance up at Köthen stopped her. She seemed surprised to find him still there. She gathered herself, sniffing. "What kind of help? What could I possibly do?"

"Convince him to change his ways. You're the only one he'll listen to. The only one he must listen to."

"He'll come after you! All of you!"

"He'll try."

"He'll find you!"

"He hasn't so far."

"And of course, we'll have you as a hostage," said Constanze.

"What?" The priestess looked at Cauldwell. "Hostage?" He nodded, somewhat apologetically.

"Luco! How could you?"

Constanze ticked items off on her fingers entirely without

apology. "And we've cut off food and goods shipments to the Citadel, and evacuated our people from the towns and farms as best we can."

"Life's going to get real hard at the Citadel, Paia. You're better off here with us."

The priestess lidded her eyes, folded her hands in her lap, and took a deep, shuddering, and hopeless breath. "I always knew you feared the God, Luco, but I thought you loved him, too. Or, at least, believed in him."

"What's to believe in?" Constanze demanded. "What does he offer but the end of the world? There's a better way, Paia."

"Amen!" breathed Luther, from out of the shadows.

"There's One who offers hope instead of despair."

"She walks in light," someone murmured.

"Ah." The priestess glanced up. "You talk of helping the people, but I see what this really is. Just another heresy. I'm surprised at you, Luco, having put down so many of them yourself."

Heresy. The word alone gave Erde a chill, but Cauldwell only sighed. "Not just another, Paia. The Beast is not the only force of nature abroad in the End of Days." He settled himself again in front of her and held out his hand. "By the way, may I introduce myself properly? My name is Leif Cauldwell. Your father was my uncle, Paia. We're cousins."

She looked at him dumbfounded. "Cousins?"

There was a sudden commotion in the corridor.

Cauldwell paused, listening toward the door, as the guards moved swiftly out into the hall. "Mick? What's up?"

"Visitors," said one of them.

Erde feared the angry damaged woman from upstairs had armed herself and her cohorts. But it sounded more like children, a lot of them. And it was! A wild pack of children, spilling, bursting into the room, squealing and laughing, racing around the adults as if in the middle of a mad game of tag, most of them younger than Mari and Senda. Erde's hands were grabbed, her arms pulled. She felt like an ancient grown-up among them. Where did they all come from?

"Gotta come! Gotta come!" they chanted. "He wants yu come now!"

A blonde little girl threw herself at Cauldwell's knees. His impatient frown vanished. He bent, scooped her up, and swung her in the air. "Young one! Hello! What is it?"

"Gotta come now, Da! Gotta come now!"

"He wants to see me?"

She shook her head. "He wanna see dem!"

"Who, them?" Cauldwell pouted comically. "What about me?"

The resemblance between them was unmistakable. Erde saw the priestess watching, her wonder entirely transparent. Not only was her supposed priest married, he had children as well. Or one child, at least. A perfect, healthy one. And Erde was beginning to understand how rare that was in this devastated future.

The child giggled and laid her small hand on Cauldwell's cheek. "Das okay, Da. Yu kin come, too."

"Who does he want to see?"

Immediately, a child fastened itself to Erde's arm. N'Doch and Baron Köthen were similarly claimed, and the two Tinkers. A young boy, perhaps the oldest, presented himself bashfully before the priestess. His thin, dark limbs seemed to move each in a different direction. He stuck out his hand like he'd just gotten it and wasn't sure how it worked. "He say, yu gotta come special."

Cauldwell seemed surprised at last. "How could he have known . . . ?"

"Ain' a lot he doan know," remarked Luther.

Cauldwell nodded, then snugged the little girl high on one hip. "Well, off with us, then, young one. We've been summoned."

The priestess let the young boy pull her to her feet, but it was Baron Köthen's arm she sought blindly, for support. The other children had regrouped by the doorway, waiting none too quietly. "Hurry hurry hurry! He wants yu to come now!"

Summoned. This word was a final key, fitting into a lock in Erde's ears. They had indeed been summoned, and now she could hear it, inside, in the dragon's place. But it wasn't the dragon. It wasn't words, or even images. More like an articulate breeze. It distracted her from the sight of another woman on Baron Köthen's arm.

N'Doch! Do you hear it?

He shook his head like a dog. *I hear it. Comin' in loud
'n clear.*

So he's back in the crowded corridors again, with kids
hauling on his arms, and a big dragon buzz in his head,
only there's no dragon, or at least, if there is, she's not
talking to him. And he's not sure what got into him, making
him stand up like that for the priestess. N'Doch thinks
things are starting to get weird, even by his definition.

Soon the clutter's so thick in the passage that just walking has to be skillfully negotiated. Then there's a door
ahead of them, circular and armored like a vault but standing wide open. N'Doch guesses it would take several hours
and some good strong men to shift away all the piles and
nondescript electronics shoved against it. He hopes it
doesn't ever have to be closed in an emergency. The joint
looks a little derelict, but through the opening he sees console lights and screen glow. Someone's up and working.

The kids get real quiet at the door, like they've turned
off the noise faucet. Even the Tinkers hesitate, Luther especially. Though he goes in ahead of Stoksie, he moves with
the same faintly awed respect that Sedou brought out in
him. Is it for all the high tech inside, or for the person
running it?

Whadda ya think girl?

There is great power in here.

N'Doch cracks a nervous grin. He can feel it in his bone
marrow. *And it ain't just electrical!*

The big room is even dimmer and colder than the corridors. Part of it is divided into low-walled cubicles, empty
workstations with desks and small banks of monitors. But
the far wall is curved, one huge wraparound screen or series
of screens, with a big curved console at the center point of
the arc. Someone is working there, and the kids halt a short
distance away and wait silently to be noticed. Köthen lets
the priestess move ahead of him. She kind of floats into
the room with her kid escort beside her. Cauldwell's girl-

baby squirms in his arms. He sets her down, and she races off to rejoin the pack.

The guy at the console is muttering to himself. N'Doch is pretty sure it's a guy because of the hulking width of his shoulders, but its hard to see much detail. He's mostly a dark, rounded silhouette against the bright blue screen. N'Doch reads the image as a map of some kind, or aerial view, with three colored blips tracking across it. A fourth blinks faintly in a lower corner. Surveillance of some sort, he guesses, and pretty advanced at that.

The priestess woman steps away from her kid escort, still a bit wobbly on her feet, and drifts toward the screen. "What is . . . ?"

"Missus!" The kid catches her, hauls her back. She tries to shake him off, still weak and vague with the aftermath of the drug and the emotional pounding she's taken. N'Doch can see she's not used to being manhandled, at least not without her permission. But her regal air cuts no ice with this determined kid, and it looks like another scuffle might erupt.

N'Doch catches Köthen's arm halfway to his sword hilt. "Easy, man. He ain't gonna hurt her."

Then the guy at the console rises. He strips off what looks like some kind of VR headset, unwinds himself from various cables and cords. He's heavyset and seriously round-shouldered. He walks with a shambling gait as if he's carrying around a little too much weight for his years. As he moves out of silhouette into the light, N'Doch notices first how the bright blue of his loose jumpsuit matches the screen, then how hairy he is. He's got a wild head of salt-and-pepper, a full mustache, and a bushy, silver-streaked beard. His brows are so long, they veil his eyes. At first he doesn't seem to notice them. He tosses a piece of paper down, picks up another. Every surface within reach of him and his console are layered with books and disks and print-out. He searches through a stack of crackling leather-bound tomes, doesn't find what he's after. Then suddenly, he glances up. He seems astonished to find new people in the room, or any people at all. Yet, within one quick sweep of this guy's dark and piercing gaze, N'Doch feels he's been surveyed, identified, analyzed, and understood. But not, somehow, dismissed. Instead, he feels welcomed.

N'Doch! I know him!

The girl moves toward the guy as if in a daze. Sure enough, the guy opens his stubby arms to her and she walks right into them, before N'Doch can stop her.

"Gerrasch!"

Erde had given up asking how the inexplicable could come to be. It simply did. It wasn't Gerrasch, and yet it was. Less like an overgrown pond animal, more like a man, yet still Gerrasch in his essence, as well as in the connection she felt with him, had always felt, from the first time they met. At least one particular cascade of events had somehow come full circle. She didn't need to know what he was doing there. It just seemed right that he was, and that she should let him enfold her in a smothering hug. His warm woodland smell was exactly the same.

"Long! Long! Relieved. Finally. Four now." His voice was still a raspy bass. He held her away from him to eye her solemnly. "Grown!"

Erde knew a laugh would violate the gravity of the moment. One sneaked out anyhow. "Oh, Gerrasch, you saw me only a few weeks ago!"

"No. You saw. Me, centuries. Waiting. Get it?"

It made her spine tingle to think about it, but she thought she did. She took his soft pink-palmed hand and drew him toward the others. "Gerrasch, this is . . ."

"Yes." Gerrasch made directly for N'Doch and held out his other hand. "Brother. Songs of welcome. Work now. Quickly."

N'Doch said, "Huh?"

Luther watched all this with happy astonishment. "Dis heah da fren' yu bin lookin fer?"

"No, but . . ." N'Doch began.

"An old and cherished friend just the same," Erde finished for him.

N'Doch laughed. "You, too?"

"What?"

"Modern English? Not even dragon English, all of a sudden?"

Goodness. He was right. She did sound better. *Modern.* A resident of both past and present. Gazing into Gerrasch's knowing face, Erde understood there would be no language she could not speak right then, right there. She nodded at the vast blue brightness, and the strange table lit with what looked like a hundred tiny candles. "Gerrasch, what is all this?"

"Library. Librarian, me."

"Epicenter," said N'Doch.

Gerrasch beamed at him.

"What's an . . ."

He took her hand. "Wait. Four. Then talk." He guided them through the solemn ranks of children and amazed Tinkers, toward the heathen priestess. Paia seemed even more confused than she had in the other room, as if the blue-lit strangeness of this one had unmoored her further. No wonder she recoiled when Gerrasch shambled up and without preamble, reached for her hand.

"No! Don't touch me!"

Leif Cauldwell stepped forward. "I'm sorry, G. She's not in the best of form. This is the Librarian, Paia."

"Don't let him touch me!"

"He won't hurt you. He's a good and wise man. If he wants to talk to you, it's for a very good reason."

Luther added, "Da Liberian isa proffet, lady. A holy oracul. He speak fur da One who come."

Speaks for the One . . .

"He does?" Four, he'd said. Erde's eyes clenched shut with comprehension and gratitude. *N'Doch, do you hear? Do you know what that means?*

I can guess . . .

He must be!

She was sure of it. Prophet or oracle the Tinkers might think him, and he might even be, but Gerrasch was also Lady Air's guide in the world of men. She was so sure, she didn't give it further question. Would he have answers to the mysteries and unknowns that had plagued the Quest from its beginnings? *Oh, if only the dragons were here!* The fourth dragon guide! Their number was complete.

But Gerrasch was rather large and strange looking, and

the poor weepy priestess, who knew nothing of her Duty
or her Destiny, saw his friendly overture as a threat.

"Keep him away from me!" she shrieked, backing into
Baron Köthen's arms.

Since waking up, Paia's felt like she's trapped inside
someone else's skin. Someone she doesn't like very much,
but can't seem to shake. Who is this frantic, sobbing woman
who's suddenly terrified of everything, who's lost her dignity, who can only think of screaming for the God to come
and rescue her? She's not even a woman. She's the protected little girl whose world was turned upside down once
before, who never had to learn to live with change and
instability, because the God came and made the world right
again. The God saved her then. He could save her now.
She has only to call him.

But she cannot. This strange creature will not let her.
Something he's doing is blocking her summons. Her head
is filled with static. She knows he's the God's enemy, one
of them, at least. Yet he smiles at her so sweetly, as if he
is overjoyed to see her, relieved even, as if now that she's
there, his life can move onward. But Paia looks down and
sees the chasm yawning between them. She would have to
cross it to take the creature's offered hand. Why should
she, though he entreats it so gently and fervently? Who is
he, but the God's enemy? She owes him nothing. Nothing!
Yet, she is tempted.

No! A part of Paia sees the panic seize her and admits
it isn't logical. But the reflex runs riot in her head, screaming about duty. Her duty must be to the God! She must
not be tempted! She fumbles inside her layered clothing
for the thing she has concealed there. Her grip is oddly
weak, but it's a small thing, easy to grasp. She jerks it out
and points it at the enemy.

The enemy smiles again and spreads his hands, as if inviting her. She sees that his palms are soft and pink, so vulnerable. But there is a danger in him, terrible danger, if she
could only comprehend what it is. She struggles to think,

the gun shaking in her outstretched fist. The girl dressed as
a boy steps in front of the awful creature. Paia hears Son
Luco swear, actual heresy and filth. But he should understand her confusion. He also has become someone else. He
has become her cousin. Even so, he moves abruptly to stop
her, so Paia turns the gun on him instead.

"Paia, be sensible. There's a hundred villagers upstairs
thirsting for your blood. Even if you murder us all, where
are you going to go?"

"The God will save me! He'll come in a glory of light
and he'll . . ."

"I don't think so," says Luco. "If he hasn't done it
already . . ."

"Don't look for it," the tall African agrees. "He's kinda
busy right now."

He grins at her in the most presumptuous, irritating way
and dances a few steps to one side, so Paia shifts her glare
and the muzzle of her little gun toward him.

"What do you know about the God?"

"You'd be surprised, lady."

Then someone's beside her, calmly lifting the gun from
her hand, the man with the sword, to whom, in her mind,
she has already given herself. She stares at him, right into
his eyes for the first time. They are as dark as she remembers from the dreams. If the God cannot save her, she will
let this man do it. He smiles back, his devotion already
unconditional. "Tch, tch, *Liebchen*."

"Smooth move, Dolph." The African takes the gun and
sticks it into his waistband. "What the hell did you give
her, preacher man?"

Luco lets out a breath.

Now the sword man takes Paia's hand. He's leading her
toward the enemy, but she cannot resist him. His eyes hold
such promises.

The God's enemy has linked hands with the girl and the
African. Now he takes Paia's hands and places one in each
of theirs. When the tall African grips her hand, Paia hears
faint, poignant music and the sighing of oceans. The young
girl's touch brings perfumes of meadows and pine boughs.

Hungrily, Paia's senses shake off their fog and drowse,
to embrace these scents and sounds. They are unfamiliar
yet longed for. She has known them all her life. A dry,

clearing wind blows through her head. She has never felt more alive.

The African has lost his snarky grin. His eyes are anxious. The three of them stand awkwardly, joined by hands in an arc, until the strange creature takes the others' free hands in his own and completes the circle.

Then Paia learns what the real danger is.

CHAPTER THIRTY-EIGHT

And it's like being jacked in to each other's brains. Freaky. Not like his silent converse with the girl. Virtual reality. Much worse than the old dragon internet. Dragons, it turns out, know how to respect your privacy. But at least now he doesn't have to ask who this hairy guy is. It's there for the knowing. Like all the files are open. All the histories, the personal stories, the varied roads taken by each of them to this place of . . . *convergence.* A meeting that it looks like everything in creation has been trying to prevent, yet one that could never have been avoided.

. . . all of this, surging like music through his head. Close to but not completely overwhelming. He's amazed his brain is big enough. It scrolls past like program code: the lineage of the three, himself, Paia, the girl, down through the millennia, their engendering preordained. And of Gerrasch, the focal link, an eternal nexus, a lump of leaf mold and clay inspired by dragon energies, set to evolve and learn until that programmed event when, half man, half beast, he met the girl along a dark lakeshore . . .

. . . a system, a fail-safe, maintained by myth and mysticism, nurtured by kinship, functioning on automatic. But . . .

. . . what is it for?

. . . The danger is in the revelation. The chasm is not emptiness, but infinite possibility. She reels under the weight of it. Layer after layer of her ignorance peeling back like drying bark, sloughed like an obsolete snakeskin, until she knows the truth of how much she didn't know, how much he kept from her, all that her father preserved in his precious library, all that the House Computer tried (too late!) to prepare her for. Not one dragon, omniscient and omnipotent, but four who are neither, and a great and sacred Duty for which she is sadly ill-equipped. As a dragon guide, she is, so far, a failure. None of this, once learned, amazes her. It all seems . . . right.

. . . and yet, the awful choice that lies before her! The God is her . . . god. How can she betray him? She struggles to explain it. He appeared at a time of confusion and loss! His promises of security, his opulent visions lent vital strength, got things going again! She believed him for so long. What makes her believe three strangers now?

. . . but they are not strangers, not anymore. She's learned their lives. She's lived them in an instant. She's walked with their dragons and cannot imagine them the enemy. She's grown up with N'Doch as bush child (ah, lost Africa!), as street urchin, as master sneak thief, dodging smooth and cynical through the disease and drought and corruption of a century that knew no better than to gun down its best and its brightest, his brother among them.

. . . and she's come of age with Erde, in terror and bloodshed, hounded by another dragon-inspired golem. She tells them that the God, too, time travels. The pieces fall together. The mad priest in white is Lord Fire's creation, no doubt of it. But why, they ask? For what purpose? She does not know. If she did, they would know it, too.

. . . and then the Librarian, the one who frightened her, so halting in his human speech, so eloquent in this . . . joining. Both source and resource, a vibrant stream of sensual data—image, scent, sound—rich with drama and knowledge and portent. His console links the world's surviving com-nets, the sensors, the archives, even her own House Computer, yet he has kept himself invisible to them.

. . . she has longed desperately for both comprehension and friends. These three are not what she would have chosen for herself, yet they bring a sort of comprehension, and the joining of minds is a wonder. There's so much they understand that no one ever has, about living with the God . . .

. . . the past and her clinging to it have been a restraint, she sees that now, a burden she can willingly set down, so that others more pressing may take its place.

. . . ah, the relief! A joyful release into the now! Past, present, future are one continuum. Didn't the dragon try to tell her this, long ago? There's no sense of *then* in the new now, no pain at having left her past so far behind. Only a clarification of purpose, brought on by this union of minds. Four far-flung dragon guides at last united by the fourth's miraculous gift, that Paia and N'Doch have words for—"virtual reality," "synergetic," "psi"—but which the Librarian tries to explain as something, well . . . electrical. The machines are his eyes and ears on the world, but he doesn't run them. They run themselves. He only "feels" them, as she feels the surge of collective power his psi gift brings to the circle. All they lack now are their dragons, and a reason why . . .

. . . Wait. So long. Despair.

SEE: a gray curl of woodsmoke coiling up through fire-light. Beady eyes in the darkness.

SMELL: burning pitch, damp earth, the pungency of dry-ing herbs.

HEAR: the quiet lap of water against the reeds.

FEEL: a chill of waiting . . . waiting . . . waiting.

. . . visions stir up the darkness. Dreams. Inarticulate. Speak it without words. Oracle. Wait . . .

. . . and waiting is learning.

SEE: a snow-scattered farmstead, steep dark hills with a

bristle of trees. A large man with a rough black beard and an armload of books.

SMELL: damp cattle, rooting pigs, hay, and manure.

HEAR: the rhythm of the ax, the shuffing of the oxen steaming in the paddock.

FEEL: ice in the wind. Waiting. Still waiting.

. . . the visions brand him as a madman, yet he will not deny them. Loneliness. Confusion. But instinct becomes knowledge, and the library grows.

SEE: fluorescent light, a nest of cables, shelves stuffed with equipment. A wild-haired man at a keyboard, before a constellation of screens.

SMELL: the tang of hot metal, the cold coffee on the console.

HEAR: the whine of accessing memory, faint rock n' roll.

FEEL: disbelief, outrage, despair.

. . . one after the other, the screens show disaster: war, famine, plague, death. He taps a key. Overlay of horsemen, red, black, white, and pale. He slaps at the power switch. The screens darken. He buries his face in his hands.

. . . a time passes. Then . . . he sits up, alert. He has heard something at last. Still, none of it makes sense. He can feel her, not see her. Guess at her, not know her. He interprets as best he can.

. . . Four and three. Missing the One. Visions. She speaks. Work. Work. The time nears. Quickly . . .

In the circle of hands, consciousness melds but the self is not lost. There is no confrontation, no accusation, no recrimination. Perhaps those will come in time, that a Duty has been neglected, that a man loves and is loved by another . . .

But not now. For now, only acceptance of what is, a vast and spontaneous learning across cultures and centuries, and the planning of what is to be done, as much as can be without a full understanding of the task at hand.

And still Paia asks, how can I betray him?

The Librarian breaks the circuit. A gentle parting of hands, the trailing of now familiar fingers across all-known palms. The four stand with their heads bowed, eager to reclaim autonomy, reluctant to give up the bond.

Erde shows them the next step, entirely by accident.

N'Doch!

She calls. And all of them answer. The connection holds. It is not the total intimacy of the meld, but that is . . . just as well. The melding is turned inward, toward the mirror of self. There is no outer awareness. The connection is . . . more like never having to raise your voice.

Their eyes meet. They smile, bashful now. A bit self-conscious.

N'Doch says: *Hey! Now wasn't that something else?*

So what do we do now?

We must find the Lady Air. She will know. She saved me, I'm sure of it, when the hell-priest came after me.

She. The One. Imprisoned.

Yeah, but where?

Lord Fire is sure to know.

He won't tell them willingly. He'll resist, with everything in his power! Oh, how can I betray him? How can I?

No betrayal. Greater cause.

How can I know that? How can I know?

Feel how strong we are! If we call out to Lady Air together, she is sure to hear us!

Cannot. Jamming. Zone of silence. Only protection.

Just a thought but, like, all this nature stuff in the data banks? That can't just be coincidence, right?

Chapter Thirty-nine

There is no signal agreed to, yet, in unison, the four turn away from each other, directing consciousness outward into the darkened room in a show of independence.

Erde would have guessed that they'd stood in their circle for hours, but every eye is still on them, surprise still lingering. Luther is still on his knees. It's been but an instant. She catches Stoksie's inquiring look, then Luther's. She glances down, away, uncertain.

Some explanation will be required . . .

N'Doch laughs aloud, a small explosion of release. *Hey, girl! You wanna try it?*

Gerrasch unsettles the moment further by producing several complete sentences. "The circle is closed. Struggle alone no longer. The work begins."

And still they are waiting. Standing about quietly, their eyes full of questions. The vast and quiet sighing of the air is the loudest sound. Something unexpected has occurred. Something perhaps momentous. Erde realizes they are waiting to be told what to do.

As it happens, she has a plan. One, she thinks, that fits the gravity of the situation. And yes, it is risky.

Give us a second to recover, huh? Before you spring it on 'em?

But we should tell them . . . explain . . .

Yeah, yeah.

The four agree that N'Doch should tell their story. All of it. The children bring cold water and plates of dried apple, and settle down around him. It takes him slightly longer than an instant.

"I coulda sung it to you faster," he grins when he's finished.

Stoksie and Luther nod intently, mulling over all they've heard. Many of the children have dozed off, curled into balls like little animals. The rest crouch among the empty desks, playing quiet games with whatever comes to hand. Köthen, having heard it all before, has eased carefully among the teetering book stacks for a close-up study of the Librarian's console. He leans over it but does not touch.

Only the rebel leader is uneasy. The guy is no ranting rabble-rouser. He's planned his rebellion carefully. N'Doch thinks he'd be well in his rights to feel put out by this sudden left turn of events. "Huh," he says. "Huh."

Paia laughs, a rueful silvery sound that makes Köthen glance up from his detailed scrutiny. Astonishment still lurks in the corners of her eyes, but the tension and terror are gone. "Oh, Luco! I mean, *Cousin* Leif. The proverbial monkey wrench! We've disrupted your plan, haven't we!"

He shrugs, though it's more of a grimace. If it bothers him not being the center of attention in his own stronghold, he's concealing it well, even if he is wound a bit more tightly than he'd like to admit. "I'm always ready to hear a better one."

N'Doch says, since everyone's playing at being so casual here, "And we'll get to that. But there's a few things I'd like to point out first."

He's always had great faith in coincidence, but his faith is being sorely tried. The Librarian's oblique response in the meld suggested he doesn't consider anything a coincidence. It's all one big pattern to him, or maybe an endless stream of program code.

For instance, N'Doch has just learned that this facility was originally a top secret center for climatological research. Coincidence? He puts his back to the big blue screen and lays it all out, as much for himself as for the others: the Library's heavy focus on a combination of myth and earth sciences, the local belief in a messiah who will regreen the planet; four dragons named after the elements of Nature.

"Dragons don't just show up for no good reason!" He sees Erde beaming at him. He agrees. He's on a roll, even without the blue dragon to coax him along. He jabs a thumb at the readout of disaster that the Librarian's brought up on the big screen. Temperature levels, weather patterns, erosion where there's land left, salinity where there's water. "All the data his network can access—satellite instruments, ground sensors, archives, and data banks, no matter that they're all half-broke and winding down— all of them are screaming that ole Mother Earth has just about had it."

"We know all this," Leif Cauldwell interjects. "That's why we . . ."

"You know it, but you don't know what to do about it. It's too far gone, right? That's why a magical fix looks like the only solution. Well, we think that's what we're here for. Why else would we have all ended up at this particular time, this particular place?"

He has to laugh. It's like some moldy old vid, but it's probably true. They really are here to save the world. Or at least, give it a damn good try.

The girl agrees, but of course, she would.

"And now you're gonna ask me how. And I'll say we gotta leave that to the dragons."

The Tinkers are still nodding, like they're ready to get right on the problem whenever he says so. They've accepted the idea that their awaited messiah is a dragon with surprising equanimity, even, N'Doch thinks, with relief. They're not of a seriously mystical bent. They're more interested in actual help. And what better weapon to combat a dragon than another dragon, or in this case, three more dragons?

Nor do they seem bothered by the notion of visitors from another time.

"Whadevah," is Stoksie's response to N'Doch's cautious explanation.

Luther says, "Can't wait ta heah all da detales."

They do not believe you, Erde says in his head.

N'Doch knows better. He's sure they're the most prag-

matic and flexible folks he's ever had the privilege of dealing with. Leif Cauldwell, however, is still an unknown.
N'Doch waits for the rebel leader to be full of ideas and
suggestions. He just seems like the type.

But Cauldwell raises an eyebrow and fidgets silently,
waiting to see where it's all going to lead. The source of
his spiritual doctrine is the Librarian, after all, and N'Doch
is speaking with the Librarian's full support. Cauldwell may
be the rebels' spokesman and leader, but Gerrasch is their
oracle and prophet. It took the arrival of the planet's endgame to produce a population that would finally listen to
him. And Cauldwell listened, reshaping the prophet's bizarre visions into a kind of liberation theology that the
frightened farmers and villagers, and at least some of the
Tinkers, could accept. Thus Air, shanghaied by Fire, became the discorporate One who Comes, the Imprisoned
Messiah. No mention of dragons. N'Doch suspects Cauldwell's own belief. He knows a politician when he sees one.
And right now, it's good politics to hear the prophet—or
his surrogate—out.

The Librarian, meanwhile, doesn't think in terms of mes-
siahs. He thinks in hardly any recognizable terms at all.
N'Doch recalls some self-appointed egghead lecturing him
once about hypertext. He didn't bother much with it at the
time, but now he's glad he listened long enough to pick up
the basic concept. Hypertext is a handy metaphor for the
Librarian's thought structure. Keeping it in mind helps
N'Doch decipher what the dude is getting at.

"Okay, so what do we know about Air, a.k.a., the Imprisoned Messiah?" He looks to see if this gentle sacrilege
bothers his audience, but it's clear he's already preaching
to the converted. "Let's start with the fact that someone,
some*thing,* has been sending the Librarian 'visions' for
centuries."

"Centuries," murmurs Luther reverently.

"And that all those aeons he put in of tireless research
and analysis suggested an ageless and mystical source.
Eventually, he tells us, the visions narrowed the definition
for him: a dragon named Air. By now, he's convinced that
Fire kidnapped Air and stashed her somewhere because of
something she knows about the reason the dragons were
awakened in the first place." N'Doch privately refers to this

as The Big Mystery, though he's about to rename it The Big Fix. "Air can't talk to him from her undiscovered prison, but recently, the visions have been coming in via this old semifunctional communications network. How 'bout that? A cyberdragon!"

Cauldwell asks softly, "How can she be accessing the Net?"

"Good question."

Erde objects. "Do you ask how Lord Earth can transport, or Lady Water transform?"

"You bet. All the time. Don't you?" N'Doch grins at her, just to let her know he's never gonna stop teasing her at least a little. But she's learned to take it. She smiles and shakes her head.

"What does the . . . ah, what does Fire do?" Paia asks.

"Misbehaves."

"No. Please." Her lovely face clouds, and N'Doch is instantly miserable. "If each of the four has a special gift, what is his?"

Cauldwell has a ready answer. "He's a leader of men, Paia. That's a gift like any other. It's not only fear that makes so many follow him. Add but an ounce of compassion and the Beast could well be a god."

Erde frowns at him. "A miracle, yes. But not God."

"God? Singular?" Cauldwell peers at her curiously, then seems to think better of it and subsides into a tense crouch against the console. Silently, N'Doch congratulates him on his good sense and restraint. He's glad his little lecture has finally evolved into dialogue, but this is no time to get the girl going on about religion.

"So he's waiting and waiting, then suddenly he gets the sense something's about to happen. Right?"

Gerrasch nods. Because he cannot predict when the visions will come on him, or in what form, he has put himself on perpetual round-the-clock duty, for a generation or more, buried in this dark hole like a giant mole in the earth.

"You, like, sleep at the console?" N'Doch pulls up a chair from one of the desks and kicks back. "Man . . . that's dedication."

"Da kids help, y'know," explains Luther. "Dey make shur he's eatin', and if a vishun come by, up deah onda wall, well den, dey wakim up."

"The visions never come when he's napping," Leif puts in sternly.

"And they come, like, actually on screen?"

"Not then," explains the Librarian. "Now. Yes."

"Too cool! Dragon vid."

Luther is almost purring. "It wuz da One ledyu ta make yer move, Leif."

But if the visions are random in their occurrence, their subject matter is not. Mostly they focus on the dire condition of the planet, which is, of course, what's encouraged Luther, as well as Leif and his rebels, to believe that when the One who Comes arrives, she'll know exactly what's wrong with the world and how to fix it. N'Doch can only hope they're right. He's run pretty short of ideas himself.

He decides it's time to head the conversation where it needs to go. Time's awasting. He can feel it in his gut. He waves Köthen closer so he can translate, then sets Erde up and gives her the floor. When she's done explaining her plan, most everybody's still nodding.

Except Leif Cauldwell. He's dead against it.

"Drop the cordon? No. No way. I can't allow it!"

The meld was exhausting, mentally and physically. Erde's sense of time and place is entirely in flux, with the present more present than ever and her own past beginning to seem like a tale someone else has told her. But this is the least of her worries.

The discussion has hit a snag. Leif Cauldwell is backed up against a desk, declaiming like the ex-military man that he is. Her plan has vaulted him out of his wait-and-see calm. His big hands clench and unclench fitfully. She catches his anguished glance at the small girl asleep against a partition. He doesn't understand. "How can you even ask it? You'd expose our stronghold? Risk the lives of six hundred people? Of all our children? Our only chance of success rests on there being some place the Beast cannot get to! Or even know about! If he flushes us now, we'll take heavy casualties and be forced into a ground war we're not equipped to fight!"

"But this might work. And it might work now. No drawn-out guerrilla struggle." N'Doch is trying to sound rational and empathetic while he wolfs down pieces of apple.

They are all exhausted, Erde realizes, as exhausted as I am. We need rest and sustenance and there is no time for either. We must get out of this muffling cave and back in contact with the dragons!

"He'll be down on top of us in a minute!" barks Cauldwell.

"Maybe not. We'll never know 'less we try."

"Easy for you! These aren't your people!"

"It's my world, least it was. You're not exactly seeing the Big Picture."

Luther hovers, a dark silhouette against the blue screen. "Leif, we bin talkin' 'bout how we gonna free da One fer ten yeer nah. If dis bring us closa to da ansa . . ."

"We might as well open the doors and invite him in! Luther, we haven't survived this long by being reckless!"

"Lotta dem down in camp wuld wanna try it, probby," Stoksie offers. "It ain't all yer call, na."

A brave thing, Erde thinks, for a little man to say to a giant. But though Cauldwell's jaw tightens, he listens. He is bigger and louder, but this is, she realizes with interest, a debate among equals.

"Okay, it's not all my call. But I have to deal with the military consequences, and—damn it—someone's got to be the voice of reason here! Paia says he always knows where she is. So no matter how briefly the Librarian's jamming signal is down, the Beast could still hear her, and if he does . . ."

"He will hear our summons as well." Erde savors the feel of this very "modern" language on her tongue. She can at last give voice to her impatience, but she doesn't want this earnestly misled man thinking that time or space have anything to do with these matters, now that she's been freed of them herself.

"But if he's occupied with battling Earth and Water," Paia points out, "how could he come right away?"

"Right." N'Doch swallows his apple. "So we should have

time to try to contact Air. Now there's four of us, we might actually get results."

"And we can let the other dragons know we've found Gerrasch."

"And maybe just lend a hand, y'know? Right now, they're fighting this war all by their lonesome!"

"And we must do it quickly!"

Cauldwell looks assaulted. He whirls on the Librarian, who is listening quietly. "You agree with all this? Should we take this insane risk? Is it worth it?"

"Big chance. Yes."

Erde notes how this reply could easily be read two ways.

"Da only chance, mebbe," says Luther.

"Your embargo's a risk, too," adds N'Doch. "Who knows how long his people can hold out?"

"I know! I know every ounce of grain in the Citadel!"

"He's got wings! He can reprovision! You could end up starving yourselves in your precious hole in the ground!"

The rebel leader drops into a chair, his eyes wild. "If! If! This is madness!"

The Librarian gets up slowly, comes over to lay a wide soft palm on Cauldwell's head. It seems to calm him a little. "Come. Each one. A lesson."

He gathers them around his big console, then directs their eyes to the wall screen while he fiddles at his touch pad. Paia knows the blue of that screen so very well. Was it here the message on the monitor originated? It's as good an explanation as any right now.

"Mattias!" the odd creature calls. "You tell!" His voice is rough. He's unused to speaking aloud. And he moves like a man feeling his way through a fog. Paia cannot imagine how she could have thought him dangerous.

The oldest boy, the one who'd guided Paia into the room, lopes forward from the shadowed group of desks where the children have retreated. Paia chides herself to remind them of the God's repopulation program, one vote in his favor, at least. She's sorry there have been so few children around at the Citadel, but for the occasional festival. They're so bizarre and funny, so sure they're being grown-up, as she no doubt was when she was their age. Like this Mattias, who rests one skinny arm atop the console and clears his throat importantly, waiting to be taken seriously.

The Librarian taps at his pad. In the center of the screen, overlaying the blue tracking diagram, appears a map. It's an old map, the hand-drawn sort with antique Latin lettering and little drawings of castles and cathedrals where the towns are. The contours are unrecognizable, except to Baron Köthen, whose name Paia has finally absorbed even if she has not quite come to grips with his point of origin. He has seen such documents in his lifetime, and says as much, while N'Doch translates.

However, the boy Mattias has been asked to "tell," and he intends to do it himself. He puts on his best false-adult Standard English. "This is a map of Ancient Europe, centering on the German duchies of the tenth century." He glances over his shoulder, kidlike again, and catches his audience's eye. "He show us dis alla time, doan know why. He say, we gotta know dese tings."

"Mattias!"

"Yessir."

The map zooms outward. The German duchies are now a tiny glow in a larger landscape traced by fanciful coastlines and dotted with puffy-cheeked wind gods. A good deal of it is blank parchment, labeled *Oceanus* or *Mare Exterius,* or simply, *Terra Incognita.*

"A tenth century European map of the world. The second century mathematician and geographer Ptolemy did a whole lot better."

Paia suffers a brief memory quake, an upsurging of ancient history studies. The House Computer liked this map, too. She's sure it's the very same. Somewhere on it is the legend: *And here there be dragons.*

Before she can look for it, the image cross-fades to a crisp and colorful, mechanically produced map dated 1900.

"Another oldie," says Mattias. "Now, watch carefully. He'll do the overlays in ten-year increments."

Sure enough, the map begins to evolve. National boundaries appear and vanish, often to reappear two or three increments later. Names change. Empires dissolve and re-form in altered configurations.

But one element of the change is gradual and consistent. N'Doch spots it first. "Okay, everybody—check out the coastlines . . ."

The years click by in the label window in the lower right corner: 1990—2000—2010.

"There! That's me! 2013. That's my time. Can you freeze the frame? See? The water's rising already."

2020—2050—2080. The inexorable creep of blue, swallowing up the green and yellow and brown. The Netherlands. Belgium. Northern France. The Mediterranean flows unimpeded into the Persian Gulf. The Amazon and the Congo are inland seas. A whole lot of India, vanished. All gone to water.

2120—2150—2180. Entire island chains have disappeared. The contour of North America is blunted by the loss of the eastern and Gulf coasts. There is no sign of Florida.

Leif has his brow pressed tight against his fists. "I know, I know . . . but the risk! The risk!"

Luther says, "If da One can't makit heah ta help us, it woan mattah if da kids grow up or not."

2200—2210. The clock edges up to 2213 and freezes. There is so little green left, N'Doch has to search for it. 2213. No further.

"That's it?" asks N'Doch. "That's where we are now?"

There's not much more yellow and brown than there is green. The entire world is being sucked back into the oceans.

"2213. I was sure it woulda been further. To get so bad, y'know?" He sits back, looks at Cauldwell. "That make any difference in your thinking?"

"Makes me think how precious our lives are. Not to be thrown away on grand gestures and guesswork!"

N'Doch leans forward again. "But what if that's all we have?"

"Yu tellit yerself, Leif. How da One'll show us da way." Luther eyes the disconsolate rebel leader in quiet challenge. "Wheah's ya fait'?"

Paia has thought she would resist them, that she must resist them, out of duty to Fire, her dragon. A clear and present duty, even when redefined by what she knows now about the nature of their connection.

Instead, she cedes the floor to Luco—or Leif Cauldwell, as she must now learn to call him, her cousin Leif—as he resists their plan for entirely different reasons. For the cause of sanity. For "his people," who she used to think were her people, or the God's. And for the lovely sleeping child he's picked up to cradle in his arms.

But just as he's bottoming out in an agony of guilt and indecision, they both get a kind of answer. The whole room shudders gently, and then again. Paia sways, reaches out to catch her balance, and finds Baron Köthen's waiting arm. She sees he is relieved to have something to do. She smiles at him gratefully as he realigns the sword sheathed across his back so that the hilt does not point at her eyes. She'd almost forgotten he was there. She's gratified that he hasn't forgotten her.

"Quake?" mutters N'Doch. "You get those here?"

"No." The Librarian taps at his console and the tracking map reappears on the wall screen. The moving colored blips have converged somewhere over what Paia now realizes to be the practically endless ocean. The room tilts again, even more faintly.

Leif hugs his daughter closer. "Has he found us already?"

"Sir, that is Lord Earth," Erde insists primly. "Keeping him away."

The Librarian points at the blips. "Long way battle. Echo just."

N'Doch leans in. "Wow. The fight? Can you get any visual?"

The Librarian searches for a working sensor at the indicated location, a buoy, a satellite, anything. The screen splits into four, then sixteen images, a lot of them static, the rest showing open water and empty sky.

"Shud be deah somweah, ri'?" worries Stoksie.

"Look!" Mattias cries. "There!"

He points at a screen. The Librarian quickly enlarges it, but all that's visible is a faint smoke trail.

N'Doch mutters, "Hope we ain't looking at no crash n' burn there."

Erde grabs his arm. "We have to try to reach her! We have to do it now! Oh, what if they're . . ."

Abruptly, the big imagine breaks up in static, plunging the room into near darkness. Only the pinpoint lights on the console offer any sense of direction. The children cry out, a chorus of awed expectation, as if this were planned solely for their entertainment. Sure enough, the screen flashes to life again.

Paia gasps, a half second before Erde does the same. "There it is!"

It's the landscape, *her* landscape, the pristine first version. It fills the entire wall with soothing green and breathless blue and tinkling silver. It's more like a wall blown away to the outside than a picture on a screen. Now she knows what the place is. She's been there in the meld, and it looks as actual now as it did then. The meandering river makes soft music. The breeze in the branches ruffles her hair and tickles her nose with pine scent and flowers.

"Oh, Deep Moor!" the girl exclaims. "Oh, Gerrasch! Where did you find such a painting? It's so . . ."

"A photo, girl," N'Doch says. "But it's . . . wow, it's really . . . real!"

When they take a step forward, Paia moves with them. She recalls what the God said: the painting is a portal. Is it a portal here as well? It certainly looks like they could walk right into the tall grasses stirring gently where the wall meets the floor. There's a path there, narrow and curving, just wide enough for single file. It leads down a soft slope toward the riverbank, and the luscious shade of broad-leafed trees.

Behind her, the children exude a collective sigh. Paia takes another step forward, but a firm hand holds her back. *"Warte! Das ist nur eine Täuschung!"*

An illusion, he says, her lover to be, her new protector. His antique language is in her head since the meld. He eases her back against him without force or presumption. How remarkable that, having exchanged at most three words, they already have an understanding, that satisfaction postponed due to circumstances will be all the sweeter. N'Doch has reached to snatch Erde back as well, just as the image starts to break up. Paia fears it's the quake returning, but it's the image evolving, exactly as the painting did. Clouds move up along the verdant profile of the mountains, the sky darkens, the glowing vista dims. The river hardens to solid white. When snow starts to fall, Paia shivers, though she has never seen real snow before. She is thankful for the heat of the baron's body. His breath is steady at her ear. She senses him taking possession, final and absolute, and in her head, she gives herself utterly. He will never desert her or do her harm. She is as sure of him as she is of anything since waking up to find that nothing in her world is what it seemed to be.

But the comfort he offers cannot dispel the very real chill that rises in her gut as the idyllic valley is smothered in ice and snow, then racked by howling gales that whirl the flakes into a blinding whiteness. The winds drive the drifts before them in a scourge of icy needles that scour the forests and fields until the frozen land is exposed and barren. Then comes the melt, and with it, rain, in sheets and torrents, shredding the last leaf, shearing off branches, tearing the bare trees up by the roots. The little river swells to an angry flood choked with mud and boulders. The valley sinks beneath it.

Paia hears weeping, feels the ache in her chest as if it were her own. But it's Erde, huddled like the child she really is, against tall N'Doch's side.

"Is it happening now?" she sobs. "Is it happening now?"

"Now's a relative thing, girl," soothes N'Doch.

"Then what does it mean?"

Poor girl. She's had to grow up so fast. Paia understands how awful that can be. Impulsively, she moves up beside them, away from the security of the baron's aura, compelled by the kinship of the meld to offer comfort as they watch the valley flood, melt, then dry up under the sudden, searing heat of a sun as relentless as the one outside. The trees shrink and wilt, or burst into spontaneous flame. The river thins, then vanishes. The grass shrivels. As the color bleaches away, from green to brown to beige, Erde buries her face in N'Doch's arm, shuddering.

"No, please, Gerrasch, no more! Make it stop! Make it go away!"

"Cannot." The Librarian's hoarse voice startles them. He's there behind them, his stooped shoulders tight with pain and knowledge. "Cannot. Not me. The One speaks."

"She walks in light," someone murmurs in the darkness behind. Paia hears a sound she knows well, the rustle of awed worshipers falling to their knees.

The girl lifts her eyes, stares again at the screen. "Oh . . . ?"

Paia says, "I saw it, too . . . my painting . . ."

"Yes. You, too. Wake-up call."

"But why does she show us Deep Moor?" Erde asks.

The Librarian's stubby arms lift and sink back helplessly. He has only the vision to offer, not its explanation.

"Damn!" N'Doch mutters. "I hate to think of it looking just like it does around here."

"It used to be green and fertile around here, too," Cauldwell reminds him. "Once upon a time."

Baron Köthen speaks up unexpectedly, a low-voiced question, almost a growl.

"Tough one, Dolph," says N'Doch.

From his crouch on the floor, Leif Cauldwell chuckles. It's as bitter a sound as Paia has ever heard from this man she thought she knew as well as any. "No, it's not," he says.

"Whatsit?" asks Luther.

N'Doch translates. "He wants to know . . . who has destroyed the earth, God or Man?"

"Das easy," Stoksie mutters.

"Well, tell him," says Cauldwell. "It's no theological conundrum. It's not like we don't know."

N'Doch shrugs. "We did it, Dolph. A long time after yours. God had nothing to do with it."

The baron sucks his teeth pensively, as if someone's just told him that half his army has deserted. A disaster, yes, but not, in his mind, a cause for despair. "Then we should do what is necessary to fix it. Is this not what you've been suggesting?"

N'Doch grins to hide the sudden grip of fear on his gut. "Put up or shut up, huh? I guess that makes it unanimous, but for . . . well, whadda you say now, preacher man?"

Leif Cauldwell moans softly. "May the One help me. Do it."

CHAPTER FORTY

The elevator ride to the top of the mountain takes longer than Paia's memory of the trip to the heights of the Citadel. Bathed in the flat white light, both alien and familiar, she wonders if her father knew of this facility, perhaps had dealings with its builders, perhaps even rode in this very car. After the collapse of order, the House Comp has told her, contact with the outside became dangerous, even between former friends and allies, especially if you had something they lacked, like power or good water.

Her father is very much on Paia's mind, as if the memory of him might help her face the terrible choice that awaits her on the mountaintop. Her head has cleared of Leif's soporific, though there's a dull pounding between her temples, hangover from the drug, maybe, or simple exhaustion. She's hoped that settling her brain might help settle her decision. She feels a lot more like the self she recognizes, but her head aches and her dilemma remains: *how can I betray him?*

She'd snatched a moment with Leif in the communications room, while the possible backlash from Erde's plan was being hurriedly prepared for. He was in motion, distracted, giving orders. His people flowed around them, moving weaponry and children and supplies. Still, they talked, in snatches, as if both of them needed the exchange in order to move onward. They talked about the past, about her father, about his death. Paia realized that her father had broken his nephew's heart.

"He lost hope. He . . . gave up! He'd never done that! Ever! I was . . . desperate, furious. Maybe I was getting back at him for dying when I joined up with the Beast. By the time I came to my senses, well . . ." Leif grabbed the arm of a man hurrying past. "Marcus! Send someone down the tunnels to check the seals!"

She should be angry with him for drugging her, for kidnapping her, for setting all this in motion. But how could she blame him for wanting to fix things? He still cared so much. Paia studied his handsome face, so familiar, trying to place it in her childhood. "You were one of his aides then? How could I not have known you?"

He grinned at her crookedly. "I was around sometimes. Mostly I was out in the field. Shuttling from meeting to meeting. We were the ones they sent out, the young ones who didn't have families. They'd always invite him, but after a while, they knew the best they were going to get was me. Then it got hard to get from meeting to meeting. I never made it home in between. I was stuck in a bunker in South Africa when the word came that he was . . . that he'd passed away."

Leif stared at the stack of books he'd picked up absently, then shrugged and put it down. He glanced at Constanze in mute appeal as she edged past with two children in tow. She paused, leaned her head against his arm for a fraction, then moved on. Leif cleared his throat. "The com-net was badly shredded by then. The news itself was a month old. It took me seven months to get back here. By then, it was too late . . . *he* had arrived." He looked away, signaling to a woman across the room to hurry. "If I'd been there, Paia! If only I'd been there, I could've kept the Old Man alive, I know I could have! Could've kept him from sinking into despair. Together, we could've fought the Beast off somehow!"

"You don't know that," Paia soothed automatically.

The Beast. The God. The Dragon. But no longer the only dragon. One of four. The black sheep of the family.

As if she had spoken out loud, Leif waved Luther over. "You go on up there with them. I know you want to. But keep an eye on this one." He shook Paia's shoulder, not ungently. "If he shows, she'll run back to him in an instant. She won't have any choice."

And then he'd marshaled his own aides, gathered up the rest of the children, and gone down to the big cavern to be with "his people" for whatever might occur. Unlike her father, Leif Cauldwell had not given up. Except on the God.

She won't have any choice.

Paia wonders. It may be wrong, but she misses him, his edgy magnificence, his energy, even his sharp tongue and cruel wit. Will he come for her this time? A surge of ambivalence and guilt presses Paia back against the cool metal side of the elevator. She has her own darkness to make peace with. If all the tales are true, she has been abetting a monster.

Monster.

She has called him that herself, to his perfect, golden face. But wrapped in her cocoon of safety and privilege, she meant it in an entirely personal way. She never thought to extrapolate his endless capacity for emotional cruelty into a notion of how he might behave out in the world. She just didn't think.

Now she can do nothing but think, as her head pounds and the elevator continues its silent ascent.

Paia lets her aching head loll back against the metal wall. Baron Köthen watches her from across the cab, keeping a cool public distance but fooling no one. He looks concerned, as if he senses she is not entirely recovered. Paia knows their sudden and inexplicable attachment is causing Erde a lot of anguish. Paia is sorry for it, but it's like asking the sun not to shine. Did she not dream him even before he arrived? Nothing to be done, except adopt a certain decorum in the girl's presence. Because Paia is so sure of him, she has no impatience, only deep, stirring tremors of anticipation. She smiles at him wanly, as if she has known him forever, this beautiful stranger from another millennium. A quiet light blooms in his eyes. Paia's glad she's given up asking the world to make sense.

But as the elevator rises, the throbbing in her head worsens. It feels less like pain now than noise, like a great bass yowl that her ears can't hear. Perhaps it's the lift mechanism in need of oil. But Paia cannot make sense of it as machine noise. It sounds somehow more . . . organic. She is about to ask N'Doch if he hears it when the elevator hisses to a stop and the doors yawn open.

For a moment, no one moves. They are at the end of a short, sheltering tunnel that leads out into a blast of heat.

Past the opening, just visible in the gray dawn, is a broad,
exposed shelf of wind-scoured rock. An old heliport, from
the looks of it, which, when it was functional, was intended
to blend in to the mountaintop. To the east, the sky is
brightening. The full heat of day will rise with the sun and
pour down on them like molten lead. Paia is sorry to leave
the cool of the elevator cab. She's sorry to be here at all,
to be in such danger and causing such pain, and yet there
seems a certain rightness about it. As if it really is, all of
it, even the miracle of Baron Köthen, part of some Great
Inevitability, this Duty Erde speaks of with such conviction.
If it is, then Paia can tear herself apart about betraying the
God, and still there'll be no stopping Destiny's forward
momentum.

She finds this soothing. She wonders if Leif's drug really
has flushed itself from her system, or if gentle traces of it
linger to soothe her toward this oddly tranquil state of
mind. Or is it the sturdy blond man in the black T-shirt,
who calms her with a nod? His acceptance of danger as an
expected part of life shows in the set of his jaw, and shames
her into searching out her own bravery. Her headache eases
faintly. Paia returns the baron's nod. She is ready.

N'Doch and the girl move ahead down the tunnel, with
the local man they call Luther. Köthen follows. Paia falls
in behind. But the Librarian is reluctant to venture out into
the open at all. He lingers in the doorway, then takes a
few halting steps into the dim gray light of the tunnel and
stalls, shifting his ponderous weight from one foot to the
other, uttering his slow monosyllables, like the moans of
an anxious bear.

Erde looks back. *Oh, Gerrasch, I forgot! You haven't
been outside for ever so long, have you!*

Paia waves her onward. *Please. Let me try.*

She recalls her own panic of not yet a week ago, when
she left the Temple grounds. She turns back, though she is
tingling with her own sort of dread, and hooks her hand
around the Librarian's soft elbow.

"Come now, don't be frightened! A big thing like
you . . ."

"Noise," says the Librarian.

Paia starts. "Yes! Can you hear it, too?"

"The Intemperate One. He searches but cannot find."
Another complete sentence. He touches one pink finger to
Paia's temple, and the noise recedes until it is no longer
painful. Then he lets her urge him down the tunnel to
where Köthen waits, his mouth quirked with approval. Together, they venture out from under the rock overhang and
across the shattered tarmac.

The old landing pad is a circular area still oddly smooth
and clear of the brittle weeds and scrub that have taken
over everywhere else. Paia guides the Librarian to the edge
of the circle, where the others have stopped. She feels Köthen's palm, gentle against the small of her back. She wants
to lean into it, and into him, but he murmurs something
about having a look around. N'Doch rubs one foot along
the unscarred surface of the pad.

"You still got copters landing here?"

"Not fera long time," says Luther.

"It's just . . . it looks so clean an' all . . ."

"Yes. It does." The girl Erde lifts her pale face toward
the light swelling in the east. Paia detects a glint of tears
tracking her cheeks. But her back is straight and purposeful
as she turns aside to walk the perimeter of the landing pad
with slow and measured step. "A magic circle."

N'Doch laughs, but nervously. He looks around. "You'd
think there'd be, like, maintenance equipment around, or
something . . ."

To Paia, schooled so long in the God's calendar of ritual,
the circle is a heavy omen. She hopes it's a good one. Magic
or not, its formal geometry lends credence and dignity to
what they are about to attempt. Baron Köthen, she notes,
instinctively respects the aura of ceremony that clings to
this open ledge. In his alert, restless pacing about, he does
not set foot past the circle's curve. And Luther steps out
of it as soon as the Four are assembled inside.

N'Doch dusts his hands together. "Well, let's get on
with it."

Paia admires his bravado. "You're very no-nonsense."

"That so?" He ruffles Erde's curly dark hair. "This one
thinks I'm all fulla nonsense. Doncha, girl?"

Erde has a brave little smile that lights up her face as
she flashes it, briefly, gratefully. Paia wishes she had bra-

vado enough of her own to put a sisterly arm around the
girl and dry those tears, but it's too hard, knowing she is
the almost certain cause of them.

"Yup," says N'Doch, filling the void. "Once you're into
something with these dragons, there ain't no getting out of
it. I've learned that much. Best to just get it over with,
whatever it is."

The Librarian is also walking the perimeter, hands
shoved in the pockets of his blue jumpsuit, humming pensively to himself. He finishes up in the center and stands
there flat-footed, his nose in the air like an animal, searching the hot dawn breeze.

The mountain shivers, as it had in the Library, the echo
of some distant and continuing catastrophe. The swell of
light on the eastern horizon reveals a tortured profile of
roiling cloud.

"Time," the Librarian intones. He beckons the others to
him. His soft pawlike palms cradle a tiny remote keypad.

N'Doch glances behind him. "Luther? Dolph? Be cool,
eh?" He repeats it in German, and Paia wonders if he
really thinks Baron Köthen could be any more alert than
he already is.

"*Sorge dich nicht, Dochmann.*" He's drawn the antique
weapon he wears slung across his back. It glimmers icily in
the dawn glow. "*Ich gebe dir Rückendeckung.*" His eyes
meet Paia's, serious and reassuring.

N'Doch grips Erde's thin shoulder with one hand and
Paia's with the other. "Go for it."

The Librarian taps out a sequence on the keypad, then
shoves it in a pocket. As the mountain shudders again beneath them, he reaches for the two women's hands.

CHAPTER FORTY-ONE

. . . He can tell the difference right off, like he was in a soundproof room before and now someone's blasted down the walls. Like maybe if he concentrated, he could hear every sound being made at this very moment all over the world. He could hear them all simultaneously and still know each one for what it is. What a symphony they would make!

. . . then he sees, as if standing right in front of him, his grandfather Djawara's knowing face. So wise, so steady, so unperturbed by knowledge. No wonder the girl first thought he was her "mage." He's smiling, but there's a warning in his eyes.

. . . *What do you know, Papa Dja? Papa? Tell me . . . !*

. . . She senses the dragon as an accelerating vastness but cannot truly connect with him. She sees flashes of light, blurs of motion. An ivory claw. He is not, she decides, quite in this world. He is not thinking in her direction, in her time, or even in her scale. The battle still rages, somewhere far away . . .

. . . yet an image reaches her, from . . . where? A well-loved face, every wrinkle familiar, floating in a swirl of mist. Alla, her old nursemaid and tutor, dead these three months . . .

. . . *Alla? Alla!*

. . . Alla smiles, and is gone . . .

. . . He is after the blue one, the rage howling in his blood. The smaller dragon sets the pace, but she is like sound through water, deflected, diffuse, omnipresent. The other, appearing out of nowhere, slams him off-balance each time he tries to rest. Paia tastes his fury and frustration like bile in her own throat. They dance and feint. They will not confront him. He trumpets that his strength is greater. Like two crows harrying an eagle, their only hope is to exhaust him. They lead him ever farther from the inhabited lands, to keep their battle from damaging the humans. He does not care about the humans. Soon he begins to suspect some other strategy, and decides he must have one of his own . . .

. . . but this is odd. As she watches, or seems in her mind to watch, the vision shrinks until it is a moving image framed by darkness, as on a screen. Words scroll rapidly across the bottom. She has missed the start of them . . .

. . . and who will be the guide's guide in this ruined world, if not me? . . .

. . . House?·Is that you? House? . . .

. . . LISTEN! LISTEN! LISTEN! . . .

Yes! Something new in the meld. Not a voice, no, not at all, but each of them has heard it before, in what they thought were their dreams. Or in waking moments of drifting inattention, daydreams, a stirring of the subconscious. Or so they thought.

That articulate breath of wind, that sighing gust so rich with meaning. That motion of atmosphere that is more formed than wind, yet less than a voice, a word. That presence at the corner of an eye, just out of view.

N'Doch N'Djai hears it as the universal harmony.

Erde von Alte sees it as the colors of the spectrum.

Paia Alexii Cauldwell feels it as the entire range of emotion, human and beyond.

The Librarian absorbs it, collates it, interprets it. He offers what he can of the nature of the new presence: huge, discorporate, a being of vast intellect as yet unfocused, of shape as yet undetermined. More potential than actual. But the potential takes their breath away.

Ah! The magnificence! A power beyond imagining!

AIR! AIR! AIR!

Toobigtooloudtoovasttoomuch! The specter of overload. The Four draw back as if burned. In that instant, a debriefing:

Clever dude, Fire. He trapped her, like a genie in a bottle, before she'd come into her powers.

But where? Where?

Nowhere.

So we gotta go nowhere to find her?

No place that we know of, he means.

*No **where**.*

Can she be a bit more specific?

Listen! Listen! Listen!

She is there. Air. His dragon. He is made whole for the briefest of instants. A taste of totality. His centuries of waiting are . . . and then she is gone.

Ah, the ache! Ah, the loss! And yet, the gain . . .

SEE: nothing.

HEAR: nothing.

SMELL: nothing.

FEEL: the outward expansion of consciousness toward infinity.

What he would say for her if he could but find the words, the all-too-human words? He wouldn't say, he would show. Image, sound, scent, touch, taste: a tidal surge of sensation and dream and memory, washing over, around. She has seen all. She has seen what you see. She remembers it for you. A green valley bathed in the golden mist of a summer evening, resonant with bee hum. The crisp sparkle of snow on a sunlit windowsill at Tor Alte. A symphony of birds and salt water cascading along an African shore. The sweet cacophony of Blind Rachel plunging cool and crystalline from a pine-scented height.

Treasure it! Hold it in the now! Do not let it pass into memory! Is it not all that is right and good? Is it not the truest miracle? Can it be that, instead, we choose nothingness and death?

Ah, the ache! The loss! There is no gain . . .

Paia feels the message as remembered grief, her mother's death, her father's decline and fall. Yet she understands how the mutable painting has prepared her to receive this message in a larger sense. Inside her now, no lazy, clichéd notion, no old denial like she heard so often as a child: *hey, it wasn't me who wrecked the planet!*

Instead, a profound, abiding rage that her birthright has been taken from her, and from all the other dwellers on the Earth. Only through another's memories will she hear the salt roar of the African surf, or taste the pure snowmelt of a German mountain stream. All she can know firsthand is heat and barren rock and devastation.

What can be done? What must I do?

The blue screen swims again behind her eyelids.

White letters read: *DENY HIM.*

No word, no voice. A sudden avalanche of emotion. A shock wave of rage and negation shakes the Four until their bones rattle. They see shredded wings, a flash of scales and smoke and blood. The contact is shattered. They are flung apart, flying, gasping, falling, slammed down hard on the weathered tarmac, overwhelmed, tumbled, scattered like rag dolls around the perimeter of the circle.

Without the multiple voices of the meld to fill her mind and her attention, Paia knows the exact moment when he arrives.

CHAPTER FORTY-TWO

Suspended in air, he sees the ground coming up hard. He tucks and rolls, gets the wind knocked out of him but keeps his head. He comes up gasping and coughing but conscious.

And in a haze of fury. Thrashing to regain his stance. Fists nose level and clenched. Ready to strike out with nails and fangs.

His lips pulls back so tight it hurts. His jaw attempts a snarl too big for his human mouth. His hands spasm with the effort of unsheathing claws he doesn't have.

N'Doch!

Her voice is a hand snatching him back from the edge of a cliff. N'Doch reels and steadies. The haze clears. Wait. Not his. This is some other's senseless rage that swept over him like a wave and sucked him into its undertow before he knew what was what. He feels nauseous and violated. Raped.

"N'Doch! Help Luther!"

Audible words this time, even more centering. He can see again. A flash of motion draws his eye: the girl racing toward Köthen up in the surrounding rocks where he stands at the ready, staring up at the sky.

Another voice, gasping. "Dockman! Ovah heah! Now, man!"

A shadow passes over. N'Doch doesn't need to ask. He hears the ear-splitting screech. He searches around wildly. Luther is half the circle's arc away, tugging on the crumpled form of the Librarian and not getting anywhere.

"Into the circle, my lord! Quickly!" The girl's yelling at

Köthen, but N'Doch gets the idea. He staggers toward
Luther.

"Wrong way! Luther! Wrong way!" The Tinker is trying
to drag the Librarian into the elevator tunnel. A trap, a
disaster in the making. "Luther! Into the circle!" It seems
like forever until he reaches them. He grabs one of the
Librarian's stocky legs and hauls for all he's worth. The
shadow slides past them again, lower this time. N'Doch
doesn't look up. He knows what he'll see. Half the
screeching is in his own dragon-racked brain. He fights Luther briefly for control over the body, but the Librarian is
coming to now, starting up his own struggle to regain the
protection of the circle. Man, but the guy is slow!

On its third pass, the circling shadow darkens the entire
mountaintop. The scream is like a detonation. It rakes
N'Doch's nerve endings, leaving him trembling and weak.
A line of flame erupts behind them, targeting them as directly as a lit fuse. Luther gives up his disagreement at last
and together they hoist the Librarian by his armpits and
drag him stumbling over the perimeter.

The bright heat splashes upward and sideways behind
them as if it has hit a solid wall. N'Doch hears the girl's
alarm call winging out across the dragon com-net. There's
no reply. She's grabbed Köthen by his sword arm and won't
let go. He's running with her toward the circle, trying to
free up his weapon and shield her with his body at the
same time. A sear of heat explodes in front of them. The
girl squeals and ducks away blindly. Köthen snatches her
up and plunges straight through the flames and across the
perimeter. N'Doch races to meet them, tearing off his
T-shirt. Köthen's hair is smoldering. He drops the girl at
N'Doch's feet. Her long linen shirt has caught. Little fiery
tongues rise up her back. N'Doch leaves Köthen to deal
with his own conflagration and blankets the girl with his
shirt, rolling her around on the tarmac until he's sure he's
put her out.

"Where are they?" she gasps, when he lets her up.
"What has he done to them?"

"Easy, girl." It's all he can think of to say as the
screeching overhead rises deafeningly, then morphs into inhuman laughter inside their heads.

Her back is tender. She knows she's been burned but not badly enough to worry. The loose light layers of her linens took most of the damage. The dragon will soothe it as soon as he returns. When he returns . . .

She has pushed her panic aside for the immediate emergency. Now dread assails her anew. She grabs N'Doch's arm. "Where are they? Isn't the barrier down? Why don't they answer? Why don't they come!"

"Don't know, but it looks like we're gonna have to deal with this one on our own . . ."

Erde follows his horrified gaze, past the priestess woman who stands as still as marble in the middle of the circle, to the vast shining beast wheeling at eye level just past the outer ledges of the mountainside.

". . . 'cause here he comes."

The golden dragon rises, a swift muscular ascent. The first red light of the morning sun glints off his gilt scales. Reflected shards as hot as flame sear Erde's cheeks and eyes. He hovers a moment, high overhead. His great wings cock back for his stoop. He screams again, and then he is plunging toward them, in a dead fall like a rock kicked off a precipice, dropping until Erde is sure he means to dash himself against the mountaintop just to be able to kill them all in the process.

But moments before the inevitable collision, the dragon begins to glow—red, orange, yellow, white, like molten iron in the forge. At the instant of impact, there is no sound, no concussion. The dragon is a white-hot halo too bright to look at. Then the brightness winks out and out of this crucible is born . . . a man.

Even as she stares in wonder, Erde's first thought is for Hal, avid collector of dragon lore. She's sure Lord Fire's spectacular translation would astound even that good knight's fertile and learned imagination. For, unlike Lady Water's exact replications from N'Doch's memory, very little is truly human about Fire's man-form. He is huge, ten or twelve feet tall, and shining gold all over, from the writhing mass of his long hair to the sharp-clawed toes of his unshod feet. Here, then, is the fierce angel of the sword, the Archangel Michael, from the chapel at Tor Alte: inhumanly beautiful, ruthless, and cold. But this face has the yellow, slitted eyes of a reptile and a surprisingly sensuous mouth. And the Beast is boldly naked, but for a billowing cloth-of-gold cloak. It swirls around him as if alive and makes him seem twice his already monstrous size, but conceals no part of his scaled and glittering anatomy. Erde expects to see horns and a tail, for surely he is the Devil incarnate. But he has left those behind in his transformation. She would look away if she dared, *should* look away in all maiden modesty, but in truth, she can't take her eyes off him. Nor can anyone else. He is riveting, magnificent, terrifying. It's what Leif Cauldwell meant about the Beast compelling men to follow him. Foolish men, who mistake beauty for truth, and believe all his lies and promises.

But where are they? Where are the others?

Fire towers above them, turning his perfect profile to catch the sunrise just so. He fixes his gaze like a snake on his prey, savoring their awe, then slowly advances in long graceful strides. The humans gather in a protective arc around the priestess. Köthen has his sword ready, but even he seems to realize how little use it will be against such a monster. The Librarian has his mysterious little device in hand again and is muttering over it like an alchemist.

"Will it hold him?" N'Doch asks.

The Librarian looks unsure, or maybe he still suffers from the shock of being slammed about. He mutters and fiddles some more. Silently, Erde prays.

But Lord Fire halts at the edge of the circle. He doesn't even try to enter it, just draws himself up with a gloating and superior smile. His slitted stare settles on Paia as if she is standing there alone. Erde sees she is trembling, but with rage and indignation as well as fear. Baron Köthen plants himself firmly behind her. Erde sees them as a single image, a pair, a joining, and grapples suddenly with a fuller notion of why Destiny bade her bring him here. A small moan escapes her. Quickly, she stifles it. If it is necessary, she must accept it.

"Our enemies are vanquished, my priestess." The golden

giant's voice insinuates a razor's edge behind its languid, silken tones.

"No!" Erde reaches for the others in panic. *Is it true? Has he caught them?*

"Burned right out of the sky! My sister went up like a tinderbox!"

"Liar!" N'Doch bellows.

"New friends, my priestess? Tell me, rather, you are their prisoner."

Paia's mouth quivers, but nothing comes out. She puts her hand to her throat as if amazed to find it there at all.

Erde thrusts herself forward, a step past the priestess, then two. Baron Köthen reaches out to hold her back. She shakes him off and advances. He does not come after her. He has his own Duty. She knows that now. She walks as close to the invisible wall as she dares and stares up at the golden giant.

"My lord Fire!"

Fire glances briefly downward, a mere deigning to take notice. "Children! They send children against me!"

"My lord Fire, what have you done to them? How dare you threaten your siblings or seek to divert them from their holy Duty! A Duty that you share, my lord!"

"Oh, please!" He levels a scimitar nail at Erde's nose. "How dare you meddle in matters you don't understand? Lecture me, will you? Your ignorance and folly are equaled only by the gracelessness of your rhetoric!"

He looks to Paia again. His glowing eyes mock. "Come, come, my priestess. Who are all these riffraff? Surely such company cannot interest you, when you could have mine instead!" He turns to pace along the outside of the circle, smooth and agile as a stalking cat, and Paia turns with him. His living cloak swirls around him, concealing, then revealing him anew, all of him. He is not shrieking now. His voice is tuned to its most intimate pitch, yet each of them hears its inviting, sensuous tones as if he is standing next to them. "Surely you have not grown tired of your sacred duties to me? Remember how I said I was thinking on ways to bring us closer?"

He is using the power of his summons to compel her. Paia knows this. Even so, she is drawn by its inexorable gravity, like the pull of tides. She knows also what he is promising this time. He has never appeared to her naked before, and his beauty and magnetism stir her more than ever.

She won't have any choice.

But matters are different now. Paia has lost a different kind of innocence. What the God has done is unforgivable. She must prove that she does have a choice.

She wrings the paralysis from her throat, the reflex submission and the weakling excusing of his arrogance and cruelty. She steps forward as Erde has. "I am no prisoner, my lord. These are my friends, my . . . cousins in Duty."

"Duty!" With Fire's bark of contempt, a small gout of flame spatters heat against the Librarian's invisible barrier.

Paia shudders. He's never been able to manifest anything real while in man-form. Perhaps the flames are an illusion, but Paia feels a difference in him. His customary languor is now but the thinnest of veneers.

The God laughs. He knows he's frightened her. He grins nastily as he stalks slowly around the perimeter. "Your duty is to me! Dare they tell you otherwise, these new friends? You should choose your friends more wisely, my priestess . . ." He waves a hand lazily. ". . . as it seems I should better choose my lieutenants. Where is the traitorous priest, by the way? I thought sure to find him among you."

"If you don't know, so much the better for him."

"A brave speech from a silly woman!" Fire arcs his head back so that his hair stands up in writhing coils. "No matter. He'll not stay hidden from me for long, my dear disloyal son, my precious Luco to whom I trusted the secrets of my Temple. Ah, he will rue the day, my gallant soldier who's lost the stomach for battle, for what must be done. For what WILL be done! There are none left to stand against me now!" He lets his brass voice ring across the open ledge, echo in the boulder piles, then calms his rant to dulcet tones of seduction. "But you and I, beloved, when I have found the priest and riven him limb from limb, we will forget all this foolishness. Come, take me in my forgiving mood, before I lose the impulse."

Paia sees Erde glance back at her wide-eyed, both incredulous and comprehending. Behind her, the Librarian growls, deep in his throat.

The God has arrived full circle, due south in the landing pad's compass rose. He settles himself there and slowly extends one arm, palm out. Tiny pinpoint explosions dance where his curved and gilded nail intersects the barrier. His viper hair gentles into curling locks of burnished gold, his claws to well-formed fingers. His eyes plead and promise. "Come home to me, beloved."

He can stir her mind and her body from a distance. He is practiced at seduction without contact. He can slip behind Paia's eyes with the memory of his dragon tongue coiling upward around her thigh.

Paia's breath quickens. The God's call thrills in her mind and commands the beat of her heart. She sees the walls of the Citadel loom up around her, the musky darkness of the God's sanctuary. She takes a step forward, lost in her own rising heat, going willingly to meet him, to take him into her at last.

Sudden motion at her side, and then . . . a man in front of her, blocking the way. Paia tries to step around him. He moves to meet her. She ducks the other way. He is quicker than she could ever be. He closes on her gently. With a cry, Paia shoves at him, arms fully extended, but it's like shoving at a wall. There are others, in a circle around them. The God is calling. She dodges again. She is frantic with need. The man blocks her, then backs off. Abruptly, silently, a sword appears in his hand. The long blade flashes dully as he levels it at her, his other arm outstretched for balance. He steps lightly. He is being very careful. The sword's tip hovers at her throat. If she feints left or right, the blade's keen edge prevents her. Confused, distracted, the God's call dimmed by this unexpected threat, Paia freezes.

The man lifts the sword until the flat of it rests beneath her chin. It's the uncanny chill of the steel that gets her attention, so sharp it almost burns. That, and the hard, clear look on him that says he will absolutely kill her now rather than give her up to the Beast. He could do it, a quick, short stroke, before anyone—even the God—could stop him.

Paia believes this just long enough for the thought to
sober her up. The man presses the sword upward, forcing
her glazed and troubled eyes to meet his. She sees there
the same male promises that the God has offered, but
something else, more shared and lasting.

"Liebste," he says gravely. *"Benimm dich."*

His voice reminds her who he is. The Citadel walls thin
and vanish like morning fog. Fire roars his outrage and
claws at the barrier. Sparks shoot high and scatter.

Baron Köthen lowers his blade, but his gaze holds Paia
as firmly as the God's ever could. He sheathes the sword,
then steps quickly forward to cradle her chin between his
hands. She expects he will be rough with her, but instead,
he kisses her with an ardent sweetness that brings tears to
her eyes, of relief, of gratitude, of surrender. She lets him
wrap her in his arms, hoping the feel of him against her
can drown out the sound of the God screaming.

N'Doch thinks he finally understands what Erde's been
going on about when she talks about Destiny. He grabs her
as she turns away from the circle, from the spectacle of her
dream-lord so impassioned, and lets her press her face into
his side.

"Easy, girl," he murmurs.

"It must be," she intones hoarsely. "It must be!"

"Listen!" The Librarian's nose is testing the air. N'Doch
doubts he could hear anything over Fire's furious ranting.

Erde jerks away from him, her anguish tossed aside. She
points in two directions simultaneously. "Look! Oh, look!"

N'Doch's glad whoop echoes across the circle.

"It's a trick. An illusion!" bellows the golden giant.

"No, my lord Fire! It is not! Your vanquished enemies
have returned!"

N'Doch appreciates bravado as much as the next man,
so he feels himself seized by a shameless fit of admiration
for Fire's sleight of hand, thrown up like dust in desperation, in hopes of luring Paia back to him before the others
returned. N'Doch has seen such performances before, even

been guilty of a few of them himself. He's interested to learn that this dragon is not all screech and brawn. There's a lot of bluff in him, too.

He tries to see surprise in Fire's lizard eyes as the vast, stony bulk of Earth appears on the rock ledge at the eastern compass point. There is none, and Fire knows to look exactly to the west to find the changeable spot of wings and glare that is the blue dragon perched on an overhanging ledge. What N'Doch would swear that he sees instead in the giant's glance is a shadow of exhaustion and despair.

What is he hiding? Something big. N'Doch is sure of it.

The returned dragons do not fly at Fire in immediate attack. They salute the Librarian with solemn respect, and receive and return the fervent silent welcomes of their guides. But they ward off all questions after asserting that both are well and whole. They hunker down on the periphery of the ledge to regard their black-sheep brother impassively. A peculiar stillness falls over the landing pad. Fire stares back at them with the appearance of arrogant nonchalance, but N'Doch reads the effort he's putting into it. It comes to him that most of the dragons' warring will not be physical.

The lovers relax their desperate hold. The humans drift together into their loose unconscious circle to wonder, and wait. The Librarian gazes at Earth and Water with longing.

Finally Water stirs, flaring a rainbow of gossamer. N'Doch drinks in her difference. He's gonna have to get to know her all over again.

We know where she is now, brother.

Where?

WHERE?

HUSH!

Fire seems buoyed by Water's challenge. He has made her speak first. "The least of victories, honored opponent! It's a clever device, you must admit. Without her help, you lack the very power required to release her. Without her, you cannot defeat me."

The how is only a matter of time. And we wish not your defeat, but your strength on our side. Will you continue this wrongheaded resistance?

Fire holds his man-form as if relishing the distinction it affords him, and the excuse to indulge in the spoken word.

"A matter of time? Time is what I am trying to win for us, sister. Soon enough, none of your meddling will matter." He lowers his gaze to the priestess sheltering in the curve of Köthen's arms. "You claim I've forsaken my 'holy duty'? Look on this mawkish spectacle before you, and consider the perfidy of these weak-willed creatures. Consider them in all your wisdom, then tell me for what reason they deserve our service . . . or our sacrifice!"

He levels his gleaming nail as if it could spout fire and annihilate the lovers on the spot. "This woman was sworn to me through the thousand generations of her blood."

AND YOU ABUSED THAT PRIVILEGE! A PLEDGE MUST WORK BOTH WAYS.

"I acted as I saw fit and necessary, given the extremes of the times! But see how she holds to that ancient vow! She'll not even do me the honor of denying me to my face!"

N'Doch thinks, *Oh, be careful what you wish for.*

Erde scolds him for giving the giant the slightest share of his sympathy.

And sure enough, Paia stares solemnly into Köthen's eyes, then gently disengages herself from his embrace. She turns and takes a few unsteady steps toward her accuser. "My lord Fire, I have been loyal to you past all reason. Do not blame me now if reason reasserts itself."

The gilded nail curls into a claw aimed at Köthen's neck. "You call that a reason?"

"Reason of the soul, my lord."

"The soul?" His voice is soft, incredulous. "Oh, no, beloved. So wrong. So very wrong. The body perhaps, but not the soul. Your soul belongs to me. To me! If you have been restless in my care, then I must, I *will,* work harder to satisfy. And look how much I will sacrifice to content you: you may keep your concubine. Come with me now and you're welcome to him, as the Suitor we've been searching for, for so long as he amuses you. A pretty thing, I admit, but just a man, after all. The interest will pall." He leans forward, and Paia's body shifts in his direction like a reed in water. N'Doch is amazed to see actual hope soften the giant's glare. His hand is out again. He is almost singing to her. "Come, my lovely priestess! Come, my most beautiful beloved! They cannot stop you. It's ah . . . against the rules.''

Paia sways, toward Fire, away from him. N'Doch is surprised when Köthen backs up a step to give her room. He knows something N'Doch isn't sure of yet, until Paia reaches out within the circle.

Is my cousin right about this? Can the bond between this dragon and myself compel him to change his ways?

WE HOPE IT WILL BE SO.

You are our only hope of winning him to our cause.

IT WILL NOT BE EASY.

No.

Will you try it?

It seems I must.

Way to go!

When Paia moves forward this time, her step is firmer. "How poorly you perceive the truth, my lord, when it's not in your own interests." She advances slowly, in almost ceremonial step. "You speak of honor. Tell me, where is yours? Have you forgotten it? Mislaid it? Or simply put it aside? When you find it again, I will keep that pledge laid on me by my ancestors. Until then, my lord Fire . . ." She stops a mere pace from the barrier. The golden giant looms over her as she draws herself into her formal Temple stance: head up, arms out, palms at right angles. "I do deny thee."

"NO! YOU WILL NOT DENY ME!"

Fire lashes out, smashing his clawed fist against the barrier. Sparks explode through it, catching in Paia's clothes and hair, driving her backward. The barrier itself seems to catch flame. N'Doch has seconds to wonder if the fire is real, and how could a force field or whatever it is be burning, before he feels the heat and hears the roar above his head.

"YOU WILL NOT DENY ME!"

"Kill it! Kill it!" N'Doch shouts frantically to the Librarian, who's already tapping at his remote. He grabs Erde, drags her behind him. They're all about to be suffocated and broiled alive.

Then the barrier is down, a hissing release of air, and suddenly water is falling around them, sheets of it, cool and quenching, then a rising curtain of steam and a bronzy mountain of scales and claws is between them and the raging giant. N'Doch swears Earth gets bigger every time he sees him. He shoves Luther and the Librarian into the dragon's protective shadow. Water, newly winged, hovers above. Erde follows, calling to Köthen and Paia to hurry.

For Paia has stopped, long paces away, to gaze back through the smoke and mist at her errant dragon.

"YOU WILL NOT DENY ME!" shrieks Fire. He is a whirl of flame and smoke and motion. He spits magma with every word, but he keeps his distance. "Listen well, my reckless kin! You can hold me at bay, but you cannot defeat me! Without the Fourth, you are nothing! NOTHING!"

He stalks them around the perimeter, as if the barrier is still in place. Water hovers, hissing showers of mist at him in warning. He ignores her. He pulls up opposite N'Doch.

"You boy. You have . . . a favorite grandparent. And a mother, as I recall." He points at Erde. "And this presumptuous child has a circle of women she cherishes. Do you not, brat?" He laughs at Erde's stricken look. "Did you truly believe you are strangers to me? Even the puny man-thing there has a friend he would die for. We all can play at the hostage game!"

Then Fire swivels his heated glare toward the dark and huddled figure of the Librarian. "And you! So quiet there. Still hoping to hide from me? You've hidden very well, all these years. Too well. But for you, my plan would have gone undetected. This requires proper recompense . . . one day soon."

He gestures, an abrupt arc that scatters a bright rain of embers hard into the staring human faces. Earth roars, a sound like continents shifting, and rises hugely to his feet.

Suddenly dwarfed, Fire holds his ground. "Will I continue my resistance? To the end of Time! And what do I promise you? War, with no quarter! War here, and war wherever your puny humans call home! I will harry and destroy, up and down the centuries, until not a soul known and loved by any of you is left alive!"

With a blinding concussion of light and air. Fire leaps and is sky-borne, a dragon again. His gilt-and-enamel wings beat the new-made mud into a cloud of grit and dust.

AND WHEN I WIN, MARK MY WORDS, YOU ALL WILL THANK ME FOR IT! IF THE WORLD MUST END, IT WILL END ON MY TERMS!

He circles once, dark and vast against the rising sun, and is gone.

THE BOOK OF AIR

For **Dorothy Koehler**, and all other friends of dragons.

And for **Jim Hansen**, who told it like it is.

As always, thanks are due to Lynne Kemen and Bill Rossow, literary critics *par excellence*, to Vicki Davis, to my agent, Joshua Bilmes, and to my oh-so-patient editor and publisher, Sheila Gilbert.

Apologies are due to all the readers of THE DRAGON QUARTET who had to wait so long for this final volume! Real life just got the better of me.

The Creation

IN THE BEGINNING,
AND A LITTLE AFTER . . .

In the Beginning, four mighty dragons raised of elemental energies were put to work creating the World. They were called Earth, Water, Fire, and Air. No one of them had power greater than another, and no one of them was mighty alone.

When the work was completed and the World set in motion, the four went to ground, expecting to sleep out this World's particular history and not rise again until World's End.

The first to awaken was Earth.

He woke in darkness, as innocent as a babe, with only the fleeting shadows of dreams to hint at his former magnificence. But one bright flame of knowledge drove him forth: he was Called to Work again, if only he could remember what the Work was.

He found the World grown damp and chill, overrun by the puniest of creatures, Creation's afterthought, the ones called Men. Earth soon learned that Men, too, had forgotten their Origin. They had abandoned their own intended Work in the World and thrived instead on superstition, violence, and self-righteous oppression of their fellows. They had forgotten as well their primordial relationship with dragons—all, that is, but a few.

One in particular awaited Earth's coming, a young girl who knew nothing of the secret duty carried down through the countless generations of her blood. Her name was Erde, and she knew her Destiny when she faced a living dragon and was not afraid.

Thereafter, Earth's Quest became her own, and together they searched her World for answers to his questions. Some they found and slowly, along with his memory, Earth's powers reawakened. But the girl's World was dark and dangerous and ignorant, and the mysterious Caller who summoned Earth could not be found within it. One day, blindly following the Call, Earth took them Somewhere Else.

In that Somewhere Else, they found Earth's sister Water, and her Companion N'Doch. N'Doch's World was hot and crowded and full of noise, and mysterious to Erde until she understood that she had traveled to Sometime, as well as to Somewhere. It became her task to teach N'Doch about the dragons and their Quest, for he did not know his Destiny, and did not join them willingly at first.

Water, too, had heard the Caller. She could answer some of Earth's questions about the Work, but added many of her own. Soon, the dragons were convinced that an unknown Power not only blocked their Search, but threatened their safety. Evidence pointed to the dragon Fire, but why would their own brother conspire against them?

When the dangers of N'Doch's World, both human and inhuman, closed in around them, the four in desperation returned to Erde's time, with nothing but N'Doch's recurring dream of a Burning Land to tell them where to go to continue the Search.

But in Erde's time, conditions were deteriorating. . . .

N'Doch's nightmare vision took the four to a farther Future, where the results of Mankind's carelessness and greed were only too evident. War, disease and ecological collapse had razed the landscape and brought human society to ruin. Here, the four found undeniable evidence of Fire's villainy. In the planet's final days, he ruled as a tyrannical god over a dwindling population, preaching Apocalypse and plotting against his siblings. He even boasted of how cleverly he'd hidden away their sister Air.

But the four found surprising allies in that hot and desiccated land, resourceful men and women who knew that their survival depended on a more sympathetic relationship with Nature. The most astonishing addition to the Quest was Fire's own dragon guide, Paia. Her fated bond with her fellow guides allowed her to repudiate her dragon's misdeeds, and join the efforts to free Air from her mysterious prison and Paia's people from Fire's cruel yoke.

From out of this rebellion, an old friend appeared in a new guise, and was revealed as the fourth dragon guide. But he didn't know where his dragon was, either.

Yet, was Fire merely evil, or was there truth to his claim of knowledge that only he possessed?

At last, Earth, Water, and Fire came face-to-face. A fiery confrontation on a barren mountaintop forced Fire into temporary retreat. But not before he had threatened murder and mayhem against all that the humans knew and loved. . . .

PART ONE

The Summoning
of the Hero

CHAPTER ONE

Gone. The Fire-breather is gone.

Seconds afterward, the Librarian senses a change. A difference inside. Like the twitching of muscles he'd not even known were paralyzed.

Smoke still hangs in the heated air, the Fire-breather's sulfurous trace. It's the same dry dawn on the same dry mountaintop. The Librarian is alive when he didn't expect to be, but he is not the same as he was a moment ago.

His dragon has touched him, he's sure of it. A feather-light glancing contact, almost too brief to be noticed, yet inside him now, this entire . . . what? A reordering, an enlarging—of thought, of perception, of understanding. A more *outward* focus.

And the connection felt deliberate this time. Not like it's always been for him before, at the mercy of his peculiar inner circuitry, picked out by random roving beams that stun and blind, then swing away through the fog. This was . . . almost directed. Behind the walls of the dragon's enigmatic prison, something has changed for her, too.

She knows where to find me.

The others must hear of this, immediately. But as the Librarian tries for words, none will come, aloud or otherwise. This has *not* changed. Besides, the others are not ready for another dose of revelation. Not yet. Though the terrifying confrontation passed within mere moments of real time, they're as stunned and spent as if it had been hours. Distracted. Sluggish with terror and awe. Struggling with watery knees and weakened bowels. And wondering, as he is, how they managed to come through the conflagration alive. Though urgency thrills through the Librarian's nervous system like a drug, he knows he must allow them space for recovery.

The smoke is persistent and sullen. Unnatural, like the creature that made it. Acid, like his tongue. The Librarian coughs, waving his arms uselessly. The Fire-breather's stench is not so easily dispelled. And it's a long time since he's been outside in the unconditioned air. His pampered lungs have forgotten the acrid stink of combustion and the punishment of daylight. The constant dry weight of the heat, even at dawn. The arid mountain ledges still radiate yesterday's baking. Already they're being baked all over again. Heat upon heat. Even stone has a life that can be burned away. The Librarian sways, overcome by a moment of synchronicity with the rock.

. . . *deep-anchored to slow-time, swelling sun seared, shattered, wind-battered, groaning with the revolutions of the dying planet* . . .

Motion recalls him to the mountaintop, to the dawn, to the rocky plateau that was once a landing pad. Once. When men still ruled. The Librarian sees the soldier is stirring. Has it been hours or seconds since? He mustn't let himself drift like that, not now. He must remember how to act. He must recall decisiveness, now that his eternal waiting has ended, and time suddenly matters. Events matter. The Fire-breather has come and gone. The dragon Air has touched him. Six hundred men, women, and children wait in the caverns below, anxious about the outcome of the confrontation above. His people, who have faith in him, who believe he has the knowledge to hold off the Last Days. Does he? Of course not. It's her knowledge, the dragon's, that he believes in, that he preaches about. Which is why he must . . . must . . . her touch . . . there is little time left . . . she is searching, too.

Drifting . . .

The Librarian struggles to get hold of himself. He wishes for the animal body of his former days, when the ability to shake one's self vigorously was all that was needed to feel put back in order. *Every hair in place.* He longs for the cool darkness of his den beneath the mountain, for the remote comforts of his screens and sensors and console. When his dragon finds him there, he can almost concentrate. Reflect rather than absorb. Deflect to the machines the bright roar of her energies. Keep the explosion in his senses within the limits of sanity . . . most of the time. With the expansion of her power over the years, the danger to him has grown also. This last century or so, without the buffer of the machines, his brain would have been burned to the proverbial cinder. The Librarian shudders. Though there is power to spare in her sendings, there is little coherency. Sometimes he fears that his dragon is not entirely sane.

But this time, *this* time . . . there *was* something different. Along with the usual kaleidoscope of images, there was a hint of meaning. More than a hint. As if a new circuit had opened, to run a message on an infinite loop: *Hurry! Hurry! Hurry!* No, it's not so articulate as that. The Librarian supplies the words, which barely describe the imperative within. It sighs like wind. It tumbles like water. It groans like the earth. He is eager to get back down below, to see if the machines can detect it, deflect it, interpret it.

Across the circular pad, the soldier dusts soot from his bare forearms and scowls at the brightening skies, as if to assure himself that the Fire-breather is truly gone. He lays a hand on the bowed head of the Fire-breather's guide. She who was lately so bold has slid weeping to the ground beside him. The soldier murmurs soundlessly without bending toward her, seeming to know that no mere word or gesture will console her. He is familiar with the aftershock of battles. The Librarian watches him as he quietly steps away across the tarmac to inspect the arc of scorched rock and heat-fused sand laid down around them by the Fire-breather's wrath. He is not a big man, but sturdy, with a blunt, determined jaw and a restless glance. He moves quickly, economically, unmindful of the gathering heat. The rising sun glints off the carved and gilded hilt of the sword slung sheathed across his back. The sword. The Librarian remembers that sword and this man, in a more youthful version. But the memory is from a former life, and hazy. Most clearly, he recalls the man this man once served, an elder knight. Battle-scarred, a weary idealist. One has grown much like the other, over time—not physically, for the soldier is shorter, blonder, more intent. But maturity and ill-fortune have blunted his youthful arrogance, so the Librarian's memories of both men blend in a tightening fabric. He follows the weave for a while, interested in the complex patterning of human lives. Then he catches himself.

Drifting again, Gerrasch. Not now, not now!

He flexes his pink-palmed hands, his clever fingers, his only sure anchor to the world. He sighs. His life is about to get very complicated.

The Earth-mover's guide stirs next. As if waking suddenly, she starts and staggers to her feet, then pivots in an aimless circle, running down like a spinning top until she ends up gazing numbly at the Librarian. Her dark curls are frizzed with singe. Tears streak the ash dusting her pale smooth cheeks. But though she is the youngest of them all, almost a child, she does not give in to sobs. She gathers herself again quickly. She looks away to the others, counting heads, assessing their welfare. Beside her, the Water-bearer's tall guide swears softly and at length, grinding his fists into his eyes.

In the Librarian's gut, the wordless signal steps up its urgent thrum: *Hurry! Hurry! Hurry!*

The Earth-mover and Water-bearer themselves are still hunkered down in a silent conference of dragon outrage. They, most of all, must hear of the change in him, but though he's only just met them, the Librarian knows enough of dragons to understand that they'll not be disturbed until they're good and ready, no matter what. He forgives them. They are dragons, after all. No matter the urgency, impatience is a lesson the Librarian has yet to learn. Not so the soldier, who has finished his inspection tour and has already begun to pace, though he attempts to disguise it as patrolling and limbering up, that is, useful movement. While the rest pull themselves together, the Librarian welcomes the chance for a moment of dragon study, his first since the pair's sudden arrival to save their humans from the Fire-breather's vicious tantrum. The Librarian has lived with a dragon inside him for all his life, yet he's never seen one in the flesh. Suddenly, he's seen three in less than half an hour.

Earth is vast, bronze, and plated. He crouches like a mountain of veined brown marble, rough-carved in the form of a beast. His neck is thickly muscled, his haunches massive. His tail is short and wide, and grounds him to the rock like an ancient tree root. His curved ivory horns and scimitar claws reflect the glow of the rising sun. In contrast to this unrelenting solidity, Water could be a swirl of a billion blue-green butterflies, ephemeral and phosphorescent, infinitely changeable. The Librarian understands this is only the shape she's chosen for the moment. He wonders if there is a shape she calls her own, in which her own identity rests and is at home. Earth and Water are as different from each other as they are from their fire-breathing, golden-scaled, deadly-minded brother.

How will his own dragon look, the Air-bringer, once she's set free to appear before him? The Librarian has no data to work with, only gut feeling and instinct. He's built a picture in his imagination. When he thinks of his dragon, he sees the tall cloud towers of ancient summers, the white-topped, fair-weather spires that once brought soft air and warm breezes. Clouds. Only a memory from a time when the planet's cycle of respiration was still normal. But the Librarian remembers them in passionate detail, as an icon in the landscape of Paradise. Of Arcadia. Of all that is lost.

Drifting, Gerrasch. Again, again. Focus on the dragon!

What else was new in this precious instant of contact? The Librarian replays it in his mind: reverse, fast forward, reverse, fast forward. The cloud image seems a bit more architectural than before, a sort of cloud city. An anomaly? The Librarian stores it for further analysis.

The pale girl and the tall young man have gathered themselves enough to turn to the older man behind them. Together, they ease him up from his knees and pat away his shudders of terror and outrage. For this man's sake, the Librarian at last wills his big clumsy body toward an idea of motion. Stillness would be vastly easier, but this dark-skinned man is neither soldier nor dragon guide. Only his faith in the Librarian's visions has brought him so near to death on a bleak and bitter mountaintop. He deserves some soothing and support.

No wind among the rocks, wreathed in heat and stubborn smoke, pressed down by the yellow dome of sky. No sound. Only the brittle rattle of pebbles beneath the soldier's boots as he paces out the blackened circle for a third or fourth time. No one has said a word, the Librarian notes, since the Fire-breather vanished.

Ah, good, he muses, when his feet more or less respond to his orders, and shuffle him forward. *Perhaps now the words will follow*.

The pale girl finally finds her tongue. "We have to go after him!"

In her widened eyes, the Librarian sees the stark reflection of the Fire-breather's long list of parting threats, each one pointed and personal. "Now! Before he . . . we have to warn everyone!"

Her name is Erde von Alte, and she is fourteen. The Librarian has met her before, in earlier times. The same time as the elder knight. Even then, she was given to overemphasis and passionate exaggeration, in the way of fourteen year olds, which is unsurprising since in the eleven hundred years since he first encountered her, she has aged but two months. The Librarian feels he has permission to note her overzealousness, having been a fourteen year old himself several times in his life, though never a girl. Besides, young Erde came to the present the easy way, dragon-back, while he has had to live each day and every year in between.

"Everyone! Please! If we don't hurry, he'll get to them first! He'll . . . !"

"Whoa, girl, easy." The tall youth stops rubbing his eyes and stands blinking. His lanky ebony body cuts a hard profile against the sun-splashed rock. "Can't just race on off. Gotta figure where he's headed."

The Citadel, thinks the Librarian, so sure he's spoken aloud that he's confused when none of them react to the visions of seared flesh and broken bodies writhing so vividly inside his own eyes.

The girl shoves away the dark youth's raised palms. "We'll go everywhere, then! We'll have to split up!"

"Maybe. I don't know." He shrugs, an uneasy dance of flatly muscled shoulders beneath his charred T-shirt. "Let's see what *they* say." He glances toward the two dragons and spots the soldier, still in restless, impatient motion. "Hey, Dolph! C'mon over! Battle conference!"

The tall youth is called N'Doch. He is West African, and from a time in the world's history when his homeland was not yet under water. The older man is Luther Williams, a local in the present time, from one of the itinerant Tinker clans. The soldier is from the girl's place and time. The Librarian is not yet sure about this one's preference in a name. A different version is used by each of the dragon guides. The knight's squire he met so long ago was Adolphus Michael von Hoffmann, heir to the sizable estates of Köthen. Germany, it was. Tenth century. A baron, he thinks. The Librarian cares little about such things.

The soldier glances up at N'Doch's summons. He frowns, already pondering solutions as he paces across the tarmac to join them. Gently but firmly, as he passes, the baron scoops up the Fire-breather's guide and urges her forward under the shelter of his arm. She leans into him, drying her eyes, flicking dubious and apologetic glances though damp lashes at her fellow guides. The Librarian feels shy as she approaches, uncomfortably conscious of his wild hair and his shambling, graceless bulk.

For this is Paia, after all. The High Priestess of the Temple of the Apocalypse, the Fire-breather's cult. The Librarian knows everything about her. His machines beneath the mountain are hooked to her machines in the Fire-breather's lair, though she was unaware of the connection—and of him—until their meeting mere hours ago. He's always known Fire's priestess was a beautiful woman, but he finds the reality of her . . . *go ahead, Gerrasch, say it* . . . her flesh quite overwhelming. Small wonder that Dolph or Hoffmann or Baron Köthen or whatever the soldier wishes to be called soothes her along like something precious. She is that rare occurrence, especially nowadays: unblemished, unmutated, undeformed. A perfect physical specimen. Of course the soldier is in love with her. Who could blame him?

A loose circle coalesces in the center of the old landing pad. First, all of them talk at once, a burst of babble that manages to express only their relief at being still alive. Then they fall silent to gaze expectantly at the Librarian, as if an urgent meeting has been called to order, of which he has unaccountably been elected Chair.

Not so unaccountably, the Librarian reminds himself. Not a moment to waste, and there's a major language barrier here.

He visualizes the problem as an interlinked flow chart. For him, an image is always more articulate than words, and so, words are a wonder to him. Words are his long life's study, which is why he comes armed with a solution.

Erde, N'Doch, and Baron Köthen have been speaking tenth century German. Though N'Doch's native languages are twenty-first century Wolof and sub-Saharan French, he's learned the antique German recently and precipitously from the dragons, who can download entire databases into a linked human mind, the only issue being how fast the mind can accept the input. Köthen speaks German and passable Old French, but is not dragon-linked like the guides. Still, he has a quick ear and a quicker mind, so he's fast picking up the contemporary English that is Luther's only tongue, as it is Paia's—except Luther speaks his own "Tinker" dialect of English, which sounds different from Paia's. But Paia, as Fire's guide, is mind-linked to the other guides. Translation is automatic. Maybe the worst of this chaos is N'Doch's slang-ridden English, learned watching old twentieth century American videos. It makes the Librarian's teeth itch.

The conundrum is, of course, what language to use in spoken conversation? Once Köthen is more fluent, English will be the obvious *lingua franca*. For now, only the Librarian can resolve the confusion. Hence their breathless attention.

He fishes in the deep pockets of his jumpsuit for his remote keypad and activates the translator program. He holds up his little device like a beacon, nodding around the circle. Again, they all start in at once.

"He'll go right to . . ."

"We gotta see what . . ."

"What about the . . ."

The soldier shakes his head and backs off a step.

"He'll go to Deep Moor first!" Erde exclaims breathlessly.

"Why would he?"

"Wait!" rumbles Luther. "Fust t'ing, we gudda tell da uddahs."

The Librarian is still struggling to vocalize. His voice is stuck, like an unoiled hinge. "Yes," he manages finally, grateful for any coherent sound at all.

YES.

The echo booms in his chest as well as in his head. It makes him want to cough. The dragons have ended their private conference. The Librarian feels his brain crowd up as the other guides drop into mental contact.

Earth lifts his horned head. WE MUST POSTPONE THE QUEST UNTIL OUR FRIENDS ARE SAFE.

Yes! Erde's slim fists ball up for emphasis. *We'll go now and warn Deep Moor!*

N'Doch shakes his head. *Faster if we stopped by Papa Dja's on the way!*

The Citadel is closest! We should go there first!

The Librarian recalls that he must tell them about his new difference, about his true moment with his dragon, the missing sister, and the object of their Quest. But time and minds run breakneck in the Meld. So long-schooled in waiting, the Librarian is like a timid driver on a freeway ramp at rush hour. He can't get a word in edgewise. *Need info,* he offers instead.

YES. WE MUST GATHER TO DISCUSS THE BEST COURSE OF ACTION.

A chorus of distress rises from the minds in the Meld, who know how long a dragon discussion can take.

Dear dragon, we haven't time!

So many lives are in danger!

JUST HOLD ON, ALL OF YOU. Water's music for once rings harsh. THERE ARE A LOT OF INTERESTS AT STAKE HERE, INCLUDING A FEW YOU SEEM TO HAVE FORGOTTEN ABOUT! OUR SISTER AIR STILL LANGUISHES IN CAPTIVITY, FAR AHEAD ALONG THE TIME LINE.

Where?

Farther in the future?

The Librarian recalls now what terror had pushed from his mind. In the midst of the firefight, the dragons' hasty revelation: *We know where she is!*

Erde subsides with an anxious frown. She would never contradict a dragon, not even someone else's.

But no one's been there. We can't go there dragon-back without an image to travel to.

Fire's been there. Let's send Paia to pick his brain.

WE HAVE BEEN PONDERING THIS, AND AS YET, SEE NO SOLUTION, Earth told them.

Water reluctantly agrees. YES, FOR NOW, WE'LL DO WHAT WE CAN DO. WE'LL HELP OUR FRIENDS.

ASK THOSE BELOW TO CLEAR SPACE IN THE LARGEST CAVERN. WE ARE COMING TO JOIN THEM.

The Future. An image. A future image. What if . . . ?

Can't hold on to that train of thought against the pull of a dragon imperative. The Librarian gives up and thumbs his remote, calling up the gawky boy he's left listening at the console in the complex far below. He summons words enough to be understood. Mattias is used to supplying the ones in between. The Librarian often dreams of vocalizing his thought-images. If, when he opened his mouth, the pictures just flowed out, as detailed and coherent as they are in his head, or as words are in the mouths of others, he'd have no problem communicating with the world. But what would the response be, he wonders, to his cloud-tower image of the dragon Air?

"Wow!" squeaks the remote. "Dragons?" The receding slap of bare feet is audible over the open line as Mattias abandons the console and hotfoots it down the corridor.

"Join hands!" Erde urges. "Lord Earth will take us down!"

Baron Köthen mutters a warning to Luther about the nauseating effects of dragon transport.

Luther says, "Mebbe we 'umins shud take da elevader."

"Too late," N'Doch replies.

Seconds later, the hot glare of the summit has been eclipsed by the opaque weight of the mountain. They are in darkness. Wavering points of light surround them like a sea of stars. The nervous waiting silence is broken only by the resonant, far-off thump of the circulating fans. The Librarian sucks in cool air, filtered and humidified, and expels a gasping sigh of relief. He'll be able to think more clearly now, he's sure of it. He sees the soldier shudder just once and swallow hard. Luther groans faintly. The Librarian has felt nothing, as if traveling disembodied through tons of solid rock is perfectly natural. As if he's been doing it for years. Sometimes he suspects he is not yet entirely "umin."

For instance, his nose is far too sensitive. The chill air of the cavern is redolent with the smell of humans and animals, yet he can pick out familiar individuals by their scent alone. He can still read their emotions, their lingering fear, the surge of adrenaline caused by Mattias' announcement. In the vast, high-vaulted space, the rows of wagons and carts and campsites have been hastily hauled back. The open center is ringed by lanterns and receding, dim-lit ranks of weary, worried, awe-filled faces. Hot meals and a good night's sleep have been rare down here for several days now. Their astonishment tickles the Librarian's nose— a tang of citrus. After all, six people have just materialized out of nowhere, right in front of them.

The most familiar scent of all steps out of the darkness. Leif Cauldwell—a mixed scent of smoke, leather, and a hint of cinnamon. Every eye follows him: tall and golden, head priest of the Fire Temple turned rebel leader. No living human has had more experience with the Fire-breather, except Paia herself. Right now, Cauldwell smells like a man trying hard to look optimistic. Behind his firmly sculpted mouth, his teeth worry the inside of his lip. The Tinker elder Reuben Stokes limps along at his side—brisk odors of salt and pine sap. Luther immediately goes to greet them. Cauldwell's body is in its prime and powerful, and though Luther's chin-forward stoop betrays his age, they both tower over little Stoksie. But no matter. All three clasp hands as if they'd last parted unsure of ever seeing each other again.

"Yu wudnta b'leeved it, Leif!" Luther's murmur is heartfelt and grateful. "Dey sentim packin', dey did!"

For the soldier's sake, the Librarian thumbs his translator up to max.

"No, Luther. He *left,* in a rage!" The remote unit mimics Erde's girlish stridency to perfection. "You know that's no-where near the end of it. People everywhere are in terri-ble danger!"

Luther nods, but her rebuke does little to dampen his enthusiasm.

Leif Cauldwell's worried gaze flicks toward the Librarian. "So what happened up there?"

"Left, yes." The Librarian offers his pudgy shortcut of a shrug. "Now what?" He knows what. *Hurry, hurry.* The message throbs in his chest like a second heartbeat. But he will not tell people what to do. He will not give orders. He's seen far too much of that in his many lives.

N'Doch rests both hands on Erde's shoulders, solicitous but restraining. "Yeah, that's it, chief. We got some hard decisions to make, and we gotta do it fast."

"But . . . he came? The Beast?" Cauldwell squints into the darkness behind them. "Is Paia with you? Did he take her? Is she all right?"

"She's here. She's fine," says N'Doch.

"Yes. No." The Librarian feels dragon pressure building behind his brow like a foul-weather headache. Not his dragon. It's the other two. They've been patient so far, but silent anonymity is not their strong suit. "Not. But . . ."

"It was rough on her," N'Doch supplies. "But she told him where to go."

Cauldwell spies his former superior, mute and lovely, within the curve of the soldier's arm. "Congratulations, cuz!" His smile offers both approval and awe: she has faced down the Fire-breather and lived. Then his edginess re-turns. "Mattias said you were bringing the other . . ."

"Draguns, Leif! Yu kin sayit." Luther's wide grin reflects the flicker of lantern light. "Da gud uns!" He points to a peculiar zone of darkness in the middle of the cleared area. A blue light dances at its center. "Dey's sistah an' brudder ta da One!"

A murmur rustles across the cavern, the very breath of hope and reverence. "The One!"

The One who will save us all. The Librarian ponders his mantra, and the tall cloud towers bloom behind his eyelids. *Air, Air, Air.* But now is no time for preaching on his vi-sions, even if he could get the words out right.

Because Cauldwell needs help. This brave and seasoned warrior has backed away before he can stop himself, retreating from the mysterious looming darkness and its companion glow, though he sees Stoksie and Luther smiling and unalarmed. The Librarian smells his reflex terror, and the effort it takes for the big man to plant his feet and gaze about, as if he'd merely been making room. Leif Cauldwell has good reason to fear dragons, from his long and bitter years in the Fire-breather's employ. The Librarian brushes away the phantoms rushing into his head—fire, smoke, human sacrifice—and shuffles over to stand close by the rebel leader's side. Cauldwell glances down at him.

"Ah. Gerrasch." He grips the Librarian's soft shoulder. "Ah."

Earth speeds up his metabolism toward visibility, and the huge cavern seems to shrink, relative to the dragon's great, glimmering shadow. His eyes precede his solid form, appearing as disembodied oval lamps, as tall as a man and glowing like the sky before dawn. The crowd stirs and murmurs. His head alone is as big as their tallest wagons. His curved ivory claws and horns shine with his own interior gleam. Cauldwell stares, his jaw set, as the phosphorescent blue eddy drops to hover at the brown dragon's side.

The Librarian gazes up at the rebel leader, willing him toward acceptance and calm. If it would help, he would embrace the man, and each and every one of the throng withdrawing cautiously into the deeper shadows. These are his people, who have gifted him with their faith for so long. Not all of them, to be sure, especially among the Tinkers. Stoksie, for one, has remained an unbeliever, even while accepting the more secular aspects of Cauldwell's rebellion. But Tinkers are by nature broad-minded, and Stoksie was always open to proof, so it thrills the Librarian to at last be able to offer him some. Proof of what he's been promising and preaching, that great Powers will appear to oppose the Fire-breather's tyranny, to help free the One and restore the dying planet. He couldn't warn them that those Powers would also be dragons. His visions hadn't been that specific.

He watches an entire spectrum of loathing shiver across Leif Cauldwell's handsome face as the man tries to come to grips.

An odd sound, half moan, half sigh, escapes the High Priestess. She slips out from under the soldier's protective arm. He takes a step after her, then falls back as she glides forward to grasp Cauldwell's hand.

"These are not like him," she whispers.

Her voice is hoarse. No wonder. She's just been shouting down the Fire-breather, inhaling the smoke and sulfur of his wrath. *Her dragon. Fire.* The Librarian hears grief and guilt and confusion in every word. The soldier waits, watching his woman like the hawk he very much resembles.

"Come. Meet them." Paia leads Cauldwell across the open floor toward the dragons. He tries not to seem unwilling. The blue glow coalesces into something nearer form: wings webbed with gossamer, a long neck, a shimmering fish tail, appearing, disappearing, changeable. An impression of music hovers in the air. Earth lowers his huge head. His eyes are like lighted doorways. His nostrils flare gently. Warm, sweet breezes ruffle the rebel leader's hair. Scents of moist loam and bruised grass. The Librarian cannot help but smile, though his heart pounds with that other urgency. *Leaves. Grass.* It's been far too long since he's inhaled such treasures. Paia lays her own hand and Cauldwell's on the dragon's shining claw. Cauldwell's hand trembles, then steadies.

Behind them, Luther says, "Wuz dem dat saved uz, Leif."

"Not a moment too soon, either," N'Doch agrees.

Stoksie whistles softly. "Heeza big un, all ri'."

N'Doch grins. "And getting bigger every day. When I first met him, he wasn't much bigger than an elephant."

"Yeah? Wuzza nelefant?"

"Yu know, Stokes," Luther mutters. "Yu seen 'em in pitchers."

Stoksie looks dubious.

"Later, dude, okay?" N'Doch watches Cauldwell ease a half step closer to the big dragon. "Later, I'll sing you about elephants."

The girl strays to the Librarian's side. He feels like he's being force-fed the entire world's impatience and anxiety. He sends Erde easeful messages. If he could reach his dragon, he'd send her some, too. Cauldwell's absolute trust must be won, or the forces for good will be a force divided.

Cauldwell lets his hand slide across the waist-high ivory curl of claw, broader than his own muscular thigh. "Is this what it was like?" he asks Paia, "With . . . him?"

Paia's choked laugh is the most rueful sound the Librarian has ever heard. "Oh, no, cousin. Oh, no. No. Not at all."

Cauldwell takes a breath, then lifts his head and looks the dragon in the eye: a tall, golden man caught in a benign and golden stare. Benign, but awe-inspiring. Even the Librarian finds it so. Cauldwell licks his lips. "Let's see . . . you must be . . ."

"He is Lord Earth." Erde has moved up on his other side. Paia steps back, into the soldier's waiting embrace. They move in concert, these dragon guides, the Librarian muses, forgetting for a moment that he is one of them.

"Earth." Cauldwell cannot tear his gaze away. "Ah. Yours?"

The girl wags her singed curls faintly. "Say rather, I am his. His servant, and guide in the world of men. As your cousin is Lord Fire's, only . . ."

"Only. Only?"

"It's my fault," murmurs Paia from behind. "It must be. Yet Earth tells me otherwise. He says I am meant to help the Go . . . um, that is, Fire . . . see the error of his ways."

Cauldwell's mouth twists. "He'll only see what's in his own interest."

The Librarian agrees. He worries that Earth's assessment is too generous. The dysfunction seems profound, and the dragon in question entirely intractable.

"Earth," repeats Cauldwell. His hand rests more easily on the dragon's claw. "Earth and . . . ?"

"Water," N'Doch supplies.

As Cauldwell turns, Water settles her form still further. The Librarian watches closely. When she's done settling, he silently applauds her cleverness. She's become a lovely, swan-necked blue dragon, cloaked in velvet like a seal, and no bigger than one of the Tinker mules that's whickering greetings from the far corners of the cavern. A phrase comes to his mind, from another former life: *good cop, bad cop*. The Librarian grins. Next to her looming, mountain-ous, and terrifying brother, Water is just the cutest little dragon you ever did see.

Luther's murmur is equal parts awe and delight. "Sheez a shape-shiftah, Leif. Ain'dat sumting?"

"It's something, all right."

"We should . . ." Erde urges. "Isn't it time to . . . ?"

Her anxiety brims over and swirls around the Librarian like surf. This time, he agrees. With Fire on the rampage who knows where, laying waste to who knows which of their near and dear, it's high time they got moving. He's lingered only to savor the luxury of someone else doing the talking for him. Three someones, his fellow guides, who can tap directly into his image-driven brain and translate for him. Except about the machines. That's beyond all understanding. The machines and his connection to them are his contribution to the four-way destiny. That much, at least, he is sure of, among so little else.

N'Doch and Erde snatch a brief reunion with Stoksie, asking after the rest of Blind Rachel, his Tinker crew. Seven out of ten of the local crews made it into the Refuge before Fire began torching the countryside. The Librarian worries about the fate of the other three.

He waves his arms. "We should. Now. The Library."

N'Doch grabs Leif Cauldwell's elbow familiarly. "Time to go to work, chief. See if the computers can tell us what Fire's up to."

Cauldwell eases free of the younger man's grip. "Leif. Call me Leif. There are no chiefs around here."

"Sure, sure. Whatever." N'Doch's round ebony face is open and guileless. He scuffs one foot along the polished stone floor. "But it's gonna make such a cool rhyming lyric when I get to writing a song about you."

Cauldwell stares at him.

"N'Doch . . ." Erde warns.

Cauldwell takes in the girl's prim and disapproving frown, makes a quick assessment and lets his testiness fade. "Yeah? Can't wait to hear it." He turns away to the Librarian. "Who do we need downstairs?"

"All. All."

N'Doch adds, "Everyone who can fit. All of us and all of you . . . y'know, your non-chiefs."

Erde's glower deepens. "He will not behave. Do not expect it."

But Cauldwell is already in motion, heading off into

darkness, along a path among the crowded wagons. He has no problem with giving orders. "Luther, Stoksie, you're with us. Where's Ysa? And Stanze? We'll need Constanze." He halts, scanning the crowd.

Luther joins him, smiling. "Sheez ovah deah, Leif. Lookit dat, willya?"

Cauldwell's wife Constanze, with their little daughter clasped in her arms, trails a pack of children out of the throng, heading straight for the brown dragon's tall snout, which he's cushioned comfortably on crossed forepaws in order to greet them. Cauldwell starts. "Stanze . . .!"

"S'okay, Leif." Luther restrains him with a raised palm. "S'awri'. We shudn't teach 'em all owah feahs, ri'?"

"But . . ."

"But nuttin, Leif. Look fer yerself."

One of the smallest children is already snuggled against the dragon's rough jaw. Earth is impressive, but he is not lovely like his sister. The Librarian admits that he's seen prettier horned toads. But the child's eyes are only adoring. Constanze shoots a helpless glance in her husband's direction. The child in her grasp struggles for freedom. She shrugs and sets the girl down beside the dragon's claws. The girl crows delightedly and wraps her arms around the nearest pillar of ivory. Constanze backs away, bemused, then with another shrug, she turns and comes toward Cauldwell. The Librarian notes that the water dragon has stealthily sidestepped out of child-range.

Beside him, N'Doch chuckles dryly. "They'll leave her alone. She's not talking to 'em like he is. He's still a kid despite his size, but she came into the world a grown-up. I sang her into kid-form once. My little brother. Died when he was five. Don't think she liked it much."

Cauldwell's arm slides automatically around Constanze's waist. They watch their little girl slipping and sliding as she tries to climb the dragon's claw. "Are we just going to leave them alone together?" Cauldwell asks.

Constanze leans into his side. "She told me, distinctly and even grammatically, that the dragon had assured her he wasn't eating children today."

"She said that? What an imagination!"

"No. I got the impression she was relaying what he actually said. All the children say he's talking to them."

"Really?" Cauldwell looks to the Librarian in alarm. "Is that possible?"

"Possible. Yes."

"Something you taught them? By the One, what are we raising?"

"The future," says the Librarian before he's even thought it over. And it's true that what the children have become is as much his fault as anyone's. He's been their tutor and their mascot. It's his dark den that's their favorite place of play. If he himself is not entirely human, how can he teach the children to be?

"Lord Earth urges us to action," Erde announces.

"We should get a move on," N'Doch nods. "The dragons'll listen in through us."

"Ah, if only Sir Hal were here!" Erde mourns.

"Sure, just what we need," N'Doch mutters. "Another chief."

Cauldwell gives the dragons one last glance of misgiving, then expels a long breath and leads his war council toward the elevator. The Librarian trots after him, his fingers itching for his keypad. N'Doch falls in behind, beside Paia and the soldier.

"Taking up the rear as usual, yer lordship?"

"One day you'll sass the wrong man, Dochmann." Köthen jerks his thumb toward Cauldwell's retreating back.

"Jeez, if you ain't blown me away yet, no one will. The world loves a clown, Dolph, doncha know?"

"I wouldn't bet money on it. Or your life."

"Like I'd better not sass the Fire dude, is that what you're getting at?"

The soldier adjusts the sword across his back to a more comfortable angle. "It wouldn't be my first advice."

"The God . . . I mean, Fire . . . doesn't take well to mockery," agrees Paia quietly. "He only knows how to give it out."

"Then I'm gonna be in deep shit," N'Doch predicts. " 'Cause there's one thing I just can't leave alone, and that's a guy who takes himself too seriously."

Köthen groans. "I'll rue the day I swore my sword to your safety."

"Cheer up, Dolph. You used to be one of those too-serious guys, remember, and we worked it out okay, didn't we?"

"It's hardly analogous."

"Yeah, well." At the open door of the elevator, silhouetted against the bright light from the cab, N'Doch glances back at the big, dirt-colored dragon, besieged by a pack of noisy little children.

He laughs softly. "That's one hell of a baby-sitter!"

CHAPTER TWO

N'doch is pondering that song he'll make up about Leif Cauldwell as he trails the others into the shadowed Communications Room. He lets the base rhythm of the HVAC underline the melody, and longs for an instrument to play it on.

The group piles up in front of the bright wall screen, still running feed from the helipad security camera. N'Doch stands at the back. He's taller than any of them, except Luther and Cauldwell. Besides, the image is so large and so clear, it's like he's inside of it, like he's back up there on the mountaintop, in the heat and the smoke, a sitting duck for dragon-fire. Makes him sweat just to think about it. And about what Fire might be up to. Even packed in here like sardines, it's tough to keep still, tough to fight the worry down. His grandpa's got power, N'Doch is sure of it, but is his magic strong enough to stand against the malign wizardry of Fire?

Papa Dja, Papa Dja, keep your head low, old man, he intones silently.

The boy Mattias jumps up from the console as Gerrasch approaches. N'Doch thinks the kid looks a whole lot tighter around the eyes than when they'd left him here before. No surprise, given what he's just seen, courtesy of the video feed. But he's trying to play it cool. N'Doch would've done the same at his age. Hell, he's doing it now.

"Weah's da dragins?" Mattias demands immediately.

Gerrasch elbows him gently aside and rolls into his padded chair, his soft pink hands working the keys before he's even settled his bulk.

N'Doch jerks his thumb. "Upstairs."

Mattias looks to Gerrasch, who's already hunched down and oblivious, then to Leif Cauldwell. His entire gawky-teen body pleads. "Kin I go, Leif, huh, huh?"

Cauldwell nods. A bit grudgingly, N'Doch thinks, but he's willing to cut the rebel leader some slack. A day ago, before all these mouthy strangers showed up out of nowhere, the dude was running his own show, the whole show, no matter what he says about chiefs or no chiefs. But his rebellion was doomed—ill-equipped and undermanned—and the man has the grace to see it, even if he won't say it out loud. Two dragons suddenly on his side gives him and his people a serious fighting chance.

The kid practically lays rubber scooting on out of there. N'Doch shoulders his way out of the press to wander restlessly among the rows of darkened workstations while late arrivals trot in from upstairs and the Librarian fiddles with his keypad. The walls to either side of the screen are gridded with smooth-faced, rectangular units adorned with svelte pull handles and tiny green idiot lights. Probably some sort of data storage. N'Doch wonders about the people who used to live and work here, sunk so deep into the mountain bedrock. What happened to them? What did they do while the world outside fell apart around them? He slides a palm along the slick surface. What is it? Metal? Plastic? He can't tell. For him, it's . . . well, the *future*. He can't repress a little private speculation about what all this super high-tech equipment could do if retrofitted and put to work mixing one of his songs. He doubts he'll get the chance to find out. Too much serious shit going down.

The yellow glow bathing the racks of alien equipment flicks over to blue. N'Doch pivots and moves toward the screen. The big world map is back, with its too-great expanse of hot, empty ocean and its overlay of satellite orbits. He scans for the blinking indicators.

"Uh-oh," he murmurs, and scans again.

There's the one for Air, parked off the map in the lower corner, signifying her imprisonment who-knows-where, and there's the two active signals poised over a position that looks to be right about where he's standing, only several levels up in the big cavern. "Where is he? Where's the fourth signal?"

He hears a weird chittering noise. It's Gerrasch, something he's doing with his teeth. "Gone," he says. "Already."

"Gone?" moans Erde. "Oh, I knew it! We shouldn't have waited!"

"Hold on, hold on." But N'Doch is offering comfort he doesn't feel.

Stoksie peers at the screen. "Gone weah?"

"To another time," says Cauldwell grimly, "If I understand this right."

N'Doch nods. "Question is, which one? Who do we warn first?"

Again, they're all talking at once, filling the room with more noise than there are people. Luther explains to Ysa what the blinking lights mean. Constanze asks if the indicator would change if the Beast assumed man-form. N'Doch thinks about his mama, alone in front of her vid set. Grandpapa Djawara can't be much help to her. He's an old man, living by himself out in the bush with only distant neighbors who fear and mistrust him anyway. He'll need all his witchy powers to keep his own self safe.

Cauldwell lets everyone yammer out their anxiety. Meanwhile, he leans over the Librarian's round shoulder and gets to work. "Gerrasch, call up House. What's happening at the Citadel?"

The Librarian keys in the connection. He and Cauldwell have worked together a long time. N'Doch moves in, interested. He's learned in the Meld how, when Fire awoke, he commandeered the Cauldwell family fortress as his temple and stronghold. But Paia's presence in the Meld is emotional more than visual, despite her being a painter and all. N'Doch is eager for a clearer look at this place he's heard so much about. And then there's the Citadel's sentient computer, this "House" that Leif's asking about. The machine that's been Paia's mentor in the dragon lore, like Papa Dja for N'Doch and Hal Engle for Erde. N'Doch still can't quite get his brain around it. There was no full-tilt AI back in his time. He always talked a lot of sci-fi, but he didn't believe in much of it. So he's startled by the voice that floats up from the console speakers. Doesn't sound synthesized at all. Not like the AIs in the old sf vids, which always talked like they'd swallowed a big dose of Prozac.

This sounds like just a human, and a kinda panicky one at that. N'Doch has never heard a computer whine before.

"Finally! Where have you been? I've been calling for hours and Mattias kept saying, 'they went upstairs, they went upstairs,' but he didn't know how to patch me through, or maybe he thought, well, I don't know what he thought! Really, Gerrasch, you have to train your people better! Is he there? He's not here. He . . ."

"Was here," intones the Librarian. "Gone already."

"Gone? Gone? Where?"

"Away."

'What do you mean, away? You mean, *downtime*? Is everyone all right? Is Paia all right?"

Funny how everyone keeps asking that, muses N'Doch.

"She's fine, House." Cauldwell leans in to be heard over the background din of questions and debate.

"Leif! You made it! I was so concerned!"

"Everyone here's fine. A bit shell-shocked, but fine. What's going on there? Can you put the monitors on-line?"

"Working on it. Such excitement you've missed, Leif! There's been a palace coup, just as you predicted. Second Son Branfer has declared himself First Son in your absence!"

"Branfer! That clod can't manage his breakfast, never mind the whole Temple!"

"And one of the Faceless Twelve, I forget which, has elevated herself to High Priestess."

N'Doch detects conflict on Cauldwell's sculpture-perfect face. There goes his other seat of authority, poof! Swept from beneath him. But he'd engineered that usurping himself. So dedicated to his cause, he gave up what had to be a real cushy job. Except for having Fire as your boss.

"Hope she and Branfer hate each other," Cauldwell mutters darkly.

"If not now, they will soon, particularly if I have anything to say about it. The Temple is doomed. They'll all be eating each other alive by noon!"

N'Doch marvels at the computer's unconcealed relish for violence and intrigue. Like lots of teenagers he's known. Proof enough for him that this machine is sentient.

Cauldwell is less gleeful. "Any injuries? Much damage? What about Christoff and Ark?"

"Safe. Holed up here in the Rare Books Room with the others. I was able to warn them in time."

"Can you keep them safe?"

"Until *he* comes looking for them . . ."

"Then we'll have to get them out of there before that happens."

"I'll tell them. Then we have to figure out a way to rescue me." There's a pause, entirely without static. The Librarian's typing fingers go slack. Cauldwell gnaws his lip. Finally, its voice gone flat, the computer says, "Patching through the monitors."

The big blue map on the wall is quickly papered over by a grid of smaller images: rooms, interior vistas, some populated, others not, some obscured by signal static, a few entirely blank. N'Doch sees long windowless corridors, paneled in gleaming wood, furnished with carpets and paintings and the occasional ornate, stiff-backed chair. People racing to and fro. He sees a vast, bustling kitchen, though he can't really tell if a meal is being prepared or if the food stores are being raided. He sees a huge dining hall with the tables laid out in a blatantly hierarchical pattern. He sees sun-blasted walled courtyards and a long view down the nave of an elaborate, gilded basilica he supposes to be the Temple. A small gathering huddles in noisy prayer near what must be the altar.

"Not many signs of fighting," notes Cauldwell. "House did the job right."

Paia drifts over to the console with Köthen in tow. "Look! My home. Or it was . . ."

Köthen looks, with his usual intensity. N'Doch doubts the good baron knows how to do anything casual.

"And will be again," Cauldwell insists. "We're not surrendering the Citadel. We're encouraging the Temple to self-destruct while the Beast is distracted."

Paia peers at her tall cousin as if just now registering who he is and what he's done. "You've planned this a long time, haven't you, Luco."

"Leif. Luco is past."

"Yes. I see that now."

N'Doch decides she's finally pulling herself together. This is the first unambiguous statement he's heard out of her since she confronted her rogue dragon up on the mountaintop and bravely denied him. He understands how devastated that's left her. No matter how fiercely he resisted the pull of dragon destiny at first, he'd be a hollow shell if Water was taken from him now.

Paia leans toward the console's one visible mike. N'Doch is sure it's an anachronism. The sensors in this room could likely pick up a mouse sneeze. Old Gerrasch must prefer the illusion of focus. Or maybe this future's too future even for him.

"Hello, House."

"Hello, Paia." The computer's voice goes deeper, calmer, like a new persona has kicked in. "How are you getting along out there in the world?"

Paia sinks into the chair that Köthen has found for her. "Oh, House! I wouldn't know where to begin! There's so much you never told me!"

N'Doch swallows a rueful guffaw, though it nearly chokes him. He eases over beside Köthen to study the Citadel up close. Searching for clues, both of them. N'Doch's still struggling to encompass this world he's landed in, how it got the way it is from the way it was in his time. Not just the rising oceans and the global drought, but the people, and how they coped, how they live now. As for Köthen, he's even farther out of the loop, but he's a sponge for useful information, plus he's dead eager to learn all about this woman he's fallen for, so hard and so suddenly.

"Big joint, huh?" N'Doch is taken by the sheer size and scope of the Citadel, at least as far as he can see from these images. "Whacha think, Dolph? Look anything like your palace at home?"

The baron snorts quietly. "Castle Köthen is hardly a palace, Dochmann. Attractively situated, comfortable enough, but modest by comparison. What it is, however, is secure and easily defended."

"Yeah? You ever have to do that?"

Köthen cuts him a look of amused disbelief. "If not me, then who?"

"Well, I mean, I guess . . . Yeah. Stupid question." When he first met Köthen, the man wore bloodied armor and wrist shackles. Putting a sword back in his hand was like grafting on a lost arm.

"Not stupid. Not really." Cauldwell has been eavesdropping. "I'd like to know, too."

"Hey, chief. Forgot you speak Kraut." N'Doch gives way, bringing the rebel leader and Köthen face-to-face. These two alpha dudes, he figures, have some deep shit to work out if they're gonna work together, so better sooner than later. And let them do it here, in a crowd, where nothing much can happen.

But Cauldwell's negotiating skills haven't gone near as rusty as his diplomat's German. He offers Köthen a serious, collegial smile. "Here. I'll show you around my place first." He guides the baron along the tapestry of images to point out a long view of barren red hills. "The cameras trained on the entrance went belly-up a while ago, but these ones up on the cliff face are still working. You see, the Citadel's a natural fortress. Dug deep into the side of a mountain." He nods to the next image, where the camera stares straight down into the empty inner courtyard. "It's proved impossible to take when its defense is well organized—I know. I've held it myself a few times."

Köthen folds his arms, as if listening out of mere good manners.

"But now, in the midst of a power grab," Cauldwell continues smoothly, "it'll be chaos in there. Which is exactly the point. House, can we look at a cross section, a plan? Give me a few screens' worth."

"Working," mutters the computer.

The image collage breaks down and reassembles quickly, but not before N'Doch has taken in a flash of blue overlaid with one bright word: *HURRY*.

"Wait! What was that? Did anyone see that? I thought I saw . . ."

But no one's listening. Several big diagrams replace the image and whatever had followed it. As Köthen moves in to look them over, his eyes narrow with interest.

"Like what you see?" Cauldwell taps a lower-level plan, tracing out access routes.

Köthen allows him the faintest motion, more shrug than nod. "What soldier wouldn't? Though I'd prefer to be defending it rather than taking it."

"Of course, and when you do get inside, it's close quarters for a fight. Hand-to-hand all the way. Which is why . . ." Cauldwell eyes the long sword sheathed across the shorter man's back. "You any good with that thing?"

N'Doch steps between them, planting a palm against the baron's chest. A short time ago, he wouldn't have dared to do this. Now it's Cauldwell he's worried about. "He is, chief. You can take it from me."

But Cauldwell knew that. He smiles his challenge. "Ready to use it?"

Köthen's glance flicks back to the feed from the Citadel. "Never a better time . . . "

"That's what I was thinking."

"Hey, wait a minute . . ." N'Doch recognizes complicity when he hears it, and it's caught him completely by surprise. He'd never have figured the rough medieval fighting man and the sleek high-tech warrior for such instant allies. Suddenly something about it worries him. "I mean, hold on . . . !"

Cauldwell ignores him. "I've got people inside, good ones, in computer contact. But I have to pull them before the Beast returns, or they're char and cinder, every one of them. The sooner we move . . ."

Köthen nods, though N'Doch knows for a fact that he'd never heard of a computer until yesterday. "The dragons could take us. Paia could show them the way, isn't that right, Dochmann?"

"Er . . . yeah."

Cauldwell blinks. "All of us?"

"I don't know. If they were horses, I could tell you their carrying capacity to the ounce." He offers up one of his rare grins, rueful and charming. "We'll just have to ask them."

"Like you said, there'll never be a better moment."

"What, now? *Now?*" N'Doch's sharp exhalation gets everyone's attention. Even Gerrasch, intent at the console, glances up. "You can't do this now! We've got relatives and friends to take care of first!" He glares from one to the other. "Dolph! Whadda you thinking?"

Köthen gazes back with that look of his that's so much like a shrug.

"I also have friends and relatives to rescue," Cauldwell jabs a stern finger at the screen. "In there. Men and women who've risked their lives to overthrow the Beast."

"But . . ." N'Doch rubs his eyes. "Aww, shit!"

"It does not require an army to deliver a warning or

conduct a spot rescue," Köthen observes. "And the sooner you're about it, the better."

"Me? What about you?"

Köthen looks away, as if to check on the latest events on the wall screen. When he looks back, he says nothing, knowing he doesn't have to.

"C'mon, Dolph! Don't desert me, man! I need your help!"

"We all do!" exclaims a voice from behind. "My lord baron, you can't possibly mean to . . ."

"My lady."

Erde pushes through the crowd to face him. "Surely you will come with us to save Deep Moor! Rose and the others—they're in terrible danger!"

N'Doch doesn't blame Köthen for avoiding Erde's eyes. Her pleading desperation would melt stones. Most stones, maybe. Not this one.

"My place is here. My *duty* is here."

He says it to N'Doch, but really, he's telling her, with an arch touch of vengefulness that N'Doch can't really admire. And the girl is so appalled, she forgets to temper her pre-emptory tone. N'Doch hears a fight brewing.

"Our duty is where the dragons lead us!"

"Who are you to tell me where my duty lies?"

N'Doch watches Cauldwell kick back and let it happen, like he already knows which way it's gonna go. But N'Doch can't keep his own stupid mouth from dragging him into the middle. "You brought him, girl. You lectured him all about dragons and destiny. I guess you gotta live with the consequences."

"But Deep Moor is in danger! Your sword is needed, my lord!"

"So you said when you hauled me away from Deep Moor. Now you wish to haul me back again?" Köthen rounds on her, and the flare in his dark eyes isn't warm or pleasant. "What should I care for Deep Moor? Have you forgotten, my lady? Deep Moor was to be my silk-lined cell."

"Only to keep you alive, my lord!"

"Alive for what? To win a crown for another?"

"For the rightful prince, my lord baron!" She looks en-tirely bewildered, like she can't believe she has to explain such obviousness to a man of honor such as himself. Their raised voices have carried over the noise in the rest of the room. Luther and Stoksie wander over, ever so casually.

"If he's rightful, then let him have it!" Köthen flings up an angry fist, then collects himself. "You said yourself, my lady, that I might discover my destiny here, and so I have. It isn't the one you had planned for me, apparently, but isn't that just the way with destinies? They control us rather than the other way around?"

"But my lord . . . *Deep Moor!* All our friends . . . !"

"Go warn Hal Engle. He'll see to Deep Moor and his witch-lady. He doesn't need me. He's made that abundantly clear."

N'Doch at last takes pity on the girl's stunned disbelief. "My guess is he'll think different about that, Dolph, when Fire shows up on his doorstep."

Köthen shrugs. "What's done is done."

"Not really. It may feel like we're a thousand years from Deep Moor, but remember, Time's gone all elastic on us, Dolph."

Cauldwell clears his throat. "Listen, if the man wants to fight for us, I could sure use him. What does it matter if he's here or there? We're all working toward the same end, right? The defeat of the Beast."

Luther and Stoksie murmur their agreement.

Then other murmurs rise around them, and die into sudden silence.

"Yes, but . . . !" Erde's last syllable rings loudly, alone.

The room has turned hot with reflected yellow glare. Astonished faces stare past N'Doch to the screen behind him, lit to molten gold by the surreal glow. N'Doch knows that glow, like he knows his hands, or the sound of his own voice. He turns slowly, afraid of what he's going to see.

It's what he's expected. Sun. Sand. Bright-painted fishing boats. Palm trees.

Home.

It's like the wall's been blown away without a scrap left, and what's outside is not a mountain's worth of rock, but . . . the beach. Outside the seaside African town that N'Doch always thought he'd grow old and die in . . . until he met a certain dragon.

Without thinking, he steps toward the screen.

Köthen grabs his arm. "Dochmann, no."

"Lemme go, Dolph."

He can feel the heat shimmering off the glistening white sand. Just past the bright curve of that hull, he knows, is a path through the palm grove to the town gates and the market. Köthen's hard fingers bruise his flesh as he struggles to free himself. "What's it to you? You don't wanna go, fine, but I gotta! I can go now, and warn them!"

"No. It is not real, Dochmann, remember? It's a wall, and moving pictures. You told me that, remember?"

"I can smell the damn salt! Can't you? And the fish? Can't you smell it, Dolph?" What N'Doch remembers is what Paia said, in the Meld when only the dragon guides could hear. When the wall turned up a full-screen image of Deep Moor, so real-looking you were sure you could walk right into it, she said, Well, *you could.*

It's a portal, she said. *A doorway.* Her own dragon had told her so. Why believe anything out of the slimy renegade's lying mouth? Because of the heat and the smell: the drying seaweed and the pungent smoke blowing off the kebob vendors' carts. And because of the sounds: the roll and break of the surf, and the tinny distant music from the market stalls.

"Off me, Dolph! Lemme go!" N'Doch tries a quick, breaking twist, unsuccessfully. Köthen is shorter than he is, but stronger and just as fast. "Look, this'll fix our transport problem! No dragons needed. I'm there!" He swings himself a few steps closer to the screen. "Dolph, they're sitting ducks! Please! Lemme go!" Another jerk and twist, another step closer.

Now Paia's hanging on his other side like her life depended on it. "It could be a trap! It's just the sort of thing he'd do!"

Köthen is talking and Paia is talking, and Erde's throwing her two cents in. N'Doch doesn't listen. He's so . . . *drawn.* It's . . . home, right in front of him. Only has to step through. He'll just be there, he knows it. Check up on his mama and Papa Dja, get them into hiding, then the dragons could pick him up on their way back from Deep Moor. He's got it all worked out. Save everyone a lot of trouble and debate if he just did it. . . .

Now.

N'Doch feints with his body. With his mind, he calls the dragon upstairs.

I'm taking a little shortcut, kiddo. Come get me when you're ready.

DO NOT . . . !

Too late. N'Doch leans hard into his feint, then shifts his weight and—a miracle—throws Köthen off-balance, not enough to break his grip but enough to be able to pivot toward him fast and slam in with a full body block. The baron staggers, his soldier's fists still welded to N'Doch's wrist and elbow. N'Doch pivots again and flings Köthen away from the screen. The force shoves Paia through it . . . and drags him after.

The passage is instantaneous. From dim cool to searing glare in the span of a heartbeat. The bright shock of the heat and the sudden grainy softness beneath them startles Paia into letting go. Both tumble headlong into hot, white sand and lie gasping for the briefest of seconds.

N'Doch looks up, and groans.

Why is it things never work out like he's intended? There's the High Priestess sprawled on the beach beside him, two hundred years away from the man who would do anything to keep her safe. No sign anywhere of a return portal. Just sand, palm trees, and hot, hot ocean. N'Doch's eyes squeeze shut. All he can think of is how many pieces Köthen is going to cut him into when the dragons arrive to rescue them.

CHAPTER THREE

Wide-eyed, Erde watches N'Doch flail, stumble into searing white light, then collapse in a heap in the powdery sand with the High Priestess on top of him. Her gasp is half giggle, for they do look comical, that is, until the hot beach vanishes, she's back in the darkened room, staring at a bright blue wall, and N'Doch and Paia are gone.

Erde shudders, her foolish half grin frozen. For between the brightness and the blue, for an instant so brief she almost doubts her senses, she'd glimpsed something else. She'd seen Deep Moor in flames.

"What . . . what happened?" Leif Cauldwell looks to Gerrasch. "Where'd they go?"

The Librarian rises in horror. Has he seen it, too? "There. Are. No!"

Erde blinks away the fiery afterimage and tries not to panic. "To Africa. It's N'Doch's home." She alerts the dragons. But they know already.

What do we do?

GO AFTER THEM, OF COURSE.

To Africa? Now? But I saw Deep Moor burning!

OVERANXIOUS IMAGININGS, GIRL.

IT'S FIRE'S AFTERMATH.

How can you be sure?

Cauldwell stares at the wall of blue. "You can get them back again, right?"

"Noo, noo . . ." Gerrasch is tapping, tapping at his rows of little square buttons, making soft sounds of animal distress.

HELP THE LIBRARIAN. LEND HIM YOUR VOICE.

The dragons are right, as usual, even Lady Water, always less patient with youthful folly. Erde hurries to Gerrasch's side. She must not give in to her terrors. "I think . . . it's not like a door. He can't open this portal when he wants to. It has its own . . . magic." She hesitates at the word. Notions of magic are scoffed at in this future world, despite the obvious presence of dragons. But how else to describe her intuition about the portal, without N'Doch here to help with his knowledge of what he calls "technology?"

"Can't open it?" Cauldwell repeats. "Well, that's a problem."

Baron Köthen stares tight-lipped at the empty blue expanse. "He did it on purpose."

"No, my lord, he . . ." Erde turns to him, wary of his hot temper, now that his lady has been stolen from him.

"He did! The young whelp!"

"He didn't mean to take Paia," asserts Cauldwell's wife reasonably. "Why would he?"

Erde is surprised by Constanze's innocence. Surely it's an obvious possibility that N'Doch abducted the High Priestess in order to entice Köthen away from Leif Cauldwell's military preoccupations. Now the baron will have to require the dragon to take him to his lady right away, as any devoted knight would do.

But Köthen makes no such demand. He stands with his arms folded and his brows drawn down in an inward stare. A conflict of interest, no doubt. He feels honor bound, Erde decides, having already promised his sword to Cauldwell's rebellion. If so, then Cauldwell must release him, and surely will quickly volunteer to do so.

Again, she is confounded. Both Cauldwells wait silently, observing Köthen's inner debate.

"Is Paia in any danger there?" asks Constanze at last.

"Of course!" Erde cries. "Of course she is!"

Köthen sends the Cauldwells an even glance. "No more so than here."

"Not true, my lord! It's beastly hot there, and the air is full of poison!"

"And so it is here."

"But there are guns everywhere! N'Doch was killed with guns, until the dragon healed him!"

"Healed?" Cauldwell asks Köthen.

"It's true," admits Köthen, "or so the lad tells me. I wasn't there."

"Huh. Never heard of Fire doing anything like that."

Constanze murmurs, "He'd rather destroy people than save them."

"Healing is Lord Earth's special gift!" Erde declares, though she knows that pride is a sin and that Cauldwell's interest is only in the military value of such an asset.

"My lady Erde." Köthen looses his arms as if breaking an invisible bond and bows so formally, she suspects him of mockery. "I would be eternally grateful if you and your esteemed dragon would effect a rescue at your earliest possible convenience. The whelp will keep my lady safe until you get there. He knows I'll have his liver for breakfast if he doesn't."

Cauldwell nods, and his wife relaxes against him in relief. Constanze is brown-skinned and eagle-eyed. She reminds Erde of the women of Deep Moor, and of her dead grandmother, the Baroness. Women of power. She'll not relent.

Erde gazes imploringly at the trio of Tinkers. "Help me convince him!"

"Dockman'll do it jus' gud, nah," Stoksie soothes. "Yu'll see."

Ysabel nods, and Luther merely shrugs. There is sympathy in his dark face, but no voice on her side. The crisis here and now is more real to these people than a crisis somewhere so far away, and Erde can hardly blame them. But the image of burning Deep Moor still flares in her mind's eye. Was it only, as Lady Water said, her fearful imaginings? Or was it a true Seeing? She looks to Gerrasch. His eyes are dark and round, and fixed on her as if he has shared her awful vision.

"Yes. Go. Quickly! Come back!"

"What? Must I go alone?"

The flames burn so fiercely in her head, and among them move the shadows of men and horses. Swords flash. She sees . . .

The hell-priest! Oh, dragon!

"You'll have the dragons, after all." Köthen puts out a hand to steady her. "Could you be better armed?"

Terror and outrage push Erde toward the edge of a tantrum, which only frightens her further. She's never been given to tantrums. Of course they are right to send off the least valuable fighter. Doubtless her real, her innermost reason for demanding Köthen's company is that she can't bear to part with him. Every day, for the two weeks since she dragged him unwilling into the dragons' Quest, she has been able to think of him as part of her life. His stern grace and beauty have been the chief pleasure of her days—except, of course, for the dragon. She even thrust her own feelings aside when the arrival of the High Priestess woke Köthen from his gloom, for Passion is one of the High Ideals, and Erde can recognize—and must honor—a True Passion when she sees it, even though she is not its object.

But here is Baron Köthen refusing to bow to the Ideal and let it rule him, as a True Knight should. She should not love him. And yet, she does. Nor should she waste another moment arguing. And yet, she does. Because to allow his willfulness to go unchallenged means forsaking her own Ideals.

"Adolphus Michael Hoffman," she hears herself declaiming. "Thou art not a man of honor, to leave thy lady thus endangered!"

Ah! She's touched him. He looks quite taken aback. But only long enough to study her with that dark gaze, so surprising beneath his shock of blond hair. She seems to have done something he approves of, though she can't understand what or how. Despite the faint, satirical gleam in his eyes, Erde blunders onward. "Nor is it worthy of a True Knight to send a lady unchaperoned into the wilderness!"

"Two dragons are not chaperone enough? Then we'll find a knight more honorable than I to guard your journey." Köthen lifts his head, unable any longer to subdue his ironical grin, and scans the faces crowded around. "Who's for a quest on dragon-back?"

Erde is stunned speechless. This is mockery for certain! Is the dragons' sacred Purpose mere child's play in his mind, and only war the work of adults?

A portentous silence gathers around her, but for the shuffling of feet on the hard, smooth floor. In the back, murmuring. Someone clears her throat. Then Luther Williams steps forward.

"I, fer one." He turns to Cauldwell. "S'all ri', Leif?"

Cauldwell nods, surprised. "Good choice. What d'you think, Gerrasch?"

"Yes. Yes. Go."

"Are you armed?" Köthen asks him.

Luther pats the large knife shoved into his waistband.

It's like being put up for auction. Erde cannot believe how badly her efforts have turned out. But she must get to Deep Moor somehow, and it will be good to have Luther along. The Tinkers are extremely resourceful, and Luther is a man of piety and principle. "Thank you, Luther! Will you really come?"

"Betcha!"

With that, the matter is settled. Baron Köthen turns away to talk strategy with the Cauldwells. Gerrasch bends over his keypad, the chatty disembodied voice of the machine called House nattering in his ear. The wall again fills with ranks of moving pictures from the Citadel. For a moment, Erde could almost weep from loneliness, so she calls to the only being whose love she is sure of.

Oh, dragon! I am so weary!

YOU NEED FOOD AND REST, CHILD.

And when shall I find them?

SOON.

But not yet.

FOOD, PERHAPS. BUT NOT REST. NOT YET. NO REST FOR ANY OF US UNTIL OUR SISTER AIR IS FOUND AND LIBERATED. ASK LUTHER IF FOOD CAN BE SPARED FOR OUR JOURNEY.

And you, dear dragon? How long since you've eaten?

TOO LONG. THE LAND HERE IS BARREN. NOTHING LIVING BUT HUMANS AND THE TAME CREATURES LEFT TO THEM.

Lady Water chimes in impatiently. I'LL TAKE YOU FISHING WHEN WE GET THERE!

Erde hopes the dragon can wait just a little while longer. For time is of the essence and since everyone is so sure that N'Doch can handle his situation, she plans to head to Deep Moor first. She can warn the women about Lord Fire's threats, and tell them of her vision of flames. They will understand. Then she can rush back to N'Doch's time with a clear conscience. It's a good plan. But to forestall further argument, she'll not inform the other humans of this minor alteration.

While the warriors gather to plan the assault on the Citadel, Erde draws Luther aside, fingering his thin shirt and woven string vest. "You'll need some warmer clothing when we get to Deep Moor. Would N'Doch's fit you? I think his pack is put away somewhere in your wagon."

Stoksie has tagged along to help them prepare. "I know weah dat is."

Luther says, "Cold deah, izzit? Mebbe snow, eben?"

"Snow, for sure."

"Snow. Dat I wanna see." Luther elbows the smaller man. "Yu wanna make da trip, Stokes?"

"Nah. My daddy saw't, wontime. Leas' das what he sed. But den, he sed a lotta t'ings." Stoksie grins and trots off to find N'Doch's pack.

Erde worries that these cheerful men have no real idea of the frigid dangers of true winter. Heat and drought are their only reference points. "I'm sure you have never been as cold as you will be in Deep Moor," she tells Luther earnestly.

But Luther is sweating by the time he's tried on as many layers of N'Doch's heavy clothing as will fit him. Erde shakes out her own woolens and slides her feet into her sheepskin boots. They make her feel safer, like putting on armor, or some sort of shell, though she's no longer ashamed to be seen in the scant, loose clothing that's the only sensible thing in this desiccated future. She's gotten used to being so aware of her body—and of everyone else's—all the time. For the sake of her little deception, she lets Stoksie fold all the clothing away again in N'Doch's pack. She will carry it, and Luther will shoulder the sturdy sack of food Stoksie has thrown together while up in the caverns. Blind Rachel provisions, she's sure, and gladly given, from wagons recently restocked from the sale of Erde's dragon brooch, which also purchased the fine and venerable sword that Baron Köthen wears across his back.

Does she now regret that sacrifice? She doesn't think so. Despite her failure to make events turn out the way she wanted, Erde von Alte retains her belief that what is meant to happen, will happen. Destiny is too essential a force to be turned aside by one man's stubborn perversity, or for that matter, by the stubborn scheming of a perverse dragon.

As if aware of her thoughts, Köthen glances up from his huddle with the Cauldwells. "Don't be long."

She looks for a trace of gloating or victory or whatever she imagines a man might feel. But all that is gone now. She sees only dispassionate concern, that of a commander sending his man off on a mission.

"What?" he demands, for she is staring back at him intently.

Erde blinks, looks away. How can she explain what she's just understood? How can she admit to it? She's interpreted all of Köthen's actions as meant specifically to thwart her personally, to make her miserable—revenge for having been brought away against his will. Now, as a larger vision opens up to her, she sees the entire folly of this assumption. Certainly he is not above rubbing a bit of salt into her wounds, but she is not his target. She's hardly within range of his aim at all. And if she catches an arrow, it's because he sees no need to be careful. Like a leaf to the sun, he turns toward what he knows best, what he's trained to do, what makes him feel worthy. And that is to get things moving, men and things, to maximize the use of slim resources, both personal and physical, in order to accomplish the task at hand. Whatever the task might be. Even though the dragons' Quest is not his own, and despite a foolish girl often putting herself in his way.

No. Not child's play. Not child's play at all. Rather, he's assigned her the danger she is best equipped to cope with and live through. A blush warms Erde's cheeks. Had she really thought that leadership only meant waving a sword about more skillfully than anyone else?

"What is it, girl?" Köthen asks, more forcefully.

Erde stares down at her sandaled feet. "I'm sorry. So very sorry."

"Pardon?" He takes a step toward her. "I don't think I heard you correctly."

"I said, I'm sorry, my lord."

"For what?"

"For all the trouble I've caused you."

"An apology?" He's actually at a loss for words. He glances back at the intent faces around Gerrasch's swiftly

moving fingers. The glow from the many rows of little buttons lights his profile, and Erde's heart turns over yet again.
She can't say which part of his face is most beautiful to
her, or why, but she knows she could stare at him forever,
and be happy. She cannot deny the truth of the sigh that
wells up, as if from the very bottom of her soul.

When Köthen's gaze returns, it is milder than she's ever
seen it. He grips her shoulder to shake it lightly. "On your
way, then. Grab up my lady Paia and that kidnapping
young whelp, then do what you can for the witchy women
on your way back. Be quick about it!"

"Aye, my lord."

"Luther!"

"Yeah!" The Tinker hefts the heavy sack.

"Bring them back safe!"

"Betcha!"

Erde readies the image of Deep Moor in her mind.
WE ARE GOING TO . . . ?

*Yes, Dragon. To Deep Moor first. Fearful imaginings or
not, it seems only right. Will Lady Water agree?*

IF WE DO IT QUICKLY, I'LL AGREE TO
ANYTHING.

Erde grasps Luther's arm. "Hang on tight!"

CHAPTER FOUR

When it's clear she's off-balance and falling, Paia gives in and lets the momentum take her. The instant the sun-bright image came up on the screen, she'd known what it was. The portal had opened again. So she is not surprised to find herself thrown flat on burning sand with the breath knocked out of her. Nor is she surprised to find the tall young African's limbs entangled with her own. Serves her good and right. She shouldn't have hung onto him. She looks for the soldier, but sees he's been left behind. When panic wells up, she fights it down easily enough. He'll be worried about her, but maybe it's all right to be without him for a while. A good thing, to be on her own. For the first time ever. In her life.

Catching her breath, Paia contemplates this sudden urge toward solitude. The air is heavy, as if it would take less of it than usual to fill up her lungs. It leaves the oddest taste of salt on her tongue. She's aware of a certain inner numbness. Her brain is a slow-turning maelstrom. Better just to concentrate on what to do for the next few seconds. Like, get out of the sun and the punishing heat. Then she sees the ocean, and the parts of her scattered self draw together. She scrambles to her knees like a worshiper at the altar.

"Steady, now," wheezes the young man, though he hardly sounds steady himself. He frees his leg and arms and edges away, then gets up to scan the beach warily.

"The water! Ah! It's so . . . beautiful!" Blue from side to side. Water as wide as the sky. The hot light dancing off a billion shifting surfaces. She's seen the ocean on computer screens, more of it than she's seen dry land. But the reality is overwhelming. It's awe-inspiring. It's so animated, so very . . . wet. The rolling of the surf is hypnotic. Paia has only known still water, like the Sacred Pool in the Citadel. Immediately, she wants to paint it, to try to capture that dance of reflected light, to work with all those colors she's never had use for before. "Are we in . . . ?"

N'Doch nods as if he had something to be ashamed of. "My place."

The western coast of Africa, then, in the year 2013. Half a day ago, she and N'Doch were total strangers. But they have been in the Meld together, and know everything there is to know about each other. By contrast, she knows almost nothing about the soldier, Adolphus of Köthen, except that they are fated together. But this sharing of minds, what a gift and privilege! Paia recalls that N'Doch at first felt invaded by his fellow dragon guides, but at least he's come around enough not to resist entirely. A sense of the merging still lingers, like an intimate scent. Intimate enough to be compromising, but N'Doch won't take advantage, even if he'd welcome the chance. It's too much like incest. Even better, he doesn't believe in running other people's lives—unlike most of the men she's met. Paia smiles up at him. He's as beautiful in his own way as the soldier is. It would be comforting just to flirt a little, as she used to with Luco, in the security of knowing nothing would come of it. But she senses it would upset this young man, at least until they know each other better. Delicately, she offers him a hand, asking to be helped to her feet.

He looks away, frowning. "He's gonna kill me, y'know. Just absolutely murder me."

Paia laughs, picturing the soldier's handsome, rough-hewn glower. Like a rock at sunset. A bright block of un-polished marble. The memory of his beauty distracts her momentarily. "I won't let him. I promise."

"Easy for you to say."

He's watching her like she's a bomb primed to go off. Waiting for the weeping and panic. But Paia's had enough of all that. For now, she prefers her numbness. It allows her to get on with things. She rises on her own, brushing sand from her long white shirt and soft pants. The open beach is as hot as a griddle. She's sweating already, and knows she must look a sight. In the Temple, looking ugly and concealing her body was her idea of rebellion. Now she's glad for the protection of long sleeves and pant legs. The sunlight may be as lethal here in 2013 as it is in her own time. Paia doesn't recall her history lessons all that well. What's the point of history when you know the world is ending? Besides, whenever she wanted actual information, she could always ask House. But House is two hundred years away. Ignorance, she realizes, can be a dangerous liability.

Farther along the beach, she sees an unimaginable thing: children running about naked, their dark little bodies as shiny as wet stones.

"Look!" she cries.

"Shhh! What? Keep it down!" N'Doch's eyes dart about. "Oh. That's just kids. Nothing to be worried about."

"But they're out in the sun! What are their mothers thinking?"

"That they might get a moment's rest if their kids have something to keep them busy." He shades his brow to study a group of colorful boats beached a short distance away. "Don't see anything that looks like a return portal, do you? How does this thing work?"

"I don't know. The God . . . I'm sorry, I mean, Fire. He never said. But the other dragons will know where we are, won't they?"

"More or less. And they're not going to be too happy with me either." He probes the sand with his toe, unearthing a mean-looking scrap of metal. "You're taking this very calmly."

"Shouldn't I be?" Paia wants to smile, but that seems to make him suspicious, like he's afraid he'll start smiling back. Will he understand if she tells him she's not feeling much of anything right now?

He's scanning the beach again. "Not the safest spot in the world."

At least there's no golden dragon spitting his fire and venom in your eyes. At least, not yet. "After this morning, nothing could scare me."

"Gotcha." His grin flicks past her like a shard of light reflected off seawater. "And just let me say, girl, you were awesome!"

I did what I had to do, Paia thinks. So why don't I feel better about it?

She realizes she's waiting for him, for the God, as she always has when he's not around. Waiting for him to appear in a wreath of flame to mock and upbraid and flatter and pamper her. How will she learn to live without him? She must root out every lingering shred of devotion and desire, and let only her fear and hatred of him flourish.

She calls up the soldier's face to banish the God's forbidden image. She studies the slender, swaying trees that raise a tall gray wall across the top of the beach. Palm trees, a memory suggests. Paia would have expected them to be greener. She imagines touching their stiff fronds into the landscape with the edge of her palette knife.

Beside her, N'Doch straightens, listening. "Quick! This way!"

She looks up, instinctively searching for dragon shadow. But the sky is still empty and blue. Then she hears a low growling from behind the palms. "What's that?"

He grabs her arm. "Cover first, questions later!" He pulls her across the superheated sand toward the beached flotilla. The boats looked like painted toys from a distance, but as N'Doch hauls her into the shadow of the nearest one, its bright prow towers over them in a rising curve, its mast at a crazy tilt.

"Hunh. That's strange." N'Doch runs a palm along the planking. Paint falls away like peeling bark. "Doesn't look like she's been out in a while." His hand snags in a rough spot, then another and another. The tip of his finger disappears into the scarred wood. "Aw, no wonder! Bullet holes."

Paia's nose wrinkles. "What's that awful smell?"

"Fish. That's fish, girl. You never smelled dead fish in your life?"

"Where would I find a fish in the Citadel?"

"Damn, woman, you need to get out more!"

The growling sound is louder. Nearing, Paia realizes, and rapidly. N'Doch draws her around the pointed end of the boat, putting a stinking pile of crates between them and the noise. Paia needs no urging to hunker down behind the smelly barricade. She knows what that sound is. Engines.

She hasn't heard engines since she was a child. They were a rare event, and usually they brought bad news.

"Jeeps," N'Doch mutters.

"Who is it?"

"No one we'll want to know, you can bet on that."

He ducks behind the curve of the boat as four dusty green vehicles roar through a gap between the palm trunks and out onto the beach. They fling up long arcs of sand as they turn and speed down the beach, swerving left and right, horns blaring. Paia hears a popping sound, like gunfire. The children scatter, screaming. Raucous male laughter echoes up the beach, over the boom and whine of the motors.

"Muthafuckahs." N'Doch slides a hand down the long knife sheath on his belt. "Let's get out of here. Now's when we'll wish we had the dragons with us. Step where I step, and don't you linger! Watch out for the shit in the sand."

Paia wonders if the danger in the sand is living or dead. She scoots after him along the line of boats, from hull shadow to hull shadow, away from the mayhem down the beach. Using the crates and the few ragged shacks as cover, N'Doch heads for the tree line. Shards of rusting metal and sun-bleached plastic are scattered everywhere. The beach might as well be mined with knife blades.

"Where did all this come from?" Paia asks.

"Folks just leave things where they fall. The Tinker crews could live for a year off this beach!" Hardly slowing, he stoops to snatch a rusted metal rod out of the sand.

"What's that?"

"A perfectly good tire iron."

"Is it a weapon?" She sees how neatly it fits into his fist.

"It is now." He glances up as they near the line of palms. "Man, these trees have seen better days. Guess I wasn't looking, last time I was out here."

Most of the palm leaves are stiff and brown, the source of the dry rattling that Paia has heard under the roar of the engines and the roll of the surf. Dead fronds lie in spiky heaps at the base of the trees.

Another burst of gunfire erupts down the beach.

"C'mon, keep moving! We're almost there." N'Doch hurries her forward, shoving her into the speckled shade between the slim, curved trunks just as the jeeps wheel around and head back toward the boats. Three of them race side by side, jostling each other with a great revving of engines and the squeal of bruised metal. "Don't let 'em see you!"

Pressed behind a palm trunk, Paia asks, "Why are they doing that?"

"Because they can." He's gripping the tire iron like a club.

His bitter tone makes Paia stare curiously after the careening vehicles as they smash heedlessly through a stack of crates. "They must be very rich. I mean, to be able to waste fuel and vehicles so recklessly."

"And it's your kids and mine who'll pay for it, girl!" N'Doch's dark face relaxes into momentary confusion. "Well, I mean, mine already have. If I even had any. If I ever had the time." He waves the tire iron irritably. "Never mind. Let's go find Fâtime."

"Who?"

"My mother."

He strides off through the palm trunks, heading inland. Within five minutes of struggling to keep up, Paia is winded. She feels awkward, running full tilt. Arms and legs all over the place. The hot grit in her sandals rasps painfully against her soft indoor soles.

"N'Doch! Please! I can't . . . !"

Startled, he glances back, then stops to wait. In his haste, he's almost forgotten her. "Sorry. If there was any place safe, I'd leave you there."

"No!"

"I mean, to rest, while I find Fâtime."

"I'll be okay," she gasps. "Just please don't leave me."

He grins sourly. "You're in luck. I can't."

Paia slumps against a palm trunk. She doesn't want to be a burden to him. But being High Priestess of the Temple of the Apocalypse did not involve a lot of physical labor. She's had a life of being merely decorative, at least since the God . . . no, she must, must call him Fire . . . since Fire arrived at the Citadel. Before that, she was her father's protected little girl.

She tries a rueful sort of smile. "I'm out of shape, I'm afraid. But if Fire is here, I'm your best chance of dealing with him."

"Your shape looks just fine to me." N'Doch grins down at her, then looks away sheepishly. "Sorry again. It's habit. Don't mean anything by it, y'know. He'd have my head if he heard me."

He. The soldier. For a moment, she was sure he meant Fire. "Does it matter so much to you what he thinks?"

"Well, yeah. I guess it does. He's the dude, y'know?" He chews his lip, considering, then suddenly he's off again through the trees.

Paia pushes herself harder, breathing more deeply, imitating N'Doch's steady stride. It's easier now that they're not slogging through deep sand. She studies his lean, muscular frame moving ahead of her. What would it take to acquire his strength and endurance? Paia envisions her soft curves bulked up with muscle. She rather likes the idea. Certainly, being so very decorative gives her a kind of power. But it's mostly the power to manipulate others—men, of course, but not only—into doing things for you. Paia would like to be able to do things for herself. Like the girl Erde—still a young teenager, yet so confident in her role as dragon guide, so totally in tune with her dragon. Paia wishes she had so clear a view of life. She wishes for a truer dragon.

Musing distractedly with her body on autopilot, Paia slams smack into N'Doch's back. He's halted, with the tire iron at the ready. They've jogged into the middle of a village without even noticing. Or perhaps it's more of an encampment. People are milling about, aimless and slow, as if exhausted. Smoke rises among them in pale columns like ephemeral palm trunks. Ragged blankets are spread on the ground and tied between trees. Small piles of possessions are strewn here and there, but Paia sees little in the way of shelter. The people are ebony-skinned, like N'Doch. Her own café-au-lait looks pale by comparison. She hears babies crying, and a murmur of argument and desperation and other kinds of prayer. Somewhere among the palms and hanging blankets, a woman is wailing. Long thin exhalations of grief.

Paia shivers. "What's happened here?"

N'Doch shakes his head. "Things are . . ."

"Are what?"

"Don't know . . . I mean, this is the *bidonville*. It's always been here, but it's . . . different than it was. Stick close. I mean it, okay?"

He waits until she nods her agreement. When he starts forward, she hooks a finger through one of his belt loops, so that she can peer around without losing him.

She sees mostly women and children. And old people. As they move into the settlement, makeshift tents appear, and lean-tos cobbled together out of scrap wood, rusted sheet metal, and corrugated plastic. There's sickness everywhere, and lassitude and injury. Moaning bodies sprawl in the shade with no one to tend to them. The children are dull-eyed and malnourished. An old man with no legs is propped up against a nearby palm trunk. He spies Paia, and stretches out a stick-thin hand. His scabbed lips mouth unintelligible beseechings.

When N'Doch elbows her along, Paia realizes she's been caught by the old man's desperate gaze. Her memory, stirred by horror and disgust, again offers up a reference. During the collapse that isolated her family fortress, the Citadel's communications links provided news, more news than anyone could want, except her father, who watched the global video feed compulsively, obsessively, in those final days. In addition to storm devastation and killing grounds, there were all those awful refugee camps, crowded with starved, exhausted populations forced to flee the rising oceans, the waves of plague, the tides of war.

Is this the beginning, or is the collapse already at full throttle?

Paia notes the change in N'Doch's body language. Wary but confident before, he has lost his bravado. His eyes flick about restlessly as he walks. She wonders if he's taken a wrong turn.

"I don't get it," he mutters.

"What? Tell me." His unease is contagious.

"It wasn't like this . . . before. It wasn't this bad."

"This is the same . . . the right place?"

"Oh, yeah, I know exactly where I am. I grew up here." He veers slightly left, avoiding a cluster of children fighting over the unidentifiable contents of a bloodied sack. One of them looks up, and Paia recoils at the feral greed in its stare. N'Doch adjust his grip on the tire iron. "See? Here's the road into town."

The road is a potholed swath of dry red dirt that swirls up with the hot gusts off the beach and sticks at the back of the throat like a thousand tiny pinpricks. Like the dust off the plateau behind the Citadel. For the first time since falling through the portal, Paia feels uncomfortably right at home. This dry landscape is one she would know exactly how to paint, but the familiarity is unwelcome. Ahead, the palm trunks thin out onto a flat orange plain, the hard blue sky like a painted ceiling. The red road disappears into heat shimmer, where low rectangles dance in and out of visibility and a wide, dark smudge rises above the bright horizon.

N'Doch shades his eyes from the glare, squinting into the mirage. A strangled moan escapes him. Without warning, he takes off at a dead run.

"N'Doch!" Paia bolts after him. A vision of wandering alone in a strange time, strange place lends her speed, but she cannot catch up. She's forced to halt in the middle of the road and holler like a lost child. N'Doch turns, his arms beating a mad rhythm of frustration. He'd like to lose her. It's as plain as if he's said it out loud. But the image of the murderous soldier must linger in his mind, for he races back, grabs her hand without a word, and drags her stumbling behind him.

The mirage steadies as they approach, into the shapes and structures of a town. The red road passes through a formal opening in the stout stucco walls, but the tall metal gates hang twisted away to either side and the walls have been breached in several places by something large enough to crush stone. Columns of smoke rise from the taller buildings. People are climbing through the ragged gaps and streaming out between the gates, limping, coughing, weeping, with their possessions stuffed into whatever was handy, or strapped to their backs. The broken walls echo with shouts and sporadic gunfire. The town is in ruins.

Before the bent gates, the road is choked with refugees and rubble. N'Doch grips Paia's elbow and uses his body as a ram to shove them both upstream through the milling and confusion. He breaks the tightest clots with a threatening gesture of his tire iron.

Startled by a close-by burst of shooting, Paia shrinks against him. "Are we going in there?"

"Have to. That's where Fâtime is."

His cool determination is a surprise to her. He didn't seem like the implacable type. Paia has a thousand questions but asks him none of them. Her memory is hard at work again, this time assailing her with an image House showed her just before she left the Citadel. It was a live feed from a local farmstead that had been unable to pay its monthly tithe to the Temple. She saw a woman with her fist raised at the sky, tears of grief and outrage streaking her sooty cheeks. Behind, a landscape of smoking wreckage.

He's burning villages, House had said.

It's like a blow to the belly. Tears of a different sort of grief and outrage start in Paia's own eyes. She fears that she recognizes her dragon's signature.

"I have to find a way . . ." she mutters.

"What's that?" N'Doch glances back, notes her dampened face. "What's up? You crapping out on me?"

Paia reaches for the more resilient pose that will make him feel comfortable. "No, I just love strolling through a war zone when I know my dragon's responsible for all the mess."

"Don't say that."

"But I think it's true."

"Then that means he's been here before us."

With renewed vigor, N'Doch shoulders them to the edge of the throng and turns off the main thoroughfare, into a rubble-strewn side street where the crowd is thinner and no one pays them much attention. They're just one more empty-handed couple fleeing for their lives. "Of course, he's only encouraging the bad shit that was going on already."

"Or maybe he began it in the first place."

"What? The whole damn cycle of human violence? C'mon!"

"Why not?"

N'Doch slows at an intersection to scan the narrow crossing alleys. Smoke obscures the distance in both directions. Two young men race by with their arms full. An old woman shrieks curses from an archway. Three sweating men struggle to topple some kind of machinery onto a half-burned cart, blocking most of the street. N'Doch edges Paia past them.

"Looters," he snarls. "As if all this wasn't bad enough already."

"Why not?" asks Paia again, but so softly that only she hears the question. Why should N'Doch believe her? He doesn't know Fire like she does.

Several blocks farther, a wrecked van burns in the street. The driver is dead at the wheel. Another body lies half in, half out of an open door. Paia veers toward them in sympathy.

"No! There's nothing you can do!" N'Doch grabs her arm. Just past the van, two green jeeps are parked cross-ways in the road. Half a dozen armed men are stopping all passersby. Before N'Doch swerves aside, dragging her into the nearest alley, Paia sees a tall youth spread-eagled against a wall. The men are jabbing at him with the butts of their rifles. The youth looks a lot like N'Doch.

In the alley, shade brings some relief from the heat. Screams follow them as the buildings close in, and a racket of gunfire, ricocheting along bare, pockmarked walls of faded pink and orange. The barred windows are set high, out of reach. A rectangle of smoky bright light yawns ahead, an obstacle rather than a goal. At the edge of the narrow concealing darkness, N'Doch peers cautiously around the corner, then ducks back, pressing himself and Paia against the wall. A huge six-wheeled armored truck thunders past, grinding up clouds of dust and grit. Already breathless, Paia inhales enough to set her coughing convulsively. N'Doch is panting, too, but will not let her rest. When the vehicle roar fades, he leads her into the searing light.

A big square spreads to their right, lined with shuttered, ruined shops. All across the open space, wood and canvas canopies are collapsed and burning, stalls shattered or overthrown.

"This was the market."

It's the first local information N'Doch has offered. Paia guesses they are nearing his home territory. The devastation has become more personal to him. Bodies lie among the flames and ruins. It looks as if a fiery hurricane has descended without warning into a busy, crowded square. Just how it would look, Paia muses, if that hurricane was a fire-breathing dragon. Furtive shapes dart through the smoke, snatching up whatever's left to be scavenged.

N'Doch's luxurious mouth thins to a grim line. He scans the burned-out square but does not linger. "This way," he orders.

A soot-faced girl with an armload of charred electronics pushes off from the wall she's been lounging against, into their path. She suggests several things in seductive tones in a language Paia does not recognize.

N'Doch brandishes his tire iron. "Scram."

They see no one else but the dead for several blocks and several connecting shadowed alleyways. Just when this sector of town appears to be empty and N'Doch is moving ahead less cautiously, they nearly run into a second, sudden roadblock. More green jeeps, more men with assault rifles. N'Doch turns aside in the nick of time, sprints down a long passage barely wide enough to be called an alley, and they are out in the light again, carrying the reek of garbage on their clothing.

"Those bastards are sure looking for someone," N'Doch observes angrily.

"Maybe it's us."

He scowls at her over his shoulder. "Girl, you are paranoid. I did a lot of stuff I'm not so proud of a while back, but I was never Public Enemy Number One. Besides, how would anyone know we're . . . Oh. I see. The Fire dude."

Paia nods.

"But how would he get men mobilized so fast?"

"If he knew, somehow, that we'd be coming . . ."

"Phew," breathes N'Doch. "Now you're really scaring me."

They hurry past rows of small houses, squatter and more widely spaced than the buildings in the center of town. Tiny plots of tilled ground shelter the desiccated remains of kitchen gardens. There is less destruction here, and N'Doch is walking faster, muttering in hopeful distraction. On the other side of a building with its roof caved in, a row of cinder-block structures fronts an unpaved road. Windowless boxes with open doorways, hardly houses at all. A few look burned out, but all are still standing. At the far end of the row, a man slumps on a stoop with his head in his hands.

N'Doch makes eagerly for the fourth house down the line. Instinct holds Paia back as they reach the door. It's pitch-black inside, despite the white glare of the sun.

"Fâtime?" N'Doch eases into the darkness. "Ma? You there?"

Alone on the dirt street with the pop of distant gunfire, Paia's terror suddenly blossoms. Only the need to keep moving has kept it at bay. She's sure she hears a jeep approaching, or the tramp of running feet, or the swoop of giant wings. A dull metallic clatter echoes inside the house.

"N'Doch?" Paia backs into the doorway, tripping over the tire iron, which lies just inside the door. It's not as dark in the house as she's expected. A shaft of light from a high side window cuts across the interior. N'Doch stands in the middle of the room, backlit by the narrow dusty beam. He's gazing at a woman sitting in a chair against the opposite wall. His shadow obscures the woman's face but for a glimmer in her eyes. Paia wonders if the woman is weeping. She sees no damage anywhere in the room. A few battered pots and pans sit in logical places. An ancient television rests on a rickety metal table. So, it must be relief that sags N'Doch's shoulders, his whole slim straight back letting go into a slump.

But the only sound is the buzzing of insects and N'Doch's soft keening, not a sound of relief at all.

"N'Doch?" Paia goes to him quickly and takes his arm.

He turns his head away, out of the light, and the woman's face is lit instead. She's an older woman, with dark skin and graying hair, thin with starvation and fatigue. Her eyes are open, but Paia sees no tears, only a neat, dark hole in the center of her forehead. The wall behind her is crawling with flies.

"Ohhh." Paia leans into N'Doch's side. "Is it . . . ?"

"Yes."

After a moment, she says, "He did this, somehow. I'm sure of it."

"Yeah, probably. It sure was no accident." He eases out of Paia's grip. As deliberately as a sleepwalker, he crosses the room to close his mother's eyes. His fingers linger on her thin shoulder. "My fault, Ma. My fault."

"No," insists Paia. "No. How can you say that?"

"Because I was never there when she needed me before, and I wasn't there now."

She understands his muddled syntax. But must the child take care of the parent? This is a new concept for Paia. Were there things she could have been or done for her father that would have kept him from descending into drink and despair?

"What should we do?"

His sigh is more like a shudder. "Go find Papa Dja, ASAP."

"I mean, with the . . . with her?"

"Nothing much we can do. She's gone. No place nearby to bury her."

Paia imagines digging a grave as the bullets sing above their heads. If Fire keeps doing things like this, it will be easy to hate him.

"I mean, Papa Dja might still be okay. We gotta warn him if we can."

"So we just . . . leave her?"

"She's in her house. That's where she liked to be." N'Doch lifts his hands to his face and scrubs his forehead, then drags his palms hard along his cheeks. He paces away from his mother's body, then back to touch her shoulder again. "Hey, Ma. This is me leaving. Like always, hunh? Might not be smart to stick around here right now."

"I will know if he's approaching," Paia says quietly.

"Yeah, but will you know the hand that actually pulled the trigger?"

"Ah. Right." In dragon-form, Fire could neither have managed a gun nor fit inside this tiny house. And his man-form is an illusion born of manipulated energies. It can be whatever size or shape he wants, but an illusion cannot hold an actual gun or press an actual trigger. "Someone else was here with him."

"To do the deed. Yes. Had to be." N'Doch moves away from the body and around the room, picking things up and putting them down, as if taking inventory of his mother's scant possessions. He stares for a moment into a small, blackened pot. When he sets it aside, his eyes are full and moist.

"Someone from the Temple?" Paia can't really believe it. She says it mainly to distract him.

It works. "Can he do that? Haul people around, like Earth can?"

"I'm not sure. He'd always threaten that if I didn't behave, he'd fly me off to a foreign land and abandon me. But he never took me anywhere."

N'Doch stops short. He bends over abruptly. When he straightens again, each fist is grasping one end of the tire iron. "Baraga!"

"Who?" Paia whirls, certain that someone is in the doorway.

"That's it! Sonofabitch!" N'Doch slashes the air, right, left, right, left. "Fire doesn't need to bring anyone from anywhere. He's got his own big toady right here!" He takes another swipe at nothing, and another. "Just the sorta guy who can get his thug into a burning town to do the job, and get him out again. Damn! Sonofabitch!"

It would be easy and obvious for N'Doch to spend his grief trashing his mother's home. Paia is glad when he lowers the tire iron, and chooses not to.

Within the next heartbeat, the room fills with a rich blue radiance. The old-fashioned video set has flicked on of its own accord. N'Doch's fighting stance collapses. They both turn to stare into the sudden glow.

Paia shivers. It's like the aged monitor that appeared so suddenly in her studio, dust-caked and battered as if it had been there forever. It showed this same empty blue screen. Foolishly, she ventures, "House? Is that you?"

But there's no answering crawl of white letters across the bottom of the screen. Just blank blue, and then, abruptly, an image.

"Hunh," says N'Doch.

"What is that?"

"Looks like a city of some kind."

Paia nods. She's never actually been in a city, but she's seen them on the vid and in her history books. This city looks brand new, as white and clean as if it had been finished yesterday. As if it has no history. Broad, smooth, empty boulevards. Terraced buildings topped with pale, shining towers that rise against a sky of the same blank blue that had filled the screen a moment ago.

N'Doch leans forward. "Where's all the people?"

As suddenly as it came, the white city vanishes, and is

replaced with blue, as if the sky behind has swallowed every trace of street or tower. And now a message does appear, in big unadorned white lettering.

It says: HURRY.

CHAPTER FIVE

S ilence in the crowded com room, awed and uneasy. The girl and Luther have vanished right in front of their eyes, without even the illusion of a place to have fallen into.

Next, a burst of querulous chatter. The Librarian glances up from his console, beginning to comprehend impatience. He has no time for wonder. Humans ask for miracles, then are upset and disbelieving when they get one. He could offer them a rational explanation, as rational as it gets with dragons, but it would take him too long to articulate it. Time he can't afford right now. He clicks his teeth irritably and bends back to his work.

Hurry, hurry, insists the imperative in his brain.

Hurry how? Hurry at what? He's doing all he knows how to do, what he's always done: search for the source. Where is this farther future, where his dragon is waiting, as desperate as he is to make contact? Desperate. He longs for it with every molecule of his being.

If only she'd send him an image of the place, or a signal coherent enough for him to pinpoint its source location, temporal as well as geographical. But she does not send coherent signals, and he is besieged at his console. Too much noise. Too many people. Too many demands. Constance wants to know what's going on inside the Citadel. Leif and the soldier require updated military data. House is in a fit of anxiety about Paia's disappearance and will not stop distracting him with suggestions and queries. The rebellion is crucial. The Librarian has aided and abetted it, but it is not his True Work. He'd like them all to get on with it, and leave him to his task: locating his dragon. If Air is not found, the rebellion—won or lost—will matter little.

But because he's so ruled by compassion and temperance, because so many of his lives have been given over to the service of causes—whatever cause . . . in the end, they were all the same: the survival of the planet—because he doesn't know how to make the demands go away, the Librarian grants them his attention for a while longer.

He transfers House to the private channel plugged into his ear, and convinces him to try a power-up of the deactivated surveillance cameras trained on the Citadel's front entrance. After a few false starts and some creative rerouting, two front-on views of the imposing Temple facade appear on the screen. A cheer goes up among the watchers. The Librarian takes a look himself. He's not seen the Citadel's exterior since the Fire-breather took over. The elaborate, overscaled columns and friezes, so sharply delineated by the harsh sunlight, are the dragon's addition. The Librarian notes an echo of styles affected by other, human, dictators in times gone by. Human, but not humane. What a difference a single letter can make. The Librarian smiles, drifting again, content in a celebration of the power of language.

But soon Leif Cauldwell is back at his elbow. "See what he's got on the Grand Stair. There's a camera still working there, I'm sure of it."

The Librarian keys in the request. To accede is much easier. Refusal would require a considered explanation. The Citadel's Grand Stair flashes up on the wall. Meanwhile, House is murmuring anxiously in his right ear.

"But how did this happen, Gerrasch? How *could* it? Why didn't anyone *stop* her?"

"Accident."

"No such thing!"

Taking the very long view, the Librarian is inclined to agree. There are no random events. In the short term, however, humans are definitely subject to them, mostly due to the thoughtlessness of their own actions. "Accident."

"Will she be safe?"

"Will any?" counters the Librarian, as Leif looms over him again.

"House, can you give us floor plans, level by level?"

"Original or revised?" House is more terse on the public channel. "Leif, how could you let this happen? You promised to keep an eye on her!"

"Revised. Don't fret, House. We'll have her back in no time."

The Librarian is not so sure. He has an uneasy feeling about how quickly their united force has been divided. If he was the Fire-breather, that's exactly how he would begin his final conquest.

A row of neatly drawn plans marches across the wall just at eye level.

"Thanks, House. That's perfect!" Leif beckons the soldier to the screen, and Stoksie wanders over for a closer look. "Here's what makes the place so hard to break into. You've never been in the Citadel, have you, Stokes?"

"Nevah bin close, even," the little Tinker replies gravely. "Das Scroon Crew's territory, y'know? But dey ain' bin too close, lately, cuza da Monsta."

Köthen traces out potential patterns of access to the Citadel from the surrounding countryside. Each route leads his finger to the same spot: the stone staircase leading up to the Temple's high outer courtyard.

"Five hundred very tall steps," Leif tells him.

"The only entrance?" Köthen asks.

"The only. In my family's day, there was an elevator, but the Beast is technophobic. He replaced it with something he could understand, something that looks more intimidating."

"Elevator. The room that moves?"

Leif nods approvingly, then taps the image of the Stair. "A perfect bottleneck. If we take it, they lose the advantage. This big gateway here leads to the Inner Court, and then directly into the Temple. And from there, into the complex."

Köthen studies the long view of the Temple facade. The Librarian marvels at how quickly this tenth-century man has mastered the concept of a live video feed. "For how long did your family rule this stronghold?"

"Rule it?" Leif chuckles. "Not rulers in name, not by your definition, but I guess it was sort of the Cauldwells' little kingdom. Our great grandfather saw the handwriting

on the wall while most people were still in total denial.
Entire governments, in fact. He sold off the other family
holdings and added to his land in the Adirondacks. Bought
up a big chunk when the country went bankrupt. Moved
his wife and kids up. Other relatives followed. The Citadel
began as an out-of-the-way vacation compound, then a family retreat. My father's generation was forced to turn it into
a fortress."

"It was a bad time, then," Köthen remarks.

Leif's laugh is a bitter retort. "You could say that, yeah."
But there is recognition and empathy in Köthen's tone, not
a lack of understanding. "You've had some hard times of
your own, I gather."

"So I imagined, until I came here." Köthen turns back
to the screen. He lays his palm on the long view of the cliff
face as if to measure it in handspans. "This is . . . high. Is
the courtyard within range from the top?"

"Not with the weapons we have."

"What do you have?"

Cauldwell makes a sour face.

"Wait, nah, Leif," Stoksie says. "Betcha we cud come up
wit sumpin."

"What sort of something?"

"Doan look so doubty, nah. Yu bin buried up in da palace a long time. Der's stuff bin goin' on yu don' know
'bout. Stuff comin' up frum da Sout'."

"Stokes, we need serious, working ammo."

"Yu kin git it, if yu got trade enuff."

"Huh." Leif runs a hand through his long auburn hair.
"Well, that's news." To Köthen, he says, "We have a big
cave full of long-range weapons, you see, and nothing to
put in them, not for years."

"Long-range. How long?"

"Plenny long, Doff," says Stoksie.

The Librarian sighs as the past rears up and ricochets
around his head. So many years, so many pasts, so many
of them dominated by guns, large and small. He knew when
he set this rebellion in motion, that there'd be fighting,
there'd be deaths. So why is the idea suddenly so exhausting? His other revolution, the reshaping of the people's hearts and minds with a new idea of how to live . . .
it's taking so long, oh, so long. Longer, he fears, than the

world has time left. The data and the computer models
have been in sync for a century, since the climate change
became irreversible. Worse still, recent sensor readings indicate that the final decline is accelerating. His new idea
came too late. Only the One can save them now. His
dragon. Air. He must hurry. *Hurry*.

"Gerrasch? You all right?"

Leif bends over him solicitously. The Librarian blinks,
lifts his head from the keypad, where it seems to have
fallen. In his earphone, House is complaining about incomprehensible commands. The Librarian rubs his eyes and
murmurs an apology.

"Time you took a break, G."

"Later." Mere sleep will not cure this particular
exhaustion.

"You know best." Briefly, Leif massages his shoulders.
"Can you get me a print-out of the floor plans, small
enough for Dolph to keep on him until he's got it memo-
rized? And print out the area map, too."

The Librarian nods. Leif strides away, head high, back
straight. The group at the wall screen watches him approach, moves aside to make room. It makes the Librarian
smile. Leif Cauldwell has waited for this moment for over
a decade. He is thrumming with strategy and resolve, and
his ardor translates into those who look to him for guidance. The Librarian can smell their anticipation. Even Köthen, the outsider, has caught a whiff of it. He sets himself
apart from the group, but is not in contention with it or
with Cauldwell, its obvious leader. Separate but equal, and
ready to fight.

The Librarian sighs. Perhaps now they will leave him
alone for a while. And he'll give House a really challenging
task to perform, so the computer will stop its whining. He
requests a trace on the source of the portal image of
N'Doch's Africa. It came up on his screens, so it must start
as a signal somewhere. Just as his visions are signals, his
dragon's mad sendings propagated through time and space.

He can feel their minute physicality as they enter his brain, lapping like waves on a lake shore. No magic, and not just his imagination. Rather, some unknown physics. The Librarian sets his electronic trackers to work.

Hurry, hurry. But he needs time. Time to think. To analyze. Where is this new future? What's the exact nature of the change in him? His dragon touched him and left him altered, but how?

He imagines the Fire-breather, racing up and down the centuries, covering all his bases, making good on all his threats. Even for a power like Fire, this will be a strain on his resources. Good. He'll be distracted. The perfect time to move on the Citadel, but also the perfect time to find and rescue Air. Is this what he's meant to understand? That he must reassemble the four dragon guides, as soon as possible. Strength in unity. Only together will they find Air.

He sees Stoksie beside him, watching blunt fingers play the keypad like a piano. How long has he been there? The Librarian cannot remember seeing him approach. The little man looks pensive, uncomfortable, like he's been standing too long on his bad hip.

The Librarian gestures. "Chair?"

"Nah." Stoksie props his elbow against the side of the console and leans his chin into his cupped palm. "Kin I ask yu sumpin?"

"Ask."

"Dat place dey wen', das like sumkinda time masheen?"

"Sumkinda." The Librarian slips unconsciously into the Tinker dialect.

"Luta, he be okay, nah?"

"Hope he will." Does even Stoksie believe he has some mystic power over life and death? To his right, the plotter spits out the printed plan and map. The Librarian passes the stiff rolls to an outstretched hand, without noticing whose, and hears the crinkle of paper being spread across a nearby table. He worries that the stockpiled reams will be too dry to use long before his supply is exhausted.

"Yu cud go anyweah, den?" Stoksie pursues.

"Theoretically." The Librarian takes a breath. So many syllables all at once. "With control."

Stoksie grunts. "But we doan have dat. How cud we git dat, dya t'ink?"

"Working on it," the Librarian mutters. Wait. What is that? There's a new humming in his earpiece, something that isn't coming from House. What is it? Too much noise in the room to be sure. Too much noise and too much busyness. He can't focus. He can't hear himself think. He waves his arms distractedly. "Quiet! QUIET!"

No one hears him except Stoksie. "Yu gotta raise yer volume sum, G."

The Librarian frowns. Wasn't he yelling at the top of his lungs?

"Heah. Lemme do it."

Stoksie limps away, moving from caucus to caucus, debate to debate. The Librarian doesn't pick up what he says, but the hubbub dies back a bit, and groups begin to drift toward the door. Soon the room is empty, but for the cluster of warriors around the printout.

". . . four days' direct march, if the dragons can't take us." Leif delineates a route across the area map, between spidery contour lines and the broken traces of old roadways.

"With how many men?" asks Köthen.

"People," says Constanze.

"Meaning?"

"Meaning the force won't be all men. The women will fight, too."

"Ah." Köthen's shrug suggests that if all the women are as staunch as Constanze, he has no objection. He straightens away from the map and turns to study the screen again. "*Herr* Stokes," he calls out, waiting for the translator to catch up. "Are those mules of yours saddle-broken?"

"Mebbe. Why yu askin'?"

Köthen seems to take this ambiguity for an assent. He nods. "Give me ten men of my choosing, Leif Cauldwell, armed with these wondrous weapons you speak of. I will take the heights, and clear the courtyards."

"Hmm, it's a good idea, but you'll be totally exposed up there when the Beast returns. And he will return, no doubt of it."

"The risk is no worse than that of an ambush in the lightless bowels of these unfamiliar warrens."

"Not entirely lightless."

"But well-known to you. In there, I would be a hazard to my men."

"I see your point." Leif nods. "Okay, you're on. The heights are your job."

So the soldier prefers to fight his battles in the open air, the Librarian muses. Better him than me. Hours later, his cave-adapted lungs still feel the dry sear of the mountaintop.

"When can we expect our dragons back, Gerrasch?" Leif asks.

"Unsure." The Librarian is not well-versed in the issues of real-time relative to dragon travel. It's not the sort of information you can easily find in books or data banks. He suspects that elapsed time in the past is not exactly equivalent to elapsed time in the present. Besides, time, as in a specific chronological goal, is not Earth's main parameter. It's *place* that draws him. The fact that places have their associated times is apparently coincidental. But standard time paradox should dictate that the physical dragon can't be in two places at once. So his return can be expected at any time *after* the moment he left. Could be seconds, could be days or weeks.

"Well, say, an hour or two, maybe?"

"Maybe. Yes." What will be, will be. The Librarian doesn't want to burden Leif Cauldwell with worries he can do nothing about.

"Let's say an hour, then. Time enough to talk to the folks upstairs."

"We do need a head count," notes Constanze.

"Let's get on it, then." Leif rolls up the printout and hands it to his wife for safekeeping. "Stoksie, can you stick around down here and keep G company? Anything important comes through from the Citadel, you can let us know."

"Betcha," the Tinker agrees.

And at last the room is truly empty. Silence settles in like a gentle rain. The Librarian remembers rain. He allows himself a moment to savor the precious memory, not wanting to waste it. Stoksie noses about for a comfortable seat, then drags a battered swivel chair up to the desk nearest the console. He props his feet on an open drawer and leans back into the cracked plastic with a sigh.

"Ain' slept sinze yestiddy."

The Librarian nods sympathetically. He feels like he hasn't slept in years. Centuries, maybe. How will any of them get rest enough to fight this war? He peers at the readouts stacked to the left of his keypad. The tracking routines are in their third loop, still without a result. He plants his elbows on the cushioned wrist pad and rests his head in his palms. Just for a moment, he tells himself. Just long enough to clear his head of the residue from the morning's noise and crisis . . . but that humming is back again. He can hear it clearly now, in his ears, in his mind. He can feel it in his gut. Is it . . . physical? Is something going on out on the mountainside?

The Librarian stirs, lifts his head. His neck muscles are cramped. His eyelids seem fastened together. He has no feeling at all in his hands. He's been asleep, and the humming has woken him. There's something different about the light. For a moment, before he is fully awake, he imagines that the sun has risen. But the sun does not rise when you're a mile underground.

The Librarian shakes himself upright.

The room is bathed in a pure white radiance. Every corner, every detail is softly delineated. In memory of his former animal self, every hair on the Librarian's body rises to attention. He lifts his dazzled eyes to the wall screen. Instantly he understands. The portal has opened again.

The darker walls and ceiling frame the bright vista beyond. Light spills in a long rectangle onto the scuffed flooring of the com room. A glowing path, leading right to his console. He is inside, looking out onto a shaded terrace, bounded by delicate columns and a railing of translucent stone. Like alabaster, the Librarian decides, but without alabaster's depth. This stone is as smooth and white as the paper from the plotter. Past the railing is a blue void, neither sea nor sky, but a seamless both. The white terrace continues out of sight to left and right, its hidden spaces beckoning.

What does it mean? It's not a place he knows or has ever been, or has ever seen. Yet it seems . . . familiar. How can this be? He's a librarian, after all. His memory is encyclopedic. If this was a place from any of his many pasts, he'd remember it. And he doubts it could be an unknown from his current present, unless there still exists some impossibly sheltered corner of the world, where such a terrace could show no sign of destruction or wear.

But he knows . . . he *knows* that a city lies concealed below the white horizon of the terrace railing. Images flood the space behind his eyes: tall glass towers reflecting the unchanging white light. Wide boulevards and open plazas. An empty city that calls to him. Is this to be the next phase of his search?

He has only to walk the width of the terrace to find out. It isn't far. Not far at all.

The Librarian lurches to his feet. Refusing to let the image out of his sight, he fumbles over to Stoksie's chair and wakes him with a clumsy, flailing arm.

"Easy, nah! Easy!"

"Stokes! Look!"

Stoksie's eyes flick open. "Whatsit?"

"What do . . . wachu see deah, Stokes?"

"Weah?"

"On da screen."

The Tinker sets both feet carefully on the floor and squints into the light. "Dunno, G. Wachu t'ink it iz?"

The Librarian is wary of admitting what he thinks. It's too impossible, too crazy, that after so long, the moment could have actually arrived, so suddenly and without fanfare. He hopes Stoksie's determined skepticism will help him think past the exultant hammering of his heart. "I t'ink . . . think it's *her* place. Why else would it come to me? She's in there somewhere."

But Stoksie seems less inclined to doubt him since the other dragons appeared. He levers himself out of his chair and takes a few stiff steps forward. "Her? Yu mean, da One?"

"Yes."

"It's da portal opin agin, den?"

"Think so. Yes. Sure of it."

Stoksie rubs his stubbled chin, runs a hand over his bald head, then limps into the shaft of surreal light, right up to the edge of the opening. The Librarian follows, a long step behind. There is a faint line across the floor, a subtle change of tonality, like a borderline between here and there. Slowly, Stoksie extends his arm, up to and past where the screen should be. He waves his hand up and down, meeting no resistance. "It's da portal, all ri'. Wachu wanna do, G?"

The Librarian swallows. Physical courage has not been much required of him during his eternal waiting period. Endurance, persistence, patience, resourcefulness, and intelligence, yes. Those are his major qualities. But his body is thick and slow, his hands agile but not particularly strong. "Gotta go deah, Stokes," he whispers hoarsely.

"Nah. Bad ideah. Stoopid."

"Got to." What if the portal closes, and she can't open it again? What if it's only Fire's current distraction that's allowed her to do it? "Got to, Stokes. Can't miss the chance."

"Now? Ri' now, yu got to?"

The Librarian nods.

"Den lemme run tell Leif an' da othas."

"No. Please. They'll try to stop me."

"Shur dey will, an' gud fer dem!"

"No. Not good. Got to do this." The Librarian shakes his head. He takes a half step forward, until the change in the light falls across the middle of his toes. Is this the difference, then? That he can actually walk off into the unknown without quailing in panic?

Stoskie moves up beside him. "Den I gotta go wichu."

"No."

"Oh, yeah. Betcha."

The Librarian shudders. His last chance to refuse the summons has just crumbled. Now he has to go. But he doesn't have to go alone. Often he's convinced that the Tinker crews are the treasure-house of all that was once admirable in humanity. "Thank you," he gasps.

Stoksie laughs, a reckless sort of cackle. "Da lame an' da halt, nah? Fine peah we make ta go aventurin'!"

No random events, the Librarian reminds himself, a litany to bolster his courage. "Let's go, then."

He rests his hand on the Tinker's shoulder and, together, they step into the light.

PART TWO

The Journey into Peril

CHAPTER SIX

After only an instant in the snowy yard at Deep Moor, Erde knows that her Seeing has been a true one.

The white ground is churned up and stained with frozen mud. Acrid odors pinch her throat and nostrils, not the warm scent of cozy fireplaces, but the stench of burning. Black smoke billows beyond the surrounding pines, toward the barns, toward the house.

"Oh, no! Oh, no!" Erde flings the sack of woolens into Luther's arms and races across the ragged snow in her sandals and leggings. The path through the trees to the house is ashy and trampled. At the base of the stone steps, she collapses with an anguished wail.

The house is a ruin. Scorched stone. Charred timbers. No sign of life.

She can hardly catch breath enough to cry out her grief and horror. The dragons, appalled as always by humankind's potential for disaster, offer what little comfort they can.

Luther rushes up, shrugging into the last of his winter layers. "Watsit, gal? Watsda matta?" He stops short at the sight of the ravaged house. Gently, he hauls Erde to her feet and presses her boots and sheepskin cloak into her arms. She throws them down, wailing.

"We're too late! How can we be too late?"

Patiently, Luther retrieves the clothing from the dirty snow. "Put dese on, nah. Yu'll freeze ta deat'."

"I don't care! How could we let this happen!"

The dragons are exploring the rest of the farmstead. Lady Water's tone is tight and furious.

THE BARNS ARE BURNED OUT AS WELL. THE ASHES ARE STILL HOT.

Earth's outrage is quieter. HE HAS BEEN HERE, OUR BROTHER.

HE, OR HIS AGENTS.

The hell-priest's armies! It must have been!

Away from the aura of the dragon's heat, Erde is soon shivering as much from cold as from horror and outrage. Guillemo's men in Deep Moor! It's sacrilege! A desecration! She lets Luther help her into her boots and heavy cloak. She notes his wary sidelong glances, at the mounded snow, the tall and blistered pines, the grim lowering sky— the habit of a man used to hidden dangers.

"Git yer stuff on," he urges. "Den we'll take a look 'roun'."

Erde forces her numbed fingers to tie up icy bootlaces. She must get hold of herself. She owes it to Luther and the dragons. "Is anyone here? Do you see any . . ." She can't bring herself to say it, so Lady Water does instead.

NO BODIES. SOME DEAD LIVESTOCK, BUT FEWER THAN MIGHT BE EXPECTED, GIVEN HOW TOTAL THE DESTRUCTION IS.

Luther climbs the terrace steps to peer into the smoking ruin. "Doan see anyone . . . yu know . . . leas' not heah."

"Then where is everyone?"

Water offers an answer almost worse than death. NO DOUBT HE HAS TAKEN THEM.

"No! Maybe they escaped. We'll search till we find out what's happened!" Erde's tears are freezing on her cheeks. She fights back a hiccuping sob and musters a more determined expression. "Look at me, weeping over an old house, when Raven and Rose and the others need our help!"

But, oh, how she did love that old house! Nestled in the leaves like a bird's nest, low and cozy and so full of life! Now her little bedroom among the eaves is gone and the massive stone chimney stands alone amidst the smoking embers of the roof. Rose's beautiful garden courtyard is a tumble of blackened sticks. The kitchen's long, sturdy, well-used table, the center of the women's lives and fellowship, is reduced to a heap of cinders clogging the charred stone sink.

Erde had come to think of this house as home, as if it had been her true home all along, and her earlier life in her father's castle was only a waiting time until she found Deep Moor. To keep herself from bursting into sobs again, she turns her back on the wreckage and her face into the frigid wind.

"Howya doin?" Luther asks.

"I'm all right now. Let's go see what we can find out."

She leads him back to the churned yard and across it, following Earth's wide, slushy trail through the pines and past the burned-out barns.

"These were big and warm and beautiful once, Luther."

The Tinker nods. "Yu kin always builda house back, y'know, gal."

"Yes, I know. Yes, of course you can." But it will never be the way it was, Erde mourns. It will never seem so perfect and protected, so . . . invulnerable. Perhaps that is the most devastating thing of all, that destruction came so quickly and so easily.

They find the dragons in the big farmyard, where it opens out into the flat meadows of the valley. Both are nosing among the smaller outbuildings that have escaped the flames. The yard is a chaos of mud and ice, trampled and refrozen, with a confusion of tracks leading off in all directions. Earth crouches at the center, the snow melting around him. He's reluctant to move his great horned bulk about and disturb the scents and signs he is taking such careful inventory of. Water has assumed a smoothly furred pragmatic shape. The dull late light glimmers in the velvet of her coat. Erde sees this particular shape has hands of a sort, for the dragon is clearing aside the remains of the henhouse. Luther hurries over to help.

Erde takes stock hastily. The duck pen is more or less intact. The hog sty sags and a burned tree has fallen on the goat hut. All the doors have apparently been flung wide. She's relieved to discover no dead animals inside. The rabbit hutch lies turned over. Luther nudges it with his foot.

Erde moans. "Did they steal *everything*?"

Earth's gaze is steady and sad. THERE IS FAMINE IN THE LAND, REMEMBER.

"I know." She relays the dragon's words to Luther, and for his sake, speaks her reply out loud. "But I hate to think of Fra Guill's men eating up all of Deep Moor!"

"Dey's all sortsa tracks heah," Luther's dark face is intent. "Like heah—dat's da rabbits runnin' away." He points across the snowy field, then straightens out of his habitual stoop to take in the long valley and the tall, pine-shrouded hills.

"You think so?" Erde squints to follow the trace until it vanishes behind a distant pile of brambles. She finds this small mercy enormously comforting.

"Betcha. We raiz'em at Blin' Rachel. Still had 'em wild, wen I wuza boy." Luther studies the ground again. "An' dis heah, das a mule."

"A mule!" Hope against hope! "Dragons, did you hear? Maybe it's Sir Hal's mule!"

OR IT COULD BE A HORSE. Lady Water noses at the tracks.

I don't recall any horses at Deep Moor.

SOMEONE ELSE'S HORSES, THEN.

Erde shudders, recalling the thick-limbed white chargers favored by the hell-priest's monkish bodyguards, trained to maul and trample. "She says it could be a horse."

"Mebbe so. Ain' nevah seen a horse. Yu gottim heah?"

"Oh, yes. The knights ride horses to battle."

Luther frowns, turning back to stare into the distant surrounding hills. "Yeah? Wonda if dey's gone yit."

What if it was not just his men, but the hell-priest himself? That might account for the rampant and needless destruction. Fear and horror rise like gall, so physical a sensation that she clamps both hands to her mouth to keep the material glob of terror from spewing out of her gut.

IF HE WAS HERE, YOU WOULD KNOW IT.

She takes a breath, swallows, and lowers her hands. "Yes, dragon. I would. I always do." But it's hard to have faith in the face of such catastrophe.

WAIT! Lady Water's sleek head shoots up. LISTEN!

"What? What is it?" To Erde, the cold air seems as still as a tomb.

DOGS.

"Dogs barking?"

RUNNING.

"Yu heah dogs? Weah? I saw wona dem onct. He wuzza mean one!"

"What dogs, dragons? Can you tell?"

But because neither of these dragons' preternatural sense is sight over distance, it's Luther who spots them first. "Lookit! Look deah!"

Dogs: Even while she sees Luther casting about for a stout stick, even though she knows that hunting hounds travel with the hell-priest's armies, hope stirs again in Erde's heart. She can see the dogs herself now, half a dozen dark ovals flying silently toward them over the snow. She wonders what Lady Water could possibly have heard.

Luther brandishes his weapon. "Yu git behin' me nah, gal!"

"Wait, it might be . . . there are dogs who live here at Deep Moor. At least, there were . . ."

"Dey doan call a bad man a dog fer nuttin!"

"No, Luther, not all . . ."

IT IS THEM.

Leaping over rubble piles and snowbanks, the dogs are suddenly among them, long-legged, bristle-haired dogs, tall and gray, with amber eyes. They race around the farmyard in tightening circles, panting, dancing, still without making a sound. Then, abruptly, as if on command, they tumble into a ragged phalanx and drop to their bellies in front of Earth's foreclaws. Only now does Erde see that they are badly battered and beaten. Their lop-ears are torn and their bearded muzzles scarred and bloodied. Despite the energy of their arrival, several seem about to collapse from exhaustion and loss of blood. One, she sees, is missing a paw.

Luther lowers his cudgel. "Dey bin fightin' sum."

Fresh tears warm Erde's cheeks. *Oh dragon, help them!*

THEY WISH US TO GO WITH THEM FIRST.

Lady Water crouches among them. JUST LIKE A DOG. IS IT FAR?

DISTANCE IS NOT PART OF THEIR VOCABU-LARY. ONLY DIRECTION AND URGENCY.

"What do they want?"

FOR US TO HURRY. I HAVE TOLD THE WORST TO COME TO ME. THE OTHERS I WILL HELP LATER.

The dragon lowers his huge head. A dog with rough

gashes on her hips and ribcage stumbles over to lean against a claw taller than she is. The dog with the icy, bloody stump struggles to get up, then falls back. His belly, too, is bleeding. A whine escapes him, and he rolls his eyes apologetically.

"Luther, help me!" Together, Erde and Luther lift the suffering dog and lay him beside Earth, who goes to work on him first, nearly wrapping him entirely in his vast, soft tongue. The other dogs watch expectantly.

"Lookit dat, nah!" The wounds close and heal before Luther's very eyes. He lowers himself to one knee in the damp snow. "Da One be praised!"

The dog shudders with relief and gratitude. He lies panting for a moment, then struggles up and shakes himself weakly. The dragon moves on to the next. Erde presses herself into the dragon's side to send him messages of love and appreciation. Here, even in the midst of horror, there are miracles.

As soon as the second dog is on her feet, the rest of the pack spring up, quivering with mission. The least battered of them sprint ahead into the meadow, then circle back expectantly.

Luther rises from his knees, dusting away snow and ash. "Dat way, dey're sayin'? Der's a big trail leadin' owt dere, seeit?"

"Let's go, then!"

"Slow, nah. Mebbe da bad guys wen' dere! Yu know wat's down dat way?"

Erde squints along the wide, roughed-up track leading out of the farmyard, then across the meadow and down along the valley. "Just fields and . . . wait! I know! The Grove is that way! Do you remember, dragon?"

OF COURSE. A GOOD DESTINATION. AND THE DOGS AGREE. I WILL TELL THEM TO MEET US THERE.

"We're going dragon-back again, Luther. Are you ready?" Erde shoulders her pack and conjures the entrance to the Grove in her mind, revising her image with the several feet of snow fallen since she'd been there last.

Her next breath fills her lungs with biting cold. They're in the middle of the valley with the tall oaks of the Grove rising before them. A sharp wind has been reshaping the drifts around the trees, but a recent disturbance is still visible. The snow is deeper here than in the farmstead, but it's been trampled in a wide area in front of two massive trunks that mark the path into the Grove. Erde sees blood and hoofprints, paw prints, bootheels.

"Ben sum fightin' heah, fer shur," Luther shrugs his woolens closer. He looks miserable, warmed only by courage and his righteous outrage. "Intrestin' how da trail goes 'roun' da sides, but not much goes in."

Erde is too cold and anxious to speak. It feels dangerously exposed out here in the open valley. She's uneasy past any rational assessment. The dog pack can be heard behind them now, no barks or howling, just their breathy scudding across the snow.

HERE'S HOW I READ IT. Lady Water turns back from a quick inspection of the trail curving off to the right. TWO GROUPS CAME HERE, ONE PURSUING THE OTHER. ONE OF THEM ESCAPED INTO THE TREES.

THE TREES TAKE CARE OF THEIR OWN. Earth sounds a note of optimism.

"Yes, that's it!" Erde exclaims in relief. "The Grove is a refuge! Gerrasch took shelter there, remember?"

Lady Water is not so certain. SHELTER FROM HUMAN ENEMIES, PERHAPS, BUT FROM OUR BROTHER FIRE?

WE SHALL SEE.

The dogs catch up, circle the big dragon once, then charge in among the trees and disappear. Now a great baying can be heard.

Luther peers after them, frowning. "Why're dey singin' nah?"

"To let our friends know that help is on the way?" Erde recalls her own confusion upon first encountering the magic of the Grove. The thick-trunked oaks look comfortably spaced. Room enough for even a dragon to pass between. Yet the dogs have vanished, within the first few ranks of trees.

"Shudn't jest walk in der, nah. Cud be a nambush."

"The dogs would know. They would warn us somehow."

WELL, LET'S NOT JUST STAND AROUND IN THE COLD, EVERYONE . . .

Lady Water takes the path between the trees. She'd
sounded so exactly like N'Doch that Erde feels a sharp
pang at having abandoned her fellow dragon guide for so
long. And Paia, too. She'd nearly forgotten about the
priestess. Thoughts of Baron Köthen inevitably follow, and
Erde hastily shoves them away. There's nothing to be done
about any of it until the present emergency is dealt with.
She plunges anxiously after the blue dragon. She might find
the women of Deep Moor, and still find disaster.

Inside the Grove, her uneasiness increases. The light is
dim under the spreading branches. The air has gone oddly
still. The leaves have shriveled, but have clung stubbornly
to their perches. They make a softly ominous rattling, directionless and steady like the sound of water over stones.
Scattered signs of flight appear along the path: a shawl
dropped in haste, a basket emptied and tossed aside. Erde
swerves, gasping, around the remains of a brown duck,
trampled into the snow. Thoughts tangle in her head. The
women would never be so careless . . . even though they
were in the greatest haste, running for their lives . . . still,
they would never have . . .

Dragon, could the soldiers have intruded into the Grove?

Erde hears the dogs ahead, and the snap of branches
behind that describes Earth's much slower progress. When
she and the dragon first arrived at Deep Moor, he fit easily
beneath the branches of the Grove. Clearly, his increasing
size will not always be an advantage. For instance, it's
harder now for him to feed himself adequately. Lady
Water, her size conveniently under her control, trots easily
along the path far ahead, thoughtlessly urging her brother
to hurry.

At last there's brighter light ahead. Between the dark
oak boles lies the pale reflective oval of the central pond,
the pool that never freezes. No touch of wind disturbs its
surface. Erde knows she will find green shards of grass
springing up around its verge. The Grove's magic is gathered here. Here's where the women would have come. But
no one's there. Erde spies Gerrasch's little hovel, mounded
with snow. The sight of it unmoors her further. Such confu-
sions of then and now. Gerrasch's rough shelter always
looked more like a pile of sticks than a home, but now all
sense of dwelling has gone out of it. The pile has been torn

apart and scattered. Where was Gerrasch when this violation occurred? Here, or thirteen hundred years from now?
Would the dragons have an answer? Or do they feel as she
does, like a tiny leaf whirling on the tides of Time?

Erde stops beside the pile to catch her breath and let
her brain stop spinning. Lady Water wades into the pool
as if entering her own bedchamber. She takes a long drink,
then plunges her head into the crystalline water. In an instant, she has flung up a large silver fish and snatched it
neatly out of the air.

Luther pulls up beside Erde, panting. "Ain' usta all dis
walkin'!" His grin is rueful and bright, but his eyes are
busy scanning the dark trees and the wide stretch of snowy
meadow beyond the curve of the pond. His grin fades.
"Dere's bin fightin' heah, too."

"No! Not here!" Only her intent denial has kept her
from seeing it. But the drifts around Gerrasch's shelter are
as torn up as the farmyard. The damp leaf litter lies exposed in great russet swaths like clots of frozen blood. Erde
fears suddenly that the dogs have brought them to be witnesses to death, not to prevent it.

"Rose?" she cries out. "Raven? Is anybody here?"

Luther hushes her. "Der's plenny yu doan wan' hearin'
yu, gal."

"But they must be here somewhere! Where else could
they be?"

"If dey ain' shown demselves yet, der's probly a reason."

The big Tinker chews his lip and looks away. Erde knows
he fears the worst and doesn't want to say so. But never
having met Brother Guillemo, Luther doesn't know that
death is not the worst that could happen to any woman of
Deep Moor who falls into the hell-priest's clutches. Just the
thought brings on the old chills, the sensation that Fra Guill
is nearby, watching her. Erde shudders. Then she notices
the dogs.

"Look. What are they doing?"

The dog pack has gathered at the very far end of the
clearing, a cluster of gray blurs against the roiled snow.

Lady Water swallows another fish, then flips a huge one
to her brother as he halts just at the water's edge. THEY
SEEM VERY BUSY ABOUT SOMETHING.

WE ARE TO FOLLOW THEM. BUT I WILL EAT

FIRST. WHO KNOWS WHEN THE NEXT CHANCE WILL BE.

Erde is torn between the dogs' urgency and her dragon's hunger. Certainly, he will need all his strength. But peering ahead, she sees that the pack has split to form two rows, facing one another. A single large dog runs back and forth in the space between, baying for attention. "Look!" she insists. "They want us to hurry!"

The two rows lean toward each other, like the sides of an arrow. At the arrow's point, two giant oaks wind their upper branches together to form a natural archway. To Erde's distant eye, the inside of the arch seems darker than the surrounding forest. Since the dragons refuse to listen, she shakes Luther's arm and points.

"See that?"

"Eyah. Dey shur tryin' ta show us sumpin."

"Oh, I pray our friends are still alive! Dragon! Please! Or shall I go without you?"

PATIENCE. WE ARE THERE.

And instantly, they are. Across the long meadow in a blink. The dogs cry with delight and crowd around Earth again, as if their job is done at last and all they wish for by way of thanks is a swipe of his healing tongue. He goes to work on them while Lady Water investigates the darkness between the twining trees.

THE DOGS ARE COMPLAINING ABOUT BEING LEFT BEHIND.

Left behind? Then, everyone's gone somewhere?

WAIT . . .

Erde gasps as light blooms within the archway, as soft and colorless as the snowy meadow. The blue dragon gleams like silver in its glow.

WHEREVER THIS IS, IT'S PROBABLY WHERE THEY ARE.

Erde peers around Water's silky side. She blinks, then looks again. The space between the ancient trunks is . . . somewhere else. No doubt about it. To left and right, the trees march off in unbroken ranks, but between these two mossy giants, a city lies.

A city?

THAT'S WHAT IT LOOKS LIKE, ALL RIGHT.

A city between the trees. Nearest to them, a shaded overhang. Beyond, a view past delicate, translucent columns, out onto a broad white plaza dotted with fountains and stone benches. No snow, no wind. As if there was no weather there at all. Only the soft white glow. Across the pale plaza, entry porticoes lead into tall white towers that rise up beyond the range of view. Between their perfect sides, as sharp as sword blades, Erde glimpses slim blue shards of sky.

THIS HAS TO BE WHERE THEY WENT. Lady Water steps up to the opening. Snow and dead leaves scatter across the seamless white marble just past her toes. WHAT DO YOU THINK, BROTHER?

Earth lifts his head from his healing work. He has waited until he's finished with the last dog. His response nearly blasts Erde senseless.

AH! THE MAGE CITY! AT LAST!

Water regards him primly over her velvet shoulder. I THOUGHT WE'D DECIDED THERE WAS NO SUCH THING.

YOU INSISTED THERE WASN'T, SO I AGREED. BUT THERE IT IS! RIGHT THERE! THE CITY I DREAMED OF AS I SLUMBERED, AND AFTER I AWOKE.

"It does look like the city we dreamed of." Erde frowns gently. "Is it another portal?"

NO DOUBT.

NOT JUST ANOTHER PORTAL! THIS IS THE PORTAL WE'VE BEEN SEARCHING FOR!

The big dragon edges into the path of the light, as close as he can get without tangling his horns in the branches overhead. The dogs pace about behind him, grown anxious again.

WE MUST ENTER THIS PLACE. WE'LL FIND ANSWERS HERE.

HOLD ON! WHAT ABOUT . . .

"What about N'Doch? We can't just desert him! What if Fire's there?"

NO DOUBT HE IS, BUT HE CAME HERE FIRST, SO THERE'S STILL TIME.

THERE ARE ANSWERS HERE! WHY ELSE WOULD I HAVE DREAMED THIS PLACE? THE DREAMS WERE A MESSAGE FROM THE SUM-

MONER WHO AWAKENED US, AND NOW, HERE WE ARE. WE CANNOT LOSE THE CHANCE!

"Dey wanna go in deah?" Luther asks.

"Yes, but . . ."

"Well, gud, cuz it's eidah dat or da trees, an' bes' be quick aboudit! Dere's summun commin'. Yu heah?"

"Where?"

"Lissen!"

The dog pack has gone stiff-legged and still. Water puts her debate with her brother aside, and listens with them.

HORSES. A LOT OF THEM.

Though Erde hears nothing, a helpless whimper blooms in her throat. "Maybe it's Sir Hal! He's got word that Deep Moor has been sacked! He's brought his own army!" But the familiar choking chill has returned in force. Her uneasiness was no mere reflex. The hell-priest has found them.

Oh, dragon! He's here!

She will not say his name out loud. She is the beacon the priest has homed in on, she knows it. It's just as before. She can see his avid, evil face in her mind's eye.

Earth rumbles his outrage. The dogs throw in their support with a chorus of snarls and growling. Lady Water's aspect is suddenly edgier and harder.

PAWN! MISBEGOTTEN TOADY! SHALL WE TAKE HIM, BROTHER?

WITH WHAT? THE ONLY WEAPONS WE HAVE WOULD WRECK THIS HALLOWED GROVE. AND TO WHAT END?

REVENGE, OF COURSE—FOR THE RUIN OF DEEP MOOR, AND FOR WHATEVER HE'S DONE TO OUR FRIENDS!

A DISTRACTION, A DIVERGENCE. PROBABLY INTENDED AS SUCH BY OUR BROTHER FIRE. REVENGE IS PETTY. OUR DUTY IS TO FIND OUR SISTER AND PROSPER OUR PURPOSE.

Water snorts. Erde notes the predatory gleam in the blue dragon's eyes.

PETTY PERHAPS, BUT SATISFYING.

WE HAVEN'T TIME! WE MUST FIND OUR SISTER FIRST!

"Waddevah we're doin', we oughta do it fas'!"

The approach is undeniable now, a thudding and crashing among the trees. The dogs fall silent and alert, like a small gray army awaiting orders.

Erde reaches for dragon reassurance. Lady Water is nearest. She buries a fist in the blue dragon's velvet hide. "What if he tries to follow us through the portal?"

PROBABLY THAT'S WHAT HE'S BEEN HOPING, FOR SOMEONE TO COME ALONG AND OPEN IT FOR HIM.

THAT WOULD NOT BE GOOD.

"When N'Doch went, the portal closed up right after him."

"Dere's da ansa, den! Hurry on up!" Luther urges dragon and girl toward the archway.

"Wait! The dogs!"

A gust of wind screams through the clearing, rousing the drifts into billows. The first horse thunders out of the forest through an unnatural wall of white. The dog pack scatters and streaks across the meadow to charge at the horse's heels under cover of the blowing snow. Another horse appears, white on white, and then another. Erde recognizes the heavy war steeds of the hell-priest's retinue. More come behind them. The dogs race and nip, duck away and charge in again. The horses shy and startle. Their white-cloaked riders yank hard at their mouths and dig in with iron-pronged heels. Erde looks for Guillemo among them, but the snow curtain conceals their faces. The dogs circle out and close in again. One of the riders draws his sword.

"They'll all be killed!" Erde shrieks. "Dragon, call them back!"

WE MUST NOT REVEAL OURSELVES. OUR BROTHER MUST NOT KNOW WE'VE FOUND THE MAGE CITY.

The big dragon has gone immobile, and vanished against the tree line. Water stomps at Erde's side in a convincingly horselike shape and gait. The meadow is a swirl of white: snow, horses, men.

But surely the hell-priest has seen us already!

THEY FOLLOWED TRACKS. THEY MAY NOT KNOW WHOSE. HURRY! THROUGH THE PORTAL!

"We can't leave the dogs!" Fra Guill knows who he pursues. Erde is sure of it. She can see his mad eyes, feel him bearing down on her, and she's frozen to the spot, like a mouse before a viper.

'Heah. Lemme try.'' Luther whistles, high and clear, as he would to his mules. The dog pack hesitates. They fall back, gather, and charge in once more. Then, as a horse stumbles and goes down, they peel away victoriously and fly back across the snow to rally, leaping and baying, around the tall Tinker.

Erde gathers them all into the image in her mind.

NOW?

Now, dear dragon, and quickly!

The transport is barely a flicker, a bird shadow across the sun. But Erde feels like she's been flung hard against a wall and been left to lie there several days. Luther is sprawled facedown on the polished white stone. As she watches, he stirs. He pulls his knees up to his chest, clutching his stomach, and groans. The dogs stagger to their feet and wobble over to lick his face and hands.

Dragon?

HERE.

Are we safe?

WE ARE. AT LEAST FOR THE MOMENT.

She sits up slowly. She needs both arms to keep herself upright.

I think, Dragon, that we've traveled a very long way this time.

CHAPTER SEVEN

"**Y**eah? Same to you!" N'Doch's gesture is the worst one he can come up with on the spur of the moment, as the ancient bush taxi rattles past, full throttle. Teeners and old men are perched on the bumpers and clinging to the dented sides of the bus with their arms hooked around the window dividers. The children and older women are mashed together inside with all the family possessions they could carry. "Glad someone's getting a ride the hell out of here!"

He drops his arm and lets it swing loose, as if he couldn't care less. Truth is, he'd been thinking about Baraga as he'd raised his fist. If the Media King is after him again, he should be scared, good and scared, given what the man did to him last time. But he's too angry to be scared.

From the sound of it, the fighting's heavier now, toward the center of town. N'Doch heads for the perimeter, along the dusty, rutted street, gesturing Paia to follow. He's glad she hasn't asked him who's fighting who, 'cause he hasn't a clue. Never did, half the time, even when he lived here. "Might as well start walking."

"But you said it's thirty kilometers!"

"Might be a bit less. I ain't not going, okay?"

"Okay," she says meekly, and N'Doch realizes he's yelled at her.

"Sorry. Don't worry. We'll catch a ride before we go that far."

But the truth is, he's not so sure. He was a fool to come without the dragons. Used to be, any driver with an inch of room would stop, 'cause the rider would always pay. Not much, but something. Now, no one's even slowing down.

Plenty of folks on foot, hurrying out of town weighed down with kids and chickens and their favorite lamp or prayer rug. There's traffic on the road, but a lot of it's military. N'Doch pulls Paia behind whatever's available when he sees them coming. Mostly they're heading back toward the center, where the action is—muffled explosions, bursts of gunfire and now, the sharp quick report of the sniper's rifle. Another palace coup, or something worse? The stuff coming from intown—trucks, bush taxis, an occasional private car—is already overloaded and moving as fast as it can. He wonders what those guys are saying to get past the roadblocks.

"You doin' okay, then?" he asks Paia. He's trying to be business-as-usual, but this hard lump of rage in his gut is as indigestible as spoiled lard. Things don't usually get the best of him, but this is real brand new, knowing your mama's been murdered and there ain't jackshit you can do about it. "Never thought I'd be *wishing* for dragon transport," he grumbles.

Paia takes two steps for each of his long ones, sticking close beside him. No dawdling now. "Are you surprised the dragons haven't come to find us?"

"Yeah, a little. You'd think Dolph would've made 'em come, for your sake."

"Something might be keeping them. Something might have gone wrong up there."

"Don't even think about it, girl." He doesn't mention the anxious emptiness he feels, in the inside places that grew to make room for the dragon. She probably feels exactly the same.

A vehicle approaches from intown. N'Doch turns, his thumb already out. A battered pickup roars past, churning up a moving envelope of dust. He turns forward again, blinking away grit. A huge explosion rattles the shutters along the wall beside them. Maybe they're bringing in the artillery. He tries to set a slick pace, but it's hot as blazes and they've got a long way to go. He can't afford to use Paia up within the first five klicks. He should've thought to bring water from his mama's house, if there was any. Should've looked around, at least, if he'd been thinking straight. He knows where water used to be, along the way to Papa Dja's, the shops and water-sellers' carts. But that was then. Who knows where he could find it now. Lots more has changed than the beachside *bidonville*. He'd like to get a look at a newsfax or just a calendar, to tell him what month it is, what year? Some very serious shit has obviously gone down here, stuff that'd take a lot longer than the two weeks that have passed for him, real-time. Two weeks! He can't fathom it. It feels like half his life.

Or is it just that he never noticed how bad it was, when he was living here day to day, intent on his own gigs and his own survival? He never saw how played out the people are, abject and sick, and stuck in a landscape that no longer supports them.

Doesn't matter, really. N'Doch knows now what it's all leading up to. He's seen the result, been there in person at endgame. Maybe it was too late already, by his time. But what if the right world leaders had seen what he's seen, had really faced the truth—could they, *would* they take the right steps to stop the downward spiral toward the end? If they'd known the truth, if they'd *believed* it, would they still have let the planet die?

You could test it, he muses, if the rules of dragon travel were more flexible. If only the big dragon could go any-where in Time, not just to places he can see or that can be immaculately imaged in the mind of a dragon guide. It wouldn't be too hard to figure out when the irreversible decline began, then just go there and warn them. Snatch the key people forward, like he was snatched, and shove their noses in the inevitable results of their greed and shortsightedness.

But it ain't gonna work that way, is it. That would take hope, and in this part of the world at least, hope is obvi-ously dead. Besides, we'd rather have everything we want, now, now, now, and to hell with future generations!

"What?" Paia asks gently, walking beside him.

N'Doch realizes he's been muttering. His fists are clenched again, so tightly that his wrists ache and his fin-gernails are boring holes in his palms. He shakes his head. When did he get to be such a raging bleeding heart?

"Nothing. Sorry." One day, he'll write a big angry song about it, for all the good it'll do. Make him feel better, maybe, but that's for later. Right now, he doesn't feel much like singing.

She peers up at him compassionately. He can see this priestess woman has a talent for empathy. Probably she needed it in the Temple, for dealing with her flock.

"I'm fine," he says, trying to sound less irritable. He considers turning back for the water, back to his mama's house, but then he'd have to look at her dead face again, so full of reproach. Instead, he speeds up, paying more attention to the rubble on the street than to what street he's on. He glances up finally to check his bearings, and sees he's nearly run them into yet another roadblock.

Idiot! He's been thinking about Baraga again.

This checkpoint's at the edge of town. Luckily, there's a line waiting in front of it. N'Doch yanks Paia behind a trio of anxious women whose heavily loaded baskets are balanced neatly on their heads. Should he try to bluster his way through? He wishes Paia was better dressed to blend in. Her plain, pale clothing stands out among the bright and busy patterns worn by the women ahead of them. The soldiers have a big APC blocking the street. They're checking papers, and matching faces against data relayed on their handhelds. The old people and kids, he notices, are being waved right through.

"C'mon," he mutters. "This ain't gonna work."

Turning aside, he hurries Paia through another maze of back streets, his stomping grounds from his bad old days. Who knew his sneak thief's knowledge would come in so handy? But the next road out of town is also guarded, and the houses and walled courtyards form a solid barrier in between. Just as it's occurring to N'Doch that they might be trapped, he hears the one sound he's been listening for all along, the one he truly fears: the thwock, thwock of 'copter blades. Paia hears it, too. She glances up, then quickly at him. He nods, and instinctively, they both shrink against the nearest wall.

"Coming in low and slow," he says. "Observational speed."

So it's not a troop transport. He could tell that by the sound of it anyway. In times past when he was chased by police 'copters, N'Doch would head for the market, to lose himself under the cover of the stall canopies. But the market is a burned-out mess.

He urges Paia into one doorway and he takes the next, as the bird makes its pass. He risks an upward glance as it glides by. It's small and sleek and white, not the olive drab of the military 'copters. Its engine noise fades a bit, then N'Doch hears it turn and head back in their direction. He gestures Paia to stay in her doorway for the second pass, which is slightly more toward the center of town. When it's gone, he waves Paia forward.

"He's gridding," he explains, pointing upward. "Search pattern."

"For us," she remarks quietly.

This time, N'Doch doesn't tell her she's paranoid. He vows silently to listen harder when she talks about Fire. "We'll go doorway to doorway. It's our only chance, till we find a way outa town."

The 'copter thwocks past on a third run, low enough for its rotors to stir up the dust in the gutters. N'Doch can just make out the insignia on its side: MediaRex Enterprises. He glares after it as if his furious stare was weapon enough to bring it crashing to the ground.

Paia tugs at his sleeve. "If we stay in the alleys, there'll never be a place big enough for it to land."

"Yeah, but if it spots us, it can radio the ground troops to close off whatever street we're in. C'mon, let's move."

They've just turned the next corner when the 'copter heads back their way again. But this alley has no doorways, not even a window, just tall, faceless walls all the way to the end, where it empties into a little square. N'Doch listens to the approach, and decides to make a run for it. But the 'copter swoops past sooner than he's expected. By the way it pulls up sharp and wheels around, he knows it's seen something interesting enough to investigate. Suddenly the sky between the walls seems very close.

"Quick! We gotta get outa this slot!"

He's tried not to drag Paia around too much, so he doesn't have to get physical. But now he's got no choice. He grabs her arm and sprints for the little square, praying for some sort of rabbit hole they can dive into. As they streak past the first few houses fronting the square, N'Doch's head swivels. He pounds to an abrupt halt. Paia slams into him. He's got to catch her in his arms to keep her from sprawling flat on the pavement. Her body feels great, pressed against his, but he hasn't time for that right now. He's just seen the weirdest thing.

The 'copter is nearing. N'Doch lets Paia go and backs up several steps. She watches in confusion. The square is lined with the older-style houses, with little high-walled courtyards out in front, entered through tall wrought-iron gates. A few of these gates are still fastened tight. Most have been beaten in or wrenched entirely off their hinges. But one orange stucco archway is closed with a pair of wooden doors, old paneled doors with flaking blue paint. It's amazing that the wood is still intact, and that's what caught his eye, but it's not what stopped him cold. One more back step, and he's in front of it.

One of the doors is slightly ajar. The courtyard inside must be catching some rogue patch of sun, because hot light streams outward through the crack like water from a bilge leak.

"What is it?" Paia glances from the noisy sky to his face and back again. "What?"

N'Doch puts the end of his tire iron to the unlatched door and shoves it open. "Omigod."

"What?"

"Omigod," he says again.

Paia hurries up beside him to stare through the doorway. "Ohh . . . !"

"Someone's sure got us on their radar, and it ain't only that 'copter."

Just past the doorway, the dry bush country stretches to the horizon and the blue, blue sky in all directions. A dry yellow landscape dotted with scrub, pursued by dust devils, hammered by the sun. They're at the edge of an abandoned peanut field, scattered brown weeds still marking out the rows. To the left, a faint red trace of a road leads off and behind a distant straggle of brush, crowned by an unlikely stand of trees. Tucked in its shade is a patch of mustard-colored stucco.

N'Doch has to shout over the scream of the rotors as the 'copter settles in to hover right over their heads. "See that, under that taller bunch of trees? That's Papa Dja's homestead." He wonders what the 'copter sees.

Paia pushes the other door wide, flat against the inside wall. Except there isn't any inside of the wall. Her hair is blowing loose from her thick braid in the 'copter's downdraft. "We're going in, right?"

"Oh, yeah. This is gonna save our asses!" N'Doch has given up resisting the bizarre things that keep happening to him, but he can't give up being amazed. Could the old man have done this himself? Or the dragons? Maybe they're in there, waiting in Papa Dja's courtyard.

A bullhorn blares intimidations at them from overhead. N'Doch quick-scans the sky inside the doorway. Baraga could have his birds out looking here, too. Once they're in, the portal will close behind them and they'll be stuck in the middle of an open field until they reach the scrub around Djawara's house.

It must be something about being home. He's seeing himself as a vid character again. Like where the hero takes the beautiful girl by the hand and steps calmly out the door into certain danger. Or in this case, from one danger to another, and this hero doesn't feel anything like calm. Conjuring a ghost of his old rakish grin, N'Doch glances up and waves to the 'copter pilot. "See ya 'round!"

The rust-hued bush wind slaps them full in the face as they duck through the archway. Curious, N'Doch holds on to the doorjamb, and looks back. The wooden doors and their framing arch are there, and through them, the rubbled square whirling with flying grit and rotor roar. Elsewhere, for 360 degrees, nothing but red dirt and scrub, and the windy silence of the bush.

He lets go of the door. The portal vanishes. He and Paia stand breathless for a moment, absorbing the sudden change in their surroundings. N'Doch waits for that filling up of the empty spaces inside him that'll tell him the blue dragon's around. But the ache remains. He swears softly and strikes out across the empty peanut field. "Better not hang here in the open for too long."

He sees nothing moving around the distant compound or in the fields around. Not surprising, as it is pretty much midday, when anyone with a brain in his head gets out of the sun. Probably some of the mutts will be lying around the gate, though, just keeping an eye on things.

But no mangy critters leap up to confront them as they round the corner of the yellow wall. No flocks of blackbirds explode from the trees.

"Look," says Paia. "The gate is wide open."

"He always leaves it like that." But this is not strictly accurate. Papa Dja leaves it *unlocked*, not all bent askew and off its hinges, just like the big gates back in town. The tire iron hits the dry roadway with a dull clatter. N'Doch bolts for the opening, then sags against the gatepost, clutching the bent ironwork. He shuts his eyes, murmuring a prayer he didn't even know he knew.

When he looks again, the trees are still there, gathered in a green and inviting corner of the yard. And there's the neat little garden plot. But his grandfather's house is a pile of rubble. It looks like giants have stomped it into chalk and gravel. N'Doch feels like howling, madly, inarticulately, but even in the grip of fury, he's aware this might alert pursuers. He wishes he could just puke up the bile and blind rage tearing his gut apart like a school of sharks. His distant third choice is to push off the gatepost and slam his fist against the peeling stucco. Pound, pound. Loose paint and plaster fly like shrapnel. Pound. Pound. Again. Again. Where is the damn dragon when he really needs her?

Paia wraps both hands around his forearm. "Stop that! Stop that right now!"

The momentum of his strike swings her around and smacks her against the wall. N'Doch doesn't notice. "I fucked up again!"

"It's not your fault!"

"I should've been here!"

"You didn't know!"

"I did! We all did! The bastard told us what he was gonna do, and he went and did it while we stood around and fucking *talked* about it!" He lifts his fist for another pound, but she's on him again, grabbing at his arms. N'Doch shoves her aside and tears into the ruined compound.

Paia chases after him. She catches up as he stops to stare at the rows of wilting tomatoes. This time, she keeps her hands to herself.

"Papa Dja used to water his 'maters twice a day."

"I know, I know," she murmurs. "N'Doch, listen to me,

please! You know why Fire's done this! Not because your mother or your grandfather were any danger to him. It's all about you. He's done it to disable *you*!" She reaches up to lay her palm against his wet cheek. "Don't let him do that, okay?"

N'Doch shakes her off and walks away. He doesn't want her seeing his tears. Halfway between the garden and the rubble pile, he's stopped by the sight of Papa Dja's metal garden chair, flung over on its side under the lemon tree. "The mutts must've all run off," he notes bitterly. "Cowards."

Fallen lemons roll around his feet as he stalks over and sets the chair upright. Then he sees the plastic water jug sitting at the base of the tree. His own old water jug, that he'd brought when he arrived with the dragons and got Papa Dja mixed up in this business. No, that's not exactly true. Djawara claimed to have been waiting for the dragons all along. To hear him tell it, he'd been mixed up in it before N'Doch was even thought of.

N'Doch feels the chill even before he picks up the jug. It's full of clear, cold water.

"Paia!" It may be the first time he's said her name, at least to her face.

"I'm here," she says, from right behind him.

He shoves the jug at her. "This was just sitting here."

She cradles it, sniffs at the open top. "Smells okay."

"It's *cold*. How could it be cold, sitting out here in the sun? I mean, long enough for the tomatoes to wilt."

She glances about. "Is someone still here? Hiding?"

"Hiding?" N'Doch bellows. He gestures furiously around the tiny walled enclosure and at the flattened house at its center, turning, turning, with his arms spread wide. "Where the fuck could anyone be hiding?"

"Under those trees?" she suggests, wary of his sudden raving.

N'Doch rolls his eyes. Can't she see? The trees are nothing. It's only because the landscape's so flat and the scrub so stunted that these trees look like anything at all. There aren't more than five or six of them. Okay, so their branches bend low. Even Paia couldn't walk under them without getting a face full of leaves. But the ground past their slim gray trunks is visible all the way to the wall behind, except for that little patch of shade way back in the corner.

And then he recalls the night when two dragons vanished into that patch of shade. Completely vanished. They'd even invited him in, but N'Doch was too creeped out to venture in there. This was before he'd accepted the fact that the dragon biz wasn't going to go away any time real soon.

"Maybe the trees . . ." He's amazed to see Paia holding out the rusty tire iron. She must have picked it up outside the gate. He takes it with a brusque nod. Maybe it's not such a bad thing she's come along.

He takes a long, delaying-action swig from the jug, then approaches the little grove. He can't picture Baraga's business-suited thugs hanging out in the brush. Why would they bother? They're armed to the teeth with a lot more than tire irons. And it's just as hard to imagine the Fire-breather soiling his shiny golden scales with all that leaf litter. Still . . .

He ducks under the outermost branches. He sees no one—and nothing. But it's much cooler among the leaves than he'd expected, and he has to admit that it is unusually dark in that way-back corner. Not just dark . . . indistinct. As if a tiny black fog has settled there.

A sudden flapping nearly stops his heart. He recoils with a string of muttered curses.

"N'Doch?" Paia calls from the sunlit yard.

"A . . . bird. It's only a bird." He hates being startled. It's embarrassing.

"A real bird?"

"Of course a real bird! What'd you think?"

He ought to feel ashamed. He ought to apologize. He knows she's probably never seen a live bird before, but this lump of outrage he's carrying just under his skin keeps popping up, raw as a blister. It won't let him be easy and reasonable right now.

The bird has dropped out of the upper branches and is boldly stalking about right at his feet. It's an ugly, scrawny black critter with one wing half-cocked, not much of a bird at all. It peers at him brightly, and then it opens its beak to utter a sound so musical, so lovely, that it halts N'Doch in his tracks. It's like the sound pure silver might make if it could pour like water.

"What?" For a moment, the ache in him eases. He forgets his rage. "Say that again?"

And the bird does. Then it walks off into the deeper shade, turns around and comes back, fixing N'Doch with first one amber eye and then the other. It warbles at him again, repeating itself several times.

N'Doch calls out softly, so as not to spook the bird. He's grateful to it for showing him how to speak more gently. "Hey, Paia? You oughta come in here. Kinda slowlike."

She slips in behind him. She's got the water jug tight in her hand. Sensible woman. She knows to leave nothing useful behind. The bird doesn't spook. It studies Paia briefly, as if to say, what kept you? Then it treats her to a particularly passionate chorus of its lyrical song. Paia clasps the water jug to her breast like it was a child. "Oh! How wonderful!"

This time, the bird hops to the edge of the shadow and stays there, regarding them both expectantly.

"Is it a raven?" Paia asks.

"Damned if I know. Why?"

"In this book I read in my father's library, ravens are often the bearers of messages and omens."

"Messages from who?"

"Someone with the power to compel a raven."

"Well, if it's telling me a message, I don't speak its language."

"But you do," Paia murmurs. She kneels in front of the bird and holds out her hand. The bird shakes its head and warbles. "Its language is music."

"Huh," says N'Doch. He is thinking of another Raven, much more beautiful than this one.

"Wouldn't you say that it wants us to follow it?"

"I'd, um . . . yeah, I'd say that."

Together they peer into the oddly shifting darkness.

"We should hurry up, then, shouldn't we?" says Paia. "Remember the screen in your . . ." Her voice drops. "In your mother's house."

Who's leading this expedition, N'Doch asks himself. "What about Papa Dja?"

"It seems clear, don't you think, that he isn't here . . . ?"

N'Doch grits his teeth, and looks away. "No. He sure isn't."

"Could he have gone someplace safe, and left this bird as a message?"

"Some place like . . ." He jerks his chin toward the foggy shadow. "In there? Does that look safe to you?"

Paia shrugs, sitting back on her heels with her hands folded in her lap, the very picture of acquiescence.

N'Doch sighs and rubs his eyes. Nothing in the world is less likely than anything else, he decides. "You win," he says. "You and the bird."

CHAPTER EIGHT

"**I**t's a strange place," Paia observes later. "But not too scary so far."

When they arrived at the dead end, N'Doch stayed quiet for a while, watchful and waiting. But when the place just went on being what it was, with no visible way in, or even back out, he began to pace and mutter.

"I'm just as happy to rest a little," Paia offers agreeably, mostly to invite a more useful conversation.

"You rest. I'm looking for a way out."

Paia tries a smile, since smiles seem to render him more tractable. But the gesture is so mechanical that even she finds it irritating. Instead, she sets the water jug down on the nearest raised surface and drops beside it with a sigh. Who wouldn't want a moment or two to recover after being chased halfway across Africa by a demon helicopter? Besides, N'Doch is the problem solver. He's used to being able to figure his way out of things.

As for me, I'm just used to letting other people do the figuring for me.

Not particularly cheered by this admission, Paia wets the hem of her shirt with the tiniest slosh of water and dabs at her face. The pale fabric comes away ruddy with dust. "You want some water?"

N'Doch paces over, grabs up the jug for a long and noisy swig, plops it down again, and paces away. "It's a trap," he growls. "Now the dragons'll never find us!"

"It won't help if you wear yourself out storming about."

"I'm walking. I'm thinking on my feet."

"Well, I'm thinking, too. And all that useless motion is distracting!"

"Oh, great. Just when I'd decided it wasn't a total drag having you along!" He jams his hands on his hips. "You must've got real used to telling people what to do in that Temple of yours."

"Why do you say that?"

"Because you keep trying it on me. Except you're always pretending you're not. So, quit it, okay? I don't like it."

"But I was only . . ." Perhaps she had sounded a bit bossy. She hadn't meant to. And he does deserve some extra patience and compassion, after the shock of losing his mother. "Sorry."

N'Doch kicks at the thing she's sitting on. "What are these, anyway?"

There are two of them, set opposite each other: pale, smooth rectangles exactly the height of a chair. "Benches? They look like benches."

"They look like gravestones. What are they doing here?"

Paia flares. "How should I know?"

"Maybe you should give it some thought." He stalks away, unrepentant.

The bird, who has been hiding from N'Doch since narrowly avoiding a well-aimed kick in its direction, hops up beside Paia with its eye fixed on the water jug. She feels responsible for it now, as if she's acquired a pet. She looks around for a way to give it some and there, at the end of the bench, is a shallow, round container about the size of her palm.

"Well, bird, look at that." Paia slides over to pick it up, but it's either glued to or a part of the otherwise unbroken surface. Odd that she hadn't noticed it before. She shrugs and pours an inch of water into the odd little cup. The bird warbles, and moves in for a drink.

"I'm not sure you deserve it," she scolds, watching it dip and swallow, dip and swallow. "Look what you got us into."

But it had been her idea, after all, that she and N'Doch should follow the black bird into the fog at the back of the tree shadow. The fuzzy blinding darkness went on a lot longer than it should, given the high wall enclosing the compound. Perhaps they'd descended without being aware of it, and somehow tunneled under the wall. Whatever the explanation, they met no wall, just an enveloping darkness, which lightened gradually through several shades of luminous gray. When the last of it dissipated, they were in this very peculiar place.

It's a big, open-ended room, smooth-floored, high-ceilinged, and as featureless as a blank sheet of paper, but for the two white slabs in the middle. Looked at more closely, they're not like gravestones at all. They're obviously benches. Paia can't imagine why she thought otherwise. They have cylindrical legs and a thick polished top, subtly veined like white marble. There is one thing odd about them. Stone in the shade is usually cool, even at the Citadel, where almost nothing is cool. These benches match Paia's body temperature, as if someone has just gotten up from where she's sitting.

"Creepy," she says to the bird. "Some sort of plastic?"

And what about the walls? They're not so blank as she'd thought at first. A faint tracery of tall windowlike shapes angles away in sharp perspective toward the dark opening at the far end of the room. And there, where there should be a way out, Paia's study stalls. Here's the really peculiar thing about this place. There's nothing there. Not night or darkness, but *nothing*. Void.

N'Doch stands halfway between Paia and the void, staring into it as if willing it to explain itself. Paia doesn't blame him for letting sorrow and frustration make him so irritable. Her father'd had that way of dealing with his feelings sometimes. And surely, once N'Doch agreed to follow the bird, he'd really let himself hope he'd find his grandfather waiting for him.

The bird finishes drinking and waddles along the bench to hop up on Paia's knee. She's entranced by its bright glance and forthright manner, and by its obvious if alien intelligence. She forgives it for looking so much the worse for wear. After all, it's her first real live bird, and if it's not as lovely as all the pictures she's seen, it's certainly much more interesting. She used to know the date when the last bird died, at least in North America. Her father often reminded her of it. She regrets that she's forgotten it, and even more that she did not grow up with such interesting creatures in her world.

She extends a hand to the bird, experimentally. It lets her stroke its dusty feathers until a bit of sheen reappears.

Then it crooks one scrawny yellow leg and grasps her fore-finger firmly. Paia gasps, then giggles nervously. "Hello, bird," she says, wiggling the leg gently up and down. She's relieved when it releases her and stands back. She'd like it better if its feet weren't so reminiscent of dragon's claws.

N'Doch slouches over and slumps down on the far end of the bench, sending the bird scurrying to Paia's side.

"Look out . . ." she begins, but the container of water is no longer there.

"What? What?"

"Nothing. It was . . . I thought you might sit on the bird." But she almost orders him up again, so she can see the spot where the little cup fit so neatly back into the bench-top. Pressed down by his weight? She'd like to know. But she doesn't want him to think she's telling him what to do.

"I don't get it." He fists one hand restlessly inside the other. "All the other portals went somewhere. How come there's no there here?"

"It's like a waiting room." Like the benches in the halls outside her father's offices at the Citadel, where people seemed to wait forever.

"Waiting for what?"

"For an idea. For a way out. For something to happen. Like we are." Paia wishes he wouldn't glare at her so accus-ingly, as if she's said something unpardonably stupid. She's not stupid. She's just more accepting of their situation. In fact, she feels curiously numb, as if she's repressed her anxi-ety all the way to affectlessness. How totally sheltered she was in her family fortress! As long as she remained inside, she had nothing and no one to fear—except, of course, the God. In the outside world, apparently everything is a threat. Just as her father—and the God—had always warned her.

"Except you, bird," she murmurs. "Isn't that right?"

The bird regards her expectantly, as if it, too, is bored with waiting.

"Sorry. Not much I can do." Paia turns away to study the windows along the opposite wall. If only she could see through all that cut glass and heavy drapery! There might be a light behind. She's not sure, but the beveled patterns in the glass seem to sparkle with a different sort of light than the cool, even glow of the room they're sitting in.

They could knock on a window, perhaps, even open it, or . . .

"What's over the railing?" she asks N'Doch.

"What railing?"

"The balcony railing."

He gives her that same accusing glare.

"Well, look." She points. "Down at the far end."

He turns toward the void. The railing is a waist-high band of white stone, supported by cylindrical balusters. "That wasn't there before."

"Yes, it . . . wait, no. You're right. It wasn't. Why did I . . . ?" Paia suffers a moment of vertigo. Because the bench wasn't a bench either. Not at first. She can picture it clearly: a plain white block. It's like waking up when you're not even aware you've been asleep and dreaming. "What about those windows?" The detail of their casing and mullions seems richer than a moment ago. "Those weren't there either, were they?"

"No. They weren't." N'Doch stands up. "Something's happening."

At least he didn't say, "What windows?" "Are we asleep?"

The accusing glare is slightly milder this time.

"Well, we might be. How would we know?" There's another possibility that Paia doesn't even want to mention.

" 'Cause I know, that's how."

The bird suddenly emits its musical cry and takes off in a dusty flurry. It soars once around the room, then flies straight out into the void, its call fading with distance.

"Hey, look at that!" N'Doch sprints after it. "If it got out, we can!"

Paia hurries to join him at the edge, and finds him gripping the balcony railing as if it might try to escape.

"Okay," he says. "This is weird."

To the left and right of the opening, long flights of stairs have materialized. The broad white railing leads downward like an arrow into darkness. But shapes are coalescing out of the void, a landscape rising from the fog. Or rather, a cityscape. As they watch, tall straight-sided towers appear, bathed in a cool, even light. Puffs of storybook cloud obscure their heights. Their feet are planted within an infinitely receding grid of wide, clean streets.

"Now where have we got ourselves to?" N'Doch murmurs.

"It's beautiful," Paia breathes, mourning the drowned and ruined cities of her own time. "It's huge. Are we supposed to go down there?"

"Where else?" N'Doch slides his hand along the railing, testing its solidity.

From high above its pale streets, the city looks motionless and deserted.

"Which way should we go?"

"If I had a coin, I'd toss it."

"The bird flew that way." Paia points vaguely toward the left. The sky between the towers is now a clear, flat blue. The puffy clouds seem permanently moored to their tips.

"As good a guess as any. Ready?" With a hint of returning bravado, N'Doch squares his shoulders and starts down the left-hand staircase. She can tell he's glad just to be moving again.

The first part of the descent is more like mountain climbing than walking. The steps are dangerously high and deep, and the stair goes straight down without a turn or landing, as if built for giants. Paia is reminded of the Grand Stair leading up to the Citadel, specifically designed to be difficult, in order to repel invading armies, but also to provide the worshiper approaching the Temple with an opportunity for penance. She doesn't question the oddness of such a stair until, after several minutes of perilous stumbling and a lot of awkwardness, the going gets easier and the steps are not so tall or wide. The farther they descend, the easier it gets, until the steps are the perfect height and width for speeding downward. N'Doch slows his pace voluntarily, to keep them both from tumbling headlong to the city streets.

The staircase spills them out at the edge of a vast, paved square. Paia glances back up the long run of steps, climbing the side of a windowless building as sheer as the face of a cliff. Who would build such a precipitous stair on the structure's exterior? The balcony is a vague smudge, a mere brushstroke in the upper distance, wreathed like the tower tops in clouds that to her painter's eye look as if they've been laid on top of an existing canvas.

"Are you sure we're not dreaming this?" she asks plaintively.

"Sure, I'm sure," replies N'Doch, with the intensity of one trying hard to convince himself. "What's your problem, anyway?"

"Look at this place!"

"What's the last city you were ever in?"

"I've seen pictures. Lots of them. Cities have people, but this place is empty. There's no one here!"

"We don't know that yet." He stands with his arms akimbo, gazing ahead down a wide street that vanishes into the distance without a crook or bend. His dark, mobile silhouette rests uneasily against the pale background of faceless buildings and streets, as if cut out with scissors and pasted on. "Wonder where the damn bird went."

Rather than striking out across the open square, N'Doch chooses the long way, around its perimeter. The pavement is as smooth and white as polished tile. The facades of the buildings are peculiarly blank, with tall arched niches wrapping curls of thin shadow around opaque windows and doors. Rather as an Impressionist might paint them, Paia notes. No detail, just the effects of light. But a painter's surfaces would never be so flat and lifeless. It's like there's an entire dimension missing from everything she sees.

"If there are people here," she asks, "how do they get in and out of these buildings?"

"What d'you mean, if? Who ever heard of a city with no people?"

"There's lots of them. Most of them, in my time."

N'Doch shakes his head impatiently. "Concealed entrances, probably. For security reasons."

As he says this, there's a shivering in the ground. A buildup of static in the air raises the hair on Paia's arms. N'Doch has moved off toward the nearest doorway for a closer look.

"You feel that?" she calls.

He steps up on a sidewalk she hadn't noticed before and peers into the archway. "Feel what?"

The sensation passes. Paia hurries to catch up with him. "You didn't feel that little . . . quivering?"

"Nope. Not a thing." He runs his palm across the blank space where the door should be. "You'd think maybe there'd be a sign or something. You know, like: dragon guides, ring here."

Paia is relieved to see his humor resurfacing. Her laugh echoes thinly, as if the buildings have absorbed most of its wavelengths. N'Doch moves on to the next entryway, which is flanked by a pair of white columns, but offers the same lack of access.

"I'd feel better if there was someone around," Paia ventures.

"Ha. Be careful what you wish for. Who says that some-one would want us around?"

"But wouldn't you prefer an enemy we know about to one we can't even see?"

"I'd prefer no enemies at all. Enemies do things like blow you to pieces and murder your ma."

"Oh, N'Doch. . . ." Paia slips her hand around the crook of his elbow. His tensed muscles are more honest about his state of mind than his face is. She squeezes him gently. "I'm so sorry."

"Yeah. Me, too."

She's glad he can finally admit it aloud. They walk arm in arm to the end of the block, where a side street enters the square. But N'Doch disengages himself uneasily when they reach the curb. He looks out across the broad expanse of open pavement. "Y'know, the folks who made this city didn't have much of an imagination. Those buildings on that side are exactly the same as these here."

Paia allows his escape to safer subject matter. "And the other two sides match each other, too. An advanced appreciation of symmetry, perhaps?"

"Symmetry is boring."

"Always?" She glances up at him, risking a smile. "You'd look very odd without matching arms and legs. Or eyes."

N'Doch snorts. "Maybe. But I knew a guy once with one brown eye and one blue one. Made a shitload of money on it, 'cause people thought he was a big magic man." His grin is sour, but Paia is happy to see it. "Point is," he continues, "I wouldn't want to meet the people that live here. They'd be the people who gotta do things a certain way. I wouldn't likely fit into their mold. Maybe if we got off the main drag a bit . . ."

He turns to peer hopefully down the little side street. The ground shivers again, a tremor like a tiny earthquake.

Paia's vision blurs momentarily. Either that, or something odd is happening to the surfaces of the buildings. And then, it's as if nothing had occurred.

"There! Did you feel that?"

"Was that it before? I thought it was me phasing out for a nanosec."

"No, it . . . look! Ask, and ye shall receive!"

On the corner of the building across the side street, a little above headheight, is a sign—the first they've seen, the first detail of any sort. Paia's eyes fall upon it hungrily. It's a bright sky-blue rectangle with a neat white border and white block lettering. Familiar looking, but she can't quite place it.

" 'As the crow flies . . .' " N'Doch reads with a puckered brow. "Huh. I guess it could have been a crow."

"What's a crow?"

"A bird. Like the one that got us into this mess in the first place."

"Ah." Paia stares at the sign, trying to tease out further meaning. Of course! It reminds her of a monitor screen. Amazing, she muses, the significance letters can assume when they're the only ones around. There are very few signs in the Citadel, and no books at all, save the antiques in her father's library. There's no one to publish them anymore. The God requires literacy for the Temple priesthood, but only to enable them to carry out the day-to-day administration and to keep track of the tithing and finances. She wonders how many of the children in the villages that pay duty to the Temple are being taught to read and write. Why bother, if there's nothing for them to read? On the other hand, how will there ever be anything to read again, if no one is taught how to write?

Paia realizes that N'Doch is staring at her.

"You gonna read that sign right off the wall, girl?"

"I was thinking about books."

"Books? I've read one or two." He shakes his head. "You're weird. C'mon. This way. This little street looks promising."

At first, Paia is not sure she agrees, and she's glad when he chooses a cautious pace and sticks to the middle of the pavement. The street is narrow, and shaded rather abruptly into dimness by the tall buildings on either side—all the horizontal confinement of a cave without the vertical comfort of a roof. But, in the distance, several vague projecting shapes promise a change in the monotony of the facades. They gain specificity as the distance shortens, and are finally resolved into objects familiar to Paia only through pictures. In colors and stripes, they hang out over the sidewalk, which is less well-maintained on this back street than out in the main square. Long cracks spiderweb the concrete, and the curbstones are worn and broken.

N'Doch points. "See those awnings? Must be a little business district."

Awnings. That's what they're called. Paia thinks they look very cheerful, especially after a long trudge through a dull gray city. Urged along faster, she can soon see little tables under the nearest one, covered with red-checkered cloths. The black metal chairs have rounded, filigreed backs. Paia feels a sudden urge to sit down.

But N'Doch's eager pace has slackened. Abruptly he stops, in the middle of the street. "Oh, boy."

"What is it?"

"You wouldn't understand."

"I might, if you give me a chance."

"I know this place."

"What do you mean?"

"I *know* it. I've been there. Bunch of times, when I was a boy."

Paia has met many strange notions in her life, but for some reason, this one gives her a chill. "Oh, N'Doch, it just *looks* like some place you've been."

"No. It is." He jabs a finger at the scrawl of lettering on the green-and-white striped canopy. "See what it says? *La Rive Gauche.* That's what the place was called. It was Papa Dja's favorite hangout when he was still living in town. Okay. I'll reconsider the possibility that I'm dreaming . . . !"

"*We're* dreaming."

"We can't both be . . ."

There's movement among the tables. A large brown animal rises from the shadows and stands at attention, looking their way. Paia encounters her second extinct creature in less than a day. It's a dog, and the sight invokes a sharp twinge of nostalgia. Her father had tried to breed dogs in the early days of the Collapse, but feeding them became too difficult when the humans around them were starving. The feudal system of tribute-in-kind that keeps the Temple denizens so healthy and well fed wasn't put in place until the dragon arrived. This dog does not look well fed at all. Even at a distance, Paia can see that its raggedy coat is patched with the matted darkness of dried blood. But it looks alert and capable of being threatening. Paia doesn't know if she should be afraid of it or not.

"It's one of the mutts!" N'Doch waves at the dog, then whistles. "Damn! It's one of Papa Dja's old mutts!" He whistles again, but the dog stays right where it is, dancing from paw to paw and panting foolishly. "Okay, boy, wait there and we'll come to you." N'Doch breaks into a trot.

And is flung to the ground by a sudden shifting of the pavement. Paia stumbles as the street jerks sideways, left, then right, and left again, as if meaning to keep her tumbling. Scrambling to her feet, she hears a crackling and roaring, rolling down the canyon of buildings behind them. Grit swirls in the air, blinding her. Where did it come from? The streets are spotless. N'Doch is yelling over the roar. He grabs her under her arms, yanking her to her feet. The grit is sharper now, biting at her skin like a swarm of insects. The gusts tear at her hair and clothing.

"Inside!" N'Doch screams in her ear. "We've got to get inside!"

They race toward the café, the street bucking beneath them, the wind like a giant's vicious sidearm punch. The crackling is behind them, approaching, nearing, deafening.

"Faster!" N'Doch bellows. "It's after us!"

Paia can't think about what "it" is. She can only run, as fast as she can, a frantic mouse scurrying for the baseboard. They gain the shadow of the canopy. The scalloped edges of the awning snap in the wind like the repeating crack of pistol shots. Empty coffee cups and butter plates are sliding, crashing to the pavement. The dog has vanished. N'Doch hauls Paia through the shifting maze of tables and chairs toward the door, shattered glass crunching beneath their feet. Paia fights off a flying tablecloth that's wrapped itself around her face and breathes a little prayer of thanks, because there is a door here and it's opening, just in time to receive them as they stagger blindly through. It slams abruptly shut behind them.

The silence is almost as deafening as the roaring had been outside. The floor is steady and level. The air is still. Paia inhales the long-forgotten dark scent of coffee and the earthy sweetness of fresh bread. The dimly lit room is full of dogs, scattered about on the black-and-white tiles. Several of them thump their tails in greeting.

"There you are! Took your own sweet time as usual."

An old man is standing behind them, silhouetted against the wall of windows fronting the café. His hand is on the doorknob. Paia cannot see his face. On the other side of the glass, tables and chairs are skidding and colliding in space like elementary particles.

N'Doch whirls. "Papa Dja!" He starts toward the man, then stops. "Damn, you're a sight for sore eyes!"

"Glad you made it in one piece."

Paia wonders if a penchant for understatement could be hereditary.

"A close thing, too," N'Doch exclaims. "You oughta stand clear of all that glass."

"We're safe in here. It can't come in."

"It?"

The old man glances behind him as a wind-borne chair crashes twice against the door, like a giant's knock. He lifts both arms in a gesture of resignation. "There is great evil abroad in this city, my boy." He moves away from the door as if exhausted, and lowers himself into a chair by the window. A tiny white cup and saucer rest on the marble-topped table beside it.

"Man, it was . . ."

"I know. I don't go out."

N'Doch drops to a crouch beside the chair and grasps his grandfather's knees, giving them a little shake. "Damn, when I got there and saw . . . I was sure you were . . . !"

The old man pats his grandson's hands awkwardly, and then the head that drops to press itself against him. "So was I, for a while there."

He is slight but elegant of manner, what Paia's father would have called an old-world gentleman. His hair has grayed in tight curls like a woolly skullcap pulled back from his high forehead. He's wearing white, a floor-length tunic with full sleeves and gold embroidery around the open neck. Paia takes to him immediately, especially when he offers her a warm and intelligent smile, and his dark, slender hand in greeting.

"Who's this, now? You're showing off with a different woman every time I see you."

"Not *my* woman, Papa." N'Doch sits back on his heels with a damp and weary grin, one hand still resting on the old man's knee. "This is Paia. She's a dragon guide, too. Paia, this is my grandfather Djawara. Pay no attention to anything he says."

N'Doch's grandfather peers at Paia without a trace of myopia. "Hmmm. The Fire-breather's, is it?"

"Yes, sir." Paia doesn't ask how he knows. She can see that this family likes to spring their knowledge on you sideways, to see if you'll startle. She hasn't called anyone "sir" since her father's diplomatic colleagues stopped coming to the Citadel, but the old gesture of respect comes back automatically with this man. She returns his handshake firmly. "We're so glad to find you alive!"

Djawara raises an eyebrow at his crouching grandson. "Nice girl. Beautiful, too. Why isn't she yours?"

N'Doch shoots a glance at Paia. " 'Cause somebody else got there first."

"And you're honoring that? Good lad. Your manners have improved."

"Funny. I'd have said I was losing my touch." N'Doch's hands are working patterns on Djawara's bony knees, soft musical rhythms of distress. "Papa. Papa. I got some bad news to tell you. Real bad. Fâtime's gone."

"Gone?"

"She's . . . um, she's dead, Papa."

Djawara's smile drains away like the color going out of a sunset. His chin lifts. He turns his face away to gaze through the dusty window. Outside, the windstorm has passed, leaving behind a rubble of broken furniture. "How?"

"Shot. Murdered."

"Murdered? Why? What for? For the house? For that ancient black-and-white TV? She had nothing worth killing her for!"

Paia pulls a chair over beside Djawara. She sits down and takes his hand. His skin is darker than hers, but just as soft.

N'Doch stands, walks in an aimless little circle, then goes to the door and leans his forehead against the glass. "Not a thief, Papa. It was too clean . . . like a hit. I think it was Baraga."

"It was the dragon," Paia says. "It was Fire. He's the one to blame."

"Who came after you, Papa? Your house is a pancake."

Djawara nods. "My lovely, loyal house. Men, for sure. There was a lot of shooting. Maybe the dragon as well. It all happened so fast. But I saved the dogs, or I should say, they saved me. Dragged me into the trees, and poof! Here I am. I always knew there was something lurking beneath those boughs. Just couldn't ever find it before."

"There was a bird," Paia murmurs.

"Oh, yes. He's around somewhere. They all are."

"But, Papa, why are we here in the Rive? No, strike that. Why is the Rive here?"

Djawara shrugs. "You don't know?"

"Not a clue."

"I thought maybe the dragons might . . . where are they, anyway?"

"On the way, I hope. We sort of got started without them." N'Doch turns away from the door to regard the café in all its richness of detail: the cracked plaster walls hung with faded posters advertising travel to cities that Paia knows were under water long ago; the dark polished oak bar with its glimmering mirrors behind shelves stocked with bottles and glassware; the towering espresso machine in the corner, surrounded by stacks of white china. He spreads his arms wide. "But why are we here? Is it . . . an illusion?"

"I worried about that," Djawara concedes. "I wandered for what seemed like days in this faceless city and suddenly, there it was, with a fresh cup of espresso sitting right there on the table, and the old horse trough full of water for the dogs."

"Suddenly? You mean, like it hadn't been there before?"

"Well, I don't know that, do I? Every street in this city looks alike. But when I spotted that old familiar awning, I'd just been thinking of how restorative a good shot of espresso would be. I walked in and everything, the whole room, was like the Rive, but not quite. Like a sort of sketch. Except for the steaming cup of espresso. That was so real, I burned my tongue." Djawara pauses to moisten his lips as if testing for lingering tenderness. "That was several days ago, and I haven't been hungry or thirsty since. And the place gets more like the Rive every day. If it's an illusion, I doubt it could feed me so convincingly. The dogs are so pampered, they're getting positively lazy." He sighs, leans forward and sips at his cup. "Sometimes I think tea would be nice for a change, and there it is. If it's an illusion, it's not your ordinary kind."

N'Doch walks to the bar, pats it, then leans against it and looks back at Paia. "This couldn't all be Fire's doing?"

She considers this nervously. But *La Rive Gauche* just does not seem to be Fire's sort of place. It's too pleasant and understated, too . . . democratic, and she says so.

"But," counters N'Doch, "the weather can be a real bitch."

"That was no simple windstorm," Djawara says. "There are monsters roaming the streets, make no mistake about it. I don't go out. Neither do the dogs. Not since we lost three of them. That's why I sent the bird. For some reason, they can get through."

"But, Papa, we gotta go out sometime. Can't just sit in here for the rest of our lives. Much as I love the Rive, and all. Remember, when I was little, you always gave me one of . . ." N'Doch looks around, then strides to a table to grab up a glistening brown lump from a white porcelain bowl. He holds it up, triumphantly pincered between thumb and forefinger. ". . . one of these! And sent me home to Ma." His grin fades. He returns the lump to the bowl. "Papa, I couldn't even bury her or anything. The whole town's a war zone."

"It was more important to find you," Paia adds softly. "Alive."

"We're all the family we have now, boy."

"You got it, Papa."

In the silence that visits uninvited, Paia's relief and exhaustion draws up around her like a warm blanket. She yawns, wishing for a more comfortable seat than the rickety metal chairs around the tables.

"Can I get you anything, my dear?" the old man asks.

There is a pitcher of water on the table now, with three glasses beside it. Lemon slices float among the ice cubes. Paia lets Djawara fill a glass for her. She's too tired to eat. N'Doch wanders about the little café, poking into cabinets and corners, lifting lids and uncorking bottles. Djawara sips his coffee silently and lets his grandson wear out his restless energy. Finally, N'Doch comes back to the table and drops heavily into the third chair.

He pours himself a glass of water and drains it. "Okay. Now, let me get this straight. You think real hard about what you want, and it appears. It does this right in front of you?"

"No." Djawara sets down his cup. "I always come upon it, as if it's been there all along. And asking for silly things doesn't work. Apparently, it has to be something I really need."

"Like coffee?"

"Well, need is evidently relative in this situation."

Paia yawns again, laying her head on her propped-up palm. "Maybe you just need to think you need it."

"What happens if I do it?" N'Doch asks.

"I don't know. Try."

N'Doch closes his eyes. In her sleepy stupor, Paia finds this comical. She giggles. N'Doch's eyes pop open in a glare, which makes her giggle again. "Why don't you try it?" he growls.

"I'm too tired."

He closes his eyes again. "I'm imagining a big plate of steak and *pommes frites.*" After a moment, he opens his eyes. All three survey the room. Nothing has magically appeared on any surface. N'Doch tries again. Nothing.

"What the hell? What am I doing wrong?"

"Maybe it's like making a wish," Paia offers. "You shouldn't tell us what you're asking for."

N'Doch makes a rude noise. "What does it care if I tell you or not?"

"Interesting," Djawara says. "That you say 'it.' I also find myself personifying these appearances, as if they are a gift from some entity, rather than an inherent reflex of the landscape."

"Perhaps *you* must make the request," Paia suggests.

"Go for it, then, Papa. I'm getting hungrier just thinking about it."

"Or perhaps," Paia amends, not sure what has made her think of this, "N'doch should sing it."

"Hey, off my back, huh?"

"I'm serious!"

"It's not such a bad idea," Djawara adds.

"What, sing about food? Oh . . . you mean like . . . oh, man, I gotta make up a song about steak, *pommes frites*?"

N'Doch shifts his chair irritably, allowing Paia a new angle of view that reveals an informal seating area in a far corner, with sofas and easy chairs arranged like her mother's reading parlor in the Citadel. While N'Doch fulminates about singing for his supper, Paia gets up and drifts across the room to the nearest sofa. A worn patchwork quilt like the one from her childhood lies folded over one pillowy arm. The cushions receive her softly as she throws herself among them, sinking gratefully toward sleep. The last thing she hears is N'Doch's musical mutterings resolving into a melodic hum. But what ushers her into delicious slumber is the homey odor of potatoes frying.

CHAPTER NINE

The white-tiled terrace holds his weight as he steps out onto it. The Librarian had been worried about that. The surface looks insubstantial, transparent, like the reflection on a still pond at dawn. He remembers such a pond, from his earlier days. But that pond was sanctuary. This is . . . something else.

Stoksie appears beside him, apparently untroubled by issues of solidity. He assesses the situation with quick Tinker pragmatism. "Dull sorta spot, G."

"Humming. Hear it?"

"Doan heah a t'ing. Watsit?"

It's a background noise, not the soundless imperative that's been urging him to speed for so many hours. It's like static or the steady breathing of circuitry. The Librarian shrugs. Maybe his ears have carried the sounds of the com room with him out of mere habit. He peers around. Stoksie's right. It is a dull sort of spot. The walls and roof enclosing the terrace are plain enough to suit the most rigid minimalist, a Bauhaus patio before the decorators arrive. The Librarian sighs. All his metaphors are archaic lately. Minimalism is no longer a choice. It's all that's left. He is unsurprised when he looks back at the portal, and encounters a blank gray wall.

Stoksie follows his gaze. "Heh. Guez we're heah fer a while, den."

The Librarian nods. Was it foolish to let himself be drawn so easily through that opening, and his good friend with him? Did he really have a choice? The hum is louder. He shakes his head. It doesn't vary or go away. But he's sure it's not his imagination. Just in a frequency the Tinker can't hear.

Stoksie ambles up to the terrace railing, with its expanse of blue beyond. The Librarian notes that the little man favors his bad hip all the time now. He wonders if the dragon Earth could fix that for him, in a spare moment, if any of them are to have any spare moments, ever again. At the railing, Stoksie leans out and looks down. "Weeeooo! C'mon an' lookit dis, G!"

The Librarian quails. Something about the light glinting off Stoksie's bald brown head as he leans over the edge. Something inexorable in its cool white glow. He knows suddenly that he'll never see his console again. Another refuge has served its purpose and become obsolete. His own evolution could be charted by the dens he's made over the centuries, and then outgrown. He suspects this is why he feels so different since the morning's confrontation on the mountaintop. Time for the next step forward. Maybe the final step.

"C'mon! Yu gotta see dis!"

As always, the Librarian's first instinct is to resist. He'd flee back to the familiar shelter of that console if he had half a chance. But his Destiny knows him well enough to make sure he doesn't—by the destruction of a home, by the pursuit of enemies, by an outbreak of war, by the slamming of a door. Always impelling him onward. Resigned, the Librarian shuffles across the terrace. The pale insubstantial tiles still hold him up. Isn't this why he came, after all? To confront the inevitable, whatever it may be? The humming, constant in his ears, suggests that the inevitable is near. But then, he's often thought that in the past, only to see the distance to his goal again become elastic, stretched toward infinity. Long practiced in the exertion of will over reluctance, the Librarian gains the railing and gazes out over the white city he'd known would be there since the moment the portal opened.

The terrace perch is astonishingly high off the ground. Even in the old days of the skyscrapers, the Librarian was never so high, except in an airplane. And this city is a forest of such towers. Clouds gather around them like luminous, upside-down shrubbery. The expanse of blue is not empty sky, but endless ranks of towers fading into blue distance. An artificial Himalaya. The Librarian's knees go weak, partly in fear, partly in admiration. It is a magnificent creation, an urban architect's wet dream.

"Yu t'ink da One is down deah?" Stoksie asks.

"Hoping. Hoping."

"How we gonna git down?"

"Elevator," murmurs the Librarian, knowing they'll find one. It doesn't take long: a rectangular outline on the nearest wall, like a box drawn on a blueprint. The Librarian approaches it, and it opens with a willing hush. He's confused for a moment, for the cab is identical to the elevator back at the Refuge. Has he misunderstood? Is Destiny leading him back to the com room, his journey over before it's begun? The Librarian shrugs, renewing his commitment to inevitability, and steps inside. Stoksie hurries to join him, and the doors whisk shut. There is a brass placket on the wall right where it should be, but no buttons to press. Time passes, without any sensation of movement. Stoksie whistles absently under his breath.

"Itsa long way down, aftah all," he remarks finally.

The Librarian chuckles. He'd love to be as firmly moored to reason as this staunch little man.

Without a warning tone or chime, the doors whisper open. It's like stepping through the portal all over again. It requires the same resolve. The Librarian's agoraphobia assails him. The space beyond the doors is so vast, so bright, so white. So empty.

"C'mon, G." Stoksie takes his arm.

Grateful, the Librarian lets himself be led.

He's expected a lobby, or an atrium at least, not this abrupt delivery out into the open. It's unsettling, architecturally, to be dropped without transition at the brink of this enormous and light-drenched plaza. Light, not sun. It's too white for sunlight. The Librarian recalls Tien-an-men, in the ancient city long destroyed. But the buildings surrounding this square are infinitely taller. To his agoraphobe's eye, the towers seem to be falling inward, toward the ground. But the Librarian is used to compensating for this old deficiency. He steps bravely forward. What brings him to his knees on the blank white pavement is not terror. It's the sound of that sunless light.

The sound!

Deafening, breath-shaking, a steady excruciating pounding on his head, his back, his ears.

"Whatsit, G? What?" Stoksie wheels back, struggles to help him up.

"The light . . . out of the light." He fumbles the speaking. He's barely able to complete the thought. He stumbles backward, blinded by noise. "Must get out of the light."

But there's no shade to back into, no retreat, no shelter. The elevator door has closed behind them and vanished into a gray wall as flat as painted granite.

"Okay, yu gottit. C'mon dis way!"

The Tinker is stronger than he looks. He guides the Librarian into the shadow of a tall, arched doorway. The hum still vibrates in his ears, but the pain subsides to a bearable level, and the Librarian can catch his breath. He tries to explain his predicament.

Stoksie sucks his crooked teeth. "Yeah? What kinda soun' duz da light make?"

The Librarian has not tried to identify it. He's been too focused on resisting it. His hands flutter. Words seem more elusive than ever.

"Izzit, y'know, like muzik?"

The Librarian shakes his head. He almost expects to hear loose parts rattling around. "Hum. Growl. Snap. Whine."

"Nice kinda soun', dat," Stoksie retorts disapprovingly. "Soun's 'lectric, like."

The Librarian has taken this for granted. But what's the source? And how will he manage to go about this huge city, searching for his dragon, if he's disabled from the start by the very daylight?

As if reading his thoughts, Stoksie says, "Y'know, G, if we go along in da shade a da bildins, mebbe yu'll be okay."

It's not a perfect solution. The flat facades fronting the square don't offer much shade, just the occasional recessed doorway. And none of the recesses have actual doors in them. No chance of retreating inside. But it will get him moving. The Librarian suffers through regular sound-beatings as Stoksie leads him from recess to recess. He tries plugging his ears, but the screaming, growling light invades his body, storming up and down his nerves. It drowns out all other voices, all other thought. Finally, they reach an

intersection, where the height of the buildings lays a strip
of deeper shadow along both sides of a narrow cross street.
The Librarian is too relieved to question this directionless
anomaly. He wishes he could sit down, just for a minute.
Even at only bearable, the cacophonous light tires him out.

"Heah, G. Take a load off yer feet." Stoksie drags up a
stout wooden crate. The Librarian notices there's only one.
Otherwise, the streets are entirely empty, and clean as if
newly made. The Tinker leans against the flat gray wall,
shifting the weight off his bad hip. "I suspected da One
wud be ina greener sorta place."

"Greener?" He's amazed to hear that Stoksie has
thought about the One at all. He was never a professed
believer.

"Yah, like yu say da wurld'll be 'agin, wen she come.
Y'know, ta fixit."

"Patience," he says, hating his inadequacy with words.
But how can he say 'have faith' to a man who's always
insisted he had none? Does Stoksie's question indicate
some sort of conversion, based perhaps on the arrival of
dragons? Or is he still humoring his mad old friend, as he
always has?

"Mebbe wen we find'er, it'll be green dere."

"Mebbe." He hopes so. He can't imagine a less green
place than the one they're in, unless it's the desiccated
world of 2213.

"So howyu wanna do dis serch, sizdammaddic-like, or as
da win' take us?"

The Librarian is at a loss. He had no plan when he
stepped through the portal. If he'd waited for a plan to
occur to him, he might not have gone. Perhaps he'd assumed that the dragon would find him, once they were both
in the same place. This is still theoretically possible, if indeed she is here. But will she know he's arrived? Is his
mere presence a sufficient announcement? The task ahead
is not as simple as he'd imagined when he stepped through
the portal. Any search should be systematic, of course, but
how to accomplish it in a strange and inexplicable city,
away from all his equipment, his electronic eyes and ears
and brain?

"Systematic," he says anyway.

"Den we gotta mark as we go, so we'll know weah we bin."

Leave it to a Tinker to come up with a plan. "How?"

Stoskie pulls a small jackknife from a hidden pocket. He unfolds a blunted metal spike and tries a few experimental scratches on the wall beside him. The awl leaves a clean line as bright as chalk. Stoksie grunts in surprise. He rubs his palm across the scratches and they disappear as if erased. "Mus' be sumkinda soff stone, dis."

"Convenient," the Librarian agrees dryly.

"Betcha." Stoksie draws three short parallel lines with a circle to the right of them, then stands back, grinning. "Dat's Tinka fer '*we wen' dattaway*.'"

The Librarian grins back. "Yer a gud man, Stokes."

They set off down the side street. He's tempted to haul the crate along with him, but he's slow enough already. He'll sit on the sidewalk if he has to, or maybe another perfect crate will appear when he needs it, as this one did, apparently out of nowhere.

"Big, emptee place," Stoksie observes, when they've walked several blocks and seen exactly the same rows of opaque windows, punctuated by the same doorless doorways, repeated over and over and over.

"Big, empty, boring place." The Librarian worries that the hum is getting louder again, though he's made sure to keep to the deepest shadow.

At the next intersection, the boredom is finally broken. Around the corner, in the middle of the wide street, sits an enormous hunk of machinery. Though it does not look rusted or broken, the Librarian knows right off that it's derelict—it has no working 'aura.' Stoksie would prefer to avoid it, as a large and alien device of unknown purpose, but the Librarian approaches it without scruple and lays his hands on its smooth surfaces, offering it solace for its untimely end. It's an awkward, ugly machine. He feels an instant kinship, grateful that he's not yet been cannibalized for parts, as this machine has. He can see the raw gaps and vacant connectors, empty housings for circuit boards and sensors. Clamps and cables have been ripped out. Its wheels have been removed, along with all their mounting hardware. He details the destruction to Stoksie at great length until curiosity overcomes the Tinker's scruples and he moves in closer.

"Mebbe gud salvage heah," he jokes. "Gud trade, huh?"

"If there was anyone to trade with."

Stoksie's shrug suggests there's always someone to trade with. "So wadda we know so fah? One, dere's masheens heah. Two, we know dey break doun. An' t'ree, we know dere's no endlis supply a parts."

Three useful observations, the Librarian agrees.

"But watsit fer, G? Yu know?"

The Librarian shakes his head. It had wheels, so it was mobile, probably under its own steam instead of being driven by an operator. It has no structure to support working arms of any kind. It has no decorative or protective carapace. With all its parts exposed, what's left of them, it looks complex. Yet it could have been something as simple as a street cleaner. With that thought, he glances at the street. What need could there be to clean such already pristine streets? But because he's looked, he spots something his sharp nose would have alerted him to, if he'd been paying proper attention. He jogs Stoksie's elbow and points.

Along the gutter behind the machine is what appears to be a trail of animal manure, spread out as if the creature dropping it was still moving forward. Its organic nature is a screaming anomaly against the faceless pavement. The Librarian can't believe he'd missed it until now.

"Da first sine a life!" Stoksie crows delightedly. He hurries over to scoop up a drying lump. He sniffs it studiously, then crumbles a small bit between thumb and forefinger. "Not long sinze. Mebbe a day, mebbe less. Funny kinda mule, seems."

"Cow. Cattle. Some kind of." The Librarian has dealt with all kinds of domestic animals in his time.

"A cow?" Stoksie's world-weary eyes go as eager as a child's. "I'd likta see dat!"

"Follow it?"

"Betcha!" He looks off in the direction of the trail of droppings. "Yu go fust, G. Yu da one wit' da killah nose."

A machine and a cow intersect, puzzles the Librarian. Maybe this pile of salvage really was a street cleaner. He wonders if whatever cannibalized the machine had its way with the cow, too. Animal scents are pungent. Easy to follow. This rich spoor is all the more articulate for being laid down in an otherwise odorless environment. The Librarian applies his nasal analysis.

"Cow. Cows, yes. Goat also. Sheep, maybe."

"Sheep! A 'hole farm, den? Wadda 'bout sum peeble?"

"Some also. Yes." The human scents are several, and they tickle the back of his brain with a feathery familiarity. An older knowing. It'll take him a while to search through the centuries of records archived in his head. Forgetting is never the problem, just locating the appropriate layer. In a few more blocks, he'll probably remember whose scents these remind him of.

The trail leads them in a path as random as the route they've already taken, a few blocks in one direction, a few in another.

"Dese folk doan know weah dey goin' needer," Stoksie decides. "Explorin'. Lookin' fer sumpin."

"Like us."

Stoksie nods. "Dey woan hab no ansers, den."

"Answers?"

"Aboud weah ta find da One."

"Guess not." Still, following a living trace seems more purposeful than wandering about at a total loss. The Librarian stays on the scent, down the next block, around the next corner, down several more blocks. More abandoned machinery turns up along the way, some as big as the street cleaner, most of it smaller, but all of it as unidentifiable as the first. Other than their dismantled state, the machines look out-of-the-box new and spotlessly clean. Stoksie shakes his head, disapproving of the waste.

"Not wasted. Recycled," the Librarian offers, to humor him. But really, in a city where the buildings or pavements show no sign of age or wear, why should its machinery be any different? *It's as if there's no weather here.* The idea stops the Librarian short. He stumbles, halfway into his next step. No weather. Of course!

"Yu alri', G?"

"Artificial," he mumbles.

"Wat iz?" Stoksie has on his humoring tone again.

"All this." It has to be. He does a full turn with his arms spread, and is proud of not tripping over his own amazement. "All."

Stoksie frowns, struggling to take in his meaning. "Da hole ciddy, yu mean?" He cranes his neck toward the narrow slice of blue between the surrounding towers. "My da tole me onct 'bout dis ciddy undah a reel big dome, like on da moon. He nevah seenit, bud he heerd aboudit. Das wat yu mean?"

The Librarian nods. Maybe a dome is what he means. He isn't sure. The insight came to him as they often do, without all its attendant evidence and explanations. He has learned to accept such understanding as visitors from elsewhere, from his dragon perhaps. At least, he's always hoped she was the source.

The hum in his head is getting louder again, except this time, it seems to be outside his head as well.

"Yu heer dat?" Stoksie asks.

"Betcha. You, too?" The Librarian is ecstatic to have the vagaries of his unruly senses for once confirmed.

"Frum 'roun' da nex cornah, sounds like."

They steal up to the mouth of the intersection. The crossing street is wider than usual. To the left, it travels for a short block, then passes through an open square. The external hum is coming from that direction. They forsake the livestock track in order to investigate.

"Git aginst da wall, nah," Stoksie advises.

When they're halfway down the block, the strong black-and-white design of the square's paving stones comes into focus. The Librarian squints at it eagerly. At last, a bit of visual interest! He fondly recalls the transformational geometrics of the twentieth century artist M. C. Escher, which this very much resembles.

In the middle of the pattern, two sprawling machines move in perfect tandem across the square. The exact nature of their work is not immediately apparent, mainly because what they're doing, while obvious to any eye, defies normal logic.

"Dey doin' wat it look like der doin'?"

It looks like one machine is pulling up the intricately laid tiles and piling them behind it according to shape and color. The other is taking up the neat piles and laying the tiles right back down again, in the same exact pattern.

"Routine maintenance?" suggests the Librarian, only half seriously.

"Das preddy weerd."

"Indeed." He listens for some hint of malfunction in the hum, but hears only smoothly functioning components. As with the derelict street cleaner, the Librarian is drawn to these devices. At least these are still functional. His inner hum is less chaotic now, he notices. He can detect patterns, a few more coherent lines among the general noise and static. While Stoksie hangs back, he moves out into the bright, hard light. The volume is deafening. He suffers it, like a man in a hailstorm, for the sake of curiosity. Hunched against the aural hammering, he totters up to the nearest machine and around it. It pays him no mind, but out of the agonizing clangor, two signals gradually resolve. This bit of ordering lessens the Librarian's pain. The signals coalesce into digital mutterings. Machine mutterings, about process and pattern and instruction. He senses no consciousness, no awareness. Less than in a barn he'd once had, where he would listen to the nighttime animal music, the murmurings and munchings, and learn entire histories of the day just past. He watches the mechanical pavers pick up tiles and put them back again, pondering their inchoate mysteries, until Stoksie edges up beside him.

"Yu bearin' up, G?"

"Not so bad, now."

"Wat nex?"

These machines have given up all their answers, if indeed they ever had any to offer the likes of Reuben Stokes, hardened rationalist. The Librarian turns away, regretful to leave them but glad to slink back into shadow, away from the discordant light. They retrace their steps to pick up the livestock trace. It moves straight ahead, block after block without turning. They pass no more machinery, abandoned or functional, for a long while. Then the quality of the trail changes. The Librarian slows to analyze the difference. Does adrenaline have an odor? He's sure he can smell it, just as he can smell fear.

"Running now." He points ahead, along the trace.

"Runnin'?"

"Running *away*."

Stoksie peers at the ground as if it might show footprints. "Wat frum?"

The Librarian is tempted to remind his friend that he's not clairvoyant. How different many things would be if he was. He's saved by the view at the next intersection: another black-and-white square, another audible hum. Here, the machine is stationed at a corner of the pattern, slowing and meticulously cleaning invisible dirt from the grout lines between the tiles.

"Wudn't be dat one, I guez."

The Librarian grunts his agreement.

"No wondah dis town's so clean!"

"Disapproving again, Stokes?"

"Me? Yah! Watta waste, yu know? Cud be doin' sumpin useful."

"Like what?"

Stoksie scowls at the slow, oblivious machine. "Doan know, G. Jes' sumpin beddah dan dat!"

The next square has a machine in it also, but this time, no new hum has announced its presence. It sits in the center of yet another elaborate *trompe l'oeil* pavement, intact and shining, and seems to be doing absolutely nothing at all.

They study it from the shade at the perimeter of the square.

"Das a big one, nah."

The Librarian nods. Bigger than any they've seen so far.

"Nobuddy bin stealin' dis one's parts. Yu t'ink its workin'?"

He shuffles to the edge of the shadow. "No sound from it."

Stoksie plucks at his sleeve. "Less leevit, G. Doan like dis one."

"Why? Arachnoid?"

"Waddevah. Jes' creepy."

The Librarian waves him back and ventures out into the light alone. Actually, the machine has only four supports, not eight. But its peculiar crouched-up position makes it look like a spider ready to pounce. Unlike the others they've encountered, this design is definitely based on an organic model, differentiating body parts to form a torso, legs, a head, even several protuberances that call to mind mouth parts, like jaws and teeth.

The Librarian pads across the pavement, once again braving the pounding light for the sake of his heedless curiosity. He's standing within four meters of the machine when he hears it switch on.

A click, a hum. The sighing of hydraulics.

Some miraculous instinct fires his usually somnolent reflexes and he's stepping backward and sideways before the crouching machine has fully raised itself, first on four legs, then on two. The front and smaller pair lift as arms, equipped with pincers jointed as precisely as dragon's claws.

"Run!" he yells at Stoksie.

The machine's head swivels. It aims itself directly at him, moving slowly. He doesn't hear its processing, as he'd heard the others'. It seems to be warming up. For the Librarian, who has never met a machine he didn't like, this one's aggressive stance has yet to be interpreted. He's not afraid. Not yet. Backing away at the same deliberate speed with which the machine is waking, he studies it with inadvertent delight. Several of his later boyhoods involved a fascination with dinosaurs. The organic model for this device just had to be *Tyrannosaurus Rex*. What is it for, he wonders? Who would build such a thing? If it decides to speed up, there's no way he can outrun it. It stands about six meters tall. Its powerful rear legs are streamlined for rapid travel. He's dimly aware that Stoksie is shouting at him. Why is the man still here?

"Run!" he bellows again.

"*Yu* run!" Stoksie bellows back.

He can't imagine himself running. Besides, in a city without doors, where could he run to that would shelter him from such a monster? The four facades fronting this little square are each as blank as a sheet of paper. On the other hand, if he did try to run, he could lead it away from Stoksie who, with a bad hip, stands as little chance of escaping as he does.

Step by step, the Librarian eases backward, spiraling toward the far side of the square. The *machina rex* turns with him, keeping him within range of its small but beady visual sensors. It's taking in his data, reading his every detail. He's surprised that it doesn't attack. Perhaps it thinks it can just frighten him to death. Perhaps it doesn't think at all. It saddens him that someone might create such a magnificent folly, and withhold from it the means of self-determination. The Librarian opens his hand to it, a gesture of sympathy.

He's almost to the edge of the building shadow, directly across the square from where Stoksie dances in helpless horror. For a moment, he fears the Tinker will do something suicidal and heroic, like charge in among the machine's hind legs to distract it. But Stoksie has found the limits to his courage. He fears both the saurian form and the machine nature of this monster. It's too much like a dragon. His pleading stare demands that the Librarian produce a miracle that will save them both. The Librarian rues anything he's ever said or done that's given rise to such unrealistic expectations. He backs up a few more steps. He's in the shade now. He can think more clearly, but he still has no idea what to do. The *machina rex* advances, servos whining.

Away from the punishing light, the Librarian becomes aware of another coherency emerging from the ubiquitous noise. This one's directional, like the signals from the paving machines, and it sounds like a summons. All other options gone, he backs toward it. Soon, he's flat up against the side of a building. His palms brush a surface as hard and granular as stone. The *machina* takes a long step forward, then another. Now it's looming over him. The sharp light glitters on its rows of metallic teeth. It eyes him with articulate intent, then throws up its silvery head to roar in convincing imitation of its ancient prototype.

The Librarian focuses on the new signal. He's certain it's calling him. Or at least offering direction. It's behind him. In the wall. No, in the building. Inside the building. The building *has* an inside. The Librarian imagines the signal as a path. It draws him sideways. A little more to the right. There.

The *machina rex* snaps its jaws like a cartoon predator and lunges for him. The Librarian retreats another step backward, where a step should not be possible. He backs into an open doorway. The metal jaws clash in front of his nose. Two more steps back. He's in a dim space, undefined except by the wall in front of him and the door opening where the hard light pours in. It silhouettes the machine as it rakes its steel claws against the stonework and tries to force its bulk through the narrow opening.

The Librarian breathes again, amazed to be still among the living.

Now, that's what I call a proper fire wall.

The door slams shut, enveloping him in darkness.

CHAPTER TEN

When she can stand without wobbling, Erde hurries to help Luther sit up. "Oh, I'm so sorry! It's all my fault!"

IT IS NOT YOUR FAULT.

Earth's great head looms over them. The dogs look on with concern.

"I mean, it's my fault he came at all!"

Luther's eyes flutter open. "We dere yet?"

"Yes, yes, we are. Somewhere." Kneeling beside him, Erde gazes around at the Mage City. The portal has winked out of existence without admitting a single white rider. She cherishes the thought of Brother Guillemo gnashing his teeth in frustration in the snows of 913.

Just try to find me here, you filthy man!

DO NOT MAKE RECKLESS INVITATIONS. IF HE IS FIRE'S CREATURE, HE WILL KNOW WHERE YOU ARE. ALWAYS.

But how? I don't even know where I am.

REMEMBER THAT YOUR SENDINGS ARE OFTEN STRONGER THAN YOU INTEND.

Her Sendings. Yes, she had forgotten. Or perhaps willed herself to forget what she'd done on the hill at Deep Moor.

But it was just that once, and never again!

NOT BECAUSE YOU COULDN'T . . . BECAUSE YOU WOULDN'T.

Yes. She'd hated how it felt, and the pain it caused Rose, the most Sensitive of the Deep Moor women. She likes even less the dragon's implication that her ability could betray her, nay, all of them, to the hell-priest. What if she was the cause of his coming to Deep Moor?

It's too much to think about. Too much worry and confusion. Erde glances up at the bronze mountain beside her and changes the subject. "Dragon, you've grown again!"

YES. I FEEL . . . I FEEL . . .

EXPANDED? Water has reappeared in her flock-of-butterflies incarnation, a glimmer of color and motion against the pale, static cityscape.

YES! AS IF ENLARGED BY EVERY BREATH. DO YOU FEEL DIFFERENT, SISTER?

The blue flutter of iridescence shivers and dances. NOT REALLY.

Erde is still contemplating the problem of Brother Guillemo. *Fire's creature.* It's a relief to think of the hell-priest that way. To explain her uncanny link to him, the way he can pick her out of a crowd, the way she always senses when he's near—all this is Fire's doing, and not some fault, or even evil, inherent in her own nature. She's glad to be rid of that guilty suspicion. She's been plagued by it for too long. If it's Fire's fault, she can deal with it.

She scrambles to her feet, flushed with new resolve. She plants her hands on her hips, like she's seen the men do in the practice yard, and gives the much-sought-after Mage City a long hard look. Its scale is daunting. Such topless towers could only be held up by magic. But what she finds most intimidating is the city's formal blandness, the total lack of welcome. If she were the Mages, she'd never choose to live in this hard, bright, silent place that seems entirely devoid of life.

"There aren't even any trees!" she exclaims to Luther, who is fending off the ministrations of two particularly earnest hounds. "Not even a blade of grass!"

Luther blinks, still gathering his senses. "Itsa neet cleen place, alri'."

"It's too clean, Luther! It looks like nobody lives here!"

"Leest it's warm agin." Luther peels off the first of his heavy layers. One of the dogs grabs his sleeve. "Git off me, yu mutt!"

Erde giggles. "She's trying to get your attention. Look, they've all gathered again."

THEY WISH US TO KEEP FOLLOWING THE TRAIL.

"Oh, my goodness, of course! Dragon, shall we?"

WE CAN LEARN LITTLE BY STANDING STILL.

As large as Earth has become, the wide white streets are larger still. It's a city made for giants. So where are those giants? Erde notes that the dog pack does not bound ahead on the scent as they had at Deep Moor. Though they seem confident about the direction of the trail, they are less bold, unwilling to lose sight of the dragons and humans, as if at each corner, they are fearful of what might be around it.

After several blocks for each of several changes of direction, Erde realizes that the city is not just huge in vertical scale, its spread is enormous as well.

"A city as big as a kingdom," she complains to Luther. "The streets are so straight, like the squares on a chessboard. And not a bit of green anywhere! You'd think there'd be a weed or two at least!" She recalls the only other great city she's been in. "There were lots of weeds in Big Albin."

Luther rolls his eyes at the featureless walls rising to either side. "Nah, gal. Big Albin's a reel city."

"This is a real city. How else could we be walking in it?"

Mid-stride, he taps his foot on the smooth white pavement. "Well, I doan know 'bout dat. But first, it doan look like a reel city. An' two, doan it stand ta reezin dat if dis is a *magic* city, it otta be sumplace diffrint an' speshul?"

"Of course, but special can be real, can't it? Deep Moor was special, a secret, special place, until Fra Guill nosed it out, may he die a thousand deaths and rot in hell for what he's done!"

"Hey, nah," admonishes Luther gently. "Speekin' evil kin bring it to ya."

"I think my fear of him brings him to me. But you're right." Chastened, Erde studies the blank building facades rising like canyon walls about them. "I've never seen a really big city, except Big Albin, and it was all in ruins. This isn't the way a big city's supposed to look?"

The dog pack races ahead, then circles back to run ahead again. Luther watches them as they approach an intersection several blocks away. "I'm jes' sayin' it doan look like eny city I evah bin in. Okay, I ain' bin ina lotta dem, but lookit dese walls, nah. No doahs or windahs? How yu gonna git inside anya dese places?"

"It could be a fortified city." Erde's personal idea of a

wall is tightly laid stone with only the smallest of openings, to hold in the heat and keep out the enemy. "I remember thinking in Big Albin that the dwellings were all full of holes. So many doors and windows! And such big ones. It seemed so . . . exposed, compared to what I'm used to. When you're from a different time and place, you arrive with all sorts of different definitions and assumptions, remember. I mean, this city is probably as real to the people that live here as Big Albin is to you."

Luther rakes a hand through the silver forelock that falls nearly to his nose. "Yu t'ink we'ah in sum odda time agin, den?"

"Oh, I should think so. Most assuredly. And a long way from my time, too. That's why we felt so bad when we got here. The distance."

"Long wich way? Inta da fuchah, or inta da past?"

Erde considers, then asks the dragons' opinions.

I CANNOT TRAVEL TO ANY TIME BEFORE MY AWAKENING. WHERE A PORTAL CAN TAKE US IS ANYONE'S GUESS. THE RULES MAY BE DIFFERENT.

Luther shakes his head when Erde relays this. "Dis kint be da past. I ain' no expert, but I seen pichurs."

"Then it's the future."

"Fuchah to wat?"

"To your time. And mine, too, of course."

"Dere ain' no fuchah afta my time, gal. We're in da lass days."

Now Erde must tread lightly. Among the Tinkers, Luther is one of the most devout believers in the faith that Gerrasch has been preaching. Her own and the dragons' understanding of the situation might not completely coincide with Luther's expectations for the world's salvation by "the One."

"Perhaps the very last days will come a bit later than you've feared."

"Wize dat?"

"Because we're here. So there must be some future at least, after yours." She doesn't ask the dragons to weigh in with their ideas on this issue. She's positive they'll agree with her, and she knows herself well enough to admit that if she's sure she's right, she'll want to push Luther until he accepts her version over his own. She really must learn to

allow other people their opinions. Only a child, Erde reminds herself, assumes that its perception of the world is
the only correct one.

Still . . .

No. Erde scolds herself and lets the subject drop.

The dogs have stopped at the intersection up ahead.
They're milling about uncertainly while four of them search
out the trail in each of the possible directions. Earth has
been lagging behind as usual, so Erde welcomes the chance
for him to catch up.

Lingering at the corner, she spots something down the
side street: a flick of motion, a dark shape against the bright
pavement? It's gone when she looks for it, leaving only an
afterimage of memory.

"That's odd . . ."

Luther's looking in the opposite direction. "Watsit, gal?"

"I saw . . . like a person, maybe."

"Yeah? Weah?"

Erde points, down the pale, empty street. "It's gone
now."

"Doan worry. I'll keep my eyes opin."

She lays a hand on the dragon's claw as he looms up
behind her.

*I'm sure I saw something. Some*one.

Earth rumbles comfortingly. Water has hitched a ride
between his ivory horns, so that he seems to be wearing a
diaphanous crown of iridescence.

You are very quiet, dear dragon.

I AM TROUBLED.

WE BOTH ARE.

Erde is impressed that Water's voice can remain so present and coherent when her physical being is so ephemeral.

Why?

Earth answers reluctantly. SAY NOTHING TO LU-
THER. DO YOU PROMISE?

Yes, of course. Why? What is it?

OUR SISTER IS HERE.

What? Really? Are you sure?

WE SENSE HER VERY STRONGLY.

*How wonderful! Why didn't you say so? It's all we've
hoped for!*

YES.

But the dragons are not rejoicing as she would expect them to.

Well, where is she? Let's go find her!

Instinctively, she turns toward Luther.

SAY NOTHING!

But he'll want to help!

IT'S NOT THAT SIMPLE. WE KNOW SHE'S HERE, BUT WE DON'T KNOW WHERE.

WORSE THAN THAT. IT'S AS IF SHE'S . . . EVERYWHERE. SO . . . DIFFUSE.

But, Lady Water, so are you, and that doesn't seem to be a problem.

Water's dancing motes draw closer together. IN SHAPE PERHAPS, BUT NOT IN MIND.

Diffuse of mind. Erde tries to imagine it, but while her imagination might be far-ranging, her sense of self is very firmly rooted inside her head. Her thoughts all emanate from a central location. She watches Luther encouraging the dogs to settle on a single trail to follow.

Can you explain this another way?

Water's shape shifts slightly to reflect her words. HER PRESENCE IS VERY STRONG BUT IT'S NOT . . . ORGANIZED. LIKE THE PARTS OF HER CONSCIOUSNESS HAVE BEEN SPLIT AND SCATTERED.

Oh. Is that so dire? Dreams seem like that sometimes.

A VERY GOOD ANALOGY.

Down the street, Erde sees another flicker, the slightest bit of moving darkness. She decides to ignore it.

Could she be asleep and you're listening in on her dreams?

WE DO NOT KNOW.

Earth's great head sways side to side. He's unhappy with his own ignorance. But Lady Water, as always, has a plan.

WE'RE WASTING TIME WANDERING ABOUT HERE AT RANDOM. WE SHOULD GO BACK, GATHER THE REST OF OUR FORCES, AND PLAN OUT A LOGICAL SEARCH.

I DO NOT ENTIRELY AGREE, BUT NOW THAT WE'VE BEEN HERE ONCE, IT SHOULD BE EASY ENOUGH TO GET BACK AGAIN.

Erde judges this information safe enough to relay to Luther.

He nods, patting the dogs, who have gathered around him uneasily. "I wudn't mind sum reinforcemints. Dis place iz creepy."

"What about the hounds? We can't desert them."

"Bring 'em. Blin' Rachel cud use sum gud dogs like dese."

As if inspired by his praise, one of the scout dogs announces a trace worth investigating. Her sharp barks bring the rest of the pack racing to confirm her discovery.

"Look, they have the trail again!" Erde cries. "Oh, dragons, let's stay with them a while longer! Surely we'll find Rose and the others soon, and if anyone's hurt, Lord Earth can help them! I know N'Doch could get into trouble away from your sensible and steadying influence. But he's also quick and resourceful on his own."

IT'S PAIA THAT WE WORRY ABOUT. SHE IS THE MOST VULNERABLE.

Erde sees she will have to beg. "Please! Just a little while more?"

UNTIL THE NEXT TIME THEY LOSE THE SCENT.

The pack surges ahead, as if held back until the dragons relented. But despite their high excitement, the dogs do not risk getting out of sight. They double back expectantly in twos or threes, with long loping strides and lolling tongues. Erde hurries after them. Yes, the town is creepy, but most of her deepest fears involve darkness, so it's hard to be too afraid in the middle of an empty street in broad daylight. Still, like the dogs, she glances back. She's left Luther and the dragons farther behind than she'd intended. She slows to wait for them, and notices a difference in the facades just ahead. Slight, but a point of interest in this bland landscape. One section of wall is slightly recessed, creating a band of shadow and a shallow courtyard. The recess contains a bank of windows, five tall rectangles. Intrigued by the possibility of seeing inside one of these endlessly blank buildings, Erde drifts over. But she finds the windows entirely opaque, a mere outline scratched on the solid stone.

Except for the one in the middle.

Erde moves closer. Here, the featureless gray is less solid, less flat. Like a very dirty window. She rubs the smooth surface gently with her palm, and the view through it does sharpen, but less because she's cleaned it than as if her action has stirred something within, dissipating a shrouding fog. A shape appears, the hooded head and shoulders of a man. By the time she's recognized the silhouetted profile, the figure has turned to stare at her.

Erde shrieks.

It's the hell-priest. Smiling.

She whirls away blindly, crashing into Luther who has run up at the sound of her scream. She flails in his arms, then backs against him in panic.

"Look! Look! It's him!"

Luther looks. He sets her aside and goes up to the window to press his nose to the now opaque surface. "Ain' nobuddy deah, gal. Kin't see nuttin'. Yu say yu look'd inside heah?"

"Yes! Yes!"

But Luther sees nothing, and Erde begins to doubt herself. When the dragon arrives, she retreats into his shadow to find comfort in his warmth. "Am I imagining things?" But it persists, like a bad smell in the air around her, that horrid intruding presence that makes her feel dirty and violated.

YOU ARE, BUT THEY ARE TRUE THINGS.

"He's here? Brother Guillemo is here?"

NOT IN BODY, NOT YET. BUT YOU SENSE HIM WATCHING. AWAITING HIS CHANCE.

"Even in the Mage City, he can come after me?"

I AM RECONSIDERING MY ASSUMPTIONS ABOUT THIS PLACE.

The weight of his tone is unusual, even for a dragon somewhat given to gloom. Erde catches her breath. "How so?"

THIS IS CERTAINLY THE CITY THAT I SAW IN DREAMS. BUT IT MAY NOT BE WHAT I THOUGHT IT WAS. WHAT I HOPED FOR.

The dragon's voice in her mind is so disconsolate that Erde shoves her own terrors aside. *But you must not give up that hope, dear dragon! Never!*

PERHAPS WE MUST LEARN TO GO FORWARD EVEN WITHOUT HOPE.

There's always hope. Probably we haven't yet come to the part of the city where the Mages live.

Water's mote-cloud swells with sudden impatience, chittering like a swarm of disturbed insects.

THERE AREN'T GOING TO BE ANY MAGES! IT'S

AS I'VE SAID ALL ALONG. YOU MISTOOK THAT PART OF YOUR VISION. BUT IT DOESN'T MATTER. IT'S ENOUGH THAT YOU DREAMED THIS CITY, SO YOU'D KNOW IT WHEN YOU SAW IT THROUGH THE PORTAL. THAT'S WHAT GOT US HERE. SO STOP WORRYING ABOUT MAGES. MAGES ARE A MYTH.

Leave him alone! Erde flings a quick glare at Water, then looks away, ashamed at having reprimanded a dragon.

NO, LISTEN! WE ARE THE MAGES. IF OUR SISTER IS HERE, AND I'M SURE SHE IS, WE ARE THE POWERS WHO MUST SEARCH HER OUT AND FREE HER. WE CAN'T LOOK FOR ANY HELP OTHER THAN OURSELVES.

"Dese dogs're getting' antsy," Luther warns.

"In a moment, Luther!" Erde tastes her own irritation like a mouthful of bile. She's torn in too many directions, and feels Earth's hurt and indecision as if it was her own.

TIME TO MOVE. AS LONG AS WE STAY HERE, WE MUST KEEP FOCUSED AND ON THE SEARCH.

GO SEARCH BY YOURSELF!

BROTHER, LISTEN TO YOU!

The big brown dragon has hunkered down stubbornly. His plated hide has lost its bronzy sheen. Erde thinks he looks like a mountain of mud.

I NEED TIME TO CONSIDER!

LISTEN TO ALL OF US! HOW DID WE GET SO DISAGREEABLE ALL OF A SUDDEN?

"You mean, it's not just me?" Erde asks.

WE'RE PRACTICALLY DROWNING IN IT. IF IT WEREN'T FOR THE DOGS, WE'D HAVE BEEN BROUGHT TO A COMPLETE HALT WITH POINTLESS ARGUING.

Earth lifts his head to gaze around as if to locate the source of this contagion of despair. YOU'RE RIGHT. IT IS POINTLESS.

IT'S EXACTLY WHAT OUR BROTHER WOULD WANT—FOR US TO BE AT ODDS WITH EACH OTHER. DIVIDE AND CONQUER.

THEN WE SHALL DENY HIM SUCH SATISFACTION.

Earth rises out of his crouch with an alacrity that astonishes even Erde. He is a force again, a glimmering mountain rolling between the towering buildings, a crown of light between his horns. The dogs gain courage to range farther ahead, yipping and crying. Their chorus ricochets along the walls, back and forth, until the faceless blocks are alive with dog voices.

Luther shrugs uneasily, then moves after the dragons. "If dere's anyone about, dey shur know we're heah."

Sure enough, from far off along the canyons of stone, a whistle sounds. The dogs pull up to listen. The whistle comes again.

Luther nods. "Summun's callin' 'em."

"But who? Oh! It could only be . . ." Erde plunges forward as the dogs streak away after the call. "Wait! Don't run away! We'll never find you!"

As if they've understood every word, half the pack splits off and circles back, dancing and bounding with impatience at the glacial pace of the dragons and humans hurrying after them.

They are led down a long, straight roadway, discovering occasional evidence of the passage of other animals. Erde finds this soiling of the perfect streets very cheering. Signs of earth, signs of life, in a lifeless city. Hope warms her heart again. She'd been lacking it so desperately. How clever of Lady Water to recognize this dark disabling mood, and alert them in time.

The dog pack wheels right, into a district of narrower streets and rougher pavements. The trail grows crooked, evasive. It curves and crinks and cuts aside here and there at sharp angles, where buildings have been placed oddly, in the middle of a road. The light is dim, and the shadows deeper. Erde shivers. Is she belatedly feeling the effects of the transport, or is simple exhaustion confusing her perception? Several times, a street that has seemed clear and open is abruptly a dead end, with a hidden escape leading off at a sharp angle, barely wide enough for the dragon to pass.

"This is a mysterious sort of place," she murmurs. "it's like a maze or something."

Earth complains that he's scraping his hide against rough walls on both sides.

Luther drags his hand along the face of a building. "Dis look like old stone, nah. Da reel t'ing. Not like before."

Erde agrees. The city does feel more like a real place here, more rough-hewn, less impossibly perfect. More like the towns she knows from her own life. The doors and windows are smaller. Because they seem more real, they frighten her. Out of any one of them, after all, might spring the hell-priest. And in the confines of these torturous alleys, there'd be no escape.

What am I thinking? I have two dragons and a strong man beside me! The despair has crept back to wind itself around her like a rampant vine. Erde rips it loose, resolving to resist it. As she makes this promise, the twining streets seem to open out. The hard edge of the shadows eases. There is moisture in the air, where she had noticed none before. She can breathe again.

"Phew!" Luther mutters. "Das bettah!"

"You felt it, too?"

"Wat's dat, nah?"

"The despair again. Closing in."

"Guez I did, den," he replies thoughtfully. "Gotta keep da fait'."

"Yes. I shall have to be more vigilant."

WE MUST ALL BE.

UH-OH . . .

Erde wonders at Water's tone—half alarmed, half ironical—but not for long. Paying such alert attention to their emotional states has disabled their external awareness. They have come into a surprise cul-de-sac where the only way out seems to be the way they came in. They're surrounded by high curved walls, like the walls of a castle yard. Dark water drips from between the huge dry-laid blocks, striping the stone with moss and green slime. In the silence, Erde hears it flowing into the drainage well in the center of the courtyard. It seems to fall a very long way before it hits the surface of the water below.

"Outa heah, quick-like!" Luther turns, then freezes. The big knife he carries is already in his hand.

Blocking their escape are two scruffy, grim-faced archers and a pack of alert and snarling dogs. Erde is sure they've been betrayed. But she can't imagine how she could mistake the hell-priest's hounds for the dogs of Deep Moor. Then she feels Earth's dragon laugh gently rock the ground.

"Margit? Lily?" She barely knows them through the dirt

and blood darkening their faces. She races to embrace
them, but is stopped by their raised and loaded bows. "It's
me, Erde!"

"Prove it," growls Margit, squint-eyed over the shaft of
her arrow.

"What? Have I changed so much?"

"Not enough, is more like it," Lily calls. "We need to
know it's really you!"

They're both much gaunter than Erde remembers, with
a cruel angle of hardship and suffering in their shoulders
that was not there before.

"Of course, it's me! Who else do you know who travels
with dragons?"

"What dragons?"

Erde gapes at them. She can understand them not knowing Water for a dragon, but they'd have to be blind to miss
Earth, with the size he's grown to. But when she turns to
point him out, she sees he's stilled himself and gone invisible. No wonder.

*I think you must show yourself, dragon, before these good
women will believe me.*

Earth agrees, and flicks back into visibility.

Lily lets out her breath and lowers her bow. "Erde? Is
it really you?"

Margit looks Luther over carefully. "Who's this one? Another dragon?"

"This is Luther, who came along to help me."

At last, Margit eases back on her bowstring. This releases
the dogs, who bound about in animal joy, untouched by
whatever horror has darkened the lives of the two brave
scouts. Their tunics and riding leathers are in tatters. Margit's gold-red braids, her glory, are dull and streaked with
gray. Lily's head is bound with a stained linen bandage and
a livid scar crawls down one side of her face.

"You both look awful!" Erde blurts.

"Well, thanks for that high compliment." A brief flash
of tooth hints at Margit's old ironical grin. "We've seen
some strange things since we've been in this demon-ridden
hellhole. How did you get here?"

"We followed the dogs from the . . . oh, is everyone all
right? Where is everyone?"

Lily purses her lips and looks down. Margit's grin fades

behind the shadow of more recent sorrows. "You'd never believe it if I told you."

"What, is the news that bad? Oh, if only we'd come sooner!"

"It's bad, but what I mean is, you'll have to see for yourself."

"Now? Can we go now?"

The women exchange a glance. This time Margit looks away.

Lily says, "I'll take them."

She turns, beckoning toward a doorway in the wall behind her. Erde did not recall it being there before. Its rough stone arch is supported by more smoothly shaped pilasters topped with capitals in the form of leaves. Through the opening, Erde sees a stone walk crossing a surreally bright grass sward dotted with flowers. Warm sunlight shimmers through leaf shadow across the path.

I know this place. But it can't really be where I think it is. What new wonders await? What new terrors?

She eyes the narrow door. *Dragon, you will never fit.*

"Must Earth stay outside?"

Lily smiles wanly. "There's room enough for all."

Then I'll call for you when I get there, dragon.

Erde takes Luther's arm and escorts him through the archway, into the courtyard garden at Deep Moor.

CHAPTER ELEVEN

Alone. Alone in darkness. Not something he's ever minded. Likes it. Particularly the alone part. Or maybe it's just the relief of darkness. It feels like home.

But the Librarian knows he'd never have gotten this far alone. So he worries about Stoksie out there with his bad hip and a murderous machine on the loose. Perhaps the machine won't notice him. He hopes the little man has shown his good Tinker sense and gotten the hell out of there.

Darkness. Like a den. One of the many he's inhabited over the span of his years. Warm. Safe. At least in his later stages, once the body he wore had evolved to a size and strength that made threats not worth the trouble for most sorts of predators. The body heat of darkness underground. Later, the dim smoky fires of his hidden hearths, in caves and hovels and cottages. Eventually, the electric warmth of machine components stacked high in shuttered rooms he hardly went out of. He hated all those dying cities. The invention of the telephone was a godsend. Only a short leap, then, to ordering takeout.

Those were all his waiting places, where invisibility was a necessity. Now the waiting is over. So he mustn't slip back into the old passive modes. He must act. He must move.

But first, he listens to the darkness. Is it the same as the light outside, but with its volume turned near to zero? Sound no longer disables him. In the darkness, he can concentrate. He sits down and crosses his legs. He forgets about Stoksie and the *machina rex*. The smooth floor is the same temperature as the skin on his soft pink palms. He opens himself, tunes his array of inner sensors to the humming darkness, takes the tamed rush of signal into his mind as if gathering up a bundle of cables. Sort through the lot of them. What goes with what? What colors match? What frequencies? Some are obvious as code. Some have patterns that might be code. There are likenesses, pairings, sets, and subsets. But there are problems, too. Discontinuities. Dead ends. Nonsense loops. The Librarian grins and licks his lips. Familiar territory at last. He's doing something useful for the first time since he blundered through the portal. Something he's good at. Something he's trained for. With effort and luck, he'll make sense of it. He'll be able to map the city's ebb and flow of signal. If one of these webberies of current is his dragon's, he'll find it. Then all he'll have to do is follow it back to its source.

Alone in darkness, the Librarian chortles with anticipation.

CHAPTER TWELVE

It's a clear and perfect summer morning in the garden at Deep Moor. And of course, that of all things is impossible.

Surrendering to the irrational, Erde follows Lily through the gray stone arch into a sonata of birdsong. She inhales the fragrance of sunlight on pine and sweet fern, and the flowering thyme creeping between the flat stones of the walk. Entering behind her, Luther stops short in amazement. Erde sets her anxieties aside long enough to stand with him and drink in the beauty, to gaze at the crisp blue sky and the grass so green it vibrates. Just a brief stolen moment to savor it all before her heart breaks again, thinking of what's been lost, and reality intervenes. Dozen of women are scattered like broken dolls across the shade-dappled grass: sitting, lying, sprawled on blankets, bloodied, bandaged, some stirring in pain, some not stirring at all.

She sees the healer, Linden, paler than the torn strips of muslin in her hands. She stumbles with exhaustion as she bends among the wounded. Against the central stone well, one of the redheaded twins, Margit's daughters, sits rocking the other in her lap, weeping silently. In the deeper shadow of an old maple tree, two frail shrouded bundles lie side by side.

"Oh, Lily," Erde whispers. "What has happened?"

But she already knows. She was there in the ruined farmstead. "Where's Rose? Where's Raven?"

"Raven is with Rose," says Lily. "Come, I'll take you."

"Yes. No, wait! Let me call in the dragon. He can help. Remember how he saved N'Doch."

Linden looks up in stunned relief as Earth's great bronzy

bulk appears in an empty stretch of lawn. It hadn't looked nearly big enough to Erde before she sent him the image, but either her eye didn't measure well, or the space itself has expanded to suit. Erde hurries over and grasps Linden's hands. The healer's eyes are raw. She's thin to the point of wasting. Her grip is still firm, yet Erde feels as if she's holding the woman up by the strength of her own arms.

"Dear Linden, help has arrived. How long have you been without rest?"

"I hardly know anymore. This time, a few days, maybe more." Linden's voice is faint, as if she barely has breath to speak. Behind her, the weeping twin gently lays her sister down on the grass, and Erde understands the hard glint in Margit's eyes, and why she stayed outside.

"We'll hope it's not too late," she tells Linden. "It won't be too late! Lord Earth will do all he can!"

Luther watches silently from the dragon's side. Erde beckons him over. "This is Luther Williams. He's seen some hard times, too. He can help carry the wounded, but he doesn't speak our language. I'll help, too, after I've seen Rose."

"Yes. You must see Rose. I'm so glad you're back." Linden offers Luther her hand. His earnest and obvious compassion draws from her a wan smile of welcome. "Come with me, please."

Luther nods and follows the healer briskly across the grass. He picks up the limp redheaded girl easily, and carries her to the dragon.

Erde whispers, "Please let it not be too late!"

"Amen," murmurs Lily from beside her.

"Is Sir Hal with you, Lily?" The senior knight had been storm-bound at Deep Moor when she'd left it last. No, the time before last. Already her anguished brain is trying to deny the awful reality of her most recent visit. "And what about Captain Wender?"

"They were long gone, back to the war. Too bad, too. We could've used two more good fighters."

"Long gone?"

Lily looks back at her oddly, then away. "Of course. No point in Hal sticking around once you'd relieved him of the problem of Baron Köthen. Oh, Kurt would've stayed, but

Hal piled on the pressure until he gave up and went with him."

"Kurt?"

"Captain Wender."

"Ah. Yes." Erde would swear she detects a blush in the other woman's wounded, weathered face. It seems, even in the midst of war and disaster, there is companionship to be found. *For everyone but me.* "Lily, how long has it been since I was last at Deep Moor?"

Lily frowns. "I don't know. Long time."

"No, really . . . how long would you say?"

"Months, at least. I'd say a whole winter, if we'd had anything but winter. You don't remember?"

"It's only been two weeks for me."

Lily stares at her, struggling with this notion.

"Can I see Rose now?"

She follows Lily around the impromptu field hospital and through a blossom-laden arbor into the paved inner courtyard nestled within the half-timbered arms of the house. The welcoming house that in reality was no more than a blackened ruin. How wonderful to find the thick thatch intact, and the stone chimney unstained. And she is relieved beyond measure to discover Raven and Rose at the stone table under the old apple tree, both upright and apparently unharmed. What a serene and pretty picture they make, sitting in the dappled sun: Rose's determined back and her short curls of russet and gray, Raven's more youthful lilt, her lovely face of high contrasts, bright and soft, dark and light. There are early apples scattered on the table, one of them neatly cored and sectioned. Raven is at work on a second. Hastily, Erde brushes away tears of joy.

Raven looks up. With a cry, she drops her knife and apple. She leaps up, hands and long hair flying. "Erde! How wonderful! Is it really you?"

Erde notes her hesitation, her quick and worried glance at Lily.

Lily nods. "Seems to be, all right. She's brought the dragon."

"It is me, Raven, truly!" Erde rushes to embrace her. "Oh, it's so dreadful what's happened! I'm so glad you're both alive!"

"If you call this being alive," mutters Lily, hurrying away again. "I'm due back on watch. See you all at supper."

Erde releases Raven and turns eagerly to greet Rose. But Rose is still sitting quietly. Her back is erect. Her strong gardener's hands rest on the worn stone table, her fingers spread as if braced to rise, the sectioned apple untouched in front of her. Her warm brown eyes are open, but fixed on some far more distant point than the mosaic of the garden wall she faces.

"Rose? Rose, it's me, Erde."

"She won't answer," says Raven quietly.

Unheeding, Erde crouches at Rose's side and takes one of her hands between both her own. She rubs it gently as if to relieve a chill. "Rose, I've brought the dragon. He'll heal everyone he can!"

"I'm not even sure she hears us," Raven says.

"But what's the problem? She looks . . . well, tired, but . . . fine."

"I know. But she isn't."

"Rose? Rose!" With a soft moan, Erde rises abruptly, spinning away in panic and despair. Raven catches her deftly and wraps her in a tight and calming embrace that lets her be a child again and sob out her great load of pent up sorrow and outrage.

"Oh, Raven, it's all so awful! Everything is!"

"I know, sweetling, I know. We've all cried our hearts out, every one."

Erde hasn't wept so hard in many weeks, and she feels much better when she's done with it and has caught her breath again. "So tell me, what's wrong with her? How did she get this way?"

"Come. Settle for a while. You look as played out as the rest of us. I'm sure you've had to be very brave." Raven hooks one arm about Erde's waist and steers her toward a high backed wooden bench in a slice of sun falling on the courtyard wall. Potted herbs scent the air as they brush past. Raven drops wearily onto the wide seat. Shoving back her cloud of dark hair as if it were the cause of all her troubles, she tilts her face to the sun with a sigh. "At least it isn't winter here. I'd forgotten what it felt like to be warm."

"Lily says it's been months since I saw you last." In the

brighter light, Erde sees the bruises on Raven's cheek, and the tightness of the skin across her jaw.

"An eternity of winter, sweetling. Then Deep Moor was attacked. If that hadn't happened, we'd have all starved to death anyway."

"There are a lot more of you than there were."

"And fewer," nods Raven sadly. "Between the blizzards and the deep freezes, women would stagger into the valley from the surrounding farms and villages, and beg our protection. Or Lily and Margit would find them, half frozen, fugitive from the soldiers' foraging parties, and guide them to safety." She pauses, then sighs. "Or so we thought. Bringing so many in is probably what betrayed us. The valley's magic was spread too thin."

"Did you know he was coming? Did you have any warning at all?"

Raven's glance slides toward her, sideways. "You know, then. Did Lily tell you?"

"I was there. *He* was there. We went back to warn you . . . I told them we should . . . but we were too late. But, Raven, it's not just the hell-priest we're dealing with. The dragon Fire is behind him. That's who we're really fighting."

"The renegade you were worried about?"

"Yes." Later, she can explain how worry has escalated into terror.

"Ah. And then . . . ?"

"The dogs found us and led us here."

"Really?" Raven's finely arched brows contract, as if mere thought is an effort. It pains Erde to see her looking so drawn and tired. "And do you have any idea where 'here' is?"

Erde offers what little she understands about the portals and Time and the white city outside the walls.

Raven shakes her head. "Between one step and another? To the future, just like that? Doritt will be glad to hear it. She's convinced we've all died and gone to hell . . . or someplace like it. I said, don't be silly. Just because we haven't lived the way others do, doesn't mean we deserve that." She smiles faintly. For a moment, her eyes drift shut. Then she rouses herself with a cough. "But who could create these magic doorways?"

"I hadn't thought of them as being created. More that they just . . . were."

"Such devices are not the way of Nature, sweetling, as marvelous as she is. For one thing, there's too much purpose implied by a portal that opens just when it's needed."

"And closes, too, when needed. I'd say it was dragon magic, but the dragons claim to know nothing of them. But they do say their sister Air is here, somewhere."

"In this nightmare landscape? Then I'm sorry for her. But perhaps the portals are her work."

Erde clasps her hands. "Of course! That must be it!" Then her face clouds again. "No, it can't be. If she can make such portals, why didn't she make one for herself and escape Lord Fire's dungeon long ago?"

Raven gently brushes curls from Erde's furrowed brow. "If she could, she would have, so we must accept that she can't, and hope to learn why."

Erde nods pensively. Gerrasch should be here instead. He'd understand it all so much better. "But now, please, tell me about Rose!"

"She's . . . well, I guess the best way to say it is . . . she's gone inside. As if she went into her room and locked the door."

"But how? Why?"

"Utter exhaustion, is my guess." Raven gazes sadly across the soft blooms of oregano and sage to where Rose sits unmoving at the table. "Let's see, where do I start? With the attack? We did have some warning of it. Both Rose and Doritt sensed that a great evil was headed our way. We'd already planned an escape route into the Grove, with all the animals. There wasn't much left to carry—our food stores were nearly gone and we'd shared out all our extra clothing with the refugees. But we were just so weak and tired . . . well, when the attack came, we didn't quite make it to the Grove in time. Margit and Lily and the dogs drove off the first thin wave—Fra Guill hadn't expected so stout a resistance from women! But we lost Esther then, very nearly lost Lily. We fled into the trees, and for a while, the trees kept the soldiers out. Then Guillemo himself turned up. He must have wanted us very badly."

Erde shivers. "For the stake."

"No doubt. The Grove's good and ancient wardings

weren't strong enough to hold up against the dark determination of the hell-priest. So in he comes. It was Rose who discovered the portal, and urged us through it. Ordered us, I should say, in the end. There were some who'd have rather stood and fought than walk through that inexplicable doorway."

Raven lets her head loll against the carved bench back, and takes a deep ragged breath. A small, bright bird lights on a branch just past her reach and begins to sing. "And then we were in . . .that awful place out there."

"The City?"

"City? A lifeless, terrible place to bear such a noble name. More like death or bad dreams. We arrived cut and battered, totally spent. The half that could walk carried the other half. One of our new women bled to death before Linden could save her. No food or water to be found. And then we were stalked by roaring phantoms and clanking giants. Through it all, Rose kept us going, moving, insistent that a safe place could be found, certain that something—some*one*—was guiding her there. We took all our hope from her. Our two oldest ran out of their life-spark and died, within a day of each other. We wrapped them and carried them with us, loath to abandon their poor starved bodies without burial in such an ungiving, soulless place.

"Finally, Rose decided that a Seeing might help her know our path more clearly. None of us had the presence of mind to advise against it. Rose always said it was foolish to undertake a Seeing from a state of exhaustion or despair. We were, she was, both. She went into her trance, and never came out of it. But when the rest of us looked up from the Circle, we were in that grim castle yard outside the gate, and the doorway into the garden was before us."

"As if she . . ."

"Yes. Because it looks like Deep Moor, even feels like Deep Moor, but it isn't." Raven pats the warm stucco wall behind them. "There's no house behind the facade. I think that, somehow, Rose made it happen, and the garden and courtyard were all she could manage before she gave out."

"The garden? Is there . . . ?"

"Food? Yes, and water—that's the wonder of it. Edible. Delicious. We're all getting well again, those of us who made it this far." Raven sighs deeply, guiltily, toying with

the stained and shredded embroidery on her skirt. "Of
course we were grateful. We can feed ourselves and the
surviving animals, and nothing bothers us. But Rose . . .
has been as you see her ever since. Occasionally her lips
will move, as if she's talking with someone. But it's never
with us. It's as if we weren't there. She won't eat or drink,
or even sleep. She'll never get her strength back this way!
I fear she'll just fade away."

"Rose, poor Rose!" Erde wraps her arms around her
chest and rocks back and forth miserably. "The dragons
will know what to do! We'll ask them immediately!"

But then a glad cry rings out on the other side of the
garden wall. Raven sits up. "Oh, listen! What a lovely
sound! I haven't heard laughter in a long, long while."

Lily runs up through the arbor. "Come quickly! Come
see!"

Raven's eyes move to the still figure at the stone table.

"You go," Erde says. "I'll stay with Rose."

She follows Raven to the end of the arbor. From there,
she can keep an eye on Rose and also have a clear view
down the bright green lawn. She sees the women gathering
near the dragon's crossed foreclaws, in the shadow of his
huge head. As many as can walk or be assisted are huddled
in excitement around Margit and her twins: three redheads,
all three, alive and well, tearfully embracing.

A life saved! Well done, dear dragon.

THERE WERE OTHERS I COULD NOT SAVE.

May God rest their souls.

Erde repeats the usual benediction by habit, but she can't
help but notice how empty it sounds, how inadequate.
What kind of god would create a good and beautiful world,
then let it be overrun by such evils as Fire and the hell-
priest? She can't see the sense in that.

She'd much rather put her faith in dragons.

NOW THAT WE'VE FOUND OUR FRIENDS, MY
SISTER SAYS WE MUST GO AFTER N'DOCH.

*Yes, we must, of course. But first, there is one more rescue
here to attempt, dear dragon.*

Water has been listening in. AND AFTER THAT,
THERE'LL BE ANOTHER DISTRACTION, THEN
ANOTHER AND ANOTHER, UNTIL FIRE'S DONE

HIS WORST EVERYWHERE! DON'T YOU SEE THE
PATTERN? IT'S HIS MEDDLING, I TELL YOU!

BUT STILL, WE MUST DO WHAT WE CAN FOR
LADY ROSE.

As if to prove Lady Water's prediction, a new and louder
commotion breaks out at the stone arch leading to the city.
Part of the dog pack streams in, howling an alarm. They
sweep around and pile back out again, setting up such a
racket in the outer castle yard that it echoes through the
gate like the baying of a thousand dogs. Margit abandons
her celebrating immediately. She kisses her daughters,
grabs her bow, and sprints for the opening with Lily quick
behind her. The other women pull back toward the house
in a protective circle, shoving the weakest into the center.

What could cause the dogs to raise such a ruckus? Erde
fears the worst. She shrinks against the arbor entrance,
praying that Fra Guill hasn't found a way to bring his
fiendish army through the portal in the Grove. For surely,
then, all will be lost.

CHAPTER THIRTEEN

The sofa is soft and deep. Paia sinks into it as into warm bathwater, giving in to its soothing, enveloping suspension. But her sleep is restless. She'd hoped for oblivion, the luxury of not thinking. Instead, she gets dreams.

She dreams of all the baggage she's left behind, way too heavy to carry on this perilous journey. Her habits and life in the Temple fill several sets of matched leather luggage. The longings she's denied barely fit into a giant trunk. The fears she's buried, so as not to be a burden in this crisis to those around her fit neatly into a metal attaché case, but it's so leaden, she can't even lift it. Stepping around the mountainous pile, she's back in the closed safety of the Citadel, pacing its red-lined corridors, walking the cool stones of the Temple floor. She dreams of the routine of ritual, which she'd chafed at in boredom, and which now seems alluringly secure. She dreams of sheltering darkness, and of the rich comforts of her personal chambers. She dreams of being clean and fed and dressed and petted and cared for by a legion of servants and acolytes.

Her dream is a nostalgic review of her life with the God.

"You could have it all back again, my love. Exactly as it was before."

His voice purrs in her ear, rough velvet sliding over steel, the most intimate of whispers, as if he lay next to her. It thrills her to hear it again. Despite all, she has missed him. Paia tries to turn her head, to look at him. She can better gauge his true mood by what form he has taken. But this dream is the sort that prevents speech or movement. In her dream paralysis, she can only listen.

"You've had your little adventure now, my sweet. Youthful rebellion, and all that. I've kept you too close to home, I see that now. But I knew I must guard my most precious treasure. I feared for your safety, my darling."

My darling. He's never called her that before. *Treasure.* Paia can feel the warm stirrings of his breath on her ear, on the soft skin of her neck. Delicious. It distracts her from his casual dismissal of her soul-wrenching denial, from the accusations she should fling at him: liar, murderer, destroyer. How is he managing a true physical sensation?

"Yes, my love, I am here beside you. You've missed me, come now, admit it. You know where you truly belong, don't you?" His tone is endearingly unsteady, as if poised to say things he might regret, unguarded confessions of his need to have her back with him. "I won't speak of Duty or the Devotion that you owe me as your God. I'll speak of destiny. *Our* destiny, not the foolish plans of others. We are paired, you and I. Fated together. We have a kingdom to rule, once we defeat our enemies, and you shall rule it with me, not as my Priestess, but as my Queen."

Yes, but he talks to me as if I was still a child. And yet . . . *his Queen.* Images of pomp and splendor parade before her eyes. His lips enclose her earlobe. Paia cannot move away from or toward him. Her breath quickens.

His laugh is boyish, boastful with delight. "Ah, did I not tell you I'd thought of ways for us to become closer? So much closer, my darling."

The long weight of his body moves against her, fitting its nakedness to hers. Broad hands touch her, a man's hands, without scales. But she feels the delicate drag of curved fingernails across her skin. Poised between astonishment and delight, Paia wonders fleetingly if they're gilded, as his always are in man-form.

"It's so simple," he murmurs. "I can't imagine why I didn't think of it before. In life, I cannot manage substance in any form that would . . . ah . . . fit with yours. But in dreams, ah, in dreams I can provide any sort of satisfaction. Unimaginable pleasures, my darling."

He begins his sensual ministrations with his mouth and tongue. Still she cannot move or return his caress. She can only respond with the rising clangor of her body, as he wakens it to ecstasy.

How like him, she thinks, in the moment before delirium

drowns out reason. How like my beloved, broken God, my Fire, to invent an idea of lovemaking that only works one way. In that moment, her most profound feeling for the great golden dragon, the scourge of the world, is pity.

CHAPTER FOURTEEN

Paia stirs, and N'Doch moves away hastily. He realizes he's been humming faintly, under his breath. She shouldn't know how close he's been watching. Watching and humming. What's that tune? He's lost it now. He glances toward Djawara, snoozing in his straight-backed chair by the window. Old people and babies, he marvels. They can fall asleep anywhere.

He folds himself into an overstuffed armchair. He doesn't recall there being any furniture like this at the Rive. The upholstery is a maroon cut-velvet, like some rich matron's boudoir. Big, soft cushions—supposed to be comfortable, but if you're as tall as N'Doch is, they make your arms and legs stick out all over the place. He plants his elbows on his knees, which feel too close to his chin. He feels gawky and aroused, a combination he's not at all happy with. He's humming again. Is this some new nervous tic? Paia's eyes open. She blinks at him, still sensuous with sleep. In the dim, shuttered light of the café, she is unbearably lovely.

"Musta been one hell of a dream you had," he says for openers. He adds an evil grin to hide his self-consciousness.

"Dream. Yes." She seems to be struggling to remember.

"Dreaming of Dolph, I bet."

She looks away, down, then back at him. Despite her moist aura of slaked desire, her regard is bleak. N'Doch might almost say, tragic. "It wasn't."

He laughs and wriggles his eyebrows, trying to cheer her. "Maybe it was me, then."

She smiles sadly, as if he's offered the sweetest sort of false compliment, and then the smile is gone. She sits up, brushing back her damp hair, straightening her clothes as if surprised to find them there at all.

"Okay, I give up. Who's the lucky man of the hour? Was it . . . Papa Dja?"

She will not be jollied. He can see there's a war going on in her head, and his questions are a distraction. But maybe not entirely unwelcome. "Not a man at all."

N'Doch takes about a half a second. Then he gets it. Uh-oh. No wonder her eyes looks so haunted. "You have dreams like that about *him*?" he blurts before he can stop himself.

Her glance slips toward Djawara. She's clearly relieved to find the old man sleeping. "Was it so obvious?"

"Oh, yeah." Now it's his turn to look away. "Oh, yeah. Phew. Complicated relationship."

Paia stares down at her hands, lacing and unlacing her slender fingers, soft and well cared for but no longer so clean. "It was his dream, really. He's trying to woo me back to him."

Again, it takes him a while. He's not usually so slow on the uptake, but often Paia speaks as if, since her history has been revealed to him in the Meld, her moment-to-moment thought process will be equally apparent and understood. "You're saying the Fire dude sent this dream? Ordered it up and sent it?"

"I could never have invented it on my own," she murmurs.

He tries his grin again. "Lot of women have told me their dreams are way better than the real thing."

"But I know nothing of such things!" Her cry is raw with both shame and regret. Her hands wring themselves into tightening knots. "He never let me have *real* lovers. In this dream, I wasn't even allowed to participate! He just did things to me!"

"Hey, every once in a while, that's a nice way to go."

She glares at him. He sees his attempts at humor are coming off as insensitive. He tries to figure out how he could gracefully slide over onto the sofa next to her. But it's the wrong time to take advantage of a girl, when she's so worked up and vulnerable. He reaches over to untangle the furious maze of her fingers and ends up holding her hands instead. "Easy, now. At least it was only a dream."

"But that's just it!" She grasps his hands as if she could force a fuller understanding into him by the strength of her grip. "I don't know that. I could feel him . . . touching me. I could really feel it!"

"Dreams always seem real while you're dreaming 'em."

"No, at first it was like it always was. Like putting your hand in a flame. Heat, no substance. Then it seemed that the more I wanted him to touch me, the more real he became. In the end, he . . ."

N'Doch frees his hands, holds up both palms. "Whoa, girl. I don't wanna hear the details. I'm no kinda saint, y'know."

"N'Doch, please, don't you hear what I'm saying?" She leans toward him as he pulls away. Beneath her soft shirt, her breasts mound invitingly between her hunched shoulders.

"Yeah," he retorts. "The Fire dude made love to you long-distance, and you feel bad 'cause you liked it."

"No! Well, not only. It's . . . what if it's my desire that makes him real?"

"Okay. Lemme think about that." N'Doch is struggling to master his own desire. He knows it's making him stupid. He wishes she'd sit back and leave him alone. "Why should it matter, as long as it's still a dream?"

"But what if it isn't?"

"Isn't what?"

"Just a dream." Not only does she not sit back, she slides to the floor in front of him with her hands on his knees. "What if my desire acts as another kind of . . . portal? Allowing him to physically manifest in human form? He's never been able to do that before."

N'Doch doesn't move a muscle. There's a song rising in the back of his brain, for the first time since he left his dragon behind. "So what you're saying is, Fire comes to you in a dream, transports you to the heavenly spheres, then when he's done, he gets out of bed and wanders over to the bar to have a beer with me." And all I get to do is watch, he thinks, but doesn't add.

"Except that having a beer is not what he's most likely to do with you!"

N'Doch remembers the gilt-scaled giant in his cloak of fire up on the mountaintop, his scimitar claw aimed at Köthen's neck. "No, I suppose not."

"And he'd be able to do it this time. He wouldn't need a proxy hit man like your Kenzo Baraga."

Now there's an image that's a real turnoff. N'Doch feels his lust seeping away, allowing room in his brain for the fuller implications of what she's said. The inner music he's been hearing fades. He scrubs his face with his hands. "That might not be good."

"No." Paia slumps back against the base of the sofa as if she's spent herself in struggle. The bleakness is back in her eyes again. "Maybe you should make love to me. Then I won't be so lustful anymore."

N'Doch stares at her through the web of his fingers.

"I mean, of course it should be Dolph, but he's not here and . . ."

Her gaze lifts to meet his, veiled by shining hair and luxurious lashes, sultry with promise. N'Doch drops his hands, struck breathless by the hot flush of desire racing through him, searing away his will. Then he sees the bright tongues of flame leap in her eyes. He's not so stupid after all. He understands who he's really staring at. Like a dry wind in the desert, the presence resonates in all the hollow spaces his own dragon left behind.

"Whoa," he says. "No way."

Her face twists. The flames flare defiantly and die. He knows he's had a close call, but there's no struggle. N'Doch senses the shadow departing, like a whiff of smoke, and understands another, more puzzling thing. The bleakness in Paia is not her own. It's Fire's.

Paia shakes her head as if she's just dropped off to sleep again and waked with a start. "What?"

"You're asking me?" Suddenly he's glad that his friend, his hero the good baron, is a time warp away from this woman. She could eat the man alive. She carries a dragon within her. N'Doch should know. So does he. At least, he hopes to, soon again. But there's a difference. Paia's dragon feels he has nothing left to lose. "Didn't quite leave him behind, did you."

She flicks a wary glance around the café. She doesn't ask who. "Why? What happened?"

"An interesting little sleight of hand. Well, sleight of body's more like it. He tried to woo us both at once."

"He?"

"The Fire dude."

She starts, convincingly. "He was here?"

"Don't you remember?" He's sure she does, but he humors her, to spare her pride. "Seems he convinced you it might be a bright idea to seduce me." He sees her whole body recoil. With shame, he hopes, not with horror. Maybe she really doesn't remember. "Hey, don't worry. It didn't go far. He gave himself away too easily."

She looks like she's afraid to ask. "How?"

"He was in your eyes. Did you know he could do that? I mean, you know . . . use you that way?"

"I, ah . . . he never has before. At least, not that I . . ."

N'Doch watches what's left of her self-possession collapse. Body, face, her entire being goes limp. All her actions, past and present, are suddenly up for question.

"How . . . how will I ever know?"

How will any of us know, he wonders. Not just about Paia. About ourselves. Four people bonded to mythical creatures driven by alien agendas and protocols. He recalls the exact instant he let his dragon into his soul. The song he sang then wasn't an act of love or selflessness, though he did it to lend her his strength. It was more like surrendering to an inevitability. "You'll know 'cause I'll tell you," he says. "That's why there's four of us, I guess. So we can keep each other honest."

He's grasping at straws, but Paia seems grateful for the effort. She stops shuddering uncontrollably. "I can never be alone, then."

N'Doch has a leap of intuition that skews his take on things abruptly enough to leave him faintly dizzy. And hating it that once more he has to buy into all this mystical symmetry of events. "And that's why Dolph came along. So you don't have to be."

She smiles wanly. "I wish he was here now."

"He probably does, too." He says it to reassure her, but it makes him nervous again for Köthen, who has no dragon to protect him. Then he takes another leap. It's like a lyric writing itself in his head. Part of the epic he could sing about the dragon renegade and his beautiful priestess. Colorful. Dramatic. Even, in a perverse sort of way, romantic. Villains have been some of his most inspiring subjects. "He's not real happy, your man Fire." It sounds silly, now that he's said it, talking that way about a devious, inhuman, fire-breathing murderer. "I mean . . ."

"I know." Paia seems eager to talk about her dragon. She hasn't had much of a chance, N'Doch realizes, to download how she feels about all of this. "He's never been reasonable. He's angry all the time. I just took it for granted." She looks up, caught in an insight of her own. Her tears reflect the gray daylight. "An angry god. I guess it just seemed fitting, after all the horrors of the Collapse. What other kind of god could you believe in, after that?"

"He's like the black sheep younger son, maybe?" A little like me, N'Doch admits privately. "The one who's sure the older ones got something he didn't get, so he figures he's got a right to go out and take what he wants to make up for it."

Paia tilts her head. "What an interesting notion." She grasps the fat arm of the sofa and levers herself up onto the seat. On a side table is a crystalline glass of iced water that N'Doch is sure wasn't there a moment ago. Neither was the table. Neither was the gleaming acoustic guitar that's leaning against it, like it's been listening in on the conversation. N'Doch stops breathing. Paia drinks deeply, collecting herself. When she sets aside the empty glass, N'Doch lets his lungs fill, and waits for it to vanish. He waits for the guitar to vanish, too. But both just sit there. This magic, he decides, won't happen while anyone's watching. So as long as I keep this baby in my sight . . .

He grasps the guitar casually by the neck, then drags it into his lap and thumbs the strings. It's real and sleek, and in perfect tune. He nearly hollers for joy, but he's wary of upsetting Paia's delicate state of balance.

But maybe she's not so delicate. She allows the sudden instrument into their universe without batting an eyelash. "You must think I live my life entirely at the whim of my handlers," she says.

"No, I . . ." But of course, this is exactly what he's thought. Petted, spoiled, but ultimately the dragon's and the Temple's tool. He picks out a quiet little riff to let himself off the hook. Cocktail music. He glances at the deserted bar. *Wonder if I could sing myself up a drink.*

"To some extent, that's been true. But I feel like I've been waiting for the moment when it didn't have to be."

"This could be it, girl," he says lightly, the same tone as his fingers on the singing strings. He hopes he'll never have to choose between holding a woman and holding a guitar. He's pretty sure he knows which way he'd go.

Paia's on her own sort of roll. "With all that's happened, so much and so fast, there's a lot I haven't had time to really take in. Like, the existence of the other . . . dragons." She laughs softly. "I was never allowed to say that word, you know. He was 'the God.' Only 'the God.' When he spoke of his enemies, he never hinted at them being his own kind, especially not his own . . ."

"Family."

"Yes. Do they have something he doesn't?"

Besides a sense of decency? N'Doch shrugs, damping the guitar with his palm. "Young Erde and her dragon would say he lacks belief in the rightness of their Destiny. He's sure made it clear he wants none of that, even if no one knows exactly what it is."

Paia says, "He's always given me the impression he knows what it is. Otherwise why would he be so against it?"

N'Doch peers at her. The café is growing shadowed, as if dusk has fallen. But on the other side of the windows, the light is as harsh and bright as ever. Best as he can, he replays the confrontation on the mountaintop in his mind. "Didn't he yell something about humans not being worth the sacrifice? What'd he mean by that? The way he's been living, it doesn't look to me like he's sacrificed much." He shifts his lanky body within the velvety grip of the chair. Not room enough in here for himself and the guitar, plus the song that's taking shape, even the first few bars. Or maybe it's the notion he's hatching that's making him so uncomfortable. "I think we gotta find out what's bugging him."

Paia laughs, eyeing him sidelong.

"No, really." The edge on her laugh surprises him. Bleak, like Fire. He hikes himself forward on the puffy cushion, elbows draped over the sinuous curves of the instrument.

He's amazed to hear his own voice sounding so earnest. He has to keep himself from turning the words into a lyric right on the spot. "Whatever's this Big Fix the dragons are supposed to pull off, they're convinced they can't do it without Fire. So we got to bring him over to our side. And you know they're looking to you to do it."

Paia shakes her head hopelessly. He guesses she doesn't hear the music.

"Well, of course you can't do it alone. You're too close to him. Too much of an insider. The problem is, who else is there?" His fingers go to work on the accompaniment. "Gerrasch is too busy finding his own dragon, even though we gotta have him. Earth and Erde don't really give a shit about the whys. Their gig is doing what's right and proper according to the Big Rule Book. And we need that, too, I guess. But nobody's gonna get Fire to mend his ways by quoting him chapter and verse." The ending chord is harsher than he'd intended. "You agree with that?"

"Of course. His only real motive is self-interest."

"Right. So we find out what he wants, and if there's any way we can give it to him, we do. At least enough so's he'll play ball."

"We."

"Yeah. You and me." Now the background line is ticklish. He's thrilled by the subtle complexities of his improvisations. "You're connected to him 'cause you're his guide. But I might be able to help figure him out. 'Cause of my own history, I mean. I had all these grandiose plans, like he does. And I haven't done so well by my family either, have I? Ever since that blue dragon showed up, I've asked myself, why'd she pick me? If it was just to bodyguard young Erde into the future, she'd have better chosen someone like Dolph, or your cousin Leif. So maybe this is why." N'Doch grins at her. " 'Your mission, if you choose to accept it . . .' "

She gazes at him blankly.

"From an old vid series." He tosses off a few notes of the theme song. "Way, way before your time. Before mine, even. Anyhow, what do you say?"

"I'd say what he wants is power, luxury, and me, probably in that order. It's not all that complicated."

"But you're back into whats, not whys. Even a dragon's

got to have his whys. And when you know a person's whys, then you've got power over him." He stops, shakes his head, then throws both hands in the air and flops backward into the chair. The guitar lies prone on his stomach like a resting limb. "I can't fuckin' believe this! I'm talking about making deals with my mama's murderer."

Near the front, a chair leg rasps against the tile. "What sort of deals?"

N'Doch jerks upright, cradling the instrument. "Hey, Papa! Sleep well?"

"Not a chance." The old man walks toward them stiffly and pulls up a straight chair from a nearby table. "There's too many voices in the air here to get any rest. What sort of deals?"

N'Doch just knows he means voices other than his and Paia's. But he'll elaborate when he's ready. There's never any rushing Papa Dja. "I'm telling Paia here how it's likely our job to try to turn Fire."

Djawara nods gravely, approving. "Was a time, lad, that I'd have had to point out that sort of duty to you. Then grab you before you had a chance to escape."

N'Doch cackles. Just like Papa Dja. Always knowing better. He plays the up-tempo intro to a traditional folk tune. "So how we gonna pull it off, O Great Shaman of the Tribe?"

Djawara crosses one knee over the other and nests his hands in front of him. "In my day, when two sides had irreconcilable differences, they met to discuss them in neutral territory, where neither could do harm to the other. Some place like the beach or the market square . . . or here."

"Here? How we gonna bring him here?"

Paia clears her throat delicately. "You just told me I did."

"Almost. Papa, why you so sure this is neutral territory?"

"Instinct, my boy. Intuition. Trust me."

The old man's gone woo-woo on him, just like the old days. To punish him, N'Doch turns away to Paia. "So you dream him here, and *afterward* . . ." He leans on the word and wishes it was light enough to see if she's blushing. The guitar is growing warm in his arms. "Afterward, I offer him that beer and say, hey, dude, just what is your problem?"

"I don't think I'd have to dream him here," Paia replies steadily. "I think he would just come if I called him."

N'Doch looks to his grandfather. "Is this insane or what? I'd sort of had in mind sneaking up on him."

"And how were you planning to do that?"

He bends low over the strings, picking delicately. "Dunno. Hadn't got that far yet." He moves into a more familiar melody, his own this time.

"If nothing else," Paia adds, "we could keep him distracted while Cousin Leif takes back the Citadel."

"And the others go looking for Air. Oooh, he's just gonna love that idea." N'Doch can smell the Rive burning already. His thumb pats out the rhythm of the flames on the guitar's polished box.

"Negotiating with him was your idea in the first place," she reminds him.

"Hey, are we arguing? Ain't gonna get nowhere if we're arguing." But he's encouraged to see a flash of spirit out of her.

"Were you thinking of attempting this on your own, without the others?" Djawara asks.

N'Doch spreads his hands, balancing the guitar on his knee. "If we put them together with him, there'll just be another big fight. End of discussion. You know how families are." But it occurs to him how good it would be to have his brother Sedou at this debate. The old political hand. If the blue dragon were here, he could sing her into that uncanny transformation: half Water, half Sedou. A winning combination. N'Doch hums the tune wistfully. He can't believe he's about to do something this drastic without her pushing him into it. "Are you both really up for this gig?"

Dread and eager anticipation chase each other across Paia's face. She's wringing her hands again.

"There's a time and a place to be proactive." Djawara uncrosses his legs and places one hand carefully on each knee. "And there's no time like the present, I suppose."

Paia says faintly, "This may take me a few moments."

N'Doch's hum grows into a song.

CHAPTER FIFTEEN

He's fine for a while, cross-legged on the smooth stone, caught up in the work. One bright line of signal attracts his eye: bits of silvery chain with intervals of silence, sequences iterating with progressive changes. Music, he guesses. He wishes he could hear it, but he can only see its patterning. It seems to be searching, but it keeps running into dead ends and flowing back along itself until its lyrical orderings eddy off into chaos.

The Librarian has often imagined code as the soft and tensile cotton twine that's best for handweaving and knotwork. In dreams, he has created magnificent tapestries of electronic macramé. So, because the place he is now feels like a waking dream, he attempts a few simple manipulations, just for the fun of it. He nudges the glimmering chain toward a less congested route. To his delight, it finds an open path and speeds along toward its destination unhampered.

By then, his pudgy body is complaining, longing for the comforts of his ergonomic desk chair, and for the back and elbow support of his streamlined, waist-level, black matte console. He can't concentrate. He can't fly along the retreating lines of code and signal when he's cramped by such a vivid awareness of the strained sinews and tense muscles that anchor him to physical reality.

The Librarian sighs. He's never had a superior body, but at least it was fit at one time, for quite a long time in fact, until he retreated into the sedentary life of a cyber-jockey. He understands this now as the careless relaxing of an appropriate if noisome discipline. He should have adopted a hobby that got him up and moving around.

In the womb-temperature darkness, the Librarian sticks his legs straight out and props himself from behind on his palms. He feels like an overgrown teddy bear, and just about as useful. Surely *somewhere* in this void-space, there's got to be something better to sit on than the floor.

Also, action is definitely more interesting than self-pity. The Librarian looks around. The darkness is very, well . . . dark. A particularly felty darkness, stippled with textures of Brownian motion and incipient light. His gaze is drawn to an area of the darkness more mobile than the rest. More transparent. He groans to his feet and shambles in that direction. The darkness seems to have substance, a dense granulation that gives way before him in a tubular passage. He can't put his hands on this substance. Nothing solid meets his outstretched arms. But he can feel the *idea* of it enclosing him. He senses the direction in which it's leading him.

Then his shin whacks something hard that rolls away from him with a sharp plastic chatter. The Librarian bellows in pain and irritated surprise. *What fool left that there?* He always shoves the chair well in under the desk, in case he has to find it in the dark, as happens so often in these days of brownouts and power outages. He moves forward, finds the desk first, then fumbles for the errant chair. And then he remembers there's no way he could be where he thinks he is.

He stands motionless for a long moment, searching out an explanation. He grips the back of the chair. It creaks under his pressure as he leans against it. Its smooth handworn metal frame and torn padding mended with peeling layers of duct tape are entirely familiar. Even though his hands haven't touched them for two hundred and twenty-three years. He sees the indicator lights on the surge protectors, just where he'd expect them, pin-point eyes in the velvet darkness. The Librarian takes a breath, reaches, and switches on the desk lamp.

The cool halogen glow illuminates a beige keyboard, a bulky monitor and system case, flanked by racks of extra memory, modem, speakers, printers, tape storage, all linked by a spaghetti mass of cable. Books and manuals to right, left, and below. Above, just inside the lamp's small circle of light, a weather radio, a row of world maps, a list of satellite flyovers. And more books, with declarative, earnest titles and stacks of *Nature* and the *JGR* as bookends. It's all there, even a half-filled cup of coffee, cold but not spoiled, as if he had left it yesterday.

The Librarian moves slowly around the chair without letting go of it. He's afraid he'll collapse if left without support. He sits, and hauls himself automatically up to the desk. He flattens his palms on it. The very desk, the very equipment that delivered up his first undisputed signal from the dragon.

What is going on?

He has never felt so rattled, so close to believing that he's finally slipped his moorings. But there's only one logical thing to do. Only one. His hand hovers, then flicks the toggle to power up the system.

Chapter Sixteen

Erde clings to the arbor post. Rose petals drift around her like fragrant snow. Voices are raised at the gate. Outside, more frantic barking. Whatever's out there is coming in. The dogs spill through the gate again and out across the lawn in a blur of teeth and hackles. Erde grips the post so tightly, her knuckles crack. She prays that the hell-priest and his white-robed minions will not be next.

Then Lily and Margit stride in, forcibly escorting a small, dark figure by both scrawny arms. They shove their prisoner roughly to the ground. The figure curls up defensively in the thick green grass and lies there, unresisting. Erde goes up on her toes for a better view. Some captured denizen of the city?

Margit's voice floats up from the lawn. "Caught this one skulking about!"

Erde squints to see more clearly. "Oh, my!"

She bolts across the lawn, forgetting Rose entirely, and arrives just as Luther has shoved his large body between the two snarling scouts and the hapless intruder.

"Leave 'im!" Luther shouts. The dogs mill about, barking.

"Lily! Margit! Wait!" Erde pleads. "He's a friend!"

The women back off only enough to give her room. Erde throws herself down beside the curled-up ball and pats it urgently. "It's all right, Stoksie. They won't hurt you!"

"Too late fer dat!" Stoksie uncoils warily, glancing about. "Hey! Wachu doin' heah?"

Luther bends to help his friend to his feet, gently brushing him off. "Yu okay, Stokes?"

Stoksie nods, shooting a grim look at Lily and Margit. "Yu prizners, too?"

"No, no. It's all a misunderstanding. You're with friends." Erde takes his arm. "This is Stoksie, everyone. He's one of Luther's countrymen."

Stoksie looks to Luther and gets his nod. "Well, den. Das diff'rent." He straightens his clothing, then bows around, as if calling on all assembled to notice how forgiving he's being.

Erde is seized with giggles, but swallows them. She knows how the plucky little Tinker dislikes being bested. "Stoksie, how did you get here?"

"Well, nah, I cud ask yu da same questchun."

"Margit says you were sneaking about out in the yard."

"I wuz lookin' fer help!" He claps his hand to his bald head as if suddenly recalling his errand. "Hey! Doan mattah how I got heah! We gotta run help G! Dere'sa monsta afta him!"

"A what?" She's heard this term before from the Tinkers. She beckons Raven and the scouts to listen. "You mean Fire? Is he out there?"

"Nah. Dis sum kinda vishus masheen!"

Machine. Erde pictures the elevator at the Refuge, and the sleek humming furniture in Gerrasch's workroom. She knows these are machines, but it's hard to imagine them being vicious. Then she remembers the flying machines of N'Doch's time, and the wagons that rolled without horses. The one N'Doch called a *tank* truly was a monster. She saw it break down stone walls. "Is it coming here?"

"Doan know, but we gotta go afta G. Yu know how he kint run much."

"What's going on, sweetling?" asks Raven, less patiently than usual.

"Oh, forgive me!" Belatedly, Erde translates. She'd forgotten that none of the women would understand a word of the Tinker dialect. Nor do they know what a machine is, but they all recognize the description.

"We saw such horrors during our journey here," Raven agrees.

"But they didn't chase us," says Margit. "They hardly noticed us, but we had to be on our guard all the same. They'd flatten anything in their path."

"Often," Lily adds, "they were fighting each other."

"We gotta hurry!" Stoksie breaks in. "Kin yer frens help us?"

Erde passes the request to the women.

"Gerrasch?" exclaims Raven. "Our Gerrasch? Here?"

"Not quite as you remember him, but yes, it's our Gerrasch."

"Did he flee through the portal, too? I saw his house was destroyed, and I feared the worst!"

"I'll explain everything! After we've rescued him!"

Lily and Margit agree. Lily hurries off to recruit a few of the stronger refugee women.

Dragon, should we go with them?

I MUST SEE TO ROSE. BESIDES, I'D ONLY SLOW THEM DOWN. SISTER, WILL YOU GO?

PHYSICAL STRENGTH IS NOT MY GIFT, BROTHER. AS SOON AS YOU HAVE SEEN TO ROSE, WE MUST GO AFTER N'DOCH.

Then I'll go, and call you to come when we find him.

I WILL WANT YOUR HELP WITH ROSE.

I HEAR MUSIC. DOES ANYONE ELSE HEAR IT? MUSIC, I'M SURE OF IT!

Erde feels their attention languishing. *Dragons! Are we to desert Gerrasch? Your sister's dragon guide? Surely not!*

THESE STRONG WOMEN WILL BE HELP ENOUGH. WE MUST ALL USE OUR TALENTS ACCORDINGLY.

Guiltily, Erde relays all this to Margit, but the older woman seems unsurprised that the dragons are preoccupied with their own concerns. In fact, Erde decides, Margit is flattered that the great beasts trust her to get the job done. She nods tightly and whistles up the dog pack.

"The hounds won't be much use against a machine," Erde tells Stoksie. "But they know Gerrasch from the old days. They'll help you track him down."

Stoksie marvels over them, real living dogs that crowd around to lick his hands instead of attacking. "Dey wuz nicer ta me den doze two wimmen."

"Those women are good fighters, Stoksie."

"Fighters, all ri'," the little man grumbles.

Luther negotiates the loan of two stout pikes from Margit. Erde is relieved to note that the women of Deep Moor did not flee their burning homestead entirely unarmed. She smiles hopefully at the party assembling at the gate. "Bring him back safely!"

"Betcha!" Luther replies.

She watches them out of sight. Then, calling the dragons, she follows Raven back to the garden courtyard, assailed by the conviction that events are happening much too fast. Faster than usual, she's sure of it. She leaves Earth to hunker down outside the rose arbor. Water joins the women inside. Raven watches her flow in and out of the corners and niches, exploring the garden.

"Like a flock of butterflies this time. But humming, like bees."

Erde listens. The tune sounds vaguely familiar.

"Could she become Sedou again?" Raven asks. "Rose was very taken with Sedou."

"She would need N'Doch to sing her into that shape. His memory. His song, not hers."

"Ah." Raven nods soberly. "A pity."

Water completes her circuit of the garden and comes to hover over the table where Rose sits, exactly as she had been. As slowly as the petals falling from the arbor, Water settles onto the motionless woman until Rose is blanketed by a cloud of scintillating blue motes.

Erde queries the dragon. *What is she doing?*

MY SISTER GREETS THE LADY ROSE AND OFFERS HER OUR AFFECTION AND SUPPORT.

Does Rose respond?

SADLY, SHE DOES NOT.

Lady Water, can you tell what's wrong with her?

The blue motes withdraw from Rose and gather at the arbor entrance. THAT'S FOR MY BROTHER TO SAY. I ONLY WISHED TO PAY MY RESPECTS BEFORE I LEFT.

You're leaving?

N'DOCH IS SINGING.

But he's in Africa.

THE MUSIC I'VE BEEN HEARING JUST NOW ORGANIZED INTO A SONG. HE'S SOMEWHERE NEARBY, HERE IN THE CITY.

But how could he be?

Erde blurts this in total disbelief. But on second thought,

it makes perfect sense that N'Doch is in the city. Symmetry demands it because Gerrasch is also here, delivered by yet another portal, to judge from Stoksie's description. Erde believes in symmetry, especially as regards the destiny of dragon guides. Eventually, she'd have worried if N'Doch had *not* shown up.

Is Paia with him?

I'LL FIND OUT WHEN I GET THERE. I'LL KEEP IN TOUCH. CIAO.

Water doesn't wink out as the dragons do when Earth is providing instant transport. She flutters away under the blossom-laden arbor. Peering after her, Erde sees her flit across the outer lawn and through the stone gate into the city as if heading off on an afternoon stroll. Erde sighs. The scent of flowers and bruised grass and the warm softness of the breeze belie the dire realities they all are facing. And then Earth's deep rumble reclaims her wandering attention.

NOW LET US TURN OUR MINDS AND HEARTS TO HELPING LADY ROSE.

CHAPTER SEVENTEEN

Paia listens to N'Doch's song, glad for the excuse to put off her summoning a bit longer. His voice is strong and pure, and the melody murmurs of loss and longing. By the second verse, in a happier vein, he's left off his guitar accompaniment, so that the song drifts entirely on its own through the thickening dusk. Paia imagines it like water, flowing into the darkened corners of the room. Where it's been, it leaves a new glimmer behind. Chandeliers flare softly overhead. Etched glass sconces glow to life. The darkness retreats a little.

N'Doch is still singing when the front door opens and shuts with the throaty rattle of thin glass in an aging wooden frame. N'Doch falls silent in the middle of a word. Paia fears to look. She's sure the God has somehow pre-empted her summons. But how has he managed the doorknob?

Djawara's back is to the door. He turns, then rises with a quick, stiff jolt and a gasp. His chair clatters to one side.

"Easy, Papa," says N'Doch quickly. "It's not who you think."

A tall black man stands in front of the closed door, re-connoitering. As tall as N'Doch, maybe taller, and more broad-shouldered. A big man. But Paia immediately sees the resemblance. It's in the smile, the great transformation from a glower to a grin.

N'Doch wrenches himself out of the overstuffed arm-chair. One fist shoots into the air angrily. The other clutches the neck of the miraculous guitar. "Whacha trying to do?" he yells at the man, "Give Papa Dja a heart attack?"

"Nice welcome." The newcomer frowns, and the heated air in the café chills noticeably. "Papa," he says gently. His voice is deep, like the roll of distant thunder. "I didn't know you were here."

Djawara finds his own voice, but barely. He looks so frail and overcome that Paia worries for him. She puts her hand out, and he grasps it gratefully. "Sedou? Sedou, my boy?"

N'Doch hugs the guitar against his chest. "Nah, Papa, it's her. It's the dragon. Will you please just sit down and take a breath?" To the big man, who hasn't moved from the door: "You oughta be ashamed of yourself!"

"Be cool, bro. I didn't know. You should have warned him before you sang me."

"I didn't . . ." N'Doch notices the guitar in his arms. "Did I? Shit, guess I did. What was I thinking?"

"I guess you weren't. Nothing new there."

"Glad to see you, too."

"The dragon?" murmurs Djawara.

Paia is amazed. Water in human form has none of Fire's charged, holographic glitter. The dragon has simply become the man, the older brother that N'Doch was singing about. The *dead* older brother, she now recalls. No wonder Djawara is so distressed.

"The dragon?" the old man asks again.

N'Doch is busy squabbling with his pseudo-sibling. "How did you find me here?"

Paia sets Djawara's chair upright and urges him to sit. "His dragon. Water. She's a shape-shifter."

He knows this, but had for the moment forgotten. She sees comprehension return as if a mist has cleared from his eyes. "Ah, yes. Shape-shifter." He looks away from the apparition of his dead grandson, then back again. "Remarkable likeness, really." He smiles at Paia and pats her hand. "Remarkable. Though now that I look more closely, not exactly as I remember him. Sedou was not so . . ." Djawara's hands sketch out height and breadth. "Not such a giant."

"He's the Sedou that N'Doch remembers," Paia offers quietly.

"I am what he sings me." The big man moves gracefully among the empty tables, snatching up a chair as he passes. He sets it down in front of Djawara and sits, his eyes level with the old man's. They regard each other for a long moment, while N'Doch hovers uneasily in the background.

"Ever since she showed up," he mutters to Paia, "I always thought it should be Papa Dja she came for. He's been expecting dragons for years."

"I am very sorry for the loss of your daughter, good sage," says the dragon. "But happy that you are alive and well."

Djawara's round face crinkles, caught between joy and sorrow. "Had I never met a dragon before now, I'd never have thought to look for salvation in a grove of trees." He pauses. "What shall I call you?"

- "Whatever makes you easy, Papa."

"Sedou, then. In honor of."

Paia tries to imagine Fire ever putting someone else's comfort before his own. She offers her hand, mostly for the chance of convincing herself of the dragon's material presence. "Sedou. I feel I should introduce myself."

N'Doch's fist descends on the big man's shoulder, beating out a soft repeating rhythm. "So, you're here. Did you leave the Big Guy outside?"

"Not here."

When the dragon has explained about Rose and the destruction of Deep Moor, N'Doch begins to pace. "We're all here, then, here in the city. Even Gerrasch. Damn, that's got to mean something."

"Still missing one," Paia reminds him.

N'Doch levels a knowing glance. "Not entirely missing, though."

Sedou sits back, swinging his arm over the curve of his chair. "Yeah, what about that? I'm picking up vibes about this little project you all have in mind. Seems like I got here just in time."

N'Doch frowns. "You mean, time to tell us to forget it, huh?"

"No. No." Sedou looks thoughtful. "Brother Earth certainly would. But I'd kinda like to hear what Fire has to say for himself when he's not trying to incinerate me." The man/dragon lets his eyes roam the shadowed length of the café. "Perhaps this civilized and casual setting will be more conducive to rational discourse than a barren mountaintop."

"He's often most deadly when he's rational," Paia warns.

"But in this zone of safety, his only available weapon will be his tongue," Djawara points out. "The only real power in words is what we give them ourselves."

Paia is surprised that this old man should be so willing to meet the dragon who has just murdered his only daughter. She's also surprised that Water is willing to go along with N'Doch's mad scheme. But she nods, accepting the inevitable. The idea seems less crazy with another dragon in the room.

"That's it, then?" N'Doch tightens his hold on the guitar. "We're still good to go?"

Sedou stands. "The sooner, the better. Before our less devious colleagues get wind of this."

"Come now." Djawara puts on a fey grin. "What's devious about a little negotiation?"

PART THREE

The Call to the Quest

CHAPTER EIGHTEEN

The Librarian flicks the switch, and nothing happens. Despair surges through him, like the rush of a bad, cheap drug. His heart pounds. His fingers rattle against the noisy, antique keyboard. *Shame, Gerrasch!* He's too smart, too experienced to rest his entire future on the outcome of a single action. And yet, he did, he has. He's secretly hoped she'd just . . . be there.

Then the rising whine of the drives drowns out the blood roar in his ears. The flood of returning joy nearly knocks him flat.

What doesn't kill you makes you strong, the Librarian intones silently. He vows to settle down. Get a grip. He is unused to being tideswept by the force of his own emotions.

Okay. Where am I?

His tiny crash pad in Frankfort. His desk and chair. A few books. His battered ham radio. Other than that, there was just a mattress on the floor and a crate for his clothing. Is the mattress out there also, lumpy and dank, in the darkness that, now as then, surrounds his desk? He's sure that's its sour smell he detects, mixing with odors of boiled cabbage and crumbling plaster. The old-fashioned mechanical keys feel both strange and familiar. He cocks an ear for the sounds of traffic and footfalls outside the cracked basement window. A single monitor shivers to gray life at eye level, and coughs up the DOS prompt. The cursor flashes at him balefully. The Librarian never liked cursors. He knows already that this system will be inadequate to his uses. Can it even do as much as he's already doing (miraculously) on his own, without the aid of machinery? Unlikely. Meanwhile, it's here, so there must be a reason. The dragon's reason, he hopes. He'll have to scour his memory for all the tricks he used back then to tease power, speed, and flexibility out of third-hand equipment. In those days, his ingenuity was fueled by necessity as well as obsession. He's tickled by the image of his burly neck and shoulders as solidly built shelves of a library, the required architectural support for all the information he carries inside his head. He stares at the cursor, pondering his course of action.

He considers what he knows, what he's sure about: the dragon Air is somewhere about. Instinct tells him this, not hard evidence. But trusting instinct has won him through many situations where rationality proved dangerously misleading. Assume, then, that she's close by, but either cannot or will not speak to him directly. The Librarian opts for *cannot,* since he feels still and always the pull of the dragon's desire to communicate. It's the bright star by which he's navigated through his many lives. He can't believe, he *won't* believe, that it would fail him now, when he's so close to his goal.

So she's here, she can't speak to him, for whatever reason, but there's all this signal in the air, which his peculiar ear perceives as sound, and his particular brain as code. *There are no accidents.* He now recalls that, back when, he'd rigged this system to do primitive cryptography, once he'd given up asking his geek acquaintances about the mysterious binary sequences that kept showing up in his system. There'd been equivalent incursions during his ham radio years, even on his CB, but he rarely mentioned these, lacking the material evidence to back up his claim. It became a very private matter. Either his friends began to suspect his sanity, or they got much too interested and insisted on burdening him with reports of their own communications with space aliens. He had no desire to admit to being one of them, and yet, there were these "messages." Not sentences. Not even words. Only their elegant patterning indicated intent on the part of the sender. But the intent was mysterious, and the sender never identified. Looking back, the Librarian is proud that he kept the faith for so long, his faith in his preternatural senses, and never let himself be convinced that he was imagining things. Eventually, in desperation, he'd developed his own private array of listening devices, but none of them was ever a channel for the mystery signal. It didn't use his devices. It just . . . arrived. And, doggedly, the Librarian would attempt to decode it.

So now, reverting to the habit of the location he finds himself in, he calls up a menu of active frequencies and chooses one at random. He squints into the monitor as the numbers scroll past.

The keyboard feels different when he sets his hands back on it: sleeker, more compact. He glances down and recognizes yet another old friend, from a slightly later time when he began to wear out his keyboard every six months. More books, piled at his elbow, his single shelf having overflowed. The familiar bibles are there: *Silent Spring, Limits to Growth,* the report from Rio, mixed in with his deep ecology journals and action alerts from Greenpeace and Earth First. For a moment, he's distracted by the hopefulness of all these pages of horrifying statistics and earnest prose. *If only we can get the word out, the people will listen!* The Librarian sighs and rubs his eyes. He believed that, then. He looks up again to find a bank of three monitors, each showing the processing of a different line of code. On the right-hand screen, a familiarity in the sequencing catches his eye. It's the signal he'd monkeyed with in order to free up its logjam. He types briefly, then waits for what seems like a lifetime. *Too slow, too slow,* he fumes. At this rate, the world will be burned to a cinder before he gets through to his dragon. At last, the screen offers him several options. When he lowers his fingers, the keyboard has become a chunky but functional laptop. The Librarian taps in his choice, and music enters the void like a friend walking into the room. A single plaintive guitar, and a voice he's sure he recognizes, even though he's never heard it singing before. He doesn't ask why he's hearing N'Doch sing. It's a pleasant and appropriate accompaniment to his work. And when he finds *her,* she will explain it all.

He calls up the frequency list, marks this one as identified, and moves on to the next. He ceases worrying about the limitations of his equipment. Each time he complains of a particular shortcoming, the machinery evolves to compensate. More memory, more speed. The CD-ROM drive. The emergency fuel cells and storage batteries. The voice recognition capability. And none of it is an illusion. Nothing so simple. The Librarian shrugs. No common standard of credibility can be applied to this situation. He believes in the material reality of place and machinery, equally, in each succeeding incarnation. It occurs to him after the first few mutations that it might all be a metaphor for processes actually taking place in his head, a sort of visual aid to help ground him and move him forward. Otherwise, wonder and disbelief might bring him to a dead halt. The Librarian can't afford wonder or disbelief. Not right now. Time, he knows suddenly, is of the essence.

He's in his loft in New York by now. He recalls the big steel desk and the double banks of monitors. It still smells old, but not so decrepit. Better digs, more add-ons, now that computing skills can equal an income. He has the Internet, and a hacker's access to the databases. Software engineer by day, eco-terrorist by night. The decoder works faster, almost as fast as he can think. He checks off several more signals. One sends instructions to the street-cleaning machines, simply and traditionally written in a long loop, so that when each machine has completed its assigned task, it will begin the process all over again. Another resolves easily into a video image: an elderly black man drinking espresso in a quaint twentieth century café. *Must be an old movie clip.* The Librarian lets the illogic of this notion pass, along with his temptation to watch for a while and see what happens next. He marks the frequency and moves on. The next several signals seem to be associated with the city's air quality maintenance and power routing. Another is a more complex set of machine instructions, but appears to be somehow damaged or degraded. *Tampered with,* the Librarian amends, then wonders why this conclusion came to him so surely and suddenly. He cannot quite make sense of it. In the next signal, the tampering is more obvious, like a text broken up by commentary from a nonnative speaker.

He sits back, glowering at the screen. N'Doch's song has ended. The silence is hollow and unfriendly. So far, the Librarian has judged all the code he's looked at to be of human origin. The additions strike him as something quite different.

What now?

The Librarian rubs his eyes some more, a habit he never has been able to break. He feels incapable of thought. His back is stiff with cramp and his well-padded butt is nearly fused to the chair. How long has he been at this? It doesn't seem like . . . but then, how would he know. He works life into his lower limbs, then gets up for a stretch. There's a bit more light to see by than before. When he turns away from the desk, his breath catches in his throat and he grabs for the chair again. Which is lower than it was. He starts, and almost tumbles sideways from the force of memory.

The space around him has evolved along with the equipment. Compact fluorescents dangle from the crossbeams inches above his head. He's in the first real bunker he'd built for himself at his vacation home in the mountains, once he saw the way things were going. He'd hired a local excavator to dig it into a steep hillside, claiming a fancy for a really big root cellar. Small for a large person, however. Dank and claustrophobic, exactly like an oversized grave, once the door was closed. The Librarian's animal origins kept him from panic, but as it turned out, he wasn't in it long. It had been unwise to let anyone know about a facility whose proper functioning depends on secrecy, no matter how far in advance of actual need the location is prepared. The excavator's family apparently had a long memory. The Librarian squeaked out of that crisis alive enough—they hadn't expected the "tree hugger" to be armed—but he'd made damn sure to dig the next hole by himself, when no one was looking.

Inhaling the earth-damp scent of the remembered burrow, he glances uneasily over his shoulder. How far does this memory world extend? What will he see if he undoes the several locks and dead bolts, lifts the steel crossbar, and shoves open the heavy wooden door? Wood. That had been the Achilles' heel. He couldn't see how to explain to his neighbors the need for a reinforced steel door on a little old root cellar. Eventually, they'd burned him out.

Interesting, the Librarian muses, *how many of my life-threatening events have involved fire. Just how long has this sonofabitch been at this?*

He stumps over to the door and lays a hand on the thick, rough planks. He doesn't really want to open it and see those lovely, lost pines, those fresh-scented hills rolling green over green over blue into a misty horizon. Dead now. All dead. Chopped down, wind-torn, bulldozed, burned out, poisoned, drought-killed, worm-eaten, pest-chewed, disease-ridden. The evergreens were the first to go. The Librarian sucks in the breeze blowing in his mind: the springy perfume of the needles, the sweet fern carpet beneath, the faint crush of wintergreen, the trailing whiff of wild stock from the meadow's edge. He's not easily given to weeping, never has been, but he knows that if he opens the door and sees those trees, he will be unable to hold back his tears.

He decides to be hungry instead. He goes looking for the refrigerator.

He'd installed one in this first bunker, using a buried power line. Later, what should have been obvious before became all too clear: he'd need his own power source as well. By the next time, solar techology was available to the rich, and the Librarian's cleverness with his keyboard had made him a lot of money. But this first, optimistic bunker lost power after the first three hours.

A tall white rectangle hums up out of the darkness in front of him. He flips open the door and finds exactly what he'd shoved in there so hastily when the time came to pull inside like a tortoise into its shell and barricade the inadequate wooden door. He finds ham from his pigs, and cheese and butter from his cows. Two loaves of bread. A roasted chicken. Eggs. Several bins of greens from the garden. Optimistic, indeed. How long did he think this would last him? How long did he think it would *need* to last him? Could he have guessed then that no length of time he thought of would be long enough? He'd been so sure he was well prepared.

He closes the refrigerator quietly. There'll be bushels of carrots and cabbage and potatoes stored away somewhere, and a row of tomato vines heavy with fruit, ripped out of the furrows in the last moments of his pack up. He feels around in the darkness behind the fridge and knocks his head against the hanging root balls, still moist from the ground. Soil cascades around him in a fragrant shower. The sharp green smell of bruised tomato leaves accomplishes what the Librarian has hoped to avoid by not opening the outer door. He slumps against the humming refrigerator and buries his face in his hands.

The tragedy was so fresh to him in those days. He had

nothing to offset his despair. He hadn't yet worked out the purpose of his dragon-haunted existence, of his miraculous many lives—which were a tragedy of sorts in themselves, in that they forced on him a very, very long sort of view, and the fullest realization of how much, how terribly much, has been lost . . .not the least of which was any remaining faith he might have had in humanity. Each generation carries forward a part of the experience of the generations before it, but these recollections fade and mutate with time, even among such experts at oral tradition as the Tinker crews. Stoksie, for instance, with all his tales of what his father and grandfather said and saw, has never known a century-old oak tree, a real winter, or a truly green spring. He has only a borrowed, mythic notion of the truth, the real, entire truth which assails the Librarian yet again as he inhales the odors of his vanished hilltop garden.

How could such a clever species be so stupid, so short-sighted? No sensible animal fouls and destroys its own nest! Only the human animal.

Cast up on the sharp rocks of despair as if for the first time, the Librarian gives in at last, and weeps. Each time he has wept, he has sworn to be strong and never weep again. But always, always, the loss is too devastating, the ache too profound.

And this time, he seems to have lost his ability to haul himself back from the brink. This time, along with despair, there is doubt. The doubt is sudden and spreading, like a fast-working virus, like the oxygen being sucked out of his lungs. He's drowning in salt water and snot. What if . . . what if there is no dragon, no purpose, no rescue? What if he's made it all up, all of it: a tall tale to defend himself against his paralyzing grief and hopelessness? What if he didn't really live all those past lives? The Librarian hears a high-pitched mewing. He wishes it would stop, but it's him making that pitiful noise. What if he's met no other dragons, never actually confronted one of them on a sun-bleached mountaintop?

Wait.

The Librarian halts in mid-motion, massaging his taut brow. His damp hands drop to his sides. He turns toward the door. He smells smoke.

Smoke?

Is that it, then? The portal was a trap after all, and he's to be forced to relive the very nearest of his many near-death experiences? Well, he didn't panic the first time, so he refuses to panic now. He goes back to the door. The hardware, he remembers, transmitted the heat of the fire outside long before the wood began to burn. He flattens his soft palm against the strap of a hinge. The smooth metal is cool, room temperature at most. And the scent of smoke is fainter by the door. The Librarian pads back to the refrigerator, sniffing studiously. Nothing. Just his imagination, as it were, overheating? He believes his nose is more reliable than that. He replays the moment in his head, calling up the odor again. Not the smell of wood burning at all. More like molten metal, or rock. Magma.

Ah. Him. The Librarian has managed for a long time to keep below the Intemperate One's radar, or so he'd thought. But now, those days are over. He glances about, expecting to see a different kind of glow in the darkness, but the acrid tang is gone from the earthy air of the burrow.

He was here, I'm sure of it . . . if only for a moment!

What let him in? The vividness of the memory? If simply the recollection of burning allows the Fire Dragon access, the Librarian swears to banish all such thoughts. He yanks open the refrigerator door and fumbles among the vegetables until he finds the object of his search, smooth and slim and chill. He hauls it out, trying to remember how many he'd stashed back there and how long he can hold out before going back for the next one. He hasn't had a real beer in decades. He twists it open as he walks, but waits until he's seated again at the desk before taking his first long swig. *Ah. Much better.* Until the return of the hops blight, he'd brewed his own. No wonder he was so fond of the stuff. Giddy with nostalgia, he swivels his chair a few times, working up speed, then shoves off with his toes to see how many rotations he can manage in free flight. As the chair spins him around, he spots a reflective glimmer in a direction he hasn't explored yet. He drops his feet, dragging himself to a halt. Oh, yes, there was an old television over there. As the memory sharpens, the object clarifies and brightens. Just like manipulating a digital image. The TV is a slim-lined table model. The Librarian sets his beer down. He goes over to the television and brushes dust off the screen. Wasn't it broken past all repair? He'd never used it much even then, but for the hell of it, he tabs it on.

To his astonishment, he gets a picture. Immediately. He's further astonished when he recognizes the location. It's the Citadel. Somehow, this broken-down television is broadcasting the feed from one of the Citadel's security cameras. He's looking at a long view down an interior corridor. A still image, or maybe the hallway is empty right now. No, here comes someone hurrying past, huge and close to the lens at first, then quickly diminishing down the dim tunnel. The Librarian sees only shoulders and a back, large and male and carrying a spear. He rocks back on his heels pensively, then stabs a finger at the channel selector. Obligingly, the image blanks and a different camera comes online.

"Hunh," grunts the Librarian, and is startled by the sound of his own voice. He backs up to where he can feel for his chair without taking his eyes off the screen, then hauls it over and plants himself in front of the television. He shifts through the channels, bringing up each of the functioning cameras in succession, with static or blue-screen for the dead units in between.

"Hunh," he says again. Has his subconscious been screaming to know what's going on back home? He sits up suddenly, then swiftly backpedals to the desk. No reason why it should work, but he tries it anyway. His laptop has become a touch pad. He taps in the address he uses to call House at the Citadel. He gets an error message. He tries a few more times and gives up, but on a whim, keys in his own address at the Refuge, adding the command for voice transmission. The call goes through.

"Hello? Hello?" A boy's desperate query.

The Librarian clears his throat. "Mattias?"

"Who's there? Who is this?"

"Gerrasch, Mattias. It's Gerrasch."

"G? *Where are you?*" The boy's yell seems to penetrate the darkness at the Librarian's back. "I come back, you're *gone*! Just gone! Where are you?"

"Pipe down. My ears." Illusion or reality? He can't believe this is happening.

"I bin waitin' forever!" The boy's Tinker accent rises with his pitch. "Weah are yu?"

"Difficult to explain. Not where you are. What's 'fer-ever?' What's happening there?"

"Yu okay? Yu alri'?"

"Yes, yes. What's up? Is Leif there?"

"Nah, he's gone! Dey're all gone, 'cept da little'uns! T'ree days, nah. Wuldn't let me go wit' dem! Said I gotta stay an' wait fer yu!"

"And here I am. You say Leif left three days ago?" It doesn't seem possible that three days have passed since he walked through the portal.

"Leif an' da 'hole army! Day shud be 'bout dere by nah."

The Librarian glances sidelong at the television. No sign of any action yet. That is, if what he's seeing on that screen truthfully represents the facts. "Food and water, Mattias? All you need?"

"Yah, shur. Dey lef' us ev'ryt'ing. But dere's nutting ta do heah. Yu commin' back soon?"

"Hope so. Listen, Matt. Boring, yes. But stay, okay? More important than you know. Safer if I can reach you."

"Safer yu, or safer me?"

"Both. The world."

Mattias groans, but it's only for show. "I be heah, G."

"Good. Now, patch me through to House."

"House! Oh boy, kint do dat, G. House wen' off-line yestiddy."

This news convinces the Librarian that he's talking in real time. "Why?"

"Doan know. He jess blanked."

The Librarian reviews the list of the Citadel's surveillance cameras. There are none in the library or in the computer room. How can he find out what's happened to House? Meanwhile, there's an avalanche of code waiting to be sorted through and analyzed. Can't let himself be distracted from his search. He must bend his mind to the issue of the differing interpolations. House will have to take care of himself.

"Mattias. Stay on station. Keep trying House. I'll get back to you soon."

"Wait, G. Tell me whachu bin doin'."

"Can't right now, Matt. Later, okay?"

"Okay," concedes the boy heavily. "I guess. See yu soon den?"

"Hope so." The Librarian cuts the connection with no real conviction that he'll be able to establish it again at will. But soon he should be able to witness Leif Cauldwell's assault on the Citadel, at least from certain points of view. He wheels back to the television and tabs through to the camera trained on the Grand Stair. The landscape is sere and barren. Dust swirls off the wide, steep steps and is lost in curtains of heat shimmer. At the head of the stair, two Temple guardsmen huddle in the slim shadow of the terrace railing, their eyes slitted against the glare and wind-borne grit, fixed on the distant pale gash where the mountain pass empties onto the valley floor. When something happens, he'll notice. The Librarian leaves the channel tuned to that view, and returns to his code analysis.

He misses the boy's eager, trusting voice the second it's no longer with him, warming the darkness. He wishes N'Doch had not stopped singing. He needs no more eruptions of despair putting him off his course. He decides to attempt to trace the song's origin. At its current stage of evolution, his equipment should be able to go back and pinpoint a signal's location anywhere in the world. Of course, the difference in time-location may intervene. He runs the inquiry anyway. A bloom of cool light draws his glance upward. A window-sized wall screen has succeeded the monitor bank. On it, a brightly colored schematic: a vast and repetitious grid. A map, the Librarian decides. Of this very city. But not a map of streets. A map of power distribution. A flow chart of signal. He studies it with the eager anticipation of a lover who's discovered his beloved's diary, as if it had secretly been written for him only.

Certain things are immediately obvious. A green dot marks the origin of the signal he's inquired about. A red dot marks his own position. According to the map, they're only a few blocks away from each other. This is convenient but inconceivable. The Librarian knows N'Doch is in twenty-first-century Africa.

On the other hand, I don't know exactly where I am, do I? Or when.

He runs the inquiry again and gets the same result. He sets this conundrum aside as currently unsolvable, and goes back to the flow chart. A deeper perusal tells him that even this trove of information will provide no easy answers.

Nowhere does he find the central nexus he's hoped for, pointing to a master control. If the dragon draws from or imparts energy to this network, she is not currently announcing her presence. The Librarian downloads his disappointment into three long, deep breaths, and returns to his methodical analysis, signal by signal.

He chooses a random city block for closer study, one of countless seemingly identical squares. He enlarges the scale by a factor of ten, and discovers that what he has taken to be mere digital texturing in the image is actually an underlying layer in the grid: more power lines, myriad and tiny, almost too small to be seen as individual signals. He increases the magnification by another factor of ten, then sits staring at the screen, trying to make sense of what he sees. He zeroes in on one line and magnifies it until a pattern reveals itself. More code. Infinite and infinitesimal beams of instructions, blanketing the entire city. Every meter, every centimeter, every millimeter, every . . .

The Librarian shoves back his chair and lurches to his feet. He glares around wildly. Comprehension lurks like a treasure in the darkness. It awaits him, rich and gleaming, if he's willing to make the leap. But it's a big one, and he fears the chasm in between. He starts to pace.

The space is smaller now, walled in by maps and monitors and wall screens. The void beyond exists only as stripes of darkness between. It's the Refuge. Not as he's recently left it, but as it was when he first came to it, sixty years earlier: raw, freshly painted, still smelling of wet concrete. Paia's grandfather was renovating the Cauldwell family compound fifty miles farther west. "Hardening," as it was called in those days. The Librarian stalls his epiphany with a moment of nostalgic revisiting.

His office down on the fourth level monitored the sea level rise. Next door to the left were the ozone boys. To the right, the Storm King, the scowling head of Meteorology whose office was always on high alert. The Librarian and his fellow post-docs told themselves how lucky they were to have wrangled jobs on high ground and in a secure location, away from the chaos in the cities, the food riots, the epidemics, and with all the hardware they could want. Let's watch the planet go into the toilet on a hundred different screens in gorgeous living color! But of course, they all assumed the need would be temporary. With the horrors of the final collapse yet to come, they still thought their work had meaning, that civilization could be saved if there was somebody out there doing good science. And it could have been saved, if anyone in power had cared to listen. But Power has a very, very short view, the Librarian learned. It's just down the block to the intersection of Profit and Job Security. Daily in his office at the Refuge, it was someone else's turn to shove open the door and exclaim, "You're not gonna believe what they've done now!"

The Librarian is sorry not to see those weary young faces around him again. Long dead, most of them, or vanished back into the maelstrom in desperate search of family and loved ones, or for a reason to continue living. The Librarian has hoped for one or another of them to resurface among the Tinker crews, but sadly, none ever has.

He pads up to the old map he'd pinned to the wall next to the door, a huge, laminated USGS composite of the Adirondack counties. His red-penciled scrawl spiders the contour lines, notating an inked-in overlay that detailed the successive backing up of the Hudson River into the flood-plain of its tributaries, and after that, into the lower valleys. New York City had gone under around the turn of the last century. The Librarian sets his toes against the base of the wall and brings his face up to the map until the tip of his nose is nearly touching the surface. The pale green-and-beige shapes blur out of focus. The thin red letters waver like splashes of blood. In his mind, he sees the machines in the city square, tearing up the patterned pavement and setting it right back down again.

"I know what you're made of," he murmurs to the map, suddenly willing to admit it. Not a dream. Not his imagination.

Nanotech. It has to be.

Nanotech. Still science fiction in those early days at the Refuge, but close enough to being a reality, if the resources for R&D hadn't dried up entirely. After the Collapse, the Librarian just assumed that technological development had ceased, and it was all downhill from there. He must have been wrong.

Nanotech.

He feels a big, involuntary grin stretch his face, his body

responding to the news before his brain has registered all its implications. His feet shuffle out a little two-step. He wraps his arms around his barrel chest and gives himself a hug. Somehow, somewhere, progress has continued. The reign of the God of the Temple of the Apocalypse is not the Last Days. There is a future after all.

And . . .

The Librarian stills as the last insight drops into place. There is a future, and he's probably in it. Now. Right here.

Nanotech. How long did it take to develop? No wonder each remembered place has looked, felt, and smelled so real to him. They *were* real, as real as matter ever truly is. Built, then rebuilt upon the instant. A numberless submicroscopic legion of machines, working at the molecular level. A whole city created and maintained by their constant labor. Worlds of memory, remade as reality. Just add water.

The Librarian lets out a slightly mad cackle. He staggers back to his high backed, high-tech chair and throws himself into it. It absorbs the force of his weight and rebounds gently. He feels it mold obediently to the curve of his back. Creepy, but astonishing. He tries not to shiver with awe.

Nanotech.

Now that he's sitting down again, he can ask himself the really scary question. The existence of nanotech is a minor miracle compared to the really big mystery: how do all the little nanomechs have access to his personal memories? From where or whom are they getting their building instructions?

The Librarian is fairly sure he knows.

CHAPTER NINETEEN

Erde returns to the garden and slides into a seat at the stone table. Looking into Rose's distant stare, she is convinced that a terrifying darkness lurks within. Much more than exhaustion has driven Rose of Deep Moor into retreat from the world.

"Should we bring her to him?" Raven asks.

"He says it would be better not to move her," Erde replies.

"I'm glad to hear it. Linden thought a change of scene might help, but I've been resisting that."

There's a third chair at the stone table under the apple tree, directly opposite Rose. Erde can't recall it being there before, but Raven takes it without comment. Rose's uncanny stillness doesn't mar the compassion and intelligence in her features. She is not a beautiful woman, like Raven, but certainly the one you would turn to in a crisis. Now, the crisis is hers. Though Rose's face is suffused with calm, it's the calm of withdrawal, not of being alert and in command of one's self. Erde is sure that some terrifying darkness lurks within that distant stare. Much more than exhaustion would be needed to drive Rose of Deep Moor into retreat from the world.

Erde seats herself, then signals Raven to join her at the table.

"Are you sure?" Raven has been holding back in the fragrant leaf-shadow of the rose arbor. "I won't be in the way?"

"Of course not. The more support we offer, the better, wouldn't you think?" She wonders if Raven expects a grand gesture of some˙sort. Whatever healing the dragon can manage, it will be a very quiet event.

Now, dragon . . . how shall we proceed?

I WILL NEED SOME BODILY CONTACT WITH HER IN ORDER TO DETERMINE IF THERE IS ANYTHING PHYSICALLY WRONG.

Erde is utterly certain that Rose's healing will not be so easily accomplished, but she is equally certain that things done properly must be done as the dragon requests. So she takes Rose's strong, mute hands in her own and quiets her mind to give the dragon room to do his good work. She pictures Rose busy and smiling, and lets the music of the garden fill her awareness: the birdsong, the hum of passing insects, Raven's shallow, anxious breathing. But all too soon, Earth has completed his exploration.

THE DAMAGE TO HER BODY IS NOT THE CAUSE.

But there is damage?

I MADE A FEW . . . ADJUSTMENTS THAT MIGHT BETTER NOURISH HER HEART AND MIND. BUT I DARE GO NO FURTHER.

Erde sets Rose's hands back on the table, side by side.

"What does he say?" Raven whispers.

"That the problem is in her mind."

"Can he heal that?"

"Do you remember at the Seeing, when I first came to Deep Moor and was still mute, how Rose could hear the dragon in her head?"

"I remember it was very painful for her."

"Exactly so. He worries that he'll make matters worse if he intrudes upon her thoughts, whatever they may be."

"So . . . ?"

"It will require a human touch to help her."

"A human touch in her mind?"

Erde nods. She is reaching her own understandings seconds before she must convey them to Raven.

"Would that be . . . yours?"

Erde nods again, less confidently. "So he says."

Raven settles back a bit, throwing one arm over the back of her chair. "I also recall Rose commenting on the power you would come into, once you found your voice." She tilts her dark head playfully, though her tone is serious. "I assumed she meant the voice you speak with."

"So did I. And so when I could speak again, and I didn't feel very different, I guessed she had misjudged, and put the whole thing from my mind."

"And now?"

"And now, I think it was I who misjudged. If only I could ask her. I feel that I should know, that I *need* to know."

Raven smiles. "Why so worried? I'm sure she meant your self, when you find your self. There's nothing wrong with growing up, even if you have been forced into it a bit prematurely."

"There is if you're not sure you like what you're growing into."

The terror comes at her in a wave, not like the surf of the African beach where she first faced an ocean, but as she's always dreamed of it, sudden, towering, inexorable, and cold. "Oh, Raven, I'm so frightened!"

Raven leans forward. "Sweetling! Why so?"

"I feel like there's something . . . coming. Something I have to do."

"Then power will be a useful attribute."

Erde takes a long, slow breath. She is inches from hysteria and has no idea how it's caught her so unawares. She loves Raven, but Raven is cheerfully fatalistic, rather like the dragon. What happens, happens . . . and then one copes as best one can. Rose's insight is the sort Erde needs to help interpret this lowering cloud of portent. "When have you ever seen power put to use where it didn't hurt someone?"

"Power is a good thing when it's properly employed."

"No. No, it isn't."

"When your dragon heals someone, that's power put to a good use."

Erde shakes her head. She needs to be unreasonably stubborn until this terror and confusion make sense to her. "No, that's his Gift. Something he gives. Power is something that's imposed on people, whether they like it or not. Like my father tried to impose his will on me. Like Fra Guill wants to on all of us. Like the dragon Fire . . .".

"Easy, child. You're working yourself up into a state."

Raven pats her shoulder, rubs her arm. "Have better faith in your own good nature."

"Rose didn't say powerful, she said 'dangerously charismatic.' *Dangerously!*"

Raven laughs, a rueful tinkle entirely without mockery. "I think she was being poetical, sweetling."

"No, I wasn't," says Rose. "I meant exactly what I said."

The other two stare at her in astonishment. Raven finds her voice first.

"Rose? Are you back with us? Are you all right?"

The awful insight that Erde was just on the point of realizing flies from her mind. "Rose!" She leaps up to envelop the older woman in a hug. "We were so worried!"

"Whatever for? I've been right here all along. Did I doze off?" Rose smiles and shrugs, raking her fingers through her graying curls. "Well, perhaps I did. I feel quite refreshed. But a good thing you called me. It's the first sign of age, you know. You're in your garden, with a spare hour finally to devote to the pruning and weeding, and you sit down to take a moment's peace in the sun, and off you go! The Land of Nod." She laughs and plants both hands determinedly on her knees. "I'll have to delegate one of the twins to keep an eye on me so I don't start sleeping through supper." Her eyes light on the sectioned apple in front of her. The edges are browning already, but Rose doesn't seem to care or notice. She grabs one and shoves it into her mouth.

Erde's hands have lingered on Rose's shoulders, but she lets them slide away as she meets Raven's sober glance.

"Supper," says Raven hopefully. "You must be starving. You haven't eaten since . . ."

"I had lunch, just like everyone." Rose brandishes a second section of apple. "Don't fuss! Why are you both fussing so? All I did was doze off. Goodness, I think I'll survive."

"That's our Rosie. Get her going and you can't shut her up." Raven's laugh lacks her usual contagious glee. Rising, she fans herself elaborately. "How about something cool? Oh, this heat. I'll just run for a celebratory pitcher."

"Wonderful," agrees Rose. "What are we celebrating? The berry harvest? A new arrival in the barn? Is somebody pregnant? You both looked so somber a moment ago, I thought something awful had happened." Her face brightens. "Ah! Is it Heinrich? Is he coming? Is he back from the war? You should have woken me earlier!"

Raven reaches the end of her inspiration. Her arms float upward in a helpless shrug. "Rose, darling . . . we tried." To Erde, she says, "I'm going for food and to tell the others. You try to explain to her."

"What? Wait. Me?"

But Raven has whirled away through the arbor, leaving Erde alone with Rose, who calmly reaches for another section of apple and offers up her wisest, most sympathetic smile. "Explain, eh? Tch, tch. Sounds dire. What mischief have you been up to now? Has Lord Earth eaten one of Doritt's precious breeding ewes?"

Erde's eyes widen involuntarily. In an instant, she is a child again. "He'd never do that! Never! At least, not without asking!"

"I know, I know. I'm only joking. But you're up to something, I can see that much. Come on, out with it!"

Erde can see Rose preparing to be stern if necessary. She wonders what storybook day in her life at Deep Moor Rose believes she is living. She hates herself for being the one who must drag this smiling woman out of her dreamworld into a present where Deep Moor lies in smoking embers. "Raven wants me to explain where we are."

Rose blinks. Her shoulders lift and tighten, as if to ward off a blow. Then she slides back her chair, rising, leaning over the table to sweep apple cores and stems into the palm of one hand. "I'll just clear up a bit here, so Raven will have room for the tray."

"Please, Rose . . ."

"No, no, I must. You know how Raven hates a mess, especially when there's food around." Rose's hands are busy, busy at the tabletop. Her eyes dart everywhere, except at Erde.

Dragon, help me!

YOU KNOW I CANNOT. NOT WITH THIS.

Why has Raven left this awful task to me?

PERHAPS SHE BELIEVES YOU ARE BEST SUITED FOR IT.

No! Not me!

Erde longs for Raven's speedy return. If she won't help,

she'll at least bring Linden, who'll know much better what to do. "Rose, please sit down and rest yourself."

Rose carries the apple cores to a corner of the garden. "Rest?" She uses the little paring knife to scratch up a section of dirt. "I've never felt more rested! I wasn't really napping just now. I was thinking, while you girls just chattered on and on." She buries the apple cores neatly and comes back to the table, dusting her palms and still refusing to meet Erde's gaze. "On and on."

"What were you thinking about?"

Rose's shoulders tighten again. She turns away, frowning. "I really must find more time to work in the garden. The weeds are positively taking over!"

Erde cannot spot even the trace of a weed. In Rose's reconstruction of Deep Moor, there wouldn't be any. "Tell me what you were thinking about."

Rose's hands weave patterns of warding in the air, but her reply is casual. "Oh, it was nothing. Just a dream I had."

"A dream?"

"A nightmare, if you really want to know." Rose bends to the flower pots clustered around the apple tree, dead-heading barely spent blooms. "I have them all the time lately. Too much red meat, Linden tells me."

"I'm sure she's right," murmurs Erde, thinking exactly the opposite. How peculiar—she has become the elder, and Rose has become the child. She recalls what her beloved nurse Alla used to say when she woke up paralyzed by night terrors. "Maybe if you tell me about it, it won't bother you anymore."

Rose snorts. "Maybe if I tell you about it, that will remind me what it was. Can't really recall it now, so it can't have been too important."

"Are you sure? You can't remember anything about it?" Terror beats birdlike at the inside of her ribs, roused by the recollection of childhood. Which is ending, Erde understands. It can only mean that her destiny is close at hand. But why should the very thing she's looked forward to and fought to attain cause her such sudden palpitations? She looks up and catches Rose gazing at her. Before the older woman can glance away, their eyes meet and Erde is staring into the eyes of Death itself: raw, despairing, ravaged by horror and guilt.

"What is it?" she whispers hoarsely, but the moment is gone.

Rose turns away with a dismissive shrug. "No, can't recall a thing about it. I had a book out here a while ago. Have you seen it?"

"No. I haven't."

"Come into the library a moment while I look for it." Rose's hand is already on the latch.

"Rose, you can't . . . there isn't any . . ."

Rose unlatches the door and swings it wide. "Might as well let some fresh air in anyway. It's such a perfect day! Isn't it wonderful, after all the rain we've had?"

"Rain?"

But Rose has disappeared inside. Erde hurries after her, and finds herself in the cool, wood-paneled shade of the book room—which, according to Raven, should not be there. Leaf-scattered sunlight filters through the many-paned windows along the outside wall. Erde glimpses the rolling spread of the valley through the branches, a glint of silver water, and the green hills beyond. She sees she will have to be extra vigilant. There's no place she'd rather be than in this perfect vision of Deep Moor, existing first in Rose's mind, and now all around them as Rose reconstructs it. It will not help Rose or anybody if she is drawn into Rose's world, instead of the other way around.

Rose is at the end of the room, searching among the piles of leather-bound volumes scattered across the big reading table. *Piles* of them! Before arriving at Deep Moor, Erde had never seen so many books in one place that piles could be made of them. Big books, used so often that they were left lying about, instead of hidden away under lock and key. Her father's castle had no library. It would have been unseemly for Baron Josef von Alte to be seen indulging in unmanly pursuits such as reading and study.

Rose picks up a book and leafs through it, seemingly at random.

"Did you find it?" Erde tries to sound casual. "What were you reading?"

"Oh, something about . . . something . . . I forget."

BE FIRM, the dragon reminds silently.

Erde folds her arms and plants her shoulder resolutely against the doorpost. "Rose, doesn't it seem odd that you can't remember anything? You are not a forgetful person."

Rose flicks a wrist and reaches for another book. "Getting old, like I said." She sets the book aside and begins to rearrange the piles.

"But you're not. And it's even odder that you, the calmest person that I know, suddenly cannot sit still even for a minute!"

"Do you need me to sit still? There's so much to be done!"

"I need you to listen . . . and remember."

Rose sighs and rolls her eyes. "Remember what, dear girl?"

"Where you are. Where you *really* are."

Now Rose's protest is faintly irritable. "I'm here. Where else should I be?"

As a child, Erde wasn't known for her patience. Impetuous, impulsive, stubborn: these were the accusations commonly hurled at her by her chambermaid, who felt that little girls should sit in the corner and sew. But even this self-knowledge does not prepare Erde for the force of the impatience that boils up in her as she sees Rose turn back to her useless tidying and stacking.

"Rose!" Her summons fills the entire room, though she has hardly raised her voice. She almost steals a look behind to see who has spoken with such authority.

Rose goes as still as a startled deer. "What is it, child?"

As soon as she has Rose's attention, authority fails her. *Oh, dragon! Now what?*

YOU'RE DOING FINE.

"Please, Rose, let's sit down."

Rose sidesteps obediently to the nearest chair and settles herself with her hands folded neatly on the table. "You're upset."

"I am, but only because I'm so worried about you."

Erde takes the chair beside her. Perhaps this will seem less confrontational. She detects a desperate sort of defiance in Rose's posture, uncharacteristic in a woman normally so confident in herself and in everything she believes in. It will be an unforgivable cruelty to force Rose to remember the terrible events that drove her into this state of forgetfulness. But it must be done, or Rose, the real Rose, wise and present, will be lost forever.

THE ROSE WHOSE GIFT IS SEEING THINGS AS THEY TRULY ARE.

Yes, dragon, I know. But it will be so painful to her.

IT WAS PAINFUL TO N'DOCH WHEN YOU DRAGGED HIM AWAY FROM THE LIFE HE KNEW AND FORCED HIM TO ACCEPT HIS ROLE IN THE QUEST.

I didn't . . . how did I force him? Surely Lady Water did that.

IT WAS PAINFUL TO THE WARRING BARON YOU KIDNAPPED TO FIGHT BATTLES NOT HIS OWN.

Because we needed him! And it saved his life!

TRUE, AND TRUE. BUT BOTH AGAINST HIS WILL.

This accusation she cannot deny, though Köthen might feel differently about his suicidal urges now. Erde is shaken by the realization that she's been bending others to her will all along, while excusing her actions as childish impetuosity. All she's done has been in the service of the dragons, always, but it's been willful nonetheless. Even though her understanding of the Quest has been imperfect, as it has several times proved to be.

THIS CURRENT DUTY IS PAINFUL TO YOU AS WELL, SO YOU RESIST IT. BETTER TO ADMIT TO THE NEED, THEN TAKE FULL RESPONSIBILITY FOR YOUR DEMANDS.

Full responsibility. The dragon's tone is mild, but it carries the power of a warning. Her willful actions were necessary, of course, but there'll be no more laying the blame on accident or the dragons or the forces of destiny. Destiny, presumably, is something that happens whether you act or not, but it takes no account of human feelings. Neither has she, because she's seen herself as Destiny's tool. Erde bows her head. Perhaps this explains her high failure rate at predicting human behavior.

I understand, dragon . . . I think.

When she looks up again, Rose is staring at her, trembling.

"He's here, isn't he?"

"He? Here?" Erde is sure she means the hell-priest.

"Earth."

"Oh. Yes. Of course. He's right outside. Why should that frighten you?"

Rose covers her face with her hands. "He'll make me See it again."

Erde slips an arm around Rose's shoulders. "He won't make you do anything, you know that. He's here to help you."

"He will require the truth."

"He will *ask* the truth, *expect* the truth, but only as you're able to give it."

"How can I say no to a dragon?"

Erde smiles, seeking some way to put Rose more at ease. "That's what I've always said. But you haven't met Lord Fire yet."

Instead of relaxing, Rose shudders, muttering into her hands. "Perhaps I have, or at least his handiwork."

The image of the smoldering, blackened farmstead hovers invisibly between them. Erde bites back her own outburst of grief and rage to allow Rose room to maneuver. "Is Deep Moor the truth you fear?" she murmurs. "The dragon knows it already. We were there, too late to warn you."

"Ah." Rose's hands slide away from her eyes, as if concealment is finally pointless. "Then let him be satisfied with that. Enough truth for any heart to bear, even a dragon's."

THERE IS MORE.

What more can there be? Can't we let her be for a while?

THERE IS MORE. YOU MUST PRESS HER FURTHER.

But it's like torturing her!

AND YET, YOU MUST ASK.

"Rose, dear, the dragon asks . . ." She's doing it again, blaming the dragon, but surely his requests will carry more weight.

"No." Rose twists her head away like a recalcitrant child. "No more. There is no more."

"He says there is."

"No no no no."

"Please, Rose. What further truth did your Seeing reveal?"

Rose flings both arms out and away toward the sunny window as if yelling for help. She struggles to rise. Erde holds her fast, and is surprised to learn that she is the stronger.

"Truth about what?"

"No no no nonono!"

"Rose! Whatever it is, running away will never change it!"

Rose cries out, the hoarse helpless wail of the lost, and collapses against the back of the chair, into Erde's encircling arm, grabbing at the edge of the table and hanging on as if she might fall or be dragged away. Shivering as if being flailed by an invisible hand, she gasps, "The truth about what I Saw!"

Look what we've done, dragon! Is there nothing you can do to help?

I CAN ONLY BE, BUT THAT MAY OFFER SOME COMFORT.

Erde feels his presence draw in around them, as the trees in a glade, or the tall grasses in a meadow. Gently, in a secret zone of safety and warmth and the sweet scents of summer, Erde rocks the quaking, sobbing woman, soothing her with whispered nonsense, until Rose has exhausted herself and at last lies quietly with only the occasional shiver. Erde contemplates the miraculous medicine of bodily contact, parent to child, friend to friend, lover to lover, the surest antidote for the loneliness of despair.

With a last shudder that rumbles through her like a small earthquake, Rose gets hold of herself and releases her death grip on the table. "Oh my oh my oh my." She sits up, weakly brushing at her cheeks. Erde offers the corner of her linen tunic. Rose waves it away and gathers up the length of her skirt. When she notes its stained folds and its frayed and dirty hem, she laughs ruefully. "Oh, dear. I guess this should be proof enough for me."

"Proof of what?"

"That I'm not where I'd like to pretend to be. Not at Deep Moor, whole and safe. Isn't that what Raven wanted you to explain to me?"

"Yes. Yes, it is. Oh, Rose, I'm so sorry!"

Rose nods, her lips tight. "Of course. But it's a war, child, and we must keep at it, or evil will triumph."

"Never! And that's why *the dragon* needs you to tell us what you Saw."

"You are persistent, aren't you!"

Hope blooms like a sigh in Erde's chest. "And you are at last the Rose that I remember. The Rose who can face anything!"

"Apparently she can't, or you wouldn't be suffering through all of this."

"Dearest Rose, it's you who's been suffering."

Rose sighs, a great heaving release and giving in, and wraps her arms around herself, rocking with shuttered eyes, gathering resolve. Finally, she says quietly, "It's more possible to speak of in recollection, but even now, I . . . I can hardly believe . . . it doesn't seem . . . it can't . . . yet I know the truth of what I Saw!"

Erde settles her features into a facsimile of patience, though she feels Rose's barely restrained dread seeping like ice into her own veins. "Maybe if you begin at the beginning? At Deep Moor?"

"No. No, child. Even in the safety of tale-telling, I've no heart to relive that awful journey. The flames, the screams, my dear friends and companions felled and dying, Guillemo's death's-head grin . . . he'd reached his transcendent moment, and I . . . I had to take whatever escape was offered."

Erde wonders if she means the portal or her fantasy-trance of Deep Moor. "Of course, and you did right."

Rose shakes her head. "Death might have been more merciful."

"How can you say that! Fra Guill has no mercy! He'd have put you all to the stake!"

"No doubt. And yet . . ."

"Rose, Rose, what can be worse than the end of life?"

Rose's gaze is the bleaker for being so calm. "The end of *all* life."

"What?"

"I know you think me melodramatic, but that is what I Saw."

"I don't understand."

"Nor do I. I only know it was true. Is true." Rose sits up straighter, suddenly insistent, indomitable. "I Saw . . . that everything is gone. It's all an illusion."

Erde frowns, still missing the meaning. "What is?"

"This . . . this . . ." Rose's hands scribe airy circles. "This place."

"This house?"

"This house. That garden. That absurdly lush green lawn. And the awful city outside. All of it. All."

"The city is an illusion?" Luther, Erde recalls, had expressed a similar opinion of the city's clean and empty streets. "But we walked in it."

"Oh, yes." Rose gives the tabletop a trio of sharp raps. "It seems real enough. Or at least, solid and material. But it's not . . . true. I can't explain it. I did not See *how* the city is, I Saw what *is*, what the whole world is, behind the illusion."

Erde hesitates, appalled. Should she trust the word of a woman who's been sunk for a week in illusions of her own? "What . . . what is it?"

Rose plants her palms on the table, the same defiant pose she held for so long out in the garden, holding at bay the temptation to turn away again from her horrific vision. "The earth is . . . empty. Barren. Everywhere. Lifeless. Bare windswept rock. Oceans of sand. Desert. No sign left of the works of man, except for mountains of shattered stone, and the gaping pits left from the digging of it. Nature, too, has been defeated. There's not a tree, a blade of grass, not even a weed, anywhere. Only dust and dead rock and howling wind."

Rose squeezes her eyes shut, shivering with memory, then opens them and turns her gaze on her companion. If asked, Erde would have said that her eyes are a warm brown, but now they seem as vast and black as a starless sky.

"Perhaps this is Hell," Rose murmurs. "Perhaps that's where the hell-priest has driven us."

"I don't know. Can it be?"

Dragon, what do you say to this? What if this is not our future world after all, but some magical other place we've come to through that portal?

I SAY THAT THIS EXPLANATION AVOIDS THE

TRUTH. THERE IS ONLY ONE REALITY, DESPITE
APPEARANCES, AND WE ARE IN IT.

Erde shoves rising terror down with a mighty effort. No
time for terror now. She must be adamantine, or else give
up entirely. "The dragons think the city is our far future,"
she tells Rose, as if it was the most reasonable idea in
the world.

"It could be our future, and still be Hell," Rose replies.
"If Hell is any place without life or hope, then we are in
it. Not the hell of the Church—you know I don't believe
in that. I tried to pretend it was a nightmare or a vision of
warning. But, limited as it is, my Gift has never failed to
provide what it promises: knowledge of what is. So I had
to believe it. Outside the illusion of these walls, that city,
the world is a lifeless place."

Then I must believe it, too.

But if she does, what is left? The implications of Rose's
Seeing are too vast and terrible for her to encompass in an
instant. Erde has listened to N'Doch rail about the destruction men worked on the world. She's seen the results of
that destruction in the devastated landscape where the Tinker crews struggle for survival. She's heard Luther's sermonizing about the coming of the Last Days of the Earth,
but all of it seemed like a story, a cautionary tale that she
could take to heart and move away from. Until now. She's
abruptly aware of the silky wood beneath her damp and
shaky palms, of the homey creak of her chair's leather seat.
How can reality be both material and an illusion? And
where does the illusion come from?

*If it's the hell-priest's illusion, dragon, why would he give
us back all that we've lost?*

SO THAT WE MAY SUFFER ALL THE MORE IN
THE KNOWLEDGE OF WHAT WE'VE LOST.

Ah. Yes.

No wonder Rose retreated from the knowledge, pulling
the comfort of a lie over her head like a favorite quilt.
Erde would do it, too, if she could be a child again, and
crawl into Rose's lap to be comforted. But she will have to
live without comfort, they all will, from now on.

*Is it the end of the world, then, dragon? Have we come
too late? Has our Quest failed?*

I SAID THERE WAS ONE REALITY. I DID NOT SAY IT COULD NOT BE CHANGED.

But how?

THAT'S WHAT WE'VE COME TO THE END OF THE WORLD TO DISCOVER.

Of course! And while we live, there's hope. Is it not so, dragon?

IT IS SO. THE BATTLE IS NOT ENDED.

Erde slides her arm around Rose's slumped shoulders to offer a comforting hug. "Well, then, we shall just have to think of what to do next."

CHAPTER TWENTY

"So . . . are we good to go?" N'Doch asks again. The guitar, he notices, has a colorful woven strap on it now. He slings the big instrument across his back, reminded of Köthen and his sword. Not such a big stretch. Music can be a weapon, too.

Now there's *something to write a song about.*

N'Doch grins. Tight and wide, stretching the muscles in his cheeks. It's what, in his gang days, he called his "fighting grin," almost involuntary, showing a lot of teeth and fueled by anticipation and adrenaline. "Are we ready set?"

Djawara nods. "As ready as we'll ever be."

They both look to Paia, who looks down and away, then quizzically to the only calm face in the room. "I can't believe I'm doing this."

Water-as-Sedou smiles, catlike. "We'll be safe here, for the time being."

N'Doch rolls his eyes. "Doesn't exactly inspire confidence. . . ."

"You'll be safe," says Paia, "but will I? Just as I can summon him against his will, he has the same power to compel me."

Sedou nods. "That very connection is our greatest hope of winning him over. Be strong, and keep our true purpose in mind."

"Easy for you to say," mutters N'Doch.

"Not really. I'll retire to a corner to begin with. It's sure to be useful if he can be kept unaware of my presence at first." Sedou studies the long dim room for possible darkened corners, then his eye lights on the bar with its shelves of glimmering glassware and mirrors behind. "I'll be . . .

the bartender." He moves away with a rapid blurring of profile and slips behind the counter. When he turns to face them, he's wearing a classic bartender's shirt and apron. He flips a towel over his shoulder and leans against the gleaming wood as if born to the trade. "What can I get you folks?"

"He'll nose you out soon enough," says Paia.

N'Doch is inclined to agree. "Just don't look him in the eye. Yours are a dead giveaway."

"Maybe so." Sedou turns to Paia. "But he won't be thinking about me at first. He'll be thinking about you." He drags the towel off his shoulder and polishes the top of the bar. "Something to drink?"

Djawara rises stiffly. "A little cordial might be fortifying."

"Hey, I thought you were kidding! You got a Spark Orange?" N'Doch strides over hopefully. "Girl, you want something?"

Paia shakes her head numbly.

"Gimme two of 'em!" He brings the sweet citrus concoction to her anyway. Paia turns the bottle in her hand like a foreign object. "Go on, try it! I bet you never had soda in a glass bottle before, right? Guess what? Neither have I. But Papa Dja always used to tell me how it was much better in the bottle than in the box." He salutes his grandfather and lifts the bottle to his lips.

Paia watches dubiously. "I've never had a soda at all."

"Don't swill it down like he does." Djawara sips delicately at his slim-stemmed glass as if to underline his point.

N'Doch drains his soda and sets it aside with a satisfied belch. "Now, how do we go about this?"

Paia's tone is more collected than her body language. She fusses with her hair and straightens her clothing. "I just call him and we see if he comes."

"Shouldn't you be sitting down or something?"

His solicitude raises a wan laugh, which was exactly his purpose. If he has to play the clown in order to lighten things up a little, N'Doch doesn't mind. "All right, then. You go, girl."

She perches on the rounded arm of the sofa, more like a girl waiting for her date to show up than a woman about to conjure a fire-breathing killer. She takes a breath and seems to turn her awareness inward. The rest wait in silence for a minute, for two. Then Paia says, "Ah," and N'Doch is aware of a difference in the room, as if a wind has shifted or the temperature's risen very suddenly. He tenses, expecting smoke and fireworks of the sort he's seen up on the mountain. He wishes he had a more obvious weapon in hand than a guitar. Seconds later, there's a sharp rap on the front door.

"Oh, that's excellent," Djawara murmurs.

"What? The door's locked?"

"No. This one can't come in unless he's invited. A good sign. Remember? The other walked right in."

The rapping sounds again, louder, more preemptory. The shadow on the frosted glass is human-shaped but larger than human size.

"If I don't let him in, he'll be furious," says Paia, as if she wishes someone else would volunteer.

Interesting, N'Doch muses, that she looks to Djawara for permission, not Sedou or himself. "Can't we just yell at him through the door?"

The old man sets down his glass. "Allow me."

"Papa . . ." N'Doch starts forward, but Djawara, steely-eyed, waves him back. His first few steps are cramped and slow, but he's striding along briskly by the time he reaches the door. The flat daylight falls through the glass onto his dark face and erect back, making his grizzled head and white robe shine.

And the angel let in the devil. The lyric is already writing itself in N'Doch's head. He pulls the guitar around in front of him, fingers fitting themselves to the strings. *Now the devil said, open up, open up. So the angel let him in.*

Djawara opens the door and stands beside it. "Lord Fire. Please join us."

Fire fills the opening, shimmering gold and red, a haze of smoke behind him. Pale, questing tendrils approach the doorway and draw back. The man/dragon is forced to duck under the lintel, making it awkward for him to sweep through the doorway as he has obviously intended. Once inside, his glitter fades slightly, as if he's walked into shadow. Irritated, he pauses, squinting into the dim room beyond.

Djawara holds out his hand. "Welcome. I'm . . ."

"I know who you are." Fire brushes past him. "Where is she?"

At the bar, Sedou has turned his back to the door and is busily wiping down the espresso machine until its chrome and copper gleam.

Paia steps into the pool of soft light from the nearest chandelier. "Here. I am here."

She and Fire stare at each other—rather hungrily, N'Doch thinks—across the scattering of empty chairs and tables.

"You are looking well, as always, beloved," Fire croons.

"You are looking . . . odd."

"Odd? Odd?" She has startled him. He preens defensively.

"I mean, why are you . . . aren't you . . . what are you wearing?"

What's really odd, N'Doch decides, is that she looks so disapproving. Having only seen the Fire-breather buck-naked except for a sinuous cloak of flame, he assumes that full parade dress is the dragon's normal clothing in man-form. Besides, why should she care what he wears? Back in 2013, all the power brokers are in uniform. Except for Baraga, whose personal drag is silk, a designer business suit. Fire's uniform is close fitting and smoothly tailored in a rich blood red. Gold glints at his high collar and across his chest. With his half-scaled skin and his furious red-gold locks, he looks like a battle-weary alien commander stepping off his starship. Either that, or a rock star, whose faintly dimmed post-concert luster makes him seem more approachable. N'Doch wants to find the Fire-breather vile and grotesque, but instead, the bile he tastes is envy. He can't help thinking the dude looks absolutely splendid.

Fire tugs invisible wrinkles out of his sleeves. "My estates are under attack, may I remind you? And the Temple is in a shambles. How devious of the traitorous Son Luco to neglect the training of a competent successor! I am at war wherever I turn, thanks to you."

Paia's chin lifts. "The Temple's command structure was loyal to their head priest, not to you. And my cousin seeks only to regain what belongs to us. Remember that the Cita-del was mine before you seized control of it."

"Seized?" Fire snarls. "You welcomed me gladly! I

brought order to chaos! Where would you and your ingrate cousin be now if I hadn't come along? Dead. Both of you. Starvation, disease, attack from squatters or war bands, you name it. You would owe your life to me even if you weren't bound to me by Destiny!"

"That debt was paid by our years of servitude in your temple! And how dare you invoke Destiny when you're so busy denying it?"

N'Doch feels like he's at a grudge match. Fire hasn't stirred from his position of power by the door, and Paia has refused to go toward him. Already they're yelling across the room at each other. He sees how it is with these two. Together much longer than the other dragons and their guides, their years of contention have compounded until every conversation starts at an inflated level, so weighted by emotional baggage that any possibility of amity is doomed from the start. His stance is aggressive, hers as sullen and passive as a child. They're like a married couple who don't get along, but just can't imagine divorce. The most archetypal of the dragons turns out to exhibit the most human failings? There's a lesson in this, N'Doch muses, as he risks a glance toward the bartender.

Maybe this wasn't such a useful idea.

NO TALK. HE MIGHT HEAR.

And Fire lifts his magnificent head, listening. N'Doch moves toward the bar. Hide in plain sight, he tells himself. He leans back against the fat ogee softening the counter's edge. He has to crane his neck upward to meet Fire's reptilian eyes. He knows he should feel driven to spit in his face, shout "murderer." Or ram his fists into actual flesh, spew venom, acid, flame, anything to destroy the dragon's awesome supercilious beauty. Instead, strumming the guitar flung across his chest, he says, "Can I get you a drink, general? What's your poison?"

The distraction works. Fire tosses off a sneer as sharp as a shuriken and returns his attention to Paia. "Why have you called me here?"

Paia says nothing. N'Doch is alarmed by how obviously shaken she is, how she can't keep her eyes off the glittering giant. But her silence seems to mean something else to Fire.

"I suppose you hope to lure me from the defense of my

kingdom. But you'll be disappointed, beloved. Time is in my favor. I am able, no matter how long I am here, to return to the battle mere seconds after I left!"

N'Doch recognizes a vainglorious boast when he hears one. He's been guilty of enough of them himself, and a few times he's been caught out because of them, having given up too much information in the boast, thereby making himself more vulnerable. *So get him to brag and run his mouth*, he decides. Something useful is bound to turn up.

"I wasn't thinking about your battles," Paia replies.

Fire throws his weight back on one foot and crosses his arms satirically. "Then perhaps you've come to your senses and wish to be rescued. The company you're keeping since you left me gets less interesting each time we meet."

"I need to talk to you."

"Talk? *Talk?*" He flings his red-clad arms wide. "My Temple is burning, my Faithful are being slaughtered, and you need to *talk?*" He makes a great show of gathering up his patience. "All right, then. What is it? Shouldn't we go somewhere more private? I don't see your new concubine hanging about." He tilts his head, a lampoon of sadness. "Oh, is that it? He's ditched you already?"

"Is the Citadel really burning?" Paia stands up a little straighter.

The golden eyes narrow. N'Doch notes the quick calculation: which answer is more likely to rouse her sympathy and interest? Despicable as he is, his goal is to win her back. "Not yet, but every second that I am away from the line of defense brings that possibility closer. So state your business, and let me be on my way."

Shrugging off her pout at last, Paia mimics his stance. "I thought it didn't matter how long you're away."

"Impertinence is unbecoming in a woman, beloved. What do you wish to talk about?"

"Your sister Air."

Fire stares at her as if she's said the unpardonable, then looks away, out the window into the empty street. "I have no sister."

"A lie. You have two."

"My enemies feed you lies. I say I have no sister."

N'Doch thinks it's time to provide a little reinforcement.

"Too late for that, general. You already admitted to it up on the mountaintop. How 'bout this: you have an enemy . . ."

Fire's glance at Paia is venomous. "I have many enemies."

"Well, we'd like to negotiate for the release of the one called Air."

It sounds right to N'Doch, like they do it in the vids: no beating around the bush, if you want to sound serious. Besides, what else can you say to the creep who's murdered your mother? Small talk just doesn't cut it. But Fire ignores him, driven at last into restless motion. He paces around the café, his knee-high boots clicking smartly on the little black-and-white tiles. He takes in its details and full measure, as if he was thinking of buying it. He studies the posters on the cracked walls. He pauses before the narrow door that says *monsieurs*. He stares up at the glass-and-brass chandelier just inches above his head until, apparently, curiosity gets the better of him. "What is this place?"

"My favorite café back home." Djawara accepts the diversion as if happy to share a pleasurable nostalgia. "An exact replica."

"I leveled your home."

"Indeed you did. I meant, in the city back home."

"Your favorite?"

"I spent many fond hours there."

"I shall seek it out and destroy it immediately."

The old man snorts gently. "No need. The politicians did the job for you long ago, when N'Doch was still a boy. One faction pulled down the old place to build themselves an expensive office building. As soon as it was finished, another faction blew it up. It's a pile of rubble now, like much of the city."

Fire looks interested, perhaps nosing out a weapon he hasn't yet considered. "How sad for you."

Djawara shrugs, nodding.

Fire wanders a bit more, smoothes a gilt-nailed hand along the length of the bar as if enjoying actual contact with its material surface. He gives the bartender's muscular back a long moment of consideration, then moves on. "And how does your café come to be here, in *my* city?"

"Is it your city? I wondered."

"It is, since the day I claimed it. This was not here until now."

"It was not here until I created it."

"Really? Aren't you clever?" Fire jerks his thumb at the bartender. "Did you create him, too?"

Djawara beams. "I did! Isn't he convincing? After all, can't have a bar without a bartender."

"Of course not."

N'Doch is sure the Fire-breather has a tactical reason for this satirical display. Is he hoping to catch us off guard with his willingness to banter and admit ignorance? Or hoping to figure out how much we know? Or both? N'Doch senses his grandfather mulling over how much ignorance to admit to in return.

Scowling, Fire begins a second circuit of the room, studiously avoiding Paia, too impatient to wait the old man out. "A dull sort of place, to spend the rest of your lives."

"I don't expect it will be that long," Djawara replies.

Fire grins at him, as if they were becoming fast friends. "How pleasantly ambiguous, old man. Should I take you for an optimist or a pessimist?"

"Take me for whichever you wish. And I will take you for a renegade and a murderer."

"Tch! Insults!"

"What are your terms for the release of the dragon Air?"

"Oh, that old song. I liked the quaint little café better."

"Your terms?"

"No terms. Prisoners do not negotiate."

"Be nice, general," says N'Doch. "You're in our space now."

"The instant you walk out that door, you're in mine, and you *know* what I will do to you. So . . . prisoners." Fire starts his third circuit, this time staring at Paia all the while. Paia tries to stare back at him, but soon gives up to gaze in confusion at the floor.

"But that's not entirely true, is it?" Djawara continues. N'Doch admires his grandfather's speculative tone. It's as if nothing more was at stake in this debate than a proper understanding of the argument. "This was just another blank city block until I created the Rive in its place. Or should I say, until something allowed it to be created from my memory. . . ."

Fire gestures grandly around the room. "You wish to disavow this charming bit of magic?"

"Not I. I have no magic. But magic there is. It appears that we have a protector."

"You put great stock in mere illusions, old man."

"Can an illusion keep me fed and safe? Was it mere illusion that required you to knock before entering? Perhaps when I walk out that door, I will create the Rue Senghor, further neutral territory, which will allow me safely to create the Marché, which will lead me safely to create the . . ."

Fire halts his circular pacing. "Try it, then!" He stabs a forefinger at the door. "I dare you! You escaped me once in your own territory. You think you can manage so well in mine?"

"As long as my protector is listening." Djawara moves toward the door.

N'Doch leaps to stop him. "Papa, no. You see what he's doing, right? Turning it into a pissing contest, just to get us off center!"

"I have no need to waste my energy," says Fire. "I am merely pointing out that there's no possibility of negotiation, as you have nothing to negotiate with. Life in here, or death out there. Those are your alternatives."

"No. There's me," says Paia.

All eyes turn to her, even the bartender's.

"There's me to negotiate with," Paia continues resolutely. "I offer myself in return for the release of your sister Air."

"No, girl, you don't. . . ."

Paia shakes her head. "I do. He's right. We have nothing else."

"It just seems that . . ."

"If we're to accomplish anything at all, we must work with what we're sure of."

Fire's languid gaze flares. Probably he's searching out the way he can take the offer without delivering the goods, which makes sense to N'Doch, since he's doing exactly the same. But meanwhile, he also sees how stirred up the big dude is, as revved as a lover. See him that way and he begins to make sense: as a proud, obsessive, jilted lover who can't imagine why any woman wouldn't want him, and who lives in the belief that it's only a matter of time or the right words before he has her back. So Paia's heated dreaming wasn't some one-way fantasy. N'Doch is ashamed he'd given this thought even a moment's notice. And it's faintly slimy to be hoping to use the bad guy's only good intention against him. Or if not exactly a good intention, then a true passion, at least. Like a junkie who craves his fix, Fire's need for Paia might render him willing to bargain.

At least that's what the dragon Water has in mind.

"Maybe you're right," N'Doch is unable, though Paia is a coconspirator, to quite look her in the eye. The apparently oblivious bartender has moved on to polishing glassware, but N'Doch senses Water's quick and absolute assent to Paia's offer. This spooks him as little else so far has. Not a moment's consideration for the sentimental gesture, now that the game is in the final innings. Not even the pretense that another solution should be sought. Even Papa Djawara does not speak up in protest.

Are we all expendable then?

HUSH, NOW! LATER!

Despite his initial resistance to his dragon destiny, whatever it may turn out to be, N'Doch has assumed since his miraculous resurrection that a protected status comes with being a dragon guide. But what if the dragons prove willing to sacrifice whomever it takes to achieve their Purpose? What if the only privilege of being a guide is being saved to be sacrificed last? Or maybe he's got it all wrong. Maybe Water is a better bluffer than he's realized.

"Of course," he continues, since no one else seems willing to, "we won't deliver Paia until you've given up Air."

Fire focuses on him directly, advancing a few steps in his direction as if just now noticing he's there. It's like being drilled with a laser. The dragon's gaze is contemptuous and bleak, the sort of look that says because you are such an idiot, there is no hope left for the world. "Not that it matters, really, but . . . why do you do their dirty work for them?"

"Who's what?" N'Doch blurts.

"My oh-so-innocent siblings. You've bought their entire line, haven't you. Surely your wise old shaman of a grandfather could have advised you otherwise."

"Hey, mother-killer, you're the one who's. . . ."

Fire glides another step closer, dropping his voice to a more intimate range. "I mean, you seem like a likely fellow. What's in it for you, being at their beck and call?"

N'Doch glances helplessly at Djawara. This is too close to his own former thinking for comfort.

"The satisfaction of a destiny fulfilled," offers the old man gracefully.

The man/dragon laughs.

Djawara crosses one knee over the other and peers up at the red-jacketed figure looming over him like the shadow of death. "If you have another idea, perhaps you might care to enlighten us."

"What?" Fire spins away with a toss of his head. "And spoil the fun?"

For once, N'Doch misses having Erde around to act as the mouthpiece for the dragons' Purpose. No one speaks of it as earnestly and eloquently as she does. The fact that the goal of the Quest is not yet entirely understood by human or dragon makes him queasy about trying to sell it to the main dude standing in its way. But what better way to pump the Fire-breather for his implied superior knowledge than to throw down a few cards he can't resist the pleasure of trumping?

Fire strolls among the chairs and tables, chuckling gleefully to himself, but N'Doch sees no real joy in him. His laugh is just a release of nervous energy. N'Doch looks for that vast underlying calm he's come to expect from dragons, even his own busy meddler, Water. He sees none of it in Fire's restless meandering, only frustration gathering like a storm. He should be more scared of the Fire-breather. He knows that out on the sidewalk, he'd be cooked mincemeat before he could even think to run. He knows that the situation in the Rive is artificial, and the dragon's man-form only a temporary limitation. Still . . .

STILL WHAT?

Is there something you haven't told us?

"You humans," Fire sneers. "Wave a few big words around, like Duty or Destiny, and you come running like sheep. You lose all common sense."

"What's sensible by your definition?" N'Doch retorts. "Murder and intimidation? Despotism?"

"Survival is sensible." Fire stops by the window, gazing outward again. "It's the only thing that does make sense."

Erde would have a heroic comeback for that remark, but N'Doch can't make his mouth say the words.

"But you're tired of mere survival, aren't you?" Paia asks suddenly. "And of the price you have to pay for it."

Fire laughs. "Price? What price? I've had everything I want."

"Except me."

A warning rises in N'Doch's throat, hovering stillborn. What is she up to? She moves toward the Fire-breather, her gait slow and sensual. She's become the seductress. Is it to lure him into divulging information, or because she can't help herself? N'Doch thinks this is a very dangerous game to be playing here and now. He considers whether to intervene. Fire is still turned away at the window, but he senses Paia's approach and turns to meet her just as she stops in front of him. They stare at each other, and Paia crosses her arms beneath her breasts so that they are presented to him roundly, a sweet and teasing gift.

"Isn't that so, my lord?"

"Yes, beloved. Except you." Fire looks down at her. With a faint but knowing smile, he lifts one gilt-scaled hand and places it gently against her cheek. "Until now."

Paia gasps and recoils, her own hand flying to her face. "How did you . . . !"

Fire says nothing. He holds himself utterly still, his hand poised in the air where her cheek has been. By the bar, the others start up on instant alert.

"What'd he do?" demands N'Doch.

"He . . . *touched* me."

It takes him a moment, then he gets it. "You mean, actually touched?"

The bartender calmly lays aside his towel.

Paia stares at Fire. "How did you do that?"

"Because you wanted me to." Fire lets his hand drop slowly. "You did want it, do want it, don't you, beloved? You always have before."

"No!" Paia steps back, but wavers in mid-stride and stalls in confusion.

"Why are you frightened? You wish to speak of Destiny?

Then admit we are bound by it. You and I. I only want
what's best for us. All I've done has been for your sake."
Fire holds out both hands to her, like a father to a child.
"See? Let me show you."

Paia's body sways toward him, though her feet do not
move.

"Come, a joining of hands at least. You owe me that
much, after all these years."

Paia shakes her head, but her hand floats toward his.

"Don't do it, girl!" N'Doch is only guessing that touching
will give the dragon power over her. But he can't bear the
longing in her eyes, and in Fire's. They are a matched set
of long-frustrated passion. Köthen should never have let
this woman out of his sight. But, then, he didn't. He
wouldn't have.

It's all my fault, even if it was by accident.

THERE ARE NO ACCIDENTS.

As Paia's hand lifts to meet Fire's, the bartender vaults
up and over the bar. Chairs and tables whirl aside. In a
dizzying blur and sprint, Sedou is a large black mountain
between the Fire-breather and his guide.

"No!" He shoves Paia behind him. "You shall not take
her from here!"

"You!" Fire's yearning gaze cracks into a mask of fury
and hatred. His outstretched hand lashes back, then forward, his gilt nails lengthening into claws. Sedou grabs that
wrist, and then the other, as it swings up to join the attack.
Fire snarls, held by both arms. He doesn't struggle, but the
tang of hot metal invades the rich coffee aroma of the café.

"Not too practiced at the hand-to-hand stuff yet,
brother?" Sedou grins. "It's a man-thing, you know? Yet I
congratulate you. This new manifesting must be exhausting.
Careful, or you'll wear yourself out utterly."

"You cannot prevent her if she wishes to go!"

"If she wishes, and only if. Or else . . ."

Fire's snarl deepens. "I am as safe here from you as you
are from me."

"True enough." Sedou releases him abruptly and steps
back. "So, brother. Let's talk instead of fight."

"There is nothing to talk about."

"Oh, but there is." Sedou reaches behind him to draw

two chairs out from the nearest table. "Shall we sit down? You can sit, right? A chair is a marvelous mechanism. You should try it."

"I have nothing to say to you."

N'Doch slides over to urge Paia away to the rear of the café. She shakes him off silently.

Sedou sits, kicking the second chair closer to Fire. "For instance, let's discuss these lies you accuse me of, or the information you claim your brother Earth and I are withholding."

Fire folds his arms across his broad red chest. "So confident of human loyalty? Very rash. It's not too late, you know, for them to see the wisdom of my way."

"Then tell us what your way is, as you see it."

"You know what it is."

"No. Truly. Tell me. It's what I came to hear."

Fire frowns, furious to have been trapped into any sort of discussion at all. "I have said it plainly enough: survival."

Sedou nods, easing back in his chair. "All right. None of us would take issue with that."

"Oh, come now."

"What? Why would we?"

Fire looks away contemptuously.

"Well, then I will amend that slightly. Given that anything worth doing inevitably bears some risk, I'll say we seek survival *as well as* the accomplishment of our Purpose. Which is yours also, since you are one of us. So, explain it to me again. Why have you set yourself against us?"

"Such endearing earnestness!" Fire bends a satirically pleading gaze toward Paia. "Release me, my priestess, I beg you. Don't ask me to sit still for this mawkish spectacle!"

"You are free to go any time, my lord, but without me."

"Why so impatient?" Sedou asks.

Fire flings both fists into the air. "Because this is so *boring*!" He paces away from the window, then stops, arms and fingers spread. "Do you really suppose that because Paia is here, I'll be a party to your lies and deceptions simply to spare her? Well, you suppose wrong! If I'm tired of anything, I'm tired of the hypocrisy that lurks at the heart of your so-called Quest! It's time she knew the truth. It's time they all knew!"

"Lies, brother? Deceptions? A dragon cannot lie."

"Ah, granted, a dragon cannot lie. But we can manipulate the truth to the same effect."

"I assume you are speaking from personal experience," retorts Sedou sharply.

"What truth?" asks Paia, and N'Doch is grateful. He senses a drawn-out dragon debate in the offing, and he'd rather they just got on with business. "What truth?" she asks again. "If I should know it, tell me."

Fire gives her a long, tragic look over his shoulder. N'Doch can't decide if it reflects the Fire-breather's true mood or the aura of high drama he prefers to surround himself with. "If I'd thought you should know it, beloved, I'd have told you long ago."

Whatever its intent, this performance brings Sedou angrily to his feet. "Oh, please! Has all this sabotage and destruction been merely for your own amusement, brother? You have a big secret, but you can't tell anyone what it is? It's a childish game, and a waste of your talents! I believe there is no secret at all!"

Fire smirks. "If it were our poor innocent brother Earth saying this to me, I could almost believe he doesn't know. But you? The clever, meddling one? No wonder you're so at ease in man-form. You should have been created human to begin with."

"Enough!" bellows Sedou. "What is it you have to tell us?"

"Whoa. Easy, bro," chides N'Doch. He sees his dragon/brother's shape wavering in the heat of rage. If both dragons take their own form in this confined space, the humans will be done for. "He's the one supposed to be the hothead, not you."

Sedou's eyes show green and golden against his ebony skin. He collects himself and subsides, but not before kicking one of the café chairs the full width of the room, sending it smashing against the wall. As the shattered pieces rattle across the tiles, N'Doch laughs softly, his heart aching. So much, so very much like his real brother.

In the impasse that follows, Djawara breaks his long silence and steps forward, hands clasped peaceably at his waist. "May I make a suggestion?"

Fire rolls his eyes. Sedou grunts and throws himself into the nearest chair.

"Go for it, Papa," says N'Doch, fed up with both dragons now.

"I propose that there is no deception. I propose that you both believe the truth of what you're saying."

"Huh," says Sedou sulkily.

Fire sighs theatrically, but his gaze drifts back to the big man slouched in a chair much too small for him. His stillness expresses his doubt better than any words could, or his constant avid reckoning of whether what he has to say will win him new friends or further enemies. "Proof, old man?"

"A dragon cannot lie."

"I told you what . . ."

"Listen to him, my lord," puts in Paia. "I beg you."

Fire laughs soundlessly. "Ah, beloved. You hope for me to redeem myself with reasonableness? Me?"

"In my eyes, if in no one else's."

"Then what choice have I?" He flashes her a sultry, resentful grin. "Let me then entertain the possibility that I silenced my sister Air before she was able to pass her knowledge on to my other siblings." He stalks to Sedou's table, pulls up a chair, and seats himself with elaborate formality. He rests his chin on steepled fingers, arch and condescending, and faces his fellow dragon. "Look into my eyes and swear you do not know."

"Know *what*?" Sedou growls.

"If you and our brother are truly ignorant of the final Destiny laid out for us, then your mindless pursuit of it is all the more tragic. But I suppose I must actually consider this possibility."

Sedou meets Fire's calculating regard. "Consider it well and quickly! Tell me what you know!"

Again, Fire glances back at Paia. Her return gaze is fervent and hopeful, so bright that even the Fire-breather seems to shrink from its glare. *Guilt*, ventures N'Doch. Maybe even a trace of remorse?

Nah, can't be. Remember who we're dealing with here.

Fire sits back and rakes his gilded nails through his hair, which does nothing to tame its mobile energy. "Then I will tell you, because I must. Because my priestess requires me to." He looks nervous and intent, like a performer about to go on stage. His big moment, N'Doch realizes. The unloading of his secret weapon, his last hope to win Paia back to him, and perhaps even a sibling to his cause. "But don't hold me responsible for the results. Because I warn you, you with such faith in the rightness of Destiny . . . my news will destroy that faith, as it did mine."

In the waiting silence, N'Doch finally understands why the Fire dude has been so civilized, so tractable. Not just to please Paia, his priestess, though obviously that's what he'd like her to think. No, the guy thinks he's won, and he's just having fun jerking our chains.

Must be one hell of a piece of news he's about to lay on us.

CHAPTER TWENTY-ONE

Hard thinking has always made him ravenous.

The Librarian piles rye bread and cheese, cold chicken and tomatoes and lettuce beside his keypad, and uses an obsolete mouse pad as a cutting board. Rye bread with caraway. And mustard. What a luxury! He lets himself concentrate entirely on the elaborate architecture of the sandwich, offering his brain a brief rest. But only the conscious part accepts the holiday. While he's slicing his precarious tower neatly in half, then in quarters, his mental subroutines are clipping away a meter per millisecond. *Per nanosecond,* he amends, filling his mouth with sensual distraction.

Nanotech. He still can't quite believe it. A whole city of it. Mind-boggling. But he figures it could work.

For instance: he's connected to the dragon in the way of dragon guides, even if the lines of communication are interrupted, and function randomly at best. So, sporadically, his memories are open to her. Assuming she has control of the city's infinite population of submicroscopic mechanisms—a big assumption, but it makes sense—and she's instructing them to re-create selected portions of his past in dimensional replicas.

How she does it is interesting enough, but the real question is, why? Why not just speak to him directly? The Librarian takes another huge bite of his sandwich. He's gone over this territory a million times. She doesn't because she can't. He has to be satisfied with a half-baked answer. But building memories around him is apparently something she *can* do. So maybe she's doing it in order to attract his attention. She's trying to communicate, and he should see each of these apparitions from the past as a sort of coded message. The dragon is telling him something general about the past, or about a specific aspect of his past . . . or maybe it's something about the nanomechs that can so easily re-create it.

The Librarian lets himself focus for a moment on the pure pleasure of Swiss cheese. Like the beer, it's something he hasn't tasted in a very long time. A thing of the past in 2213. And the dragon has created it for him. So maybe it is the past she wants to talk about. But what about it? The nanomechs seem like a better bet. And at least he has an idea of how to proceed with them. He can look at their programming.

He sets the last quarter of his sandwich aside. Brushing crumbs from the desk and then his chin, he centers the keypad in front of him. Before he sets to work, he glances over at the old TV sitting at the edge of the darkness. The Grand Stair to the Citadel is as hard and bright on the screen as the Sahara at noon, and still just as empty, except for the two Temple guardsmen, who appear to be sleeping. Or perhaps they are just too heat dazed to move. The Librarian offers them his sympathy, then turns back to his search and forgets about them entirely.

It doesn't take him long to discover anomalies in the nanomech programming, the same sort he'd seen with the larger devices like the street-cleaning machines. Are they accidental corruptions, or intentional interpolations? The Librarian reverse engineers several of the modified nano-mechs, and decides that their functions have been pur-posely altered, and then linked, so that they form a sort of broadband signaling device. Very broadband. He can't get the signal to play over his human-ear-specific speakers. But as soon as he activates the device, the signal is there, shout-ing in his head. And not just noise this time, but articulate with meaning.

AWAKE! COME! YOU ARE NEEDED!

The voice of the Summoner. The Librarian has been hearing this call all his lives, ever since . . . well, it began by the lake, didn't it, when the elder knight arrived with his squire in tow. Only the squire was a girl, disguised and on the run. And if that wasn't interesting enough, she traveled with a dragon. The knight, an old lore-hound, announced it proudly: *a dragon!* As if he was responsible.

The Librarian chuckles. Good old Hal, doing his preordained duty by jump-starting the Quest, considering it a minor part to play and consequently feeling sidelined, never realizing how crucial he'd been. For on that very day, the Librarian—or the creature he'd been then—took the young girl's hands in his own and saw Destiny written across her palms. Hers, yes, but his own as well.

The girl's dragon was following a mysterious inner "summons." The Librarian—not a librarian then, just Gerrasch, half man, half beast—stared into her eyes and heard the Call himself for the first time, though it was several lives before he understood that it summoned him as well.

The Librarian blinks. He's been dragged into memory again, as irresistibly as if with a block and tackle. Some important message waits, abandoned in the past. Some understanding he should have recognized then and carried with him. What? *What?*

There were questions asked that day. He recalls that much. What were they? Hal paid him good king's silver for the answers. The Librarian retrieves the abandoned quarter of his sandwich and munches it pensively, searching for the mnemonic hook that will haul that memory out of the shadow of a millennium.

Bread and cheese. Hal had brought some of that as well.

The answers come to him stripped of their questions. They flare into his brain like bright meteors, inexplicable but sure.

The first answer: *The Purpose is to fix what's broken.*

Well, that's clear enough. The question was: What is the purpose of the Quest? And what's broken is obviously the Earth. The whole ecosystem is on the verge of collapse. But was it then? Who in 913 had any inkling of the horrors to come? The Summoner must have known, and therefore, the purpose of the urgent Call that woke the dragons.

The second answer: *The Summoner is not here.*

No, not there in 913. Because the Summoner was here, in . . . wherever here is. The Librarian has long assumed that the Summoner is Air, his dragon, but he'd never guessed the mechanism. A million nanotech voices calling down the centuries.

The third answer, for three was all he'd had time for, with the girl's pursuers fast approaching: *Ask them about the City*.

He knows he meant the women of Deep Moor, but what was the question? Does it even matter?

For here we are in it, millennia later. The long-ago Gerrasch saw the City that day, this city, in the girl's frightened eyes. Which explains the déjà-vu he was assailed with the moment he stepped through the portal. The Librarian rubs his forehead vigorously. He needs his brain to work faster, deeper.

The Purpose is to fix what's broken.

Those few words could be said to describe the entire arc of his life, of all his lives. It's always been his purpose, and there's always something broken: a bird's wing, a man's spirit, an entire ecosystem. Or this city, for instance. He thinks of the crippled street-cleaning machines, and the mangled lines of code he'd repaired to let N'Doch's song take flight. So much of everything now is broken.

But why is the dragon directing his thoughts backward? What was there to fix in 913, except the hell-priest's wagon? Now, at least, there is no shortage of candidates.

The Librarian's strong thumbs are wearing bruises into the soft skin of his temples. He shifts to massaging his head, his fingers twisting in the salt-and-pepper thatch, as thick as an animal pelt. There's some connection he's not making, he's sure of it. Something so obvious that any child could see it, but not a full grown, super-educated, overcomplicated man. It's the reason the dragon has brought him here. Something he's meant to fix, might actually be *able* to fix, unlike the sad old broken planet. That's beyond his abilities. *She's* the one who's supposed to make that happen, but she's . . .

The Librarian goes still.

That's it. Of course. It's the dragon herself that's broken.

He has, since he was aware of her, conceived of Air as a storybook sort of prisoner: shut away, gagged and bound in some dank dungeon, perhaps physically, perhaps by magic. Whatever the mechanism, she's been denied the normal means of communication, has only occasionally been able to slip a message past the barricades. But her messages, when they arrive, are never whole and coherent. And besides, what are the *normal means* to a dragon? Now that the Librarian has met a few more of them, he realizes what an imperfect scenario he'd constructed. Just the sort of notion born of living with your nose stuck to a computer screen. Even if forcibly restrained, a dragon should be able to speak to her guide through barriers of any sort. The breakdown must be within.

What sort of breakdown? Is she mute, as Erde was when he first met her? That would make little difference to a supposedly telepathic dragon. Besides, dragons are not equipped for human speech, unless they're in man-form.

The Librarian releases his aching scalp. He swings up and out of his chair to pace, and sees that the confining details of his office in the Refuge have vanished. Only his console remains, an island in the void, its brushed chrome gleaming, its idiot lights shining like the eyes of forest creatures in the night.

He has to fix his dragon? Not just locate, free her, and do her bidding, but *fix* her?

How? How? How? His hands stray to his hair again. He has to repair her like some sort of machine? He's never felt more helpless.

Machine? Nanomech?

He has an unwelcome vision of the dragon as a benign version of the *machina rex* that chased him into this memory-haunted darkness. He sees her as a collection of parts spread out on the machinist's workbench, or as countless invisible specks of nanomech. A hateful notion. It makes the Librarian abruptly nauseous, which he recognizes as panic. Because if any of this is true, there'll be no eureka, no golden breakthrough of mutual recognition as he bursts through the walls of her prison to find her whole, waiting and material, ready to save the world. The Librarian swallows convulsively, banishing his panic to gnaw invisibly at his gut. Well, it was a silly romantic notion anyway.

Sudden peripheral motion distracts him. The old TV still lurks at the edge of the circle of light, its bright screen hovering like a window in the darkness. The somnolent view of the Grand Stair has erupted with frenzied preparations. Soldiers are racing to the parapet, taking up battle stations.

"Not now! Not now!" the Librarian pleads. He can't lose

the many threads of his elusive and still-developing epiphany. But he throws a quick glance at the screen anyway. He has to. Leif Cauldwell's army has reached the Citadel. The security camera shows the view down the long final flight of steps from the midway landing to the ramshackle buildings clustered at the bottom. The long dry road is a pale scar down the middle of the village and out across the valley. But past the edge of the village, details blur with distance and heat shimmer. If he had House on-line, the Librarian could ask for a satellite close-up, maybe even sound. He gets up and shuffles nearer to the screen, but he can only squint and guess at how much of that broad dust cloud inching across the arid plain is actual and how much is mirage. Running a few numbers in his head, the Librarian estimates that even if Leif took with him every adult in the Refuge, he must have doubled that number in order to throw up a cloud that size. The Librarian is not surprised that the Temple-ruled towns and hamlets along the army's route have proved less loyal to the Fire-breather than they're sworn to be.

And where is Fire, while all this is going on? The Librarian sees no vast winged shadow gliding across the barren flatlands or sliding down along the parched swell of the hills. No sign of burning wagons, or men. At least not yet.

It'll be an hour or more before the rebel army reaches the foot of the Stair. He has to get back to work. Grunting with the effort, the Librarian manhandles the big television closer to his console. He's amused by its lack of a power cable. How convenient if we could edit reality as readily as we do our memories. He throws himself back into his chair. No more casual sorting. He'll have to scrutinize every signal, every line of code for hints of the dragon's presence, guessing at the outline of the whole by the shape of the parts.

Hands poised above the keypad, he hesitates. Should he try to contact Mattias again to let him know that Leif is at the Citadel? Maybe the boy has managed to raise House in the interim. As he ponders the wisdom of this further delay, the Librarian hears the oddest sound. It's so anomalous that he turns in his chair, expecting to find himself in some new memory place, a much older one this time, judging by the sound. But past his circle of light, there's only darkness.

And the baying of hounds.

Perhaps all hounds bay alike, but the Librarian is certain he knows those dog voices. The memory that goes with them includes a rough stick dwelling by a pond in a grove of ancient oaks, where the verges were always green and the water never froze, even in the deepest winter. The void ahead is thinning now, but it's not tree trunks the Librarian sees. It's a paneled door and a row of tall windows with sills as high as his chest. The walls have reappeared, and through the windows, the paved city square is visible past the looming shadow of the *machina rex*.

Damn! It's still there.

How much time has actually gone by while he was indulging himself along memory lane? No, not indulgence. Important information was gathered, passed on by the dragon, in the only way she can.

And the baying is not a memory. It's outside, filling the square.

He goes to the window farthest from where the *machina* is mindlessly raking the facade around the door with its claws. The jointed, meter-long spikes don't seem much the worse for wear, and neither does the building. But suddenly the squeal of metal on stone is deafening, perhaps because the dogs have fallen silent.

Certainly some time has passed, because Stoksie has managed to escape and return, somehow, with reinforcements. The Librarian spots the little Tinker at the entrance to the square, pointing at the Rex. Inexplicably, he's got Luther with him, two women and a pack of dogs. This is disorienting, and for a moment, the Librarian is forced to question what he sees. He doesn't recognize the women at first, but the dogs help jog his memory. It's the two scouts from Deep Moor, he's sure of it, though he can't retrieve their names. What are they doing here?

Looking for him. He can tell that much from Stoksie's wild gesticulating. And not finding him anywhere, they will assume that the Rex has eaten him, or pounded him into a red smear on the otherwise spotless black-and-white pavement.

The Librarian doesn't want the distraction of company just now. He needs to get on with the work. If they find nothing, will they go away? Or, not knowing he's alive and well, will they tangle ˙with the *machina* to recover what's left of him?

Lily and Margit. That's what they're called. How did they get here, they and their dogs, so out of place in this high-tech city? And Luther here also, who'd left with Erde and the other dragons to warn . . .

Ah. The Librarian remembers N'Doch's song, and how the signal locator had placed him a few city blocks away. If N'Doch is in the city, very likely Paia is, too. If Luther's here, probably Erde and the other dragons aren't far away. All the players are here. Lily and Margit he'll figure out soon enough. The Librarian sees it now. The forces are gathering. He's always assumed that the Citadel would be the final battleground, but the campaign heating up there might be only the misdirection. Then who's the magician, Air or Fire?

Ask them about the City.

Perhaps he did know, even then in 913. Because the dragon told him. He just didn't take in the full meaning of her only partially coherent message.

Across the square, Lily and Margit assess the situation with the hard-eyed squints of seasoned warriors. Margit shakes her head while Stoksie argues and Luther attempts to run interference. The dog pack is gathered in tight formation, ears erect, all eyes fastened on the stupid clanking hunk of metal that's trying to tear down a building. It occurs to the Librarian that as fast as the Rex rips away layers of brick and stone, the dutiful little nanomechs are building it right back again, like the two machines that were unpaving and repaving the nearby square. Perhaps it's the best a machine consciousness can do by way of a metaphor for human birth and death. If any of these machines have a consciousness. The city as a whole has a kind of consciousness, perhaps. But certainly not the Rex. It clearly hasn't a thought in its titanium alloy head. It seems to be working on a single instruction: *get Gerrasch.*

This is brought home more forcefully when the Librarian, watching the increasingly heated debate across the square, steps sideways for a better view. He drifts into the Rex's line of sight through the window nearest the door. It spots him, and immediately shifts and redoubles its abuse in his direction. To the Librarian's horror, cracks appear in the featureless gray wall. Long snaking fissures etch the smoky glass with patterns of dead tree branches. But the cracks are knit up as soon as they're made, over and over, birth and death. He decides that the Rex will not get in. But neither will he be able to get out, definitely not through the door, and he sees no way to open any of the oversized window sashes, even if he could do it without drawing the Rex down on top of him. He's safe, but trapped. He tries jumping up and down at the farthest window, waving his arms to attract Stoksie's or the women's attention. The Rex is there instantly, battering away and blocking the Librarian's view of the preparations across the square.

Now he's worried. Because he's no longer sure who the Rex is answering to. Fire is the obvious answer, but the Librarian hasn't lived this long by assuming the obvious. What if Air has sent the Rex to keep him confined to the building and his console until he figures out a way to rescue her? Could she be that impatient, after all these years? The good news is that this could mean he's actually close to a solution. The bad news is that, though he wouldn't willingly sacrifice his friends' safety to the interests of the Quest, the dragon might not be so choosy. The Librarian has few illusions about the altruism of dragons where their Duty is concerned.

A handful of other women appear around Lily and Margit. Not Deep Moor women, at least none of the ones he knows. Margit issues instructions, her hands indicating positions to right and left around the square. Lily huddles with the dogs, as if coaching a football team. The *machina rex* has noticed none of this. The Librarian recalls that he walked within four meters of it before tripping its proximity alarm. Maybe its range really is that small. He offers it another moment of sympathy. It reminds him of athletes he's known, or career soldiers. It's a handsome, scary machine with no brain and one skill—intimidation—at which it excels. Sneaking up on it will not be difficult, but sooner or later, the women's activity will snag its dim awareness, and what they'll do then, the Librarian cannot imagine. He wishes he saw more weaponry spread among the eight

women and two men sidling along the bright building facades. The sketched-in doors and windows offer scant refuge. Only speed will save them if the Rex attacks, and the
Librarian can neither warn them nor help them. He's always refused to carry a weapon, except his brain and his
two clever hands.

He's gazing guiltily at his hands, pink-palmed and soft as
a baby's bottom, when he gets his idea. It sends him stumbling back to his console. If only he can do it in time!
Fingers pounding the keypad, he sets up a series of searches
aimed at picking up signals from machines operating within
the immediate vicinity. He asks for red locators on a map
of the surrounding blocks. Outside in the square, the
hounds are baying again. The Librarian glances toward the
windows just as the Rex pulls away from its destruction of
the facade and turns to face the new intruders. His fingers
thrum against the console. The search is taking longer than
he'd hoped. When he looks up at his map, the entire screen
is hazed in red.

He whacks his forehead. He's forgotten to exempt the
gazillion building and maintenance nanos from the search.
Or maybe there are two gazillion. Whatever. He taps in
new instructions, and the map clears. A dozen possibilities
remain, six of them on his side of the square. What could
they be, smart street lights and sewage drains? He'd seen
nothing in the square but the Rex.

A crash outside nearly catapults him from his chair. The
dogs are barking now, their high-pitched, got'im-cornered
bark. The Librarian hears a yelp, and a soft, wet thud
against the window glass. He groans, and lines the six signals up, one below the other, looking for hints.

He picks it out right away, so quickly that he double-
checks himself. It shouldn't be so easy. But it's the only
constant signal. The others are intermittent: loops of regularly scheduled basic instructions. The Rex, or what he
hopes is the Rex, has to go back to base every time it
changes its direction or its target. The Librarian needs to
follow the signal back to the Rex and capture enough of
its code to be able to create a new instruction to send along
to the machine. What he wants to do is turn the damn
thing off. Fast. Soon. Quickly.

He thinks he hears Lily whistling off the dog pack, but

maybe she's actually urging them forward. He can't worry about the skirmish outside. He closes his ears, and bends his fingers to the chase. Once he locks onto his target, he's inside the Rex soon enough. It's like breaking into a big, empty, and echoing warehouse, with a few crucial items left prominently in the middle of the floor. The Librarian is delighted to find its programming so simple. It'll make it much easier to mess with.

Now that he's doing a block by block analysis, the Librarian is struck by how similar the big machine's code is to the tiny nanomechs. As if the Rex is the giant sibling to the nanos, somehow grown up way out of proportion and scale. He shoves this insight aside for future analysis. No time for it now. He's on a mission of life and death. Still, in his frantic search for an on/off button, he can't help noticing that the places in the Rex where its code differs the most radically look like the same sort of later interpolations that converted a big batch of nanomechs into the voice of the Summoner. He slows the rapid scrolling of ones and zeros. No, in this case, it looks like repair work. Rather artless repair work, at that, like a tapestry that's been worn, then rewoven. The transition from original to restored is not entirely smooth. The reweaving looks to have been done by an unimaginative student, one who only knows how to go by the book.

Like it's been done by another machine.

The instant the notion comes to him, the Librarian knows it's right. Machines repairing machines, just like they constantly make and unmake the city. Because there's nothing else for them to do, and no one else to do it? There'll be no human population to look for, then, except those the dragon has managed to import. Was there ever, or was the city made for as well as by machines? The dragon will be able to tell him, when he finds her.

He studies the repaired sectors again. The damage was extremely random. This may have confounded the logic-driven nanomechs, and made their reweaving awkward. Which introduced anomalies, which affected the broken device's development, as if a fungus had invaded its originally clean and functional structure. Essentially, the repair nanos created a mutant, a machine mutant that grew into the *machina rex*.

So the Rex isn't his dragon's creature, at least not intentionally. He'd like to know what caused this odd kind of damage. It's not what he'd find if someone had gone into the programming and purposefully taken stuff out. The breaks aren't that clean. It's more like the result of physical damage, to the actual hardware. Like smashing the processor, or cooking a memory unit.

Cooking. Fire damage? The fire *dragon's* damage, that is? Could be. It's widespread enough throughout the code he's been looking at to be due to one major incident.

The Librarian chews his lip. How would Fire, a proven technophobe, go after a sibling who's so at home in the ether? Would he smash her electronic toys? Burn everything in sight? He's dealt with all his other problems with flame and violence. It would explain why Air can't communicate using normal electronic means. But not why her *dragon* means aren't functioning. Unless . . .

Circular thinking brings the Librarian back to his vision of the dragon as a machine. He doesn't, he *won't*, believe it. It's too . . . inelegant. But it's certainly possible that the Fire-breather went on a rampage at some point, among the city's machinery. One reason he might do it is to contain or disable Air.

A shout, a scream, and another crash from outside penetrate the Librarian's haze. The Rex! He's forgotten it entirely, with its code still staring balefully at him from the screen. He'd prefer to shut down the machine rather than wreck it, that is, write the instruction that will tell the Rex to turn itself off. But he hasn't time now for the clean solution. His friends are out there being murdered. He flexes his fingers and starts deleting entire blocks of code, whole hog, grimacing as he does so. When he's done what he hopes is enough, he sends it along and waits, hands lifted scant millimeters above the keypad. He doesn't race to the window. He just listens. Soon there is a horrid grinding as the Rex tries to execute two conflicting motions at once. Joints squeal. Pistons bind. The Rex shudders to a halt. The Librarian hears a wan cheer from the forces in the square. He relaxes. Probably they think it's something they've done that stopped the monster. So what. At least they're safe.

Or are they? Motion on the screen draws the Librarian's

gaze upward. In the spaces where he has deleted code, lines are reappearing one after the other, as the nanomechs rebuild the *machina*. No telling how long before it goes online again, but at least he's bought his friends some time to escape. Which they'll only do, he fears, if he can manage to let them know he's still among the living.

They're doing something out there. The Librarian hears a slow muffled banging, like wood on metal. The rhythm is too irregular for the Rex. He shoves back his chair and goes to peer out the high windows. The rescue party is standing about glum and bloodied, inspecting the stilled Rex. All but Stoksie, who is beating furiously at its huge foreleg with the shaft of a pike while Luther attempts to reason with him.

A pike? Where did he get a pike?

Time slippage is making the Librarian dizzy. Several dogs lie dead or dying beneath the Rex's belly. One woman is down and another is nursing a limp arm. Luther tries to draw Stoksie away from his raging and is abruptly shaken off. Voices resonate through the glass, not clearly enough for words, but the Librarian can tell they all think he's dead. He pounds on the window, and again jumps up and down, waving his arms. He bellows at Stoksie and Luther until he's hoarse. No response on the other side of the glass. He might as well be watching them on television.

He decides that if he can't open the window, he'll smash his way through it. He whirls toward his console for a suitable weapon, a book, a chair, anything portable. But his console has vanished. No desk, no chair, no circle of light. Nothing but darkness. He turns back to the window, and it, too, has disappeared.

A small animal moan escapes him. He wraps his arms around his chest and stands swaying in the void. He's emptied of conviction. How can he not question the reality of all he's just seen? Did Stoksie really return with the Deep Moor scouts? Did he really manage to subdue the Rex? Is he being played with, tested, tortured? Or is he just living through the city's version of daily random event?

He rotates slowly, arms outstretched. One full three-sixty. No sound, no break anywhere in the velvet black. The only sure and solid thing is the floor beneath his feet.

And perhaps he shouldn't be so sure about that. Yet the darkness is somehow full of meaning, of *intent*. The Librarian stands listening, waiting for it to speak to him.

And it does. *Hurry! Hurry!*

CHAPTER TWENTY-TWO

The women gather murmuring at the library door. How odd, Erde reflects, that they don't just come piling in. She imagines a charged aura of magic in the room that keeps them at bay, awestruck by Rose's marvelous restoration. Or perhaps it's the wonder of the room itself, appearing so suddenly and in all its details where it hadn't been before, a room they all know lies in ashes in their home time. She looks down the long narrow space, past the shelves full of old books and the dark, low-slung beams and the bright slashes of sunlight from the windows. She realizes with a shock that it's not Rose they're staring at so searchingly.

Do I look strange to them? Erde's hand strays up to rake at her dark scrawl of curls. She smiles at the women self-consciously.

"May we come in?" Raven asks.

"Certainly!" Erde turns to Rose. "I mean, if . . ."

But there's a rush through the door already. The chorus of joy and welcome overwhelms Erde's hesitation. The women surround Rose to hug and pet her, and proclaim their vast relief until Rose laughingly shrugs them off. Raven stands aside with Erde, and gives her shoulder an encouraging squeeze.

"Well done, sweetling."

"But I did nothing . . ."

Raven arches an eyebrow.

". . . much."

"Whatever it was, it was enough, and more than any of us had managed so far."

"It was the knowledge Rose carries that broke her spirit.

But she found her strength again and came back to us renewed." Erde grips Raven's arm. "Oh, such tidings, Raven! So terrible! But Rose must tell it in her own way."

Raven smiles and ruffles Erde's hair. "Do you know how lovely you've grown? I just realized it, standing there at the door. All this racing about dragon-back must be good for you."

Erde blushes, confused by how delighted this compliment makes her, as it comes from the most beautiful woman she knows. Yet her delight stirs the ache beneath it. What good is being beautiful if the one she loves has already given himself to another? Köthen's face fills her mind's eye until she has to shake her head and blink it away.

"Sweetling? Erde?"

"Forgive me, I was just . . ."

"Thinking?"

"Yes." She hasn't thought about Köthen for several hours at least. Perhaps that's a good sign.

"Such sad eyes! Must be very deep thoughts you're having."

Erde shrugs shyly. What a relief it would be to tell Raven everything, to be able to talk with another, more experienced woman about her unrequited passion. "It's just . . ." She can't make herself continue. There are so many more important things to worry about.

"There, there," Raven soothes. "If Rose brings bad tidings, it won't be the first time. We've lived through disaster before, and we can do it again. It isn't the end of the world."

Except that it is.

Erde chokes back a very N'Doch-like laugh. His smart-mouth graveyard humor must be contagious. Instead, she nods. These women have a true reason to celebrate. She will not dampen their joy until Rose herself decides that the moment has come.

Standing in darkness, the Librarian wonders if he should trust his senses.

HURRY! HURRY!

Is it an actual voice whispering through the void this time, from a source outside himself, or is it the old neurons firing, sparked by some inner signal?

Or does it matter?

It's like the bet he took once, several centuries ago. For the winner's choice of pizza and beer, he proposed to outlast a colleague in the psych lab's sensory deprivation chamber. The Librarian won handily, understanding beforehand that the contest was essentially rigged. Who's more comfortable with the infinite, after all, than a man who's lived many lives? The void is not so disorienting, so soul-swallowing, if you're willing to just sit still and listen to the universe. The music of the spheres, the ancient conceit that claims that inaudible, holy music surrounds us all our lives. It's a lie, of course. It's not inaudible at all. The Librarian is hearing it now.

Hurry! Hurry!

In the sensory dep box, after the first few hours, the Librarian had felt himself growing, expanding outward. Not in a defined way, like the swelling shell of a balloon, but like a dissipating gas. Space flowed into him, easing all his molecules apart. An equal opportunity expansion. Remarkably, he lost no sense of self. He did not "become one with the universe." He had no religious epiphanies. He just lay there listening, growing and listening. And he remembers feeling—even after he climbed out of the box and toweled off, even as he wolfed down the victor's super-large with mushrooms and extra cheese and went about his life—he recalls that he experienced no contraction. The added space remained inside him, like the air that never leaves your lungs. He was, still is, expanded matter masquerading as ordinary flesh.

And he's never been more aware of the extra space than he is right now. Because Nature abhors a vacuum, and inevitably that space will want to be filled.

Hurry! Hurry!

He's been listening to this appeal for hours, who knows, maybe days, and he's not yet asked himself the obvious question: hurry up and do what? *Fool, Gerrasch!* It's not hurry up and get *somewhere*. That's much too simple. Or that may have been the idea once. But now the entity—

the dragon, he believes—appears to have him exactly where it wants him, and is keeping him there. Hurry up and do what? Get me out of here? Hurry up and . . . understand what I'm telling you?

And suddenly, he is not alone.

If the void was to clear, and the Librarian were to find himself in the center of an arena filled with thousands avidly watching, he would not be surprised, so profound and pressing is the sense of presence in the darkness surrounding him. So insistent the anticipation. Crowding him, demanding . . .

There's an idea in the air. He hears it spoken.

Entrance.

Demanding entrance? The Librarian throws his head back with a gasp as understanding comes, and the panic that never touched him in the dep tank takes hold with iron fists. Entrance. In order to fill the space inside him. *She, inside me.* The Librarian's integrity of self seems suddenly precious to him. The dragon is knocking at his door.

Hurry! Hurry!

This is the crucial detail he's never intuited, never reasoned out. Has she kept it from him intentionally? It's the explanation for his many lives, for the peculiar way his brain works, for the mystical expansion of his matter. It's his particular destiny.

He is to be the dragon's vessel.

And lose his self in the process? If he lets the dragon in, will she erase him? Will Gerrasch cease to be anything more than the name pinned to a carcass inhabited by another?

The Librarian has waited all his lives for this moment. And yet . . . and yet. . . .

"Your only faith is in yourself, and that seems as intact as always." Paia's quiet scoff shocks even her. It's the closest thing to a snarl she's ever let out of her mouth. Fire's lip curls, but he only looks away.

N'Doch nudges her. "Maybe we need to hear what he has to say."

"Oh, yes," Fire returns. "I think you do. After all, why perish in ignorance?" He adjusts his chair to put his back to Paia, facing his fellow dragon. "My tale begins with our wakening. Or mine, I should say. I was waked earlier than you or Earth, due to my den's chance proximity to the chronological end of humankind. Or perhaps it was . . ." he grins slyly, ". . . because I was always Air's favorite."

Water-as-Sedou sniffs. "Certainly our sister would have trusted you to aid with whatever crisis awakened her. A trust you then betrayed."

"Define the nature of the betrayal."

"Subversion of our ancient duty."

"By your terms. By mine, I've chosen the much wiser path. My intention was to save her, to save us all."

Sedou crosses his arms and leans back, as if weary with incredulity. "So you locked her up?"

"Yes!" Fire bolts out of his chair. The chair teeters and topples against its neighbor as he stalks away from the table. "You're always so sure you're right! I see no reason to proceed with this charade!"

Paia moves after him. She's sure Fire will slam out the door. If he can move a chair about in his newly material form, he can open a door. But N'Doch grabs her arm, and Fire's not ready to leave quite yet. He plants himself by the window, hands on hips, gazing outward with an air of wounded dignity. The flat daylight limns his golden profile with an icy edge.

The dragon-as-Sedou rocks his chair gently. "Then why do you stay?"

Djawara clucks his tongue. He walks over to stand beside Fire as if he's been invited to enjoy the view. "It's the shape she's taken, you understand. My grandson Sedou . . . you never met him, but . . ."

Fire casts a knowing eye at the old man, and Paia shivers. Either the dragon can't bear to admit to any sort of ignorance, or he's been interfering fatally with N'Doch's family for longer than any of them have guessed. She's glad that Djawara's gaze is fixed on the street outside.

". . . he was a magnificent man. Bravehearted. A dragon of a man. But impulsive. Rash. Headstrong. A bit like you." Djawara clears his throat gently. "So perhaps you will pardon . . ."

"She is neither rash nor impulsive. She's merely insufferable, and always has been. She gets no pardon from me."

"Nor needs one," Sedou interjects.

"Tell *me* your story. I'd like to hear it." Djawara clasps his hands behind his back, his slight, erect form so vulnerable-seeming beside Fire's towering bulk. "You were saying that you waked early . . ."

Fire sighs, not the satirical exhalation that Paia is familiar with, but a long hissing release. "I find myself in need of someone to run my temple, old man. Are you available?"

Djawara chuckles politely.

"I take that as a 'no.' Pity. Perhaps you'll reconsider when you hear what I have to say."

"Please do continue."

But Fire is growing restless with human interaction. Paia knows the signs. At home, in this mood, he would bellow at a subordinate or two, resume dragon-form and swoop off to terrify a few villages. In a rage, he'd do much worse. He's not in a rage, not yet, but she can see the darkness gathering in him. He turns away abruptly from the window and his moment of quasi-intimacy with Djawara, and announces flatly to the room at large, "It's very simple, really. Our Destiny requires our death. That's the short explanation. Air, of course, gave it to me in endless painful detail at the time, but I . . ."

"Come now," says Sedou. "There is always risk with . . ."

"Listen to me! I said, *requires*. The concept of accident is not involved. But I wasn't having any of it then, and the same goes for now."

"But what . . ."

Fire whirls back to the table to loom over his sibling with his palms planted to either side of Sedou's elbows. "Shut up and listen!"

Sedou's chin juts and his nostrils flare, but he stays seated and quiet.

"Fortunately for all of us," Fire continues tightly, "the final fulfillment of this absurd plan demands the presence and more crucially, the cooperation of all—four dragons, four guides—within a certain time frame. Which, of course, will not be revealed by me, and is otherwise known only to the missing fourth of our number, who you have been unsuccessful at locating."

"So far," Sedou hisses.

"Perhaps." Fire looks down, flicking a trace of ash from the gold braid circling his cuffs. "But the point is, like it or not, I'm saving your lives. Now tell me how that constitutes betrayal?"

. . . and yet, he must.

His genes decree it. Every atom spiraling in his cells is arranged to obtain precisely this result. His will, even if he wills otherwise, is secondary.

She, immaterial, an ephemeral impulse, a *signal*. He, physical. She has need of his voice, his hands, to move in the world of men. To move at all. And she is the One. There is work that must be done, and quickly. If there is hope yet for the planet, it's her. The dragon. Air.

Hurry! Hurry!

The Librarian tells himself that he's had more lives than any ten men could hope for. Perhaps that's what his recent trip down Memory Lane was intended for—to remind him of that. Now it's time to let the dragon live . . . if only he can find the courage. So hard to let go. Never once, down along the centuries, has the Librarian ever contemplated suicide.

But now he searches his overstocked data banks for images of his most beloved places. A difficult choice. He's had so many. Though his physical body will continue without him—former occupant moved, left no forwarding address—he imagines it enshrined in earth, a final resting place, at each favorite site. He chooses one.

It's the mirrored, dark-rimmed lake where he first met a fellow dragon guide, and got his first whiff of Destiny. He sees his stick hovel deserted, the worn plank door thrown wide, the chimney clear of smoke. He see the oblong pile of smooth lake stones that marks his grave. He lets the clear orange sun sink past the far shore, toothed by spruce and pine, and just as the moon is rising behind him, the Librarian says . . .

Yes.

CHAPTER TWENTY-THREE

He doesn't . . . *cease,* as he's expected, as he's prepared himself for. But very soon, the Librarian suspects that oblivion might have been easier.

His mind is eclectic, wide-ranging. It has made for him, over the centuries, a commodious and varied inner space. But the dragon is vast. Like a mighty ocean tide, she rushes in through the opened locks of his consciousness, into every bay and inlet, every nook and cranny, until there's little room left for his smaller, more finite, self. Pressed flat against the curve of his skull, he's near to suffocation. The dragon is unpracticed at sharing even an ephemeral geography. She has no sense of how to keep her mental feet and elbows and breath and volume to herself. Crushed, jabbed, stomped on, deafened, the Librarian quails.

He could blank on her. Overstretched, overwhelmed, he could choose a painless voluntary oblivion. Put his besieged brain to sleep. But he worries that the dragon has no idea what to do with this physical body she's so abruptly claimed. He can sense her testing its mechanisms, without any concept of its limits. She's playing with his heart rate, speeding it up, slowing it down, dilating his pupils, stimulating his muscles into spasm, inflating his lungs past comfort or reason. Stretching him like an elastic band. Deep, primal agony. Lightning bolts of pain. The Librarian imagines a teenager climbing into his first car. The dragon could kill him out of sheer ignorance, before she has a chance to make use of his body. His miraculous serial lifetimes, wasted in a moment of clumsiness.

Stop! Stop!

But begging for mercy has no effect. The dragon isn't

listening, or can't. Or rather, she's listening at such a cosmic tuning that the Librarian's faint human pleadings go unheard. Suffering, helpless as a laboratory rat, he knows he must, somehow must, resume his task of calibrating the lines of communication. But this will take time, time he may not have if he can't wrest control of his limbs and metabolism from the dragon before she carelessly tweaks him into cardiac arrest. And this means giving himself to life again, after having made his quietus. It means rejoining the fray.

Life. Okay, perhaps. But can he do it?

His fists open and close. His fingers and elbows stretch and recoil. His legs twitch. He's stumbling about in involuntary dizzying circles while his features twist through a series of grotesque grins and grimaces. What does a dragon know about human expression, after all? Or human balance? The Librarian's ankles tangle. He goes down hard, shuddering, breathing in gasps, and still the dragon, in her perilous curiosity, seems intent on jerking his strings like some demon puppet master until every last one of them snaps.

Writhing in the dark on the smooth, chill floor, the Librarian fights for a hairbreadth of elbowroom in his beleaguered consciousness. Grasping at straws, he sends out a fervent SOS. A bit of signal snatched at random, its code rewritten and released, like a messenger pigeon taking wing from the walls of a besieged castle. A demand for recognition, a request for dialogue. He thinks of it as a dove. For clarity's sake, he images its diagonal, white flight in his mind. The bird flies home, from one sector of his brain to another.

This is insane, the Librarian muses. It's like pleading with myself. But it works. The puppet master eases off abruptly, leaving him limp and panting on the invisible floor. But the Librarian is wary. The dragon's urgency has not faded. She's still there crowding him into the farthest, tightest corner of his self. He can see that a simple giving in, giving over, is not how this is going to work. A more active partnership will be required if they, man and dragon, are to accomplish anything at all. He dispatches another dove, requesting a parley.

The dove returns. He can see it this time, a pale, faintly glowing, fully dimensional bird. It lands silently on the floor beside him. He takes it into his hands, astonished, and gently picks the slim curl of paper from the capsule banded to its leg. He unrolls the tiny scrap. It's thin, almost translucent, and totally blank, but its message comes to him loud and clear.

SORRY.

The Librarian chuckles, half amused, half for joy. Well, now, that's better. A bit awkward, birds and paper bits and all, but who cares, if it works? It seems he doesn't have to actually write out the minute print with his big, soft hands and lack of any sort of writing implement. He has only to think his words, and there they are.

A second dove lands beside him, announcing itself with a soft salvo of flapping. The Librarian extracts its message.

NOW? HURRY!

Ah. Back in familiar territory at last. He's relieved, but no more enlightened. Hurry, yes, of course, but where and how, not to mention why? What exactly are we meant to do? He has so many questions. Too many to fit on a tiny scrap of onionskin.

Perhaps a larger messenger? The Librarian pictures the big crow he'd once rescued from a trap. After it healed, it stuck around, apparently because the life he offered it was more interesting than the one it had known before. He smiles at the thought of it, and out of the darkness ambles the very bird, its bright eye fixed on the pile of raisins that have appeared in the Librarian's palm. By now, the Librarian is incapable of surprise. He greets the bird, then lays half the raisins on the floor and nibbles the rest himself, pondering his next message. What questions will win him the most information in return? Meanwhile, a shorter query goes out with the dove. He doesn't really care if she answers, but he'd kind of like to know.

Why me?

HAS ALWAYS BEEN.

What is my part in all of this?

HANDS. EARS. EYES. FEET.

I know! I know all that! Though to tell the truth, he hasn't thought of being her feet before. *What am I supposed to DO?*

HURRY!!

The Librarian takes a breath. Perhaps he can inhale a

measure of patience from the very air. Finding a common language is not always the same as finding a common basis for reasoning. The dragon is as circular as ever. Random access. Well, fine. He knows how to deal with that. He sends the crow out into the ether, its tightly rolled scroll black with printed code.

And so, painstakingly, and strained by the effort of staving off the dragon's single-minded urgency, the Librarian extracts the outlines of the history he's lived, but has never understood. Finally, it's no longer a mystery why he's felt the need to live so many of his centuries in hiding.

In the beginning, he and Air were one. She, a discorporate entity, deaf, dumb, and blind to the material world. He, an animal body, canny, clever, and secretive, willing but hardly self-aware. The perfect physical vehicle for an ephemeral power. He existed while she slept, keeping himself alive and ready, should the need arise for the dragon to walk in the world.

But when the call came, the aeons of separation proved a desperate disadvantage. Air woke still wrapped in vast and cosmic dreaming. In her waking confusion, her sibling Fire saw an opportunity. He stole her physical vessel and stashed it away down the timeline, far from the forward point in the world's history that Air had chosen for her den. And so her den became her prison. A prison not of walls but of silence. Marooned far forward in time with no way to communicate either her dilemma or her whereabouts, except by the faintest of beacons, as likely to reach their goal as signals from another galaxy. No way, that is, until her kidnapped guide had lived long enough to evolve a brain capable of recognizing her distant transmissions, and figuring out how to reestablish their connection.

Kidnapped! The Librarian lets the memory surface, so long buried beneath the sediments of time and terror. The sharp grip of the golden dragon's claws, the fury and heat of his presence. The horror of abandonment in a cold, wet world full of unfamiliar threats and vicious two-legged predators. Why didn't the Fire-breather murder him right then and there?

Either he couldn't, or he . . . wouldn't.

The Librarian decides that an answer to this particular mystery could prove a crucial key in dealing with the renegade. Perhaps Fire was simply being lazy. Probably he believed the vast gulf of years between Air and her guide would be enough to suit his hedonistic purpose. But how ironic that the technophobic Fire should resort to such a high-tech prison. He may not even have recognized it as such. Considering it further, the Librarian is sure he did not. Certainly, Fire could never have predicted the development of an electronic means by which his imprisoned sister could amplify her calls for help.

The Librarian formulates another bird: *What is this place, this city? Why did you choose it for your den?*

Instead of birds, an abrupt and shocking downloading of images. The Librarian reels, clutching his temples. The entire history of the White City in pictures, neatly packaged in sequential files for storage in his capacious memory.

FOR LATER STUDY. LATER.

This last message comes through strong and clear. The dragon has no time now for education.

Basic information! Necessary!

Hastily, the Librarian opens the first file. A holographic video of the city streets, full of sunlight and green trees and living people. Immediately, his hands and legs spasm with involuntary motion. While he wrestles with his rebellious limbs, a peculiar sensation, an entire flock of white-and-gray pigeons settles down around him, feathers flying like snow.

HURRY! HURRY!

The Librarian knows he's gotten all the information he's likely to for a while. But he's learned that once, humans did inhabit the White City. Pondering their fate, he hoists himself awkwardly to his feet and tests his legs for control. He sends several of the birds back expressing his total willingness to serve but pointing out in no uncertain terms the absolute requirement for a physical body such as himself to follow a linear plan of action.

First one foot, and then the other. He images himself walking. *Get it?*

Air images her other siblings, and the Librarian is briefly distracted by how aware he is of her accessing his personal data banks for the necessary visual information. Item: one large bronzy-plated dragon called Earth. Ivory horns. Stubby tail. And so on. She pictures the four dragons coming together, the fourth image being himself. A gathering of dragons. He's always suspected that would be the plan. But Air seems unaware of all that Fire's been up to since she saw him last. After he stole her guide and left, he's apparently managed to avoid the temptation of coming back to gloat. But does Air suppose that her guide has been missing for centuries by accident? The Librarian explains. A single goldfinch delivers a minuscule reply.

OH, THAT.

Even behavior as unforgivable as the Fire-breather's is not vast enough to register on Air's cosmic scale. The dragon seems sure that her wayward brother will show up, once the other three have gathered. The Librarian is a whole lot less convinced, but for now, it seems pointless to argue.

Where should we gather?

This time, letters appear in the air in front of him: ANYWHERE. FOR NOW.

He understands that she does mean *anywhere,* in time or space. And he knows that it's his own brain supplying the alphabet. But, good, excellent. Further progress. The birds were getting very cumbersome.

WHEN ALL HAVE GATHERED, THE RIGHT PLACE WILL BE KNOWN.

Practically a paragraph. And there will be a right place.

Now we're getting somewhere. Except . . . how do we get there? How do we get out of here? And how do we contact the others?

He hopes she will confirm his guess that Earth and Water are in the city, somewhere nearby. Perhaps she will even explain how they got there. Instead, he gets confusion and impatience and a storm of grackles wheeling and arguing overhead. Not a one of them bothers to land. The Librarian gets the idea that locomotion and communication are solely his territory. He feels stolid and clumsy. He's tempted for a moment by exhaustion and despair. He hates taking action based on so little knowledge, so imperfect an understanding of the whole picture. But, after all, he's come up with the necessary solutions so far. One problem at a time. He must trust his dragon and get . . .

Of course! The Librarian enacts the cliché. He slaps his forehead.

Escaping this darkness isn't about bashing his way out. He'll just program a few nanomechs to build him an exit. He glances behind him, for the vanished windows looking out on the square. He's sure a faint towering shadow of the Rex lingers there, like an afterimage burned into the inside of his eyelids. The *machina* will be reviving soon. Better make his exit on the opposite side of the building. Then he'll rescue Stoksie and find out how the Deep Moor trackers got there, and then . . .

Already the darkness is thinning, and the door is forming in front of him, a pale rectangular outline floating in the void like chalk on a blackboard. He waits for the knob to complete, then grasps it and gives it an experimental twist. The door cracks open and flat, bright light spills in, the light of the city. But when he hauls the door fully open, eager for air and space, he's not where he expects to be. He's on the edge of the huge empty plaza where the elevator left him when he first arrived, with Stoksie, after coming through the portal. He's stymied, but only briefly. Perhaps the dragon has sent him this new insight, or perhaps he's figured it out on his own. No matter, he understands now that the city, like the dragon, cannot be counted upon to be linear. It has a random access geography. He remembers his schematic map of the power lines, and how he'd marked the source of the signal carrying N'Doch's song. He'll start there, with an address he knows. He shuts the door on the empty plaza, calls up the map, and reprograms his door to open across the street from that source location. He opens the door again.

There is a street this time, narrow and cluttered. The potholes surprise him, a hint of the texture of real life. If he had any doubt of his data, he'd wonder if he was still in the city. Across the cracked pavement sits an old-fashioned café, complete with a worn striped awning and metal tables and chairs. The furniture looks like it's been recently thrown around. The tall windows are fogged with grit and condensation, but the Librarian detects light and the motion of bodies inside. If he's guessed correctly, one of them will be N'Doch.

He's about to venture out across the street, when inexplicable paralysis assails him. A weight in his chest, like a boulder crushing his heart. Panic first, then realization: it's the dragon, holding him back.

What? Why? You were in such a rush before.

He spots a flock of bright blue finches perched along the sagging rim of the café awning. Though he's never thought of birds as having expressions, these little critters look distinctly reluctant.

NOT YET. NOT ONE BY ONE.

The Librarian is reminded of other long-sentenced prisoners who, when released, find it difficult to walk through the open door into freedom. The weight on his heart eases but does not go away.

ALL MUST GATHER. ALL AT ONCE.

It's something about the news she bears, the Librarian senses. She wants everyone to hear it at the same time. He doesn't ask why again. She will simply turn vague and prod him to get on with his part of the job, collecting their allies, simultaneously, in one place.

As the Librarian ponders this new logistical challenge, another understanding blooms inside him, like a flower captured by time-lapse photography. Inspired, perhaps, by the tired but insistent reality of the café across the way, he asks himself: *If I can program a door that leads anywhere in the city, could I not also program the place it leads to?* If the initial gathering can be *anywhere,* he can create, or better still, re-create a site of his choosing. A place of safety and comfort from which to plan the rescue of the planet.

The Librarian deliberates issues of security and size, even familiarity. Urged to quick decision by his dragon's implacable impatience, he settles on a place he recalls most fondly: the Grove at Deep Moor. And since he can set his own parameters, he'll tweak it a little. He'll make it an Urgrove, a haven of peace and beauty. The Grove the way it was before the dawn of man.

That accomplished, he will set about providing transportation. The Librarian takes a last, hungry look at *La Rive Gauche,* certain he detects the sharp fragrances of espresso and fresh-baked *brioches.* He sighs, shuts the door, and gets down to work.

CHAPTER TWENTY-FOUR

N'Doch thinks maybe it's time to pour himself a *real* drink. Normally, he's not much for alcohol, but the mood in the café is beyond tense. The very air has darkened, humming like a plucked string. Or maybe it's the guitar he's got clutched in his arms, responding on its own in some kind of celestial angst. *Our destiny requires our death.* N'Doch's sure he's not the only one who'd like to know exactly what the Fire-breather means by that.

Water-as-Sedou has taken a dragon's own time to consider his reply. He's holding very still while Fire leans over him. N'Doch can see the effort in it, both for the dragon and for the man whose identity she's borrowed. "I repeat," Sedou says at last, "betrayal is the subversion of your given duty."

Fire drops his head between his outstretched arms, the very picture of exasperation. "Have you even been listening?"

Sedou nods, a new and scary resignation deep in his eyes.

Fire snorts. He gives the metal table a rough shake and shoves himself upright, folding his arms. "I did not volunteer for that duty, and made no promises to it."

"Betrayal is also doing harm to those who've accepted the responsibility you seek to avoid."

"I've hurt no one."

Sedou's eyes widen. He turns half away in his chair. "Brother! Please! We all know better!"

"Things! I've destroyed things!" Fire snaps. "Stuff."

"People's homes and livelihoods!"

"What about my mother?" N'Doch finds himself suddenly nose-to-nose with the Fire-breather instead of challenging him, as he'd intended, from the comparative safety of the bar. The guitar vibrates in dissonant sympathy from the countertop. "You threaten her up on the mountaintop, and next thing, she turns up dead! I call that hurting. I call that murder! What do you call it?"

If it's possible to look bored and furious simultaneously, Fire has managed it. "A regrettable accident."

"Accident?" N'Doch can feel the dragon's heat, standing so close. A human this hot would be dead of spontaneous combustion, but it matches the heat in N'Doch's heart. "You called in your hit man! Remember your man Baraga? Remember what he did to me?"

"Kenzo Baraga is very much his own man," Fire replies, without taking his glare from Sedou's. "I only offered him what he craved already. Besides, you look alive and well enough. Are you a ghost?"

"Woulda been, if it weren't for the big guy Earth. Shot to pieces. You don't call that hurting?" N'Doch almost grabs the Fire dude's gold-braided lapels, but a quick hard NO! slams through his brain. He backs off like he's been hit. The dragon can pack a wallop when she wants to.

Paia has worked her way around to stand beside Sedou. She lays a very visible hand on the man dragon's broad shoulder. "You can lie to others if you must, my Fire, but don't try to tell me I haven't seen you burn men to cinders before the altar of your own Temple!"

Fire watches Sedou lean back into the curl of Paia's arm. "I am not lying! As my sister has agreed, a dragon is incapable of lying."

"Dissembling," Djawara murmurs from the side, like a helpful referee.

"No! Take an honest count! I've hurt no one who wasn't in harm's way already, or who didn't willingly put themselves there to honor me, or for fanatical reasons of their own."

"Fanaticism that you created and encouraged," Paia pursues.

"For your sake, beloved! Always for your sake, to have servants around me to help keep you safe!"

"An elaborate and delusional denial, brother," growls Sedou.

"I can't be expected to answer for the bloody deeds of humans, suicidal or otherwise!"

"I doubt my daughter Fâtime understood herself to be 'in harm's way,'" Djawara observes quietly.

"Really, old man?" Fire gazes at Djawara sideways, framing his incredulity in theatrical scale. "Though she lived in a dying town in a dying country on a collision course with the end of the world? Though she suffered in poverty and lost all but one of her sons to the greed and violence and corruption of the time? Not in harm's way? Really? Could a sage like yourself have birthed a fool?"

"Enough!" Sedou rises, taking Paia gently by the shoulders and setting her down in the chair he has just vacated. "Give us something more creative than a coward's whine of denial! You are steeped in blood, my brother, be it by your own hand or otherwise. Not a one of us doubts it. The only question is *why,* and you haven't yet made that fully clear."

"I told you . . ."

"But you didn't *convince* me."

Fire watches Water-as-Sedou place both hands on Paia's shoulders. Longing and reluctance shine through the veil of irritation shading his golden eyes. "Must I?",

"Do you mean, must you, with the humans present?"

Fire's jaw hardens. "And you consider me heartless."

"It's only reasonable that all of us know the fate all will share."

Fire's lip twitches in an unborn snarl. He says, slowly, deliberately, "All right. If you insist. Does the phrase 'mutual annihilation' bring anything to mind?"

N'Doch thinks it brings a lot of things to mind, and none of them good. But his repeated subliminal calls to the dragon for an explanation go unanswered. The sense of foreboding he's been shoving aside for a while comes flooding back big-time. His grandfather takes a half step forward, as if unsure he's heard correctly. Paia shifts slightly in her chair, maybe because Sedou's grip has tightened. Protection or restraint? N'Doch can't be sure, for the big man's outward manner is completely calm.

"How? Why?"

"Ask our sister Air, if you can find her. Which you never will. A shame really, since she appears to be in possession of all the facts which have been hidden from the rest of us."

"But some of which she shared with you."

"When she sent me off to collect you and our brother."

"Perhaps you misunderstood. She's not the clearest . . ."

"No. It was unequivocal." After this suddenly reasonable and direct exchange, like actual conversation among siblings, Fire seems uneasy under Paia's expectant stare. He turns away. "So I took other steps . . ."

"Ah," says Sedou. "Ah."

A moment follows that's so still, so lacking in purpose, so much as if the entire world has stopped, that N'Doch wonders if it means a stalemate. The two dragons have reached some sort of understanding, that much is obvious. But the light seems different, and there's a new rigidity in Fire's red-clad back as he lifts one clawed hand to the misted glass. Thin curls of steam rise as he swirls his palm against it to clear his view. N'Doch would swear he's seen Fire shudder. Quick and hard, like he's gotten a bad shock but mastered it instantly. His hand drops like dead weight to his side as he moves back from the window, one step, then two, and turns on his heel.

"Well, I think it's time I left. A delightful diversion, but I really must get home. I have a war to fight."

N'Doch is disappointed. Is the Fire dude really giving up so easily? Sidestepping the central issue? N'Doch has expected him to be bigger, badder than that.

Fire's glance slews sideways toward Djawara, but slides on past to rest intently on Paia the whole time he's talking. "Are you sure you won't reconsider my offer, old man? The religious life can be very rewarding, I assure you. A measure of comfort and luxury to ease your old age? I know my priestess would appreciate your company. Far more stimulating than any she's had up till now. Myself excepted, of course."

Something's happened. N'Doch feels the change blow through the room, as palpable as a storm gust off the Atlantic, but he's got no sense of what it means. He glances at Sedou, sees him straighten, watches his attention move outward, past the café walls, into the street and beyond.

"And of course," Fire continues, "I can promise a bevy of lovely ladies to decorate your days and nights."

Paia shakes her head, her tone almost as mocking as Fire's. "Shame, shame! How do you ever expect to win any credibility if you go on like that?"

A long look passes between them. Then the satirical light blooms as wildly as hope in Fire's eyes. He lifts his sculpted chin and pounds his chest like a cartoon despot. "Because I am the God."

Paia smiles sadly. "But you're not. You're only a dragon."

"Yes, and you are my guide."

N'Doch's glance swivels from one to the other. *What is it? What's happened?* They could be errant lovers, reconciling.

Sedou shakes his head, listening, but not for any sound audible to human ears.

Paia sighs, rising from the table, politely disengaging Sedou's grip. "If only you'd let yourself be guided by me."

"We could work on that," says Fire agreeably.

She laughs, as if he's made a frivolous joke.

He returns a charming, deprecatory smile. "Of course, I'm not making any promises."

"No. For then, you might be forced to make good on them."

"I see you understand me now." Fire holds out his hand. His gilded nails gleam in the light from the window, which seems warmer than before, as if the sun has risen. "It's time, isn't it?"

N'Doch sees the tide turn in the priestess' eyes. It spooks him badly.

What the hell is going on?

LISTEN!

To what? I don't hear a thing!

"Unless you mean that humming," he says aloud. Getting no response, he turns to his grandfather. "You hear anything weird, Papa Dja?"

Djawara is grinning like an old fool. "I believe the 'never' has just become a 'now.' I wonder how that happened."

"What are you talking . . . oh."

And now he hears it, too. Voices. A flurry of voices on the dragon internet. New voices. *What does it mean?*

HUSH!

Fire says, more urgently, "Are you coming, beloved?"

"It seems that I have no choice." She looks to Djawara.

Djawara nods. "You are our only chance."

Fire barks a laugh, a desperate, uneasy guffaw. "Ha, old man! You're convinced she'll convert me?"

Djawara smiles up at the towering man dragon, then very decorously lays a hand on his glittering cuff. N'Doch tenses, ready to spring to the rescue, but smoke does not rise, and there's no stink of burning flesh.

"Here is my hope, lad," says the old man earnestly. "That she will help you to see reason and accept the inevitable. And if more can be expected, that she will lead you to find that deep place in your dragon's heart where compassion and honor lie waiting in chains, and convince you to set them free."

Paia nods, and places her pale hand in the dragon's red-and-gilt palm.

"No!" N'Doch cries out, but too late. The pair has vanished before the protest leaves his mouth. "No!" He spreads his arms to his grandfather in fear and loss and frustration. "Why? How could she? Why did she go with him?"

Djawara's face is solemn and shining. "She knows it's only a matter of time."

CHAPTER TWENTY-FIVE

The carved wooden beams of the library at Deep Moor resound with the glad laughter of unsuspecting women. Though warmed by Raven's cheerful affection and the women's awed and grateful smiles, Erde is sure that she's never felt lonelier. Deep Moor is not the home she hoped it would be, and tried so hard to make it. Even if the real Deep Moor did not lie in ruins, it could never be.

Not now. Now that I've been where I've been, seen what I've seen, know what I know.

Deep Moor stands for all that's good and right about humanity. But her life has become—*she* has become—something not quite human. Something only her fellow dragon guides can comprehend.

My home, my fate, whatever it is to be, is with them.

As she is contemplating all this and feeling sorry for herself, which she admits is one of her least favorable characteristics, a sudden imperative from the dragon outside banishes all other thoughts.

WE MUST GO.

What? Where?

A NEW SUMMONS. FROM THE GROVE.

A trill of fear roughens Erde's reply. *No, dragon, surely not there!*

YES! WE MUST LEAVE IMMEDIATELY!

For the Grove? But Fra Guill is in the Grove! And all his minions! Have you forgotten?

MY SISTER AIR IS THERE.

Erde is so astounded that her mind blanks momentarily, like a mill gear slipping its cog. *Impossible! We would . . . you would have known!*

I DIDN'T SAY SHE WAS THERE BEFORE. I SAID SHE IS THERE NOW. I HAVE JUST RECEIVED THE SUMMONS. WE ARE ALL TO GATHER THERE.

Surely there is some mistake! Did she say the Grove, exactly?

OF COURSE NOT. HER SUMMONSES DON'T COME IN WORDS. BUT I KNOW THE GROVE WHEN I SEE IT.

We can't go back there, thinks Erde desperately. We just can't!

"Erde? Sweetling? Are you all right?" Raven laughs. "You really have become the most distracted child!"

"I'm sorry, I . . . I was just talking with the dragon. He . . ." Erde knows she cannot share this news with Raven. She might insist on coming along. "Will you excuse me for a moment? I think I'll go speak to him in person."

"By all means. Give him my best."

Erde puts on her best calm face as she eases casually through the throng of celebrating women, receiving their thanks and congratulations as she goes. So many of them now! What a refuge Deep Moor had become in her absence, for the battered, mistreated, and misunderstood. Erde wishes she better comprehended the nature of the illusory Deep Moor that the City has created here. It would do her heart good to be able to promise these women a permanent place of safety, though surely even an illusion is better than the horrors they fled from.

Erde's heart pounds as she imagines those horrors: starvation and servitude, beatings and witch burnings. It could have been her own life, but for the coming of the dragon. She gains the library door, hurries across the dappled garden courtyard and through the shaded arbor, wrapped in the heavy fragrance of roses.

She finds the dragon lumbering up and down the open lawn, the closest thing he can manage to pacing impatiently.

"Look at that, dragon!" she scolds, hoping to lighten his urgent mood at least a little. "You're wearing a great mud track in that tender green grass!" But she also notices, to her amazement, that the bruised grass at the farthest extent of his pacing has healed itself completely by the time he returns to it.

ARE YOU READY?

Ready?

TO LEAVE. WE MUST GO IMMEDIATELY.

Dragon, please. We must think this one over carefully.

She has never refused him before, never withheld from him the mental image he needs to guide his transport, or as N'Doch would say, his "homing device." She can sense his surprise.

WHY ARE WE LINGERING? MY SISTER CALLS!

But Fra Guill . . .

PERHAPS SHE HAS VANQUISHED HIM.

But are you sure it's her? How do you know?

Earth halts in his tracks and pulls his massive bronze body up to its full monumental height. HOW CAN YOU ASK SUCH A THING!

He towers over Erde like a rugged cliff face. His scimitar horns could almost tangle with the clouds and brush the dome of the sky.

That is, she muses, if it was the *real* sky . . .

He lowers his great head, letting his horns sweep through the sunlit air like the vanes of an ivory windmill. His plated snout swoops toward the ground and settles inches from Erde's toes with a hearty snort. The warm gale of his breath tousles her hair like an unseen hand.

"Dragon!" she exclaims fondly. "You did everything but roar! Are you trying to intimidate me?"

Earth's fierce demeanor wilts. AM I NOT SUCCEEDING?

Of course not! Now, let's discuss this new summons of yours.

"A matter of time, sure, but after all the trouble we went to, getting her away from him? I can't believe this!" N'Doch scrubs his face with both palms like a sleeper waking. Surely he *must* be dreaming. "What's Dolph gonna say? What am I gonna tell him?"

Sedou stands at the window with his back to them, as the Fire-breather had done before. "The knight has already played his role. It's endgame now."

"Endgame, huh?" N'Doch laughs nervously. "Sounds a little too much like 'mutual annihilation' for me."

"I mean that it's time for the major pieces to do their part."

"Easy for you to say, bro. It's not your head the good baron's gonna be after."

"Hush, boy!" Djawara hisses. "It's no time now to be playing the fool!"

"I'm not. I was only . . ."

"You are. I know it's only your apprehension babbling away, but now's not the time for it."

"Yeah?" N'Doch glares sullenly at his grandfather, who always manages to hold a man's face to the mirror just when he's least interested in looking at himself. "What time is it, then?"

"Time to meet my sister." Sedou turns back to them with an elated grin. "We've been summoned!"

"Just now? You heard . . . ?" Djawara clasps both hands as if in prayer.

"Air? She got out? She's free?" N'Doch exclaims. "Wow! How?"

"Unclear," Sedou admits. "But we'll find out soon enough!"

N'Doch puts two and two together. "So that's why the Fire dude split so suddenly." He rounds on Djawara. "How'd you know?"

"It seemed the only logical explanation."

"Nah. C'mon!" N'Doch doesn't want it to be so simple. Truth is, he doesn't want it to be so at all. If it's so, if the last dragon is out of the hatch, it means they're on to the next stage of the Quest, the stage Fire's been working so hard to prevent. It means finally finding out what he means by "mutual annihilation." "You got some kind of magic, right, Papa?"

Djawara ignores him. "To where are we summoned?"

Sedou gazes at the far wall, as if the message was printed there. "Now, there's the problem. No words, only images, and it *looks* like . . . the Grove at Deep Moor."

N'Doch offers his grandfather a brief explanation, then shrugs, hoping his relief isn't too obvious. "Well, that's a no-go until we hook up with the Big Guy again. He's our only mode of transportation."

"Easily done. He's only a few blocks away." Sedou heads for the door. But the instant his hand touches the knob, the gale starts up again outside, as if it had been lying in wait until someone ventured into the street. Violent gusts lift and tip the café tables, and slam the chairs against the base of the facade. Then, louder than the wind, a roaring and pummeling sound. The door and the windows vibrate in their frames. Sedou clears a circle of condensation and peers through the glass.

"Hunh. Not so easily."

Djawara quickly joins him. "Oh, my."

And then there's nothing left for N'Doch to do but follow. Besides, he'd like to know what all the noise is about. He clears his own little view port, and looks out on a hail of stones. Not hailstones, which he's only seen once in his life anyway. These are actual stones. Rocks the size of chicken eggs, falling from the sky in a steady downpour, like petrified rain. More than just falling, each stone seems to have been flung downward by force, so that when they hit the street, they bounce. N'Doch sees there are two hazards out there: the stones coming down hard on your head, and the stones careening back up in your face. The quaint old striped awning that had led him down the street in the first place is already in shreds and tatters.

"That'd lay us all flat in a second," he observes with as much neutrality as he can muster. So they won't be leaving the safe haven of the Rive for a while yet. He strolls back to the bar and picks up the guitar. He'll want to take it with him anyway, when the time comes. "It'll stop, probably. Let's just kick back till it does."

"I can go, and come back for you." The outline of Sedou's body shimmers as the dragon contemplates a shape change.

"But is that wise?" Djawara asks. "From what you've said, separating us seems to have been his most successful delaying strategy."

Sedou scowls, shimmers again, then retreats from the window and flings himself disconsolately into a chair. "What, then? We can't just sit here! Earth will be summoned, too, but will he think to search us out before he goes?"

Djawara settles beside him quietly, as if keeping vigil over an ailing relative. "We'll think of something."

Suddenly, a knock at the door. N'Doch nearly drops the guitar. Three evenly spaced raps, neither demanding nor impatient. Formal, N'Doch decides. "Who's it gonna be this time?" he wonders unnecessarily.

Nobody moves, as if all of them expect the door to burst open of its own accord. Finally, Djawara nods and rises to answer it. "Seems I'm the Gatekeeper here . . ."

An ordinary looking man in a plain gray uniform, neatly pressed, waits beneath the shredded awning, his billed cap in his hands. The stones are still falling, but none of them seem to be falling on him. "Your car, sir," says the man helpfully.

Djawara's impeccable poise finally wavers. "My . . . car?"

"Yes, sir." The man glances down at a slip of paper tucked inside his hat. "Says here, two passengers for the Grove, sir."

"Did you say, the Grove?"

"Yes, sir." He skins a look past Djawara's shoulder at the two staring faces inside. "Will that be three, sir?"

N'Doch comes up behind his grandfather. Out in the narrow street, a long, gleaming, sky-blue limo waits with its engine running. The stones aren't hitting it either. N'Doch shivers.

Djawara rolls marveling eyes toward Sedou. "Will we be three?"

Sedou nods.

Djawara turns back to the man with a courtly nod. "Three. Yes." He gestures casually at the rain of stones, as if stones fell every day of his life. "Would you care to come inside while we gather ourselves for the journey?"

"Oh, no, sir. Thank you, sir. I'll just wait right here, sir. No rush. Take your time."

No rush. Yeah, right. N'Doch can hear the urgent imperative hidden in the man's implacable courtesy. "She sent him, hunh? Hey, you didn't tell me your sister had style! And we're going?"

"Oh, yes." Sedou laughs. "I would say so."

N'Doch looks back at the sleek blue car. Its unblemished finish shines as if with its own light. It's the perfect embodiment of all he'd ever thought he wanted out of life. *But that was then.*

He sighs. *Hey, I've died once. How bad could it be a second time?*

He wraps grateful arms around the foundling guitar, puts his ear to the box to hear it hum its quiet, consoling song. It appeared just when he needed it. Like magic. Now, he's as ready as he'll ever be.

CHAPTER TWENTY-SIX

Paia cannot say clearly what makes her grasp the hand of the intemperate, murdering bully she had denied with such conviction not twelve hours ago. Or was it twelve days? It could have been weeks, for all she knows, she's so entirely lost track in this place where time seems somehow irrelevant. What she does know is that she's exhausted, dirty, hungry, and overwhelmed by a longing to be home again, no matter what the situation there might be.

I can do nothing useful here, she tells herself, reaching to lay her hand in Fire's palm. *At the Citadel, perhaps I still can.*

Paia has had little experience of life outside the narrow sociology of the Temple and the Citadel, but she's consumed enough of the House Computer's large stock of classic novels to understand at least secondhand that a young woman's first taste of freedom can result in a reckless plunge overboard. In the safety of Djawara's quaint café, as her dragon defiantly justifies his bloody deeds and flagrant dereliction of duty, Paia suddenly sees his actions as mirrored by her own. At that moment, her connection to him has never seemed more real or poignant. For what was leaving the Citadel if not a dereliction of duty? Or a denial of her proper destiny? Fire is her dragon. She is his guide. Her responsibility, her life's duty is to him, not to some stranger lord from a distant past. Nor even to the other dragons or their guides. If both she and Fire do owe allegiance to some larger Purpose, her best way to serve that Purpose is to fulfill her duty to her own dragon, in her own place in the continuum of time. Ironically, Fire would agree, the only difference being how that duty is defined.

And it's a major difference, she realizes, now that she's clear about it, but not so much in its particulars of behavior as in its intended result.

I had to come all this way to figure it out.

Paia consoles herself that her little rebellion was not entirely pointless. Of course, she fears what might happen should she meet Adolphus of Köthen again, face-to-face. Or even see him from a distance. Perhaps she gave in to her attraction to him with girlish abandon, but the attraction was real enough and certainly mutual. This is probably on her dragon's mind as well, which will make Köthen either a prime target, or someone to be avoided at all costs. It's a shame, Paia muses, that they must be rivals. For wasn't it Köthen's dragonlike qualities that made him so desirable? The perfect stand-in for the dragon lover she dreamed of but couldn't have. But now . . .

Paia recalls the heat of Fire's fingertips against her cheek. Now everything is different. Now she might actually have some power over him.

She lays her hand in his outstretched palm.

The sensation of falling goes on forever, falling not toward or into, but away from, falling until fall becomes flight, without up or down. The rush and lift of the wind beneath her wings is so thrilling that she soars deliriously for more endless moments, drifting in the thermals that rise off the dry, red cliffs. Then self-awareness stirs, and exhilaration gives way to fear.

!!

Her flight falters. Speed fading, altitude lost. A spinning plummet into a dive. Confusion and terror. Then amazement and gratitude as the great dragon body—hollow bones lighter than air, vast and glittering wingspread—turns back into the wind, catches a strong updraft and rises, exultant, laughing.

I SEE YOU'LL NEED SOME FLYING LESSONS.

It's as if he's right beside her. Not inside her head, but as if this scaled and gilded frame is a vehicle they both are driving. He's just taken over the wheel to save them from disaster.

!!

Speechless still, even inside herself. Sorting out identities, separating the physical entities. Words are useless until she's sure whose self they've come from. Is she the dragon, or merely resident inside the dragon's body? Is this a temporary manifestation, Fire's own mode of dragon transport, which he's never invited her to experience before, except as a threat of deportation and abandonment? Or is it some more permanent arrangement that she's unwittingly agreed to by placing herself, literally, in his hands?

As she struggles to form the question, Fire distracts her with a breathtaking surge of speed, wings billowing and snapping like the sails of an ancient galleon. Her heart fills with air and sky and freedom. Joy gives her back the words.

Could we have done this before?

ALWAYS.

Why not, then?

I DIDN'T TRUST YOU.

And now you do?

NOW IT DOESN'T MATTER.

Paia has had this thought also, without knowing where it came from, or exactly what it means. It wasn't just the dragon's touch. In the café, something changed, and now all things are different.

Why doesn't it matter? What happened?

DON'T THINK ABOUT IT NOW. THINK OF ME. ONLY OF ME.

The great wings pump. Higher, higher, past the soft mist of clouds into the darker blue of the sky, and then into a spiraling roll, as if tunneling through the air itself, or swimming, in water the temperature of blood. At once aware of wings and claws and scales and flight, and of two more human bodies within, rolling together, skin slick and hot, rolling entwined, pillowed by the wind, his forked tongue in her mouth, his gilded arms cradling her hips. Paia sighs and takes him inside her as they roll and soar and rock in ecstasy.

"It's all an illusion, of course," says Fire later, as the dragon body rests on an isolated windblown crag.

"My body doesn't think so."

His murmur suggests a self-congratulatory smirk. "Your body is an illusion. As is all matter."

Paia recalls her physics lessons only vaguely. "Some more so than other, then."

The illusion now is of their human bodies lying in the softest of beds, limbs entangled, slack with release. No sight, only sensation. Damp skin and whispers. And desire, so intense. Already, she wants him again.

"I mean our lovemaking is an illusion."

"I know." It's like receiving his thoughts, Paia notes, rather than sharing them. He still holds part of himself aloof.

"And yet, it's not. My energies have absorbed yours. Therefore, we are joined more fully than any normal lovers could be."

"Hush," she whispers, stroking him. "Don't talk."

"But I could as well have been describing this outer body. That, too, is an illusion, its design derived not from some magical genetics but from the darkest corner of human imaginings. Shaped to rule the souls of men."

The outer body lifts its reptilian head to arch and preen. Paia is the dragon again, showing off her sleek and sinuous neck, her magnificent form, proud of her powerful legs and tail. She stretches gilded wings and extends curved claws to whet their razor tips on a handy rock. Then the dragon settles down again and closes its eyes. Paia is released to a single consciousness. She doesn't mention how she prefers the shape of the man-body beneath her hands, the one she feels but cannot see. "You're trying to tell me something."

"My siblings and I are made of elemental energies. Our physical form is determined by the genetics and evolution of the human mind. We have no DNA of our own. So which came first, the dragon or its myth?"

"Is it a riddle?"

He pulls away slightly. "A basic truth."

"Does it matter? You are here." Now she's sure he's working his way around some bit of information he doesn't want to come right out and deliver. What now? She'd thought he'd told her the worst already.

"It matters to some. But in the long run, well . . ."

"Your siblings have different shapes." She had been about to say "kinder."

"No accounting for taste," he quips, but she senses an attempt to redirect her line of questioning.

"Why take any shape at all? I mean, why does it matter what shape you take? You could be one shape today, another tomorrow, like some people change their clothing. Water does it."

"No." He stirs brusquely, as if recalling some old grudge. "It's not my gift. Water *actually* changes. Her power is over matter. Mine is over minds. I had a choice and I made it, and that was that. Because . . . no, never mind. We have better things to do with our time."

"Because? Because?" She pushes his hands and mouth away with mock severity. "You can't leave me hanging!"

"Better for you if I do."

"I am you now, or so it would appear."

"Beloved, you always were."

"Then I should know what you know." She stretches against him like a cat. "You were saying, because . . . ?"

He rumbles his irritation, reminding Paia how very recently she feared doing anything that might displease him. Now what's left to fear? He's dissolved her already, and her consciousness appears intact and fully capable of sensation. Yes, fully indeed, she muses, as another tsunami of desire sweeps over her, rolling her against him. Astonishing, how desire can animate a body all of its own accord. Astonishing and wonderful. Still, she wishes she could see his eyes. They were always the surest gauge of his true mood. But his eyes are now her eyes, those great golden orbs lidded against the scouring winds of the heights. To test the extent of her control over the dragon body, she focuses her awareness of it and lifts one lid, thinking of it as a kind of giant window shade. The flood of light is blinding. The cold air sears. Fire growls in protest, and Paia closes the eye. Some control, then. But whose eye is it really? A perplexing dilemma.

"Am I to have my own body back, my own . . . self?"

"Is that what you wish?"

Just like him to twist a question into a complaint. "Whose choice is it?"

He shifts again. Another flare of silent irritation. Finally his voice comes muffled, as if from the depths of pillows. "Yours."

"Ah. You didn't want me to know that, did you? Among other things."

Silence. Yet, in their old days together, she got nothing at all from him if he didn't want to tell her. So even this little is progress. Wishing she knew more about the art of seduction, Paia puts her hands to work, and when it seems she has him pliant beneath her, she murmurs, "It's a lovely shape. It fits just right. But explain to me: why take any shape at all?"

He is a creature with a long habit of illusion, so bedsprings creak faintly as he twists away from her and up, to pace invisibly. Only the air moving across her cheek marks his passage. "Because," he says in a voice she recognizes, his angry voice, the voice of the God. "Because men need to be controlled! Because men are Nature's suicidal impulse! Because the history of the world would be so much shorter than it is to be already if terror and awe had never been given form and articulation!"

"And you did that?" she asks meekly.

"I am that!" His voice booms as if he's grown to fit the scale of his rage. "I am the terrible image of Nature uncontrolled and uncontrollable! The hint of awesome Powers beyond their ken! The threat of the dire consequences of misbehavior! A deterrent against greed and selfishness, against mankind's wanton thirst for power and taste for destruction! Terror and awe! Before there were gods, there were dragons!"

Now Paia is glad for the unnatural darkness around them, for how could she possibly conceal her utter dismay and disbelief? He cannot be unaware that most others, human and dragon, would level at him exactly the same accusations he's just thrown at mankind. Is this some new strategy of self-justification, an art she knows he's already well-practiced in?

"But what about the innocent humans? Not all can be blamed! All those innocent lives you've . . ."

"There are no innocents! All humanity is complicit in the death of the Earth, by inaction as much as by intent!" His volume dims, as if he's turned his back. "Besides, intimidation is not the same as murder. How often must I make this point? Count the dead, I tell you! You'll find that either their lives were willingly offered here in my own time where I can physically manifest, or they died in other times at the hand of some human gone out of control! If human nature is weak and corruptible, am I to blame?"

"But surely there are other myths you could have personified!" Part of her curses and accuses him, but another part accepts the tragic truth of all he says. "More . . . hopeful ones."

"That was my brother's theory, and Water's, too. And you see how successful they've been at keeping mankind in check. If it weren't for me . . . !"

Paia waits, for what seems an abnormal length of time. Perhaps there's a part of him that's lost faith in his pitiless rhetoric. "What?" she asks finally, and hears him sigh, long and dry, like a wind off a wasteland.

"Well, no method is perfect, when you're working with such fallible material as the hearts and minds of men. Sooner or later, some human or other wants his own piece of the terror and awe. And then there's no controlling them. They lose all respect for the natural order of the world, and the long doomward spiral has begun."

Paia thinks of the girl Erde, able at the direst moments to find an optimistic angle of view, or an excuse for positive action. *I am not that girl,* she decides. I have seen too much of the destruction men have brought about. I have lost my family to it, and the life I once knew. What convincing arguments can I pull together to counter his, when the evidence in his favor lies all around the Citadel, in the greedy hearts of its merchants and in the scheming minds of the Temple's priests and priestesses?

"I always wondered, even as a little girl, when you first arrived . . . I always wondered why the God was so angry all the time."

"Not *all* the time." His growl from the darkness is half-denial, half acknowledgment.

"Yes, all. All the time. Even in your most generous or frivolous moods, it was always there, that underground simmer of rage. I thought you were just mean."

"I am mean. I am the . . ."

"I know. The God." An uncomfortable pressure is building in Paia's chest. She reaches for a sheet to pull up around her shoulders, and finds it right there beneath her hand. Silk. "So you came to the Citadel to punish mankind for all they'd done?"

Fire laughs bleakly. "The world they've made seems punishment enough. Let them suffer in it. I came to the Citadel to enjoy myself while the planet still lives. And because you were there, dragon guide. You might say I had no choice. Perhaps a bit of revenge seemed excusable, under the circumstances, and since there was nothing better to do with my time . . ."

"But you became all and everything that you despise men for!" she cries out suddenly, and bursts into tears.

"Don't do that. Don't *do* that!"

"I can't help it! It's so . . . such a terrible waste!"

"Maybe I became what humanity deserves!" he shouts. "It's too late to change things now. Stop crying!"

Does she detect some faint stirrings of regret? Or does he simply mean it's too late for *him* to change? Paia hiccups and swallows a sob. "Earth and Water tell a different story."

"And I have told them, and you, the truth of that story. And a dragon cannot lie." He sits down beside her and draws the sheet aside. "Come, beloved, why concern ourselves with the fate of undeserving men? My siblings are fools to do so. I refuse to join them. My clever ingenuity has made a way for us to be together, at least for a while. Shouldn't we enjoy it while we can?"

A new concern saps Paia's resistance: wouldn't a dragon guide inevitably share her dragon's weaknesses as well as his strengths? "I suppose a little while longer can't make any difference. But do you think, my Fire," she adds only half playfully, "that you will be able to accept the responsibility of an actual relationship?"

He kisses her in reply, then fills her again, and again, and somewhere in their endless excess of orgasm, Paia realizes that they've had the argument he was willing to have, but meanwhile strayed completely from the questions she most wants an answer to: *Why now? What made me know to come to you so willingly? What's happened? What has changed?*

Chapter Twenty-Seven

The Librarian programs a tiny window through the blankness around him to watch the sky-blue limo glide away along the narrow, pitted street. He's programmed a longer journey than necessary for its passengers, a guided tour of the White City while he takes the time to rescue Stoksie and the others from the *machina rex,* and discover what Luther knows about Earth's whereabouts.

Now that he has a method, he works quickly and efficiently. He'll gather up the next ones in a group. He calls up the power grid diagram to trace out the Rex's location. He hunts up the nearest paver machine, and sends it a long set of radical instructions. Just before leaving, he remembers his video feed to the Citadel. He turns to find the old TV waiting behind him, like a patient family retainer. The screen frames a bright view of the Grand Stair and a great deal of commotion. The Librarian reflexively reaches for the volume control, then recalls that this signal has no sound. In the dust and pitiless sun, armed men are pouring up the steps toward the Temple. The Librarian can't even think of staying to watch, but he lingers long enough to observe that the vanguard of resistance has already crumbled. The soldiers guarding the stair have thrown down their weapons. Some seem to be greeting Leif Cauldwell's army as if they were old friends. It's possible, the Librarian muses. As if famine and epidemic weren't enough, the Firebreather's tyranny split families, estranged neighbors, destroyed the fabric of entire communities. There is a sporadic hail of arrows from the walls of the upper plaza, but perhaps Leif will have less of a battle than he was prepared for. All for the best . . . and still no flash of gold from

above, no vast dragon wing darkening the sky. What can
be keeping Fire, the Librarian wonders?

HURRY! HURRY!

Yes, yes, I will. I am.

When he opens the door this time, he's around the corner from the Rex's square. His transportation and rescue
vehicle is already waiting for him.

It's tall, gleaming, and yellow. Yellow like daylilies, or
the sun before global warming. It makes the Librarian
smile, something he's felt the need of for a while. It's a
replica of Luther's Tinker wagon, as accurately as he could
remember it, having only seen it in the lantern-lit darkness
of the great central cavern at the Refuge. Of course, he's
taken a few liberties. He's enlarged it substantially, to have
room inside the cargo box for a crowd. He's also beefed
up its armor to withstand potential Rex attacks. And if the
nanomechs had any real grasp of organic forms, they'd
never have produced a nasty looking mutant like the Rex.
So the Librarian has avoided replicating Luther's sturdy
mules. Instead, he's restored the old truck's propulsion system, substituting clean nanopower for its original filthy-
dirty internal combustion engine.

He shuts the door behind him and walks around his creation admiringly. Even the chipped paint and faded signage
is bright and new: *Schwann's Ice Cream.* The Librarian licks
his lips. He remembers ice cream.

HURRY! HURRY!

He's never been one to rush about. How did he get
matched with such an impatient dragon? He sighs, and
climbs up into the cab. It's been half a century since he's
driven a vehicle of any sort, but since the last one was an
armored personnel carrier, he figures an ice cream truck
should be a piece of cake. It'll come back to him quickly
enough. There's a key in the ignition, not bright and new,
but a match to the one Luther wears around his neck as
personal amulet and talisman. The Librarian grasps it
boldly and fires up the engine. Its nearly silent nano-hum
is so different from what he's expected that for a minute,
he's sure nothing's working. Then he feels the soft and
steady vibration. He slips into gear, gingerly presses the
accelerator, and the old/new truck rolls obediently forward.
Down the length of the street, the Librarian gains

confidence . . . and speed. Enough to come careening into the square with some doubt still in his mind that he'll find the Tinkers there with the women and dogs. But he's proved to himself that N'Doch's song was not imagined, so probably the women and dogs are real, and Luther, too. As real as anything can be said to be in the white nano-city.

And there they are. The Rex has rebuilt enough of its damaged circuits to begin a random, self-protective flailing of knife-edged limbs. The women have wisely drawn back, hauling their dead and wounded to the square's perimeter. He counts two bodies at least. Stoksie and Luther turn at the approaching squeal of tires as if sure it's a new attack from the rear, then stare dumbfounded as the Librarian screeches to a halt in front of them. He tumbles out of the cab, pointing madly without explanation. The Rex is waking, waking!

"Get in! Get in!" he shouts. Later, he'll tell them all that's happened, if he can find the words.

Stoksie is stunned to immobility. "Weah'd yu cum frum, G? I t'ought yu wuz . . ."

"No! Not dead! Quick! Hurry! Get the women!" He grabs Luther, who stands entranced by this altered vision of his beloved and familiar wagon, and hauls him around to the rear. "Open it! You know how!"

No strangers to wonder or emergency, the Tinkers spring into action. As the Rex rediscovers coordination by gnashing its jaws and retracting and extending its claws, Stoksie enlists Lily and Margit with nod and gesture to help him herd the others toward the big yellow vehicle. They're willing to trust the dark little stranger, whom they've lately seen bashing the metal monster with a pike. The dogs are less willing, however, and Lily, burdened with one of their wounded, is forced to be stern with them before they'll leap blindly into the dark cave of the rear cargo box. The Rex finishes testing its systems. Its sensor-laden head swivels toward the source of sound and motion.

"Hurry!" the Librarian calls. Or is it his dragon's urgency he's giving voice to? The borderlines are blurring.

Luther and Margit insist on delaying long enough to load the dead.

"Mebbe he'll fix 'em," Luther says. "He did sum al'reddy."

He means Earth, the Librarian realizes. "Yes! Hurry!" The Rex is moving toward them, gaining speed fast. He leaves them to finish up, and stumbles for the cab. He's just started the engine when he hears the rear doors slam. Luther vaults into the passenger seat, just ahead of the Rex's vicious sidearm slash. He ducks, grabs for the door, and pulls it tight. Steel claws rake the window, screech across the armored side. The truck sways wildly.

"Go!" Luther yells.

The Librarian floors it.

The Rex pursues them for a while, swift on the straightaway, but tending to madly overshoot its turns. Taking evasive action, the Librarian gets lost several times, with the Tinkers hotly debating the route and Margit and Lily swearing up and down that the streets have changed since the trip out. The Librarian offers them the minor consolation that they're probably right. No knowledge is permanent here, and nothing is to be trusted. Also, he's noticed something else. The city's machined perfection seems to be breaking down. Entire townhouses disintegrating. Highrises developing gaping holes in their upper reaches. And, here and there, as they've sped past, he's seen places where the nano repair machines are not replicating the bland building facades as they were before. Instead, the new portions reflect a much more alien geometry, as if the nanos' memory of buildings designed by and for humans has failed, or stranger still, been jettisoned intentionally. The Librarian wonders if he needs to start worrying about the city's life-support systems.

"Yu gottit! Lost 'im, I t'ink." Luther hangs out the side window, searching for signs of the Rex.

Stoksie pokes his head through the hatch between front and back. "Yu gotta turn back leff, nah."

The Librarian accesses the grid map to locate a concentration of nano power lines in the general direction that all describe. Eventually this guides them to the dank courtyard and the stone archway that all agree leads to Deep Moor. Here, too, in the fabric of this nano re-creation, the Librarian sees anomalies: blank spots in the drystone masonry, or patches of circuitry mingling with mossy cobbles in the court.

He pulls up in front of the iron gate. Luther jumps down to open the cargo doors. Lily and Margit pile out and through the arch, calling for help. But Margit is back soon, too soon, and Raven is with her, her lovely face tense with worry that eases with surprise and delight when she sees who's come.

"Gerrasch! Oh, it's you! I mean, it's you and yet it isn't. Just look at you! What a marvel!" She smiles, holding out both hands. "Quite the figure of a man you've become!"

The Librarian presses her fingers between his soft palms, and blushes.

Margit says, "He's not here!"

"He's not?"

"Gone!" exclaims Margit desperately.

Raven grasps the scout's sleeve. "Shhh! Don't tell them. Don't worry! Linden will do all she can."

"She can't bring back the dead!"

"Shhh! Shhh, dear!"

"You should have kept him here!" Margit jerks her arm free and stalks away to help unload.

"Had I known, I . . ."

"Where is he?" The Librarian has definitely planned on Earth being here.

Raven's eyes follow the wounded being carried through the gateway. "Gone again. Both of them. Without a word to any of us."

"Why? Why?" His demand is more to the dragon inside him than to poor, distraught Raven, who looks further stricken anyway.

"Why, indeed! I can't fathom it! Especially when they knew the rescue party had been sent out after you!"

Should have acted sooner! Should have got here faster! The Librarian knows his reaction time is down, way down. But it's hard, after so many millennia of waiting, of living in slow motion. He vows to work on it.

"I'll find them," he promises, to whomever's still listening.

"And odd things are happening here, too," Raven continues. "I mean, the whole place is odd to begin with. At first, we were constantly finding more and more of Deep Moor. You'd go through a gate or a door and discover a garden or a room that hadn't been there moments before. But now, parts of it are disappearing. There's less and less of it. What do you think it means?"

"I don't know," the Librarian lies. Then he climbs back into the yellow truck to concentrate on programming a new sort of search.

CHAPTER TWENTY-EIGHT

With enormous misgivings, Erde pictures the Grove in her mind, paying proper attention to its most telling details. She has failed to talk the dragon out of answering this latest summons, though she tells herself she shouldn't call it failure, since that would imply that she'd had some vague chance of succeeding. As gentle and diffident as Earth appears at most times, when decided on something, he's as stubborn as a rock and cannot be dissuaded, however foolish she might consider his chosen course.

Erde's final warning concerns the stretch of years from this far future to her far-away past, and the risk of arriving in the midst of a dangerous situation already half-felled by weakness and nausea from the long journey. The dragon promises he will protect her, and how can she insult him by questioning his ability to do so? It's a shame that the law of dragon transport does not permit her to travel any farther back in her own time than she has already lived in it. She cannot, for instance, send the dragon to the Grove as it was when she first saw it. It must be to the Grove of snow and ice and cold, and the black ashes of Deep Moor. At least she has thought of a backup plan.

So, sensing doom in every nerve ending, Erde tells the dragon she's ready, then offers up her image of the Grove: solemn, majestic and, even in the smothering snow, heart-breakingly lovely.

She has chosen a smaller side clearing as their specific destination, away from the central pond and the broad, open meadow where the portal to the city had opened. Given his ever expanding size, the dragon will just barely fit under the arch of the great spreading limbs, but there they might manage to arrive undetected if Fra Guill and his forces are still about, at least for long enough that she might recover her balance. But when they arrive, though Erde's travel illness is mild this time, the trees are much thinner than she's remembered. She barely has a moment to catch her breath and stand steadily on both feet, when a cry goes up from the meadow.

Dragon! We are discovered!

Hastily, she tells him her backup plan.

NO. NOT YET. WE MUST WAIT FOR THE OTHERS.

But surely you can see! There's no one here but white-robes and soldiers!

Brother Guillemo's army is encamped across the meadow, and all around the sacred pond. Their equipment and personal kits are strewn across the snow like garbage. Their heavy-footed warhorses have trampled the once-flowering verge of the pond into mud. Their boots and tents and lumbering supply wagons have crushed the delicate forest grasses and flattened the meadow into a field of rutted ice. And now Erde sees why the thick lattice of branches did not conceal them. Raw stumps protrude through the dirty snow where several vast and ancient giants have fallen to the ax. Cook fires and campfires dot the clearings, blackening the tender earth and sending up dark billows of smoke to blur the air.

Oh, the trees! They're killing the trees! Oh, dragon, what are we to do?

The dragon, too, is stunned.

How could such sacrilege have been allowed to happen? Could not the Grove protect itself? Is the hell-priest's power so very great?

In her grief and horror, Erde for a moment forgets her own peril. The alert soldiers who'd spotted them spring up and reach for their weapons. They kick dozing neighbors awake and send word of intruders down the line. Messengers race toward the cluster of tents, blindingly white, taking up the center of the meadow. The nearest men brandish their pikes and glower, but they do not advance. They glance behind, awaiting reinforcements.

They fear you, dragon, but you'll see. Once their numbers give them courage, they'll be on us like a swarm!

OR THEY WILL WAIT FOR THEIR LEADER TO APPROACH.

Their leader. Erde can feel him there, sniffing her out. She could point directly to the tent he hides in, not the biggest—the decoy—but that scruffier one off to the side.

No! We can't wait for him! We can do nothing here without the others. Let's go! We must wait until they come!

The first reinforcements have come up. At a shouted signal, the soldiers lockstep toward them, pikes and lances leveled. The dragon is hemmed in by trees. There is no possibility of retreat. For once, Earth is sensible, and relents.

An instant later, they are on a wide stone ledge high above the valley, overlooking the old downward trail. Once this was a faint and secret track that kept Deep Moor hidden from the world of men. Now, it's trampled raw and wide, obvious even to the unskilled eye. An icy wind scours the ledge, but Erde has her old woolen clothes and the dragon for warmth. She leans against him disconsolately and knuckles away tears she can't control. From this ledge, she'd beheld Deep Moor for the very first time. She wonders if she can bear any more sadness, any further loss.

Ah, dragon, I feel as if nothing good will ever happen again!

Earth lifts his horned head from a perusal of the battered trail. THEN LOOK OUT THERE, AND BE GLAD!

Far out in the middle of the valley, where the snow-flecked trees nestle in a bend of a silver ribbon of river, a further army spreads in a closed circle around the Grove. A protective circle, Erde assumes, the overflow of Fra Guill's numberless legions. She cannot imagine why the sight of more tents and men and wagons littering her beloved valley should make her anything but horrified, and tells the dragon so between her sobs.

THEN LOOK CLOSER.

She does so, if only to please him, then sags against his foreclaw with a gasp. *Do I see it right? Is that the king's standard flying above that red and gold pavilion?*

The dragon assents gravely, as if this joy might be too fleeting to admit to.

Oh! And do you see . . . ?

A LITTLE TO THE LEFT. He helps direct her gaze, not so keen as his over distances.

"I see it!" she cries aloud, grasping Earth's claw to keep from pitching wildly over the ledge. The red dragon crest of Baron Weisstrasse flutters bravely among a cluster of smaller tents. "Hal! Sir Hal! Oh, listen to me! As if he could hear me! You see? I told you he would come to rescue Deep Moor!" She says nothing of him arriving too late, after Deep Moor is already in ashes and its women fled. That he is here is enough to lift her spirits. "Let's go to him immediately!"

THESE SOLDIERS WILL FEAR ME MUCH AS THE OTHERS DID.

Then take me partway, and I'll walk in alone to find him. We'll let Sir Hal introduce you to his men. Imagine how proud he'll be!

PERHAPS.

Now it's Earth's turn to be dubious, but he sets her down along the icy road, a decent distance from the encampment, then instantly stills himself to invisibility. The wind cuts cruelly across the valley floor, but Erde gathers her woolen layers about her, and with as much grandeur as she can muster, marches toward camp.

The outermost pickets are too cold and battle-weary to offer more than a halfhearted challenge, plus a few perfunctory leers. Erde does not offer her name. When last she was here, her father was the king's enemy. But when she asks, with the grace and dignity learned from her grandmother the baroness, to be directed to the compound of Baron Weisstrasse, the three guards are intimidated into silence and pointing.

Only when she is walking away does one sneer, "'*Compound.*' Get her, willya?"

"Likes 'em old, I guess," mutters another.

"And crazy," adds his friend.

"You'd be better off with me," the third calls, now that her back is to them.

Erde lets it be that way. She can't blame these broken soldiers for their lewd assumptions. No lady of her station would travel on foot in such weather, never mind without her lady's maid and several stout retainers for escort. No lady would dress as she is dressed, with her short curls unbound to the wind beneath her sheepskin hood. She tries to see herself as those men had seen her. She's grown quite tall, she realizes, measuring her height against the soldiers, who'd seemed dwarfish by comparison, battered and underfed. She has forgotten her lady's mincing steps, and now strides like a boy. No wonder they jump to the only conclusions they have definitions for. To them, she must be a camp follower. She's an exotic, a freak. If she looks them in the eye, and doesn't smile coquettishly or flinch, perhaps she is even a witch.

But the surprise is, she's beautiful. At least, to battle-weary soldiers, she is. She can see it in their eyes. It makes her stand straighter and walk along with a more confident step, if only not to disappoint their expectations, as their stares follow her down the road.

The second round of sentries have a tent and a sputtering fire built in its lee to huddle about. These have strength enough to stop her and question her more fully about her business. There are also more of them, and they leer with more serious intent. One tries to rub his hands on her, under the pretext of searching for weapons.

"I do have a weapon," she declares, revealing but not unsheathing the heavy dagger she's worn since she traded her ancestral brooch for Sir Hal's sword in a dusty market town far in the future. Köthen now carries the dragon-hilted sword. In its place, she got the dagger, which had belonged to his captain, a man called Wender. Erde thinks of Köthen now, as she says sternly, "And I will use it, in the king's name, if you do not stand aside and let me pass!"

The soldiers laugh uproariously. Her defiance only whets their appetite. Four of them form a ring around her and smack their lips over all the "favors" they'll extract from her, which they describe in lingering detail. She should be terrified, but she knows she can call a dragon down on them in seconds flat. She stands still, waiting with exaggerated patience while the men argue, with increasing heat and distraction, over which of them will "have" her first. Finally, she sees her opportunity. She shoves hard at the shoulders of the two loudest and shocks them into momentary recoil. In a breath, she's past them and drawing her dagger, rounding on them threateningly. As soon as she's done it, she's amazed at herself. Little Erde, throwing her weight around. For the second time that day, she tells herself: *Won't Hal be pleased!*

"The king shall hear of this," she rebukes them haughtily, though she has never met her infirm and elderly liege, who might have little sympathy for the daughter of his enemy, Josef von Alte. "Or Baron Weisstrasse," she adds. "If you will direct me in his way now, nothing more shall be said of this."

A couple of the soldiers snicker.

"Yeah?" says one beefy guard, "And what's that crazy old coot gonna do to me?"

But his smaller neighbor elbows him warningly. "Wender," he mutters. "He'll do it to you, and you won't forget it."

Some of the others nod their agreement. Erde is delighted to hear Captain Wender mentioned. It must be the same man, she's sure of it. She can see their enthusiasm for her has dimmed. She's looking like too much trouble to be further bothered with, and so, she presses the advantage. "Well, then, if you haven't the decency to direct me to Baron Weisstrasse, will you tell me at least where I can find Captain Wender?"

The smaller man steps forward, but only to send her farther along the road. "You'll want to go on down that way, milady, and take the first right."

Erde thanks him graciously, as if no unseemly incident has passed between them. She leaves him smiling, quizzically and much against his better judgment, and continues onward, trying not to rush. There are tents and wagons rising to either side by now, and soon she is passing the taller canopies of the minor nobles, more spacious and artfully decorated, with clusters of warhorses tethered alongside. But these finer tents are as stained and many-times mended as the lesser ones, and the poor horses are hunched together against the cold and look as starved as all the men.

She takes the turn as directed, narrowly avoiding being run down by a young man on horseback whose armor looks much too big for him. Finally, in the distance, above a row of shorter canvas shelters, Erde sees Hal's silken banner stretching boldly in the hard north wind. Now she can't help but quicken her step, with her gaze downcast as much for seeming modesty as to keep her balance among the icy wagon ruts, which are wide and treacherously full of half-frozen mud. Surely there must be a few women of virtue among this spread of apparently lawless men! Who else, she wonders, will care for the sick and wounded? Who will say prayers for the dying?

With this mournful thought, Erde glances up to be sure of her path. Ahead of her, a tall man is flinging orders at a scurrying group of unwilling boys, squires, perhaps, or scullery lads. She is reminding herself that there is no scullery to be had for leagues about, when she realizes with a shock that the faded tunic that the big man wears over his battered mail was once the sky blue and gold of Castle Köthen. Quickly, her memory sorts out the man's broad back and burly frame.

"Captain Wender!" she calls, though she knows it's hardly ladylike. "Captain Wender!"

The man has been shouting at the boys. His scowl lingers as he turns, then evaporates abruptly as he recognizes her. To Erde's surprise, an even fiercer expression replaces it, a sudden and desperate bloom of hope.

Erde quails before its brilliance. *Oh, dear. He thinks I've brought his baron back.*

"Milady!" Wender banishes the boys to their errands, then hurries toward her. His frown has returned. "Milady! Alone, and on foot?"

She gazes up at him for a long and helpless moment. "Alone. Yes."

Wender's mouth sets in something like despair. "Then how came you . . . ?"

"I came. . . ." Then it comes to her. It's the *dragon* he's hoping for. "I left Lord Earth a ways away, so as not to frighten the soldiers."

Wender sags as if every breath has gone out of him. "Then he is with you? The . . . the dragon?" When she nods, puzzled by his vehemence, he rushes on with little of his usual deference. "Then you must bring him, milady! Quickly! The knight has need of him!"

"Sir Hal? What? Why?"

"Cut near to death a day ago, milady, and won't lie still! If there's even hope of his mending, he won't give it a chance! I beg you, milady, call in your creature!"

"I doubt even Lord Earth could convince Hal to lie still if he doesn't wish to," Erde says.

"I mean to heal him! Please! Quickly! He's dying!"

"Dying?" Finally, she takes in Wender's haggard look. She's been so wrapped up in anticipation of a fond reunion with her elder knight that she hasn't properly listened. "*Dying?* Oh, sweet Mother, help us! Take me to him, and we'll summon the dragon immediately!"

CHAPTER TWENTY-NINE

The limo's ride is the smoothest he's ever known . . . not that he's actually been inside one before, so okay, it's smoother than he's ever imagined. N'Doch tunes the interior lights up and down on their dimmer just for the hell of it, then lounges back on the soft, dark blue leather, so real you can smell it. Room enough for his whole body, plus the guitar. Room enough between the seats for the full stretch of his legs. He grins at his grandfather, perched opposite him.

"Okay, now, Papa, why don't you just pop open that cooler beside you and see what's inside?"

Djawara is still regarding his tall grandson as if he's not sure they're related. He glances at Sedou next to him, for support. But the man/dragon is gazing out the window, frowning in thought.

"C'mon, Papa! Maybe there's nothing. You oughta look, at least!"

"There'll be water," Sedou murmurs from the depths of his brown study, as Djawara bends disapprovingly to search the compartment between their seats. And there is, but only water. Three chill blue bottles bright with tiny bubbles. Djawara passes them around. N'Doch takes his and inspects the label.

"You were expecting something stronger?"

"Nah, Papa, you know me. Not much of a drinker." He doesn't jump to the bait like usual. Feels like he's done arguing over small stuff. Can't see the point anymore.

The car purrs forward though identical streets, and the men sip their water in silence. The driver's head never moves. N'Doch knows this 'cause he has the forward facing seat, and he's been watching. The dude's as still as glass. Like he's a robot or something. N'Doch strums the guitar absently, picking out a mournful little tune. Finally he says, "So, I'm waiting, bro."

Sedou stirs. "Waiting?"

"For that explanation I figure you owe me." N'Doch shifts his gaze, which he hopes looks accusing enough to win him an answer. "Or maybe you can tell me, Papa, since you seem so tuned in on the dragon hot line."

"Hardly, my boy. I just pay attention."

This time the bait is hard to ignore. N'Doch shoots a look back at Sedou. "Is he in on this 'mutual annihilation' gig, too? 'Cause if he's not, I think he oughta just . . ."

"Look!" Sedou leans forward, his attention caught by something outside the window.

It might be a diversionary tactic, but N'Doch checks it out anyway. Between two faceless building facades, he sees a flash of rock and darkness. Then the limo has rolled on past, and it's just the usual bit of boredom out there.

"What was that?"

Sedou is frowning again.

"You notice how it's never night here?" The uncanny blackness between the buildings lingers in N'Doch's mind. "I mean, we got to have been here long enough for it to get dark out, doncha think?"

"I suspect," says Djawara, "that if you asked for night in the right way, you would get it. If you actually *needed* night, for instance."

Sedou nods silently.

"Like you needed your espresso?" N'Doch laughs, though none of this seems particularly funny right now. "It's like a big hologram, isn't it? Like, y'know, the holodeck." He's remembering the old vids.

"More material than that." Sedou turns the blue bottle in his hand. "More *actual*. But my real concern is, why is it breaking apart?"

"Is it?" Djawara asks.

Sedou gestures at the buildings gliding past. "That . . . space we saw. An anomaly. Like a hole in the fabric of this particular reality."

"A hole?" N'Doch looking hard, now, to find another one. "Where does the hole go to?"

Sedou shrugs. "To another layer of the illusion? Or, I suppose, it could be to . . . actual reality."

"I challenge you to define that satisfactorily," Djawara chuckles.

"You mean the world outside?" N'Doch goes for a more literal interpretation. "It looked awful . . . y'know, empty."

"Barren. Airless, you might almost say."

"What's airless?"

"Lacking an atmosphere," Sedou supplies patiently.

"I know that! I mean, why?"

"Look!"

They all stare as another 'hole' slides by. This one is taller and wider, exposing a brief but definitive glimpse of a raw, red landscape, dust and rock, illuminated by a hard white light. Not a single speck of relieving green.

"Sky's a weird color," N'Doch observes. "Not black, exactly, but . . ." He thinks of the old photos of lunar landings, ancient history in his day. "That's what you mean by airless, huh?"

"That's what I mean."

The weirdest thing, N'Doch decides, is that right after the facade bordering the hole, there's a crossing street, which extends away from the intersection as if the city had turned a corner around this "anomaly," as the dragon called it. The contrast blows his whole perception of three-dimensional space.

No, wait, that's not the weirdest thing . . .

N'Doch's head slews around, trying to stay level with the view down the next intersection, where he's just seen, or thinks he's seen . . .

Nah. Can't be. A Tyrannosaurus Rex? *Now I'm really losing it!*

It was remembering those vids, that's what did it. Like when he first laid eyes on Water and was so sure she was a special effect. He decides not to mention this, to her or his grandfather.

The glass panel between the driver's seat and the rear compartment whispers aside. The driver leans sideways to speak through the opening. "I beg your pardon, sirs, but I thought you'd like to know: there's been a destination change."

"Really?" asks Sedou. "Who says?"

"My principal, sir. Straight from headquarters."

N'Doch rolls his eyes at his grandfather.

"And our new destination?" Sedou pursues.

"Says here, 'Deep Moor,' sir."

"That'll be fine. Thank you."

"Thank you, sir. You're welcome."

"Robot!" mutters N'Doch, as the glass panel slides shut.

"Quite possibly," Sedou agrees.

N'Doch stretches back against his seat and regards the man/dragon owlishly. "Well, going back to Deep Moor's all right with me. Might get some answers there. Those witchy ladies know a thing or two. 'Course, we gotta worry about them being okay. Wasn't only my people the Fire dude was after." He says it lightly to ward off his shiver. He'd really rather not find any more good women with holes in their foreheads.

"I'd give you answers if I had any," Sedou growls.

"And you don't."

"Don't sound so dubious."

"Something passed between you and Fire back at the Rive. And don't be telling me you were just catching up on old times."

"It was my sister . . . when we both sensed she was free. It blew his mind, and he couldn't quite keep it from me. Beyond that, I have innuendo, half-truth, implication, and guesswork? No."

"Never mind." N'Doch slumps back and draws the guitar across his chest like a shield. He's thinking how like Sedou the dragon's become, how . . . human. Like the taking on of a human biology has changed her more than just physically. She didn't used to hold back on him for the sake of his feelings. "Hey, bro," he calls softly across the chasm between the seat banks. "You gonna need a song any time soon, you think?"

Sedou gives him a long, deep look, the dragon gazing at him through the man's dark eyes. "Might be, bro. Might be."

"Now here is an interesting neighborhood," remarks Djawara suddenly.

N'Doch feels the car slowing. They're into another district of narrow streets. Narrow and twisty, with twin ruts worn into the paving stones, and dirty water flowing in the gutters. And animal signs: the occasional manure pile, though none of it looks very recent. N'Doch tries to lower the window beside him, and runs into the first thing about his dream car that doesn't work. Broken? He somehow doubts it. Probably if he tried the door, he'd get the same result. Is it a trap, or just a safety precaution? He's just about to air this latest anxiety when the car rounds a particularly tight corner and turns into a circular courtyard, dark and dank, and bounded by high stone walls. At least most of it's stone. Here and there, N'Doch sees odd patches of what looks like electronic microcircuitry, enlarged a billion times. He squints as the car sweeps past a nearby one. It's big, taller than he is. Maybe it's some kind of art, set into the walls.

He's distracted as the driver pulls around and stops beside the only other vehicle N'Doch has seen since setting foot in the city. He lets out a snort of recognition. The thing is twice the size he remembers, and a whole lot brighter, but he knows what he's looking at, sure enough.

"This sure ain't Deep Moor, but hey, check it out! There's Luther's old caravan. Looks like he got himself a new paint job!"

When he tries the car door, it works just fine. The driver's already popped out of his seat to open the door on Sedou's side. N'Doch wonders idly if the robot will expect a tip. But as soon as they're all out and standing expectantly on the broad, wet stones paving the yard, the driver tips his cap neatly, climbs back into the limo, and drives off. N'Doch stares after it. He misses the blue leather seats and the soft ride already.

"This way," Sedou calls. "She's this way."

Making a quick inspection tour around the big yellow caravan, N'Doch sees the man/dragon vanishing through a tall stone arch. Its nasty-looking iron grille is partially ajar. Djawara waits at the opening, his calm eyes not entirely able to contain their amazement. Is it what's inside, or what's outside, or the contrast between? N'Doch cups the old man's elbow and escorts him through the gate. He's getting more than used to walking through strange doorways into unexpected places. This time, he finds a rich green lawn and a cluster of old trees, half-concealing a low-slung dwelling. The house he recognizes, with its big stone chimney, and some of the outbuildings and barns. But others seem to be missing, and it had been deep winter at Deep Moor when he was there: bleak, leafless, and monochromatic. This symphony of green and bloom and fragrance stops him in his tracks by the gate. He liked the place enough before, but now . . . ! All his senses go on overdrive—eyes, ears, nose, bathed in lusciousness. The air is sweet in his lungs, and the touch of the sun on his cheeks is gentle, like a caress. It's all he can do to keep himself from racing off and rolling in the grass. No wonder the girl always talked like this place was paradise!

Djawara gently jogs him out of his daze. "We're waited on, I believe."

There's a big crowd up by the house, full of people N'Doch recalls, and some he doesn't. He's relieved to see Raven and Rose, and most of the women he'd known there, alive and well. He sees Luther and Stoksie and heads their way, not even bothering to ask himself how the hell they got here. He looks for Erde and the Big Guy, but they don't seem to be around. The real surprise is Gerrasch, who N'Doch thought would never willingly leave his technohaven in the Refuge. He's got mirrorshades on, and he and Sedou seem to be having some sort of reunion, which is interesting, since N'Doch can't recall Gerrasch ever having met Water in his brother's shape before. What's more interesting, everybody else is watching, with near-breathless anticipation.

"Whazzup?" He eases in between Stoksie and Luther, short and tall, as if he's left them only yesterday. Fact is, it *could* have been yesterday, for all he can tell.

"Itz her! Itz da One!" Luther is beaming.

"The one? You mean, Air? Where?"

Stoksie nods at Sedou and Gerrasch. "Itz G. He's gotter in 'im. Or so he sez."

"In him?" N'Doch knows he can test the truth of this. He can ask Water on the old dragon internet. He can ask Gerrasch, for that matter, guide to guide. But they both look pretty busy, plus he's even more reluctant than usual. If it's true, Air will be there, too. A whole new dragon voice to contend with, a whole new variety of invasion. And this one's the one they've gone through all this to find, the one who has, everyone keeps assuring him, all the answers. He tells himself he oughta let the dragons do their catching up in private anyway.

"How'd she get loose?"

"G diddit. Sumhow."

Luther's sigh is soft with admiration and awe. "He tuk her spirit wit'in 'im."

N'Doch can't think of anything worse, but he respects Luther enough to keep that irreverence to himself. Besides, Gerrasch is different from the other guides. He's already half dragon, so maybe it doesn't bother him as much. "But he's still . . . he's still, y'know . . . still Gerrasch?"

"Yah," Stoksie marvels. "Seems like it."

"Huh. So where's Erde and the Big Guy? Looks like everyone else is here, and I wouldn't think they'd want to be missing this."

"Gone." Stoksie shakes his head, then scrapes his hand over its shining baldness. "Gone. G's not reel happy 'bout dat."

"You mean they were, but . . . gone where?"

"Doan know fer shur. Dat lady . . ." Stoksie points out Raven, N'Doch's fantasy woman, who looks more worn and anxious than he's ever seen her. "She t'inks dey wenta . . . weah izzit, Luta?"

"Da Grove," Luther intones solemnly.

"Makes sense. The summons. That's where we were headed." N'Doch would love to spin out the tale of the sky-blue limo, but he senses this just ain't the time for it.

"Da reel Grove," says Luther, grimmer than before.

"So? What's the problem?"

"Dat wacko preechur iz dere. An' heeza bad'un, all ri'. I saw 'im."

"Didja? Fra Guill?" N'Doch is curious. "I ain't had the pleasure yet."

"Well," drawls Stoksie darkly, "I t'ink yu gonna gettit reel soon."

CHAPTER THIRTY

It seems a very long and languid time before the novelty of actual lovemaking wears off, and Fire recalls that he has a war to fight. But though his mind returns to the subject increasingly, he is still easily distracted by a caress or a heated glance. In between, he is content to expound at length about his superior strength and winning strategy, more willing to boast of the dedication and ferocity of his loyal followers than to rush to join them on the field. Paia is bemused by how easily she has conquered. It cannot be her shapely body and her loving alone. She's not that good at it yet. Observing Fire from as clear-eyed an angle as she can manage, she would swear she detects signs of exhaustion in the slow way he gathers himself at last to return to the fray.

"Well, they will be looking for me to claim the victory. Make a few decorative passes over the battlefield. Incinerate a few prisoners."

"You won't!"

"Why not? Think how much it will cheer the priestlings to see their old chief go up in flames."

She pulls away from him, wrapping the sheet around her shoulders. "Do you plan to carry me with you to this battle?"

"I can hardly leave you here on this barren mountaintop."

He draws suggestively on the sheet, but Paia holds it fast. "You cannot expect me to war against my own cousin!"

"You won't be fighting him, I will."

"But it will be as if I was fighting him." Perhaps an argument can be her next delaying tactic.

Fire lifts an arm over her shoulder and draws his sharp nails lightly down her back. "You would not fight him to reclaim your exalted status as my priestess? To regain your ancestral home?"

"I hate being a priestess." She tries to sound prim and disapproving, when all she wants is to press herself against him. "And Leif wants the Citadel for all the Cauldwells, myself included. From there, he can provide help and shelter for all who come to him in need."

"Very noble," murmurs Fire into the curve of her hip. "But a waste of valuable and vanishing resources. With so little time left to us, I have no intention of allowing my hard-won luxuries to be shared out among the worthless and inept who can't find a way to take care of themselves. Death to the weak," he says, taking her nipple in his mouth.

"But fighting wastes resources, too."

"Ah, but it results in fewer mouths to feed."

Paia summons a vastness of will and pushes him away. "Listen, my Fire. Couldn't you work out some sort of truce? That way bloodshed could be prevented and the resources be conserved. If you swore on your honor as a dragon not to harm anyone . . ."

Fire falls backward on the bed, spread-eagled in a cascade of helpless guffaws. "On my honor?"

"But I'm serious. I could ask my cousin. I'm sure he . . ."

"No." He looks up at her, his laughter fading. "Come now, beloved. You're not actually suggesting that I share my palace with a legion of dregs and riffraff? That I live at the sufferance of my former slave?"

"Not a slave! He . . ."

"Subordinate, then! Servant! Stop splitting hairs!"

"The Temple ran smoothly due to my cousin's inspired management! You'd never have been able to carry it off without him. You should be more grateful!"

"GRATEFUL?" Fire is on his feet and pacing before Paia can blink. "But for me, he'd have starved with the rest of the riffraff! He's the foulest of traitors! He destroyed the Temple! He betrayed me and all who believed in me!"

She can offer him no denial on that count, and the usual excuses and explanations will only enrage him further. But

Fire seems to have lost his relish for impassioned debate, as if even he senses that his accusations are growing repetitive and stale. Instead of heating up his diatribe against the ex-priest, higher and higher to the point of threats and invective, he slumps and turns away with a hiss of frustration. "Besides, even if Cauldwell did let us live in peace until the end comes, my siblings will be after me soon enough. With the end so near, they'll never let me rest."

"They're well occupied with the search for Air, my Fire." Paia has seen for herself the other dragons' capacity for obsession. Though its focus differs radically, it is the match to his own.

But Fire, wandering in the shadows, shakes his head. "Not anymore."

"What? Why not?"

He turns away again, waiting so long to answer that his reluctance is finally obvious. "My clever sister has found her own way to freedom."

"You didn't tell me."

"No. I didn't."

Because you're ashamed, guesses Paia. *Because now there's a real possibility you've failed. It's three against one now.* That's *what's changed.*

"How did she get out?"

He flicks an impatient hand. "What does it matter?"

And Paia thinks, *His real shame is that he doesn't know. She's outwitted him.* "So, then . . ."

"So there'll be no deals. No truces. What's the point? It's all or nothing now."

"But why?"

"Because!"

"Really, my Fire. You sound like . . ." She can't find a stinging enough comparison. "Well, you're being completely unreasonable."

"And this surprises you?"

"I thought perhaps . . ." She falters, knowing the words will sound foolish.

"Perhaps what?' He stalks out of the shadows to loom over her with his hair wild and his arms folded across his chest. He is looking less . . . *human,* she notes. More like his familiar scaled and gilded man-form. "You thought I would give in? Give up? You thought you'd *tamed* me?

You and that sage old fool back in the café: you expect me to wax suddenly reasonable for the good of humanity? Humanity doesn't deserve my charity. Besides, what's the point of reason at the end of the world? Beloved, you forget who you're dealing with!"

Paia droops. She smooths the silky bedsheet with her hand. She is not disappointed. She has done the best she could. She only hopes it will be enough. "No, my Fire. I do not forget."

"Good. See that you don't! Enough of this. I'm bored. We're off to war! My faithful are waiting!"

And she is aloft again, instantly, her protest swept away by the wonder of flight. Again she is the great winged beast gliding over the ragged hills, where the only color is the red and yellow and gray of stone and the dust-thick windblown sky. Having now walked a landscape softened by trees, even one as sparse and dry as N'Doch's Africa, Paia looks for green and feels a lack she never did before. The endless barren rock seems unfinished, lonely, somehow . . . tragic.

She hasn't seen the Citadel from the air since she was small. Besides, things look different through the eyes of a dragon than they did from the passenger seat of her father's hover. Or maybe things are different: drier, more scrubbed, more beaten down by heat and scouring winds. Either way, they are nearly on top of it before she recognizes the wide sweep of valley, cut by the straight bright line of road. And there, in the shadowed curl of the upthrust cliff face, the walled courtyards climb like stacked boxes to the gilded facade of the Temple.

Paia would prefer to swoop and glide though the hot gusts of the heights, aloof from the struggles of priests and warriors, exulting in the glory of wings. She could observe the interesting dynamic of human geometry imposed upon the more random patternings of rock and sand. A juxtaposition once strong, now fading with the weakening of man's hold over the Earth. Paia often tried to capture it in her paintings. She could learn the newer patterns, like the intruding fingers of blue, not as distant as she'd thought, and beyond and around, the infinite spread of ocean.

Perhaps she could exert some control over this magnificent body not her own, through sheer delight with its speed and agility, with its gleaming skin and taut muscle. She knows how the dragon responds to flattery. But Fire, having avoided the battle for so long, is now impatient to be at it. He banks and drops, chasing his own broad shadow across the wasted valley floor, toward the Grand Stair where dust and smoke rise and mix in an unnatural cloud. Clots of figures appear as the cloud thins or shifts, then vanish again behind a thickening billow. Running to and fro, the figures look like scurrying ants, dark against the red dirt but indistinguishable as to sex or age, or loyalty. Fire stoops out of the pale hot sky to wheel over the courtyards, his shadow scudding across the cliff face like a cloud crossing the sun. The ants are resolved into soldiers and priests and villagers, mingling in a common melee. Many halt as the dragon passes, to stare upward. Their gesticulating could be fearful or defiant. Paia cannot tell for sure. Even if she tries to deflect the dragon's attack, which way should she turn him? She sees no neat and comprehensible battle lines. Apart from the occasional red flash of an Honor Guard's tunic, it's impossible to tell the sides apart or determine the course of the fighting. Leif Cauldwell's army marched to war in the same clothes they farmed in or cared for their livestock, and the villagers loyal to the Temple would be no better equipped. They could be fighting a wildfire down there, instead of each other. The dragon offers no comment, but she senses his victorious mood plummeting like the pressure before a storm. His silence speaks his dismay and disbelief. He circles out over the valley and heads back for a second pass, lower this time, his roar crashing like wild surf along the cliff. He's searching for patterns, too, a direction in the movement of bodies, a focal point, a leader. Some sign that his forces are rallying. They're close enough now to see actual fighting, sprawled bodies here and there, the wounded being dragged to safety. But it seems that the motion is mostly toward the Temple, a steady inward flow meeting only sporadic resistance, passing eddies of stillness formed by groups of guarded prisoners, sullen in the heat or relieved to be out of the fighting. One large group near the top of the Grand Stair is entirely uniformed in Temple red. Several of them are chatting amiably with their peasant guards.

It is the red-coats, not the rebels, who duck and quail as the dragon's shadow sweeps over them.

The dragon hisses deep in his throat. COWARDS! TRAITORS! THEY'RE SWORN TO FIGHT TO THE DEATH! HAVE THEY FORGOTTEN? WHERE ARE MY FAITHFUL? WHERE IS MY VICTORY?

As they glide past, only meters above the fighters' heads, Paia tries to direct Fire's furious disbelieving glare. There are men and women, Tinkers and farmers, fighting side by side, some of them wearing little more than rags. Where is Leif Cauldwell, she wonders. Up at the front lines, or at the rear, directing the attack? Where is Dolph Hoffman?

Ahead, the tall plate-metal gates to the Inner Court are closed against a steady onslaught. Fire slows, spinning tighter circles above the sun-baked plaza where the remnants of the Honor Guard and a handful of priests and priestesses battle for control of the entrance to the Temple.

HERE ARE MY HEROES, MY FAITHFUL! HERE THE INVADER WILL BE TURNED BACK AND DESTROYED!

Can he really believe that, Paia wonders? She knows little of war, but she can tell a rout when she sees one. Siege ladders are being relayed hand over hand up the Grand Stair. Reinforcements have arrived, probably from the outlying villages that suffered so under the dragon's tyranny. Fat metal tubes are carried up on men's shoulders, gleaming dully in the sun. Guns of some sort, Paia is sure of it. Who could have guessed that the rebels would be so well armed?

With another thundering roar, Fire sweeps low over the gates. His rage and his body are a united force. Paia feels his chest expand with his fury to exhale a long fiery breath. Flame splashes across the heads and backs of the attackers. A few trailing screams as the beast wings by, but most of the fighters duck, then just move onward. They're wearing some sort of shielding, a wide-brimmed helmet flexing into riveted plates down along their backs, like a turtle's shell. *Or the scales of a dragon.* Paia reflects on the difficulty of defending the Citadel from the very man who held it against all attackers for so long. Leif Cauldwell has not sent his rebels into battle unprepared.

The ladders swing up against the walls. The defenders scale the inner sides to shove them away, but the weight of the rebels swarming upward holds the ladders firmly in place. Inside the courtyard, three red-robed priestesses scurry out of the Temple, their arms loaded with the gold ware from the altar. Paia assumes they're saving the Temple's treasures from the marauders, but as they race past the fighting into the tunnel to the Citadel, their guilty backward glances tell her otherwise.

No, they're looting. Under the Temple portico, in the shade, she sees two priests arguing. She wonders what political dispute could be more important than fighting for their lives.

The dragon wheels, shrieking, and swoops in for another searing pass. As he reaches the gates, a sharp popping sound rips the air. Several of the defenders pitch forward silently and topple into the mass of rebels climbing the siege ladders. Paia has seen this before, watching the news feed during the endless days of the Final Collapse. Projectile weapons, primitive compared to the little laser pistol the dragon gave her, but effective, nonetheless.

Where is it now, that pistol? She follows the thought in order to distract herself from the continuing murder of the Temple staff. Men and women she has spent most of her life with. It doesn't matter that she never befriended any of them. The God—no, the *dragon*—always discouraged that. It doesn't matter that she considered them fools. Or that the ones she did like turned out to be rebels undercover, like Son Luco, aka Leif Cauldwell, and are probably the ones out there gunning down their former colleagues. Death is awful and final, no matter whose side you're on.

Another rattle of gunfire. This time, it follows the dragon's flight, falling around his body and gilded wings like a scatter of hail.

Falling. Gunfire from *above.*

As Paia comprehends this, so does the dragon. He tilts his fiery glance upward. A line of dark shapes, the heads and shoulders of men, roughens the worn profile of the cliff top. Again, the popping, then the sharp clatter against his scales. The dragon bellows and pumps his wings, soaring upward and away, then wheeling back, aiming himself like a missile at the heights. He skims low above the plateau, laying down a line of flame hot enough to scorch the rocks, but the sharpshooters have taken cover beneath deeply protruding ledges. As Fire passes, Paia hears a shout, a man's voice raised in command. Another rain of metal chases the dragon's tail.

For the first time since they joined the battle, Paia is afraid. Not for herself, but for the man down there, with the voice she recognized. The dragon banks sharply, turning back. One man stands higher than the rest, his blond hair and broad shoulders exposed, silhouetted against the sky. In his raised fist, an ancient weapon. Paia knows it well. The dragon-hilted sword.

Fire knows it, too.

HA! THAT ONE!

She'd cry out to Köthen if she could. *Get down! Get down! Your guns cannot hurt him!* But she has no voice now but the dragon's. Panic swirls around her, floodwaters. She will drown in it. Then she recalls Köthen on the mountaintop, how his steadiness and calm lent her the strength she needed to deny Fire the first time. Not a physical strength. A strength of mind. Too late now to wheedle, seduce, or beg. She must find that strength again, immediately. She must bargain with the devil.

Fire pulls up, then settles slowly onto a wind-carved pinnacle of rock. He stares at Köthen, considering. Köthen gestures to his men to stay under cover and hold their fire, then lowers his sword to the ground, point first. He leans easily against the hilt, and stares back. Paia feels the dragon shudder with outrage. She bends all her will against the hard wall of his innermost being.

You will not hurt him, my Fire!

I WILL!

He cannot hurt you. An unequal fight would be cowardly.

WHO CARES? I'M AT WAR! HE'S MY ENEMY!

If you harm this man, I will know that your siblings are right. That all you've told me is lies! That you are a coward and a murderer and you care for nothing but yourself and your own pleasure!

HE IS YOUR LOVER!

No, though he might have been. Instead, you won me back again.

YOU BETRAYED ME WITH HIM! YOU LOVE HIM STILL! HE SHALL NOT *LIVE!*

Is it love she feels, gazing at Köthen's sturdy, imperturbable stance, or gratitude?

But I chose to follow you instead.

HE DARED TO CHALLENGE ME! HE SHALL NOT LIVE!

Her own person is her only currency. The threat of leaving is her only weapon. Such as they are, Paia knows her Duty is to use them.

If he dies, you will lose me again, and this time, forever! You can only hold me if I come to you willingly!

The dragon screams, his tail carving the air like a giant's scimitar. Flame spews across the seamed and broken granite but dies at Köthen's feet. The hot wind ruffles his hair. The men cry out from their shadowed refuge. Köthen doesn't stir.

Spare him, my Fire, and I will not desert you, ever. If you kill him, you kill me also.

Fire's rage and incredulity burn through her like a fever.

MY FAITHFUL DESERT ME! MY ARMIES SPLIT AND SCATTER! MY FORTRESS IS TAKEN! AND NOW YOU . . . AGAIN? GIVE ME A REASON I SHOULD SPARE HIM!

What good is reason, my Fire, at the end of the world?

NO! TELL ME! WHY THIS ONE?

Let your own standard apply. Spare him because he is worthy. Because he is not weak. Spare him because he is what you would have been, had you been human. Because he taught me that love is possible only between equals, and that to love you, I must cease to fear you.

Paia feels the molten light of the dragon's rage fade just slightly. Köthen waits, puzzled and wary. Why doesn't it attack, this enemy he does not comprehend? But Paia thinks that man and dragon actually understand each other very well. She'd like to be able to explain it to him, how they are alike. How loving the dragon does not mean loving him less. How she is a creature of Destiny, and must follow its call. With no language between them, it would be a daunting task. With a language, it would be heartbreaking. Paia is grateful to be spared the pain. Köthen stands defiant on his rock, a brave man facing down a dragon. The absurdity of it makes her love him all the more. He'll never know she's saved his life. He doesn't know she's there.

In her heart, Paia bids the soldier good-bye, and wishes him well.

Come, my Fire. There's no place for us here.

His swift agreement leaves her feeling dizzy and confused.

YOU'RE RIGHT! THERE ARE OTHER PLACES. BETTER PLACES! WHERE MY SERVANTS ARE STILL LOYAL! WHERE THEY'LL WELCOME AND WORSHIP US! LEADERS OF MEN WHO'VE NOT YET LOST THEIR FAITH IN THEIR GOD!

But that's not what . . .

AND THERE WE'LL RAISE A REAL ARMY AND BRING IT HERE TO CHASE THIS FAINTHEARTED BAND OF MARAUDERS BACK INTO THE HILLS THEY SPRANG FROM!

And keep on fighting and fighting? When will it ever stop?

STOP? Inside his pause, a returning echo of exhaustion. A longing or despair. IN THE END, BELOVED, EVERYTHING WILL STOP. AT LAST. THE CYCLE WILL BE ENDED. UNTIL THEN, WE MUST PERSEVERE. PREPARE YOURSELF, MY PRIESTESS, FOR ANOTHER JOURNEY!

CHAPTER THIRTY-ONE

S now blows up again, mixed with needles of sleet, and
Captain Wender bellows for a horse. One of the chas-
tened boys materializes from behind a stack of firewood.
"A horse for milady!"

Erde lays a hand on his muddied sleeve. "No, Captain,
we should not wait. I can walk perfectly well. I've walked
this far, after all. The dragon will follow as soon as we've
made room for him."

"As you wish." The captain peers at her to be sure, but
he's anxious enough not to stand on ceremony. "Hot water,
then, lad. And clean cloths, if you can find any!" He sends
the boy packing with a gesture, and offers her his arm. "If
you will allow me. It isn't far."

Erde is relieved that he sets a stiff pace. She'd be dragging him along herself if he felt it necessary to observe a
more ladylike stride. "Are you fighting in the king's name
now, Captain?"

Wender grips her elbow to guide her past a crowd milling
around the chirurgeon's tent. The moans from behind the
stained canvas make Erde shudder and quicken her step.
The dragon could do much good here, though it would
exhaust him desperately. And where would food be found
to fuel the recovery of his strength?

"I serve the Knight now, as my father did before me,"
Wender replies solemnly.

She glances up at his stern, ruddy face. A weathered
face, weary but without complaint, though frost rimes his
mustache and his eyes are slitted against the biting snow.
"I didn't know."

Wender nods. "I was apprenticed at the armory at Weiss-

trasse when my young lord of Köthen came to squire in
the Knight's household. Being just a few years older, I was
assigned to look after the boy, keep his horse, spar with
him in the training yard, back him up in fights. The usual
sort of thing." Conversation with a lady is clearly not the
captain's favorite exercise. He seems glad for a subject he
can pursue without discomfort. "But we were . . . a good
match, you might say. And his lordship was still young
when he was called home to assume his title. The Knight
judged he could use some backup while the power issues
were being sorted out. So I came to Castle Köthen. And
I stayed."

"An excellent match, indeed," says Erde politely, while
her mind's eye fills with the dark dream-vision she'd had,
little more than a month ago, of Baron Köthen, Wender,
and the bloodied body of the murdered prince. A month
for her, perhaps, but not for Wender.

The captain paces in silence for a moment, then asks
humbly, "Can you offer any news of his lordship, milady?"

"Oh, forgive me! Of course you will be wondering! The
Baron is well, Captain." She will not mention how changed
Köthen is, or how he'd refused her plea to return with her
to Deep Moor, alas too late. "He's fighting the dragons'
battles now."

One small portion of Wender's anxiety seems relieved
by this knowledge. "The Knight will be glad to hear it. And
so . . . we are nearly there."

Ahead, smoke rises damply from a large cook fire, cano-
pied against the snow. Men huddle close around it, while
their horses stamp in the cold. Several canvas-draped wagons stand like a barricade between the fire and a faded red
pavilion set a bit apart. The pavilion is larger than the tents
clustered on the other side of the cook fire, but shows no
other sign of luxury.

Erde expects to find men hurrying about, servants or
healers caring for the wounded knight. But the door flap
hangs flat and still, and silence lies like a pall around the
pavilion. Perhaps the knight's retainers are respecting his
slumber, but Erde senses something chillier than that. As
they pass the cook fire, Wender calls to some of the gathered men. They mutter, and answer him as sullenly as the
boys, but a few leave their place at the fire to do his bid-

ding. Erde shivers, watching them approach. Their hands and faces are chapped raw, their postures lank and suspicious. Brusquely, the captain orders them to clear the area in front of the red pavilion.

"It's fear keeps them away, milady," he tells her, correctly reading her questioning glance.

"Of sickness?"

"Of him, milady. When the battle turns, they blame him now. He's . . ."

"He's what?" Disfigured? Delirious? Can it be the captain was not exaggerating? Is the dear old knight really dying?

"Well, you will see for yourself." He strides to the flap, then hesitates. "Your pardon, milady. Let me go in first and prepare him."

"Captain, let us not delay! I'd rather . . ."

"A moment only, milady." Wender ducks through the loose canvas as if intent on concealing the pavilion's interior from all eyes. Shivering now from cold as well as dismay, Erde gathers her woolen layers about her against the snow and icy wind, and reports all she's seen and learned to the dragon, waiting far out in the drifted meadow.

Wender soon reappears as promised, but remains at the door, blocking the way. "Milady, you will find him . . . most changed."

"Of course, Captain. He is weak from the wound, I suppose. Is there fever?" This, of course, would be the worst: the wound inflamed.

"Fever, yes, and more." Still, he hesitates. "Even before the wound."

"Surely I'll not be in any danger?" she demands in a shocked whisper.

Wender's gruff face twists, with doubt or caution. Or it could simply be grief, Erde decides. Without further comment, he steps aside, gathering the limp canvas in one hand for her to pass.

After the bleak gray of the snowy afternoon, Erde expects a greater darkness inside. Instead, her gloom-adjusted eyes are stunned by the glare of a score of lanterns, oil lamps, and candles, arrayed about the interior of the pavilion as if for some saint's day celebration. Their many points of light are misted by smoke from the braziers set at the corners. Squinting into the brightness, Erde doesn't see the knight at first. She see books, piles of books, as well as loose sheaths of parchment and the rolled scrolls of vellum maps, piled on rickety camp tables, spilling out of trunks, scattered across the muddied rugs that only partially cover the frozen meadow grasses matting the ground.

"Has he brought his entire library?" she exclaims.

"Most of it." Wender has come in behind her and closed the flap, pulling it tight against invading wind and snow, and prying glances.

"My lord? Sir Hal?" Erde looks for a sickbed and finds it—rumpled, mud-stained, bloodstained, and . . . empty, but for a litter of books and occultish charts. "Are you here?"

"He's here."

She thinks Wender's tone is very dire. She steps farther in, her eyes adjusting to the flickering, smoky light. She sees motion among the candle flames, and then, a stooped old man, thin past all reason, his gray hair unkempt, his chin ragged with bristles, totters toward her with an armload of leather-bound tomes.

"Is that you, girl?"

She knows the voice only because she expects to hear it. But it was never so cracked and wheezy. *He* was never . . .

"Yes, it's me." She is numbed to a whisper.

"Good! Kurt told me you'd come back."

She clears her throat and tries again. "Yes. I'm back."

"Well, I've got one of you at least! And not a moment too soon!" He dumps the books onto an unoccupied corner of the nearest table and stands breathing hard. When he seems more confident of his balance, he snatches the top book off the stack and shakes it at her like a fist. "Come! You must help me call the others! There's not a moment to lose!"

Wender murmurs, "He won't sit still even long enough to let me shave him."

Surely this is some imposter! Where is her tall, stern, red-leathered knight? Erde cannot comprehend how a man so strong and vital could have aged so greatly in so short a time. Could the injury alone be responsible? Didn't the captain say he was wounded but a day ago? She notes the flush of fever on his cheek and in his eyes. His skin is stretched taut, as if from a wasting sickness, or from the denial of constant and agonizing pain. Beneath the masking scents of burning tallow and charcoal, Erde detects the sour-sweet odor of decay. She turns wide, horrified eyes back to Wender.

"Oh, Captain, go bid your men to hurry, I beg you! I'll be all right here with him."

Wender nods briskly, and ducks out.

Erde turns back to the knight with the most encouraging smile she can muster. He has thrown the book down where a small cleared space is ringed with the golden cylinders of altar candles. He props himself against the table and leans in to study the pages. His arms quiver with the effort, and he bends so low that she fears his scrawl of untrimmed hair will catch in the circle of leaping flames. He appears to have forgotten her entirely.

"Sir Hal?"

Without looking up, he beckons her over impatiently, as if she's been away but a minute, not the several months that she calculates have actually passed. Winter should have been gone long ago, but she knows from Raven that it went on and on. How long actually? She must remember to ask the captain. Weather so freakish cannot provide a reliable calendar.

"Come, child! Look!"

As Erde approaches, the musty stench grows sharper. He is wearing a rumpled but clean tunic—the captain has managed that much, at least—but the right side, across his shoulder blade and down along his ribs, is damply stained: rouge, yellow, russet. Erde struggles for composure, and a steady stomach.

"Look here!" Hal insists. His finger trembles on a brightly illuminated page. "See here where it says . . . well, the translation is clumsy, but this passage . . ." He shoves several smaller books aside, reaching for an older, tattered volume stuffed with torn strips of parchment. He fumbles with the markers. "Where is it? Where?"

"My lord, you needn't tell me now. . . ."

"No, we must . . . Here! Here it is! The same, you see? The very same passage reoccurs, encapsulated within this earlier text!" He holds the ragged little book out for her perusal. Every inch of margin is crammed with his carefully inked annotations.

Erde nods weakly. His bright mad grin has brought her to the verge of tears. "What does it say, good knight?"

"Listen!" He brings the page up close to his eyes, then peers aside at her apologetically. "My own translation, you understand. An improvement, but . . . well." He turns back, clearing his throat and squinting to read his notes. " 'In the beginning, four mighty dragons' . . . four, my girl! You hear that? It speaks of them. It must be them! It goes on, ' . . . raised of elemental energies, were put to work . . .' " He stops to cough and ends up gasping for breath.

"No more, dear knight, I beg you! You will kill yourself with this!"

"But the text breaks off there! It's a fragment only!" He turns to her with crazed intensity. "A damned illusive fragment! But then, I found . . ." He fumbles again among the many books, but his fingers seem to have lost the will to grasp. He gives up and leans against the tabletop, shuddering and heaving.

"Dearest Sir Hal, you are not well!" Now Erde cannot keep the horror from her voice. "Has the chirurgeon seen to your wound?"

He waves his hand, a jerky half-controlled motion. "Yes, yes. A fool. I called for Linden, but . . ." He frowns, having lost his train of thought. "A fool! He'd have me drugged on my couch if I let him!"

"With good reason! You're sorely hurt and should be resting!"

"No time for that, girl! No time!" He reaches for another book. "It's here somewhere, and I shall find it."

"What is?"

"Did they tell you? The hell-priest is in the Grove. Cursed be the day I took that devil into my household!" He drops the book convulsively and grips his head with both hands. "Aiii, I am to blame! I am to blame! The priest is in the Grove and we cannot pry him out!"

"You are not to blame," she protests, but uselessly, for he isn't listening.

His hands fall back to rustle among the books and papers. "It's his damned black magic, of course. Like he's done with the weather. Somehow the Grove's own magic has been subdued. I've been searching for a proper conjure to lend it strength, but you will help me find it. Now that

you and Lord Earth are here, we shall . . ." He looks up,
and then wildly around the tent, his whole body sagging in
a seizure of doubt. "He is here, isn't he?"

Erde nearly rushes to catch his fall. "He is, dear knight!
He surely is, and the first task he must undertake is to
make you well again! Then we shall worry about the hell-
priest." She moves closer, to take his arm and lead him
from the distraction of his books. He tries to wave her
away, but there is no strength in him. His wrist is as frail
as a willow twig beneath his fevered skin. He shudders as
if her touch is agony.

"No time, no time! The answer is here! I had it, almost,
and then . . . !" He coughs, a dire rattle clogging his throat.

Erde panics. "Captain Wender!" Hal's face is rigid with
suppressed pain. "Captain! Will you come, please?" She
sees that the knight's every breath is an effort, a battle
won. She cannot imagine what's keeping him upright. She
will not ask what answer he seeks so desperately, for he
will try to tell her and only wreck himself further. "Please,
dear Hal, time for answers when you are well! The dragon
will be here soon. Let him see to you, or there'll be no
time for you at all!"

"Milady?" Wender appears at the tent flap, then hurries
in to help her support the old man's lanky, sagging frame.
He grabs up a soft and thickly woven blanket and drapes
it over Hal's stooped shoulders like a cloak.

Hal struggles within the enveloping folds. "No! Leave me!
My work is not done! I'm so close, Kurt! Let me go!"

"Good, my lord," Wender murmurs. "Behave yourself
now."

"Will you not come out and greet the dragon?" Erde
asks brightly.

The fever-glaze in Hal's eyes clears long enough to let a
ray of his old joy and awe shine through. "The dragon!
Yes! He will know! Wender! My sword!"

"No need for that, my lord."

"My sword, I say! I must make my obeisance!"

Wender sighs. Balancing the knight on one arm, he
reaches behind him for the sword hung by sheath and belt
on a tent pole. Erde catches just a glimpse of the familiar
dragon-shaped hilt before Wender presses it to Hal's chest,
then wraps sword, sheath, and knight up soundly in the

woolen blanket. "We've cleared as large a space as we're likely to get, milady. I'm hoping it will do."

"It will have to, Captain. Let us hurry! I'll go outside and call the dragon now." She stays a moment to stroke Hal's bruised hand. "Soon, dear knight. Soon all will be well."

"Soon all will be over," Hal mutters.

"Not at all! You mustn't say so. It's only the fever bringing you to such madness and despair!"

"And a good thing, too," he continues. "It's the only way. The texts are very clear in that regard." He begins to cough again, so racked by it this time that his mouth is stained with blood.

Wender gently wipes it away with a corner of the blanket, while Erde turns her glance away. "You go ahead, milady. Go call in your magic beast."

Outside, Erde steals a moment to compose herself, to brush away the tears she's allowed herself only once she's turned her back, to breathe in air—no matter how icy cold—that's free of smoke and the rank stink of infection. The wind has died, and the snow falls more gently, like a caress rather than a punishment.

Oh, dragon! Just when I think I've known every sadness possible!

DO NOT DESPAIR.

Never! Not while you are here. They've made room for you. Will you join us? You are sorely needed!

She gazes across the rutted stretch of field in front of the tent. Wender has ordered the supply wagons drawn aside, and several of the smaller tents and lean-tos moved farther down the line. Word of a happening has obviously been passed through the camp. A sullen throng of infantrymen and squires has gathered around the perimeter to speculate and stare. Erde does not feel particularly welcomed. She has never called the dragon into a crowd of strangers before, except at Erfurt, to snatch Margit from the stake. The men have brought their pikes and crossbows, she notes, but these are soldiers, after all, and they are at war. It is their duty to be armed. Swallowing her dread, Erde images the trampled field, the tents and all the onlookers, clearly and in precise detail.

Are you ready, dragon?

I AM . . . HERE.

And he is. Crouching neatly in the center of the space, with little room to spare. The ranks of the curious gasp and draw back. Prayers and blessings are mumbled. Weapons rattle as their owners' fists tighten on them in terror. Horses neigh and the dogs bark or quickly slink away. The dragon looms over the camp, a bronzy mountain. The squared plates of his hide shine as the gloomy daylight picks out its concentric ridges, like the coffering in a cathedral ceiling. Erde's heart warms to see him, so vast and magnificent, but her joy is not shared by those around her. She hears the words "witch" and "antichrist" muttered around the field. She'd like to scold them all for their foolishness and superstition, but men do not like to be told they're wrong about something, especially by a girl.

The dragon, too, is nervous. He's never liked crowds. Nonetheless, he is soothing the panicked animals, smothering the fright signals they've picked up from the humans with calming messages of his own. Soon, the dogs and horses are quiet, but the men have grown restless, ashamed of their fear and resentful of the dragon that caused it. Emboldened by his placidity, several of them step forward, halberds gleaming wickedly. Erde sees crossbows armed and cocked, and guesses herself to be the most likely target, though enough arrows shot at close range could do serious harm to the dragon as well, perhaps before he could stop them or remove himself from danger. His legend has followed him, she surmises. They've all heard he doesn't fly or breathe fire.

Can't they see we're trying to help them?

THEY COULD . . . IF THEY LOOKED FAR ENOUGH.

Erde decides she might actually be in danger. She glances back at the silent pavilion. She tries to sound casual. "Captain Wender?"

The men with the halberds advance more boldly. One of them mimics her call to the captain in falsetto.

"That's it!" calls another. "Bring the damned turncoat out here!"

Behind them, the crowd murmurs encouragement. Erde understands that her arrival has fanned the flames of an already existing animosity toward Wender and the man he now serves. What has become of the king's once noble army? She'd like to give them a piece of her mind about the nature of duty and loyalty, but recent months have taught her the value of discretion. Instead, she strides to the tent flap and draws it aside. "Captain?"

Wender stoops out from under the gathered canvas with the limp and shrouded knight cradled in his arms like a child. He looks anguished, and Erde sees no sign of life on Hal's slack face.

"Oh! Is he . . . he isn't . . . ?"

"Collapsed. But there's still a breath. It's very close, milady."

The emboldened soldiers are moving in to cut the pavilion off from the center of the field and the dragon.

Wender scowls at them. "What's going on here? Out of my way! We have vital business to attend to!"

"The devil's business!" snarls one, stepping forward and leveling the point of his halberd like a spear. "There's no denying your witchcraft now!"

The crowd calls out its agreement with raucous threats and cheers.

"This man is dying!" says Wender angrily.

"Let him, then!"

"Then maybe our luck will change!"

Wender growls, "If you fought with more heart, you'd change your own luck! Out of my way, I say!"

Small wonder these men resent him, Erde muses. He's brought with him some of his old master's arrogance. She hears shouts in the distance, and the pounding of hooves. She prays it's not more bad news. The crowd's grumble rises like a nest of hornets. A string thunks and an arrow slams into the mud at Wender's feet.

"I am unarmed!" Wender fumes, his arms sagging with the knight's dead weight.

"So much the better," calls the man with the halberd, advancing another step. The shouts and hoofbeats are nearing.

Dragon! We need your help!

He could transport the three of them to safety, but she needs to be touching him. And where would they go? Four more foot soldiers have moved to stand beside the man with the halberd, blocking the way.

· I WILL COME FOR YOU.

Earth slews his giant horned head toward the pavilion and lumbers to his feet. Simultaneously, the approaching shouts resolve themselves into audible words. "Make way for the king! Stand aside for His Majesty!"

The king! The crowd parts hastily as two mounted knights trot into the open. Behind them, Erde sees another pair of knights, a flurry of banners and color, and a flash of gold warming the dull air. Then the entire throng is kneeling, herself included. Even Wender manages to sink to one knee while holding his unconscious burden well above the snow and icy mud. Erde is more than grateful for the interruption, which has probably saved their lives, but Sir Hal's failing health is of equal concern. His Majesty has heard about the dragon, no doubt, and has come to see it for himself. She is glad that the ailing old monarch is well enough to travel on horseback, but she prays that he will not require too lengthy a show of ceremony. If Hal is to live, the dragon must get on with his healing.

Her head bowed with the proper respect, she hears horses approaching, murmured commands, then a single horse coming nearer. It halts and two pairs of muddy boots race up to catch its bridle. She hears the soft clink of mail and the creaking of harness. The rider dismounts, more easily than she'd expect from a sick old man.

"Well, little sister. We meet again at last."

She forgets all the protocols drilled into her as a baron's child. She looks up, gaping at the man standing in front of her, helmetless, a thin, bright band of gold embracing his brow. He looks older, less by the march of years than with the maturity gained from the weight of his royal responsibilities. He is still tall and thin, but his boyish beauty has sobered into something more august, as befits a king.

Dragon! It's Rainer! Alive!

"You . . . Your Majesty?" she splutters.

Rainer grins down at her, enjoying her astonishment, then spreads his hands apologetically. "You see? I have regained my heritage. Are you surprised?"

"Yes . . . no . . . I . . ." *I'm just so glad to see you well!* A thousand memories come flooding back, not all of them comfortable. "So you are . . . ?"

"I am. The lost prince." His shoulders twitch in the faintest of shrugs. He lowers his voice. "Or so they believe. In that case, what does it really matter?"

She stares at him. Why does he greet her with such ambiguity? Does he fear she'll challenge his legitimacy? "It matters not at all . . . my liege."

Rainer smiles, satisfied. "You're looking well, little sister."

Erde recalls her reasons for urgency. She must put her discomfiture and wonderment aside for later. She gazes up at the new king imploringly, gesturing behind to Wender and the man in his arms. "Please . . . it's Hal . . . he . . ."

Rainer frowns. "Yes, I was in to see him yesterday when they brought him from the field. Is he worse?" He offers her his hand, not so that she might kiss the royal ring, but outstretched to help her up. "Is it true your dragon is a healer? Hal has told me some amazing tales. Can you help him?"

"Lord Earth will do what . . ." she begins weakly.

But Rainer has moved past her to Wender, waving him also to his feet. "How is he, Kurt?"

"It's very bad, Sire."

"We must hurry, then!" Erde blurts. "Oh, forgive my rudeness . . . Sire."

"No, we must. You're right." For a moment, the king looks very young again, and at a loss. "What do we do?"

"Bring him here. Oh, Captain, hurry!" The way to the dragon is clear. Erde shows Wender where to place his burden, between Earth's massive forelegs. Rainer paces along beside them, silencing the mutters of the crowd with a few well-placed scowls. But between the scowls are precautionary gestures to his men. A dozen or so of the king's knights take up stations around the perimeter.

Dark times indeed, Erde mourns, when the people will not bow to the word of a strong, young king. And Rainer will be a strong king, and a good one. She is sure of it. No matter if he's Otto's true son or not. Even further in his favor is that he knows how to greet a dragon. He halts where he can comfortably look up at the huge jaw and golden eyes. He bows slightly, not a subservience but a paying of respects.

"Lord Earth," he declares, in a voice he intends to carry into the surrounding throng of doubters and dragon haters.

"I never thanked you properly for saving my life back there in Erfurt. But for you, there'd be a priest on the throne today! Our gratitude is boundless!"

To further his point, he rests his hand easily on the curve of the dragon's foreclaw. Wender watches apprehensively, still cradling the dying knight. He's never stood this close to the dragon before. His jaw works as he masters his fear.

"You may set him down and step back, if you wish, Captain," Erde tells him. "Lord Earth will keep him warm."

"I'll stay." Wender kneels, eyeing the stout pickets of ivory enclosing him on either side, taller than his head. "He's grown some, all right, milady."

Erde allows herself the ghost of a smile. Perhaps even in the midst of horror and crisis, a touch of wonder will lighten the heart of this stalwart and deserving soldier. She kneels beside him to murmur, "You must expose the wound, Captain."

Wender stretches Hal out on the frozen mud, with the blanket under him and the dragon-hilted sword clasped long-ways on his chest. Erde shudders because he so resembles the funerary statues of her ancestors in the crypt of Tor Alte. The dragon lowers his head.

Dragon, is it bad?

VERY BAD INDEED.

Oh, but not . . . you can help him, can't you?

I CAN HEAL THE WOUND AND QUIET THE FEVER, BUT HE HAS DONE MUCH INNER DAMAGE WITH HIS GUILT AND WORRYING.

But he will live . . . ?

HE WILL, I THINK. BUT HE MUST REST, AND TAKE BETTER CARE OF HIMSELF. HE IS NO LONGER YOUNG.

Just like you to be worrying about the long term, when all I can think of is, will he live now?

HE WILL.

Erde's eyes squeeze shut against a threatened flood of grateful tears. If only this was to be the end of it, and the revived Sir Hal could ride off home to Deep Moor to rest and recover in the care of his loving lady Rose. Happily ever after in Deep Moor. A vision rises of Erde's vanished paradise, so sweet that it pierces her heart like love, and the hot tears prick her eyes again.

Not to be, not to be. Not ever. Deep Moor is in ashes, and Fra Guill is cutting down the Grove!

And then she is dragged from her mournful reverie by Wender's glad cry. "He wakes!"

The exclamation is repeated among the watching soldiers, passed around the circle like a prayer and a prophecy. Hal's chest heaves as if drawing his first true breath in days. He coughs but the sound is functional rather than strangulated. He opens his eyes. He's staring straight up into the dragon's golden gaze. "My lord Earth! You've returned at last! Thank good Providence for that! There's not a moment to be spared!"

He struggles to sit up, brushing the sword aside in his haste and confusion. Wender supports the elder knight with one arm, and snatches the sword up from the mud with the other. He cannot repress a quick accusing glance at Erde. "Is it the fever still?"

Erde rests her palm on Hal's brow. "I feel no fever now."

"Fever? What fever?" Hal's eyes narrow in suspicion, then clear, and he gently lifts her hand away. "I recall. I took a blade." He looks to Wender.

"Indeed you did, milord."

"And it went bad."

"Aye, milord. And before that . . ." Wender reconsiders and falls silent.

"Before that, what?"

"You've . . . been unwell, milord. For a while."

Hal rakes a thin hand through his hair, his habitual gesture of bewonderment. "Well, I'm fit as a fiddle now, and a good thing, too. We have much to discuss! I beg you, Kurt, help me to rise."

"You mustn't . . . !" Erde and the king speak simultaneously.

"But I must," replies Hal. On his feet but tottering, he grabs the dragon's claw for balance. He squares his starved shoulders, lifts his stubbled chin. "Lord Earth! At last I can repay you for the many favors you've done me and my king! I believe I have uncovered the final purpose of your Quest!"

CHAPTER THIRTY-TWO

The Librarian is grateful to Water for retaining her human shape while in the garden at the Ur-Deep Moor. It reflects an empathetic understanding of human sensibilities that his own dragon appears incapable of. And it gives him something to do while the two dragons greet and debrief, strolling up and down the lawn: the tall black man and the stubby bearish one, walking side by side among clusters of sober observers without speaking. N'Doch and the two Tinkers can easily imagine the silent conversation going on at light speed, but it must look peculiar to the Deep Moor ladies, who aren't so used to dragon oddities. The Librarian listened in on the dialogue eagerly enough at first, and then with waning concentration as he realized that, despite Water's obvious advantages, the process of communicating with Air is not a whole lot easier for her than it has been for himself. If all these avid watchers have expectations of immediate answers, they will be disappointed.

So the Librarian listens with a part of his brain, and concentrates on his balance and footing with the rest. He constantly has to counteract Air's tendency to let her intensity spill over into his physical being. Twice he has nearly slammed his elbow into Sedou's ribs. Without warning, any one of his limbs might be flung suddenly outward, or his head made to nod violently, as the dragon struggles to convey to her sister a certain crucial point. In sympathy, Sedou/Water now grips his arm, for support as well as gentle restraint.

So the Librarian is not the first to see it happen, though

he is the most likely to comprehend what it means. It's the murmur that snags his attention, beginning as an ominous undercurrent to the hushed fits and starts of conversation across the lawn. Soon enough, however, it rises to a descant of wonder and dismay that can no longer be ignored by man or dragon.

Beside him, Sedou lets out an involuntary grunt of surprise.

The Librarian glances up from his stumbling toes. The women are staring and pointing. Above the sloping roof of the Deep Moor farmhouse, the background profile of barns and trees is mutating, sector by sector. Leaf, branch, and human architecture are being replaced, three dimensions by two, organic by inorganic, natural randomness by abstract symmetry. The new is no less beautiful than the old, the Librarian observes impartially. But it's not human.

"Ask her," he suggests to Sedou. "Would she keep the nanos in line a while longer?"

Sedou frowns, but does not say, "Why don't you ask her?" He's silent for a space, then his mouth draws tight in concern. "She feels it is not important."

"But the women are frightened. They have no understanding of this."

"I've little more myself. But I mentioned the ladies. And actually, my sister didn't say it was unimportant. I said that. She just refuses to focus on anything peripheral to her central priority: gathering the eight. The only words involved in this transaction were . . ."

"I know. *Hurry, hurry.*"

Sedou nods. "Perhaps this is her way of forcing us into action. She's going to let the city fall apart around us, and we'll have no choice but to go where she wishes."

The Librarian is not surprised. He's concluded already that the dragon inside him is heartless. As in, lacking any sort of human pity. Or if she has any heart at all, it's his. Not the physiological organ so much as the awareness of a connection to others, to life-forms that it might be one's duty to protect. If she were human, she would be called driven, obsessive, perhaps even autistic. But Air is hardly even a dragon, in the organic sense. She is an impulse, an eternal intention housed in pure intellect. A force not entirely immovable but requiring his constant surveillance and direction. Otherwise, she would mow down everyone and everything in her path.

The Librarian accepts this because he must, but he finds it perplexing in the extreme. He has supposed that the dragons' great Purpose of saving the Earth inevitably involves the rescue of humanity. Yet because she has no further use for it, Air is letting the White City disassemble itself. She has withdrawn from its systems, now that she has his own organic circuitry to inhabit. Her energies no longer direct the nanos' programming, so the nanos are taking the city back. They're reassembling it according to nanomech standards, which will soon render it inhospitable to human survival. What need, after all, have the nanomechs for the sort of life-support systems that once served the City's human population? Nanomechs can function quite successfully in lethal doses of ultraviolet, or in the thin and poisonous vapor which, in this far future, is all that remains of Earth's atmosphere.

It's a delicate line he has to walk, the Librarian reflects. He can't allow Air to ride roughshod, but neither can he point her too boldly away from the line of her Purpose. It will seem to her like resistance or rebellion, and she has no time for that. She'll simply hijack his body again, and get him and everyone else killed in the process.

What is it, then, that she's so hell-bent on saving? Is her concern only for the Earth itself and its ecosystems? If so, it seems to the Librarian that the chance for that rescue has already long gone by.

And what is he to tell the others, who are turning to him now with frightened, questioning eyes? Where will he find the words? He looks to Sedou, and breathes a sigh of relief. The engaging black man whose shape Water has borrowed is already busy soothing and explaining, revealing little that might distress, without ever seeming to conceal, all this far more articulately than the Librarian could ever manage. At last, a dragon that can speak for itself.

Meanwhile, if Air will not see to the welfare of the humans she has dragged to this fatal place, he must do it himself. According to Luther, the Grove is currently a perilous location in its own right. But if Air insists on going there, the Librarian will not be able to stop her. Still, a little resistance is in order. He must put the dragon off long enough to prepare everyone for the journey. Then he must make sure that the portal stays open long enough for all to pass through it safely.

Most important, he must let them know that they'll have to be ready to fight the minute they get there.

CHAPTER THIRTY-THREE

The sultry heat is familiar, way more humid than the Citadel. The ruddy skies are what reminded Paia of home the first time she came here, but it's the tired, dusty palm trees that tell her for sure she's back in Africa. The smell of dead fish and carrion is strong even this high. As the dragon soars along the curving borderline of bleached sand and ocean, Paia is assailed by the memory of N'Doch closing his dead mother's eyes. She'd weep for them if she could, tears of rage and guilt. But a dragon has no tears. Especially this dragon.

Fire materializes in man-form in a deserted hallway of a vast marble palace, in full dress uniform, his most stunning confection of red and gold. Paia finds herself beside him, corporeal, separate, as if her moment of despising him so totally has flung them apart. She lays her fingers to her cheeks in wonder. Her own skin, her own being. A sigh of relief escapes her so audibly that Fire stares down at her and scowls.

"You're to be gorgeous, quiet, and submissive. This will indicate my high honor and status, as well as assuring your safety. Can you manage that?"

Paia nods, distracted by the joy of being herself again.

"All right, then. Two steps behind me always. So they'll see you as a virtuous woman, not for sale, and belonging to me. Understand?"

She makes a face, gazing up at him impudently, and curtsies. "Yes, my Fire."

"You used to call me 'my lord.'"

"Yes, well . . ."

He turns on his booted heel and strides off down the

hall. Paia hurries after him, but her surroundings are a distraction. Double ranks of polished marble columns support heavy gilt cornices and a long coffered vault stretching toward a distant pair of gilded doors. The marble is heavily veined in rich reds and blues, so gaudy that Paia wanders closer to see if it's painted. This is architecture on a grandiose scale, built with one intention in mind: to impress. Paia has only seen its like in picture histories of ancient empires. Between the columns, arched panels of beveled mirror reflect the glimmer of crystal chandeliers. She's reminded of old videos of Versailles, in her day half-submerged by the rising water. This is how it must have felt to walk its glittering corridors during the reign of the Sun King. But there's also a lot that Louis would not have recognized. Surveillance cameras swivel to keep the intruders in sight as they pass. Hidden speakers fill the long arching hall with sound and music. Huge video screens are set into the mirrored panels between every other column, a different image playing on every screen. Paia lags behind. She hasn't seen advertising since the earliest days of her youth, and the only actual programming she's known is what's archived in the House Computer's library. Very little of it looks like this. She slows in front of a graphic battlefield scene. A cacophony of screams and explosions leaps at her in stereo from behind the columns.

"So real . . ." Paia stares, fascinated. Perhaps it's actually a news report?

Down the hallway, Fire glances back, then stops, his tall silhouette perfectly reflected in the shine of the marble floor. He hisses at her to hurry. Paia trots dutifully after him. Along the way, she glimpses nude bodies intertwined on one screen, and some indescribable carnage involving small animals on another.

"Where are we?" she demands, catching up. Her whisper dances like soft light across the gilded coffering to join the bellows and moans of the mingled sound tracks.

Fire waves her back. "Two steps behind, remember! If anyone sees, I'll lose face immediately!"

Paia complies, trying not to sulk. "What *is* this place?"

"You like it?"

"Not really. I think it's creepy."

"Get used to it. We'll be staying a while."

"But what is it? Did you see what's on those screens?"

"What do you expect? We're in the headquarters of the Media King." Fire gestures grandly around. "A gallery of his current work, I assume. A new addition. And the decor is much improved since I was here last. My minion has obviously come up in the world. You see? There are still places where my favors can make a leader out of an ordinary man." He pauses, irritably adjusting the high tight collar of his tunic. "It's hot here."

Paia stares at him. Is that sweat beading on his red-gold forehead? "What did you say?"

He looks amazed and vulnerable for about a nanosecond, then snaps, "I know, I know. Permit me the discovery of climatic discomfort, now that I'm actually embodied."

She can't keep the wonder from her face, and the hope from her eyes. "You actually feel the heat?"

"What's so wonderful about that?"

"Well, it's so . . . so human."

"Damned inconvenient."

Paia shakes her head, and then, very deliberately, she goes to him, slides her arm up around his neck and draws his head down to hers to kiss him deeply and lovingly. She feels his astonishment, his delight, the rising of his desire, and then his fury and resistance. He breaks the hold of her arm and pushes her roughly away. "Not here! You'll ruin my image!"

Smiling to herself, Paia keeps pace with him as he turns away, following respectfully in his wake. She's made her point, and she doesn't want to be left behind in this salesman's palace. Despite its luxury and scale and the omnipresent security cameras, it doesn't feel safe.

Just short of the gilded doors at the end of the corridor, a wide crossing hall intersects. Fire wheels right, his sharp heels resounding with military precision. Paia represses a grin. How the dragon must be enjoying this new ability of his man-form to make sound in the material world! Another tool of intimidation added to his arsenal, to compensate for his sudden vulnerability to the heat. She follows him cheerfully around the corner.

A broad staircase rises ahead of them, its elaborately carved newels sporting twin logos in polished brass. The bottom step is flanked by two beefy guards, smartly dressed, despite the humidity, in close fitting black and gray. Their collective gaze is fixed on one of the nearby wall screens. Their jaws are slack with fascination. Paia cannot see the screen from her sidelong angle, but she hears cries and weeping, and a woman's desperate begging. The sentries snap to quick attention as Fire cruises to a halt in front of them.

"General! Sir!" exclaims one, saluting so abruptly that Paia is surprised he hasn't broken his wrist. "You are welcome! Sir!"

"I should hope so." Fire breezes past to mount the stairs two at a time. Only at the top does he wait for Paia to trudge up after him, by which time the sentries have returned their attention to the screen. At the top of the stairs, more guards and more wall screens, this time offering a selection of programming: the battle scene again, and a young girl being beaten, then an elaborate costume drama where only the women go without clothing. Paia glances at the final screen and away again, shocked. Surely this is far too intimate to be viewed among strangers! Worst of all are the actress' screams of pain. So convincing. The soldiers watch in avid silence, their eyes constantly flicking from one screen to the other. Behind them, several doorways lead into other huge rooms and brightly lighted hallways, with other open doors beyond that.

Again, the uniformed sentries snap to with brisk salutes. They are boys, really. Sweating beneath their chic uniforms. While the rest stare openly at Paia and make whispered suggestions among themselves, the oldest steps forward.

"Welcome, General. Are you expected?"

"Expected?" Fire offers a lofty but complicit grin. "Mr. Baraga would soon grow bored, Lieutenant, if I showed up only when expected."

The young man nods politely, but Paia can see he's repressing a frown. He can't bring himself to meet the man/dragon's glance directly, so he stares intently at the middle button on Fire's red tunic, taking another step forward to lean in and murmur, "Begging your pardon, General, but it's His Excellency, the President, now."

"Really? I'll be sure to remember." Fire turns to Paia with a sly wink. "Didn't I tell you he's come up in the world?" To the lieutenant, he says, "Yes, it's been a while.

Sorry I missed the coup, but I gather it all went as planned.
Is *His Excellency* about?"

The frown mutates into a tight and awkward smile. "His
Excellency is shooting live at the moment, sir." The lieutenant waves vaguely at the screens, then slides his gaze past
Fire's chest to where Paia has stopped the prescribed two
steps behind. "Perhaps you would care to join him."

"Perhaps I will."

The other guards have turned away from this mundane
conversation, and the passing diversion of a merely live
woman. And though the lieutenant steadfastly faces front,
his concentration is faltering, drawn away by the bright,
beckoning screens and the promise of drama. "Shall I accompany you to the studio, sir?" he asks unhappily.

"No need." Fire moves past him, beckoning Paia to follow. "I know the way."

A succession of gilt-ceilinged salons leads to a parquet-
floored ballroom and rows of gold chairs with plush maroon
velvet upholstery. A larger chair resembling a throne rests
on a dais at the far end. The ubiquitous wall screens are
even larger here, with each sound track trying to over-
whelm its neighbors with excesses of volume and pitch.

Passing out of the ballroom into another corridor lined
with doors, Fire gestures into the wedding cake of cornices
and chandeliers. "There's an entire wing down that way
I'm sure he'll be happy to give us."

Paia smiles up at him. He's looking damp and a bit disheveled. She'd like to wipe his forehead, and maybe nibble
a little on his perfect, chiseled mouth. "Perhaps you can
negotiate for air-conditioning."

"Stop looking at me like that!"

"But why, my Fire?"

He looks away. "It clouds my thinking."

Paia laughs delightedly.

Fire scowls, looming over her. "You don't realize how
limited our options are, do you?"

"Perhaps I don't."

"Then let me do what I must to find a place for us!
There's time for pleasure later."

Paia damps her seductive grin. "Forgive me, my Fire.
I will."

More corridors and rooms, then, and finally, a large door,

distinctive by being steel-plated and closed, and by the group of men who stand around outside it, drinking and smoking. A few of them watch the bank of screens that lights up the entire adjacent wall, but most of them are chatting, or playing cards or e-games. Above the door, a lighted panel reads: ON AIR.

The men glance up at the click of Fire's boots across the polished marble. These are not spiffy, boyish soldiers. They are older, and casually dressed. Their pragmatic, world-weary expressions remind Paia of the Tinkers she has met. They observe Fire's approach with mild disinterest, and yet ease imperceptibly aside so that a passage is cleared to the door without anyone actually greeting him or even acknowledging his presence.

"You see how they know me," Fire murmurs, and though Paia is steps behind, she hears him as if his lips were at her ear. "Perhaps I should have made my kingdom here."

He processes grandly through the crowd of men and stops at the metal door. By habit, Paia steps up to open it for him, as she has ever done when the God wished to pass through a closed door without the awkwardness of vanishing on one side and reappearing on the other. Then she hesitates. Perhaps he'd like the novelty of opening it for himself, now that he's material enough? But he nods, as if granting her permission.

"Let it be as usual," he says quietly. "That way, I can surprise him."

The space inside is cavernous and cool and dark, filled with the bustle of men and machinery focused like bees around a central, brightly-lit hive. Paia actually shivers in the draft from the huge vents pumping in cold air. A mist of condensation rimes the trusswork below the ceiling.

Again, space clears magically as Fire moves among the rolling scaffolds and lighting instruments and the thick bundles of cable snaking across the smooth gray floor. But soft catcalls and laughter follow in their wake, dark male laughter that Paia does not like the sound of. Hands reach for her uninvited. Not like the soft touch of the Faithful of the Temple. These hands are rougher, grasping, and presumptuous. Paia closes the gap between herself and the man/dragon until she's nearly treading on his heels.

"Don't be concerned," says his voice in her ear. "They will not harm what belongs to me."

Paia twists away and into him with a cry of pain as a stray palm cups her breast and squeezes hard. Fire turns. It's not hard to pick out the perpetrator. He's guffawing and moving in for more. Fire glares at him, and instantly, the man yowls and doubles over to cradle his arm in pain and terror. The grabbing, rubbing hands withdraw.

I AM STILL YOUR PROTECTOR, AM I NOT, BELOVED?

Paia nods, knowing it would be unproductive to point out to him his penchant for putting her into situations where she will *require* a protector. "I don't like it here," she mutters instead. "But it is cooler."

"Like I said: get used to it." He continues onward, toward the center brightness.

Peering past him, Paia sees a short but powerfully built man in a crisp white shirt, the sleeves rolled up to his elbows. He's talking to a man with a clipboard, describing something with impatient, expressive hands. The bright lights fall on him as if besotted by his hair, which is pure black and glossy and straighter than any Paia has ever seen. She knows instantly that this is Kenzo Baraga, once a big-time media baron, now (apparently) president of his country. And more significantly, once N'Doch's hero and role model, now the scourge of his entire family. She studies him carefully as they approach. The man doesn't look like a murderer of helpless old women, even though she knows he is. He's neat and clean, and looks to be stylish within the standards of his era. Nor does he look insane, as is said of Fire's other known henchman, the "hell-priest" of Erde's time. Baraga looks like . . . a businessman. Paia's father used to entertain such men—powerful and rich—at the Citadel in the days before the Final Collapse. But they were never his particular friends.

If Baraga senses the dampening of the bustle that Fire's sudden punishing of the grabber has caused, he gives no sign. He continues his emphatic explanation to the man with the clipboard, who notes Fire's advance with slightly widened eyes but keeps nodding at his boss as if nothing else was on his mind. Only when Fire has come to an august and expectant halt several paces away, does the Media King glance up.

"Well, look who's here!" He offers a faint but genial bow. "El Fiero. It's been a long time."

Paia searches for fear in him, and finds not a hint.

"Kenzo." Fire nods in greeting. "Congratulations on your recent . . . elevation. I hear you're running the place now."

Baraga laughs. "Somebody's got to maintain order around here. Got so I couldn't get any work done. And so, you see? Here I am, back in the traces." He spreads his arms to embrace men, equipment, and studio, then brings his palms together to rub them jovially, looking Paia up and down. "What have you brought me?"

"Ah, my old friend, this one is not for you. Personal property, I'm afraid."

Baraga eyes him as if suspecting a joke. He laughs, but sees no answering gleam in Fire's golden eyes. "But, your pardon, old boy . . . what will *you* do with her? A waste of a gorgeous woman, if she cannot feel your touch and thrust, eh?" He nudges the man with the clipboard, who's frozen to the spot by the man/dragon's proximity.

Paia's distaste deepens. *At least the rest of these creeps have the sense to be afraid of him!*

"Kenzo," says Fire. "You presume too much."

Baraga laughs. "I do, I do! It's your own fault, Fiero! What man could resist such beauty?" He elbows the clipboard man aside and steps past Fire to walk around Paia as if contemplating her purchase. Unlike his underlings, he keeps his hands to himself, though he does lift her chin with his thumb to appraise her face. He seems intrigued by the cool dislike in her gaze. "Hmmm. A live one! Surely you don't really mean to keep all this to yourself!"

Fire says, "Kenzo, we need to talk."

"Such perfect skin! Café au lait! My favorite! Looks marvelous on camera, you know."

Appalling that a mere thumb can feel so possessive! Paia looks away, distracted by the sounds coming from behind Baraga, in the circle of bright light. Somewhere over there, a woman is sobbing.

"Kenzo, a word in private, if you please."

"Let me guess: you've come to claim your piece of the action."

"In a manner of speaking."

"No problem." Baraga shoves gently against Paia's chin, simultaneously a gesture of challenge and dismissal. "But let's talk over dinner, when I can concentrate. Okay by you, Fiero, old boy?" He gestures toward the light and the sobbing, screened from Paia's glance by a barricade of men and equipment. "I'm right in the middle of the final sequence, the devil to get right, you know, under the circumstances. Stick around and watch, then we'll talk. You'll enjoy it. I've revived an old industry tradition to stir up those jaded pricks out there. It's right down your alley. I'd have a chair brought for you, but . . ."

"Kenzo, I need your full attention right now."

Paia is amazed by how reasonable the man/dragon is being. A flash of hot temper is more his style, rather than this calm insistence.

But either Baraga does not hear the menace building in Fire's tone, or he chooses to ignore it. "Five minutes. No more than ten. Soon as I get this shot. Time is money, y'know, and we're in a real time crunch here. I can't afford to have our star, ah . . . leave us . . . before we're finished." He walks away, waving various subordinates into line, and the crowd flows after him, opening a view into the center of the studio. What Paia sees there makes her start violently and bury her face in Fire's side.

A young woman, no, a girl, just a girl, lies naked on a blood-soaked mattress. The mattress is raised off the floor on a sturdy wooden platform so that the cameras can cozy in for close-ups. The platform also carries the metal rings to which the girl's manacles are fastened, hands and feet. A big man stands beside the bed with a knife in his hand. Both hand and knife are as blood-drenched as the bedding, but the man isn't looking at her, though she's sobbing and moaning, and has been sliced in several awful and private places. He's turned away to a mirror, gazing at himself intently while a makeup man blots and powders his face, and touches up his hair.

Paia takes refuge in the assurance that it's all make-believe, truly inspired special effects. But the cameras are currently at rest, and the girl on the bed still wears the terror-stricken glaze of a trapped animal. What did they used to call it? Method acting? And now Paia notices the two men crouching on either side of the bed, whom the first shock of revulsion had hidden from her. They're wearing white lab coats. One applies a pressure bandage to the deepest wounds, while the other monitors the girl's pulse and other vital signs. Well, the girl must be all right if the medics aren't rushing her off to the nearest hospital. But the sticky-sweet smell of carnage under the hot studio lights is nauseatingly real. In her stomach-turning daze of horror, Paia can only wonder how they've kept their white coats so clean.

Baraga strides over to stare down at the girl. "How much longer do we have?"

One of the technicians shrugs. "If you hurry, you'll get the shot."

"Good. Stay in tight until I tell you to clear." He turns to the clipboard man, who is dogging his heels. "Time?"

The man checks a stopwatch. "Commercial break ends in three minutes."

Baraga nods and turns to the big camera, which has been rolled up beside him. He adjusts it slightly, presses a few buttons. "Take the master from here," he says to the operator. He crosses to the second camera, positioned for a close-up of the girl's face. When he's arranged it to his satisfaction, he touches the nearest white-coated medic on the shoulder. "Don't let her die on me too soon. Let her go as slow as you can. We need the footage."

"Yessir, Mr. Baraga."

Die? Don't let her die too soon? Paia's elaborate rationale crumbles. Dizzy and terrified, she snatches at Fire for support, but he's not there. He's moving toward the circle of light, and Paia supposes with a sinking heart that he's zeroing in to enjoy a closer look. But his back is more than usually erect, and he glides rather than walks, a reversion to less human phases of his man-form. He stops just inside the bright circle, taller than any man in the room. The light falls on him as it had on Baraga earlier, setting his red tunic and red-gold hair aglow, glinting off his golden nails and on the faint gilded profile of the scales that have risen up like hackles on his cheeks and neck.

"Kenzo. What is this?"

"What's what?" Baraga barely glances away from the third camera's view screen as he lines up the shot.

"What are you doing here?"

Baraga chuckles into the little screen. "I knew you'd approve. It's kind of an underground thing from the early days of video. Used to call it a snuff flick. I figure people out there are tired of holos and sims. If this doesn't boost the ratings, nothing will."

"You will stop this now."

"Don't make a scene, now. You'll throw off my actors. Don't worry, I'll give you all the time you want when I'm done."

Baraga eases the camera this way, then that, oblivious to what everyone else in the big dark room sees and is backing away from: Fire's ominous glow, his increasingly towering height, the angry hiss of his serpentine curls. The bloody knife clatters to the floor as the big actor shoves past the makeup man and flees into the shadowed perimeter of the room.

"Listen to me, Kenzo Baraga. You will stop this abomination now!"

"What? What?" Baraga lifts his head from the screen at last. He sees he's suddenly alone with a bunch of equipment in a big open space. His only companions are the bleeding girl and the medic whose hands are staunching the flow. Apparently that one fears Baraga's wrath more than the dragon's. Baraga seems unruffled, except for his irritation at the delay. Paia thinks he is either very dense or very confident. He plants his hands on his hips, gazing point-blank into Fire's chill fury, and sighs. "What *is* the problem?"

"Bind her wounds. Let her go."

"What? No way. I have a ton of money invested in this."

"Do it!"

"Wait a minute!" Baraga looks incredulous. "I'm hearing this from you? My evil angel is getting squeamish? The flaming demon of my dreams is suddenly bothered by a little reality video? I can't believe it!"

Paia is not sure she can believe it either. Astonishment shoves horror into the background temporarily. What's come over Fire? Is this another of his poses, or a genuine change of heart?

"Don't argue about it," growls Fire. "Just stop it. Now."

"No." Having moved past his surprise, Baraga is getting angry. "Absolutely not. I've done nothing illegal here. The girl is bought and paid for. Now her father will be able to feed the rest of his family for the next six months, maybe even a year if he isn't reckless. She has three younger brothers who might now make it to adulthood. She's fortunate she can offer them such a gift! Besides, who are you to object?"

Paia hears strong echoes of the God's rationalizing rhetoric in Baraga's justification. She wonders if Fire hears them, too.

"This is not a necessary death, Kenzo. She is no threat to you."

"She'd have died on the streets anyway before she was twenty."

"This is torture, for the pleasure of it."

"Hey, she's not in pain. Scared, maybe, but we've got her on an anesthetic. What do you think I am?"

"A monster."

Baraga laughs. "Oh, that's rich. I'm the monster now. You're going soft, I swear. Look at you all puffed up and furious. What's going on? I've never known you to mind a little mayhem."

"I mind when you misuse the power I gave you."

"You didn't call it misuse when I took care of those little odds and ends you wanted dealt with."

"Those deaths served a larger purpose. A kill should always be *necessary*. And it should be done quickly and cleanly."

"Oh, it's predator's ethics we're talking about here? How old-fashioned. Well, this isn't about ethics, it's about money. My money." Baraga goes into motion now, pacing about, shaking an angry finger at the scaled giant towering over him. "What do you know about what's necessary? What do you know about what sells? What do you know about human tastes?"

"More than I ever cared to."

"Ah, now we're into aesthetics. Look, I'm the sales expert here, and I'll tell you what: people don't *want* a clean kill. Or a justified one. They want it the way they see it in the world: random, messy, and violent. They don't want it noble, and they don't want it metaphorical. They want it real and dirty. They want to see every drop of blood. They want to hear every last gasp." Still pacing, Baraga shrugs elaborately. "Who am I to question? I just give them what they want."

On the shadow's edge, Paia shudders in empathy. Fire cannot fail to hear the echoes now. These are his own words flung back at him.

"And I've given you what you want. So bind her wounds or end it quickly. Otherwise, I'll withdraw my patronage."

The Media King's head snaps up, and his full mouth tightens. "Yeah? Terrific. You go ahead. I can manage without you just fine."

"Kenzo, I'm warning you. No patronage means no protection. Do not take my mercy for granted."

"Threats, Fiero?" Baraga folds his arms and leans against the boxy camera in a show of swagger. "I've got the greatest security organization around."

"Indeed? And where are they now?"

Baraga waves a negligent hand. "I've only to raise the alarm."

Fire shakes his head solemnly. His bleak and implacable gaze makes the circuit of the empty room, boring into the tiered ranks of faces at the control room window, into the crowd at the half open door. "They're watching, oh, so eagerly, but they're not helping, are they? You're just another thrilling episode of reality video as far as they're concerned. The truth is, Kenzo, you've been deserted, as I was, in your last hour."

"What last hour? What are you talking about?"

"If I'm finally going to destroy the monster that is humanity, I might as well start with those of my own creation."

"Threats again? Remember, I know what you are! You can't pick up a glass or open your own door! What're you gonna do to me? You're a vision, a nonthing. Your psychic laser only hurts if the victim believes it will. You may have the rest of them pissing in their pants, but me? I know better." He steps away from the camera and stoops for the knife dropped by the frightened actor. It leaves a puddle of blood behind as he snatches it up. "You can't even stop me if . . ." Faster than Paia has time to comprehend and react, Baraga is beside her, has grabbed her and put the knife to her throat. "If I decide to use this pretty lady as a substitute when the first one's gone wasted?"

The knife is no mere prop. It's actually done the cutting so horribly evident on the dying girl's body. Paia feels its edge as a thin, cold line against her skin. She knows better than to struggle. She'd be terrified, but she knows something else that Kenzo Baraga does not.

An interesting thing happens during the suspended moment while Baraga grips her tight against him, breathing hard from defiance and adrenaline, while the knife blade warms from her own nervous heat, while Fire watches and watches, each second stretching into an eternity. As he watches, the visible signs of his fury diminish. His snarl fades, and with it, his gilded glow and his scales. The wildfires of outrage die in his eyes, leaving them empty and remote, no longer golden but as black as the eternal void. It's a look of failure, of profound defeat.

When at last he moves, it's like Time restarting. Only a pace or two between them, but this also seems to take forever until, with the speed of a snake strike, Fire grabs Baraga's arm, jerks the knife clear and crushes the Media King's wrist to pulp in his gilt-clawed fist.

Baraga cries out in pain and shock and disbelief. The knife spins through the air, away into darkness, clattering wetly against nameless machinery. Paia is flung out of Baraga's grasp, stumbling against the camera. Fire has him by the throat and he's writhing, gasping for help. But those watching from the shadows are not soldiers. Their only loyalty is to their paychecks. And if a few of them are concerned enough to alert the sentries in the outer halls, it's too late by the time those boys in uniform storm the door of the studio, automatic weapons raised before them like talismans of their faith.

By then, Fire has already taken Baraga's head between both hands, as if the stunned and struggling man was straw or feathers, and twisted once. The crunch is like sticks breaking. Fire holds the limp weight aloft for a moment, shakes it gently, then lets it drop. He steps over the corpse, man-sized again but no less intimidating. He stops beside the bleeding girl and pins the terrified medic with a surprisingly gentle regard. "Can you save her?"

The man swallows. "I'll sure try."

"See that you do."

With a deft and iron twisting of his fingers, Fire snaps the girl's manacles, then turns away toward Paia.

"Come, beloved," he says with a tired sigh. "We have an appointment to keep."

CHAPTER THIRTY-FOUR

"What is it, dear knight?" Erde cannot imagine how the old man could have succeeded where the dragons so far have failed. But she's just seen Captain Wender turn away with a grim look, and she refuses to join these men in their gloom and despair. Hal's scholarly side has proved useful before. "What is their Purpose?"

The wind has come up again, flinging snow into Hal's haggard face as he stares up at the dragon and struggles to speak.

"Milady," Wender pleads. "Let me bring him inside, out of this damnable weather, before you get him started again with theories and explanations!"

"Of course, Captain! Though he would be warm enough, tucked next to the dragon."

"And what about the rest of us?" complains Rainer, dryly amused.

"Oh! I . . . forgive me! I . . . !" Again, Erde is too flustered to continue. It seems she will never get a full sentence out in the young king's presence.

"Come, Kurt," he says briskly. "Shelter for all."

He orders the braziers stoked, food and wine brought, then gestures his knights into position around the pavilion. Graciously, he offers his own arm to support the protesting but still tottering Hal through the thickening snow into the comparative warmth of the tent. Inside, Wender hangs Hal's sword back on its hook, and draws up a circle of fur-draped camp chairs. Hal stalls at the doorway, staring in dismay at the chaos of books and papers and lanterns and jumbled furniture. Erde sees him calculating the depth of his plunge into fevered unreason. He lets Rainer lower him into the nearest chair.

"How long, Kurt?" he asks quietly.

"Milord?"

"How long was I . . . unwell?"

Wender decides to play it lightly. "Depends, milord."

"On what?"

"On where you think the borderline might be." Wender gestures toward the higher, messier stacks of books. "It all sounds crazy to me, so who am I to judge?"

"You're a patient man, Kurt." Hal's shoulders relax, and he smiles, rubbing his chin. "I sure need a trim."

"Indeed, milord."

The smile and the calmer manner bring back the elder knight of Erde's fond memory. She settles into the chair next to him once the king has indicated that he prefers to remain standing for a while. "I'm so relieved."

"No more than I." He glances at his hands, sees that they're smeared with mud and dried blood. "Kurt, some hot water, when you have the chance." Wender has it ready, and a clean cloth, and is just clearing space on one of the tables when a boy appears with food and warmed wine. Hal washes intently, as if a proper scrubbing might scour away the shame of his madness. With dripping hands, he slicks back his unkempt hair, then turns stiffly in his chair to eye his king, who leans against a tent pole, watching.

"You're very quiet, my liege."

"I'm savoring the relief of having you back again."

"You're very kind to say so. And I, of course, have no idea of how to apologize."

"No apologies needed."

"If not for the dragon . . ."

"If not for the dragon, you'd be dead of a sword thrust, in my service. And I would have lost my good right hand."

"Well . . ." Hal looks down again to study his palms, clean this time, at least visibly. "It's not all madness, you know. And I really do believe I've found some answers."

"No one doubts you, dear knight!" Erde leans toward him, her hand on his arm. "Tell us! That is, if you're feeling well enough."

Her eager concern and the warm cup of wine that Wender thrusts into his fist are all the encouragement the old soldier requires. He takes a long swig, then sets the cup aside. "You recall, my girl, way back when we pondered the meaning of the answers that odd fellow Gerrasch gave us?"

Erde nods. "You'd think him all the odder if you could see him now."

Hal looks stunned. "You've *seen* him? I thought he'd died, or gone away. Where did you see him?"

"When is actually the question, my knight. Very far in the future, where he has become . . . almost a man, but still very much Gerrasch. You'd recognize him. He is Air's dragon guide."

"Ahhhhhhh. No wonder! A sort of . . . immortal, is he?"

"A halfling creature. Part man, part dragon-stuff."

Hal's stare goes inward for a moment, contemplating this new miracle. "But, remember, when we asked what the Purpose was, he said, 'to fix what's broken'?"

"Of course."

"Well, I know now what's broken."

Erde is too concerned for his delicate health to simply declare this mystery already solved, that it's the Earth itself that's broken, and the question is how to fix it. Nor is this the time to describe to him just how broken. Can these men, for whom disaster means a really bad winter, ever comprehend the devastation that Rose intuited, outside the White City? Instead, she refills his wine cup and hands it to him, putting on her listening expression, while inside she battles with the dragon's impatience as well as her own. Now that Hal is healed to the best of her abilities, Earth wants to get back to the Grove, and it's hard for her to disagree with him. "Tell me your theory, good knight."

"It's all in the book, if only I'd read more carefully, though the understanding is a bit buried by metaphor, perhaps so that it would not fall into the wrong hands. For it is, you see, rather heretical."

"My whole life is heretical, Sir Hal. After all, I consort with dragons."

"Indeed you do." He smiles. "Lucky girl. Anyhow, according to my study, the world was not created by God directly, as it says in the Bible, but by elemental dragons. Four dragons: Earth, Water, Fire, and Air. Whether they be His creatures or not is, I believe, an article of faith."

"Yes, of course." Erde accepts the wine cup that Wender has poured for her. Perhaps sipping it will help her to greater calm.

"When these four created the world, the tale goes, it was in perfect balance. All the elements of Nature in harmony, like musical notes. Then the dragons' work was finished, and they retired to the various depths of the world to sleep. This much was easy to put together, once I accepted its heretical message." He glances at the cup in his hand as if surprised to find it there, and takes a sip. "Then I came to the question of why the dragons waked at all. It seemed obvious that something must have gone wrong."

"Yes. Something has 'broken.'"

"Well, what do you get when you 'break' a perfect balance?" Hal regards her owlishly over the rim of his wine cup.

Erde frowns gently. "I don't know. A mess? Like broken eggs?"

"Anarchy," chimes in Wender, with a sweeping gesture around the tent.

"Imbalance," says the king, with certitude.

"Right as rain, my liege!" Hal exclaims. "Acute as always. You have Nature out of balance. Freakish storms, flood, and drought, the seasons off their cycle. So the dragons' obvious Purpose is to restore that balance."

This is still old news to Erde, though she sees it a bit differently when expressed in Hal's language. "But how, dear sir, how? Isn't that really the question?"

"Of course, importunate child! I'm just getting to that!"

Erde subsides with her wine cup warming her lips. Outside, the wind shakes the heavy canvas of the pavilion so that the tent poles sway. Rainer drops into the chair on Hal's other side, listening expectantly.

"In order to know the cure, as the healers say, one must know the cause. What is the *cause* of this imbalance?" Hal gazes around the small circle of faces as though he was a tutor testing their aptitude. "What presence in the world most often works against the laws of Nature?"

"Evil," Erde declares.

"True, true. But evil in what form? Be careful, now. The evil that's done may not always be present in the *intent*." He eyes them again. "Come, come! You've all of you suffered at its hand!"

"War?" suggest Wender.

"The Church," Erde murmurs.

The young king shifts in his chair, recrossing his long legs. "It's men you speak of, isn't it?"

"Surely, it is!" the old knight crows. "Allow me to kneel to you yet again, Sire, and offer my sword in your service!"

Rainer flushes, not angry but visibly annoyed. "There are faster ways than guessing games to get at the heart of a matter, my knight."

Hal nods, unrepentant. "Indeed there are, but indulge an old retainer a moment longer. If, as you so astutely surmise, it is men who create the imbalance, it is men who must be corrected." Now when he looks around, he's greeted with glum silence. "Ah. I see you perceive the dilemma."

"People have been trying to do that since the year One."

"And before!" exclaims Hal, as if the notion offers him great satisfaction.

"But surely men are part of Nature," Kurt Wender protests.

Hal shakes his shaggy head. "Set above the rest of Creation, according to the Book. The natural world is intended for his use and sustenance. But in return, man is pledged to act as steward of these resources, to protect Nature, and sustain her. Somewhere along the line, the bargain' was forgotten."

He sits back to take another long pull at his wine cup, then collects a hunk of cheese from the platter beside his knee. "Now, here's where I begin to fly off into the ethereal heights of wild speculation. Think of it from the point of view of bridge building or barn raising. Any balanced structure will have some natural flex to keep it from snapping in the gales, or in ice heaves in the winter. So at first, the depredations of man come and go without dire effect. Contemplating this one day, it occurred to me that if I were the master builder of the 'bridge' of Nature, I'd try to build in some sort of signal that would raise the alarm if the bridge was about to fail. Let's say such a signal exists, and it woke the dragons . . . ." He leans forward, his eyes alight.

". . . at the point when the balance tipped too far for the natural flex to be able to restore it."

Erde feels a small implosion of insight inside her head. She's unsure if it's hers, or the dragon's, or both. "But that would be now . . . or, just a while ago, when . . ."

"Yes. When you found Lord Earth, and not long after, I found you."

"It's *now*," Erde repeats, aware that her attack of insight is still in process. "Oh!" She grabs her head as if her growing comprehension might split it apart. "That's why Air called us back to the Grove! That's where the balance tipped, and it's going on right now! It's Brother Guillemo cutting down the trees!"

"Among other things." Hal nods, gone suddenly solemn. "Guillemo isn't the cause himself, so much as its final incarnation."

"Guillemo!" Erde stares at him, wide-eyed. "The dragons are coming, Air and Water and their guides. Earth and I will go, too. To the Grove. What will we do there?"

"Teach the race of men to honor their bargain, or destroy them. Those seem to be the only possible options."

Captain Wender shakes his head at such grandiose imaginings. Erde can see him wondering if the old knight's mind is once again wandering. "We can't do away with the one man, never mind the whole race of 'em!"

She sees it come over them, all three of them, as visible as the shadow of a cloud over sunlight. Their shoulders slump as if choreographed together. Their mouths and brows turn gently down.

Hal says, "True enough. The hell-priest's magic has protected him damnably well." He squints at his book-laden camp desk and a hint of his former confusion returns to his eyes. "I was looking for some sort of countermeasure. It's as if he reached out and corrupted my search."

"Can't kill the bastard," Wender mutters. "Begging your pardon, milady."

"But how can it be," Erde asks, "that you have him surrounded and still cannot finish him?"

"Our forces are demoralized," Rainer admits, "both men and knights, by weather and hunger and disease. We've had victories everywhere else, but this siege has proved, well, intractable."

Hal adds glumly, "And as long as Guillemo lives, many will believe in him."

"The men are afraid for their souls," offers Wender.

"In a way," continues Rainer, the rationalist, "Guillemo's turned the trees against us. We have the advantage of numbers, but you can't send an army in there. There's no room to fight. The men get picked off from above before they're a horse's length into the trees."

"But we have to stop him! He's destroying the Grove!"

Hal glances up suddenly, remembering. "Did you say Air called you to the Grove? Have you found all four dragons, then? There are four, as I said?"

"Yes, dear knight. Though we have yet to win Fire to our cause. Yet we are summoned, all of us, so sometime soon—Lord Earth and I are unsure of the timing—Brother Guillemo will have surprise visitors."

The men exchange glances.

"An unusual opportunity," notes Rainer.

"The perfect time for a fresh offensive," Wender agrees.

"But perhaps the dragons will not need our help," Hal observes.

"Do not say so!" Erde exclaims. "All help is welcome and necessary!"

Wender drops his chin into his palms and rests his elbows on his knees. "It'll take some time to get the men ready . . ."

Rainer rises from his chair and wanders away, stretching his long back. "The barons always resist fighting in this weather."

"Again?" Erde is unable to restrain herself further. She leaps up from her chair. "Listen to you all! For shame! Will you give up so easily?" The men blink at her and glance away, and she knows they're ashamed for her breach of ettiquette. It's not her place, as a young girl, to be scolding her elders, or advising seasoned fighting men, or for that matter, berating her king. But she sees no one else around willing to do it, and something must be done to stir them out of their gloom!

She tries to moderate her voice, and keep her whirling arms under more ladylike control. "I'd think Fra Guill has put a spell on you, but I don't believe in such spells, not anymore! Cease your search for magic, good knight. There is no magic but dragon magic, the magic of the elements that made the world. If you seek to understand the success of the hell-priest, look no further. It's right here, in this camp, in this tent, in your own hearts! Your true enemy is despair! Your men won't fight because they have no faith that they can win. They and you—now, don't deny it! I can see it in your eyes—believe that evil is the stronger force, and therefore the hell-priest triumphs!"

"Little sister, little sister," Rainer chides. "You are as always passionate in your ideals. But real life is not so simple."

"No, listen!" Is it treason, she wonders briefly, to argue with your king? "Sometimes we must *make* it simple! Sometimes we must speak in absolutes! Rainer . . . your pardon, I mean, Sire . . . you think me naïve, and perhaps I am, though not nearly so as I was when you saw me last. I have seen how 'real life' wears down the great Ideals: with this excuse, that pragmatic consideration, the several 'necessary' concessions. Soon, the clean and noble marble edifice is worn and weary, crumbling at the edges so that all manner of petty evils and cynicisms enter unheeded through the cracks!"

She pauses, breathless, and the discomfort on their faces nearly stalls her momentum. She's embarrassing herself in front of them, her mentor and the young man she once thought she loved. No matter! She must finish what she's begun. "Well, all that may be 'real' and day-to-day, and we must live with it. And perhaps the smaller evils will most often triumph. But this is not day-to-day, and the greater evil cannot be allowed to triumph! Good must win, or the world will not survive!"

She faces the young king, who regards her stony-faced. "My liege! Go to your barons and your captains! Inspire them with your faith and vigor! If we believe, they'll believe!"

"And you, dear Sir Hal, whose tireless conviction in the rightness of dragons saved our Quest from early disaster . . . I know the winter has been desperate and long, and the battle endless, but surely you'll not give up when that end is now in sight?"

Then, all of a sudden, she's out of words. The last drop has poured out of the wine jug. She feels as if she's run a long foot race, and has no idea if she's lost or won. She sits down again, and lapsing into silence, she wraps her arms around herself and gently rocks. The men are silent, too, and for a while they all sit listening to the wind howl and the snow rattle against the canvas. Captain Wender sips his wine. Hal stares morosely into his upturned palms as if hoping to read his fortune. Rainer stares off into the shadow at the corners of the tent, probably wrestling with the weight of his new responsibilities.

Finally, he stirs. "Can you say with any accuracy when the other dragons will arrive?"

Erde can see the brilliance of her smile reflected in the men's eyes. "Not when it will happen, Sire, but surely we will know the exact moment when it *is* happening. If we are ready. . . ."

"Then we'll be ready." The king rises, and Wender with him, drawn upward by respect and the strength of the younger man's returned resolve. "Wender, alert the captains, rouse the men and the knights. Drag the barons from their beds if need be."

"Aye, my liege!" Wender wraps his heavy cloak about him and ducks out of the tent.

Rainer lifts the canvas door flap. "It's near night already."

Hal consults the water clock on his camp desk. "No, Sire. It's just past noon. It's an unnatural night."

"The moment will be soon, then," Erde murmurs, feeling the stirrings of a terror she cannot even name.

"So be it," Rainer replies with conviction, and follows Wender through the doorway into snow and darkness.

CHAPTER THIRTY-FIVE

N'Doch stares through the iron grille set in the stone gateway. Only this frail barrier and Gerrasch's chunky body stand between him and what used to be a dank castle courtyard. Now it looks like the insides of a computer. The nanos have been hard at work out there.

He tugs nervously at his heavy vest and leggings. The Deep Moor ladies have once again managed to outfit him against the cold, this time by giving up various layers of their own, since the fake Deep Moor neglected to include the storage closets. So, he's sweating in wool and sheepskin, but shivering in his heart. Least, that's how it feels to him. The word "endgame" keeps cycling through his brain like some kind of fiendish audio loop.

This time, he tells himself, *the shit really is gonna hit the fan.*

The truth is, he doesn't know what to expect. If this was a vid, there'd be smart nukes and laser weapons and robotic armored vehicles. But this little assault force, except for himself, is all women and old men. Well, old-ish. He knows Stoksie and Luther wouldn't appreciate the designation. As for Gerrasch, who knows what he is.

Women, old men . . . and two dragons.

He's spent the last few hours helping with the flurry of preparation, getting everyone briefed, provisioned, and armed with whatever was available, which wasn't much. Having had their way with the outer courtyard, the nanos are taking down the farmstead at an ever-increasing rate. The house is gone, but for remnants of the rose arbor. The central tree is a last holdout, as if the nanos have preserved its sinuous branches and green tapestry of leaves as some kind of museum exhibit of the extinct characteristics of organic life-forms.

N'Doch shivers again, then gathers himself sternly, leaning on the shaft of the pike he's been assigned, and grins down at his grandfather, who stands as calm and composed as ever.

"Well, it was sure great being back at the Rive 'n all, but I won't mind seeing the last of this burg."

Djawara crinkles his eyes, as if a full-tilt smile might show disrespect for this serious occasion. "All my life, I never traveled abroad, just from the bush to the city, the city to the bush. Now, in my old age, fifteen centuries in what's seemed like an afternoon."

"We ain't there yet, Papa." But he knows getting there is not the problem. It's what happens after. Behind them, the women are falling into formation. A ragtag army, but N'Doch can't help feeling proud of these women. A few of them look scared—after all, they're headed right back to the place they ran from in terror not too long ago—but no one's complaining. They're used to having to defend themselves, and they have faith in the dragons. Probably more than he does.

A big hand lands on his shoulder. "Ready to sing, bro?"

"Damn, I thought you were gonna send me in there on my lonesome." Despite his doubts, N'Doch feels a lot better with the dragon beside him. "Gettin' near time?"

Sedou nods. "G won't be able to hold her back much longer."

"What's gonna go down? You got something spectacular planned? I keep pushing to hear some strategy." He jerks his thumb toward the silent Librarian, who stares intently through the gate like he was entirely alone in the world. "But G tells me that sort of thinking's too structured for Air."

"My plan is, we'll rout the bastard." Sedou grins wickedly.

"Yeah, yeah." He tries to conjure up his old pawn-of-destiny resentment. Do him good to toss out a few anti-dragon slogans right now, just to keep up appearances. But, truth is, he's about used all that up. Given that he's pretty sure he'll never see home again, given all this "mutual annihilation" business, still he'd have to say that what he's feeling is a kind of gratitude. If he was told he could go home tomorrow, he'd probably tell 'em he wasn't interested. How could he say otherwise? Thanks to these dragons, he's had the adventure of his life.

He scratches his jaw uneasily, leveling an accusing stare at the back of Gerrasch's hairy head. Something's happening to him, no question about it. Ever since Air came on-line with the dragon internet, he's felt different. He'd mention it to Erde or Paia, if they were around, see what they say. Like, maybe they're feeling it, too. Sounds too stupid to come out and say it to anyone who isn't a dragon guide, not the way he really feels it. Which is, like he's got more . . . air . . . in him now. Like, when he looks at these gutsy women, instead of thinking how uncool they are, he feels vast and generous inside, and like he can see to infinity. The real way to describe it is, he feels more like a dragon now. But he knows if he told that to Sedou, he'd get laughed out of town.

So instead, he tucks the pike shaft against his chest and drapes his free arm around his grandfather's slim shoulders. The dragon-as-Sedou stands behind them both. Like a family portrait, N'Doch muses. One that never got taken while Sedou was actually alive.

In front of him, Gerrasch stirs, and the hand on his own shoulder tightens. "Here we go."

And through the stone gateway, the view is no longer nanomech abstract art, but the drifts and snow-laden branches of the Grove.

Erde yawns, despite her nerves being stretched taut with waiting. She'd caught a few hours' sleep in Hal's tent while the armies prepared, and was woken later in the afternoon by the dragon's rumblings. Now, at the king's insistence, she sits wrapped in a royal cloak and astride a royal horse, even though she'd have preferred to walk out to the field alongside the dragon, and even though the poor horse will be suddenly riderless when the others arrive, and she and the dragon go to join them in the Grove. Earth expects that Air will reopen the portal at the far end of the meadow. What will happen after that is anybody's guess, but Earth made sure to build up his strength by easing the death of two badly wounded horses and a starving dog, having first asked their permission to consume them afterward.

For now, the king has arrayed his men in a wide circle around the Grove, just outside the range of the archers who've been lurking among the first rank of trees. The strategy is simple: to rush in when the dragon signals that the portal is opening. He says he hears nothing specific, but senses his sibling's preparations as a very faint echo rolling down the years from the far future. When the portal opens, it will be as if the echo has become a shout from across the valley.

Earth crouches to Erde's right, huge and dark against the white snow, a wall of shadow in the afternoon gloom. Both the barons and their knights resisted the notion of fighting at night, no matter that success would rely on coinciding the assault with the arrival of the other dragons. Their young king finally won them over with a stirring paean to the value of surprise. Now each foot soldier carries both his weapon and a torch. Erde hopes the ancient trees of the Grove will forgive her for allowing this ancient enemy into their sacred precincts, but they've withstood fire before. The saws and axes of Brother Guillemo present a much more present danger.

Hal lopes down along the line and noses his horse in beside her. "Any word?" He regards the dragon eagerly, almost lovingly, for a sign. His horse dances, restless for action.

Erde shakes her head. She rejoices to see the knight hale again, washed and barbered and clad in his worn red leathers from the old king's service, looking like the warrior who taught her the skills that kept her alive once she'd fled her father's castle. He's looking especially inspired at the moment because she'd finally found the time to let him know that Rose and the other women were not killed or taken prisoner during the burning of Deep Moor—as he had assumed, swearing that this was what had driven him over the edge. Erde could privately have added a number of reasons for the knight's sanity to be vulnerable. The news in Hal's life, despite his great virtue and cleverness, has most often been bad, especially lately. Though, perhaps Hal himself would not say so. After all, one of his most cherished ambitions has been fulfilled: he's consorted with dragons. Right now he's even smiling, in his stern sort of way, as if recalling the good news she has given him, and savoring it all over again.

How wonderful to love, Erde muses, and love in return. Perhaps Rose and Hal are each other's consolation prize for not having dragons of their own. And, as visions of love always conjure Adophus of Köthen, there he is, like a mirage before her eyes. But instead of banishing his handsome visage, as she has learned to do the moment a thought of him arrives, Erde lets her memories of him fill her senses, just for now, a sort of farewell. A true love must be all-consuming, and perhaps she would not have had proper room in her heart for both a dragon and a man.

Still, she wishes he was here, less for her sake than for Hal's, to have one more agile sword fighting by their side. But he has chosen other battles, as is his right. Erde wishes him well, and godspeed.

The Librarian's arm answers the dragon's signal. Before he has time to think about it, he's gripped the iron grille and swung it wide. He's lost all sense of independent existence, of owning his own life. He is Air's conveyance, yes, but not just some mindless mechanism. That would be easier to bear. No, he's her smart-car, programmed with all the rules of the road, and the assignment of keeping his reckless driver from veering off the highway.

As the portal opens, long stored memories awaken. The bite of the cold, the dry scent of the winter trees. The Librarian sees/hears/feels the forest as the dragon senses it, as a tapestry of sensual data. He adds to that his emotional connection with this old place of safety and retreat, his first Refuge.

And then, peering into the dim late light, he sees what

has been done to it. Raw stumps, hewn logs lying scattered about like giant matchsticks, piles of broken branches, the trampled ground gouged from the dragging. The wide wounds of a road, bleeding mud, leading from the base of the meadow to the spread of tents and campfires at the farther end.

He opens his mouth, gasping like a fish on land. He'll spew up his cry of rage and grief like vomit. And then, between one despairing breath and the next, he's alone in his head again.

The Librarian nearly collapses. Behind him, Luther sees him flag and shoulders past N'Doch to grab him under the arms and drag him through the gate so that the others will not crush him, rushing through.

"Yu all ri', G?"

The Librarian hasn't a clue. Has the portal malfunctioned? No, here he is, knee-deep in snow. And there's N'Doch with one arm around his grandfather, and Sedou/Water, even now morphing into numberless and nameless tiny motes. After them, the two trackers, and Stoksie and Rose and the other ladies of Deep Moor. He has to keep count, make sure they all get through before the portal closes. But where is the dragon? Where is Air? Who wil revenge this awful desecration? A newborn child is n more innocent or worthy than an ancient tree!

"She's left me," he mutters, hearing himself rave like some old drunk who's lost his woman.

"Who has?"

"She . . ." No, there she is. He feels her now. Touching, filling, merging with the trees, with the leafless branches and the sodden earth of the meadow and the snow and the muddied rim of the pond, entering the very substance of the Grove as she had entered him, molecule by molecule.

As she flows into and through, the snowdrifts swirl up and coalesce into the shapes of woodland animals. Pale and huge, they stalk across the meadow. The barren trees writhe like a nest of vipers. The smoke rising from the campfires twists into the form of winged raptors, and the water of the pond leaps up as fish, their gaping mouths lined with teeth.

The sentries bellow their alarm. The quiet camp explodes into action, as the bedded-down troops glance up from their dice games and weapons repair. Voices cry out for light, though it is not yet night. The fires flare high as wood is thrown on in armloads. A hundred torches burst to life. The dark profiles of running men and rearing horses crisscross the brightening glare.

The Librarian hauls himself out of his tumble into grief and outrage. Knowing no other direction but forward, he raises his arm and gestures his little battalion on across the meadow, while around them the trees sway and the whirlwind snow shapes of stag and bear ride guard.

"More light!" the voices cry, now less distant and more frightened. Other commands ring out, but panic deafens the soldiers. They stumble over each other, reaching for their boots, their weapons, their helmets, striking out against shadows and blindly maiming their friends. The campfires swell into bonfires, shooting flame and spark into the thick dark air above the meadow. A man on a tall white horse circles the central fiery tower, yelling threats and encouragement. His white robe takes on the ruddy colors of the fire, and his raised sword throws shards of light far enough to flash in the Librarian's eyes.

The shadows recede before the fire's onslaught. The snow beasts seem less substantial, even flimsy in the glare. Taking heart at the banishing of darkness, the soldiers come to their senses and once again hear the hoarse shouts of their officers, and especially the mounted white-robe, who rides among them like a dog among sheep, herding them into order.

"Illusions only! Pay them no heed! Magic has no force among the righteous!" the white-robe rails, and even through the veil of centuries, the Librarian recognizes the voice of Brother Guillemo.

He glances behind him, with fleeting thoughts of retreat. He is halfway between camp and portal. The last of the women, Margit's twins, each assisting one of the older refugees, hurry through the stone arch hovering insubstantially among the trees. The Librarian grimaces at the finality of it, then releases his stranglehold on a tiny shred of Air's consciousness, which is all that's kept the portal open after his own passage through it. The gateway, its stone pillars and iron grille and its slice of view into the sun and green of Deep Moor, vanishes into snow and air and darkness.

And then, Earth arrives. Water completes her transmutation. Her numberless crystalline motes swirl up into the whirlwinds to be carried over the camp as a glittering cloud with uncanny intent. Raindrops hiss in the bonfires, the early warning of the downpour that follows, quenching the flames with a great whoosh and a belching of black smoke. New cries of dismay rise from the soldiers, blinded again by smoke and oncoming night, and another wave of terror as the ground shudders and sways, jerking them off their feet. Still the white-robed rider, Brother Guillemo, whips his frothing mount through the panic and pandemonium, one moment exhorting his troops to bravery, in the next, promising courts-martial and executions if they do not stand and fight. Many are frightened back to their posts. Even more choose to take their chances with the shadows and the spectral beasts. They flounder off into the drifts between the trees, where their retreat is cut off by a new flare of light. The armies of the king have entered the Grove unchallenged for the first time since the siege began. Surrounding the camp, the foot soldiers light their torches. Fra Guill's army is circled by a ring of bright and steady fire.

Taking advantage of Air's ubiquitous eye, the Librarian observes how, for many of those seeking to flee, the appearance of the enemy seemingly out of nowhere and at night completes the destruction of their fighting spirit. They throw down their weapons, and then themselves, begging rescue from the fury of unnatural forces, and from their mad leader as well. Fear lends others strength enough to hack a way through the enemy line. Mounted squads are immediately sent off in pursuit. But the Librarian knows this is not the real battle. He hopes that the fighting will be over soon, now that it has accomplished its purpose, which was to clear the Grove of this pesky human intrusion so that the important work can begin.

But there is one intrusion more to be reckoned with. Never having dealt with him, and despite the Librarian's warnings, Air has overlooked Brother Guillemo. Until he's done for, this king will not leave the Grove. And the priest sees this is likely his final stand, which makes him a desperate and unpredictable obstacle. Already he has succeeded in re-forming a substantial phalanx of his personal guard, his white-robed priest-knights. On their huge and spirited horses, they fill the central clearing, stirring up the pond and spilling out into the snow-swept meadow. But he does not order them to attack. He's stalling for time, the Librarian guesses. Several of the knights have dismounted to build up the largest bonfire, still smoldering damply at its heart. The flames rise high as the dragons pull back, allowing the king's armies to march away their prisoners, clear the wounded, and tighten their ring around the remaining enemy. A respectful space is left for Earth, the only visible dragon, to take his place among them. The men tip their pikes to Erde, who rides proudly on Earth's shoulder. Water glitters among the tree branches like a galaxy of stars. Air waits. She thinks the humans will be gone soon. Again, the Librarian cannot convince her that she's wrong.

The Deep Moor refugees have been spotted, and Hal is racing around the outer ring to greet Rose and draw her up onto his saddle. But he soon sets her down again, signaling Wender over to shepherd them to the safety of the camp outside the Grove. As if in evidence to the Librarian's point, Rose and Raven insist they will stay. Linden joins them, murmuring that a healer might be needed. Stoksie and Luther vow to protect them, while Margit and Lily insist that they will join the fight. Wisely, Hal doesn't argue. He shrugs, kisses Rose soundly, and rides back into the line.

Inside the ring, Brother Guillemo rides around the central bonfire as if celebrating a victory. His white-robes have drawn their mounts up around him in a second ring. Guillemo has thrown back his hood so that his pale face shines in the firelight, cut across sharply by black brows and a black beard that shelters a surprisingly full, red mouth. *A sensual face,* muses the Librarian, whose earlier collisions with the hell-priest left him little time for leisurely observation. The priest's deep voice carries without straining, as an actor's must, lending it a disturbing quality of intimacy, despite its volume and grandiose rhetoric.

"Illusions!" he is bellowing. "If you do not heed them, they can do no harm!"

"But the dragons . . . !" shouts one of the white-robes, as if speaking an assigned role.

"Dragons! A mere creature of Nature! God decrees that man's proper destiny is to rule over Nature! Nature is chaos! Chaos is the enemy! Man brings order and piety and civilization!"

The Librarian's old habits of protest stir in his gut like a nest of hornets. *If cutting down a grove of sacred trees is your idea of piety and civilization,* he wants to shout, *language has lost all its meaning. This is filth, what you've done! You are filth!* But because the dragons still wait, he keeps his silence.

"Man must bend all Nature into harness!" the priest continues, as if he stood in the pulpit of a church and not on the field about to fight his last battle. "Water, wind, the products of the earth! All are created to fuel humankind's drive toward our manifest destiny! I know this to be true and good and righteous! If you believe in me, if you believe in that destiny, they cannot stand against us!" He whirls his horse at the circle of his own men. A way parts for him, as if rehearsed, and he rides boldly into the no-man's-land between the opposing forces. Now his exhortations are aimed at the front ranks of the king's infantry, who stare back at him stonily with pikes at the ready.

"You there!" He singles out one soldier in particular, a boy with sullen eyes. "Most likely you will die tonight! You think you have the advantage of numbers, but hear me! Few can stand against my knights! What will become of your immortal soul if you die fighting for a dragon's cause?"

The Librarian notes several nods among the boy's neighbors. Heads bend together, muttering.

"You there!" The priest spurs down the line, flirting with the archers in the rear by dancing his horse in and out of their range. He pulls up across from an older infantryman. "Is it right that your stripling king forces you into battle in support of *witches,* who should be properly burned in God's name?"

More nods and mutters, even some audible grumbling.

The Librarian grinds his teeth. He's just realized what the dragons are waiting for. They're still expecting the fourth of them to arrive.

Erde shivers as Fra Guill evokes the horrors of the stake. She's slipped down from Earth's shoulder to his forearm, avoiding the hell-priest's line of sight, and hopes that the women standing in the warmth of the dragon's shadow will do likewise. Is he looking for her even now? For Rose, or Raven? As he wheels his horse in her direction, Erde shrinks against the dragon's chest, then gasps as a hand grips her ankle.

"Hey, can I come up?" N'Doch grins up at her, his teeth very white against his face and his face very dark against the snow. He vaults up beside her and ruffles her hair, which is his idea of an appropriate greeting. "So far, so good. Was that you brought in the army?"

"Sort of. I mean, they were already out there, waiting."

"Good move. Speaking of waiting, what's going on? Water's too discorporate to make any sense."

"That's what they're doing. Waiting."

"What for? Why don't they just finish the bastard?"
Erde stares at him.

"You're giving me that old surely-you-know-by-now look."
She replies as if reciting a lesson. "A dragon cannot end a life without asking that life's permission."

"I mean the soldiers, not the dragons. How can they stand to sit still for that crap?"

"Oh." Erde frowns gently. She'd stopped listening to the hell-priest long ago. "I think they're waiting for the dragons to do it."

"Well, someone better let them know they could be in for a long wait. Surely Hal knows better."

"Sir Hal answers to his king."

N'Doch rolls his eyes. "The old king thing."

"Don't be disrespectful."

He makes another sour face, tapping the ridges on Earth's chest plate. Erde sees he's anxious, a bit jumpy.

"What about the Fire dude?" he asks finally. "You think he'll show?"

"I don't know." She realizes she's disappointed, and yes, nervous, too. Earth had nearly convinced her that Fire would be unable to resist Air's final summons. But if he doesn't come, what next?

"Okay, here we go. Somebody's making a move. It's Hal. What's he up to?"

N'Doch points along the rank of soldiers, and Erde pulls up out of her defensive slouch to look. Hal has urged his horse forward from beside the king, and is riding with slow deliberation around the ring on a path that will bring him face-to-face with Brother Guillemo. His back is erect. His chin is high. The dragon-hilted sword lies unsheathed across his red-leathered thighs. Erde thinks he looks the very picture of a King's Knight.

N'Doch whistles softly. "No chance of one man taking this creep down. What's Hal gonna do, challenge him? I wouldn't trust that dude to fight fair!"

"But no one has more reason to challenge him." Erde chews her lip, worried. "And he feels this is all his fault for not seeing what Fra Guill was from the beginning, and for not putting a stop to him then."

"Hey, hindsight is twenty-twenty."

"Is what?"

"Never mind."

After a moment, Erde says, "Still, I wish he would let a younger man fight. If only . . ."

She hesitates so long that N'Doch fills in the rest. "If only Dolph was here?"

"Yes."

"Hey, I'd like that, too." He pats her shoulder. "Don't worry. If it goes bad, the dragons'll step in somehow."

There's another pause, so that the sound of Fra Guill haranguing the troops intrudes like a physical presence between them. Finally, Erde says, "We put so much faith in them."

"You're the one who taught me to."

"But what if three is not enough? What if Lord Fire doesn't come? What if our dragons can't do what needs to be done?"

"Then the world goes down the tubes, I guess. Least, that seems to be what they're suggesting."

Miserable, anxious, impatient, but grateful for his company, she leans into his side, and together they watch Hal ride to within a dragon's length of the hell-priest and stop. Guillemo ignores him, or seems to. But he abandons forward motion in favor of pacing his horse back and forth within a contained area, as if he's detected a particular source of potential converts within the enemy's ranks. He's reached the point in his sermonizing where the "witch-girl" comes up for specific mention. After a few paragraphs of choice invective, he turns his horse at the end of a pace and pretends to discover the red-clad knight who sits calmly leaning on the bridge of his saddle, not ten yards away.

"Angels of grace!" the priest exclaims. "It's the dragon lord himself! Are you resurrected, by some black magic? They said you'd fallen on the field not three days ago!"

"It's true I took a blade," replies Hal amiably.

"Then, what devil's bargain keeps you in this world?"

"None but the desire to see you dead and buried, Guillemo."

The priest looks shocked, and shoots a complicit glance at the murmuring soldiers. Erde suspects Fra Guill's spies have told him of the superstitious fears that Hal's eccentricities have inspired in some of the men under his command. "Sir, I am a man of the cloth. You will address me as 'father,' my son."

"Not a chance."

"Though you are lost to Hell for your unrepentant delving into the blackest of magic, yet I will pray for your soul."

Hal smiles blandly. "And that's the surest road to Hell I can think of."

The mutters from the infantry are clearly audible by now. N'Doch clicks his tongue. "Ease up, Hal. It's not playing too well to the troops."

Hal lifts his sword casually from his lap, letting it hang alongside his horse's flank. "So, what will it be, Guillemo? In the King's name, I can offer you surrender, to save the lives of your men, or certain defeat and no prisoners."

But Brother Guillemo has turned away, listening, as if to heavenly choirs. Erde nudges N'Doch as the dragon stirs beneath them. "Do you feel it? Something's . . . happening. Someone's . . . it's . . ."

N'Doch hears Water's subvocal warning just as the dark sky above the clearing is split by the flash of gilded wings. He's not sure if Fire's coming is good or bad, but he's relieved to have the waiting over with. Fire circles once, screaming like a jet on a runway approach. The soldiers break ranks and run for cover. Half of Guillemo's knights take advantage of the chaos to kick their horses into a gallop and leap to freedom over the heads of the fleeing men. The rest draw up tight around him, while the king's captains struggle to regain control of their army. With a great splaying of talons tipped in shining gold, Fire hovers above the central bonfire as if born out of its flames. Then he settles on top of it, scattering burned logs and embers among the loyal cluster of white-robes. Only one manages to retain his control of his mount, and his position by Guillemo's side. Two are unhorsed, but steady on their feet. The rest follow their fellows off into darkness.

"Damn!" N'Doch whispers fervently. "Another great entrance! The dude's timing is impeccable!" But Erde is staring at him with her usual mix of horror and condemnation. "I know, I know," he says. "If he's here to save Guillemo's butt, this could be very bad."

Fire hunkers down in the embers for long enough to chill every heart in the Grove with his golden glower and the curl of acrid smoke escaping through the corners of his snarl. N'Doch thinks he couldn't have scripted it better himself. After all, cliches work because they're primal.

To his credit, Brother Guillemo recovers first, his voice steady atop his skittering horse. "You see! He conjures yet another fiend from the fires of Hell!"

Hal replies dryly, "No, Guillemo. I believe this one is yours."

Now what, wonders N'Doch. He spots Water's sparkle migrating toward a gathering point. Gerrasch stands in the open several paces away, still as a statue, a Tinker hovering protectively to either side of him. The king's army is settling into some measure of order, but its ranks have been thinned by desertions, squads sent off in pursuit, and others detailed to escort prisoners back to the main camp. Guillemo's in a tough spot, and N'Doch figures it's about time for him to try sleazing his way to a surrender. He has three men left of his own, and precious few of the king's to preach to. He's likely gained a dragon on his side, but he can't welcome Fire's support without blowing his whole cover. Brandishing his sword hilt as a cross, the priest faces the dragon crouching in the fire with as much ambiguity as he can muster. "Speak, O Fiend! What is your errand?"

As if in answer, flames shoot up to obscure the dragon within a curtain of blinding light that burns so fiercely that the horses squeal in terror and those around it retreat from its sudden heat. Then, just as suddenly, it dies away into smoke and a shower of sparks. A man and a woman stand among the ashes. Or rather, N'Doch observes, a spectacular woman and a great, golden giant.

"Quite the couple," he murmurs, hoping to cheer Erde with a scandalous remark. Yet, as he watches Fire offer his hand to help Paia through the smoldering remains of the bonfire, N'Doch realizes he's not far off the mark. He knows how lovers move together.

The other dragons are still waiting.

The Librarian notes how solicitous Fire is with Paia, but otherwise, the giant's expression is grim and furious as he glares around the clearing, taking stock of who's there and how the confrontation has so far played out. He stalks toward the priest, keeping Paia close behind him. As they leave the circle of embers, the flames spring up again to light their way.

Brother Guillemo's bold facade has been visibly frayed by Fire's transformation, and the Librarian suspects he knows why: it's one thing to rant over a snarling, voiceless reptile, but another thing altogether to handle a walking, talking man. Still, with his trio of knights clustered behind him, Guillemo sits firmly erect on his horse. Only his eyes show the true depths of his terror. Good, good, the Librarian approves. At last we've found something the hell-priest is afraid of.

Fire stops at the point where a perfect triangle could be drawn between himself, the hell-priest and Hal. His towering, muscular body is wrapped in a long robe of cloth-of-gold that reflects the firelight and hisses faintly as he moves, then continues to shimmer and dance long after he's eased to a halt. His glimmering hair is braided and bound at the back of his neck, but it, too, seems to have a life of its own. Despite himself, the Librarian has to admit that if he believed in a god, he'd wish it to look this magnificent. That he has a beautiful and apparently adoring woman draped on his elbow does nothing to disturb the Librarian's notions of deity.

When the giant speaks, his voice is a modulated tenor, a cultivated voice, and in its cool formality, the Librarian hears the echoes of ritual.

"I come to claim the kingdom you promised me," Fire says to the priest.

Guillemo lifts his sword hilt higher, as if its cruciform shape might actually protect him. "Away! I know you not! Why do you speak to me?" He gestures hugely in Hal's direction. "Look there to find your master!"

"I have no master, and seek none. I come for repayment of the favors I've granted, as we agreed."

"I know you not, I say!" Guillemo lowers the sword slightly. "Unless you are one of God's angels sent in disguise to deliver the just from the enemies of righteousness?"

"Will you deny me to my face, ungrateful priest?" Fire throws his massive shoulders back. He seems to be enjoying himself, in a dark sort of way. "Again, I ask: have you prepared my palaces and lands? Is my Temple ready to be consecrated?"

"Begone, vile imagining! Or if you be a true angel, claim your heavenly form and aid me now! Do you not see? I am beset by devils!"

Fire's rigid stance unbends. He motions Paia to remain in the warmth from the bonfire, and moves in on the priest. Guillemo's horse lays his ears back and shudders, but stands admirably still as the giant looms over them. "That's the required three chances, Guillemo. Do you need a fourth? It looks like you've failed to prepare the Faithful for the arrival of their god, but if you can offer me a comfortable castle toward the south, I'll call it even."

Guillemo turns his horse, circling his three stony-faced knights. "Fear not, men of good faith! A test is sent us from above, but we shall show ourselves equal to it!" Now that he has put the knights between him and the dragon, he faces Fire again. "You! Angel! Prove the truth of your divine origins! Defeat our enemies! Destroy the witch-girl and her warlock mentor! Depose the false king! Then all just believers will bow to you as God's representative on earth!"

Fire says, "The witch-girl. Ah. There's an idea." He turns away, and for the first time, looks around at the scattered ring of watchers. The Librarian knows this is only for show. Fire knows exactly where Erde is, where each dragon and dragon guide stand, awaiting a sign of his true intentions.

Despite the bonfire, Paia is stunned by the cold and the dank sucking mud, and the cinders still half alight beneath her sandaled feet. As usual, the dragon has neglected to clothe her adequately. But this new place he's brought her to seems half familiar, even shrouded in fire-lit darkness, as if remembered from dreams. Or from borrowed memories. Memories from the Meld. For the darkness isn't empty. The others are here. The girl Erde, and N'Doch, and Gerrasch, oddly abstracted. Paia greets them, glad for the company, but only Erde replies.

Why has he come? For our side or theirs?

I don't know!

And then Fire issues his summons.

His voice rises again in its formal pitch. "I call Erde von Alte to speak for the Eight!"

Dragon! What must I do?
YOU MUST ANSWER HIM.
But why?
BECAUSE HONOR REQUIRES IT.
It helps that she feels her own reluctance echoed in his

tone. She gathers herself to climb down from the safety of his forearm.

N'Doch grabs her. "You're not going out there!"

"I must."

"Then I'm going, too. We should face him together."

They slip through the whispering crowd of Deep Moor refugees. Rose embraces Erde silently. Raven says, "You'll know what to tell him!" Erde moves into the open, N'Doch a half step behind. On the far side of the smoldering fire, Hal sees them coming.

"No!" He spurs his horse into the path between them and the waiting giant, then dismounts, sheathing his sword. "Lord Fire! If you require a life, I offer you mine!"

Erde breaks into a run. "No, you shall not!" She knows Fire will not be satisfied with just any life, but probably wouldn't mind doing away with one persistent opponent in order to get at the other he intends. She reaches Hal and brushes past him, shaking off his arm when he tries to hold her back. "Earth will protect me," she murmurs. To N'Doch, she says, "Stay with him."

But Hal has made his formal offer, and understands it has been refused. Out of the dark behind him, Gerrasch appears, and Paia moves over to join them, shuddering with cold. N'Doch hauls off his top layer and wraps it around her. What fit him as a vest shelters her as a cloak.

Erde approaches alone. Fire glares down at her from his smoke-wreathed heights. Scales glint on his cheeks. She sees his whispering robe is made of chained links of gold. She's relieved to find him decently clothed for a change. She prepares to meet him glower for glower. Yet it seems that the flames leaping in his golden eyes are fed by exasperation rather than rage.

"Do you come ready to lecture me about my sacred Duty, witch-child?"

Overhearing, Brother Guillemo cries, "His duty is to punish you! And he will, by all that's holy!"

Erde folds her arms across her chest. "You know your Duty better than I, Lord Fire."

Fire sighs. "You virtuous ones. Such a bore, really, but so much more reliable."

Erde frowns. "For what have you Summoned me? Time is passing, and the Purpose requires our attention!"

Much to her discomfiture, Fire drops gracefully into a crouch before her, so that their gazes are level. His is hot and cynical, reflecting the fire behind her. She wishes she could look away. He smiles, as if to a much younger child. "So eager for it to be accomplished, are you? You're not even sure what it is."

"I know it is right." Erde's voice catches slightly, despite her efforts to hold it steady. "Whatever else it is, I'll bear up with."

Fire's eyes lid shut briefly. "Ah. Heroics. Again."

"You shall not stir me to rage with your mockery, Lord Fire."

"Really? Then that fierce little scowl and those shoulders up to your earlobes have nothing to do with anger?"

Erde smoothes her face, and lifts her chin out of her neck.

"No, keep your anger, witchling! Nurture it. It's a proper righteous anger, after all. You'll need it for the task at hand."

"The Purpose should be accomplished with a calm and glad heart, Lord Fire. I know little, but I know that much."

"Ah, but I mean the task I have for you . . . which must be finished before the other can even be attempted."

The frown returns. She cannot banish it. "What task is that?"

"Ask my brother Earth. He will tell you."

"I'd rather you did."

"So be it, then." He straightens, shifting his glare from Erde back to Hal. "Now, sir knight. Front and center."

Hal glares back, uncomprehending. N'Doch moves to grab hold of him, but Erde shake her head gently, and Gerrasch says, "Yes." N'Doch shrugs and urges the knight forward. "Might as well see what he wants."

Shrugging his tunic and mail into order, Hal hurries to Erde's side. "Lord Fire," he acknowledges crisply.

"I have need of your sword."

Hal's jaw tightens. "My sword is sworn to my king, and to the Great Purpose. I cannot . . ."

"Oh, please! No more lofty rhetoric. I wish only the weapon itself, not your undying loyalty."

Confounded, Hal lays his hand on the sword's gilded hilt.

"Yes, yes, that's the one. Draw it and give it to the girl."

As Hal hesitates, Brother Guillemo crows to his men, "Now you'll see how he'll punish the witch!"

. "Do it, dear knight," Erde urges. But when she holds the dragon-hilted blade, so heavy that she must use both hands to keep its tip from being fouled in the mud, she says to Fire, "I will not swear to you either."

"Of course you won't. I'm not that delusional. But hear this: will you accept the gift I offer, in recompense for all you've suffered? In doing so, you will also open the way for the accomplishment of the Purpose which has been the cause of that suffering."

His silky tone alerts her. "I think I must know the gift first, my lord, to see if I am worthy of it."

"Oh, take my word for it, you are."

"Nevertheless . . ."

"By all that's eternal!" Fire snarls, while Brother Guillemo dances his horse into a gloat behind him. "No wonder you people never get anything done!" He turns, picks the stunned priest out of his saddle by the hood of his cloak, and flings him at Erde's feet. His terrified horse careens off into the trio of his knights who have pointedly not ridden to his aid. Resilient as always, Guillemo scrambles up, groping for his own weapon. But he has lost it in the transfer. Erde braces herself and lifts the point of Hal's blade. She faces the priest with the same horrified fascination that he's always aroused in her. His black eyes bore into her. His pouty red lips repel her. He is the thing that, in all of life, she comprehends least: the personification of badness. How can a being so wrong support enough life to draw breath?

"Again I am tested," croaks Guillemo, brushing snow and mud from his cassock.

"This looks like a fair fight," observes Fire to Hal, as if soliciting his approval. "He is the stronger, but she has the weapon."

"But . . ." protests Hal. "You can't . . . this is monstrous!"

Fire only laughs, though his laughter dies when Paia steps back into the glow of the firelight. "This is petty vengeance, my Fire. Do you call this a clean kill?"

The smoldering giant shrugs. "Depends on how good she is." Hal begins another protest, but Fire waves him to silence. "Of course, I could show the further depths of my generosity, I suppose . . ." Abruptly, he shoves Guillemo from behind so that the priest stumbles and falls flat. Before he can rise, Fire places one clawed foot in the middle of his back. ". . . by holding him down for her."

Erde stares at the fallen man. A sudden bloodlust grips her heart, as tightly as she grips the sword. Here, under her blade, is the evil who corrupted her father, murdered her dear nurse, set the barons against their king, destroyed the country and the people with war and famine and superstition. It's an opportunity she should welcome. It would be treason not to. And it would be easy. She has only to lift the blade, the great dragon-hilted sword, and the perfection of its edge plus the weight of it falling would sever the priest's neck with little effort on her part. The sword will do the killing, not her.

Dragon?

She hears only disapproving silence in reply. She glances back at Hal, and his eyes are also saying no. She turns away angrily. Stupid dragon! Selfish man! He only wishes to do the deed himself! She strains to lift the blade level with her shoulders. She approaches the struggling priest.

BEFORE YOU STRIKE, ASK: IS THIS RIGHT?

Memories of her first encounter with Guillemo rush back. How he ogled her and confused her and made her feel dirty and stupid. She was too innocent then to recognize that his interest in her was sexual. He was a priest, after all. A man of God.

IS IT RIGHT?

Dragon, you were not there!

IT IS DESERVED, BUT IS IT RIGHT? LISTEN TO YOUR HEART.

Dragon, you are my heart! Tell me what to do!

I CANNOT.

But why?

IT IS AGAINST THE RULES.

The rules! How can you talk of rules? This is a mortal decision!

THE DECISION MUST BE YOURS, NOT MINE.

Erde knows that if she was going to do this thing, she would have done it already. As quickly as it came on her, the bloodlust departs, leaving her nauseous and trembling.

She lowers the sword, letting the tip sink into the mud and ash and melting snow.

Fire clicks his tongue once, irritably. "I thought you of all of them might have it in you."

Erde looks up at him, spent and lost. "If a dragon cannot kill, then neither shall I."

Brother Guillemo laughs under Fire's claw. The dragon steps back, releasing him. "I give up. I've lost again."

"And righteousness has won!" Guillemo shouts, leaping for Erde and the sword. Fire is there before him, snatching the sword from her shaking hands and leveling it with a smooth backhanded stroke that catches the priest full in the throat and passes through without a sound.

"*This* dragon can kill," Fire mutters, as Guillemo topples to the ground. Paia regards her dragon with somber eyes as he casually thrusts the sword back at Erde, hilt-first. Its blade is almost clean. Cries of triumph and release erupt from the soldiers remaining in the Grove. Fire says, "Well, at least someone thought it was the right thing to do."

Hal steps in and gently takes the sword away. The king rides up to join them as they stare down at the new freshet of red flowing between the footprints pressed into the mud and snow. Then Hal calls over two pikemen to cover the corpse and haul it away. "And treat it with due respect," he growls, just as one of them is about to grasp Guillemo's head by the ear and exhibit it on its own in gory triumph.

Fire braces his fists against his back as if in pain, and starts to pace.

The king watches him, a hint of awe and distaste hiding behind his glad air of relief. He turns back to Hal. "Is our business here complete?"

Hal nods. "The business of the kingdom, yes. You may declare the victory, Sire."

"You deserve that honor, my knight."

"No, better you." Hal glances quickly at Erde. Then, having answered his lord too abruptly, he looks up into the young king's eyes, begging patience. "Your pardon, my liege. There are, ah . . . yet a few details to be settled here. If you'll permit me . . ."

Rainer frowns, thinks better of it, and gathers up his reins. "Of course. Report to me when you're finished." As he turns to go, Hal signals Wender to follow. Erde watches them canter off along the dark road through the trees, the other knights and infantry cheering as they pass, then falling gladly in behind.

Oh, yes, she tells herself again. He'll make them a good king.

Meanwhile, Fire continues to pace.

CHAPTER THIRTY-SIX

The Grove is liberated! The Librarian can hear the trees sighing in relief. Or perhaps it's his dragon, breathing into their bare, battered limbs and brittle twigs, whispering through the roughness of their bark.

HURRY, HURRY!

Ah, yes, it's Air. The trees are in no hurry. When everything Changes, the sacred, eternal Grove will remain. But it's no rest for the weary. The Eight are assembled. The Work must begin. It will start with the trees. The trees are Air's work, and Earth's. The breath of life, the healing force. The Grove will be restored.

Water has chosen to return to man-form for the debate they all know is coming. While her brother pouts and paces, Water-as-Sedou moves among the stay-behinds, those who sensed that the battle was not yet over and still wish to lend their support: the women of Deep Moor, Djawara, Stoksie and Luther, Hal. She will gather them, help them find a comfortable place around the fire. Already, she's sent Margit and Lily off to raid the enemy tents for food, wine, extra clothing or blankets, stools or kegs to rest on.

Rose sets her women to making a meal. Erde searches out deadfall to bring to the fire, refusing to burn the fresh hewn wood while Earth moves slowly among the great trees, mending broken limbs, cracked trunks, the raw scars of cutting and dragging. Paia sits quietly, letting N'Doch and the Tinkers fuss over her. But she's watching Fire pace.

Finally the purposeful busyness settles into quiet, and Sedou says, "If you wish to open the discussion, brother . . . we haven't much time."

Fire turns. "It's too late. She's already on about her usual business. She's as bad as the humans. She won't listen. It doesn't matter what any of us says." He starts to pace again, then stops in front of Erde. The Librarian sees he's not much taller now than N'Doch, as if his pacing has worn out the rage that earlier swelled his stature. But the fire lord's gaze, as he fixes it on the weary girl, is as scornful as ever. "How do you ever expect to fix things if you can't even take the basic steps?"

"Wha . . . what?"

"Ridding the gene pool of the bad ones." When she stares at him openmouthed, he bends over her, articulating each syllable as if she had trouble hearing. "Kill-ing them off."

"Which is what you'd like to do with all of us."

"Yes. The species is hopelessly flawed."

"You made Guillemo what he was!" N'Doch leaps to Erde's defense, shaking his finger in Fire's face. "You can't blame us! You made Baraga, too!"

"And unmade him as well, which is more than you can claim. But, allow me an addendum: I made them *worse* than they already were, merely by the power of suggestion . . . to prove a point."

"What point?" Erde asks.

"That the defective material was already there. And that humanity is incapable of policing its own ranks. It's futile to run these cycles over and over again. We ought to either quit it completely or start over from scratch. New genes, new species."

The Librarian feels another memory stirring. He's been remembering things, but this is a very long and complicated one. The other dragon guides stare at Fire for a moment, then as a trio, turn questioning eyes to him. "Not yet." He waves away their gaze. "Soon."

Water-as-Sedou calls from beside Rose's soup pot, "He means he hasn't remembered enough yet. But he will. You all will, soon enough."

"Cycles?" Paia asks.

Fire throws up his hands, exasperation on a theatrical scale. "Endless! Pointless! I keep trying to make them see it! We should just play this one out and let that be the end of it. No more cycles!" To Paia, he says more gently, "Your father used to breed dogs, do you remember?"

"Of course."

The Librarian can see she's surprised Fire even knows what a dog is.

"If he bred a dog as mean as Guillemo, what would he do?"

Paia's brow creases prettily. "He'd . . . put it down."

"Exactly! If that whole line turned up mean, what would he do?"

Now she looks away, uneasy. "He'd discontinue that breeding program."

"And if the entire species of dogs turned up mean, what then?"

Sedou brings a tray of steaming soup bowls. "But it's not the entire species. Look at these good people! That's the whole point."

"That's *your* whole point." Fire peers into Paia's bowl, clearly wondering if his newly material man-form might be capable of eating. "If we can't get them even as far as the printing press each time without tripping the alarm, I'd say the experiment is a failure, and I'm tired of it. I say no more restarts, no more futures. Let's all go find a comfy den somewhere and enjoy ourselves while the damn planet self-destructs. Let's stop these endless, useless efforts to help mankind get it right, because *they never will!*"

"I don't much like the sound of this," N'Doch admits.

"The Intemperate One." Sedou jerks his head in Fire's direction. "Actually, we get a little further along each time."

Fire dips a gilded nail into Paia's soup. "Not every time. It's two steps forward, three steps backward, if you ask me. Which nobody does."

IT'S NOT OUR PLACE TO MAKE THIS JUDG-MENT. OUR DUTY IS LAID OUT FOR US AND WE MUST FOLLOW IT.

"Another county heard from," Fire growls.

"He's hard at work making things better," Erde returns hotly. "All you know how to do is destroy!"

"Burn, consume, *renew*, little girl. It's mankind who does the destroying."

"Wait, wait," begs N'Doch. "Lemme get this straight. This has all happened before?"

"A billion times!" declares Fire. "Humanity fucks up, we

pull the plug and restart the cycle before they can destroy the planet completely."

A BILLION IS UNTRUE. THE ACTUAL COUNT IS . . .

"What does it matter? It's still a waste of our time!"

N'Doch lets out a breath. "Whew. Where do you restart it?"

"That depends." Sedou's voice is steady and quiet. "It's often a matter of debate, but usually, somewhere around the end of the last great ice age."

"Too late," says Fire. "They're already men by then."

"As I said . . . a matter of debate."

Along with his returning memories, the Librarian reclaims an idea. Did I mention this after the last cycle, he wonders? Perhaps he didn't have the details quite worked out. If he cannot express it articulately enough, will they listen? "An idea . . . er . . . a proposal."

They all turn to him. He worries that Earth and Air are nearly done among the wounded trees, and it will be time to move on to the next phase of the Work. He worries that the words will not come, or won't come in time. But miraculously, it's all there in his mind, recalled in full, as if he's been handed a prepared speech, or a recording to just flip on and run. "I have an idea," he begins. "What about a compromise?"

"You were our compromise," says Fire. "Don't you remember?"

"Let him speak," Sedou insists.

"How was I?" The Librarian is disturbed beyond measure by Fire's implication that he's failed at a task he's not even been aware of.

YOU ARE CRUEL, BROTHER.

"I am . . . truthful. Uncompromising."

"Mean," Erde mumbles.

"Tell me," the Librarian begs, though he thinks he recalls it now, all of it.

Sedou regards him kindly. "You were to keep the knowledge alive, from generation to generation, evolving with the world. The knowledge of what the planet needs to stay healthy, to survive. Our living library."

A DUTY WHICH YOU PERFORMED ADMIRABLY.

"But it didn't do any good," Fire points out. "Nobody listened."

"Some did," murmurs the Librarian. He'd always found allies in the ecological movement. "But not enough."

N'Doch nods. "No way. Not near enough. I'd still be one of those nonlisteners if I hadn't met the dragons."

"But that's my idea. More people. Our ideas should evolve, too. Don't restart so far back. There's too much room for error if, each time, men must reinvent the wheel."

"Literally," N'Doch puts in.

"It was thought," says Sedou reasonably, "that memories of the former, wrong ways would hamper the evolution of the right ways."

"But why not let memory work to advantage? Let's restart where some already carry the necessary knowledge and understanding. Let the knowledge persist through the Change. Make *sure* that men remember. See what they can become if there are some of us around to explain, to remind, to tell the truth, to spread the warnings."

Fire laughs nastily. "Ha. Prophets. You know what happens to them."

"But the memory of the Change will persist for a while, perhaps long enough. Even as it fades into legend, then myth, it will have its effect on men's behavior, and progress will be made."

Sedou rubs his jaw. "A good idea. But there's a catch. We won't be around."

The Librarian has remembered that, too. "No matter. Some will be." He nods toward the fire, at Hal and Rose and Djawara, listening soberly. At the Tinkers, cleaning up from the meal. At the other women, spreading canvas and blankets to curl into close to the embers. "More than just me."

Rose clears her throat. "Won't be around?"

"Sleeping," Sedou offers gently, "until the next crisis."

"Of course. But the . . . your guides?"

Sedou looks at Fire, and then away. "Why does this always fall to me?"

"Because you do it so well, sister."

Erde lays a hand on Sedou's arm. "I recall it now. I will tell them."

"Heroics," Fire mutters, walking off to the edge of the darkness.

"The guides are . . ." Erde begins. "*We* are . . . extensions of our dragons, born into human form. There are always four such in the world, though they live unaware of it until the Summons comes. To gather the energies necessary to create the Change, the dragons require all their energies. The guides must be . . . reabsorbed."

She sees the shock and protest paling their faces. "No! Don't be sad for us! It's a wonderful . . . a joyous reunion! We will be . . . *be* our dragons again! And we'll rest until it's time to go to work again. So, it is you who have the harder task. You must carry the knowledge into the world. You must struggle to remake the habits of mankind. That is . . ." She looks to Sedou. "If it is agreed to try Gerrasch's idea this time. And I do think it's a very good idea."

"It's a terrible idea," calls Fire from the shadows. "A poor excuse for one more pointless cycle."

"Doan know if yu doan try," Stoksie comes to stand beside Hal and Rose. "Shur gonna be sum supprize out deah, when da wurld getz all green agin . . ." He snaps his fingers. "Jess li' dat. Dat's what'll happin, ri'?"

Sedou nods, a smile softening his solemn gaze. "I guess it will. We've never done it that way before."

"What a lovely vision," murmurs Rose.

"That's why it's a good idea," Erde urges. "People will see a great miracle happen, and they'll be thankful and remember. And with the likes of Rose and Hal around to explain the why and how, surely no one will ever let it happen again!"

Fire's laugh is dry and weary. "There's a sucker born every minute."

Erde scowls at him. "I think I'm a lot happier with hope than you are without any."

"But why sacrifice your lives? You're all young and healthy. Do it my way, and you get to live your lives to the full, and in the end, know that you'll never have to repeat this pointless exercise!"

"You wanted us to take steps," N'Doch reminds him. "So, we're taking one."

Fire shakes his head. "I just wanted it to end."

Earth lumbers out of the darkness and hunkers down

beside the fire. A dozen or so stray warhorses wander up behind him, their tack askew.

THE GROVE IS HEALED. I HAVE BROUGHT SOME FRIENDS.

"Time," intones the Librarian. Already, he feels the pull, the dragon's substance calling back its own.

"Already?" breathes Hal.

"Oh, dear," Rose echoes him. "Not so soon!"

Sedou says, "The urgency is at the far end, uptime. There, the world is . . ."

"I saw it," Rose agrees. "Dry, barren, already lifeless. Do what you must. I understand."

HURRY! HURRY!

"Details. Still." The Librarian's internal recording has run out, leaving him terse again. He looks to Sedou to speak for him.

"Yes." Sedou beckons to Stoksie and Luther. "Guess you fellas need a ride home."

Stoksie chuckles, relieved. "Me 'n' Luta wuz shur we'd be lookin' fer digs aroun' heah."

"No way. We need you uptime, to spread the word."

"Yu gottit."

"Now?" The Librarian prepares himself for the effort of slowing Air's momentum long enough to get a portal open. "When?"

"Will you go to the Citadel?" Paia asks. "Will you tell Leif all that's happened? He'll make an excellent messenger of the word."

"Sounds like some crackpot religion," says Fire sourly.

"You oughta know," says N'Doch.

"Shur, gal, we'll go deah. Leif's gonna be wunderin' anyhow."

When the portal opens, it's a discontinuous rectangle of otherness, suspended in thin air, an opening without borders. The Librarian understands that the more formal structure of previous portals—a picture frame, a computer screen, a wooden doorway, a stone gate—has been a concession to human concepts of time and space. But Air has no patience left for the niceties. The view through the opening brings Hal and Erde simultaneously to their feet. They're looking into a richly paneled room, a high dark room lit by a single glowing lamp hanging above a long, polished wooden table. Leif Caldwell sits surrounded by papers and maps. Constanze leans over his shoulder, pointing out something on the paper currently held in his hand. A few of the Blind Rachel Crew are with them, hard at work passing papers back and forth, discussing various issues among themselves. At Cauldwell's right is Adolphus of Köthen, his head cocked with interest as he listens to what Constanze is saying.

"Now," directs the Librarian.

The occupants of the dark room glance up in astonishment as the Tinkers step through the opening. Within half a breath, the portal has closed behind them.

"Oh!" Erde's cry is a single birdlike call of heartbreak. It brings tears to the Librarian's eyes.

Hal frowns, pensive but faintly amused. "He looks more at home there than he ever did here."

Paia takes Erde's hand, squeezes it briefly. "He'll do well. He'll be happy, I think, at last."

HURRY! HURRY!

"Master Djawara!" Sedou calls, then says more fondly, "Grandfather. For I feel that you are, have been. Will you go home to the bush, Papa?"

"Nothing there to go home to," the old man says. "The Change will be welcome, but it will not restore my family." He looks at Rose from under penitent brows. "I thought I might beg shelter of the ladies, to help rebuild Deep Moor. Out of gratitude, you understand, for their hospitality to my grandson. And to live out my life in peace and quiet among people who believe in dragons."

Rose laughs, brushing aside her tears. "You are welcome, good mage!"

HURRY! HURRY!

"Good-byes, then." The human niceties are deserting the Librarian as well now.

The stray horses are commandeered, good-byes said with silent, fervent hugs and the pressing of wet cheeks. The women mount up. Passing on her way to her horse, Rose stops before Fire.

"Perhaps this time, Lord Fire, we will be better able to live up to your high expectations of us."

He inclines his golden head. "Good lady, I wish you all the success in the world."

"Satirical," she scolds him gently. "You lack faith."

"You're right. I do."

HURRY! HURRY!

Djawara declines a mount, swearing he has never yet ridden a horse and is too old to start now. He embraces Erde, then his grandson, then turns away quickly to walk toward the road.

"You be good, Papa," N'Doch calls after him softly.

Hal sees the women onto their horses, then grips Erde's shoulders with both hands. "I swear you're a foot taller than when we first met."

"That was barely a season ago, dear knight."

He smiles, then sobers. "There is no other way?"

"You of all know the answer. It is what we are."

He nods, looking quite at a loss. He brushes a ragged fringe of curl back from her brow. "If I understand this right, you're saving all our lives with this new . . . arrangement. Lives that, like a million others, would otherwise cease to exist at the moment of the Change."

Erde's sad face clears in a wide, joyous grin, as bright as summer sunrise. "Yes! I hadn't thought of that! I guess we are! All the more reason!"

Hal presses his lips to her forehead. "Our thanks to you, lady of the dragons."

Then he flings himself on his horse and leads his little band down the dark road back to Deep Moor.

The Eight are alone. Paia sighs. The wind whispers in the branches. Sedou calls down a brief shower to douse the campfires.

"Don't want the place catching *fire*, after all," N'Doch quips.

They have no further need of light. They are as aware of each other as if they stood in an open field at noon. They feel eternity coming upon them, as the inevitability that haunted Erde from the beginning, as the annihilation that N'Doch dreaded, as the Librarian's perennial sense of drifting unmoored in time and space. But fear, dread, confusion . . . all that dissipates before the anticipated coming together. Union. Reunion. The joy of oneness.

Paia slides her arms around Fire's waist and lays her head on his chest. She thinks he might push her away, not yet released of his rage and frustration. Instead, he draws her tightly against him, his breath hot on her neck.

"Alas, my Fire," she whispers, for his ears only. "I fear you would rather be human."

HURRY! HURRY!

Earth, Water, Air and . . .

Fire?

I am here.

It will be easy, Erde tells them fleetingly. *It will be just like the Meld, except that it will. . . .*

EPILOGUE

He knows they've succeeded when the pair of Tinkers comes bursting out of thin air, breathless, grinning like fools. They've barely greeted anyone before they're dragging him and Cauldwell out of the room and down the corridor to the Great Hall with its wide windows overlooking the valley.

For a while they all stare through the dusty glass, and nothing happens. Leif starts muttering about getting back to work. Stokes dances up and down on his crooked hip, insisting, "Yu'll see! Yu'll see!"

At the first hint of change, Köthen understands she isn't coming back, or she'd have come with Stokes and Luther. She'd have wanted to see this for herself, if there was any way she could have. He'll ask Stokes later what's happened to her. He'd had visions of a life, children. He doesn't want to think about it now. Right now, the only thought he's got room for is wonder.

They throw open the windows and hang out in the hot, dry gusts, gawking, pointing. The hint becomes a fuzz of amber softening the hills, which cools into pale yellow, then an undeniable haze of green. Green! As he watches the hard red rock smooth over with a patina of new life—lichens, grass, wildflowers, leaves—in his mind he's seeing the snow melting on the battlefields, along the rutted roads, on the ramparts of Castle Köthen. He hopes Heinrich is alive to see it. And the brat. The two of them. What a pair.

Though it pains him to admit it, he's grateful to the brat for yanking him out of what Constanze Cauldwell calls his "narcissistic descent into suicidal despair." He shakes his head. He likes talking with Constanze. It's like talking to another man, but . . . not quite. And these people have phrases and elaborate explanations for notions he's never even thought of.

The valley below has become a vast windswept meadow. The sky is losing its ruddy glare. Beyond the crenellation of mountains, he sees the rounder profile of approaching clouds. Perhaps it will even rain. Rain! That thought makes him smile, and once he's started, he can't hold it back. His jaw just keeps spreading, his eyes crinkling, his mouth curling up, of their own accord. He knows what it is. It's joy.

Adolphus Michael von Hoffman, Baron of Köthen, has long been a stranger to joy. But Dolph Hoffman thinks he's willing to let it into his vocabulary.

He sees what's happening, but he'll never comprehend it. He'll accept the reality of it, but never be able to quite encompass the *possibility*. Why bust his head about it? Instead, he mutters something soft and obscene. It snags Stokes' attention, and they share a winner's grin.

"Das sumpin, yah, Dolf?"

"Yah. Das sumpin."

P.R. Frost
The Tess Noncoiré Adventures

"Frost's fantasy debut series introduces a charming protagonist, both strong and vulnerable, and her cheeky companion. An intriguing plot and a well-developed warrior sisterhood make this a good choice for fans of the urban fantasy of Tanya Huff, Jim Butcher, and Charles deLint."
— *Library Journal*

HOUNDING THE MOON
978-0-7564-0425-3
MOON IN THE MIRROR
978-0-7564-0486-4

and coming in June 2009:
FAERY MOON
978-0-7564-0556-4

To Order Call: 1-800-788-6262
www.dawbooks.com

DAW 70

MERCEDES LACKEY

The Collegium Chronicles

Foundation

The first new Valdemar novel in five years!

In this chronicle of the early history of Valdemar,
a thirteen-year-old orphan named Magpie
escapes a life of slavery in the gem mines when
he is chosen by one of the magical Companions
of Valdemar to be trained as a Herald. Thrust
into the center of a legend in the making,
Magpie discovers talents he never knew he
had... and witnesses the founding of the great
Heralds' Collegium.

978-0-7564-0524-3

To Order Call: 1-800-788-6262
www.dawbooks.com

S.L. Farrell

The Cloudmages

HOLDER OF LIGHTNING
0-7564-0152-6
MAGE OF CLOUDS
0-7564-0255-7
HEIR OF STONE
0-7564-0321-9

To Order Call: 1-800-788-6262
www.dawboks.com

DAW 71

Tanya Huff's
Blood Books

*Private eye, vampire, and cop: supernatural crime
solvers—and the most unusual love triangle in town.*
Now a Lifetime original series.

"Smashing entertainment for a wide audience"
—*Romantic Times*

BLOOD PRICE
978-0-7564-0501-4
BLOOD TRAIL
978-0-7564-0502-1
BLOOD LINES
978-0-7564-0503-8
BLOOD PACT
978-0-7564-0504-5
BLOOD DEBT
978-0-7564-0505-2

To Order Call: 1-800-788-6262

DAW 75

Tanya Huff
The *Smoke* Series

Featuring Henry Fitzroy, Vampire

"Fans of *Buffy* and *The X-Files* will cheer the latest exploits of Tony Foster, wizard-in-training.... This spin-off from Huff's popular Blood series stands alone as an entertaining supernatural adventure with plenty of sex, violence, and sarcastic humor."
—*Publishers Weekly*

SMOKE AND SHADOWS
0-7564-0263-8
978-0-7564-0263-1
SMOKE AND MIRRORS
0-7564-0348-0
978-0-7564-0348-5
SMOKE AND ASHES
978-0-7564-0415-4

To Order Call: 1-800-788-6262
www.dawbooks.com

DAW 72